STRYI
HOUSE
OF SPIES

BIOLOGICAL WARFARE
ESPIONAGE THRILLER

A contemporary biological warfare spy thriller set in 1993 during the disintegration of the Soviet Union. An elite Russian scientist has developed the world's most powerful biological weapon but through glasnost his experimental facility Lyubychany near Moscow is to be decommissioned. Seeking asylum in Britain in exchange for his secretly modified killer virus, events unexpectedly tumble out of control when he unwittingly becomes the target of both the Russian and British secret services.

BY
CHRISTOPHER SPACKMAN

For Florence and Margaret.

CONTENTS

ACKNOWLEDGMENTS

G.B. Carter of Porton Down for the technical help I gratefully received regarding biological and chemical matters and for reading selected pages of my manuscript.

Thank you so much. Any howlers are truly down to the author.

PART ONE

CHAPTER 1

DUBAI

In April 1993 during the early hours of the morning at the British Embassy in Dubai, a US citizen named Stryker sat with a gun pointed unsteadily but resolutely toward his chest. His gut instinct was to remain calm and gather his thoughts, dwelling on the horrifically bizarre events of just a few hours earlier leading up to his present predicament.

It had been just another holiday for him as he lay on a warm sandy beach staring out across the blue sun-dappled waters lapping the coast of Dubai daydreaming. It was very hot – the type of heat that addles the brain – and his thoughts drifted back to the sound of ice cubes being dropped into a double shot of bourbon he had been nursing. Two large splashes – two small. And that simple thought of two large splashes brought into sharp focus the picture of two bodies. And that sound of two small splashes made his mind reel. He had seen dead bodies before, but not like this. As a seasoned detective working for the Seattle police department he had been familiar with bodies shot up with small arms weapons and even Uzis – but not like this. What were holidays for but to unwind with friends or perhaps meet up unexpectedly with unexpected people you have not set eyes upon for years – perhaps both. But this!!

***

Stryker slipped silently from the sleek deck of a motor cruiser into the warm waters off the coast of Dubai, gliding smoothly like a fish, without making a ripple, before clambering onto one of the small aquatic one man craft and striking out for unknown territory. It was pitch black except for tiny pinpricks of stars twinkling in the inky sky. Everything was quiet now after the frantic hustle and bustle aboard the vessel on which he had changed into his diving gear, the final piece of equipment being a deep water oxygen cylinder. Then he heard them, the silence punctuated by

1

voices conversing in a foreign language. After his eyes had adjusted to the darkness he turned his face toward the voices and made out the silhouettes of four men sitting in a rubber dingy dressed in frogman's diving suits. Then fleetingly, perhaps for a second, something lit up their faces framed by rubber headgear before being extinguished just as quickly. It must have been a powerful torch or lamp within the dingy. These were definitely not tourists like him. Each had a large commando knife strapped to his chest which glinted in that brief flash of light, and the occupants of the dingy were speaking in Russian. They were the USSR's equivalent of America's renowned Special Forces Navy SEALS. Stryker's own insignificant looking little dingy bobbed some fifty feet away unseen. The main vessel which had ferried him and the two other men to this vicinity was now at anchor two nautical miles or so behind the dingy, its lights having been doused long before reaching its destination. He stopped swimming, the extra-large flippers silently treading water, pulling hard against the undercurrent. His head, covered in black skin-tight rubber, stayed half submerged as he removed his goggles for a better view.

His once pink skin had been smeared with black grease, leaving only the whites of his eyes visible in the darkness somewhere out in the Persian Gulf. The tightness of his goggles left deep ridges around the temple and across the bridge of his nose. The water was dead calm, resembling a smooth black sheet of oil. Lights flashed in the distance from the faint silhouette of what appeared to be a small submersible or ROV suspended by an 'A' frame from the side of a large vessel whose own lights had been extinguished. Looking around and seeing his two colleagues he gave them a thumbs-up sign to which they responded in kind before he swam in a little closer toward the Russians. They were speaking fast, but he could now hear clearly what they were saying.

"My dolzhny podnyat ikh sevodnya. Nam nuzhno toropitsya. Ich opasno ostavlyat zdes." It must be lifted tonight. We must move quickly. It is very dangerous to leave it here.

"Khorosho, ya so glasen. Prichal korabl I astroy oborudovanie na palube dlya podnyatia gruza." Alright, I agree. Bring the vessel over and get the lifting equipment sorted out on the deck.

A third voice broke in: *"I nuzhno osvetit eto myesto."* And let's get this place lit up.

After consulting the sophisticated miniaturised satellite navigation equipment strapped to his wrist alongside his waterproof Rolex watch, Stryker pulled the goggles back over his eyes. Fitting his mouthpiece snugly into his mouth he drew deeply on the oxygen supply strapped to his back before ducking beneath the gentle swell on the surface, swiftly descending

STRYKER'S HOUSE OF SPIES

vertically like a stone. After what seemed like an eternity he switched on the powerful hundred watt torch strapped to his other wrist and almost immediately spied through the murky water the bridge of a sunken vessel.

Swimming close by, he pointed the powerful beam of his torch at the bow of the ship illuminating the name *LITTLE MURMANSK*. On the deck of this recently sunken freighter lay large wooden crates and dented metal barrels in a haphazard fashion. He estimated the size of these crates to be about two metres wide and the same in height. Some were broken, but others were still held secure by steel ribbons biting into the wooden structure making up each crate. Peering into the shattered crates he detected what looked like stainless steel fermenters as used for dairy products. Inside other wooden crates there were steel cages precariously stacked one on top of the other, some containing dead incarcerated monkeys lying spread-eagled at the bottom of these padlocked cages, their fur moving eerily with the motion of unseen water currents, and small, exotic, brightly coloured fish weaving between the metal bars. The scene looked surreal.

As he swam in closer, Stryker illuminated the side of a cylindrical container, about half the height of the crates, which bore the international biohazard symbol in carmine, the vivid red logo indicating a dangerous, hazardous cargo and the word EBOLA in Cyrillic script. Moving around to the other side of the same container he once again flicked his torch in its direction, lighting up a graphically illustrated skull and crossbones stencilled in red with Mandarin Chinese lettering below it. Yet other containers bore the words MARBURG, SMALLPOX and ANTHRAX, also in Cyrillic script, plus more Chinese writing. After spending another five minutes surveying as many crates and containers as possible, he had seen enough. Switching off the powerful beam of his torch he began his ascent like a harpoon, shooting upwards, enveloped in a thick cushion of bubbles.

Once his head broke the smooth surface of the water he strained his ears as he glanced at his watch. It had been over twenty minutes since diving and there was now an uncanny silence. Des and Terry were not where they were supposed to be and the ROV had disappeared. From what the Russians had said earlier he had been expecting to see powerful floodlights illuminating the area, but now, if that were possible, it was darker than ever.

As he continued to peer through the gloom he caught sight of the faint silhouette of the ROV as it loomed up before him against the dark sky, but this time in complete blackness. The Russian-speaking frogmen in the large dingy had also vanished. Then shattering the dead silence, four distinct splashes could be heard by the side of the vessel which only minutes earlier had held the ROV suspended just above the water line. Two large splashes and two smaller ones accompanied by the sound of voices whispering frantically. This time he could not make out what the Russians were saying, though he sensed these four men with their deadly commando knives were encroaching on his comfort zone. Keeping his head half submerged, he removed the slightly waterlogged goggles. His flippers were now working much slower to maintain his general position according to the satnav strapped to his wrist. The surface of the water remained dead calm.

He turned his head quietly to the right just before something solid hit him in the neck from behind – a gentle thump. His heart pounded as his eyes rapidly adjusted to the velvety darkness as he swivelled around in the water. What he saw next made him stiffen like a rod of iron, seeing the muscular back of a body floating beside him. He knew instinctively that it was going to be one of the others. Steeling himself, he grabbed at the black rubber-clad shoulders, turning the body over as quietly as he could. What he saw next made him realise the significance of the splashes he had heard just a short while before: Two large splashes, two small. Two bodies, two heads.

He gagged on the bile rising in his throat. It took another moment to regain his composure, then quickly readjusting his mouthpiece and goggles, he slipped silently beneath the water, swimming furiously toward where he had last sensed but not seen the four Russian Special Forces frogmen. Surfacing seconds later he made contact with the first frogman, who happened to be on top of the water swimming away from Stryker's direction. Quickly moving his giant flippers with muscular legs Stryker caught up with the black clad figure taking him by surprise, grabbing the Russian's ankles before pulling him downwards toward the vicinity of the shipwreck. But before reaching the container ship the Russian Special Forces frogman momentarily struggled furiously, involuntarily taking a great gulp of water before drowning, not having had enough time to slip his oxygen supply into his mouth for the long descent.

Stryker harpooned up again like a rocket and almost immediately hit the feet of a second rubber clad frogman, taking him so much by surprise that the blade carried on his adversary's chest was removed by Stryker in one smooth motion without the Russian even being aware of it and breaking the surface once more, he swung the large commando knife in the direction of the Russian's neck. Stryker put the full force of his musclebound arm into severing the head as though it were made of soft cheese.

Two down, two to go, Stryker thought, as he remained staring expressionless across the dead calm sheet of water desperately straining to see through the dark, his eyes just level with the surface. It was not to remain quiet for long as from his left an unseen hand ripped off Stryker's goggles while at the same time another pair of large hands grabbed at his rubber clad head and with the entire frogman's weight, pushed it down below the surface of the water. Stryker, now drinking a lot of it, hit the quick-release mechanism on his oxygen cylinder with his left hand, releasing the weight from his back as it sank. Feeling but not seeing what was causing the heavy pressure upon his head, Stryker struck out with his newly acquired razor sharp commando knife gripped firmly and came away with a severed hand. Lashing out once more he made contact with another hand grasping his shoulders, and then another. Then all was returned to quiet, like a morgue.

It took ages for Stryker to relocate his aquatic one man craft and slumped onto it in a heap of exhaustion, overcome by his exertions. It was slow going, but eventually he located the isolated motor cruiser, still shrouded in a cloak of blackness, the silence overwhelming, not a sound to be heard. Now with every second that passed Stryker was closing in on the sleek vessel before finally making out the silhouette of the cruiser's captain still sitting in the skipper's chair where he had last been sighted before Stryker and his fellow divers had set out on their terrible adventure. The water remained dead calm with just the faintest sounds of water slapping against the hull as he silently boarded the vessel using the swim ladder attached to the stern of the boat. In a loud whisper from the deck he announced his arrival but before he had reached the wheelhouse he knew something was wrong. There was no response to his presence as he entered the enclosed space, and when he was level with the motionless captain bathed in a green glow from the sophisticated instrument panel of gauges he saw that his throat had been cleanly sliced open, his body tethered to the swivel chair by rope. Stryker suspected the captain had been located on the cruiser by his now dead assassins.

Stryker scanned the deck, seeking out any threat and making sure all was secure before severing the rope that held the captain in position with the commando knife before gently manoeuvring the skipper's blood-soaked body off the seat onto the cockpit floor before quickly sitting down to study the boats control panel, comprising of a vast array of buttons and dials. Turning the ignition key to the 'on' position he pressed a large button to start the twin engines then heard them splutter into life. The throttle was opened slowly at first and he could hear the whining of the motors as they engaged, moving the vessel through the water at quickening speed until, pushing the throttle to full acceleration, and with the aid of the ship's compass, he pointed the boat in the opposite direction away from the Russian freighter, sending it skimming across the surface of the water toward the coastline of Dubai.

CHAPTER 2

"Come on old boy, I appreciate you've been through a hell of a lot and not had a wink of sleep but what you must appreciate is that these questions have to be asked." Stryker's imposed host at the British Embassy in Dubai had introduced himself an hour earlier as the naval attaché, a Mr Hughes. He was rotund and fifty something. The purple-faced man representing the British government sported a white lightweight suit and a similarly coloured walrus moustache. He also had an obvious predilection for booze. He wore an audaciously multi-coloured striped tie with his white shirt even though it was halfway through the night and the heat was oppressive, giving an indication of his fastidiousness. He had what Stryker would call a lilting Welsh accent, equating his singsong inflection with that of the Welsh poet Dylan Thomas, whom Stryker had listened to on tape whilst at college back in his hometown of Seattle years before. After that cursory introduction and a string of questions which included enquiring as to which hotel Stryker was staying, he had promptly disappeared, leaving the American in the safekeeping of someone whom the naval attaché had referred to as Stephen the Duty Officer.

This dishevelled young man was patently not pleased with having been roused at such an early hour of the morning and who kept his distance by sitting across the room from Stryker, staring in total silence with a pistol obtained by Mr Hughes from the Keep clenched firmly in his hand, fervently wishing he could pull the trigger and toddle off back to bed. In this intervening period Stryker's insomniac host, for it was now well into the early hours of the morning, had obviously been gleaning as much information as possible from other British Embassy staff who had escorted Stryker from the docks after improvising a discreet cordon sanitaire around the Omani registered yacht before removing the skipper's body using a nondescript Embassy van. But the other embassy staff had little to impart due to the fact that Stryker had refused to speak to anybody except someone in authority and now the naval attaché was back, to the obvious relief of his young subaltern whose face, to Stryker's mind, bore all the signs of the first flush of youth and looked barely out of kindergarten. He also figured his initial interrogation would now be rekindled.

"Once again you ask me to begin at the beginning. Well as I keep telling you buddy, I am on holiday from America. I live in Seattle actually." Here

Stryker digressed by requesting to see an American consular official but the request seemed not to have been heard. Stryker gazed distractedly at a framed photographic portrait of Queen Elizabeth II upon one of the walls which had been signed with a flourish in her inimitable signature and felt like an intruder upon some important meeting to which he himself should not be privy.

"Mr Stryker or whoever you are." As he spoke the naval attaché was staring at Stryker's American passport and leafing through its pages. Stryker wondered what else this servant of the British state had retrieved from his luggage. "You arrive on board a hired vessel off the coast of Dubai, a vessel fitted out for diving and exploration and ostensibly used for entertaining tourists who enjoy such seafaring pastimes. You say you went to explore a shipwreck with two old friends who you accidentally met up with just the day before whilst you were here on a diving holiday and who you had not seen for quite a few years. You say a large Russian vessel was near the scene of this shipwreck and whilst you were beneath the water exploring this shipwreck the Russians killed your two friends, at which point you yourself got into what sounds to me like the fight of a lifetime and managed to kill some of these Russians. After this you returned to your own vessel where you discovered the ship's master with his throat cut then promptly reported the incident through the ship's radio telephone to the night duty officer here at the British Embassy, for which we shall remain eternally grateful; mentioning the deaths of these two British nationals to him. Heads hacked off, to quote. I appreciate that there was no way for you to call anyone else using that particular radio telephone because of course as you may or may not know it had been permanently set onto that particular waveband. And after organising a welcoming committee for you at the docks you were escorted back here. This place by the way is under British jurisdiction so you really have to play by our rules I'm afraid. None of your Miranda rights afforded to you here my good friend."

"Listen fella, I'm not interested about Miranda and all that bullshit. My buddies and I worked together on Special Operations years ago when I was a U.S. Navy SEAL." Stryker broke in with a tetchy tone to his voice. "I was then a diver working for the American military and my two buddies were from the British SBS. That is the Special Boat Service. Top secret stuff you know – covert operations, that sort of thing."

"My dear boy, I'm in naval... well I certainly understand precisely what all that entails."

"Yeah! Naval Intelligence. Is that what you were going to say? Well anyway, it was natural for us to go diving together: back in the day if we weren't diving we were like fish out of water. We hadn't seen one another for quite a few years as I say. No big deal. They said they too were on holiday and it would be like old times if their mate – that's me by the way – would like to join them for this dive. They mentioned something about a wreck; possibly a dive of a lifetime, they said. They were right about that, poor fellas. And that's the very expression they used – mate! Why wouldn't I want to explore a shipwreck with my two old buddies? Why, what are you suggesting? That I murdered them myself in the middle of the Persian Gulf and calmly returned to the boat the three of us had left barely an hour before? What motive would I have? And that's assuming it would have been possible for me to decapitate two of the West's best trained Special Forces just like that?"

"Mr Stryker, I will pose the questions. Is that clear? Besides which, if your story is true you seem to have excelled in the matter of decapitating a Russian Special Forces sailor and killing three of his comrades in God knows what manner. Unfortunately we have lost two valuable men and I wish to establish the circumstances."

"How do you mean valuable?"

"There you go again, asking questions."

"Look. We were old friends. Drinking buddies." Stryker's mind reeled back to when he had first made their acquaintance at a pub within minutes of setting foot in Portsmouth whilst embarking on a course at Fort Monckton – training H.Q. for MI6 personnel, Britain's foreign intelligence service. From what Stryker remembered Portsmouth was not exactly the most exciting place to spend more than a few hours and that was a few hours too long. He could picture it now – the middle of winter, a seemingly endless grey windswept promenade and accompanying stony beach; the bleak vista broken only by an empty, forlorn looking amusement pier jutting out into the sea, shuttered up against vandals and the inclement climate, its rusting iron legs being eternally battered by the unforgiving waves. A lonely, desolate place, low grey clouds and the cold white mane of sea horses rushing in from the Solent. He shuddered, much preferring the temperature in Dubai which had been hovering around the 120°F mark. It was true that he was not a spy but had been seconded by the American government at the time to learn a few tricks of the trade from close allies – swap ideas, that sort of thing. But he was not going to tell this goon any of that. Let him go to hell.

"It was to be a piece of cake; a night dive – fun. I love diving – that as I say, is why I was here, on a diving holiday. We all do… correction, did. From my hotel we left the Jumeirah Beach Road, pulled onto the Mina Road where we headed for the Dubai Cruise Terminal and Port Rashid. That was our port of embarkation." The naval attaché stared at Stryker.

"Look here dear boy." He bore a feigned expression of pained sadness in his mid-grey eyes as he spoke. "Save all this detail till we get back to London. It's late. There are other people who know the right questions to ask. Comprenez?"

Stryker did not need to feign a look of indignation as he momentarily let his composure slip. "You mean London, England? I have absolutely no intention of going to England. You must be out of your mind. I'm an American citizen here on holiday. And you have absolutely no right going through my things at the hotel."

"Sir... Mr Stryker, let me explain to you the facts of life according to our British Foreign and Commonwealth Office. You have admitted going diving with two British nationals who you say were decapitated whilst you yourself were beneath the waves in the Persian Gulf, and here I might add the bodies of your two friends have not as yet been located. Then there is mention of Russians. Now, you can see your story has to be checked out to our satisfaction. After all, to us you are a total stranger and as far as we are concerned these two divers might have been kidnapped with your assistance by your so-called Russians who may even have been of a completely different nationality. We only have your word for it after all. And until or if these bodies turn up..."

"That's preposterous."

"Come, come now, we did not say we do not believe you. It's just that these things have to be verified by our interested parties. Then there is the matter of the body of the skipper and if what you are telling us is true there are dead Russians to add to this list. The authorities here might not be so favourable regarding your predicament. Yes, you might very well ask for help at the American Embassy here in Dubai, but there is a little matter of national security, biological weapons with the Chinese and Russian language writ large on these crates you insist you saw. It might even evolve into an international incident with God knows what consequences. Anyhow, all these things will be gone into, as I say, when we get back to London."

"I see." Stryker looked thoughtful.

"There is one more thing, the most important thing of all. Something I cannot emphasise enough." The naval attaché wore a grave look upon his weather beaten face. "That thing is secrecy! I have been instructed from the very top echelon in London, and I really do mean the top – that these things which you say you saw remain between ourselves, just the three of us, so mum's the word. Do you understand the expression?" Here the naval attaché gave a sharp nod in the direction of his young subaltern still wielding the pistol in Stryker's direction. "And that means you as well Stephen. This is just between the three of us. Do not speak to anyone of

9

anything you may have heard or seen this evening – or should I say morning. Not to any other member of staff, neither in this embassy nor anywhere else. I have been instructed from London that all that passed between us this morning is to be classified on a need-to-know basis." The young man gave a sombre nod of his head and continued holding the pistol in Stryker's direction, not letting it waver a millimetre.

CHAPTER 3

LONDON

"Four days ago someone claiming to be a Russian scientist based in Moscow and experimenting with highly toxic biological warfare agents manages to surreptitiously contact our Secret Intelligence Service – from somewhere in London in fact, although his whereabouts continue to be a mystery to us. The telephone call was so quick we could not trace from where it was coming even using triangulation except as I said, the call came from somewhere in London in the region of Victoria train station. His stated aim apparently is to apply for political asylum in Britain in exchange for his supplying us with classified information. That's what he told us. To lend credibility to his story of being a top level Russian scientist he supplies us with a snippet of information i.e. the coordinates of the shipwreck of the *LITTLE MURMANSK*; in retrospect, with disastrous consequences as you yourself can confirm. When we learnt of these coordinates from our Russian scientist – no mention from him, mind you, of a sunken ship, just a cryptic set of points on a compass – a few hours later information had come to our attention from a reliable source that a recently sunken Russian cargo ship was suspected of causing contamination in the waters off the coast of Dubai in the Persian Gulf. This information was all kept very close to our chests so to speak. Very hush-hush. The coordinates were pretty much the same as this would be asylum seeker had given us. Now it doesn't take much imagination to realise that our Russian friend – if that is what he turns out to be – has obviously a fast track to some very privileged information. Our staff had already established through the shipping agents Lloyds of London that the embarkation point of this sunken vessel had been from one of the southern states of Africa in which..."

"The Russians maintain a substantial presence. Yeah, I know."

"You are obviously a very well informed chap."

"It doesn't take much. I read the newspapers."

"Well, anyway, our man in Dubai had specifically requested two operatives from what we call The Increment. These are men drawn from the Special Air Service and SBS, both of which are part of Britain's Special Forces, to which those two men who were your former buddies had belonged. Like the owner of the vessel you prepared to dive from they were

11

also working for British Intelligence, sent to Dubai to confirm the veracity of our potential Russian defector's information."

"Go on, I'm listening."

"Now I understand you speak fluent Russian mister Stryker. That might be of value. You also have a physical defect." The officer nodded in the direction of Stryker's head. "I regret having to be indelicate but such an impediment would normally rule our agents out of the game. Generally speaking, one has to be one hundred per cent fit to work for us. However in your case it might work in our favour; help with you not being suspected of being in collusion with our Intelligence Service."

Stryker took exception at being described as not one hundred per cent fit but thought now was not the time to raise his new found host's hackles. It is true he bore the faintest of a scar relating to a run-in with some criminal but that did not detract from his being very efficient when it came to tracking down and gaining prosecutions against most of those whose misfortune it was to cross his path. The particular problem alluded to had occurred in Seattle while Stryker was still in the police force. He was attending the scene of a shop robbery when he was shot. He had lost an eye whilst throwing himself in front of a woman who just happened to be pregnant with the result that he was decorated for showing exceptional bravery in the line of duty and then been promptly retired on a police pension against his will. But he had kept his detecting abilities honed by becoming a bona fide licensed private detective. He also consoled himself that the prosthetic eye he now sported was pretty well undetectable thanks to his uncle, Richard Truman, a top consultant cardiac surgeon also based in Seattle who had good connections within the medical fraternity, and Stryker's prostheses was the best that money could buy. The only thing that drew any attention to this so-called physical defect now was a tiny, almost undetectable scar running just beneath his lower eyelid, but from Stryker's point of view it was nothing to become paranoid about, especially since the ordinary layman untrained in medical matters would not necessarily notice anything at all.

"For the sake of your two comrades you lost and for the safety of our two countries will you help us track down this scientist? He may be a Russian SVR agent luring us into a trap or he might be a genuine victim of the Russian State who simply wants out. But whoever he is we must locate him. After all, he certainly has confidential information about that sunken vessel which it would seem the Russians thought it worthwhile attempting to keep secret by killing two of our men. He could be an invaluable asset for both your country and mine."

"When will he be in contact with you again?"

"That Stryker, I do not have an answer to, though he did give us a cover name: 'The Red Chameleon'. As soon as we hear from him you will immediately be put in the frame. You must therefore be available twenty-four hours a day at a moment's notice."

"Mm. Twenty-four seven! I can handle that but it will cost you. Don't forget, I am a private detective now." Stryker gave a sombre nod of his head. "And I guess that would be Red for Russian? And the chameleon part of his epithet? This joker obviously enjoys playing games – thinks he's a master of disguises does he? Blends into the background without being noticed – sounds ominous. Anyhow, besides my being this Nemesis to avenge my good friends' deaths, why would I put my life on hold and possibly in considerable danger to work for your security service?"

"Listen carefully old boy; by working with our organisation you don't get charged with being an accessory to murder."

"And what about the owner of the vessel which took us into that danger zone; could he not be posthumously charged with being involved with their deaths? After all, he was the one who initially took us to the place where they were killed."

"I very much doubt that sir, for he was one of us before he had his throat cut – he was one of our agents."

"Oh yeah, so you intimated earlier." Stryker was caught off guard so thought about this last response to his question for all of a nanosecond. "When do we begin?"

"Well, our opening gambit is to draw this Russian fellow with a penchant for theatricality out into the open by explaining to him how the information he gave us first time around was not good enough and that we require something more tangible. If he is genuine we don't want to frighten him off by explaining that his information about the sunken freighter led to the deaths of two of our own side – of which, I hasten to add, he might or might not be aware. We just tell him it was not good enough information for us to grant him political asylum. We tell him that if he really wants to change sides and work for the West he has to supply us with something more concrete. I know it sounds awkward for him, but he'll go along with it I'm sure."

Stryker's interrogator, who had now turned into his confessor, let a moment's silence intervene. "You would be expected to carry on the work of these mates of yours by attempting to locate this would-be Russian defector."

"What about your own men – can't they do the job you require?"

"Well, of course they could, but you have something that none of our own operatives possess – you were there on the spot; first-hand knowledge of the shipwreck – that's invaluable. You tell me you even saw four faces in that dingy."

"But that means jack shit for there are probably thousands of Russian Special Forces on active service. Sure I'd recognise their faces again if I saw them but I think there is more chance of winning the Lottery because they're dead as a dodo."

"Well that's as may be, but you still saw more than any of us."

"And you've no idea where this guy who calls himself the Red Chameleon resides?"

"Mr Stryker, we are looking, but if we knew where we could contact him there wouldn't be any need for you to become involved. If you like, you should view yourself as what we call a *cut out*. That is to say, you will act as a buffer between our Secret Intelligence Service and this would-be Russian defector. The Russians will not have any background on you if you have not carried out any spying activities in their sphere of influence... you haven't, have you?" There was a long pause while Stryker digested what he now supposed was in reality an obvious question.

Stryker stared in disbelief at this middle-aged Brit with some sort of regional accent who was attempting to recruit him in a non-too-subtle way for a job on behalf of the British Security Service, before answering in the negative. He was not stupid. You do not get an invitation to work for any country's intelligence service just because you were in the vicinity of two horrific murders. He knew they had him by the balls and that if necessary they could throw him to the Russians any time they liked if it suited their purposes. No country had a monopoly on morals – even the British. He guessed life was not full of hail fellow well met people in the spying business – and that, he conjectured, is all it was to them, a business.

"You are ideal for this particular job because of your language skills and as I have already said, because you were there at the kill so to speak." Stryker gave his would-be saviour a hard look before the British secret agent ameliorated his sentence. "You are the only one who witnessed the sunken vessel and its interesting cargo and therefore we would like you to become familiar with this particular facet of biological warfare as this knowledge might somehow come in useful if the balloon goes up. So if you agree I should like to introduce you to someone whose brains you can pick regarding biological weapons of mass destruction and who will help put the things you saw below the waves on that sunken vessel's deck into some perspective."

"But as I have already told you, I'm no spy – if you really require someone from my homeland, use one of our CIA men. I'm not CIA, I'm just a run of the mill detective," Stryker broke in.

"Good try Stryker. But that's not what a certain Captain Billy Stoker, a Seattle homicide detective tells us."

"You spoke to my ex-boss?" Stryker looked dumbfounded.

"Mr Stryker, we spoke to more people than you can imagine – our American cousins for instance. They are willing to go along with our suggestion that you work with us. You see, we are closer than you might imagine; all this stuff about rifts within the two services working with one another... just aren't true. Believe me; your compatriots are as willing as we are to sort this matter out to our mutual advantage. That is why it has been sanctioned from your embassy in Grosvenor Square, London, and from Langley, Virginia. We have permission to run you as if you were one of us. And as for your working with Captain Stoker, I think you are twisting the truth slightly Mr Stryker. He tells us you are like a son to him. Vouchsafed for you – gave a glowing report, good references, all that type of thing."

"Well, I'll be... Huh. But thanks for reminding me that as I have said before I have to work for my living and therefore I would expect to be paid my usual going rate for services rendered plus expenses."

"Don't worry about that Stryker. All that will be sorted out just as soon as possible."

"So when do I get to meet this biological weapons specialist of yours?"

"You'll meet him soon enough. But first we must find you somewhere to live. However let me make it clear that on the off chance, for whatever reason we send you to Russia, it is always safer to assume you will, once inside that country, be watched by the Federal Security Bureau, formerly known as the KGB – that is Russia's Counter Intelligence Service for your information. Assumptions are not generally our stock in trade but this is the exception to that particular rule. Though for our particular business I always like to quote the saying that the one golden rule is that there are no golden rules. Anyhow, be that as it may, the one thing above all others a good secret agent requires is anonymity, the ability to merge into the background – a 'grey' person if you will, who no one would notice or look at twice. As I mentioned earlier, if it is true that you do not have any track record with the Russians then that is something in your favour. We must get you a cover story as soon as possible on the off chance, as I say, of your travelling to Russia. We will also furnish you with a new identity or legend as we call it, you know – false documentation, driving licence, job description, that sort of thing – but that will take a little time. I have one immediate surprise for you however. Just sit tight while I get someone to fetch you a cup of tea."

Stryker had not had any sleep since his disastrously impromptu diving expedition, having been escorted from the British Embassy in Dubai to London via a very uncomfortable military flight to Brize Norton, no business class travel here, just basic seating meant for soldiers and SAS forces alike, and was therefore not up for any surprises just at that particular moment. He was also no great lover of tea but couldn't be bothered to say so. The house he had been taken to was obviously somewhere in central London. On the way there the heavy traffic had been very noisy but this house, or at least this particular room he was now sitting in, had double glazing because you could hear a pin drop. He assumed this soundproofing was to assist the concealed microphones' delivery of a good quality reproduction of his conversation with the security man who had been introduced to him as Noel, but to Stryker's ears sounded very much like Know All which perhaps was nearer the truth than it might have at first appeared.

As Stryker re-ran the last twenty-four hours through his head there was a particularly sharp knock on the sturdy wood-panelled door. The question of who gasped first was discussed over dinner at some length later that evening. Stryker insisting that she was the last person in the world he had been expecting to set eyes upon. But the old familiar greeting – "My favourite American hunk," came as no surprise – she had always said things like that.

And for Stryker one particular phrase sprung into his mind and as quickly translated to his lips: "My sweet Patootie!"

***

"I expect it was as much a surprise for you as it was for me," said Caroline Lambton, a tall girl with intelligent eyes and light chestnut-coloured hair framing an angelic looking face. Slim, fit and barely out of her teens she stared into Stryker's deep blue eyes. "I just did not connect the surname Truman with you. Of course they knew all about our relationship," she murmured with a coy look, "otherwise I suppose I should not have been asked to accompany you to Hampstead to show you this flat. Just been vacated by another spook. Posted abroad I guess. Mind you, the powers that be never *actually* tell you anything like that. Would you like a chocolate? After dinner liqueurs, they're very good – I adore them – my favourite!"

Stryker explained that he was not a 'spook' as she very well knew, declining the chocolate as Caroline set to work on the complementary pound box found on top of the sideboard and settling herself into one of the comfortable armchairs opposite the detective by kicking off her shoes and furling her long legs beneath her. "From my limited experience this box was not left here by chance by the last occupant you know. Once a place is vacated the special cleaning mobs go through the abode with a fastidiousness most employers would envy. I'd recommend them to Mummy if they were not so hush-hush." Caroline laughed. "You knew Dad was a scientist didn't you? I assumed you knew that, being a private dick." Stryker ignored the jibe about his being a private dick, disregarding her childish attempt at humour.

"Yes, of course I knew your dad was a scientist, but I didn't know Doctor... err... Professor Lambton was Deputy Director General of the government agency at Porton Down – that's the place that deals with Biological and Chemical Warfare weapons isn't it?"

"You're spot on there, Stryker. But don't worry about that this evening... this evening is for us – to catch up. I hope you like pasta because that is what I'm cooking for you. It's one of my speciality dishes. I'll be introducing you to Daddy soon enough. That's what I've been instructed to do by those people we dare not mention." Here Caroline gave a sweet girlish laugh reminiscent of a peal of bells. She was so much younger when Stryker had last set eyes upon her while studying languages at one of the Oxbridge colleges, and now she had grown from a runner bean of a girl into a very attractive young woman in her early twenties. To Stryker's mind she could very well have been a model straight out of one of those top fashion magazines – slim and slinky – which is what she had in fact been. "When Mummy divorced Daddy and married your Uncle Richard... well, you know how I felt about that don't you? And then after it all fell apart I just wanted to disappear forever because that was the second time Mummy had screwed up her life – and mine." Here she gave Stryker a meaningful look.

Stryker was not in the right frame of mind to listen to his uncle's former stepdaughter going on about family affairs when he had far more important things to worry about. Neither was he over the moon about her innuendoes regarding her non-existent relationship with himself.

"Years ago I used to tell Mummy she should have married someone like you instead of your uncle. Of course I'm a lot older now so the situation has changed."

"Situation?"

"Well, that's what I'd call it anyway. As I say, I was just a kid then."

"And of course you're all grown up now."

"Well aren't I?"

"I'm not going to argue with that."

Stryker attempted to change the subject. "Do you still live at home Caroline?"

Carol smiled broadly. "You know you're the only person who ever called me Caroline. All my friends call me Carol. But no – I have a place close to where you were initially taken this morning. It's in Pimlico – moved in just a couple of weeks ago actually. Living at home with Mummy didn't matter when I was a fashion model because I was never at home anyway. It's a standing joke between us that whilst living at home I was also flying to Rome, Milan, and I suppose halfway around the world to all those dreamy locations as well. Don't like Pimlico much though, bit of a dump to be honest." Then as an afterthought she added… "But it's cheap – though the money doesn't matter because I made so much working as a model you wouldn't believe. I'm financially secure for the rest of my life so my accountant tells me." She had a cut-glass English accent, like one of those actresses in old British movies, very upper class. But what would Stryker know about that? "Do you know what Mummy told me us Brits said about Americans during the Second World War?" This last sentence took Stryker by surprise, coming straight out of the blue.

"No! But I'm sure you are going to enlighten me."

"Well, during the war when so many of you were over here helping with the war effort the British people said, to quote Mummy: 'They're overpaid, oversexed and over here.' So which are you Stryker?"

"Well, if we really have to play this silly game, I'd say I'm definitely over here as you can see."

"And that's it? What about the other two things?"

"O.K. I'm definitely not overpaid and I'm definitely not overwhelmed at being coerced into being here. It's a shame as you say," he carried on, attempting to change the subject "that you don't like where you live." Stryker felt happy that he had made at least a modicum of an attempt at empathising with Carol's housing situation.

"The S.I.S., and that, if you don't know, it means Britain's Secret Intelligence Service, keep safe houses around that area for just such an eventuality as yours, and also a few staff flats, or condos as they say in your funny American lingo."

Stryker frowned. "Shouldn't this sort of information be kept… well… secret?"

"Oh, it's alright Stryker; I'm part of the organisation too, don't forget. I might only be a rookie as they say in the States, but being a probationer with MI6 I am covered by the official secrets act as much as you are which I hear you were coerced into signing before anything of real importance was explained to you. Isn't that right?"

"You're dead right Carol," Stryker replied, making his uncle's stepdaughter smile at his newly truncated version of her name. The Seattle detective was also smiling, but his amusement was unfortunately at her dress sense, he not being able to equate a bona fide member of the British spy service with the outrageous silk lime green suit coupled with floppy black hat and elongated black jade earrings dancing about her face as she gesticulated in her inimitable way when conversing with him.

"Would you not take just one of these delicious chocolates? I simply adore them."

"No thank you. Not keen on them. I'm rather curious though as to why if those chocolates were as you say, not left here by chance, why my recruiters should possibly think that I might be given a box of them."

"Oh Stryker, you really are naive. Those chocolates were not left here by chance as I said," Carol laughed, "because I myself was asked by the Department to buy some little token to make you feel at home."

Stryker smiled. It was the first time since setting foot in England that he truly felt at ease with himself, remembering just what he had been missing in his home town of Seattle. It was the little jovial things like this which made the world seem a much better place. But he began to wonder just how much Carol knew about the task he had been assigned, and at the same time wondered if she knew about the gruesome circumstances which had led to him being coerced into working for the Brits. He figured she must have been taken into their confidence for after all, was it not her dad, Professor Lambton, who was going to explain to him the wonders of biological warfare which might help put into perspective what he had seen lashed to the deck of that sunken cargo ship in the Persian Gulf, and which might also be of assistance in leading him to the scientist whose shared compass reference was, however unwitting, instrumental in the killing of his two buddies? Carol's next sentence answered his unspoken doubts about both things.

"Stryker, I'm so sorry you lost two of your friends in such a horrific manner. It makes my skin creep. But as I told that stuffy Mr Hughes from Six, if anyone can locate this Russian chap, you can." Stryker hoped Caroline's faith in him was not misplaced, knowing that if it was in his power he would obviously be only too happy to avenge his two buddies' deaths. His seeming reluctance to become involved was because he had an aversion to being coerced into anything. He watched her sashaying in the green silk figure-hugging outfit toward what he took to be the kitchen as if she was on a catwalk modelling the latest designer outfit. Then moments later her head popped into view again from the doorway.

"This lipstick – is it too red? I bought it just today. Tell me the truth Stryker, is it?"

Stryker looked at Carol and also wondered why she had taken a job with the British SIS. "What's the attraction Carol? Why join a mob like the British Secret Service?"

"Well, like you Stryker, I have more than one language to my name and the Service like linguists. I did modern languages at university. They also said that I have other attributes." Then she gave that girlish laugh once more, adding archly, "I can't think what they meant by that, can you?"

CHAPTER 4

The flight on Aeroflot, the Russian state-owned airline, from Moscow's Sheremetyevo International Airport to London Heathrow had still not taken off and the passengers were becoming restless. They had been sitting on the runway for over an hour and there had not been any communication between the crew and their fare paying charges. Along each row of seats the same antics were being played out; feet shuffling back and forth in the limited leg room, handkerchiefs constantly removed from pockets and handbags, dabbing at perspiration from around their faces and necks, then being replaced in frustration.

The air inside the aircraft was stale and becoming hotter with every minute that passed. Eventually, one and a half hours after boarding the aeroplane, instructions came to fasten seatbelts. Everybody was by now feeling frantic, wondering why there had been such a long delay. There was however one passenger who appeared unperturbed.

It was a Russian by the name of Anatoly Grachev. He was lost deep in his thoughts. Time at this moment meant nothing to him. Dr Anatoly Grachev, to give him his full title, was a Russian scientist. He had been a communist all his life, but now communism had been destroyed and his security with it. He worked at the top secret research institute, Biomedico, just a few kilometres north of Moscow, dealing with what might possibly be classified as some of the most virulent of killers: modified bacteria and viruses. Now his job was on the line.

Working at the secret Biological Germ Warfare Unit as a microbiologist and geneticist as well as being something of a force to be reckoned with in the world of epidemiology, operating under the auspices of the Soviet state pharmaceutical agency Biopreparat, like many other research scientists in so-called civilised countries, his task was to create microorganisms so powerful that they would have the power to kill millions of people by infecting them with disease.

Russian bombs had already been designed with the sole purpose of replacing nuclear weapon warheads on Intercontinental Ballistic Missiles. These bombs would break open in mid-air and using sophisticated aerosol delivery systems, shower chosen populations with an invisible and more often than not, undetectable, fine mist of deadly organisms. Although Russia had consistently denied at the highest political level over the years

21

any such research of this nature, this was in fact a lie and had remained a lie.

In late 1989, a very senior Russian scientist named Pasechnik, director of a secret research institute directly linked with the biological warfare company Biopreparat, went on a scientific trip to Paris, ostensibly accepting an invitation to visit a pharmaceutical company there. Within days of arriving in Paris he had fled to England as a defector. Within months of Pasechnik being debriefed by the British and American security services and their learning of the aggressive and illegal nature of the Soviet Union's biological warfare programme, a joint Anglo-American scientific delegation, at the reluctant invitation of Moscow, visited some of the sites in the Soviet Union where they suspected the 1972 Biological Weapons Convention, which actually came into force on 26th March 1975, was being deliberately ignored. In 1990, when Glasnost – openness – was in full swing and the Soviet Block was in its death throes, Moscow, on the orders of Mikhail Sergeyevich Gorbachev, had artfully convinced the West that only defensive biological research allowed within the treaty had been carried out. The United States and Britain gave the Russians the benefit of the doubt. Then in October 1992 another Russian defector, this time to America, had explained that a huge programme of producing and stockpiling biological weapons was continuing, even under the guise of a new relationship with the West. This defector's name was Dr Kanatjan Alibekov.

In September 1992, a month before Alibekov become a defector, Russia had once again signed yet another agreement with America and Britain to put an end to its biological warfare capabilities. This agreement had been pre-empted when Yeltsin signed an internal decree in April six months earlier, banning offensive biological weapons. This decree from the highest, the most powerful person in the Soviet Union related to the Biological Germ Warfare Unit where Dr Anatoly Grachev worked. The orders were to close down the research programme. Russia wanted money and other assistance badly and had to dance to the tune of the Western leaders if it was going to be able to carry on with the democratic reforms started by Gorbachev, such as Glasnost – *open government* and Perestroika – *restructuring of the political and economic system* – as first suggested by Leonid Brezhnev in 1979. Gorbachev had resigned in August 1991 after the failure of an attempted coup against him. The reform programme was then taken over by Boris Yeltsin who succeeded Gorbachev, thereby assisting the top Russian echelon to stay in power.

Quite why there was any more belief in this recent 1992 agreement with Moscow than there had been in the old one – Biological Weapons Convention, signed on 10 April 1972 – will never be known. This 1972 convention signed in Moscow, Washington and London, which was intended to ban the acquisition of biological weapons, although not banning the possession of equipment for producing them, led to Britain and America naively destroying their biological warfare stocks whilst Russia reneged on the agreement to stop working on these offensive weapons of mass destruction and actually stepped up production. Thus this convention, in retrospect, turned out to be not worth the paper it was written on. At the end of the day it had obviously been a very bad political decision for the signatory countries in Washington and London which now had dire consequences for the whole world.

As opposed to this flouting by the Russians of the Biological Weapons Convention however, it had been fortunate indeed that the 1972 US-Soviet anti-ballistic missile treaty had stood the test of time and become the raison d'être of subsequent arms control agreements.

It was against this pervasive backdrop of suspicion, traitors and spies that Dr Grachev found himself working under in early April 1993, nearly a year and a half after the sudden collapse of the Communist regime and for whom, it seemed, time was running out. His Institute had dragged its heels over the past year with regard to the decree aimed at closing down its biological weapons facility but the excuses put forward of technical problems relating to its shutdown could not delay its demise forever. It had not been easy for Dr Grachev to get where he was and he now felt a grievance toward the West.

In the last five years Dr Grachev had travelled widely, attending scientific conferences in Europe and America, he being trusted to a degree other Soviet citizens could have only dreamed about. However, this situation was beginning to change. Because of the two Russian high ranking scientific defectors to Britain and America respectively, and Dr Grachev's high security risk status relating to top secret work on biological warfare, on two recent occasions he had been strip searched and x-rayed at the airport and the scientific papers he carried were meticulously gone through, *before* leaving Russia. Nevertheless he had put up with these indignities without complaint so that he could continue to enjoy the privileged lifestyle which he had carved out for himself by his own industry. He had made many acquaintances in the global scientific community, but now Dr Grachev felt the Western Powers were unwittingly destroying his career by leaning on the Russians to stop his and his colleagues' research work. He visualised his whole scientific life crumbling away. To him, that was not an option he was willing to tolerate.

Yet he had ambivalent feelings toward the West. He loved the Russian culture and scientific achievements which he felt in many ways were far superior to the Western states. But he also knew that the generation of computers in his country had for years lagged behind that of Britain and

23

America. There again, he felt proud of his country – proud that Russia had been the first country to put an object into orbit around the earth: Sputnik. That had been the greatest triumph of mankind, opening up the way for Yuri Gagarin and all the other cosmonauts in the wake of that triumph. Now, following the demise of communism and with it the prospect of losing his coveted job, Dr Grachev was at a crossroads in his life. It appeared that if he was to attain a lifestyle commensurate with his own scientific achievements, he must flee the country of his forefathers to begin a new life in the West. For him that was unequivocal.

Travel, as the saying goes, broadens the mind, but to Dr Grachev it meant much more; it had wetted his appetite for the good things in life. Yet he felt torn between the spiritual and the material, feeling in many ways that the West was morally bankrupt. Though who was he to speak of morals? Had he not been working on the most infectious, the most deadly bacteria known to man – anthrax, and plague? Was he not also modifying strains of virus which were invisible to the naked eye, such as Ebola and smallpox that in very small doses had the capability to kill, scar and blind millions of people in the most horrific and terrifying way ever conceived by man? Was he not offering the possibility of such suffering on an unimaginably massive scale never before seen on Earth?

This type of rhetorical argument had been well rehearsed over many months and now he had finally made up his mind. A new leader of the Soviet Union had recently emerged in the form of Boris Yeltsin, and events and changes were moving faster than ever in a country that had been under the stifling yoke of ideology for too long. Who knew how events would turn out in the turmoil of upheaval now taking hold of the country?

He was a pragmatist. The defector to America must have given everything he knew to the Americans, but even he didn't know what Dr Grachev and his unwitting team had been working on. And not only working on, but what he, Dr Grachev, thanks to the co-operation with the Chinese working in the field of xenogeneic research dealing with human tissue and cell implants, was now on the verge of actually bringing to fruition. It was not too dramatic to claim that because of its special characteristics, his breakthrough with the virus upon which he had been working would change the whole nature of warfare forever, and only he had the knowledge to reveal its inner secrets.

Dr Grachev was also only a mere matter of months away from being able to produce a potent sample of the killer virus – and though only a sample, a sample nevertheless. And it would be a live sample. The challenge for him was that he had just a few months remaining to put his plan into operation before his research facilities were closed down and therefore time was running out. Once he had produced this living sample, it would be used as a bargaining chip, a passport to a new life in the West. It would be a good life where he was respected, which he felt he had never truly been in his own country. Hopefully he would be able to convince the authorities, once safely inside his country of choice, that they should fund his work as a research scientist so that he could continue to pursue his career, except that he would be free of the fear and petty restrictions that one suffered in Russia. And freedom, the antithesis of the Soviet political system, was in essence what it all essentially boiled down to.

The one seemingly insurmountable problem to be solved was how, once Dr Grachev had produced such a sample of this specially constructed, highly contagious and lethal virus, would he be able to smuggle it out of the country? If he were caught trying to smuggle such a valuable military scientific breakthrough out to the West he would spend the rest of his life rotting away in some Siberian labour camp, at the very least; more likely he would be shot as a traitor. And the State security police might very well find anything he attempted to hide on himself as he fled to freedom, because of the now very real possibility of being subjected to a strip search and x-rayed at the airport as had happened recently before letting him leave the country.

Because of these fairly recent defections of the Russian scientists – Pasechnik who had defected to England and Dr Kanatjan Alibekov who had defected to America – the Russian organs of the state responsible for such security matters were now becoming more paranoid by the day and determined that no further secrets should flow out to the West. Superficially the old order of communism may have collapsed but the KGB – superseded in 1991 by the Russian post-Soviet Foreign Intelligence Service, now known as SVR or *Sluzhba Razvedki,* were as ruthless as ever when guarding its state secrets.

Making contact with someone through one of the Western Embassies also posed its own problems for Dr Grachev, a life and death risk as he saw it because of being constantly followed by the FSB – Russia's internal Counter Intelligence Service operatives, or members of the GRU, the Soviet arm of Military Intelligence. And even if Dr Grachev did succeed in Moscow in passing his sample virus on to someone from the West, how could he trust them not to leave him in Russia whilst they exploited his discovery? Even worse, what if they got caught with the virus before they could spirit it out of Russia? He was not prepared to place his life in the hands of someone within his own country whom he didn't even know. No, once he had his viral sample, he would have to work out an ingenious and fool proof way of spiriting it out of Russia without incurring too many risks. Although risks would undoubtedly have to be taken, they would have to be calculated to the nth degree.

Dr Grachev's thoughts drifted back to when he had just turned twenty. A fresh faced young man strolling through a park in Minsk. It was early summer and the midday sun was filtering through the tall pine trees. However, the delights of summer was the last thing this young man was concentrating on at that particular moment, for along the narrow track up ahead of him was a group of men, badly dressed even by Russian standards. His pace slowed as he drew close like a moth toward a flame, but he could not, would not change his course.

There were about ten of them of similar age to Grachev, but he could see they had nothing in common with him; they were like a band of wild animals with feral looks upon their faces. As he approached and attempted to pass he was surrounded. Out of pure instinct, self-preservation, he walked up to the one immediately facing him and taking his adversary by surprise, punched out hard, his fist making perfect contact with the youth's stubbled chin. As Grachev's would-be attacker's body hit the hard dirt track, and before his adversary's friends could do anything, the young scientist had leapt over the motionless figure, fleeing as fast as he could. He did not stop running until he arrived back at the university campus where he was studying.

"Anatoly, why are you so out of breath?" one of his colleagues had called out as he staggered in the direction of the lecture rooms.

"Oh, it's nothing," he answered falteringly.

That particular event had lodged like a thorn in his mind, becoming a turning point in his life. It engendered within him a strong sense of self-belief and confidence which no amount of adversity had been able to destroy in the intervening years.

As a young man Anatoly Grachev had been a very serious student and he liked nothing better than to be studying the laws of physics. He loved science and knew Einstein's Theory of Relativity off by heart when he was just ten years old. He also knew of Einstein's mentor, Russian-born German mathematician Professor Hermann Minkowski, Einstein's one-time tutor and inspiration for his Theory of Relativity, Einstein using Minkowski's mathematical description of space-time as part of that now world renowned hypothesis. Grachev was what is known as a child prodigy and already had one degree to his name by the time he was fifteen. This was in Biology. At the time of this incident in the park he had been at the tail end of a degree in Chemistry and Molecular Biology and everyone knew he would come top of his year as he always did.

Now, years later, as his career was being threatened, he knew he would beat anyone or anything that stood in his way and put the life he had created for himself in jeopardy, just as he had beaten the odds of getting out of that circle of hooligans. And once again there was only one way of accomplishing that feat, and that meant doing it solo. He saw himself as someone only too happy to face the challenge of an uncertain and dangerous situation on his own, in other words, what would have been described by his old university colleagues studying psychology as a philobat. What his colleagues at university would not and could not have known was that he also had a latent tendency towards another psychological term – psychopath.

CHAPTER 5

"Mr Smith, would you like to follow me." It was a command rather than a request, but either way it was totally ignored by the person it had been aimed at. The grey-haired middle-aged woman, who gave more than a passing impression of a determined looking man in a dark brown suit repeated the command a second time with an air of irritation in her voice, before the penny dropped and Stryker responded to his new name given him by the MI6 powers that be, this time quickly rousing himself from his reverie.

MI6 operated out of sumptuous postmodern offices at Vauxhall Cross, situated on the south side of the River Thames adjacent to Vauxhall bridge, a building known by its detractors as Ceausescu Towers if the people who operated within its interior were old enough to remember the deposed tyrannical communist president of Rumania, presumably because of its high profile, pretentious grand scale and kitsch exterior. An architectural oxymoron because of the top secret work carried on behind its theatrical façade – younger members of the secret service called it 'Legoland'. But it was not the architecture that Stryker had been dwelling upon as he waited for yet another briefing regarding his forthcoming undercover work.

Stryker had been re-christened Smith for the sake of his fledgling spying activities and was now in possession of a new meticulously created identity to cover him should he ever travel to Russia, including a bona fide passport which had been especially produced for him, his legend describing him as a dealer in Russian icons. To this end private lectures had been laid on regarding the finer points of this subject together with his being tutored as to what to watch out for when dealing in such precious objects. This tutoring included visits to museums, galleries and specialist salons dealing in such artworks as well as trips to churches and auction houses so as to sound like an expert if or when engaged in conversation regarding his specialist knowledge of Russian icons, a mantle he was beginning to wear with some aplomb. But Stryker had still to be introduced to Carol's father, professor Lambton, for instruction as promised, on the much deadlier art of biological warfare.

There was a lot to learn and he had not as yet exploited his new identity, though there had been an opportunity on the preceding Friday night, but on that particular occasion he had retained his own name. Even so, unexpected consequences would flow from this episode at the London based Russian Orthodox Church.

*****

Carrying his small flickering candle around the boundary of the Cathedral Church of the Russian Orthodox Church in London's Ennismore Gardens, Knightsbridge, he had felt spiritually uplifted, and why not? Surely that was what religion was all about. He was not what one might call a proselyte, being a non-believer as he was, but Stryker reasoned that did not preclude him from indulging in such practices as attending a Russian Orthodox Easter service.

It might have been the beautiful singing. It may have been the intoxicating perfumed incense released from the censer in the form of puffy white clouds swirling around the altar, reminiscent of some great Renaissance painting, but whatever it was, he felt moved. More than once Stryker had spoken of the spiritual strength he had derived from attending this particular service and which he believed could only be fully appreciated if one were fluent in the language.

He enjoyed the ritual of the Russian Orthodox Church, especially at this time of the religious calendar. He also had that perception that there was not the cant and hypocrisy in this church as there was in some of the other persuasions. The service in the Orthodox Church had not changed for over two thousand years and he liked the idea of that – a sense of stability in a very unstable world. And Stryker knew, being a detective from Seattle, more than most just how unstable that world was.

The icons and tradition filled him with awe. The altar with its precious religious objects and the congregation's chanted response in Russian to the Easter greeting:

"Khristos Voskresye." – 'Christ is risen."

"Vo Istinu Voskresye." – "He is indeed," – echoing around the high ceilinged church, giving him a sense in a spiritual, and yes, an emotional manner, of being closer to God – of being wrapped up in this metaphysically protective shroud.

What his newly acquired bosses in the British Secret Intelligence Service would have thought of one of their agents – even if only an agent on a temporary basis – attending a Russian Orthodox service, he shuddered to think. They would probably choke on their vintage port at the Athenaeum club. But he needed the freedom to believe in the things which appealed to him and not have to follow some rule book which told him that because he was fighting the enemy he shouldn't take on board some of their culture, no matter how valid that culture was. He had also used the Russian church service in Seattle to keep up old contacts and cultivate new ones, but then that was his particular game and it had proved useful on more than one occasion. Here in England he actually began to feel he was defending freedom, and yet he was far from free himself. Stryker still chafed at the pressure brought to bear so as to keep him working for the Brits with the implicit threat of being charged with his two buddies' deaths hanging over him. Sometimes he would ponder on such irony and chuckle loudly to himself. Yes, tonight, he thought, would be the start of a new beginning. At the time he did not realise just how perceptive that thought would prove to be and how his visit to this seemingly benign institution would presage such unforeseen consequences.

As Stryker walked cautiously around the outside of the building, cupping his large left hand over the symbolic tiny bright flame so as to shield it from the stiffening breeze, and following in the footsteps of others in the congregation who carried venerable icons depicting the many saints who played such an important role at this august ceremony, he became aware of a voice with a deep, heavy accent enquiring as to whether he might re-light his wind extinguished candle from Stryker's. After obliging his newfound acquaintance, Stryker continued to be jostled around the church perimeter by a congregation of a few thousand, most managing to keep their candles burning brightly in the dark. The symbolism illuminated the darkness and minds of the congregation in such a dramatic way that to Stryker nothing else could quite match it.

The Easter service finished at three thirty in the early hours of the morning and Stryker anticipated a clear run back to Belsize Park, Hampstead, where his newly acquired condominium awaited his arrival. Slowly emerging with the crowds of other worshippers he felt a light tap on the shoulder as he was about to climb into his other new acquisition – his pride and joy. The car was a bright red Morgan in daylight, but in the street's halogen lighting it appeared the colour of purple.

"I'm sorry to trouble you again, but do you know where I can pick up a taxi? My name is Anatoly. Dr Anatoly Grachev."

"Everyone calls me Stryker," the detective replied. "Where are you headed for?"

"Well, I'm checked in at the Normanhurst Hotel on Park Lane. Are you an Englander?"

Stryker baulked at the suggestion but played along with the idea as it appealed to his sense of mischievousness. "English, why yes, yes I am. But the hotel is on my way. Hop in and I'll give you a lift."

"Thanks, that's very kind of you." As Dr Grachev spoke, Stryker noticed the doctor could not avert his eyes from Stryker's tiny imperceptible facial scar. For some inexplicable reason he bridled at the Russian's insensitivity.

"Does this bother you?" Stryker enquired, pointing to his cheek.

"No, no my friend, I am sorry. As I told you I am a doctor, to me it is nothing. I was just admiring the virtually invisible scar; almost certainly metal stitches were used – very neat, very impressive."

On the short journey ferrying Dr Grachev back to his hotel, Stryker discovered that they had a common passion for chess, both great admirers of Gary Weinstein, now better known as Gary Kasparov who dethroned another Soviet Union world champion Anatoli Karpov, to become the youngest ever world chess champion at the tender age of twenty-two. Dr Grachev also professed to be something of an Anglophile. He then posed the very obvious question as to why an Englishman should attend an Orthodox Church service. Stryker replied that beside the fact that this particular religion appealed to his innate sense of history and theological leanings, he was also a businessman who frequently spent time in Moscow, and so the service also helped him brush up on his Russian accent. This final piece of the explanation was in fact a complete fabrication, for Stryker's mastery of the Russian language was second to none, quite often having been taken as a Russian national. After dropping his newfound friend off at the hotel he mused on the fact that Dr Grachev had requested his telephone number.

"To return your favour we'll get together sometime to have a drink. By the way, I admire your choice of transport." Those were Dr Grachev's final words as Stryker watched him walk off in the direction of the hotel entrance hall, the back of his head bearing a distinctive birthmark in his hair in the form of a tiny white cross. *How fitting*, Stryker thought, having just made the acquaintance of his newly acquired Russian friend within the precincts of a church.

Driving home in the darkness, Stryker turned the conversation with the Russian doctor over in his mind. He had learnt that Dr Grachev was thirty-five, being seven years older than himself, and that he was attending a conference on genetics here in England at Imperial College, London University. Dr Grachev was only slightly taller than Stryker but of a skinny disposition. He was also very friendly.

Climbing out of the Morgan after pulling up at his basement flat in Hampstead, Stryker raised his head to the sky, now beginning to show the first glimmer of light as a grey stain spread slowly over London. Within a minute he would be ensconced within the cosy confines of his pied-à-terre, concentrating on his more immediate requirements, a mug of coffee laced with a liberal measure of rum to bring the warmth back into his frozen limbs. There was just one thing to do before that. He raised his head above the railings to the street and noticed that the small black car that had been trailing him all the way from the Russian Orthodox Church service in Ennismore Gardens had now disappeared. It did not matter though, for Stryker had its licence number engraved firmly in his memory.

Opening the basement street door to his flat, Stryker quickly entered so as to get out of the cold, walked through the lobby into the sitting room before tossing his jacket over the back of one of the armchairs and made his way quickly into the darkened bedroom. That is when he saw all the stars in the firmament light up as in a brilliant firework display.

CHAPTER 6

For Dr Anatoly Grachev this was the second scientific conference he had attended in London within the past six months. His host in November had been Imperial College, part of the University of London. This present conference, like the one in November, held a very special interest for the scientist because its subject matter related to genetics, and that he regarded as his baby. He was also a regular visitor to the conference on genetics held at the University of Washington in Seattle and the one held in Venice. He had once even been to a symposium in the Caribbean. The organisers certainly knew where to set these things up. The cuisine was usually of the highest standard, and why not? These were important people. He was important. He knew this and he let it be known to others. He was not exactly arrogant but had a certain way with people below his own perceived intelligence, and that unfortunately, was most people. To coin a favourite phrase of his, one he had pinched from the English and never tired of using was, "I do not suffer fools gladly."

The hotel food in other countries certainly beat the usual fare at Dr Grachev's own scientific institute back in Moscow. It was true that he ate in a separate dining room from the main canteen. A carpeted area where there were white linen tablecloths instead of the regulation red plastic Formica. There was even waitress service, the waitresses being dressed soberly in black dresses and showing due deference by speaking in hushed tones, but the food was the same – mediocre.

Travelling abroad always made him feel good, a man of the world. A man to be respected at the many conferences he graced with his presence. Not so with his colleagues. One of the few things in life he could not fathom out was why no one at the Institute actually liked him. He worked hard, that could not be disputed. He was the one who could always be relied upon to come up with a brilliant solution to a problem regarding his scientific work. Had he not had more papers published over the last four years than any other member of the Institute? Yet he felt an outsider just the same. This may well have been just because of his success with having so much of his work published – that is the nature of the beast – jealousy. He suspected that. He was respected, yes, but it was a respect for his work, not for himself. He knew it, his colleagues knew it, and he did not like it.

Dr Grachev's special subject, that of genetic engineering, had worked in his favour for some years now, because unbeknown to the West, a secret pact of mutual co-operation between the two most powerful communist countries in the world, the Soviet Union and China, included within its remit the science of genetics, which for Dr Grachev meant the opportunity to extend his knowledge of the subject. The recent techniques garnered from the Chinese, who were now light years ahead of the West with regard to manipulating DNA, the so-called building blocks of life, had been invaluable in his particular field of research.

His most brilliant colleagues could not conceive that the possibilities of marrying together the two sciences he had been working on for so many years, that of Genetic Engineering and Biochemistry in relation to Biological Warfare, had been carried out by Dr Grachev in such a seamless way that the jigsaw constructed within his mind of creating a super new biological bomb, comparable in its outcome in many ways to the American Manhattan Project, which had led to the detonation of the first ever nuclear weapon, was near completion.

Yet even as Dr Grachev dared hope he had found the missing piece of that jigsaw as an outcome of his regular visits to Beijing, the truth was that holding onto it without declaring its significance, like some recalcitrant child who did not want to share all his toys, served his purpose well. He was on the threshold of discovering a key he likened to opening Pandora's Box, a key able to release a pandemic of truly unimaginable proportions onto mankind and Dr Grachev very definitely wanted to keep that key for himself. Not for Mother Russia, his homeland, not for China, but for himself. It was his secret breakthrough and he intended to keep it that way. He knew the secret of success. Knowledge is power and he knew he could trade on that knowledge.

Being a geneticist as well as an expert on the science of biological weapons made him something of a unique one man band, and that was one of the reasons why so many of his colleagues held him in such high esteem. However, Professor Anton Cherenkov, chief scientist at Biomedico, did not share the same feelings toward Dr Grachev, his protégé and second in command at the Institute.

These disjointed thoughts vied with one another shortly after Dr Grachev had been dropped off at his hotel in the early hours of the morning by his newly acquired friend Stryker after attending the all-night Orthodox Easter vigil.

CHAPTER 7

MOSCOW

It was much colder in Moscow than in England and the day was fading into night. Darkness was fast encroaching as the cafés, restaurants and bars began to fill up for their evening trade. The antiquarian bookshop was situated in the Ulitsa Arbat, a street branching off the Arbat proper, a renowned tourist area in the middle of the city.

A dim yellow luminosity spilt from antiquated light bulbs, looking as if they were pre-revolutionary, in the vain hope of illuminating aged books lying on dust-lined wooden shelves reaching up to the ceiling, lending the place an air of genteel decay. A musty odour of decomposing paper foxed with age clogged the nostrils and grabbed the throat. To add to this suffocating atmosphere of times long past was a distinguished looking gentleman, well into his eighties. He possessed a flowing mane of white hair touching his stooped shoulders and a pair of pince-nez glasses perched precariously upon an eagle-like nose, lending him the appearance of a distinguished elderly academic, which indeed he was, or rather had been, at the University of Moscow. Now, long after having been retired against his wishes he was doing what he liked best, spending his remaining years with the books which had sustained him all through his youth and adulthood. Through the turbulent years of the early twentieth century and the frightening decades of Stalinist and post-Stalinist rule.

In the summer months the bookshop was busy with many tourists and locals alike but now the steady stream had dwindled to a trickle, the occasional visitor bringing half the snow filled street in with them, leaving trails of slush between the many wooden cabinets. It was behind one of these cabinets that a young man with yellow tousled hair stood browsing, occasionally surreptitiously examining his watch. He looked every inch the English gentleman in his Burberry raincoat and tweed jacket peeping from beneath the collar. His brown Brogue shoes appeared out of place in the inclement weather he had just trudged through to be here – he also looked every inch the foreigner.

As the Englishman stood scanning the books in front of him, the white-haired elderly gentleman walked through the now deserted shop and closed the sturdy door, sliding a large metal bolt across from the inside, giving it an obligatory tug to make sure it was locked securely. Moving behind the counter adjacent to the entrance, he furtively reached down and extricated a small leather bound book by Mikhail Lermontov. Then disappearing out of sight of prying eyes he proffered it to the tall, fair-haired young man who was still concealed behind the bookshelves. The elderly scholar spoke with a stilted English accent and phraseology garnered from some ancient tuition recordings of spoken English.

"How are you my good man...? Page one, one, and one." These were the somewhat archaic and cryptic words muttered under his breath as the old scholar handed over the small novel without looking up into the clear complexioned face inset with pale blue eyes staring down at him. When this instruction had been passed on they both self-consciously moved away from one another without another word being spoken and again, without acknowledging one another at all, whereupon the pitted metal door bolt was once again drawn back, emitting a muffled screeching noise, letting the young man out of the shop tightly clutching his newly acquired possession. As he moved out into the snow-lined street he gazed at the gold embossed spine: *A Hero of our Time.* The young man grinned wryly as he made his way on foot back to the embassy, thinking how nice it would be if he were on holiday in Scotland from where this particular novelist's ancestors had hailed, instead of working incognito as second in command under the British Embassy station chief here in Moscow. That said, no matter what guise he worked under, the one trait he could not change was that half-forgotten quintessential Englishness of manners, imbued at an early age, perhaps at boarding school, but which he now trailed around the world as he worked undercover like some favourite battered old suitcase. It was a touchstone or point of reference to be adhered to with unswerving loyalty, an ambassador of the old public school system.

It was the only novel Mikhail Yurevich Lermontov had ever published, all his other works having been in a poetic vein. But the story Lermontov had penned was of no particular concern for the embassy official who had so carefully turned the pages until, as the elderly scholar in the bookshop had instructed, he reached page one hundred and eleven. It took a little more time, meticulously searching with an outsize magnifying glass, before he found what he had been searching for. Carefully, with the aid of an eye dropper and a steady hand bestowed by a youthful aspect, a special solution was released upon what until then would have been construed as a full stop terminating one of Lermontov's beautifully constructed sentences. This piece of material, known as a microdot, would soon be enlarged to that of an A4 sized sheet of paper, upon which was a mass of information detailing the secret location and designated areas of a factory tagged with the abbreviation ES 205. Anthony Lovejoy-Taylor was feeling elated, thinking he deserved a pat on the back for another successful mission completed. It was always easier when working out of the British Embassy under the umbrella of diplomatic cover, feeling safer beneath the guise of his diplomatic status. *Out of harm's way*, he thought to himself; a piece of cake – a doddle.

CHAPTER 8

To expect the unexpected had been Stryker's mantra since being conscripted into the American armed forces and then afterwards, when he had joined the Seattle police force and the maxim had served him well – until now. His misplaced confidence through occupying a basement flat, paid for as it was by the British Secret Intelligence Service, had lent him a greater sense of security than would otherwise have been expected, and through this fact he had committed the unforgivable sin of ignoring his own advice. Thus he now found himself in a situation which appeared to him both acutely embarrassing to his professional training as well as his privacy. From where he now lay he was able to contemplate this unfortunate event at his leisure – or at least for as long as it would take for his head wound to heal and concussion to subside. And yet in a way the situation he now found himself in was none of his doing, not even in fact a premeditated act of vengeance from those who might have wished to see him in such circumstances. The situation had arisen, as he was now slowly beginning to learn from Caroline, through her own, and solely her own machinations and could therefore be laid firmly at her door – or to be more precise – Stryker being laid out cold at the foot of his own bed. Though even this final statement was moot for at the time of the happening Carol had been the one occupying it.

Had it not been for Carol's overweening thoughts upon superstitious nonsense, to Stryker's mind at least, he would not now be propped up in his own bed, relinquished, it must be said, by its previous occupant with surprising alacrity and philanthropic aplomb, with an ice pack clutched to his temple listening through a foggy haze of concussion to what he himself would have termed utter drivel. No, she had not heard him entering the flat as she had been fast asleep and no again to his close questioning, she had not thought of the consequences of rearranging the bed so as to act as a death trap as Stryker had termed it. And no again, with vehemence it should be stressed, she had not thought of the consequences of having moved into Stryker's flat without his permission, even though her own abode had been voluntarily given up that very day with ostensibly no hint on his part or even a casual suggestion as far as he was concerned of her being able to share his lodgings. And finally, no again – this time with risible contempt, to the question of her thinking she might have conceivably violated his privacy by undressing him and putting him into his own bed.

"So what the hell did you think you were doing moving my bed – my bed I reiterate, into such a ridiculous position?"

"I've already said, it was to line up the bed with the direction of the floorboards so that no bad luck should befall me."

"Oh great! So I suppose I don't count then."

"Come on Stryker, you must be able to see the funny side of it. After all, I didn't do it with any malicious intent did I? We all have our little foibles. Mine happens to be that I'm just a tiny bit superstitious that's all."

"Tiny bit superstitious! Foibles! I could have been killed tripping over this bed in the dark and striking my head on the dressing table. It's the last thing I expected, to come home to what I assumed to be my temporary safe abode and find something akin to an elephant trap set for me. God save any intruders if they ever attempt to rob your place, that's all I can say. I'll bet your mother was only too happy when she found out you were going to spend most of your time away from home on your modelling assignments."

"I hoped you would have said our place. Surely you didn't expect me to live in that terrible nondescript area did you? Where's that big tough American detective I always thought of as invincible?"

"He's in bed suffering from concussion due to your foolhardy actions, that's where. Anyhow, how come you were able to gain access to my flat? I usually lock the street door before leaving. I'm sorry but it's just one of those bad habits I picked up when living in Seattle. Call me suspicious if you like but I forgot, you obviously don't bother to close your street doors here in London."

"You're sorry! No, let me say I'm sorry – there, does it make things better between us? I truly am sorry Stryker. You know I would never do anything to harm you of all people. Though I must say sarcasm was not one of the attributes I thought you would be capable of displaying. Anyhow, to answer your question, I gained access to this flat by picking your street door lock – I'm afraid it's one of those things they teach you when working for MI6."

"Well, that's a relief. I was beginning to think you were capable of walking through walls like one of those spirits which I was practically on the verge of joining. Anyway, let's forget it. Now to change the subject, have you arranged for me to meet your father yet to discuss the intricacies of biological weapons?"

"Let's have a coffee seeing as it's still early morning, just to wake ourselves up and then we can have a heart to heart. I'll go make one." To this suggestion Stryker painfully nodded in agreement, feeling a hostage to fortune as he watched Carol move to the kitchen in her figure revealing night dress. Five minutes later she was back nursing two steaming hot mugs.

"So spill the beans. What can you tell me about biological weapons?" Carol stared at Stryker with a vacant look hovering between self-indulgence and a plea for sanity.

"I said we could have a heart to heart not a deep and meaningful discussion on killing people with invisible microbes. Surely Stryker, in this situation that's the last thing we should be discussing."

"What do you mean this situation? What situation are you referring to?"

"Well now, do you not find me just a teeny-weeny bit attractive? I mean I'm sure it's not every day you find yourself in bed with an ex-model sitting on the edge of it."

"I agree you are a very attractive and desirable young woman but as far as I am concerned there is no situation. I'd much rather you helped me out with this problem I have of understanding something of the nature of microbes seeing as it might serve me well if I am to do my job properly and possibly keep us both safe."

"There now Stryker, that wasn't so hard, was it? I like the idea of you being concerned about my safety." Before Stryker could utter another word Carol kept talking. "You must understand that it's my father who's the expert on such matters as these. All I know is that microbes can be designed to be killer viruses through mutation. That is, specifically modified into something which can in certain cases cross the barrier between animal and human species such as foot and mouth disease. Bio-warfare if you will. There is a great deal of concern that terrorists might be able to get their hands on some of these killer microbes which could conceivably be used to cause a pandemic, that is, a disease covering the whole country or even the whole world. Or maybe a dangerous virus might escape from one of the many laboratories dotted around the world and infect the population. Just think how quickly flu can race through a population. There again, think of AIDS. It has been said that particular virus has killed more people than all the people who died during the Second World War. That makes you think doesn't it? I just thank God that AIDS is not spread through aerosol transmission. That is, you cannot catch it through coughs or sneezes. There again, a rogue state might wish to invest in these invisible killers for all sorts of reasons. Quite frankly Stryker, I'd prefer to think of something else wouldn't you? Anyhow, as I mentioned before, I'll arrange a meeting with my daddy just as soon as it's practicable, I promise, so don't look so concerned." Carol suggested the coffee was getting cold and went to move into the sitting room to get dressed before Stryker began speaking again.

"You forgot to ask how my Easter service went."

"Forgive me Stryker, how did it go?"

"It was interesting. I gave a Russian man, whom I met at the church service, a lift back to his hotel and noticed a car following us. It tailed me all the way back here."

"Did you get its number?"

"What do you think? Of course I got it. For me that's second nature." Stryker leant forward and handed Carol a piece of paper removed from on top of the bedside cabinet. "Would you see if Vauxhall Cross can find out who it is registered to?"

Just then the telephone rang. Stryker attempted to get up before falling backwards onto the bed, feeling dazed.

Carol dashed into the sitting room and lifted the receiver. Stryker could hear her voice but not what she was saying. After a few seconds the receiver was replaced then he heard Carol lift up the receiver once more before redialling a number then returned to the bedroom.

"Who was it? You've gone as white as these bed sheets."

"It was for you – a man's voice. He said someone was attempting to kill them. He asked for you by name and enquired if you had a secure line – said he could not speak on an open line but that it was very serious. Then the phone went dead."

"Did you tell him this landline was secure?"

"Well, I didn't have time."

"Did he give you his name?"

"No name. He just said what I've told you – verbatim. He said someone was attempting to kill them."

"Them! Was he English or perhaps Russian? Did he have an accent?"

"Yes, he had a soft Welsh accent."

"Can you try dialling back to see if we can get a number?"

"Tried that without success I'm afraid."

Stryker stared hard into the distance before speaking. "There's only one person I know who has a Welsh accent and he resides at the British Embassy in Dubai. If it was him then he's the naval attaché who interrogated me after the incident with the sunken Russian vessel. The question is – is he the one who just telephoned and if so what did he want? And what did he mean by saying someone was attempting to kill them?

And who is them? Carol, can you get me the telephone number of the British Embassy in Dubai?"

CHAPTER 9

NORTH WALES – HARLECH

The imposing granite building set down upon a craggy coastline in Harlech, North Wales, within Snowdonia's National Park, made an instant impression with everyone who set eyes upon it. Viewed from the sand dunes on a starry night with a full moon shining and swirling with mist rolling in from the sea conjured up a magical romantic air, its medieval fortification harking back to some distant past. Even the water lapping at the rocks and sandy inlets had a distinctive sound all its own. David could bring this evocative music to his ears just by lying silently upon his bed and closing his eyes.

Sometimes, on warm balmy late summer nights, he would secretly make his way over the grass strewn dunes down to the water's edge, shedding his clothes as if in a paper chase, leaving a trail for no one in particular to follow and gently let his naked body slip into the water and float out into the sooty blackness, soaking up the feeling of nothingness. At times like these he felt happy and at one with whatever was out there that made up this unfathomable universe.

The building of megalithic proportions had once been part of his day to day existence as an adult student in residence. Now he lived barely a quarter of a mile away, with the college in clear view from his small but cosy cottage situated high above on the other side of the main road, eking out a living doing odd jobs such as gardening for people who had outlived their aspirations and were too feeble to dig the neat gardens themselves. He was happy with his lot, reading anything he could get his hands on, his intellect fired by the close contacts kept up within the college. He was also heavily into complementary therapies.

Tonight, as he strolled through the portal of this hallowed seat of learning, he was keeping an appointment made the previous week with the college warden, Dr Kenneth Jones, MA, Oxon., who was at that very moment waiting there for him on the threshold. The title 'Doctor' was not because of any practical medical training but had been awarded for loftier academic pursuits. To the casual observer, the two men now seen standing together deep in conversation might have been viewed as lending a certain dignity to the occasion, and might even have been viewed as grandfather and grandson, but in reality only acted as a counterpoint to the previous evenings revelries, whereby David and Kenneth had been propping one another up in The Black Crow bar getting legless.

A less likely proponent of academia David knew he would never again set eyes upon. An unkempt man in his late seventies, of short, solid stature, Kenneth lived in a brown tweed jacket which had undoubtedly seen better days, the worn frayed elbows now failing miserably to conceal a crumpled dark blue shirt beneath. Rough labourer's hands with stained nicotine fingers up to the knuckles, Kenneth never had a cigarette out of his wet lips. A bright red beaten up face which looked as though it had been through the wars, which incidentally it had; the constant stream of nicotine having wreaked havoc with his overgrown moustache, resembling a patch of yellowed grass upon which dogs had peed with alarming regularity. All these external clues seen through the eyes of a stranger would not bode well for a character assessment.

Fortunately the computing terminology, "What you see is what you get," did not hold true in this particular instance. For beneath Dr Kenneth Jones' aged reddened face there lurked an academic mien, an air of learning which hovered chakra like, around his forehead. His fine knowledge of Shakespeare, indeed literature in general, was vast. To say he was well read would have been an understatement. He was known as an eccentric by his students; one indication being that although his rooms were crammed with books, he now had so many that after reading at great speed a new analytical tome on perhaps Thackeray or James Joyce, Chaucer or Christopher Marlow, Sartre or Tolstoy – these last two books having been read in their original language, his being something of a polyglot – they would end up in one of his outside dustbins, open to the vagaries of the elements, but which his college students scavenged on a very regular basis, thereby laying the foundation for their very own academic libraries. His scholarly output, literally, was astounding.

Dr Kenneth Jones's only other vice was drinking, and this intoxicating aroma mixed with the fusty odour of nicotine emanated from his every pore. Yet it was an odour which did not disgust, but to people within his presence, it produced an instant real or imagined recall of an old favourite learned uncle, who might have spent all his days incarcerated in the great libraries of country houses, his youth spent imbibing the knowledge of centuries and who now imparted it generously to his fellow travellers. Not for the want of other people's admiration, but for the sheer joy of doing so. That said, the Board of Governors had been trying for most of the past ten years to find a way of getting Ken to retire, but as he was only too happy to remind them with his paraphrase, "You can't put an old dog like me down," so it had seemed.

David was already standing behind the heavy oak lectern as the last adult stragglers finally made their way into the Great Hall after having received grace at table and consumed their evening meal in the refectory. The introduction by Dr Kenneth Jones in his rich Welsh accented voice having been completed, David cleared his throat with a growling noise before beginning to speak.

"No doubt many of you will have seen my ugly face hanging around the college." There was a pause, waiting perhaps for an outward sign of empathy between the students and himself. Tonight the Great Hall was unusually full and all eyes fixed firmly in rapt attention on David's fine features. He was in his early thirties and an acknowledged attraction for the female contingent spread liberally throughout the student population on campus. A disturbing hush had settled upon the audience – not a good omen for someone about to embark on a long lecture.

"Tonight I shall let you into the mysteries of the subconscious mind by way of my specialist subject... hypnosis." Now David noticed a distinct lightening of atmosphere as an enthusiastic shifting of weight on chairs and feet shuffled in exited expectation.

"But before I expound upon this subject of hypnosis I shall demonstrate the power of such a medium and for this demonstration I require a volunteer."

Within seconds a dozen hands shot into the air. "You there, yes you. Please come up to the stage." A thin young man in his mid-twenties looking every inch a student with his spectacles perched precariously upon the bridge of his nose swaggered on to the stage, looking rather too cocksure of himself.

"Have you ever been hypnotised before?"

"No, never," the volunteer responded with a hint of sangfroid belying his now obvious state of nervousness, the terror of which could be seen in his eyes as it suddenly dawned upon him just what he had let himself in for. This overt nervousness had also transferred itself down along both arms and into his hands, which had taken on a stiffness resulting in the tight clenching of his fists.

After explaining to his potential subject that there was nothing to be afraid of and that hypnosis was a natural state which all people unwittingly pass through twice a day: "What I call the twilight zone – once when we are about to wake up and the other when we are about to fall asleep." David took a couple of strides toward the young man whose name was Brocklebank, briefly coming to face him within inches of their noses touching and gazing straight into his eyes before turning to the audience, saying: "I now require another five volunteers to help me with this demonstration; preferably four hefty men and one woman. After all the volunteers had been duly assembled amidst much cajoling and banter from their friends in the audience – the woman named Lucy, being a slight-framed girl of no more than twenty – they were all given a spontaneous round of applause as David took control of the proceedings once more, producing a microphone upon a tall stand which he placed at the front of the stage and getting a couple of his male volunteers to drag two heavily padded red velvet armchairs which had just a moment earlier been sitting alongside the microphone so that they were now strategically placed centre stage, back to back four feet or so apart.

Then to the delight and mystification of his audience David disappeared to the side of the stage before quickly reappearing moments later with what was clearly a roll of silver aluminium kitchen cooking foil. Without preamble Brocklebank was stood facing the audience whereby David proceeded to tear off a strip of this aluminium foil before tightly screwing it up into a ball and passing it to his subject to hold in his right fist, instructing him: "When you feel that silver ball becoming too hot to hold you will drop it." Within ten seconds an audible gasp from the students rent the silence as the thud of a screwed up silver ball hit the floor. Amidst excited mumbling from the now spellbound audience David proceeded once more to tear off yet another piece of silver foil, but this time Brocklebank now being instructed to sandwich this particular sheet of foil between his outstretched palms as if he was praying. At this point it is only a matter of conjecture what was actually going on in the young man's head but he did as he was instructed. To those close enough and if they were very observant they would have noticed Brocklebank's eyes glazing over. After letting his subject remain in this preposterous position for another half-minute without uttering a word David stepped forward and firmly taking hold of the sheet of foil from the bottom, gave it a yank toward the direction of the stage floor, swiftly puling it away from Brocklebank's hands whilst at the same time ordering his subject to "Look into my eyes," quickly followed by the loud command – "SLEEP." Brocklebank now stood transfixed to the spot, gazing above the audience's heads into the far distance in a deep state of hypnosis, looking for all the world as though he was praying. Now a deathly hush settled upon the Great Hall right up to the exposed oak Hammer Beam rafters; the myriad of students' faces giving the impression that they too had also succumbed to that self-same trance as though at a prayer meeting. The spectacles Brocklebank had been wearing were removed and pushed into David's shirt pocket.

Two of the volunteers were now instructed to sit down upon the heavy armchairs with their backs to one another – "to add ballast" David quipped, eliciting another ripple of chuckles echoing around the large auditorium, whilst the other two men were taken to one side. "I am now going to proceed to make this fellow you see standing here before you much heavier than he might appear and you will therefore when instructed, lift him up by his shoulders and feet and carefully place him down upon these two chairs with his ankles resting on one chair and his shoulder blades resting upon the top of the back of the other padded chair…is that clear?" The two men gave a puzzled acknowledgement of David's instructions and took a step back whilst David himself now moved toward his potential victim.

As these instructions were being given the college warden, Dr Kenneth Jones, looked on smiling broadly, dwelling upon the fact that his young friend had managed to do something which he himself could only dream of doing in his lectures; that is, holding his students in thrall to such spellbinding curiosity.

David now began giving orders to Brocklebank fast and furiously as he sent his subject spinning into an even deeper trance by awakening him and putting him back into a deep sleep several times. Then the real reason for the deep trancelike state soon became obvious as he began piling suggestion upon suggestion as to how Brocklebank's body was becoming less pliable and as stiff as a wooden plank. "You can feel yourself stiffening. Your whole body is becoming as strong and as stiff as a plank of wood. You cannot bend your body for it is as strong and as stiff and rigid as a rod of steel. You can feel nothing. Your body is stiff and rigid and you can feel no pain." After a minute or so had passed in this manner David beckoned his two young helpers selected from the audience just minutes before. "The person before you will soon appear very heavy when you lift him up. What I would like you to do now is, when I give the order, is to carefully lift him up as I said a moment ago and place his shoulder blades on one edge of the chair and his ankles upon the other. Is that clear? Your two colleagues will continue to sit upon the two chairs to keep them steady. Be very careful not to drop him. I must emphasise this as he will feel very heavy, even to you strong young men."

Here there was muffled laughter from the now captivated audience.

David took a couple of steps behind Brocklebank and with his arms outstretched, made slow sweeping movements with his hands very lightly across the top of his subject's shoulders, uttering the words "You are falling backwards," at which point Brocklebank's body began swaying. This was as much for showmanship as anything else. After doing this a few more times he then suggested that Brocklebank was falling backwards NOW! As he proceeded to fall, David caught him as he fell backwards before laying him on the floor of the stage.

As David's instructions to his two helpers were being carried out in the way he had previously instructed he carefully supervised the positioning of Brocklebank's body upon the two chair backs; his shoulder blades being placed on one padded edge and his heels upon the other with his legs slightly splayed for balance with the result that a large space was now left beneath the rigid body as though Brocklebank had become a bridge between the two chairs. Then after making sure his airways were not impeded by the angle of his head yet more strengthening suggestions were made, tapping the suspended man's abdomen as they were being given. "You cannot bend; you are made of steel. You cannot feel any pain."

The slight young girl who had been invited onto the stage earlier as a pleasant distraction was now brought before the audience. "Ladies and gentlemen, let me introduce you to someone who might very well be the second most interesting person in this room tonight. Lucy, please take a bow."

Lucy, the dark-haired young lady, took a long theatrical bow in the spirit of the proceedings, fortunately not knowing what lay in store for her. After explaining to the young lady that she must do exactly what she was told and that she must firstly remove her shoes which she obligingly did immediately, without warning David grasped her by her very small waist and told her to remain still without moving a muscle as he swiftly hoisted her up into the air and placed her two feet upon the young gentleman's taught stomach. Making sure he had her hand grasped firmly in his he gave her instructions as to how to place her feet slightly apart so as to retain her balance, all the while making sure he did not let go of her hand. Slowly she straightened her back as instructed so that she was now standing erect upon the young man's unsupported stomach, the only contact he had with the armchairs was his shoulder blades and ankles. As Lucy raised her head so as to be able to gaze out at the audience a spontaneous round of applause rang out.

Before David lifted Lucy back off the prostrate body suspended across the two heavy chairs he quipped; "Be careful where you place your feet Lucy, we don't want you ruining this young man's marriage prospects do we?" Laughter and applause rang out from the now totally captivated audience. David knew he now had the students eating out of the palm of his hand.

An hour and a half later, after a coffee break, by which point many of the students had learnt for the first time of David's ability to help people through his use of hypnotherapy, questions were thrown open to the audience. A sea of hands floated around the Great Hall as if at a pop concert, the music being substituted by a low murmuring of eager voices.

"Is it true that you can get anybody to do absolutely anything under hypnosis without their objecting?"

That old chestnut, thought David, as he patiently explained to the male questioner that it might be easier and cheaper to find a prostitute for the night. A roar of laughter rippled through the students.

"By the way, I am also a mind reader." At this point there were knowing smiles all around.

"Can anyone be hypnotised?" This time the question was posed by a young man with a severe case of acne.

"Everyone can be hypnotised given sufficient time. The only people who cannot be hypnotised are very young children, drunks and imbeciles; that is, people who cannot hold their concentration – and please don't take that as a personal comment." Another roar of laughter! It was going well, and David like his audience was smiling broadly.

"Has anyone ever been murdered through the use of hypnosis?"

"Yes, I believe there was a case in the nineteen-fifties, in I think, one of the Scandinavian countries. The person was shot. It was carried out under a post-hypnotic trance. There may well be other cases which are not documented or known about." David gave a long sideways glance toward Dr Kenneth Jones, as he did so muttering loudly, "Watch out warden," accompanied by more laughter from a sea of smiling faces.

"What is a post-hypnotic trance?" The questions were coming fast and furious and David warmed to his subject.

"A post-hypnotic trance is one whereby under hypnosis the subject is given instructions by the hypnotist – instructions which are to be carried out at a specific time in the future, sometimes I might add, many years later. And this will be without the subject having been made aware of these suggestions being planted deep within his or her subconscious mind."

"And have you ever used such a technique?" This supplementary question was posed by the same questioner.

"Yes, to help people with many problems, such as insomnia, stuttering, and enuresis for example – that is bed wetting for the uninitiated." There was another round of laughter.

With regard to eeenu, whatever you said. Can children be helped and can they be hypnotised?"

"Yes, over the age of about seven years or so, if they can concentrate sufficiently then they can be hypnotised. And of course it goes without saying but I shall say it anyway, it is usually children who are the recipients of treatment for this type of complaint."

"Can you hypnotise people over the telephone?"

"Yes."

The next question was posed by a rather attractive young woman who had only recently arrived to fill the post of assistant to the college bursar. "Can you improve a person's sex life using hypnosis?"

"Come and see me later this evening." There was another round of laughter and cheering.

Another young woman interjected. "Can you hypnotise a person in bed when they are already asleep without them knowing?"

"Yes. And at risk of repeating myself, come and see me later."

"Could you hypnotise my bank manager?" came a voice from the other end of the hall.

"Well, I am guessing that does not have any relevance to the last question. If it does then you already have a very good working relationship with your bank manager. But if you are not sleeping with your bank manager then what's it worth?" David was growing tired; the previous night's festivities were beginning to take their toll. It was at this point, to the gratefulness of David that Dr Jones stepped in, bringing the lecture to a close. With applause and cheers still ringing in their ears, they both made their way to Kenneth's rooms within the college precincts for just one more hair of the dog that had bitten them the night before.

***

The rooms Dr Kenneth Jones occupied were large and airy and the living room, come study, come library, was lined with shelves on each wall groaning under the weight of books. The vast majority comprised of the great literature masterpieces from down the centuries, plus many critical works on the writers themselves, not just in English but in Russian, French and German. David always felt a little humility when sitting amongst these books, knowing that he himself could have done so much more with his own talents than what had been achieved so far.

Kenneth poured out two generous glasses of neat whisky and handed one to David whilst easing himself into the most comfortable looking armchair within the room, around the feet of which were scattered copies of *Izvestia*, the Russian daily newspaper. David chose a chair facing his host. After taking a sip of the golden nectar, as Kenneth referred to it, he carefully placed the whisky glass down upon the paper strewn side table beside his chair, and with both hands lying upon his lap closed the heavily lined eyelids. He sat like this for about a minute, David beginning to wonder if he had fallen asleep, before the silence was broken by Dr Jones' lilting Welsh accented voice.

"You didn't answer that very pertinent question posed earlier, did you?" Kenneth's face looked very old at that moment. It was the way the light spilt from the standard lamp just above his head, emphasising the deeply lined ridges across his forehead and his cheeks.

"What question was that then?"

"Can you really make people do things against their will?" He may have been perceived as the wise old sage that he really was, but to David, Kenneth also had an honest simplicity about him that was touching, rather like Christian in Pilgrim's Progress, the small leather bound book David now held in his hand, having lifted it from his own side table to make space for the glass he had not yet touched.

"If one gives a logical reason for the person under hypnosis to carry out an instruction, then yes, yes you can get them to do absolutely anything. It's all a matter of psychology really."

"And is it true that people have had their limbs removed under hypnosis without the use of anaesthetic, or is that pure bunkum?"

"That is perfectly true. James Esdaile, a surgeon from Perth in Scotland carried out many such operations in the State of Bengal in India during the eighteen-forties and fifties using nothing more than hypnosis and which, by all accounts, were stated to be completely painless. Dr James Braid was another Scotsman who used this form of mesmerism and was the one who actually coined the term hypnosis."

Dr Kenneth Jones, fascinated by the subject expounded upon by his good friend David, took another swig of whisky – formulating just one last question in his mind before calling it a day. Fortunately for the now tired David, the question beginning to form upon Kenneth's red lips never expressed itself further than making a soft whistling sound as he sank deeper into his favourite chair and nodded off. Draining his glass, David then crept silently to the door, quietly letting himself out while at the same time gazing at his wrist watch. It was now 2am.

CHAPTER 10

RUSSIAN HINTERLAND

Ten hours earlier, allowing for the difference in time zones, just as David had begun to deliver his lecture on hypnosis in North Wales, somewhere out in the hinterland south-east of Moscow toward the great Ural mountain range and Aral Sea, Marishka Petrova stood sheltering from the rain and enveloping darkness in an outhouse, one of many within the now abandoned farm's five hundred hectares. Marishka's long, wet, jet black hair tumbled from beneath a brightly coloured headscarf, a few straggling strands clinging to the upturned collar of an astrakhan overcoat. The heavy coat was the same colour as her hair, bought from one of the expensive shops set aside for foreigners and high ranking party officials in Moscow, some one thousand miles away. The wide cheekbones and big brown eyes enhanced her beauty, giving the illusion of being much younger than she really was. She had just turned seventeen.

An old battered hurricane lamp expanded the searing incandescent brilliance held within its crystal sphere, bathing everything in a soft golden glow and creating an illusion of comfort amidst the rusting farm implements; discarded horse harnesses and long handled scythes never having seen the light of day for the last half century. Bundles of hay, cut under the fierce heat of a summer sun which had grown cool with the seasons, lay scattered in a haphazard fashion on an ochre-coloured dirt floor. The only other token of rustic domesticity illuminated by the oil lamp was a steaming samovar, settled precariously within the shadows upon a bale of straw.

This was the scene which greeted Ivan as he gingerly pushed open the creaking wooden door, slipping furtively inside. He remembered to lower his head, so as to avoid a low hanging branch found earlier that week beneath one of the many apple trees dotted about the fields which had been used to shore up part of the rust encrusted roof. The tin roof which now threw a heavy torrent of rainwater outside the perimeter walls instead of within.

It did not take long for his eyes to adjust to the darkness, settling initially, as they always would, upon Marishka's expectant pouting lips. As Ivan moved forward, Marishka's arms stretched out imploringly, pulling the would-be lover tightly to her thin, girlish body and breathing a warm sigh of relief as their lips met. No word had yet been exchanged within the silence, broken only by the rhythmic beating of heavy raindrops upon the thin corrugated tin above their heads.

After what seemed like an eternity, the tension in their bodies relaxed and Ivan became conscious of a familiar aroma, the burning lamp oil pervading his senses sending his mind reeling back to childhood, memories of holidays spent with an aunt at her dacha just outside Moscow. Antimacassars smelling of mothballs lying limply over backs of antique chairs and the musty noxious odour from a box room in which his aunt stored her large-brimmed hats. It was the property which he had inherited two years previously, although only recently having been notified of this fact, and which is why the memory of it was still fresh in his mind as the oil lamp's glowing wick flared up, making a gentle hissing sound just before spitting and spluttering, jolting him back to the present, a sure signal that the fuel would soon be exhausted.

Marishka broke away first, turning her back upon the man nearly old enough to be her father, delicate faltering hands now busying themselves with the task of milking the samovar, a strong brown liquid slowly being released into two tin mugs while shadows danced frenziedly around the roughly hewn wooden slatted walls, announcing a final dying gasp of illumination. At the very moment the lamp expired, a steaming hot mug was being placed within the strong cold hands of Ivan, Marishka smiling as she did so, her white teeth glowing like fireflies through the darkness.

The rain had abated as the two co-conspirators settled down upon a bed of straw so dry it crackled beneath them each time they moved a leg or an arm, the lack of light helping to ease the awkwardness each felt by their secret tryst. Still neither had spoken, afraid to break that magical spell which had engulfed them, their feelings heightened by the closeness and heat of each other's bodies.

"How long can you stay?" It was Ivan who finally broke through the heavy silence. There was nervousness in his voice which Marishka picked up on.

"Don't worry, I shan't go for ages." Her soft, half mature voice, did not carry the conviction he had hoped for, knowing that at this hour Marishka would soon be missed, either by her widowed mother or by her younger brother Gregory, a boy far too inquisitive and outspoken to be trusted with such a secret as theirs. Marishka lay with her head resting within the nook of Ivan's neck and shoulder, her long, damp, soft hair exuding the scent of the cheap fragranced perfume removed from her mother's bedroom just before setting out on her secret rendezvous with a man known to locals by the nickname of Ivan the Terrible. This sobriquet did not however, mean that Ivan had within him a terrible streak of cruelty, far from it. He was indeed the embodiment of gentleness itself. He was quite simply known as Ivan the Terrible because of his job at the top secret factory known as Experimental Sector Two Oh Five abbreviated to ES 205, a cluster of buildings producing deadly anthrax spores and other bacterial diseases and viruses on an industrial scale.

As a scientist and GRU officer with the Fifteenth Directorate, part of the Russian Ministry of Defence, Ivan held a senior position at the factory in which he spent a great deal of his time. And although the work, known colloquially as 'Germ warfare production', was supposedly top secret, a good fifty per cent of the local population toiled within its confines, leading to half-truths and an air of mutual distrust between its workers and the rest of the indigenous population because of the frequent outbreaks of mystery illnesses.

As Ivan moved his hands toward the top button of the astrakhan coat, left behind when his wife finally abandoned their matrimonial home after years of quarrelling, Marishka placed her own childlike hands on top of his.

"No Ivan. Not now. Not tonight." Ivan's expression registered disappointment as he looked deep into her soft brown eyes, a powerful yearning welling up within his loins, filling his body with half-forgotten feelings, sensations he had not experienced for many years. He settled his back against a bale of hay, his senses overwhelmed by Marishka's wet clothes exuding a heady intoxicating aroma redolent with the secret musty atmosphere of such country pursuits. Ivan savoured the precious minutes left to them before leading Marishka through the darkness in the direction of her home, knowing that one hint of this relationship might spell disaster for both of them.

***

Much later that same evening, under the cover of darkness, Ivan made the long trek back to his love nest. This time however, there was no welcoming mug of hot tea to be pressed into his hands by the attentive Marishka. Now all was deathly silent as he switched on a small torch, throwing a narrow beam of light, just large enough to illuminate within the shed and beneath several inches of soil and wrapped in a waterproof plastic bag a bundle of technical looking papers, each bearing the heading of the department he worked for, and each marked SECRET. He meticulously worked through the papers, carefully highlighting a passage here and another there, making annotations where necessary within the margins.

After two hours he re-wrapped the papers and gingerly buried them once more. This done, he inspected his work, making sure that the ground did not look as though it had been disturbed before laying a bale of straw on top. Then in his mind he reviewed the last trip he had made to Moscow, and the Lermontov novel he had left within the sanctuary of the Ulitsa Arbat bookshop and into the hands and safekeeping of an elderly academic with a mane of white hair touching his stooped shoulders and wearing a pair of pince-nez glasses.

CHAPTER 11

NORTH WALES

The railway carriage had been vacated half an hour earlier by everyone except for a very feminine looking twenty eight year old woman with long brown hair who now sat huddled deep into one corner for extra warmth. The heating from this carriage could not compete with the wintry air outside seeping through the ventilation ducts and rattling doors, making it feel more like a cold storage container for transporting dead animals to butchers as opposed to ferrying passengers in notional comfort and style.

It was late as the train pulled into the little station in North Wales. It was also already dark, the last vestiges of light wrung from the sky hours before, so that Penny could barely make out the surrounding countryside and certainly not the coast where she had spent a pleasant two weeks earlier in the year. Nearly six hours after leaving Euston train station in London, she was now feeling very tired, having changed trains twice; once at Birmingham and then again at Machynlleth. Besides being tired she was also overcome with feelings of desolation and emptiness. It had been a long journey, giving her too much time in which to dwell upon her mother's funeral the week before and the events leading up to it.

As soon as the carriage door was flung open into the darkness she could taste the salt and heavy dankness in the air and even hear the swishing of the sea somewhere out there behind the now invisible sand dunes. Her senses were also more than usually sharp as the chill damp night enveloped her. The railway station itself had that certain depressing familiarity about it – the same as hundreds of others scattered throughout the countryside, with unseen overgrown bushes and rotting fencing.

A small ticket office was situated along one end of the platform, the line of the roof bearing remnants of Victorian tracery lovingly carved into wood now decaying with age and mildew. Tagged on to one side of this ticket office was a cold, draughty waiting room with its door missing, crumbling plaster walls hinting at a brown and green colour scheme from many years before and an old empty fireplace, which had probably not seen a fire since the time the walls had been painted. It was from this drab scene that David now appeared, beaming with excitement and half frozen to death.

"Penny, how are you? Lovely to see you arrived safely." He had a glow about his personality which seemed to give everything within his presence a touch of magic. Penny surprised herself as she ran toward David, struggling with her small suitcase and literally fell into his arms, catching her toe in a stray root which had grown through the asphalt. Without thinking, he kissed her on the forehead which proved easy, he being all of six inches taller.

"Here let me take that," he said in a loud voice, reaching out his arm and effortlessly grabbing the small suitcase as if it were empty. "Are you feeling alright? No, of course you're not, that was a stupid question. Sorry." David gave her a sympathetic look. "How was the funeral?"

"Ghastly. That's the second one I've been to and I hope it's the last. Thank you for sending the flowers."

"Least I could do. Well, you're here now. I'll look after you."

Penny's eyes had now adjusted to the darkness and she could see a small car waiting for them just outside the station entrance. Dr Kenneth Jones, a long thick scarf wound around his throat, was opening the back door of his old black Morris Minor as David strode up to it carrying Penny's suitcase.

"My dear Penny," Ken said, peering through the dark around David's shoulder. "Good to see you my dear, though not in such circumstances." He walked toward her and gave her a hug. "So sorry to hear about your mother."

Penny's eyes grew moist as she lowered her head, climbing into the back seat, hoping that the two men had not noticed. Dr Kenneth Jones released the brakes of Gwendolyn, as he affectionately called his runabout, the car rolling down the hill swiftly and silently as it gathered speed.

"I hope you'll excuse the bloody freezing temperature in here. It won't make any difference when the engine's running, you'll see in a minute."

Penny remembered the last time she had taken a ride in Dr Kenneth Jones' car after having had a few drinks with the two of them in their local bar on the last night of her holiday, when she had ventured the observation that it had been a very quiet engine, whereupon the rejoinder came back: "Yes my dear it is. Shall I tell you why it is so silent? It is because I have not yet switched the engine on. It's known as freewheeling."

"But its pitch black out there, how can you possibly see?"

"I know this stretch of road like the back of my hand. Even without lights."

Penny had persisted, having been in a rather euphoric state of intoxication: "But what would happen if you met a vehicle freewheeling without lights coming toward you in the other direction?"

"Then my dear, it would be the first miracle I should have ever witnessed, defying the laws of gravity, and I would undoubtedly be ready for conversion, both myself and no doubt the car too." The three of them had burst into uncontrollable laughter. Then it had been a warm evening in midsummer. Now the frost was biting. They continued for a while longer, rolling down along the almost invisible winding lane before the engine roared into life and the interior lights came on, illuminating the three white faces pinched with the cold.

"You and David are having dinner with me this evening so we'll take your case back to David's little house later on."

As they pulled up at the college Penny began to feel easier as the happy memories came flooding back.

"The first time I saw this magnificent building it reminded me of a castle." Her observation was not aimed at anyone in particular, just an expression of what she had felt when first setting eyes upon this very majestic seat of learning.

***

It had gone midnight when Penny Churchill finally unpacked her small case in the tiny bedroom she had been allocated. On the windowsill there were some dried flowers in a jam jar and an old antique clock in a polished mahogany case sitting on the mantelpiece, and outside the window was a wall of blackness. The only sound Penny could hear as she lay with her head upon a duck down filled pillow was the softly ticking clock and the rhythmic chirping of crickets.

No sooner had she closed her eyes than a ray of warmth fell across her face as bright sunlight streaked through the window announcing a beautiful morning. And the chirping of crickets had given way to a gentle tapping on her bedroom door.

"Penny, breakfast is served." David stood in the doorway holding a large tin tray bearing a steaming bowl of coffee and mounds of hot buttered toast and marmalade which he balanced precariously on the bedside table. From her bed, Penny clad in a pale blue diaphanous nightdress, could now see the familiar view which had been obscured by nightfall. It was not the coast of sand and sea but the dark green hills rolling away from the rear of the cottage, up toward the sky.

"You don't know how lucky you are David, living here with such beautiful views."

"On the contrary I do know, but sad to say, one sometimes becomes immune to it. I thought we might go for a walk on the hills later to get an even better view. From up there," David nodded toward the hills, "it's even more magnificent." Back in the summer when Penny had visited David, they had never got around to walking up the hill from the back of his cottage because of spending all their time upon the sandy beach and among the grass-strewn sand dunes. Penny now began to understand why David exuded so much confidence, living as he did in such a picture book environment.

***

From where they stood, high up on the hillside, the breath-taking view was as stunning as David had said. His cottage had now been reduced to a full stop, and the college which Penny had earlier described as a castle now resembled a grey hyphen just below it. Then a little further down the yellow line of sand dunes became visible snaking along the sea's edge. The wind had got up, and David suggested they move a little higher to what appeared to be the crest of the hill. As they reached the brow, the green grassy bank gave way abruptly to a slate quarry hewn out of the other side of the hill. The effect was dramatic; vast acres of grey rocks hugged the perpendicular sides threatening to tumble down the sheer cliff face, down to pools of accumulated rainwater trapped in grassy divots of outcrops above a sinister looking lake.

Penny followed in David's footsteps as they cautiously made their way along a concealed path until they came to a ledge halfway down, hanging over the azure-coloured water. David's face was wreathed in smiles.

"What do you think?"

"Are you trying to impress me or what?" Penny responded, slowly lowering herself onto her stomach. Her long hazel-coloured hair danced in the breeze as she gingerly inched forward until she could peer over the edge, down on to the lake, a dizzy vertiginous drop two hundred feet below. "My mind has just been blown away. It's fantastic!" Penny felt a tug on the waistband of her skirt.

"Do be careful, it's a long way to fall." As David held onto her she rolled away from the edge and into the safety of his arms. It was now midday and the sun was at its zenith. They lay there in its surprising warmth hugging one another; Penny curled within David's arms. Then her body began to tremble violently. Suddenly David's shirt felt damp in the area where Penny's head lay on his shoulder. As he looked down, Penny's face was staring up at him in floods of tears.

"What's wrong?" David whispered, letting his arms drop to around her waist.

"Oh David, I feel as if I'm losing my mind. I shall go mad if I don't tell someone."

"Is it something I've dome or said to upset you? Because if it is..."

"No, it really is absolute bliss being here and I'd rather not be anywhere else."

"Then what is it?" David searched Penny's face, now a picture of misery.

"You can't imagine what mental torture I've suffered over the last few weeks David. It's so confusing, not knowing about my father. I know now that my mother was lying to me. But I don't know why." Penny burst into tears once more. David felt helpless and just sat there looking at Penny, attempting to make sense out of what she was saying. The wind had now abated, letting Penny's hair fall down across her back and at the same time throwing off an ebbing radiance from the dying reflection of the sun.

David raised his head and stared out across the vast open slate quarry toward what had been a blue sky a moment before, now suddenly filled with grey nimbus clouds threatening rain. Half closing his eyes he squinted up into the dazzling greyness of light wondering what on earth to say. A silence had suddenly grown between them, slowly being built into a wall of embarrassment. A stiff breeze returned, removing with it the last vestiges of warmth from a wintry sun. It was Penny who spoke again, extricating herself from David's arms and suggesting that it was getting quite chilly; perhaps they could go back to the cottage. The couple returned in silence, neither knowing quite how to cross the self-imposed impasse.

***

Dr Kenneth Jones had a secret part to his make-up which nobody, not even his young drinking partner, knew anything about. True, there were the clues: the frequent trips to London, explained by the fact of having a close elderly uncle in need of his constant attention. Then there were also the numerous late night visitors, usually male though sometimes female. And whilst he freely acknowledged his service during the Second World War, what he failed to mention was just what that service had consisted of.

It was in fact as a young man, after having left Oxford University in the late nineteen-thirties, that he had decided to hone his language skills in the countries where they were spoken, spending a year in Germany at a time when Deutschland was obviously gearing up for war, even though many politicians all across Europe tried to ignore and accommodate the facts that were staring them in the face. He also spent a year in France and a further nine months in Russia just prior to the outbreak of war. By then his talents as a linguist had come to the notice of the Foreign Office, and via that hallowed institution to the attention of the Secret Intelligence Service.

After the war he had often been called upon to use his translating skills, making it easier for more than one Prime Minister when on their official tours abroad to understand the complex semantics of various foreign dignitaries and Heads of State. During this period he made a few very close lifelong friends, one of whom had just been on the telephone to him requesting yet another urgent meeting.

CHAPTER 12

LONDON

It was not only London that had a reputation for bad weather and yet total strangers in England seemed to have an obsession with talking about it. When Dr Grachev got caught up in this trivial type of conversation he would often think back to his grandfather who had spoken about the Second World War and of walking over frozen bodies; men who had succumbed to a treacherous freezing climate on route marches across the Russian plains. The Russians, the Germans, the Poles. He said you could see them under the ice; like looking through a sheet of clear glass. That's what you call bad weather.

These ideas drifted through his mind now as he wandered, with crowds of other people, toward the church through a flurry of snow. He had prepared himself well for this nocturnal service by taking a nap in his hotel during the afternoon. Not sleeping well, he had also taken a tablet proffered to him earlier by an Italian research scientist at a seminar. This scientist said it was something called melatonin, a substance which one of his colleagues had been working on, and which apparently had the benefit of resetting the body's internal clock, interfering with its circadian rhythm. Good for jet lag, he was informed. Now, feeling refreshed, Dr Grachev had glanced around the large throng of Orthodox Christians and caught sight of something that was to change his life, and the lives of many other people with whom he was to come into contact with – forever!

Inspiration, as Dr Grachev knew only too well through his work in science, often went hand in hand with luck. Take Alexander Fleming as an example, he mused. If Fleming had not left his culture dishes sitting on an outside windowsill in London exposed to the elements at Saint Mary's Hospital, Paddington, penicillin might never have been discovered and millions of lives around the world might have been lost. Well, Dr Grachev was inspired now and luck was on his side as a seed of an idea quickly germinated and took root. He felt elated. It was a brilliant idea and so he immediately put his plan into operation.

Pushing through the throng of people while surveying the sea of heads, he homed in on his chosen victim. This particular Orthodox service seemed to go on forever until it was time to light the candles and carry them outside. Closely following his prey, it became only a matter of time before the opportunity arose for Dr Grachev to extinguish his own small candle, thereby presenting the opportunity for him to ask his target now slowly walking beside him if he might re-light the candle from his. Dr Grachev's chosen victim, a large man with a somewhat benign look upon his face who was only too happy to oblige.

It was somewhere past 5 a.m. on Sunday morning when Dr Grachev finally slid down into the soft warm bed of his hotel room, closed his eyes and saw a clear image of his new acquaintance, a British icon dealer named Stryker now seared deep within his consciousness.

***

In another part of London, a dossier initiated just a few weeks earlier was being added to. The concluding words terminating with a flourish, read: Russian Orthodox Church, Ennismore Gardens, London. England. The front cover had two words printed on it: Dr Grachev. By this time too, Stryker had also succumbed to Hades, where some of his unfulfilled fantasies were being turned into reality in true Technicolor.

CHAPTER 13

SVR HEADQUARTERS: MOSCOW

Somewhere within the large comparatively new building housing the First Chief Directorate – (Foreign Intelligence) – headquarters, south-east of Moscow, which also housed other secret police agencies of the State and known as the Yasenevo, successor to the infamous KGB Lubyanka prison, situated on Dzerzhinsky Square with the statue of its namesake recently toppled by the fury of the masses – infamous because of its grisly past history of torture inflicted upon its unlucky guests unfortunate enough to fall prey to its secret police in the name of egalitarianism – a junior SVR intelligence officer sat in a nondescript room with a file opened before him on a computer screen, diligently adding to the contents with a slow *tap, tap, tap* of the keys. This was obviously not a man who had been hired for his typing skills.

He was oblivious to the irony that at another block of relatively equally new offices housing MI6 – Britain's Secret Intelligence Service, situated at Vauxhall Cross in central London, chores like this were also happening on a very regular basis, as indeed they were on a global scale: spying, after all, was a growth industry.

The file just amended with Dr Grachev's name writ large had been pushed into the memory bank using just two keystrokes and thus making way for this current file. Working with the co-operation of the GRU – military wing of the Russian Intelligence Services – the conclusion had been reached that one Anthony Lovejoy-Taylor, a designated political officer installed within the British Embassy in Moscow, was indeed a spy. It was through using an old but simple formula; one might even say an infallible formula that the Russians had come to this conclusion.

The premise worked upon was as follows: if one indisputable proof that an embassy official holding a certain post within that embassy was a known spy, however that classified piece of information came to be recognised, then it followed that if that particular post were vacated, the probability was that his or her successor would also be a spy. And by backtracking other unknown agents might very well be unmasked and eliminated or used as and when convenient in any number of ways. Anthony Lovejoy-Taylor was just such a successor. The ramifications were widespread and revealing. Of course this logic did not cover every spook in Christendom, especially the deep cover variety, many spies avoiding embassies like the plague. But in general it helped to flesh out what might otherwise have looked like an extremely emaciated skeleton.

A simple extrapolation of the names and associated posts throughout the British Embassies throughout the world had produced for the Russians a working map detailing any spy at any time in any part of the world. And thanks to computers, that task had now been made so much simpler and pretty well instantaneous. The beauty of the system was that once identified and if at all possible, depending on the sensitivity of the information gleaned by them, left in place, their careers could be followed and misinformation passed their way ad infinitum. Of course, this system was also used upon all other foreign Embassies as well. When one added to this equation all known associates of the suspect spy and cross referenced with all known associates of all the other spies then it is self-evident that computers, their information extrapolated and honed down to the smallest degree, all help to eliminate a lot of guesswork. Thus it was that Anthony Lovejoy-Taylor joined some of the most illustrious names in the annals of spying.

CHAPTER 14

LONDON

Six months had passed since Stryker had been coerced into working for Britain's Secret Intelligence Service and he was on his way back to Hampstead from his temporary office at Vauxhall Cross where he had been attending yet another morning briefing when at lunch time on the spur of the moment he decided to make a short detour. Ferris & Ferris was located not two steps either way, but slam bang in the middle of the Burlington Arcade, situated just off Piccadilly. With its fine polished mahogany woodwork façade, sparkling bevel-edged windows, and gleaming antiqued brass plate incorporating fancy turn of the century lettering which ran beneath the window spanning the whole length of the shop, it's ambience left no one in doubt that this particular establishment, though small in its frontage, reeked of solid service over many, many years. The fact that it had only been trading for the past four months was neither here nor there. The embellished characters chased deep within the brass work announced: *RUSSIAN IKONS*.

The window display was eye catching: Two beautifully hand painted pink cherubs sitting amidst white billowing clouds – each cherub a floating decoration upon a liturgical fan once used in close proximity to an altar in Mother Russia. Set upon an ornately gilded tripod between these two lyrical works of art was a large magnificent oval-shaped icon depicting a praying haloed Mother of God, attired in rich plum-coloured robes against a deep blue and gold background with Cyrillic hieroglyphics picked out in pink. One could well imagine the awe and inspiration drawn from such an image by followers of the Orthodox Church.

These thoughts however, were far from impinging upon Stryker's consciousness for time was pressing. Ambling through the half glazed door by pushing its heavy brass finger plate, he nonchalantly stepped past the shop assistant who was busy dealing with a client. It was a funny thing with icons. In an establishment of this calibre buyers were not customers but clients. Initially he strolled over to a beautiful icon in the Filimonov style, about two feet in height and eighteen inches wide and which had been authenticated by one of the few experts in Britain who knew about these things. Then he idled by this beautiful triptych set upon an altar cloth, admiring its workmanship, clad here and there in its silver riza ornamentation. Stryker stood as if transfixed, biding his time.

When the middle-aged woman with a pronounced English accent was in full flow extolling the finer points of icon collecting, Stryker seized his opportunity. Twisting the key which had been left in the cash till and letting the ornate drawer open slowly, counterbalancing the spring loaded mechanism with the palm of his hand, he could see that he was in luck as a large wad of twenty pound notes was revealed. Slowly and without attracting the attention of either the sales person or client, he slyly removed the money and transferred it into his Savile Row suit pocket, deftly pushing the cash drawer back into its rightful resting place, leaving both women blissfully unaware of his criminal tendency. That done, he attempted to make his way as unobtrusively as possible out of the shop and nearly succeeded in making his unannounced exit. Lady luck however, was not on his side.

"Oh, Mr Smith, this client would like to meet you. Mrs Dunhill, meet the owner of this beautiful shrine to religious art." *Ouch!*

Ferris & Ferris, the name of the establishment, was Stryker's idea – appealing to his mischievous sense of humour. Life, he thought, was a merry go round, not to be taken too seriously – much the same as a Ferris wheel. His new 'legitimate' business, pretty well instantly created so as to lend authenticity to his ruse as an established icon dealer was the importation and selling of Russian icons, of which he was in the throes of becoming something of a connoisseur thanks to MI6's contacts and one to one lectures on the subject. Sarah, another Six operative, had been assigned to help Stryker run this part of the business for reasons to quote C – "As being something of a symbiotic relationship between Stryker and Six." Ferris and Ferris would provide an excellent front for Britain's secret service to arrange meetings and collect information in many forms, acting as something of an undercover post office besides helping Stryker with his authenticity and giving him a business address. Six would bear the cost of renting and furnishing the premises with initial stock and carrying out minor changes to the façade including the upmarket brass plaque. Sarah and Stryker's joint learning curve was moving at pretty much the same pace. In his newly acquired icon business he was also helped by Caroline. His other business of course was to be the importation of 'The Red Chameleon's' secrets once he could be traced and which he very definitely could not sell though being remunerated in a miserly fashion, as he saw it, by his legitimate employers at Vauxhall Cross. Having swiftly built up his false identity using this import and retail business as a front for his proposed travelling to Russia in the course of his spying activities, he also speculated that it would help to keep his finances most definitely in the black. He would not concern himself with repairs or restoration of the mainly Russian icons – Sarah was also in the process of obtaining a few icons from Greece – but would farm the work out. Ironically, one of these rapidly acquired so-called 'experts' Stryker was going to use via his new contacts had been a passing acquaintance of Professor Sir Anthony Blunt. An establishment figure and respected art historian and director of the Courtauld Institute of Art, he had also been a Foreign Office official. Blunt at one time had held the title 'Keeper of the Queen's Pictures', though he was stripped of his knighthood in 1979 when it was disclosed he had in fact been a Soviet agent since the 1930s and a fellow traveller of the infamous British spies Burgess and Maclean, throwing his lot in with communism to fight fascism.

***

It was late as Carol sorted out their evening meal. That is to say, they prepared to visit Stryker's now favourite Chinese restaurant on Haverstock Hill, his half dozen dazzlingly white starched shirts having just been collected with another dozen items from the local laundry in Belsize Village. He was in the midst of tucking one of these shirts into his trouser waistband when the telephone rang. He touched a button on the answering machine and just as the light by the receiver came on, so did the tape.

To Stryker's surprise it was Dr Grachev, saying that he was sorry not to catch Stryker in but hoped he would remember the Russian scientist he had made the acquaintance with at the Easter Church service six months before and perhaps he would like to call back and let him know how he was placed for that belated drink he had promised. A telephone number was also left at the tail end of the message. Stryker smiled to himself as he replaced the receiver before putting a call through a secure line to Vauxhall Cross, asking one of the operatives there for background information on a Russian National going by the name of Dr Grachev to be left on his desk by morning. Stryker then recalled a verbal message that had been left for him months earlier regarding the request Carol had put through enquiring as to the owner of the car that had trailed him home from Ennismore Gardens after the Easter midnight service. The message informed him it was registered to the London Russian Embassy.

Ten minutes later Stryker and Carol were on the verge of letting themselves out of their flat when the idea occurred to Stryker that they should try once more to get through to the British Embassy in Dubai. Since receiving the anonymous message about someone being threatened with losing their lives, for whatever reason, he and Carol had been stonewalled whenever they attempted to speak to Hughes the Welsh naval attaché or his young duty officer named Stephen. Personnel at the embassy would always make some fatuous excuse about neither of them being available. Stryker was becoming suspicious and incensed and had decided not to take no for an answer. As the number was rung Carol hung onto Stryker's shoulder attempting to listen in to what was being said.

"Hullo, is that the British Embassy in Dubai?"

"This is the embassy – may I help you?"

"Yes," replied Stryker, with a firmness Carol had never witnessed before. "Would you please put me through to the naval attaché, a Mr Hughes or his colleague called Stephen I believe? I don't know his surname. It is very urgent I speak with either of them. My name is Stryker. I am calling from London. They know me."

The reply came back too glibly, as though his call had been expected: "I'm sorry Mr Stryker, but there is no one here of either name who works at this embassy. Sorry."

"But..." The line went dead. He had been cut off.

"Did you hear that?" Carol whispered, though there was no reason why she should do so.

"Yes, I did," replied Stryker as he pulled the street door firmly behind them and hurried off to the restaurant, his and Caroline's sole conversation now consisting of the strange telephone call from the suspected Welsh man several days earlier intimating that someone had threatened to kill 'them' and the startling news Stryker had just been presented with.

Two hours later they made their way back home from the Chinese restaurant into Belsize Park. They descended the steps, and let themselves into the flat before Stryker made another quick telephone call. He had decided to meet Dr Grachev on Wednesday evening at eight o'clock at the Normanhurst Hotel, Hyde Park.

CHAPTER 15

Saturday morning smiled brightly upon the London crowds as they moved around in droves, filling the streets and shops under the winter sunshine like flood water filling every conceivable nook and cranny. It was still chilly but the bright blue sky lifted everyone's spirits as they began the longed-for weekend. Dr Grachev was also in good form as he strolled up Charing Cross Road from the direction of Leicester Square, turning right into New Oxford Street, waiting patiently until the traffic lights were in his favour before making a mad dash with the other pedestrians beneath the soaring concrete Centrepoint Tower, a honeycombed skyscraper rocket ready to pierce the few wispy traces of clouds soaring amidst a sea of blue.

The Russian loved large cities because they afforded him that cloak of anonymity longed for by people who came from the Eastern Block and who had lived their lives under the pernicious forces of communism, with its all-pervading secret police listening and watching. There was a definite spring to his step as Dr Grachev sauntered along, feeling very relaxed. London can be a very daunting place for anyone not familiar with its layout as any large metropolis can be for a stranger. But for Dr Grachev it posed no problem, having walked these streets so many times before. However, he was not pounding these streets just to soak up the atmosphere of a big city. He had a very definite purpose in mind as he moved further along New Oxford Street until suddenly that purpose came into view.

The wide windows displayed a myriad of umbrellas in many different colours and styles. Some had beautifully carved bone handles, yet others had detachable handles, having the capability of turning themselves into swordsticks. Others even entertained the possibility of holding a measure or two of alcoholic beverage within their skilfully engineered shanks. However, umbrellas on such a pleasant day as this were the last thing on Dr Grachev's mind.

It took some time for the Russian scientist to find exactly what he was seeking, but as he suspected, the shop did in fact possess the object with which to lend a little authenticity to a plan laid out so meticulously many months before, and under such different circumstances as he now found himself. After insisting that the newly acquired object be wrapped securely in a decent amount of the shop's plain brown paper, Dr Grachev left the premises, only pausing to enquire as to where he might purchase some business cards. Upon being informed that if the amount required was negligible, he could instantaneously print them himself without the trouble of going to a printer and that he could carry out this simple task from a machine situated nearby for a matter of a few pounds, Dr Grachev began to feel that the day was definitely going his way.

After leaving the umbrella shop, a cynic might well have suggested that a visit to the theatrical costumiers Bermans might also be on his agenda. This would have indeed marked out the cynic as one who possessed great foresight, as within the hour Dr Grachev did indeed enter that hallowed shrine to thespians the world over.

CHAPTER 16

HAMPSTEAD

Chen Hsu could not get the thought out of his head. It had been quite late when the attack happened, just before midnight. He was still trembling uncontrollably. The evening had been normal in every respect before then. There was always going to be a certain amount of hassle when one dealt with members of the public, but Chen liked the variety of people that came into his restaurant. They were a cross section from the area. Lawyers, actors — some very well known, estate agents, businessmen, doctors, artists, writers, television personalities, all sorts, and he was on first name terms with many of them. Chen was proud of that. Sometimes in the quieter moments, he was even taken into their confidence, when some of the customers had just that one glass too many. This particular night was no exception.

It had been quiet earlier on, becoming busier around the middle of the evening. He recognised the face of a psychiatrist that he had seen on late night television a few times. Arriving with his extended family of eight, they stayed for a couple of hours and made quite a lot of noise after consuming many bottles of wine, which was not of the vin de table variety but of a much more expensive choice. It was unusual in the respect that every one of them had ordered the same dish for their main course; Peking duck, a speciality of Chen Hsu's restaurant. Then a spot of bother with another customer's credit card ended up with him paying cash. It had taken a few years to build up the business in Haverstock Hill and handling bank notes as compared to pieces of plastic always made him feel just that little bit happier.

Not that Chen Hsu had been unhappy up until the moment of the trouble. He took pride in running a restaurant that was decorated to a high standard. A large glass fish tank was the central feature of his open plan restaurant. In the tank were a variety of exotic fish which had cost him many thousands of pounds and would often crop up in conversation with the customers. Ten tables sat amidst a cosy glow of candles and soft unobtrusive music.

It was just before closing time that the two men came in and walked to the rear of the restaurant, taking up a table which had not yet been cleared. Chen told them there were vacant tables at the front by the window overlooking the street but they had insisted on remaining where they were.

He knew all the regular Chinese customers but had never set eyes on these two before. By now most of the other customers had left, except for a couple of young English men, one of whom had a little earlier accidentally knocked over a bottle of red wine, staining the tablecloth. The two Chinese men ordered enough food for four people and Chen told them as much, but the shorter one of the two had insisted and so the meal was duly served. They also insisted on keeping their dark unbuttoned overcoats draped across their broad shoulders, although the waiter whom Chen had assigned to their table had offered to hang them up.

As the evening takings were being counted and totals being checked against the duplicate bills, Chen Hsu heard the waiter shouting. As he looked over to see what was happening everything seemed to speed up. The taller of the two Chinese men had got to his feet grabbing the waiter's arm, pushing the hand down upon the pristine white tablecloth while the smaller man produced something from beneath his loosely draped overcoat which glinted in the candlelight, making a chopping motion at the waiters' fingers, expertly severing all five with one blow. Chen Hsu reeled as he looked for help from the two young English men but they had already fled. The five digits lay like some delicacy served up by the restaurant, the tip of the thumb having bounced onto the silver dish of a side order; its cuticle already tinged a delicate bluish-white, the blood rapidly mixing with the spicy sauce.

The tall man, a look of insouciance upon his featureless flabby face, still held the hand in his vice-like grip with the thumb tip and fingers now missing. The waiter was seen by Chen Hsu peering down at his hand. He was in shock, the colour drained from his face, giving him the appearance of a dead man. Then came the scream – a scream which chilled Chen Hsu's blood. A scream he could still not get out of his head. It seemed to go on and on. The man holding onto the handle of the large heavy steel meat cleaver now embedded into the wooden table top wrenched it away, displaying a neat gash through the severed fibres of the stiffly starched tablecloth itself. He then lifted up a part of the edge not covered in blood and carefully wiped clean the razor sharp steel chopper. Walking calmly over to Chen Hsu he whispered into his ear.

"We will be back... soon. Ten thousand pounds. Have it ready." A visiting card was pushed into Chen Hsu's trembling hands. After they left, he had looked down at the card, attempting to bring into focus the swirling black letters smudged with the waiter's blood: Xiang Wah Wei. It was a name he would not forget.

CHAPTER 17

RUSSIAN HINTERLAND

It was the weekend for which Marishka Petrova had been praying would arrive. The weather, growing colder by the day over the past few weeks had suddenly given way to an unseasonable break, creating the impression of autumnal days instead of the winter they were now dressed for.

Ivanovich Sobolev had unexpectedly spent Saturday morning on official business at the factory, going over production figures relating to anthrax spores to be used for the purposes of mass destruction in bio-warfare.

Back in Moscow, the military in the shape of one Colonel Oleynik had ordered that a shortfall at biological facility ES 205 over the preceding month was to be made up, meaning longer working hours for all involved, including Ivanovich Sobolev.

Marishka stood half concealed behind a copse of tall pine trees on the perimeter of the large abandoned estate, now an overgrown wasteland partially reclaimed by nature, her heart skipping a beat as the tall figure of Ivan came into view along the winding lane, hugging the boundary. His long strides lifted up a thin film of red dust lying on the track relentlessly covering everything, the strong sunlight casting hard-edged black shadows from the trees across his path. Stepping out from her hiding place Marishka ran toward him, eyes opened wide, her face wreathed in a smile of excitement.

"Ivan, I've got great news." There was breathlessness in her voice which made her seem even younger than she was. An innocence of youth which Ivan had noticed the very first time he had set his eyes upon her. As she tumbled into his long, thin, outstretched arms her words gushed out in a torrent.

"My brother, he's leaving. Off to stay with my aunt in the Urals. She said he can stay permanently and later work there when he is a little older. Mama told me last night. Oh Ivan, isn't it great news? Now we shan't have to worry about being spied upon any longer. It will make it easier to see one another. Oh Ivan, I love you."

Marishka's large dark brown eyes shone with happiness as she stood upon her toes, pushing her warm face close to his before gently planting a kiss upon his cheek. Then, searching for his hands, she pushed him back toward the copse only vacated minutes before where she had kept her stubborn lonely vigil from early morning. Beneath the tall trees the floor was littered with a bed of pine needles making the ground under their feet soft and springy.

"Marishka, my Marishka, you little kitten, I have something for you." As he placed one of his hands into a large pocket of his overcoat Marishka kicked off her well-worn shoes. Leaping up at him, she curled her bare legs around his waist, knocking him off balance, sending both of them sprawling backwards. Landing in a heap, her girlish giggles resonated softly in Ivan's ears.

"What have you got for me that is more important than my kisses?" Marishka gasped, rubbing his neck with her small tender hands. Ivan stretched out a clenched fist, so that something the colour of red and gold could be seen between his splayed fingers.

"Here, try and get it," he cried, laughing.

Marishka lifted one of her hands from Ivan's shoulders, attempting to pry his taught fingers away in a futile gesture to see what the precious object was. When she failed in this, a moist pink tongue poked out from between her red lips as she began rocking her head from side to side, her long black tresses framing a mischievous face as they tumbled down across the now bared milky white shoulders.

Ivan's clenched fist relaxed, dropping into her opened hand a beautifully carved and painted wooden figure of a peasant girl wearing a blue and yellow headscarf, the same colour as Marishka's. With a squeal of delight, she held the wooden body firmly and twisted off the upper half, revealing a smaller figure beneath. Then repeating the process, five more figures appeared, one inside the other until the final figure was no taller than one of Marishka's small fingernails. After reassembling the set of Matryoshka or Russian nesting dolls Marishka puckered up her full lips before giving Ivan a solemn look.

"I promise you I'll keep these dolls with me until my dying day. Ivan, I love you with all my being, with all my body." Gazing up at him. Marishka then slipped the scientist's large rough coat from off his thin shoulders and spread it out on the ground beneath the tall pine trees that masked the direct sunlight, allowing only a dim semblance of illumination to penetrate from above. Then, without waiting for any words to cross his lips she gently pushed Ivan's delicate shoulders back until he lay upon his own garment.

He did not move a muscle but was transfixed as Marishka, bathed in a dappled shaft of sunlight, began to remove her heavy outer clothing, dropping the woven green flounced skirt down by the side of Ivan's head. Carefully, lowering herself onto her haunches, she eventually sat crossed legged before him, revealing a soft warm rug of dark brown pubic curls below her belly, and wearing nothing more than a thick unbleached band of calico covering her as yet only partially formed breast buds. Ivan lifted himself upon one elbow, moving towards her from his supine position, his slim hands embracing Marishka's smooth, warm hips. The gentle ensuing murmurings of love-making were too far away to be heard by the voyeur who had observed them from a distance even before Marishka had initially broken her cover from the pine trees to greet Ivan only minutes earlier.

Later that day, Ivan told Marishka of his impending visit to Moscow and why she must never betray the trust he placed in her. He also explained how their relationship should, for the moment at least, remain secret, just between the two of them and why it was imperative not to mention it to anyone, not even her mother. It was a stricture Ivan bitterly regretted imposing upon her, but knew that there was no other way to safeguard their security. Marishka trusted Ivan and did not ask for any clarification of his short absence but it was freely given anyway, explaining that his aunt had left her dacha to him and that it was situated just on the perimeter of Moscow and even told her the address, saying that one day he would take her there for a holiday. Marishka's imagination was fired up, having never been to Moscow, and asked Ivan to tell her about the city, taking it all in and devouring every detail as if her life depended upon it. She also committed to memory the dacha's address.

CHAPTER 18

NORTH WALES

David knew that in these circumstances it was better to wait for the other person to decide when to speak. He knew this not just through instinct but from his training as a hypnotherapist. Penny had been quiet all through the afternoon and he hadn't wanted to intrude into what were obviously very private thoughts. Then as the light began to fade outside the cottage and David busied himself with putting together a log fire in the hearth, Penny, perhaps sensing a more intimate atmosphere developing, seemed to want to unburden herself. She sat in a small easy chair to one side of the fireplace looking forlorn.

"I'm sorry about spoiling your day with my mood. Please forgive me. The reason is that my mother told me something before she died and now I don't know what to do."

David nodded to Penny. "Go on, I'm listening." He scrunched up some old newspaper from the side of the hearth and retrieved a handful of small brittle twigs, laying them carefully over the top.

"I think I've mentioned how possessive my mother can... could be. When my father died, she grew even more so, if that was possible. She was always contacting me, threatening to commit suicide if I did not go home and keep her company. Well, staying at home was the last thing I wanted. Besides, I have my job. But Mum just wouldn't listen. She could never see it from my point of view. I needed my freedom. It wasn't a selfish attitude was it?" Penny looked to David for reassurance.

David thought back to the previous year when he had first bumped into Penny in London. It was whilst searching for some books on alternative medicine in Foyle's bookshop situated in Charing Cross Road. At the time Penny had been wearing an all-black outfit and he thought she must have been a model. He got chatting to her and discovered she actually worked at a large hotel by Hyde Park named The Normanhurst as a receptionist. After corresponding with one another he finally invited her to spend a weekend with him which she at first declined, thinking the invitation rather forward coming from someone she had only met once. Eventually though, after being asked several more times she had accepted his invitation and thoroughly enjoyed herself, happy at the thought of having overcome her reserved nature. Later that summer a two week holiday in North Wales ensued which turned out to be pure ecstasy, the two of them growing very close in the process.

"Well of course it wasn't a selfish attitude; everyone has to sever the apron strings sometime. It's probably because she missed your father. She's bound to have felt lonely."

"Yes, I'm sure that's it. You know that when we came from Russia I was quite small and we didn't have any relatives here to contact. Well, obviously we had ties with Britain otherwise we should never have seen these shores. I think it was my grandparents in fact, who had left England for Moscow initially, when Mum was barely a baby. If we'd had somebody to get in touch with in England it would have made things so different," Penny said wistfully, staring at the as yet unlit fire, absorbed for a moment, deep in thought.

"Anyway, to make settling here easier, my mother in her wisdom decided that we should change our names to English sounding ones. So we reverted to Mum's maiden name, Churchill. A good old English name isn't it? It seems so long ago now I don't even remember leaving the place where I was born, which is sad. And that's part of the problem. As hard as I try, I cannot remember anything about my childhood in the Soviet Union. It's as though I had never been there." Penny looked a picture of misery, having to pause to regain her composure.

"How old were you when you left Russia?" David placed two small logs precariously on top of the twigs.

"Eight. And my mother had only recently been prepared to talk about the country we left – my real country – the country of my birth. I don't want to sound silly David, but that's where I was born. Perhaps I should forget about it, but deep down in my heart I know that really was my country, and England is only my adopted place of residence; as much as I love it. Do you understand?"

David looked perplexed, wondering how someone who had spent all of their life, at least, all the life they could remember – how they could possibly think of a country they knew so little or nothing about, as being more important than the country they had been brought up in. He looked at her childlike features and his heart melted, thinking how beautiful she was.

"You don't understand do you? No, I suppose unless you've been in my situation you couldn't possibly begin to..."

"Do go on, I'm listening." David was now kneeling by the fireside, not daring to move and thereby break Penny's concentration.

"Well, recently, while Mum was sorting out some of Dad's accumulated bits and pieces, just before she became ill, a picture fell from between the pages of a book. It was a photograph of my mother when she was a lot younger, holding a little baby, perhaps a year old, with blond curly locks and plump cheeks, looking wide-eyed straight at the camera lens. The photograph had obviously been taken before we came to England. Anyway, when I turned it over, instead of finding a date of when the picture had been taken, which is what I had half expected, there was something written there, but not in English obviously, but in Russian. When I enquired as to what it said I knew straight away that something had upset her, she looked so distraught. And I also knew that when she did translate the words upon the back of the photograph she was lying to me. Call it a woman's intuition if you like."

"But what did your mother say to make you think she was lying?"

"She said that the message on the back meant *Best wishes from your cousin, Igor.'* She told me he had taken the photo and had scribbled this on the back when he gave it to her. I didn't believe a word of it."

"But maybe this really was what it said." David's face registered concern that Penny was making such a fuss over a trivial message on the back of an old photograph.

Penny sighed as she watched David return to fumbling with the newly laid fire. She watched him carefully as he raised the box of matches, extricating one in the process and struck it. The phosphorus match head flared noisily, breaking the silence which had descended upon the small sitting room.

"No! That was not what it said." The vehemence with which Penny had uttered the word 'no' caused David's fingers holding the lighted match to waver so much that the flame was extinguished before it had a chance to ignite the edge of the newspaper. He turned his head around to see her face flushed with indignation.

"That was not what it said at all."

"How do you know? Did you get it translated?"

"Yes."

"Well, what did it really say?"

"It said, *'My beautiful wife and daughter,'* and was signed *'Igor.'*"

"Well then, so what's the mystery? You told me that your father's name was Dimitri but he could have had a second Christian name, Igor, and signed the photograph accordingly."

"But he didn't. When I approached my mother with the translation she confessed before she died that Igor was her first husband, that she had been married twice."

"Oh! You poor thing. All these years and you didn't know that Dimitri wasn't your real father. I really feel very sorry for you."

"No, but it's even worse than that."

"How do you mean?" Penny stretched out her arm, pulling David toward her and held him close for comfort, as a child might hold a teddy bear for reassurance after a bad dream.

"David, it's the way Mum told me. It must have been because she was so ill – a bit delirious. Toward the end she would ramble sometimes. She said: '*Dimitri was not your father. Your father had died when you were just two months old.*' I said that could not be right because I was about one year old in the photograph – sitting on her knee. David, I really thought it might have been the drugs she was taking. You know, they were very strong painkillers and they made her feel a bit divorced from reality sometimes. She told me that herself. Anyway, what she said next had left me feeling sick and overjoyed all at the same time. Sometimes I burst out crying, just as I did this afternoon. I couldn't help it. My emotions just run away with me."

"So what did your mother tell you?" David's mind was now working overtime wondering what revelation was about to be divulged.

"I accused her of lying to me again, just as she had done about the message written on the reverse of the photograph. I feel really guilty now, her being so ill and everything. But then she told me something which I remember with such clarity, every one of her words engraved upon my mind like a tape recording. She said, '*No my darling, I'm not lying. You are not in that photograph.*' I thought her mind was wandering. '*But Mum, I can see myself plainly, what is wrong with your eyes?*' I was beside myself with frustration and just when I was beginning to think I would never understand what was going on she said, '*No Penny, you do not see yourself.*' That's when Mummy began crying and through her sobs she said, '*No Penny, what you see there in that photograph... is your sister.*'"

A gloom set in on what was supposed to have been a cosy reunion of two people obviously very fond of one another, seated around a blazing fire. Instead, David had not yet lit the paper so as to bring the flames through the twigs to the logs. They both sat in the small cold room, their features half concealed by the dark.

They remained like that, seemingly frozen in time for ages, before Penny spoke again, now even more distraught than when recounting her mother's revelation that she had a sister.

"What I am about to tell you next David, you must promise not to reveal to a soul. I know that I can trust you, but I just feel that I must ask you not to tell anybody. You don't mind my saying that, do you? It will help ease my mind a little."

CHAPTER 19

Villiers Street is situated adjacent to Charing Cross railway station and just a stone's throw away from the River Thames Embankment but far enough away from the Secret Intelligence Service offices based on the side of the River Thames at Vauxhall Cross so as not to be conspicuous. It was therefore in many respects an ideal venue for Carol to meet her good friend Barbara from Central Registry.

Sixty years before, Villiers Street had a reputation for housing some of London's most notorious crooks and also for the procurement of prostitutes, but now it supported a string of bijou cafés and a rich assortment of restaurants of various nationalities. It was in one of these small restaurants set deep within the dark, cloistered basement that the two friends now sat nursing a cappuccino accompanied by a large portion of spiced apple strudel. It had been at Six's annual Christmas party when the two women really got to know one another and had remained firm friends and confidants ever since. So Carol did not hesitate when asked by Stryker to see what she could find out about the British naval attaché and his companion duty officer Stephen, both stationed at the British Embassy in Dubai. She immediately thought of approaching her line manager Brenda from Registry, whom she looked upon as her friend and mentor, being a lot older than her.

It was after the waitress had climbed the rickety wooden staircase that Brenda lowered her voice to barely audible. "I've got some news for you Carol." She now looked very worried, which she definitely had not appeared to be when they were outside in the street. Carol supposed the previous façade of normality adopted by her companion just minutes earlier had been for both of their security, and that this was now the real Brenda speaking. The string of pearls peeking out from beneath a pale pink twin set gave the impression of her hailing from the upper classes and her accent, like that of Carol herself, confirmed this aspect. But unlike Carol she had gone prematurely grey, looking much older than her mid-forties.

"I don't quite know how to tell you this. It's very strange. I didn't have time to look through the whole Dubai file you asked me to scan because one of the security people came in whilst I had some of my other files out on the table so I don't think he knew what I was doing but it made me nervous – I suppose it's because I knew I was doing something I shouldn't have been. Anyhow, I think you should be very careful in what you say to your other colleagues because for some reason you have been tagged *persona non grata.*"

Carol swallowed hard but did not immediately respond to this piece of debilitating information. Brenda carried on regardless.

"In the file there was a copy of a note sent to the British Embassy in Dubai and that is what it says. To be specific it instructed all employees working within that embassy not to impart any information you might request. The file says you and your boyfriend Stryker are – to quote: *'Persona non grata.'* Brenda gave Carol a funny look which she found unsettling and coupled with this devastating news made her feel physically sick. There was only one initial response she was able to give and that was a long, drawn out gasp though Brenda's unwarranted reference to Stryker being her boyfriend was music to her ears.

"Whaaat! Did I really hear you correctly? Are you telling me the Department doesn't trust us? But that's unbelievable. How could they possibly employ me if they don't trust me? I mean, I've been through that long, drawn out process of vetting like the rest of us who work for 'Six'. And for that matter so has Stryker – in a matter of speaking."

"In a matter of speaking?"

"Well he was treated as a special case – but of course I have been forbidden to discuss such things."

"You did say that you couldn't tell me what happened in Dubai because of the need-to-know caveat, which of course applies to all of us who work for the department. But that said: *'Persona non grata!'* It's not the sort of thing Six usually bandies about lightly. Might there be some aspect of this case which warrants such an instruction? After all, the notification does only apply to Dubai per se, which on the face of it seems rather strange to my way of thinking."

The two women ceased their conversation as they watched the waitress slowly come down the rickety staircase, remaining at the other end of the tiny cellar from where they were seated as she fiddled with her order pad.

Carol and Brenda tucked into their apple strudels so as to fill in the time until it was safe to speak again. It didn't take long before the waitress saw that she was not required and once again ascended the staircase.

"I'd very much like to fill you in on what this is all about Brenda, but as you say this whole thing is on a need-to-know basis which is a very convenient catch-all phrase for the upper echelons to have at their disposal. However, because of certain circumstances relating to the Dubai embassy I suppose it is how the system operates. You know, Stryker only became involved when he was on holiday in Dubai. And it was through sheer bad luck he lost his two friends because of it. There, I've said far too much. You'll be regarding me as a blurter."

"Darling, if I regarded you as anything remotely like a leaking sieve I should not be sitting here with you now, and it is after all only an order addressed to this single embassy. The powers that be cannot possibly think you might be a traitor or the note would have been passed to all the embassies and you certainly wouldn't be let into Vauxhall Cross. And I saw with my own eyes that the order was only concerned with the British Embassy in Dubai. Anyhow I did my best and I am terribly sorry to be the bringer of such bad news. You won't shoot the messenger will you?"

Carol tapped Brenda on the back of her hand. "It's what's behind the message that worries me. I think I'm the one that should be afraid of being shot."

CHAPTER 20

NORTH WALES

David had felt that there could not possibly be any more revelations to divulge, except of course there obviously were. Yet being Penny's confidant was in itself bringing the two of them closer together, which made him feel good. He twisted his body slightly so as to hold onto one of Penny's hands. "Of course I don't mind you confiding in me. I would never divulge a confidence."

"No, of course you wouldn't. I'm very lucky to have you as a friend David." Penny rested her free hand lightly on David's shoulder.

"The last time I saw Mum alive she was in considerable agony and I had measured out her dose of painkiller, but before she took it she motioned me to sit down by her bedside. I suppose because the medication had the effect of making her feel groggy she had decided to put up with the pain for a while longer, so as to be able to speak to me with a clear head. It must have been agony for her but she did it. Her voice was not very strong so I had to put my ear quite close to her mouth so as to hear what she was saying, but she seemed extraordinarily lucid that day. I can see her head propped up on that large white pillow as if she were here now. She brought up the subject of my sister again, but only in a passing reference. I obviously wanted to discover where she was but Mum told me she would explain everything in good time and that I had to be patient.

"She then spoke of Dimitri, my stepfather, whom I had always thought of as my real father. She asked me to forgive her for getting married again, but that maybe next time she would explain the circumstances of how it all came about; but that even then I might not understand. It all sounded so cryptic. She said marrying him had become a great burden, and that she had carried a sense of guilt around with her ever since leaving the Soviet Union – as it was then. Apparently my real father, Igor, had died soon after I was born. Dimitri came along some time later, after he had been involved in a terrible tragedy. He had apparently killed someone. Mum stressed that it was an accident and that Dimitri was the kindest, gentlest person who had walked this earth. She said that when she first met him Dimitri was a broken man, riddled with guilt."

David squeezed Penny's hand, as much for his own benefit – to confirm that he was wide awake and not dreaming of such portent, an incredible story yet to be unfolded, at the same time giving confidence to his confessor for what must surely be a very difficult story to relate.

"Oh Penny, I'm so sorry."

"I suppose that's why he never worked since living in England. He always suffered from ill health – bad nerves, that sort of thing. Anyway, Mum said that a tragedy had also befallen her own family at the same time. I assumed some relative or other of ours had been involved, and that through their common misfortune they found themselves drawn to one another, eventually marrying. To tell the truth, I was more interested in hearing about my sister and discovering where she was, but my mother seemed in such agony I just went along with her, hoping to discover more about my sister's whereabouts the next time I saw her. I gave Mum the pain killers and watched her for a while until she fell asleep. Then I left her to go back to London. The next day, as you know, a call came through to tell me that she had died early that morning. Now I don't know how I shall be able to find my sister. I thought I knew my dad. I thought he was a good person, and kind like my mother said. But he was neither of those things. He was not my father and he had actually killed someone. It's a nightmare. My world has been shattered. To have your faith in someone so utterly destroyed. Someone who you loved and believed was your father. He was obviously a bastard."

David was taken aback. "Now that's not fair Penny. Why say such a thing about the person who helped raise you?"

"I say it because he should have been concerned about bringing up his own son."

"What!"

"Yes, that's right. Mum said he had a young son who was there when this person was killed. His son actually witnessed the whole event. Can you imagine, it must have left a deep psychological scar on his mind, don't you think? So anyway, Dimitri divorced his wife to marry my mother and left his son with his former wife. So I have a stepbrother living somewhere in Russia to add to my newly discovered sister. What a mess!"

David rose slowly to his feet before crouching down to light the fire. This time there was no unforeseen outburst to distract him from his singular task. The paper caught light at once, rapidly spreading to the bone dry twigs and logs which crackled loudly, spitting out unseen debris. He then moved over to wrap both his arms around Penny's body, enveloping her in a bear hug.

"David, you will help me find my missing sister, won't you?" To her mind, as sister-germane, it was obvious that Penny should feel a closer affinity to her lost sibling than that of a stepbrother. The question had already been answered by David's affectionate embrace.

"I love you Penny, like you cannot imagine." Penny looked into the now blazing fire with a fragile smile around her lips, feeling more relaxed than she had felt for the last few weeks.

CHAPTER 21

LONDON

There was a light drizzle as they departed London University campus and the reunion, which had generated so much anticipation for the last few weeks. Meeting up with so many old friends brought memories flooding back – of the sheer hard graft – often studying into the early hours of the morning, burning the candle at both ends with parties as well as work. Yet it was only now, upon returning, that they had met properly for the first time. True they had made one another's acquaintance fleetingly in the dying moments of last years' reunion – before going their separate ways once more.

Although the weather was dull, they both felt in high spirits. Tom was determined not to let another year pass without seeing Li Cheung again.

"Are you hungry?" Tom knew she must be, for there had only been copious amounts of booze to cement the friendships on the campus that day: real or imagined. It was a mystery why he had never bumped into Li Cheung when he was at university; even taking into account the fact that she had begun her studies a year later than him. He had studied biology and chemistry and had been a real swot. Li Cheung had also studied biology so they had something in common to talk about.

"I am a bit. You can come back to my little hovel if you like and we'll eat something there." Tom could not believe his ears. Here was the most beautiful girl at the reunion inviting him back to her place. He found it hard not to sound too enthusiastic just in case she changed her mind.

"Here you are Li, my old banger. You'll have to give me directions though as I don't know London all that well, except this particular area of course. Unless that is, you live just around the corner." They were standing beside a beaten up old wreck of a car. Although Tom described it as an old banger, it was in reality his pride and joy, until the next cheap second-hand car that came his way. Working in the civil service as a Scientific Officer at his particular grade paid quite well and he could have afforded something better, but to Tom, having a car meant much more than just transport. It was a challenge. He loved tinkering with engines and getting his hands dirty, He supposed it had something to do with the fact that at his place of employment, everything had to be kept absolutely scrupulously clean. At

Porton Down, the top secret government biological research centre, he worked in a sterile environment like no other in the country, with a strict protocol for keeping it that way.

As they drove through Stockwell, South London, the drizzle gave way to hazy sunshine. Soon they were at Camberwell Green and the next minute found them standing outside a large semi-detached house in Camberwell Grove; number seventy. Li Cheung's eyes lit up.

"I'm on the second floor – see – those two large windows." Her delicately formed white hand with clear-lacquered, beautifully manicured fingernails motioned to two high Victorian mullion windows, the black paintwork in need of urgent attention. From where they stood, strains of the latest popular music wafted down. "I didn't mention it before, but there's a party going on. I hope you don't mind?"

Li Cheung's long lustrous black hair glistened in the fading sunlight and Tom had never felt more like being on his own with a girl. But he smiled softly and lied.

"Of course not, I like parties."

Li Cheung's accommodation consisted of one very large room with a couple of single beds pushed beneath the tall windows overlooking the street, mimicking sofas, with scatter cushions placed judiciously. A tall chest of drawers and wardrobe stood in one corner with a heavy oak wooden dining table also set against one of the other walls. Another door opposite the window led into a small bathroom. A gas cooker had been fitted into a niche between the bathroom and the entrance. None of these features were visible as Tom followed Li Cheung into the room. It was just a sea of heads bobbing in time with the beat of thumping music, drowning out any possible conversation. Shouts of recognition from the gyrating throng greeted Li Cheung as she immediately took hold of Tom's hand, pushing a way through to one of the beds. Removing her small pink jacket she threw it down and looking into Tom's face smiled sweetly as she grabbed his other hand and started dancing in time to the music. They were pushed so close together by the other dancers that he could feel her soft body jerking against his. The sheer exuberance and physical force she was exerting on him was something he had never experienced before and he knew he was becoming incredibly aroused.

"It's my birthday next week; will you come to it?" Li Cheung had to shout above the cacophony of music and other voices to make herself heard. For Tom it just kept getting better. No girl had ever been so forward with him before and an invitation from such a siren as this was the stuff of dreams.

"You try and stop me," he replied, his face wreathed in smiles.

CHAPTER 22

An elderly gentleman shuffled slowly along Harley Street, bent almost double and leaning heavily on a black cane topped with a silver pommel. Because of his stoop he appeared to have difficulty in raising his head to scan the upper sections of the old buildings until he spied what he had been looking for. There, fixed firmly to a wall high up above eye level and pointed in his direction was a remote camera, now a familiar sight of street furniture's antipathy to democratic ideals found in every town and city in England. He slowly tapped his way, step by step, toward the entrance of an imposing-looking house. To the right of a bell push was a brass plate bearing the words: Doctor's Surgery. He rang the bell once and waited. After a gap of perhaps thirty seconds the door was opened, leading into a cavernous hall, two doors giving off to his right and one to his left. The room to the left was obviously the reception area for patients. The doors to the right led to two doctor's surgeries. The walls supported prints of hand tinted seascapes. At the far end of this hall, facing the street door was a dark wooden reception desk incorporating a modesty panel with a small modern telephone switchboard sitting on top.

"You must be?"

The elderly gentleman paused, weighing up his interrogator before answering.

"Dr Grey. I rang you earlier regarding your advertisement in the newspaper." The visitor's head was bent low, the receptionist having difficulty in making out his face.

"Ah yes, you were interested in renting a room here. Let me show you." The tired-looking middle-aged woman moved toward one of the rooms and held the surgery door handle down. "It's a month's rent in advance. You must also give a month's notice if you decide to vacate the premises. The terms were in the newspaper."

There was no charm in her voice and her lips were too thin and her eyes watery. As the consulting room door opened, a pungent odour wafted from its interior, the impression being that it had not been used for some time. As if reading Dr Grey's mind the receptionist walked over to the window and threw it open. "Bit musty in here at the moment but the air should soon be fresher." The conviction in her voice did not carry much weight.

There were two hard upright chairs for prospective patients and a much larger leather swivel chair, half hidden behind a heavy oak double pedestal desk, plus a rather worn-looking examination couch. A business card was proffered to the receptionist, an expression of surprise lighting up her face as she studied the initials after the doctor's name. They meant absolutely nothing to her. For the first time she eyed the elderly doctor up and down. He looked as though he might be in his seventies. Exceptionally long grey hair crowned a thin, pallid face topped off with thick, bushy, white eyebrows and she thought he might have sported a grey moustache but he was so stooped it was hard to make out all his features.

"That's fine mister... err, Doctor Grey. That's very kind of you." The money disappeared quicker than a magician's coin and just as deftly. "Here are three keys. Two of the keys are for the street door and this one for your consultation room. You can use the surgery on a Saturday if you wish but I am only here until lunchtime, it being the weekend you understand. You'll find it quiet at the moment because we are just in the throes of redecorating the other rooms so there is no one other than you on the premises at the moment." The doctor smiled to himself as he pocketed the keys to the building. The receptionist quickly scrawled a receipt in illegible handwriting. Dr Grey slowly made his way along the entrance hall toward the street door, a buzzer sounding as he reached for the heavy Victorian brass handle to let himself out.

***

One can be anonymous in a large hotel lobby amid a sea of faces, and this proved to be the case with the elderly gentleman as he shuffled his way toward the lift still holding the silver-topped walking cane. As the doors closed and a lift attendant pressed a button for the required floor, the old man momentarily caught a glimpse of himself in one of the ornate gilded mirrors adorning the three walls, and if a stranger was paying particular close attention to the gentleman's vanity, a thin but fleeting smile would have been detected. Once ensconced within the safety of his room however, the elderly man appeared to become rejuvenated and several inches taller, lithely tossing his black walking cane upon his freshly made bed, the brown paper wrapping in which it had earlier been brought into the hotel now having been disposed of by the chamber maid. Moving swiftly into the bathroom he stood for several seconds, gazing intently into the mirror which was illuminated by a fluorescent tube neatly concealed behind an ornate gold leafed white plasterwork frieze.

The skin beneath his eyes was far too smooth. Where there should have been wrinkles around the corners of his mouth there were none. And the eyes themselves possessed a brightness, a twinkle which the intervening years would in normal circumstances have dimmed. In truth, his face on closer inspection was not in reality that of an ageing gentleman at all but that of an imposter bearing the obvious outward sign of white hair designed to feign such an illusion. As his thin elongated fingers tugged at the fine bleached mane of wavy locks, the toupee fell to the floor, revealing a full head of healthy-looking black hair without a fleck of white in it except at the nape of his head which bore a small strange birthmark in the form of an irregular white cross. The thick white eyebrows were slowly peeled away, catching the skin where too much fixative had been applied by an inexperienced hand. And lastly, the full moustache was replaced by a clean shaven face, now displaying all the signs of healthy youth, the years having melted away in front of him. The decrepit old man who just minutes earlier had entered the bathroom no longer existed. So far the ruse had worked to perfection, and the person who now gazed back at him in the mirror was a very satisfied looking Dr Grachev; biological weapons scientist and expert par excellence.

CHAPTER 23

The spacious hotel reception area was relatively quiet. Within the foyer a dozen people attired in evening dress moved around chatting animatedly between themselves. A frock-coated doorman wearing a gold braided olive green peaked cap was beckoning a hall porter for help with some new arrival's luggage. Two young women dressed in smart silver-grey costumes stood behind the long mahogany reception desk quietly chatting. A tall young man dressed in a black suit and tie, white starched shirt and sporting a red carnation in his buttonhole also stood behind the counter writing in a large leather bound book.

A magnificent chandelier, suspended high above exquisitely crafted Louis XIV bergère armchairs scattered in an asymmetrical manner and upholstered in Hungarian flame stitch fabric within gilded frames, threw out a myriad of light, reflecting all the colours of the rainbow through the exquisitely cut glass pendants.

"Ah! Mr Stryker, how are you?" Stryker felt a hand in the middle of his back and spun on his heels out of instinct, to be confronted by the grinning face of Dr Grachev. In different circumstances Stryker might very well have instinctively struck out hard with the edge of his hand, aiming for the throat with the intention of severely damaging his opponent's windpipe. He had killed before whilst serving with the U.S. Special Forces and knew the sound of a man's last gasp as his larynx is destroyed.

"Dr Grachev – how very nice to see you again." He looked into the doctor's face and noticed the skin had a pale appearance to it as if brushed with fine white powder. *This man does not relish being in the sun*, was Stryker's first fleeting thought. The skin over Dr Grachev's face was pulled taught over high cheekbones. His thick eyebrows almost met in the middle, always a bad sign, and his lips were too red. The doctor wore his jet black hair short, almost in a crop, and his eyes were a deep brown. All of this visual information Stryker absorbed in an instant. He was used to making mental notes on the features of people, their characteristics, weaknesses and strengths. Stryker's tradecraft as a Seattle detective had been learnt well over the years and he felt very secure in his judgement and intuition that had never failed him. Except for the time he acquired his slight facial scar. But then no one was infallible – not even him.

Stryker was used to assessing other people – of sizing them up in such minute detail, so much so that sometimes they hardly seemed like people at all, just characteristics to be categorised and filed away in his head. The subjects' whole being stripped down to its barest essentials. He had always thought of himself as a master of verisimilitude, having a natural bent for giving credence to his cover stories in so many different ways when working undercover as a Seattle cop, which was why he was taking to this spying business so readily and even in a way beginning to enjoy its quirkiness, being instructed in the art of spying and the calibre of his foes, the Russians, though he had not as yet done anything of significance. Though that said, since the unfortunate disaster ending up with him losing an eye, he had begun to doubt himself sometimes and knew that could be dangerous, especially in this new line of work, however temporary. But for tonight he would attempt at least to suspend the working of his ingrained suspicious analytical mind.

"We are in luck this evening Mr Stryker." Dr Grachev put his head close to Stryker's ear in a conspiratorial manner, as if they were planning to blow up the Houses of Parliament. "The hotel management seem to have made a blunder in overbooking the restaurant, thus leading to us having been allocated a small private room for our evening meal. Are you hungry Mr Stryker?"

The American detective stood clutching his recently acquired brown trilby hat firmly by its battered rim, wondering just what possible ulterior motive Dr Grachev might have by inviting him for dinner.

"I thought we were just having a drink."

"Well, that was the idea, but I have not yet eaten and so I thought I'd kill two birds with one rock. Is that not a good old English expression Mr Stryker?" Not wishing to destroy Dr Grachev's illusion of his possessing a sound command of the English language, Stryker just smiled and nodded. He was beginning to like this Russian fellow.

Upon the ornate door being opened, Stryker was surprised at just how cramped the room was which they had been ushered into, and also how bare of ornamentation. Most of the space was taken up by a small circular table covered in a white damask tablecloth laid out with the requisite silverware. He also felt guilty about having a meal at Dr Grachev's expense until he was informed that Dr Grachev had authority to put such things on a credit account courtesy of the Russian Government. Stryker saw the irony of the Russians giving him sustenance so that he could fight his little war against the as yet mysterious Red Chameleon. He enjoyed his private little joke, thinking it a waste he could not share it with his hospitable table companion.

The two men's conversation revolved around various general points of interest of no significance, as conversations between relative strangers are apt to do. Dr Grachev then made another foray into the intricacies of his newly adopted vocabulary by attempting a stab at his knowledge of the Trooping of the Colour and warming to the challenge as he enthused about the ceremony of the 'plumed and skinned guards.'

After finishing the light meal and saying goodbye to Stryker in the hotel foyer, where the evening's meeting had been initiated, Dr Grachev made his way over to the receptionist who had arranged the small dining room on his express wishes, surreptitiously pushing five pounds into the palm of her hand as a thank you gesture. The scientist wondered how such a smart and very attractive-looking young woman could possibly be working in such a menial position. She took the tip with a beaming smile and said thank you. It was not the largest tip she had received that day, but Penny assumed the man must by his name be Russian, and coloured by this assumption therefore attractive. Looking him up in the hotel register it had given her a thrill to see that he resided in Moscow, the city of her birth. She did not inform her Russian compatriot of this fact however, for forwardness was not part of Penny's nature, whereas being discreet with hotel guests was regarded as de rigueur.

Earlier, Dr Grachev had ordered steak and salad for himself whilst a light chicken salad had been chosen to pick at by his guest without enthusiasm, Stryker not feeling particularly hungry. Coffee and cream was served soon after. Both declined brandy. It was therefore on reflection a puzzle to Stryker as to why he had but the vaguest of recollections of his journey home. Tiredness had later been put down to his lapse of memory. He could vaguely recall expounding with his host on the perceived Russian siege mentality and a hazy idea that both had agreed Russian society was in the process of fragmentation. He also had a dim memory of bidding Dr Grachev goodnight smiling broadly and promising to call upon him when next in Moscow on business, even letting Dr Grachev write down his address and telephone number in Stryker's pocket diary, something he would normally never let anyone do, neither here nor in the States, if only because of the security aspect.

A feeling of wellbeing had enveloped him as he arrived home at Hampstead in a good frame of mind, in a state of euphoria in fact and was only too happy to accept a cup of coffee made by his now constant companion who tonight happened not to be working late at Ceausescu Towers as she would sometimes refer to Vauxhall Cross.

"I was thinking about how you managed to obtain that information regarding the car which tailed me from the Orthodox Church and how it turned out to be registered to the Russian Embassy; haven't had any luck yet with the background information I requested from Vauxhall Cross on

Doctor Grachev though. Don't you find that strange?"

"Oh Stryker, you're just becoming paranoid."

"That's my detective's suspicious nature I guess. Mind you I do feel rather elated this evening. Must have been something my Russian friend slipped into my coffee." Stryker laughed at his remark before Carol mentioned that Vauxhall Cross must be getting lazy if they had not obtained the information on Dr Grachev as Stryker had requested, promising that she herself would look into it.

CHAPTER 24

Stryker's feeling of wellbeing appeared infectious, for Dr Grachev too had cause for celebration. He had just completed the necessary and very successful covert hypnotic induction of Stryker without his subject knowing anything about it, using a technique called 'confusional', whereby one may be able to hypnotise a person without them realising what is happening.

This particular technique had been learnt and mastered to perfection whilst Dr Grachev was on one of his frequent visits to America. By studying the works of the late renown exponent, Milton H. Erickson, an American and fellow doctor who had devised it, he had raised his own proficient technique as a hypnotist to a new level, though there had been many other optional techniques open to him.

When Dr Grachev set his mind to it, he knew before going ahead that almost anything could be achieved. His belief in himself was phenomenal, a man whose hubris was, even for a scientist of his calibre, excessive. He also, like Stryker, took a professional interest in people, except, unlike Stryker's new temporary vocation, it was not to figure out if they could be persuaded to betray their country. On the contrary, Dr Grachev's interest was much more basic, even though his particular perspective was seen through scientific eyes. The question which constantly ran though Dr Grachev's mind was: What would be the most efficient and cost effective way of killing people?

CHAPTER 25

OUTSKIRTS OF MOSCOW

Ivan had only recently been informed of his legacy regarding the dacha and the small piece of tree-strewn land upon which it sat on the outskirts of Moscow, notwithstanding the fact that his aunt had died over two years previously. That did not surprise him. Even post Gorbachev, bureaucracy still reigned supreme. He felt guilty not knowing about her long illness and subsequent death, having left Moscow on a semi-permanent basis many years before, not of his own choosing, but that of his superiors within the Ministry of Medical and Microbiological Industries. It was not that he never visited the city, quite the contrary; he visited it on a regular basis so as to attend meetings with his scientific colleagues at Biomedico. That is why he felt so guilty.

It was still daybreak as he moved from room to room, attempting to reconstruct the gossamer-like childhood memories of his aunt, the fragments of conversation which at the time had seemed so important to him. He found it difficult to bring to mind even what she had looked like, and the harder he worked at it, the more holes appeared within his fragile tangled web of happy memories. The gilt photo frames which might have supplied him with her image and which had sat upon an assortment of rustic tables for a lifetime were still there, untouched and gathering dust, but the photographs themselves had been removed, perhaps in some fit of pique as an attempt to erase painful memories of people lost in death, or to the vagaries of friendship. It was as if in some strange way his regular visits as a schoolboy had all been an illusion. And yet here he was, his feet echoing around the very tangible dust-strewn wooden floors, threadbare carpets doing their best to hide the years of neglect and dereliction which had stealthily encroached upon the dacha, shrouded from the outside world by unrestrained oak trees and limes, hawthorn bushes and weeds growing in fertile abundance.

Ivan shivered, furling his arms about himself, red raw hands rubbing briskly up and down upon the thick sleeves to keep himself warm, no heat having permeated the fabric of this house for the last two summers. A musty smell clogged his nostrils. Uninvited spiders had taken advantage of the intervening years to weave their cobwebs in corners undisturbed;

trapped, shrivelled, desiccated flies and insects, hanging from invisible filaments, caught in the erratic eddy of draughts and spinning endlessly. A pervading dampness of the countryside had also taken up residence, leaving everything cold and clammy to his touch.

The flight had been uneventful, except for the inclement weather, including snow, which had made his sleep on the plane fitful. In the kitchen he began clearing out the log fire stove in preparation for a hot meal, removing ashes and pieces of charred paper, his aunt's final futile attempt to destroy her personal papers accumulated over such a long period of time. Ivan knew this because of the dates on the partially burnt correspondence, some going back to the nineteen-twenties.

Then something caught his eye, a remnant of a letter bearing an address in England. It was from a Mrs Churchill. The name brought sudden clarity to his thoughts, and he could once again visualise his aunt standing by the kitchen window, her fragile features shining with a waxen luminescence, the light giving form to a bone structure cleverly developed, hinting at a certain indefinable beauty. The blonde hair interspersed with silver threads, and that same deep green dress, trimmed with a decorative bead work around her waspish waist which she always seemed to wear. She was speaking to him, but it was not in his native Russian tongue but in a language at first he could not comprehend. Then still a child, over a period of years he came to understand the language she taught him so meticulously, and to love the stories he heard in it from her lips. It was through his aunt that he made his first tentative steps at speaking in English.

He blinked, and as quickly as his aunt's image had appeared it vanished, stolen into the soft, hazy early morning light. Yet upon the door frame there was tangible evidence of their relationship, the barely perceptible marks etched into the wooden structure, made with the point of a knife, running from a height of about three feet up from the floor to approximately four and a half feet, charting the outward signs of a growing young boy, still full of innocence and as yet ignorance of the world he was beginning to come to terms with. Ivan measured the top indentation with his hand, discovering that it barely came up to his chest and figured that he must have been about twelve or thirteen. A tinge of sadness touched him, knowing that he could never retrieve those lost years, the time when he was happiest. By then of course he had his sights set on becoming a scientist and soldier, both of which inspiration had come to fruition, though his brief active military career had ended abruptly when he lost part of his trigger finger in an unrelated accident. He was still able to use a gun, but it was a slower, cumbersome affair, not equal to the task of being a competent soldier.

Eventually, after foraging for fuel, the stove was lit, allowing Ivan to make a steaming pot of coffee. Then, as tiredness overcame him, instead of preparing himself a hot breakfast, he settled for a torn off hunk of rye bread and some cheese which he had the foresight to bring along. Damp scavenged sugar was heaped liberally into the black coffee, transforming it into thick syrup.

Beginning to feel revived after his hastily prepared snack, Ivan took a stroll around the large, snow-laden, overgrown garden, carrying a slim briefcase stuffed with papers so meticulously gathered together and furtively buried in the shed used for his clandestine tryst with Marishka Petrova. After a while, he stopped by one of the large oak trees on the perimeter of his recently acquired property and surveyed it from all angles, before scraping away the heavy snowfall around its base. He then dug a shallow hole using a spade found with other garden tools lying in a shed adjacent to the dacha. The earth was rock hard and it took great effort and some time before his task could be accomplished. Then, making sure that the briefcase was well sealed in a plastic bag, he buried it, replacing the frozen brittle sods of turf before stamping it down hard with his feet. So as not to leave a mound of earth where his papers were buried, the displaced residue of soil was hurled down a steep wooded escarpment some distance away leading to the main road far below.

Making his way back toward the dacha, Ivan peered up at the whiteness of the washed out sky and saw a flock of geese move slowly overhead in their telltale chevron formation. So high did they fly and so low was the sky that it seemed possible the geese might rupture the low slung canopy with their rigid wings. Once again, for some inexplicable reason, he thought of his childhood, a wave of melancholy sweeping over him as he re-entered the building. While in the process of exploring the upper floor, Ivan discovered a well-used chaise longue upon which he threw his tired body, sending up clouds of fine dust. By the time this dust had settled, Ivan had also sunk into a much needed sleep. It had taken courage to carry top secret research documents through both airports and his energy had been sapped by the experience. The title of the Lermontov novel within which Ivan had so cleverly concealed the microdot might have been set down as his own future epitaph: '*A Hero of our Time.*'

When Ivan opened his eyes again it was dark outside, the only sound came from the rustling of a mouse scampering along the edge of a curtain pelmet, one end having become detached from the wall at an acute angle. For a moment he did not know where he was, the realisation slowly seeping into his consciousness that he was in his late aunt's dacha, and that his stomach was crying out for food. Rubbing his chin, he could feel the rough stubble where only a few hours earlier it had been quite smooth. He depressed a button at the side of his watch, illuminating the face. It was just after six pm; surely he had not slept for so long!

Attempting to stand up, his body crashed down hard upon the wooden floor, the right leg buckling under him, it having lost all feeling. Hauling himself back onto the edge of the chaise longue he waited until the pins and needles entered his dead leg, a sure sign that blood was once again flowing through his arteries. What little heat had spread from the log burning stove downstairs had long ago been dissipated by the overwhelming cold, the chill now seeping into every muscle within his lean body.

The plane taking Ivan back home was due to leave that evening, therefore little time was spared for his ablutions. He used freezing rust-stained water from the kitchen tap. The ritual of shaving in cold water which he so abhorred had become a way of life as a recruit in the Soviet armed forces. Although a serving army officer, he no longer had to endure such hardships in his present day to day life.

As Ivan dried his face he became aware of something moving around his feet. Gingerly grabbing hold of the long black rubber torch, whose light he had been shaving by, he slowly directed the beam downwards, illuminating two small bright eyes peering up at him. They belonged to what appeared to be a medium sized brownish grey cat. To his horror he soon realised that what he was really staring down at was the biggest rat he had ever seen. Rats can move fast so perhaps Ivan's instinctive reaction played a part as he quickly brought the heavy torch crashing down upon its hunched furry back, the creature making a shrill screeching noise before springing off the floor to a height of a metre before falling back motionless, its tiny eyes now lifeless. Then the reflex action took over, ingrained in all who are used to dealing with such vermin. His leather boot swiftly lashed out at the now flaccid furry lump, sending it flying from the torch's beam of light into the darkness and landing with a dull thump against the unseen wall. Ivan lifted the torch to inspect the damage inflicted upon its lens. The clear plastic was cracked from one side to the other but still held securely within its rubber frame.

***

Ivan came out from beyond the tree line and stood stock still upon the grassy verge, a wave of relief sweeping over him as a dark-coloured car's wheels swung hard against the rutted bank and screeched to a halt. *Bang on time*, he thought as a door swung open for him to climb inside. He pulled his small travelling bag in beside him and settled down within the warm interior.

"Enjoy your brief visit?" The question was framed in a way that said the driver did not care one way or the other.

"Will we make it back to the airport in time for my night flight?" It was a habit Ivan could not break himself of; perpetually answering a question with one of his own, although in this instance it was quite pertinent. He had purposefully cut down on the time his driver would have to reach the airport so as to allow him the opportunity of insisting on speeding up if necessary. This particular precautionary tactic was to allow for any possibility of being followed, thus having the option of attempting to lose a trailing vehicle without drawing too much attention to the fact. A ruse which had occurred to him earlier that morning, after suspecting that he was being followed by a dishevelled-looking man resembling a vagrant. This had happened after disembarking from the plane and whilst wandering around the airport terminus before making his way to the dacha. It appeared that wherever Ivan went, this vagrant would not be far behind. He had felt sure he was being lined up for a mugging, so he had used the well-worn ploy of entering some toilets and exiting, with some difficulty it should be said, through one of the windows before quickly hailing a taxi. To his surprise his escape had worked, but the episode had unsettled him and made him a little more cautious concerning his homeward journey.

In the end, as luck would have it, the taxi got a flat tyre, making them over half an hour late, and Ivan had resigned himself to spending the night at the airport, except that when he did arrive, as if by a miracle, the plane was still standing on the runway and he made it with only minutes to spare. Now he sat strapped into his seat ready for take-off, heading back to his precious factory and the one person who meant more than anything else to him in the whole world, his very own little petrushka, Marishka Petrova.

CHAPTER 26

MOSCOW

It was a Second Secretary at the British Embassy in Moscow, designated the political officer, who passed June on his way to Registry and gave her a knowing wink. His name was Anthony Lovejoy-Taylor. Over her manual typewriter she screwed up her face and blew him a kiss in return. June was a floater between British Embassies and Consulates around the world: not of course, in the real sense of levitation – but always ready to move to another posting at a moment's notice if required. June had been working at the British Embassy in Moscow for just over two years. To flirt like this relieved the boredom and found she enjoyed it, though it was a very close community and could be a bit stifling at times.

She knew that every time she walked out of the embassy, someone in the Federal Security Bureau – Russia's internal Counter Intelligence Service or FSB for short, would be logging her movements. She could not take a journey anywhere without being tailed by a Russian secret agent. The only really private conversation achievable would be to enter the Safe Room, but a grade ten floater would never see the inside of such a structure even if she had known of its existence, which indeed she did not. June had therefore been made aware that every conversation she held in Moscow would probably be recorded and that recording housed in the archives of the FSB and listened to carefully for any clue as to what was happening within the embassy.

It was a sobering thought then, that having an affair with Lover Boy, as she had nicknamed Anthony Lovejoy-Taylor, was out of the question, though to phrase it in her particular vernacular she fancied him like mad. Anthony Lovejoy-Taylor was a mild mannered person, a real gentleman in June's mind. Only one grade higher than herself, she felt an affinity with this young, tall, blue-eyed, blond-haired Adonis.

The problem was of course, what with his Eton and Cambridge background, and with an accent to match, it was only ever within a figment of her imagination that she stood a chance. His being a Second Secretary in truth never had a real bearing on the matter. His paltry salary could be regarded in reality as a pittance, because he actually came from a very wealthy family – landed gentry owning thousands of acres of rich fertile farmland in the midlands. It went without saying, that no one within the embassy, except for the Ambassador himself, Sir John Postlethwaite, who had been a close friend of his father when they themselves were both at Cambridge, knew any of this. There were also lots of other men of his ilk scattered around the world who were what was known as being across the water – in other words, spies.

It would therefore have come as a complete surprise for June to learn that within twelve hours, she would be lying on the floor of Anthony Lovejoy-Taylor's small sitting room making passionate love.

Anthony Lovejoy-Taylor was known by the floaters and some of the locally engaged secretarial staff within the embassy as a groper. For instance, if a floater he fancied was standing by the photocopier, he might very well approach from behind and grab her breasts with both hands. The reaction was one of either studied indifference from the secretary, which Anthony Lovejoy-Taylor would take as a signal to carry on in the same vein or, which very rarely happened, the young woman in question, whom they invariably were, would scurry away red-faced muttering all sorts of obscenities over her shoulder. This however, was not how the lithesome June came to end up in Anthony Lovejoy-Taylor's flat. That situation came about because of a signal for 'Lovejoy-Taylor, Second Sec.' emanating from London, which had arrived minutes before. June had been the one to deliver it to him in person, the communication being sealed in a thick manila folder marked SECRET – TOP PRIORITY.

After re-reading the communiqué for his 'EYES ONLY', Anthony Lovejoy-Taylor mentioned to June that he had to cancel a prior dinner in order to be available and therefore had to cook for himself, and mentioned that he was a lousy cook anyway. June had jumped in with both feet first, promising to rustle him up something to excite his taste buds.

Thus it was how June came to be having sex with Anthony Lovejoy-Taylor on the floor of his very cramped sitting room, lying across a Persian style rug courtesy of HMG's furnishing supplies department. While lying there, partially keeping her promise to excite his taste buds, the telephone rang three times and then fell silent, which uncannily mirrored Anthony Lovejoy-Taylor's performance. That was when June had become disillusioned with the fantasy of Lovejoy-Taylor being a great lover; the first part of his double-barrelled surname not quite living up to expectations, as the office gossips so succinctly and eloquently were to put it later.

Within ten minutes of the telephone ringing she had been bundled out onto the street to make her own way home alone, climbing into the embassy car which had taken but nanoseconds to arrive at Anthony Lovejoy-Taylor's flat, thus ensuring that June would arrive safely at her own destination, an equally cramped flat only a stone's throw away from his own. Meanwhile, Anthony Lovejoy-Taylor was mentally going over the routine in his mind of locating the dead letter-box and retrieving God knows what.

***

It was 2.45 a.m. before Anthony Lovejoy-Taylor arrived back at the British Embassy. An old imposing mansion, it had been built many years before the Russian revolution of 1917 on Sofiskaya Quay immediately across the river from the state apartments of the Kremlin and was now shrouded in darkness. His stout English leather Brogues echoed on the road as he made his way through the solid stone arch leading up to the beacon of light shining in the porch, which had just saved him from tripping on the steps. He could sense the watching eyes of the FSB drilling into his back from their covert observation post situated opposite the embassy. He was tired and would feel much happier when he was safely tucked up in bed.

After being let in by the night duty officer who was backed up by an armed guard, he followed a long ornate corridor until he came to a staircase. Descending to the basement, his legs began to feel like lead weights. He could not shift June out of his mind. Having to break up the evening so early, when she had clearly been enjoying the sex thing so much, annoyed him tremendously. He now felt riddled with guilt. He had known for ages that she fancied the pants off him but he had been too busy with other women up until then to do anything about it.

These fatuous thoughts skimming the surface of Anthony Lovejoy-Taylor's mind evaporated as he found himself standing before a massive steel door. He rang the bell push situated to one side.

Seconds later a cipher and SIGINT (signals and intelligence) clerk roused himself from the large table which bore a small monitor giving a clear image of the intruder. Pushing the paperwork upon which he had been working to one side, the MI6 officer let Anthony Lovejoy-Taylor enter before swiping the computerised locking mechanism with a plastic card which had the desired effect of re-sealing the room. Then the cipher clerk moved to one side as a second solid steel door was unlocked, this time by punching a series of seemingly random numbers into a keypad located just below a spy-hole, letting Anthony Lovejoy-Taylor enter what to insiders was known as the Station. This room was sacrosanct and only for the use of Intelligence Branch or IB Officers – to the uninitiated – British Spies.

Within this smaller room which engendered a sensation of

claustrophobia and to one side of it, was a sturdy wooden table containing many pieces of electronic equipment with dials and what looked like band width monitors and other paraphernalia plus a QWERTY style typewriter keyboard. It was from this smaller room that the message from Anthony Lovejoy-Taylor would be sent in a secure form of cipher, eventually reaching an agent in London via GCHQ and paged to MI6 Headquarters at Vauxhall Cross through powerful transmitters bouncing the signals off a telecommunications satellite.

When decrypted, the beginning of the cabled cipher would read:

CX *** HIGHEST PRIORITY STOP – UK SECRET: UK EYES ONLY STOP ATTENTION AGENT 32133 STOP FROM 21566 STOP SUBJECT MATTER – RECENT SINKING IN PERSIAN GULF OF RUSSIAN SHIP "LITTLE MURMANSK" LINKED TO BIOLIGICAL WARFARE STOP CHINESE CO-OPERATION TO BE CONFIRMED STOP SECRET JOINT SINO-SOVIET TREATY RE ASPECTS OF BIOLOGICAL WEAPONS RESEARCH REAL POSSIBILITY STOP REQUEST ASSISTANCE STOP

By the time Anthony Lovejoy-Taylor finally made it to his bed in Moscow, the black leather clad rider on a 1000 cc Harley-Davidson motorbike was roaring around the now cold deserted streets of North London on a mission to deliver this and other longer parts of the coded message to the agent concerned in as fast a time as possible, allowing for the fact that a recent shower had left the now black shiny road surface in an unstable condition. Moscow was three hours ahead of London. In London it had just turned midnight.

CHAPTER 27

LONDON

Before returning to Moscow after his short stay in London, Dr Grachev had decided that now was the time to act. Having turned the idea over in his mind many times during the last day or so, a plan formulated upon first making Stryker's acquaintance would now be put into operation. An audacious plan which he hoped would be instrumental in changing his life forever. He had felt too vulnerable while in his own country to attempt such a thing. Though he suspected that on his frequent trips abroad he was being watched closely by his fellow countrymen in the form of the SVR, he had to take a chance. Even at Moscow airport, he knew the telephones would be tapped by Russian Intelligence. He stepped into one of the numerous phone booths situated within the concourse of Victoria train station. His fingers grew clammy as he quickly located the telephone number he was seeking from a scrap of paper in his jacket.

"Hello. Is that the Foreign and Commonwealth Office?"

"Yes. Which department did you require?" A woman's thin, tinny voice responded to the thick heavily accented voice on the other end of the line.

Dr Grachev weighed up this question before responding.

"Err... it's about security." The phone clicked a couple of times and he guessed the conversation was being recorded.

"What was it about sir?"

"I told you, security."

"Please, one moment, sir." Pause.

"How may I be of help sir?" The woman's voice had metamorphosed into that of a man's, the timbre of which even to Dr Grachev's untutored ear sounded smoother, very cultured and languid.

"I would like to request political asylum. I'm a Russian scientist."

"Please hold the line for one moment sir."

There was another pause, this time much longer. Then a very English clipped accent rapped back, "From whereabouts are you ringing?" This time there were no pleasantries, just demands.

107

Grachev had not planned to get into a detailed conversation; instead at this early stage he had wanted to keep it short.

"I'm in London."

"Give me your name and telephone number please and I'll ring you back straight away."

Dr Grachev considered this last request but had no intention of complying.

"I'm afraid I cannot do that."

"What do you mean? You're requesting political asylum aren't you?"

Dr Grachev's voice faltered through nervousness. "Yes... but I wish to remain anonymous until I'm granted it."

A hint of frustration began to creep into the voice at the other end of the line. "Are you seriously expecting us to consider political asylum without knowing anything about you or who you are?"

"I told you, I'm a Russian scientist." Things were not going to plan and Dr Grachev began to have doubts about his whole scheme. It was not the sort of situation he could feel at ease with as it was a totally alien concept to betray one's country.

Dr Grachev ploughed on. "I cannot stay on this line too long."

"What's your name and where do you work?"

"I told you, I cannot give you these details at the moment." The Russian scientist paused. "But you will be interested in the fact that I can supply your government with information regarding Russia's ongoing experiments into biological warfare." From the other end of the line came an audible intake of breath.

Dr Grachev stood rooted to the spot with the telephone clamped tightly to his ear. He knew he could be summarily executed in his own country for what he had just suggested. The information imparted was also an enormous understatement, for the secret he held would have dire consequences regarding the whole of mankind, and that was no exaggeration in his expert opinion. This was not some run of the mill biological weapon he was referring to, produced by some third world country as a cheap alternative to nuclear weapons. No, this was the crème de la crème of biological weapons, or in layman's jargon, germ warfare. It would not just change the balance of power between nations but could irrevocably alter mankind's history forever. The people in the West did not yet understand this – how could they? The authorities had to be shown the blueprint. There was no immediate response from the other end of the line for about half a minute and Dr Grachev wondered whether he might have been cut off. Then he became aware of more clicks and yet another voice, this time in the background.

"I believe you are from Russia, is that correct sir?"

"Yes, that is correct." Dr Grachev was beginning to feel nervous.

"How can we communicate with you if you don't want us to know who you are?" This part of the conversation he had fully anticipated before making the call. The fact was, he had thought of nothing else.

"I have telephoned before but time was not on my side then – nor is it today. The last time I contacted you I gave you a name, not of course my real one."

"And what was that name sir?"

"I said I would contact you again and asked you to remember my name – Red Chameleon. But now I require a secure number I can contact you on." Dr Grachev was sweating profusely. "Oh! By the way, once I'm granted immunity I shall require a physical change of identity."

"You mean cosmetic surgery?"

"That is correct." Dr Grachev replied firmly. He had not planned to spend so long on the telephone and was getting very worried.

The very English voice came back on the line. "You said you are a Russian scientist. May I ask you if you know anything about map coordinates in the Persian Gulf?"

"That is correct." Dr Grachev thought of the coordinates relating to the *LITTLE MURMANSK* he had recently supplied anonymously to the FCO together with his non de plume Red Chameleon.

There was another pause on the line before the voice came back.

"The contact telephone number I am about to give you will be in operation twenty four hours a day. Do you understand?" As Grachev agreed he understood a seven digit number was quoted to him which he was then asked to repeat back. He was also supplied with an address in the form of a box number.

"And who should I ask to speak to?" Another brief conversation was heard, something to do with a duty officer.

"Mr Smith. Ask for Smith."

Dr Grachev fumbled for his pen and a piece of paper then scribbled down the name and repeated it back as requested.

"Smith?"

"Yes, Smith."

Without saying goodbye Dr Grachev dropped the receiver as if it was red hot. He guessed the kiosk telephone number would be traced and did not want to be around the area when it was located. He moved quickly, clutching the piece of paper with the telephone and box number together with his contact name: Smith. He was lucky and managed to pick up a taxi from a rank of taxis outside the station almost immediately. It was as his taxi pulled away from the kerb whilst settling himself low down in the back seat that he caught sight of three police cars with their sirens wailing skidding to a halt alongside the row of telephone kiosks he had just vacated.

CHAPTER 28

This time there was no frenzied music emanating from the large house, which Tom found puzzling. *A party is a party is a party*, he thought, admiring the latest model of a red Mercedes Benz sports car parked directly opposite his own offending eyesore. It was the type of car he would definitely buy if his salary was hiked by another twenty thousand a year – fat chance of that. He pressed the bell, the idea slowly forming in his mind that he had the wrong house, it being so quiet. Tom was on the verge of trying next door when the second floor window flew open.

"Hang on, I'm coming down."

It was Li Cheung and from what he could see, she was wearing a very revealing low cut red dress. By the time these thoughts had crossed his mind the door had swung open revealing the best thing that had happened to him all year.

"My god, you're stunning," he spluttered. Li Cheung had obviously been to the hairdressers, her straight black hair cut Cleopatra style, sporting a fringe just above her dark eyebrows. The contrast with the red dress was dramatic and Tom felt weak at the knees.

"Come in." She gave Tom a beautiful smile, revealing a perfect even row of white teeth framed by deep red lipstick, the colour matching her dress and contrasting with her milky smooth pale skin. "Go up dahlin'."

Tom moved up the stairs so fast that upon reaching the top he could not even remember climbing them.

"You said you were going to have a birthday party."

"Yes, this is going to be a party. I thought you would like it this way... just the two of us." Tom was taken aback. The contrast within Li Cheung's room was so different from the last time. Then it was vibrant, with bodies gyrating in time with loud thumping rhythms, whereas now the room was filled with the strains of soft classical music and resembled a haven of tranquillity. As soon as the door had closed Li Cheung caught Tom's hand and led him to the window. He remembered the last time she had taken his hand, to dance with him, the crowd of total strangers pushing both of their bodies so close together. Now Li Cheung had an impish expression on her soft featured face.

"Do you like it?"

"If you're referring to this red dress... as I said downstairs, you look beautiful." Tom slid his hand around her waist, feeling the silk beneath his fingers.

"No silly, not the red dress. Look out the window... the red car."

"I was admiring it just now. Yes, that's also beautiful." Li Cheung thought how funny it was to compare herself and the car using the same adjective.

"When we've eaten you can take it for a spin if you'd like to. My father gave it me for my birthday." Tom's eyes widened in amazement for the thought of Li Cheung's parents being wealthy had never crossed his mind. After all, living in one room, even a large room like this, did not go with having a very expensive sports car parked outside.

"It must have cost a fortune. Your father is obviously a very generous man."

"Yes – well he is my father. He's always spoilt me and I know I really don't deserve it. He's the kindest, most loving father one could ever have. I had another car before this one, but unfortunately I crashed it a few months ago. I felt very guilty about it – a complete write off."

Tom looked into her clear, dark eyes and felt lovesick. Up until the time of his leaving the party, just a week before, there had not been an opportunity to kiss her, not even when they said goodbye. It had been awkward, so many people around and he felt unsure that it would have been reciprocated. Now all that was changed. They both fell silent. Li Cheung's perfume, Miss Dior, hung heavily in the air, intoxicating Tom as he stood so close to her. They both moved silently as one toward the bed that Li Cheung had been sleeping in only a few hours earlier, Tom's hand still around her waist. Then, raising her head, she softly brushed his lips with hers. Tom wanted to express his feelings for Li Cheung, to tell her just how much he loved her and was on the verge of saying so, but Li Cheung laid her right-hand index finger upon Tom's lips. Hot, moist lips which craved the fulfilment, which only she could give. A sensuous feeling ran along his spine as Li Cheung's arms were arched above her shoulders with the grace of a ballet dancer. Releasing the tiny catch at the back of her neck, she slowly unzipped the long red dress and let if fall away, exposing a pale, smooth, taut, perfectly formed physique.

As Tom undressed, both aware of each other's self-consciousness, the fragrance of Li Cheung's body made him feel delirious with desire. Each helped the other, with soft caressing outstretched hands, gently lifting and cradling one another until they lay down upon the sheets – naked, exploring each other's sensual feelings. Li Cheung began with Tom's lips, moving her tongue between them with a softness which belied her eagerness to taste every part of him, her saliva mixing with his saliva, her lips moist as she opened her mouth as wide as possible to receive his probing tongue, their faces clamped hard together, pushing tighter and tighter so as to push their tongues even deeper into one another's mouths, tasting and licking the inside cheeks, the throat, teeth occasionally scraping, their jaws locking in the effort to prise open the void even wider. Tom's sinewy body lay beside Li Cheung, every nerve tense as he felt her hand sliding across his round, tight, boyish bottom and over his slim hips, her fingers finally finding what she had been searching for. Li Cheung's hot breath matched the warmth of her flushed face as she brought Tom to a climax. And as she did so, she slowly raised her left leg until it lay across the top of Tom's, caressing the length of his muscular thigh.

Li Cheung's smooth white breasts rose and fell with her laboured breathing. They lay there catching their breath; the aroma of Li Cheung's body mixed with that of Tom's overwhelming their senses. As Tom inserted himself with a jerking motion, Li Cheung's breath came in short bursts, squealing in ecstasy as involuntary waves of bliss began rolling across her stomach. Tom, now lying on top of Li Cheung, could feel her taught, trim belly rippling as she came with moans of pleasure, perspiration breaking out on her upper lip as she arched her body and jerked it frantically in time with Tom's.

It was some while after, when their sexual appetites had finally been sated and feeling blissfully happy, that they fell asleep in each other's arms with their bodies entwined.

***

By the time Li Cheung and Tom awoke it had grown dark. Deciding to leave their warm temple of love, constructed out of crumpled sheets and blankets, Li Cheung cooked one of her speciality quick meals, for which she had been justly famed at her university digs. After they had eaten, Li Cheung whispered into Tom's ear.

"Come on then dahlin', let's go for that drive." Li Cheung's voice was always soft.

As they reached the car, Li Cheung threw the keys in a playful fashion toward Tom, but they flew wide of the mark and slammed against one of the rear wheel hubcaps instead, scuffing the shiny chrome finish before falling into the gutter. "Sorry dahlin', my fault." Li Cheung had retrieved the keys before Tom could get to them and pushed them into his hand, at the same time giving him a furtive kiss on the cheek. The car Tom could only dream of owning roared into life, pulling away with so much power that it left Li Cheung pinned back into the contoured leather seat and Tom with a big grin on his face. Soon they were leaving the suburbs of London behind as they headed out into the countryside, trees becoming solid indistinct shapes, melded into the road's edge, one long blur, until soon the darkness had enveloped them save for the occasional village lights flashing by, creating the illusion of a strobe effect seen at rave parties, freeze framing images in an instant before vanishing once more into the blackness. Li Cheung's fingers dug deep into Tom's arm, her face a mixture of horror and excitement as they roared around invisible bends at breakneck speed.

"You're a maniac," Li Cheung shouted thorough roars of laughter, her tears smudging the black mascara against her smooth, pale cheeks. Tom carried on driving in this manner until they could just make out the straight line of the sea cutting across the base of the sky along the Sussex coast.

High up on a hill Tom had known from childhood, he slowed the car down and they came to a halt.

***

It was early Sunday morning as they lay in one another's arms staring out of the car window across the Sussex Downs. It might have been five minutes or it might have been five hours that they had lain there, holding hands, drifting in and out of sleep before they became aware of the sun rising from the edge of the sea. A great ball of orange fire slowly revealing the true splendour of the panoramic view, white sea surf laced with gold frenziedly dancing upon the restless lapis lazuli surface.

"Am I in heaven dahlin'? It is so beautiful. I want to stay here with you forever."

Tom looked at Li Cheung, her slight body touched by the rays of the fiery sun, emphasising the colour of her dishevelled silk dress and washing the smooth features of her face with a crimson glow. A clicking sound ensued as Li Cheung pushed hard against the car door, almost tumbling out before running to a large oak tree nearby and flinging her arms around it.

She turned to Tom. "I want to make a mark of happiness on this tree dahlin', for both of us. To say how much in love we are. Have you got a penknife?"

Tom knew even before looking that he did not but very much wished he had. "Is there a tool kit in the boot?"

"Probably, I'll see," Li Cheung replied, releasing her slender arms from the sturdy tree trunk. Now it was Tom's turn to ease his body from the warm leather seat, make his way around to the rear of the car and unlock the boot. Before he could begin searching Li Cheung had found a large metal bar.

"Come, we'll both do it with this," she said, waving the object above her head like some warrior from a bygone age. Taking Tom's hand she led him to the great oak. "Here, you hold onto the bar with me and we'll strike it together." Tom covered her small delicate fingers with his. Three times they hit the bark before some fell away, revealing the smooth trunk beneath. They swung the metal bar another three times, aiming at the same spot, leaving a deep scar. "There dahlin', that will be there for a thousand years as a symbol of our love, won't it?" To Tom at that moment Li Cheung looked like a little girl. An inquisitive little girl, perhaps asking for reassurance that the world will indeed go on for another thousand years. He took her in his arms, holding her tightly against his chest so she could not see his eyes well up with tears of love.

"Yes, my darling, for a thousand years."

"You are so emotional Tom. I can hear it in your voice. That makes me love you even more."

"Li Cheung, I want to ask you something,"

"Yes dahlin', what is it?"

Tom unfurled his arms from around her slender body, and with a serious look upon his face he rested his hands loosely on her hips before staring into her dark eyes. "Li Cheung, will you marry me?" He watched as she pursed her lips whilst lifting her gaze to the heavens, the red dawn now giving way to a magnificent blue sky. It was as if she were consulting her seer. She remained in this tranquil-like state for several seconds before lowering her gaze to look deep within Tom's eyes, answering softly, almost whispering the answer.

"Yes dahlin', if you want me, I will marry you."

CHAPTER 29

As the taxi glided to a halt beside the hotel's richly carved stone portico, Dr Grachev reached into his pocket and pulled out a ten pound note. Quickly pushing it into the driver's hand he muttered his thanks before moving toward the revolving doors, so successful at keeping the chill east wind from entering its sumptuous interior.

Mingling with the other guests, he made his way across the deep pile carpet to the reception desk and collected his room key before climbing into the mirrored lift. Upon reaching the designated floor he stepped out quickly, clutching the plastic access key with his right hand while with the other he searched deep within his pocket for the piece of paper containing the recently acquired details of his potential saviour.

Once safely ensconced within his room Dr Grachev locked the door behind him. Without wasting a second, he settled himself down at the writing bureau and proceeded to slip a piece of the hotel's headed writing paper out of the polished wooden rack. Folding the top two inches of paper between his thumb and forefinger he then laid it upon the writing desk, running his thumbnail deftly along the fold. When this was done he detached the hotel's letterhead from the rest of the writing paper before throwing it into the leather upholstered wastepaper bin. Only then, safe in the knowledge that this particular note he was about to write would be untraceable, did he put pen to paper.

Dr Grachev began writing quickly in a very mall hand, the telltale sign of many eminent scientists, setting out his terms for defection: protection – money – house – plastic surgery so as to disguise his identity and a request for meaningful work as a scientist, but this time on behalf of the West. Then he wrote of his scientific expertise, briefly hinting at the knowledge he had gained working as assistant director at a top secret Russian institute for biological warfare housed just outside Moscow. He explained that if he were granted political asylum he would exchange information on Russia's Biological Weapons programme plus his knowledge of experiments and inroads made into antibiotic resistant strains of virus created through genetic engineering. *"I can supply you with a living sample of a newly constructed selective pathogenic virus with no known antidote."* Dr Grachev now thought it expedient to mention at this particular juncture his pièce de résistance, the one thing he felt sure would clinch the deal; the possibility of obtaining for the British Government a sample of the most devastating biological weapon ever envisaged, which he himself was now in the process of creating. All his life he had played things close to his chest, never giving too much away, only enough to enhance his own career. That was how he had conducted his scientific work within the Soviet Union and that is how he had continued to act, with extreme caution. His approach had served him well up until now. As with his favourite pastime – chess – he liked to weigh up all the possibilities before making a move.

After having committed his bargaining strategy to paper, Dr Grachev set about memorising the telephone number, box number and name of his contact Smith, using a system of mnemonics which he had employed since his schooldays. Then, holding the piece of paper upon which he had written down these details earlier, he moved to the window and slid it open. The paper, now held at arm's length was then set alight, Dr Grachev watching the flames consume all the incriminating information before releasing his grip at the very last moment. As he watched the gentle breeze lift up the charred remains high over the rooftop of an adjoining building, he felt that he had moved relentlessly another step closer in his quest for a new life.

The letter, addressed to a Mr Smith, had been posted just a few streets away from his hotel fifteen minutes after having been written, and some four hours before Dr Grachev's plane moved smoothly over the rooftops of London. His flight was not subject to the vagaries of the weather as the charred remnants of his Foreign Office contact now turned to black ash had been, for in this instance there was only one specific destination: Moscow.

CHAPTER 30

MOSCOW

In the vicinity of the Kremlin, the bright neon strip lighting ten floors up within the tall nondescript office building had refused to acknowledge daybreak, remaining permanently on as it always did twenty-four hours a day, giving the impression of a battery hen house. The man from Military Intelligence, a GRU officer with high cheekbones and sagging bags beneath his small, hard, bead-like eyes, smiled thinly as he listened to the lame excuses being trotted out by his subordinate. The listener was dressed in an ill-cut crumpled grey suit and had been up all night. The strained, weak, watery light filtering through the office window at this early hour of the morning perfectly matched his mood of feeling more dead than alive. His red rimmed eyes had a vacant look about them as he tried to fight off the effects of sleep deprivation.

"Where is the target now?" Nicotine stained fingers fumbled for yet another cigarette, having absent-mindedly discarded the dog-end of the previous one. This charred butt now joined others, forming a mound of ash and stale smelling butt-ends on his desktop, testifying to the previous night's anxiety. It was the stress. In this early morning gloom it was ready to topple.

"I used to smoke those Peter the Great cigarettes. Don't know if he'd be impressed with that puny funeral pyre to his memory though. Maybe you're unwittingly building your own. Ever think of that eh?"

"Didn't you hear what I said? I asked where the target was."

Pyotr gave his boss a furtive glance out of the corner of his eye, having already guessed that his stab at a joke would fall on deaf ears. "He's on his way back to the Institute. Plane should be landing within the hour," he replied, hoping his interrogation would be kept short so that he could get home and clean himself up.

Pyotr had worked with Konstantin for over ten years, but had never managed to break down that fortified barrier of officialdom which kept him at arm's length. Konstantin did not have any, what one might call close friends within the service, but that did not surprise Pyotr. Neither did it surprise him that Konstantin was still single. Mind you, come to that, so was he.

"And is anyone meeting him at the other end?" Konstantin enquired through clenched teeth. The taught sinews in Konstantin's neck protruded from beneath his pale skin like steel rods, his temper barely controllable.

"Comrade Yevgeny is on the plane with him. The target shows no sign or awareness of his being under constant surveillance. Yevgeny will keep tabs on him till you decide what to do."

"And does Comrade Yevgeny know that the target... oh fuck it... let's call a spade a spade... that Ivanovich Sobolev gave you the slip for nearly fourteen hours?"

Pyotr breathed deeply, his lungs drowning in the smoke-laden atmosphere, before giving a heavy sigh. "He was filled in last night. We had to hold the plane up for nearly forty minutes, till Ivan arrived. I don't think it made any difference. Planes are always being held up for one reason or another. I don't think he would have thought anything of it." The grey suited man gave him a withering look.

"You don't think! You don't think! You idiot! That's the point. You don't think. If you hadn't lost Ivan in the first place we wouldn't be in this mess. We don't know where he went to or who he met. It's a real fuck up and if anything goes wrong now, you'll be the one held responsible."

Pyotr noticed Konstantin's hands trembling slightly – a bad sign. He furrowed his brow in consternation. "What will our colleagues at First Directorate Foreign Intelligence do if they get wind of the fact that I lost him on my own patch? Will that fact be recorded on my record?"

"You really do amaze me sometimes Comrade Pyotr. Firstly, I do understand what First Directorate deal with, and secondly no, it will not be put on your record because our arch-rivals in First Directorate won't hear about your balls up. We'll keep this operation just between ourselves if possible."

"Thanks... I appreciate that."

"No, no. Don't thank me... you've got it all wrong. It's not that I give a fuck about you and your career or how this reflects on you." Now Konstantin's face grew red with rage. "If you had carried out your assigned task correctly we might all be a little wiser now about how these state secrets are being passed over and who the contact or even final recipient is. No, it's because Ivan is a close friend of Colonel Oleynik – therefore it would be better if we kept it between ourselves, in the GRU family, at the moment, so to speak." Her Konstantin gave Pyotr a sharp look. "Apparently Colonel Oleynik and our friend go back years. The Colonel knew Ivan's father. It's true that I'd just give anything to be in the position of saying to him: 'Oh, and by the way Colonel, did you know your old friend's son Ivanovich Sobolev is a spy?' I'd love to see his face then. But in the meantime, he's the last person I want to see."

With a slight raise of his eyebrows and a smile upon his lips, Pyotr volunteered to get some coffee for them both, feeling relieved that for the time being he still had a job and that Konstantin was still on speaking terms. There were times in the past when his boss had sulked for days when something had gone awry.

"Don't bother about that now, we're off."

"Off! Where to?" Pyotr's throat was parched due to his nervousness at times like this, and was also dying for something to alleviate the effect of the smoke laden atmosphere. He had remained unshaven from the day before and was still arrayed in his disguise, feeling keenly the mendacity of his attire relating to down at heel tramps and other vagrants.

Konstantin was already pulling his heavy overcoat on as he dropped the bombshell. "We're catching a plane to visit our quarry."

"But I need to change into something more suitable. I look so shabby in these clothes."

"And you smell. But don't worry. You look fine to me. All set for retirement, which might be sooner than you expected if you don't get a move on."

Pyotr thought about this last attempt at a joke at his expense and then wondered if it was indeed a joke or perhaps some sharp insight into his future. He immediately dismissed the notion, thinking that he was becoming too sensitive. He followed Konstantin out into the depressive string of corridors which went under the name of modern architecture, relieved to be able to draw breath once more on the less polluted but still foul air which always seemed to inhabit these darker institutions of the state apparatus.

CHAPTER 31

EARLY 1993, MOSCOW

The order from the highest echelons of the Soviet Government to close down the Biomedico facility, within which Dr Grachev worked, could not be ignored. Not by the doctor, nor by Professor Anton Cherenkov, Grachev's boss and chief of Biomedico. The decree had been signed by Boris Yeltsin himself on April 11th 1992, banning offensive biological warfare research and reluctantly taken by the Soviet state pharmaceutical agency Biopreparat as a direct order to cease production of and experimentation with deadly viruses, toxins and bacteria as weapons of mass destruction.

It was now early 1993, nearly one year later, and due to the upper echelons of Biopreparat management dragging its heels on the dismantling of the many satellite factories and scientific institutes which came under its control, Dr Grachev's Institute was still operating, but the time of its demise drew ever closer as the months passed. Dr Grachev's laboratory was due to finally close down within weeks, which did not give him much time to put his plan into action. Over the previous twelve months he had witnessed not only the breaking up of the scientific institutes which he had come to know so well over the years, but also the parallel dismantling of the Soviet Union itself.

The Biomedico Institute was surrounded by barbed wire, ferocious killer dogs and armed guards from the Ministry of Internal Affairs. Not that the general public could see the buildings, which were hidden by tall pine trees. Large signs for miles around prohibited anyone from encroaching on the roughly hewn vehicle tracks leading to the top secret installation.

The entrance inside the Institute leading to Dr Grachev's own personal laboratory was secured by a large, heavy safe door to which only he had the combination. This was unusual in the extreme, even for a top highly secret research establishment, one that was surrounded by soldiers ordered to shoot first and ask questions later. This impenetrable door had been installed on the direct orders of the GRU, much to the chagrin of Dr Grachev's boss, professor Anton Cherenkov. Prof Cherenkov had been Dr Grachev's mentor in the early days when Dr Grachev was newly arrived. He had been taken under Prof Cherenkov's wing and shown the ropes. Prof Cherenkov knew straight away that he had been given an exceptionally bright scientist in the form of Dr Grachev when he was first transferred to the Institute from another research facility situated in Leningrad. However, having picked Professor Cherenkov's brains regarding the operation of the Institute Biomedico and learning its ways, Dr Grachev was soon up and running with his own ideas – ideas which were often diametrically opposed to the direction in which Professor Cherenkov had wished to move the Institute. This irritated Professor Cherenkov intensely and gradually their once jovial rapport had deteriorated into a strained atmosphere between the two scientists. What initially had been an almost father and son relationship, had now grown into an unspoken hatred for each other. In retrospect Professor Cherenkov now felt he had been used to further Dr Grachev's own career.

To enable Dr Grachev to enter his own restricted zone the combination of metal wheels on the heavy door would be sent spinning into a vortex of random numbers and letters, the door being immediately closed and secured on the other side after he had entered.

His day was split between being incarcerated within this well-equipped research laboratory and deep within what was designated Zone Three, known as the most dangerous area of the institute in which to work because of the virulence of the bacteria and viruses used for experimental research purposes.

An agenda relating to the research Dr Grachev was working on had been set between himself and Colonel Oleynik on the express orders of General Kovalyev. General Kovalyev worked for the Fifteenth Directorate which came under the Ministry of Defence. As a member of the GRU, Military Intelligence, he helped set the agenda for certain biological weapons. Colonel Oleynik had worked closely with General Kovalyev at the Fifteenth Directorate dealing with the military's own Biological programme but had been transferred to Biopreparat to act as liaison officer between the two organisations, though he was still firmly under the control of the General. Dr Grachev made only occasional appearances from outside of his laboratory or Zone Three, to enquire of his research team colleagues on how other related projects were going and to take lunch.

His particular project in the Biological Warfare Unit housed within Biomedico was top secret. So secret in fact that he literally did not exist – certainly not on paper. He was not listed in any directory within the Institute. Not in the telephone directory, nor on any staff list. In fact, he might very well have been known as the original Invisible Man. Other scientists in his research team respected his intellect but did not like Dr Grachev the man.

CHAPTER 32

He was not in the Russian Military Intelligence Directorate – the GRU, but every one of his colleagues absolutely knew he was. Held in awe by fellow scientists for his many academic achievements, he had his acolytes. However, it was an awe tinged with fear. Dr Grachev was an arrogant man. And yet when required he could charm the birds off the trees.

However, Grigulevich, the little old gentleman behind the entrance desk who checked people in and checked people out of the large anonymous building – the old man that often seemed to be nodding off behind the well-thumbed newspaper, his chin permanently covered in grey stubble and his eyes often watery from the constant smoke of hand rolled cigarettes – the one whose cherry 'Good mornings' were often ignored, and even treated with contempt by quite a few of the scientists who were more fascinated with their own ego. He was indeed an old KGB Intelligence Officer from the Third Main Directorate, and a good one at that. He resented the fact that it had, along with others, lost its former initials, known all over the world as the KGB. One of the old school, Grigulevich had learnt his trade the hard way. He had fought and killed so many Germans on the Russian front during the Second World War that he had lost count. Medals! He had two rows of them at home in his cramped modest flat, but he could not wear them at his place of work. Semi-retired, he prided himself on keeping an eye on things at the Institute. And his cover worked well.

His mind was as clear and incisive as when he was twenty. He could store the whole of the day's comings and goings in his head as if reading the details from a computer monitor. There was not much he missed and he certainly knew that when he left at eight o'clock this particular evening Dr Anatoly Grachev, man of medicine and brilliant scientist with four degrees to his name, was still in his laboratory.

This event and many other details of the day's comings and goings, as he liked to refer to them, were of course duly written up in the daily report and sent via a messenger to Moscow's Federal Security Services Headquarters, the Yasenevo, at the end of his shift. He also knew there was trouble brewing. Big trouble! Trouble that could get someone killed – that kind of trouble. He regretted it but knew it would end in disaster for someone. It was inevitable. He had seen enough trouble in his life and he realised it always ended the same way. But then, being an old soldier he understood that if you break the rules you pay the penalty.

It was Colonel Oleynik's secretary Shelmatova who had first warned Grigulevich of the unease within the colonel's department at the Ministry of Defence. The situation, as she called it, began with one of those seemingly inconsequential events when Shelmatova's niece, Anya, invited her to a little family gathering. Anya was to call at the Ministry to collect her one evening at five o'clock sharp. This was the time Shelmatova always left her office. However, no call came from the reception duty officer at five to say Anya had arrived, which was very unlike her as she was never late. So, at ten past five, to check that Anya was not waiting for her downstairs, Shelmatova picked up the intercom handset in her outer office to contact the front hall. It was then that she unwittingly overheard a snippet of Colonel Oleynik's conversation speaking in a hushed tone to someone, she did not know who, saying that he'd been informed research papers had gone missing and that he had to see General Kovalyev.

Shelmatova did not think any more about it until three days later when two men in dark suits came and settled themselves in Colonel Oleynik's office. Two large desks were installed and banks of telephones were wired up and there these two uncommunicative men remained for four weeks. The colonel could not make a move without informing them of what he was doing. Then one day Shelmatova arrived for work and they were gone, just as suddenly as they had arrived. The tables and chairs were gone and the telephones had been disconnected and removed. It was just as if they had never existed.

"And the strangest thing was that Comrade Colonel Oleynik never mentioned those two men to me once in that whole four week period," Shelmatova told Grigulevich. "It was as if he'd assumed I was blind. I mean, they were right there in the next office, and when I went in to take a letter or anything, there they sat, just listening. I tell you, it was unnerving. I've never felt so uncomfortable in all my life. I was so happy to see they'd gone."

Grigulevich of course had tried to find out more from headquarters but no one would tell him anything. Maybe it was because he was semi-retired and now looked upon as an outsider. He attempted asking people whom he'd known for forty years what was going on, but they also played dumb. For the first time he began to realise that people who he had regarded as the best of friends were nothing of the sort and it shook his confidence in his judgement. He'd always thought that being, what he termed 'a friend', for such a long time, meant something. Yet here they were, his so-called compatriots and fellow workers, giving him the cold shoulder. He was shocked and disgusted. It made him realise that human nature had the capacity to be rotten to the core.

It was then fortuitous indeed, that just as in the case of Shelmatova, a chance mistake by his own hand resulted in his discovering what the term 'situation' stood for. Spying! *Yes, spying*, he thought to himself, even now not quite being able to believe that his fellow countrymen or man – certainly not within his very own department – were actually passing Russia's secrets to the West. Every Thursday evening Grigulevich would leave the Institute early and catch a bus into the centre of Moscow city, forty-five minutes' drive away, to do a little shopping. This particular evening the usual messenger, a man called Pavel, who collected his daily report, did not turn up. The person who did turn up happened to be an old soldier like himself who Grigulevich had not set eyes upon for maybe fifteen years. It was as much a surprise for this messenger as it was to himself. Grigulevich explained that he was off to do some shopping in the centre of Moscow as usual and his old pal offered him a lift.

Tossing his government issue briefcase and overcoat onto the back seat of his friend's car, and keeping hold of the folder containing his report of the day's activities close to his chest, they'd set off. Grigulevich had never learned to drive whilst he was in the army and now being semi-retired, never would, having to get by on his much reduced salary thanks to the demise of communism. It made him angry when he saw the gangsters, spoken of in hushed tones as the Russian Mafia, cruising around in their large limousine cars when once they were the preserve of the elite of Moscow's politicians. He was an old Communist with a capital 'C' and proud of it. He knew that people had suffered privations over the years, but the Soviet Union had been a proud nation, but now, as far as he was concerned, it was going to rack and ruin. No rules and no discipline anymore. Upon reaching the point where they parted company, Grigulevich retrieved his coat and briefcase from the rear seat, placed the Institute folder containing the day's comings and goings on the front passenger seat for his colleague to deliver to the FSB headquarters, and after saying his goodbyes, carried on his way to do his shopping, dwelling on his chance meeting with an old colleague.

***

It was that time of evening when Grigulevich usually poured himself a very large glass of vodka and settled down to watch the news on television. Holding the glass in his right hand he absentmindedly placed his left hand on the top of his briefcase lying next to him on the worn out sofa. It took a while to sink into his consciousness, his being absorbed by news of yet another killing of some black marketer, but when the realisation that what his hand lay upon was not his own briefcase but one in pristine condition and not black but brown, his heart gave a judder. He had not noticed before, having had it tucked under his arm as he carried his heavy overcoat. His mind flew back to the scene in his friend's car and quickly realised that he must have lifted the wrong briefcase from the front seat.

Grigulevich now stared at the briefcase and wondered if it was locked. He knew his own papers would be safe enough but wondered what lay inside this more expensive leather attaché case. He pulled at the spring loaded catch and to his surprise it flew open with a loud click. *It's just natural curiosity*, he reasoned, as he slowly tugged at the file inside, producing a buff coloured folder with the word RESTRICTED on the front cover. Inside there was one single sheet of paper. At the top it read:

ATTENTION COLONEL OLEYNIK.

AGENTS STATIONED AT THE RUSSIAN EMBASSY IN LONDON HAVE OBSERVED ONE OF OUR BIO-WARFARE SCIENTISTS, A DOCTOR ANATOLY GRACHEV, IN CONTACT AT EASTER WITH POSSIBLE BRITISH AGENT KNOWN AS "STRYKER" USING GUISE OF BUSINESSMAN DEALING IN RELIGIOUS ICONS. AWAIT YOUR COMMENTS.

The document was signed:

GENERAL KOVALYEV.

Grigulevich's old hands began to shake as he read the piece of paper once more, hardly able to believe his eyes. Comrade Dr Grachev a spy! He quickly re-read it a third time before returning the damning piece of paper to the file and the file to the leather briefcase before going outside to a public telephone box and ringing a special number. Soon after, he was able to get his shabby briefcase exchanged for the one he had in his possession. That particular night he did something which he had not done since he was a young man in his twenties. He finished off a full bottle of vodka without even thinking, his mind too preoccupied with images of traitors and spies.

CHAPTER 33

LONDON

Striding across Hampstead Heath gave Chen Hsu time to himself; time to reflect on his troubles in a calm rational manner. Except that he could neither remain calm nor gather his thoughts into a rational pattern. He was terrified. A happy family of four – mother, father, little son and daughter passed him by, and it hurt to see such normality. He on the other hand had nobody. All his family were in China. He had not taken a wife and he was very lonely with no one to turn to for help or advice, his whole life orbiting around the restaurant. Having just been to visit his waiter at the Royal Free Hospital at Hampstead in North London was a traumatic experience. The hand had been bandaged so much it gave the illusion of it being whole again. It might even have been some trivial skin condition or an accident of a minor sort such as opening a can and cutting his hand perhaps. But no fingers, and no accident! Chen Hsu shivered as his imagination worked overtime. How could one cope with something like that? He scoured Hampstead Heath spread out before him and felt vulnerable. He felt vulnerable outdoors but he felt even more vulnerable indoors, like a trapped animal; claustrophobic. The events of those few minutes of carnage had played over and over in his head until he felt it was driving him crazy. The image of a bloody hand with truncated finger stumps would not go away.

Thirty thousand pounds; Chen Hsu was seriously considering suicide. It had been five days and they could come back at any time. He had thought of contacting the police but did not do so because there were relatives to protect back in China. The Triads have long tentacles. After years of sacrifice the business was finally ticking over nicely. But thirty thousand! It was impossible unless he could re-mortgage his property. His whole body was shaking so violently it was as if he had a touch of malaria. He could not control himself. Walking along a tree-lined footpath, strangers gave him lingering sidelong glances, thinking he might be high on drugs, or just insane. Parents passed him warily, tugging hard at their children's hands so as to give him a wide birth.

The business of totting up his assets to raise the money began. Car... the little gold he had in the form of jewellery... few thousand in the bank... some shares and other bits and pieces, maybe thirty thousand pounds could be raised, but then what? It might be a never ending problem. A frightening thought. These were ruthless people. You could not trust people like that not to demand more.

As Chen Hsu continued wandering aimlessly the trees gave way to a wide expanse of grass leading down to a stagnant pond. The dirty stagnant water strewn with broken branches created havoc on the smooth green-tinged algae surface. It was a depressing picture, reflecting the sombre sky. He knew there had to be another way, but what?

It was late afternoon as Chen Hsu, following a circuitous route, arrived back at his car. He had been walking for three hours but did not feel tired, just isolated. Isolated from the few remaining people still out upon the heath; isolated by the terrible events that had destroyed his peace of mind. Slamming the car door he started the engine, revving it loudly to blot out the thoughts spinning around in his head, revving it and spewing a thick black cloud of noxious fumes from the exhaust.

Chen Hsu's mind was now on auto pilot. He did not know where he was going but just kept on driving. From Hampstead Heath the car headed for the leafy suburbs of Finchley before making a swift about turn and headed back toward the centre of London. Crossing the Thames he eventually found himself driving through Brixton. His mind had been in a stupor, having no idea what he was doing, The remaining light was rapidly draining from the slate grey sky as he parked his car in one of the many side roads giving off from the high street. After a moment's hesitation Chen Hsu wandered into the nearest pub. The drabness of his surroundings barely made an impression on his unsettled mind as he ordered a double whisky. There were a few men hanging around the bar chatting animatedly, their arms flaying the air as if imitating some exotic dance. He moved to a circular table in the shadows. Easing himself down onto the hard bench, the energy which had kept him going on his march across the heath was now depleted, flowing from his body like water. He removed a lighter from his jacket pocket and stood it in between the puddles of spilt beer and overflowing ashtrays. As he patted his pockets with the palms of his hands, searching for a packet of cigarettes, a voice broke into his concentration.

"Here, take one of these." A large black fist held out a packet of foreign cigarettes Chen Hsu did not recognise. As he looked up he noticed the heavy gold chain hanging limply from the wrist and the expensively cut sleeve of an electric blue suit.

"Thanks." The gesture had the effect of making Chen Hsu feel human again, cutting through the isolation which had dogged him throughout the day.

"We don't get many whities in here. You're the first for I don't know how long. You look all in man."

Chen Hsu raised his head, scouring the people in this refuge of kindness and realised that true to his words, his was the only pale complexion within sight. He began to feel a little more relaxed after drawing on the now lit cigarette, until the next piece of conversation came in the shape of a question.

"What's up?"

"Why do you ask?" Chen Hsu could not decide whether to tell his story or make some lame excuse and hot foot it out of this possible awkward situation.

"Because you look as though you're in trouble. Don't need to buy a fortune cookie to see that." Chen Hsu was surprised at the bluntness of his interrogator but at the same time it gave him confidence in this newfound friend. Inwardly he wrestled with himself. Should he inform him that in the very near future there was a strong possibility of his ending up on someone's hit list? Before he had time to make a measured response he surprised himself by blurting out something which must have been in his subconscious mind all along.

"I need a gun."

CHAPTER 34

RUSSIAN HINTERLAND

The two men alighted from a taxi into the chill stiff breeze, too caught up in their own thoughts to realise just what a spectacle they presented to the outside world. The taller of the duo was smartly dressed though crumpled-looking with a pasty complexion, his down at heel companion on the other hand, sported a two day growth complementing his unkempt hair and a ripped jacket.

Konstantin insisted on being set down well before their destination, explaining that a walk would help clear their minds. "Bring a little oxygen to the brain," as he succinctly put it. They had been grateful to snatch a few hours' sleep on the plane, knowing that when they arrived they would have to play the situation by ear. It was like no other community which Pyotr had ever seen. Almost everyone they passed had a grey complexion which he had equated in the past only with slave labour camps run by the Nazis as witnessed in old newsreels. There was a vacant look behind their gaze, a vacuous expression which reeked of joylessness. He was reminded of the title of one of Maxim Gorky's novels – *Dead Souls*. Though Pyotr was shabbily dressed, no one gave him a second glance. There was a lack of interest. There was also one common feature etched within these people's faces, and that was one of fear. A fear of what, he could only try to imagine, but it was there all the same.

Konstantin was propelled down the pavement with an eagerness which Pyotr could only marvel at as he tagged along behind in his wake. The streets were fringed with utilitarian, long, narrow, flat roofed communal houses, hastily thrown up to a low standard of building specification – if there had been such a thing. The dirt strewn rutted track designated a road in better times, led them past an enormous grey brick building, perhaps erected in the nineteen-fifties but which now stood empty and forlorn looking. It was scarred with broken windows, row upon row of jagged icicle-like glass shards reflecting what little light emanated from the overcast pollution ridden sky. *Kids, same the world over*, Pyotr thought to himself. It did not occur to him that in reality, because he had never left his familiar confines of Moscow, except to holiday on the shores of the Black Sea, he could not possibly know how kids behaved 'the world over'. To one side of this building was a tall brick tower, an essential component and telltale sign for carrying out research and development into biological weapons.

"These people, some of them look as though they're on their last legs." Pyotr had twisted his head to catch a fleeting glimpse of a shadow of a man dressed in soiled white overalls as he passed them by.

"Oh, you mean the factory syndrome," was Konstantin's response.

"What's that?" queried Pyotr, with more than a little curiosity in his voice.

"It's common around here; nothing serious. It's the thing you contract when working in these places. It doesn't do them any harm."

Without breaking his pace Pyotr glared at Konstantin. "Are you saying these people are healthy?"

"Not necessarily healthy," Konstantin replied, with a nonchalance which bothered Pyotr, "but then neither was their politics or they wouldn't end up in a place like this."

"I thought the days of the Gulag were over. This is the tail end of the twentieth century."

"You have much to learn," replied Konstantin. "Have you noticed the expression on their faces? Not exactly optimism is it?"

"Why is that? What are they afraid of?"

Konstantin lowered his eyes to the ground. "I'll tell you later. For now let's just concentrate on the task at hand."

Another ten minutes and they were crossing the threshold of a much more modern building than the ones they had passed.

***

The security officer stared in disgust at Pyotr's unshaven face and ragged clothes, being on the verge of propelling him at speed out of the building before Konstantin stepped in to save the situation. After identifying themselves and completing the formalities of pinning a badge to their lapels and signing an official looking register they were led to a lift.

"Let me do the talking. I understand the mentality of these people who run the factory complex down here. They're all the same – animals." Although it had proved impossible over the years for Pyotr to break through that cold, seemingly impenetrable reserve of Konstantin, just sometimes he was apt to drop his guard and let his unsullied prejudices shine with undimmed brilliance.

A lumbering barrel-chested ursine figure of a man opened the door, ushering them into the spacious air conditioned office incorporating large comfortable black leather easy chairs dotted around the room. As he made a gesture for them to sit down with a wave of his shirt sleeved arm, Pyotr noticed that the large hands and plump wrists matching his bulldog-like neck were covered in a dense forest of grey hairs. There was also a tight wad of hairs protruding from each of his thick fleshy ears and nostrils. The voice was deep and heavy, equal to his stature, carrying a tone of authority within it.

"Ah Comrades! Captain Zhizhin at your service, I've been expecting you. I believe you wanted to know about our friend Ivan the Terrible." These were no words of friendliness, just a bored fellow GRU man going through the motions with a hint of contempt noticeable in the flat tones of his speech for the two men now seated before him, one in a crumpled ill-fitting suit, the other attired in the rags of a vagrant.

Captain Zhizhin slid his hand over the top of the desk, his index finger stabbing at a brass protrusion jutting from one side of the heavily carved edge. Then another adjoining door flew open and there stood someone they had not seen for the last twenty-four hours. The two visitors both exclaimed in unison much louder than they should have.

"Yevgeny!"

Yevgeny was a small, squat man, barely five feet in height, and with a rather unprepossessing look about him. His mouth was lopsided so that when he spoke, spittle dribbled down one side of his longish chin. Although short in stature he was very capable of looking after himself, having at one point in his violent career taught unarmed combat to recruits of Russia's elite Spetsnaz teams; the Soviet's equivalent to America and Britain's Special Forces. He had been well equipped in doing so, having seen much service in his military career, including that of the Soviet forces' withdrawal from Afghanistan in the spring of 1989. Now however, he worked for the GRU's Ministry of Defence Fifteenth Directorate – Main Intelligence Directorate – as did his two colleagues.

Pyotr was beaming, only too happy to see a familiar face. "Been rabbiting like a ferret, you old dog?"

Yevgeny ignored this hospitable greeting and just stood gazing at Pyotr, unmoved by the familiarity.

"Well, where is he now?" It was Konstantin who spoke next, his voice lacking the friendliness of his colleague.

"He's back at work. Our fellow FSB officers are watching him, monitoring his every move."

Konstantin shot a look at Pyotr. "Pity we couldn't have done that back in Moscow."

Captain Zhizhin raised his head from some papers he had been studying on his desk. "How long are you going to be here? Do you need accommodation?"

Konstantin looked at Pyotr. "Yes, just for tonight."

Pyotr felt relieved. His imagination had conjured up the idea that he might have to spend a week in Konstantin's company outside working hours, and that had been playing on his mind. "There must be someone up there taking pity on me," he mumbled to himself as he, Konstantin and Yevgeny took their leave of Captain Zhizhin.

***

Pyotr sat with a very depressed look upon his now clean shaven face, feeling sick and dwelling upon the last few hours in the company of Konstantin and their reunited colleague, Yevgeny. It had begun shortly after arriving at a recently vacated GRU flat which had been put at their disposal through the good offices of the gorilla Captain Zhizhin. Yevgeny himself had been accommodated in a sparsely decorated single room some distance away. Pyotr envied Yevgeny that privacy.

After cleaning themselves up, Konstantin and Pyotr had arranged to meet their colleague and eat something in the staff canteen at the factory where Ivanovich Sobolev worked. On the way, Yevgeny said that he would show both Pyotr and Konstantin something which would be of interest. Ignoring the fact that neither of them had yet had a meal for the last twelve hours, Yevgeny led them in the direction of the factory, going all around the world to reach their destination. Or so it had seemed to Pyotr. They had dived down many backstreets and even got themselves lost twice before coming upon the place which Yevgeny had suggested might be of interest.

A large single-storey flat-roofed building, set in the middle of a clearing, well away from the many surrounding dwellings, it was obvious the journey had not been inspired by any leanings toward architectural merit. This white nondescript monstrosity bore only two external features guaranteed to capture one's immediate interest. The first consisted of a red cross, five feet high painted on the building's façade just beside the entrance. On the other side of this entrance was painted in similar proportion a central red seed incorporating its spreading and intersecting ripples denoting the international biosafety hazard logo. There was also a very large ferocious-looking Alsatian dog tethered to a running lead. People dressed in surgical gowns and masks moved in and out of the building's main swing doors, with the intention of gaining access to a much smaller windowless building situated to one side. This smaller prefabricated structure bore a symbol of a skull and crossbones painted in black against a white ground on a large board, the word 'BIOHAZARD' beneath, picked out in red letters. Adjacent to the swing doors on the larger building was a wide entrance with well-worn plastic flaps taking the place of ordinary doors through which white ambulances would occasionally pass.

The unsettling aspect was the building's perimeter, surrounded by wire netting and patrolling soldiers toting Kalashnikov machine guns hanging loosely over their shoulders, who seemed almost casual about the whole set-up as they sauntered around aimlessly chatting to one another, looking bored. This counterpoint of military activity vis-à-vis a hospital sent shivers down Pyotr's spine. A couple of armed guards came running out of a red brick hut to inspect the trio's identification and open the tall wooden gates topped off with barbed wire.

"What is this place? It surely cannot be a hospital. And why is it surrounded by such security?" Pyotr looked to Yevgeny for an answer as he self-consciously walked in between his two colleagues, desperately wishing that he had been able to change into some normal clothes before embarking on this trip.

"Don't pester Comrade Yevgeny with such questions. You'll see for yourself soon enough." There was an edge to Konstantin's voice which grated on Pyotr's ears. Three times Pyotr had applied to transfer from the department in which he worked with the intention of getting away from Konstantin, and three times he had been thwarted by his request being denied.

"Why do you want a transfer? Aren't you happy in your job? Konstantin gives glowing reports about you." Glowing reports – ugh! What lies! The department knew that nobody else would put up with his sarcastic outbursts and silent treatment; not to mention his withering looks and barbed comments with which he used to cut people down to size.

But it was the barbs on the wire that really puzzled Pyotr. What were they for – to keep people out or to keep people in? Either way, in Pyotr's eyes, it had sinister overtones.

CHAPTER 35

LONDON

When Penny arrived back at the prestigious London hotel from her trip to Wales she had to pass through a labyrinthine maze of passages in the basement to reach her room. As a live-in member of staff she was entitled to meals as well as accommodation but it was late, and she had missed dinner with her work colleagues in the staff dining area long ago. Penny could have grabbed a cold supper from the kitchens: cold chicken, beef, eggs, milk and always a dish of prawns being left in one of the large still room refrigerators. However, she felt too tired and instead went straight to her room without making a detour. Not long after this she was lying in bed still turning over in her mind what seemed an insurmountable problem of how to locate her sister. Only one letter had been found amongst her mother's belongings, and that written in Russian, the translation having been carried out by a colleague in the hotel who spoke the language fluently. It did not offer any clues, nor even supply within the letter or on the envelope a return address, just trivial pieces of gossip from an old friend whom her mother must have corresponded with over the years without her ever mentioning it to Penny. She had obviously kept this correspondence to herself.

Penny lay there staring at the whitewashed walls, the colour however had become faded over the years, resembling old parchment. It was obvious that some of the previous occupants must have been heavy smokers. The room contained little in the way of furniture. A rickety chest of drawers upon which a cornucopia of various coloured nail varnishes and jars of creams and plastic boxes in all shapes and sizes sat cheek by jowl with books and small items of clothing mixed up with expensive-looking bottles of perfume. The furnishings supplied by the hotel were of a cheap quality, Penny having made it a little more homely by scattering a few personal items around the otherwise drab surroundings, but to her at this moment in time it represented a shrine to independence and youth.

"*No Penny, what you see in that photograph... is your sister.*" Those words of her mother span round in her mind like a carousel. Then came her own recalled response. "*But Mummy, I do not have a sister.*" As she had looked at her mother she realised they were both crying; tears of anguish for her mother's part and secret tears of hope within Penny. To suddenly discover that you had a sister would indeed be a miracle. She had not been able to get her thoughts in order that afternoon, so many ideas filling her head; so many questions that required answers. These questions were still being formulated in her mind as she finally drifted into a light, restless sleep.

***

A few days later, Penny cut across Hyde Park to meet David in a small café within walking distance of her hotel. He had telephoned the evening before, saying that an idea had popped into his head which might help resolve some of the problems becoming such a burden to her. He would catch an early morning train.

It was a bright, crisp day and Penny wore a new beige-coloured cashmere overcoat which had taken her ages to save up for. She looked stunning in it, her neck being covered up beneath the large collar with a fine wool roll neck jumper of a similar autumnal shade. She also applied her most expensive perfume which David had said he liked so much.

Strolling through the park on that late Saturday morning in early spring helped to blow away some of the cobwebs. The place was buzzing with people and David had said as much when they both met, mentioning that North Wales and London were as different as chalk and cheese. They decided to order croissants and coffee. After the two steaming cappuccinos and croissants arrived David spoke first.

"I've been thinking about our last conversation we had regarding your childhood and how, since you left Russia as a little girl, you have not been able to recall that period of your life."

"How sweet you are David, always thinking of other people."

"It's true though isn't it? Your memory is just a blank about those times. Isn't that right?" David tore a piece of croissant and dipped it into his coffee, just the way he had seen Parisians do it outside a large glazed pavement café beside the River Seine opposite Notre-Dame cathedral.

"Yes, it's true. I've never been able to remember my Moscow childhood. My memories begin from the time we arrived in England. Sounds crazy doesn't it?"

"Possibly not so crazy as you might imagine. For example, if you had some reason for not remembering."

"How do you mean, some reason for not remembering? How could I possibly decide not to remember something?" Penny sipped her coffee and moved the croissant in a circle around her plate without attempting to eat it.

"Oh! I don't mean that it's a decision of your own volition."

"But what could possibly be the reason for not remembering my childhood in Russia? After all, those would have been my formative years wouldn't they!"

"I see you've been reading books on psychology. Well, that's no bad thing." David gave a mock haughty laugh.

"Don't act so superior. Yes, as a matter of fact I have read a few books on the subject. I think it's interesting to try to discover what makes oneself tick." Penny beamed at David, displaying her very white perfectly formed teeth.

"The point is, something might have happened to you in Russia causing your memory to blank the episode from your mind – what one might call selective memory. It's quite common you know – well documented. And to answer your question regarding what could possibly have happened to cause the unconscious part of your mind to shut down your memory. Well, that's what we would have to find out isn't it?"

Penny looked thoughtful and nibbled on one end of her croissant before raising her coffee cup and taking another sip. "If I can't remember my years spent in Moscow, well... how can I possibly change that? Surely, if I can't remember, then I can't remember." A puzzled expression crossed her face.

"Penny, I can unlock your memories though the use of hypnosis. When memories are suppressed by the unconscious mind there is usually a very good reason for this to happen – a sort of protective mechanism. But what you must understand is that although these memories may be erased in your conscious mind they remain in your unconscious mind, the place you cannot consciously access. But through the use of hypnosis I can unlock that door to your unconscious, or as we may call it, your subconscious mind. It's a very powerful tool when placed in the right hands. It's like opening a safe door, the key to that door being hypnosis."

"So you think that by using hypnosis you might be able to retrieve the memory of my Russian childhood and discover if there is anything there to help locate my sister. Well, if that's the price I have to pay I'm quite willing. You shall be my Svengali darling. When do we begin?"

CHAPTER 36

RUSSIAN HINTERLAND

Amorphous flaps of skin hung down like so much bunting, not in any symmetrical way but with a form all their own. A macabre patchwork quilt made up of many shades, the spectrum running from vivid pinks through mid-greys and purples to a deathly white.

Faint twitching movements could be detected as yet another medical biopsy began on this soft tactile map covered with tiny blood capillaries, resembling some three dimensional road guide splashed here and there with pools of blood red ink.

As the green robed doctor swung his razor sharp knife with dexterity, slicing through a portion of this living organism, what upon close inspection had at first appeared to be nothing more than so much scientific fodder, now took on the vague form of a face beneath a plethora of skin and hair. Although no eyes or nose were now visible, as in Munch's *The Scream*, a black hole was discernible, within which a shrivelled tongue set deep inside could vaguely be sensed as opposed to seen as the surgeon worked quickly and methodically with an adroitness borne out of much practice.

The perceived head itself, if that is what it was, lay on the pillow without any obvious support of a body, though slight bumps here and there within the folds of sheets suggested a possible cadaver sans flesh or sustenance. Periodically the sheets would visibly heave up around the area where the chest cavity might lie in relation to the head, as though a small balloon was in the process of being inflated and then deflated in a cyclical manner resulting in a perpetual series of discordant gasps and wheezes interspersed by occasional rasping sounds.

Pyotr, unsolicited tears silently flowing down his white crumpled cheeks, was unaware of the blood he had drawn on the index finger pushed deep within his own mouth to stifle the anxiety he was feeling. He averted his gaze only to be met by that of Konstantin's, whose nether lip was also being bitten hard so as to hold onto sanity, no matter how tenuous that grip might be. Their eyes locked fleetingly, both feeling the shame of looking at another grown man cry as they fought to stem the tears. It was the first time Pyotr had felt any empathy with his boss. Instead of turning his crippled attention once again toward the desecration being carried out upon another human being, Pyotr now focussed his eyes upon the reflection in the glass window directly in front of him, staring at the semi-transparent apparition of Yevgeny.

Upon this lopsided face however, there was no response, just an air of insouciance, a frozen image of a short stocky man staring blankly, watching the operation with the divorced detachment of someone who had witnessed and participated in all manner of atrocities against his fellow man without a hint of compassion. Pyotr searched Yevgeny's long chin but could find no familiar trace of the saliva which appeared as regular as clockwork when he spoke. At this particular moment Yevgeny was keeping his thoughts to himself. If it had not been for the fact that they were all three GRU Intelligence men of a certain rank, it would have been impossible for them to enter this closed world, where the accepted rules of society had been suspended. Among the general population, rumours of all manner of horrors must have been hinted at, half-truths whispered. Fear of the unknown was a powerful tool used to keep the masses in line, except that the reality of what they imagined was actually ten times worse. These were the thoughts now stumbling through Pyotr's mind as the three men stood once more on the outside perimeter of the building, which for himself, had taken on the mantle of a house of horrors.

"I feel sick."

Yevgeny looked at Pyotr with a mocking smile. "You want to go to hospital?"

Konstantin fumbled with a box of cigarettes, but his fingers did not have their usual co-ordination as one slipped out of his grasp, becoming half submerged in the carpet of grey dust beneath his feet.

"Fuck!"

As the trio retreated from the closely guarded compound, the same two soldiers who had initially greeted them made their appearance once more, scuttling from the red brick guard hut to scrutinise their papers as though they had never set eyes on them before. Pyotr glanced at the guard closest to him and thought he detected that same mocking smile as he had seen on Yevgeny's face just minutes before.

Even though the air was the same immediately outside the compound as within, Pyotr imagined it tasted sweeter than the highest hill he had ever stood upon. Relief swept through his body as he and his two colleagues left the confines of the so-called hospital far behind them, making their way to the factory. Trailing Konstantin and Yevgeny, Pyotr fervently wished he was at home in the familiar surroundings and secure confines of Moscow.

Nobody said a word, only Yevgeny making any sound, whistling softly to himself, perhaps giving a clue to what he was thinking by the plaintive melody issuing from his tightly pursed lips.

***

The hall they sat in was devoid of decoration, the apt grey walls matching Pyotr's sombre mood as he stared transfixed into the dish of equally watery grey stew. He could not tell if it was fish or meat. Feeling nauseous again, a piece of dark bread was stuffed into Pyotr's mouth, giving his teeth something to work on as his thoughts dwelt unremittingly upon the abject horrors he had witnessed. The hospital, a word in this context which did disservice to such an institution, had been pristine in its appearance: immaculate wards with well-equipped modern operating theatres. The nursing staff, doctors and surgeons, appeared very professional in their white uniforms, their epaulettes of red, yellow or blue attached upon their shoulders added to this air of professionalism, though Pyotr could only guess at their qualifications, not having any medical background himself.

Pyotr closed his eyes, attempting to blot out the images he had witnessed, but to no avail. Ghostlike figures in bare feet, ill-fitting loose off-white gowns hanging from painfully frail bodies, their shaven heads atop faces resembling neither male nor female – half stumbling, half dragged along the white painted concrete corridors by a strong nurse on either side, holding on to their charges as if they might flee their confines, though it was patently evident that the wretched figures were in no fit state to do so.

The clattering of wheels could be heard as a long trolley glided past them, bearing nothing more substantial than a small form no larger than a child beneath a soiled blanket, stained, Pyotr thought, with urine, though he could not be sure. A ceaseless high pitched tone resembling that of a giant mosquito's perpetual whining droned on unremittingly: the cause of this sound reverberating inside Pyotr's skull was a giant air conditioning unit struggling in a futile attempt to expel the fetid decaying odour of rotting flesh. The sensation of being hastily whisked past closed doors from behind which, frightening screams and banging emanated. Then the explanation came from one of the female directors whose task it was to take them on the whistle stop tour.

Much more research was required if the full implications of biological and germ warfare could be evaluated on a pragmatic basis. At that very moment a big drive was on to delve deeper into something called Glanders, a disease found mainly in horses, but which could also be harnessed for biological warfare. As its name suggested, glands below the jawline would swell and the nasal passages fill with a terrible mucous discharge, leading to an impediment in breathing and death.

"We have some really exciting lines of research going on into this particular disease at the moment."

"Where do these people come from upon whom you are experimenting?" Konstantin had good reason to ask, for he himself had once been instrumental as a member of a team of GRU undercover field agents travelling incognito to Sierra Leone charged with the task of obtaining deadly samples of Lassa fever, a horrific virus endemic in that particular country and carried by rats. It killed thousands every year, being initially discovered only in 1969. The thought now occurred to him that a strain of this very virus he had helped to collect might very well have been used on some of the wretched subjects passing through this very same experimental institution.

The female director's tetchy reply about not experimenting upon anyone, just accessing results of modified pathogens such as smallpox, anthrax, yellow fever, Ebola and many others, sounded to Konstantin like something a politician might utter: Cold, clinical and totally devoid of warmth relating to humanity. And what was her answer to his question about human fodder?

"The people in this institution perform a great service for their country... many perhaps for the first time in their lives. The subjects we perform tests upon here, would in the normal scheme of things very likely be incarcerated in some prison serving long sentences for crimes against the state and living on meagre rations of rotting scraps. Here they get fed on a nutritious wholesome diet. We look after them very well."

Pyotr thought of the skeletal fragments of humanity wandering under escort along the hospital corridors, his appetite no longer gnawing at his stomach as he looked at Yevgeny who had commandeered his meal. The slime from it reflected a sombre diffused light as it slowly trickled down Yevgeny's long chin, and under the guise of a faint smile, those yellow teeth, as crooked as his mocking sneer.

Pyotr felt sick again, a tremor running through his body, knowing that it would be another day before he could escape this nightmarish world where everything was tainted with an ugliness he could never have imagined.

CHAPTER 37

KREMLIN – MOSCOW

Dr Grachev strode quickly through the large open doorway of the institute and leapt up the shiny dark wooden staircase taking two steps at a time with Grigulevich's enunciated "Good morning," in his high pitched voice still ringing in his ears. Grigulevich's eyes drilled into the back of the doctor's head but there was no acknowledgement from the scientist. It was the usual routine.

"Ah! Comrade Dr Grachev. Comrade Colonel Oleynik wants to see you. He says to be at his office at twelve noon." Dr Grachev gave the faintest of nods in acknowledgement to his young secretary Marina as he hurried through the corridor to his laboratory.

"What the hell does he want?" he muttered to himself, looking back toward the secretary who greeted him with a warm smile. She had long ago been made to feel second rate by this young man who was treated within the institute as a VIP. He grudgingly returned her smile before reaching the bank vault-like door bearing the combination lock of which only he held the code. Sending the metal discs spinning by rotating the numbers and letters of the alphabet in a strict sequential order enabled him to enter his own well stocked laboratory before slipping on a white starched cotton coat.

At eleven sharp, Dr Grachev revved his car, swinging right along the gravel driveway out between the institute's two tall, heavy, wrought iron gates. In his wing mirror he stared at the receding figures of armed Fifteenth Directorate guards who specialised in the security of government installations. The guards were moving rapidly to close the heavy steel gates where Dr Grachev's car had left a thick black trail of exhaust fumes in its wake.

***

The sun shining in a bright blue sky had warmed up the plastic seat covers inside his car, giving off that certain nauseous odour and making it feel stuffy. He revved the engine of his prized Trabant, which had been with him since his student days and it responded nicely thanks to the loving care with which he had tended it over many years, pulling away swiftly through the suburbs of Moscow, heading for the city centre. Soon the doctor was passing the elegant august pre-revolutionary building which was the British Embassy bristling with antennas and aerials, safely nestling within the crook of the River Moskva on the opposite bank; a constant thorn in the side of Moscow authorities, overlooking as conspicuously as it does, the Kremlin. A short time later the solid and forbidding Kremlin walls loomed up before him.

Fifty minutes after leaving the Biomedico research institute Dr Grachev found himself sitting outside the Russian Ministry of Defence building. Although Colonel Oleynik was now a bona fide member of Biopreparat he still retained his office here at the Ministry. Dr Grachev sat in his car staring hard through the dusty windscreen spattered with bird dirt. He tried to lower the windows further so as to ventilate the car but his offside one would only move halfway. He could so easily have chosen one of the official black Volga cars with a chauffeur from the pool of elite drivers, army trained in close protection tactics, and all sporting their telltale bulge under neatly cut dark jackets. Using his own small car however, was for Dr Grachev an opportunity to make an equally small statement – no matter how subtle, that he was still capable of retaining a streak of individuality, even if his reasoning went above the heads of his superiors. Dr Grachev was a man of surprising complexity. It was his small gestures of defiance to the State that had for so many years ruled his life in a very dictatorial manner. No matter that he was a senior scientist; he still had to obey the rules. And the rules were many and often seemingly ridiculous. One of these rules was not being allowed to have family photographs, even of nephews and nieces, in one's place of work. That particular rule of course did not apply to him as he had no family as far as he was concerned. Switching off the engine he sat in his token of independence for a further five minutes before swinging his lean frame out onto the pavement in one fluid movement.

"Are you trying to kill me?" It was a tall, slim man whom Dr Grachev had hit with his car's door as he swung it open onto the pavement with some force, sending him sprawling. Aged about fifty, he was dressed in a well pressed military uniform.

"Comrade Colonel Oleynik. So sorry sir!" Dr Grachev's verbal gesture of apology was ignored by the colonel. It was a bad start for the scientist as he followed the colonel into the imposing building and up the elegant spiral staircase to his office. He smiled pleasantly at the secretary Shelmatova. Her steel-grey hair was worn in a bun, reminiscent of the wire wool used to remove rust from kitchen utensils.

In need of lifting his spirits he let out a resounding "Good morning

Tanya!" Although reminding Dr Grachev of his grandmother she returned his easy greeting with a blank look, far removed from any maternal instinct his grandmother may have had. He followed Colonel Oleynik through into his office.

"Sit down. How are things going at the lab?" Any semblance of cutting through the formalities by using his patronymic was missing, being replaced by an air of coldness. The colonel was always short on small talk and without waiting for an answer, came straight to the point. "General Kovalyev wants to know how much longer this project you are working on is going to take."

Colonel Oleynik stared hard at Dr Grachev. The colonel's fine facial features bearing only one particular blemish, those cold dark eyes half obscured beneath languid eyelids. Dr Grachev felt uncomfortable in his presence. It was always the same with these GRU people. They had so much power over one! Quite often the power of life and death. He knew the stories of the terrible things they had done. The traps they had set and of the horrible deaths inflicted on quite often innocent victims. He also had first-hand experience of this particular man's incompetence and ruthlessness.

"Comrade Colonel Oleynik, as I told you the last time we met, it is coming along well. But it will take a little more time yet to get the virus to the stage where it is more virulent than anything possibly conceived by the enemies of the State." Dr Grachev chose the phrase 'enemies of the State' carefully, knowing only too well the political language which might get him into trouble and other such phrases which tripped easily off his tongue. He also knew like the next man, that no matter how bright you were, if you did not belong to the Communist Party your chosen path would lead into a cul-de-sac. Although communism was now, for all intents and purposes, dead and buried, with Russia you could never be sure. As Dr Grachev would sometimes remark, why tempt providence?

"As you know Colonel, the West ceased production and experimentation with these particular viruses under the 1972 Biological Weapons Convention whereas we carried on with our research and development, so in any race we have a head start. But these are new frontiers. Science takes time. I am working as hard as possible and appreciate all the special facilities put at my disposal by you and General Kovalyev."

"You use animals for your experiments don't you Dr Grachev: horses, monkeys, goats, sheep, and pigs? Is that not correct?

"Well, that is often the case, yes."

144

"And humans?"

"Colonel?"

"Humans to experiment upon."

"No Comrade Colonel, you know we do not use human beings. I am a trained doctor and it is against all ethics." The fact that he had heard whispers to the contrary, that suggestions had been made that human guinea pigs had sometimes been used in a multifarious number of ways was neither here nor there. Over the years Dr Grachev had learned to keep his mouth shut tight, feigning ignorance when he thought it expedient and this particular line of action had served him well throughout his career.

"We shoot spies Dr Grachev. Is that against your precious ethics?"

"That is, of course, different."

"How different Dr Grachev?"

"Well, if one commits a crime of that sort against the State, then one deserves to be punished."

"Punished? Well yes, capital punishment. Killed!"

"Colonel?" Dr Grachev was not sure what Colonel Oleynik was driving at.

"Let us not beat about the bush Grachev." The title 'Doctor' had now been dropped, which disturbed him and at the same time put him on his guard. "If things are being held up... your experiments not moving along fast enough because of ethical considerations..." The words 'ethical considerations' were enunciated with a hard tone to the colonel's voice which hung in the air just long enough for Dr Grachev to realise what was being suggested.

"We... I... can supply people who deserve to be punished." He spat out the words 'who deserve to be punished' in a loud bellicose voice, repeating the phrase Dr Grachev himself had just used. Dr Grachev felt a long cold shiver run down his spine. He cleared his throat.

"That is not the type of problem I have with these ongoing experiments. It will not take much longer now I feel sure. I shall continue to keep you informed Colonel – as usual."

"Listen carefully to what I am saying. If it does take much longer Grachev, then maybe we will try this futuristic and fantastic new virus out on you, to see just how virulent it is." Colonel Oleynik once again stared hard at the doctor before letting out a roar of mirthless laughter, his slim body becoming convulsed with the paroxysm. "Only joking my friend – only joking."

However, Dr Grachev did not breathe a long sigh of relief because he knew that Colonel Oleynik was very definitely not joking. He never joked. The Third Main Directorate, under the auspices of the Ministry of Health, had within its control certain so-called 'dedicated hospitals', the express purpose of which was to experiment upon unsuspecting Soviet nationals with the sole aim of refining deadly toxic agents for use against '*Enemies of the State*', both within and outside its international borders. This was what Colonel Oleynik was alluding to. It was a veiled threat which Dr Grachev took only too seriously. And although Colonel Oleynik himself did not work for this particular section run by the FSB, he nevertheless had close contact with this Directorate. Because of Dr Grachev's working for Biopreparat, which came under the control of the Ministry of Medical and Microbiological Industries, he also attended seminars and other meetings with fellow scientists belonging to the Third Main Directorate through their work on the human genome, a branch of science so close to Dr Grachev's heart.

As he dwelt on Colonel Oleynik's veiled threat, Dr Grachev's adversary suddenly changed his tone into something altogether more sombre as if pulling on the mantle of a sociopath, his face becoming drained of colour. "You realise that these conversations are confidential don't you? They must be kept secret. You do understand?" When he spoke again his cold eyes were focussed upon the desk top between them as if talking to himself in a detached manner.

"Do you understand?" The colonel again emphasised the interrogative nature of the question so that there was no mistaking the importance put upon such a request. Dr Grachev answered in the affirmative with all the gravity he could inflect into his voice. He also felt a twinge of nausea emanating in the pit of his stomach which had the effect of fetching up bitter bile into the back of his throat. He swallowed hard.

Dr Grachev's mind drifted back to when a similar request had been made to one of Colonel Oleynik's adjutants once before. "You must never speak of this again. It is a state secret; do you follow me? Never!"

CHAPTER 38

LONDON

It was late when Stryker and Caroline arrived at the restaurant on Haverstock Hill. The candles lent a romantic ambience and Stryker might have fallen under its charm had it not been for the suggestion of eating out at the behest and expense of the SIS. The conversation turned to travel, Carol saying that like Stryker she too had been to Moscow several times before and that she would make sure he was well briefed before they travelled.

"Why would we be travelling to Moscow, has something come up? It's the first I've heard of it."

"That's why we're here, for me to break the news to you. Anyhow my darling Stryker, I thought you might have realised that the time would come for you to do something for the department whilst waiting for our Russian friend to materialise. Do cheer up – the powers that be are paying for this meal and our trip – it might be interesting and possibly even fun." Carol lowered her voice: "They want you to act as bagman for the agency – simply collect some papers from Moscow relating to Biological Weapons."

"Oh Carol, when will you ever understand that nothing is simple when working for spooks. And I repeat, why would I be going to Moscow at this particular moment in time? I haven't even been briefed by your father on the subject of B.W. yet as promised. And another thing, would you please stop using those infernal terms of endearment. I'm nobody's darling."

"Don't be so grouchy, you're beginning to sound like my father. Nobody would believe that you're still only in your twenties." Stryker gave Carol a sharp glance and concentrated on the menu just that moment set before them. Carol softened her tone, hoping to lighten the mood.

"The other thing I wanted to speak with you about," Caroline whispered, "is a communication Six have received regarding our would-be defector, the Red Chameleon. It's in the form of a letter baldly spelling out his terms for defection. He is no shrinking violet this one I tell you. He says he will only trade information on Russia's Biological Weapons programmes and things like their advances made in genetic engineering, but, listen to this litany of requests: for protection – money – house – plastic surgery and scientific work in his own field of specialisation but this time he adds, in the interests of Britain and America. He must really hate his homeland!"

"Speaking of which, have you managed to get me the background I asked for earlier regarding that Russian fellow I met at the Easter service – names Dr Grachev?"

"Sorry Stryker, not yet. Brenda says that for some reason there is a problem obtaining this info. But she says she will also keep trying to glean any more information she can from Registry on the Dubai situation."

"Well they didn't seem to have a problem obtaining the information I requested on the car which followed me from the church service."

"I'll see what I can do. In fact, I'll do better than that. I'll give her a ring when we get back to the flat."

It was during the meal that Stryker noticed the proprietor of the restaurant Chen Hsu was not his usual chatty self and seemed to be edgy, which was completely out of character. When asked if everything was alright Chen Hsu answered in a cryptic fashion, "If you only knew how hard things can sometimes be my friend," then before saying anything else promptly fainted, dramatically slumping to the floor in a crumpled heap. Carol was surprised at the swiftness with which Stryker acted, as though he'd been trained as a doctor, going through the ritual of propping up his head and loosening his clothes and taking Chen Hsu's pulse. As waiters rushed up to help their employer, Stryker took charge of the situation.

"He's fainted, leave him where he is." Then Stryker fired questions at the staff: "Is he diabetic? Does he suffer from fainting fits? Is he epileptic?" As he was speaking Chen Hsu came round, his eyes opening wide as he stared past Stryker with a look of terror on his face. Stryker turned his head to see two big Chinese men standing behind him, long black overcoats draped over their shoulders and glaring. The tallest one of the men spoke with a calmness which belied the situation.

"He's alright. Don't get involved. Just leave the restaurant... now."

Still crouching over Chen Hsu, Stryker stared straight back into the eyes of the one doing the talking.

"He's sick. He needs a doc..." Stryker's sentence was never completed as the toe of a shiny black shoe thudded into Stryker's lower back, spinning him around still in the crouching position. Another kick aimed at Stryker's face came fast and furious. But this time Stryker was ready, catching hold of the incoming foot, twisting hard and pulling at the same time, the antagonist gliding through the air before crashing onto the table at which Stryker and Carol had been eating just moments earlier. Now the smaller of the two Chinese men bent low, aiming a karate chop to Stryker's neck which was deflected by Stryker's left arm while at the same time jabbing his stubby fingers with an upward motion deep into the man's solar plexus. The man jack-knifed, head meeting feet as Stryker aimed the side of his hand in a chopping motion at the back of his opponent's neck, this time doing what his second assailant had failed to do, making contact with a crunching sound.

The big man lay motionless, spread-eagled on the table, his head having crashed into the wall behind Carol who was by now on her feet and in tears. The waiters had fled to the other end of the restaurant, their backs and hands pressed hard against the wall as if trying in their desperation to disappear through it. Customers sat transfixed in a catatonic state, their forks and chop sticks carrying food, frozen in mid-air, while the assailants slowly roused themselves, the bigger of the two men sliding off the remains of the table, before finally fleeing the premises into the dark anonymity of the night.

Stryker grabbed Carol by the arm before dragging her out of the restaurant as they mingled with the rest of the fleeing customers. Carol had ceased crying but was in shock, not being able to make a sound. Once outside, Stryker bundled her into his sports car, driving the short distance back to Belsize Park in half the time it usually took. It was a few hours before Stryker could finally coax Carol to sleep with the help of some medication and a lot of reassurance. But before she slept, Carol insisted upon keeping her promise to Stryker. A telephone call was put through to Brenda's apartment. The conversation was kept short but for Stryker's benefit Carol repeated what her friend from Registry was telling her. "You say you will definitely try to get another look at the Dubai file and this time even possibly see who signed the papers relating to Stryker and I being classified as persona non grata? But do please be careful Brenda. For your own sake."

CHAPTER 39

MOSCOW

"You must never speak of this again. It is a state secret; do you follow me? Never!" Colonel Oleynik's reiteration sent shivers down Dr Grachev's spine as he recalled the events.

The whole story had later been relayed to Dr Grachev in the strictest confidence by Colonel Oleynik's adjutant. The colonel had been very sure of himself that day, kitted out, as all the other observers were, in their biohazard protective suits and masks. There he was giving orders without a moment's hesitation, attempting to impress all around him with his supposed total command of the situation. The experiment had been weeks in the planning and was to involve pigs and monkeys being tethered to steel stakes, leaving them exposed and vulnerable to the Russian biological attack which was to follow.

The uninhabited island, reached by plane from the Moscow region's Kubinka Military airport, had been chosen because it was separated from the mainland of the former Soviet Union by a considerable safety margin of many miles so as to counter the dangers posed by experimenting with airborne anthrax spores. This bacterium is excellent at combating hostile environments, samples of which can be found deep in the permafrost of the Russian steppes out in the hinterland, lying dormant for decades, sometime thousands of years before becoming active again, therefore making it a very dangerous biological weapon, more so because of the new strain being tested for its very virulence. There are well over 1,000 different strains of anthrax. Owing to its natural hardy character, it was also considered eminently suitable for dispersal in a weapons context, such as bombs. The virulence of this new strain of anthrax was being tested in concert was a new delivery system incorporating a cleverly modified aerosol technology, the brainchild of Colonel Oleynik himself. Not only did he work for the armed forces GRU Military Intelligence but he was also known as a scientist and engineer of some calibre.

Classified as low level, the plan was that a metal orb would break open at a height of some twenty metres and deliver pulmonary anthrax spores in aerosol form above the tethered pigs and monkeys. Meteorological conditions had been perfect; a rather dull day with no strong breezes to cause problems, nor any threat of rain.

However, the delivery of anthrax, using a system developed on the orders of Colonel Oleynik, had malfunctioned. This prototype orb-like bomb containing anthrax microorganisms had failed to split open after being jettisoned from a low flying aeroplane. Instead, after plummeting rapidly to earth it had dug itself deep into a marshy area some way off of its mark and without releasing its deadly offering onto the animals now straining frantically at their leashes. The small explosive device had not been activated according to the principles of the design and Colonel Oleynik had lost his usual suave, calm composure.

Becoming consumed with uncontrollable rage, Colonel Oleynik had blamed the engineers responsible for the construction of the bomb which had been designed ultimately to be delivered by rocket. It made him look incompetent. There was only one possible solution, and that was to re-test the bomb. Time, in the mind of Colonel Oleynik, was of the essence. The kudos of success would add to his high standing with his boss General Kovalyev and his many contemporaries; failure was not an option. It was therefore imperative for the test to be carried out as soon as possible.

In normal circumstances it would have fallen to Dr Grachev himself to supervise the safety aspects of retrieving the bomb and preparing it for the second test. With its deadly payload this was a very dangerous operation and would have taken days if not weeks. But Colonel Oleynik had insisted that time was not on their side which had resulted in the operation being rushed. Luckily for Dr Grachev he was not involved in any of this as he had to depart for one of his regular pre-arranged visits to Beijing well before work on the bomb and its retrieval could begin, and Colonel Oleynik was in no frame of mind to wait upon his return to help sort out the accident. So soldiers and auxiliary workers had been called in to locate the malfunctioning bomb without Dr Grachev being on hand with his expertise.

It had been hard work attempting to locate the bomb and then dig it out and after a while the heavy, cumbersome protective biohazard suits coupled with respirators had been dispensed with on the orders of Colonel Oleynik so as to speed up the process of recovery. The colonel himself had viewed the retrieval of the malfunctioning bomb from some distance away through powerful binoculars. The person on the spot giving orders on behalf of Colonel Oleynik was the colonel's second in command, a lieutenant-colonel, who happened to be another GRU man. The soldiers had been kept in ignorance of what type of deadly microorganisms the bomb contained and the bomb had exploded just as they were retrieving it, showering them with anthrax, one of the deadliest organisms known to man. There had been the lieutenant-colonel, seven army engineers, and dozens of auxiliary workers who succumbed to the deadly invisible cloud of anthrax spores. They were immediately quarantined on the island.

The first signs of infection were breathing difficulties experienced by all within the immediate vicinity of the biological blast. Within twenty-four hours nasty black ulcerous swellings had appeared on their skin. Within three days the lieutenant-colonel, all the soldiers and auxiliary workers were dead. On the direct orders of Colonel Oleynik a pit was dug large enough for the bodies to be pushed into before having kerosene poured over them and incinerated. There were fifty-two bodies in total. At the same time as this accident it was rumoured that the Soviet Union had accumulated not tons of anthrax, stored ready for use in a possible future war, but hundreds of tons.

Subsequently the accident had been hushed up by the authorities, like so many other incidents had been covered up over the years, and Colonel Oleynik had managed to push the responsibility onto others. Dr Grachev himself had of course been in Beijing, thereby abrogating any responsibilities placed upon him by Colonel Oleynik earlier: he having initially planned for Grachev to oversee the safety aspect of preparing the biological bomb for testing. Nevertheless, many of Dr Grachev's colleagues had suffered for Colonel Oleynik's mistake of ignoring these safety aspects and were demoted with their meagre salaries following suit.

"And now to the real reason why you were summoned here," said Colonel Oleynik, his voice breaking into Dr Grachev's private thoughts. "No doubt you will be pleased and perhaps even a little surprised to learn, after you nearly caused me a heart attack with that bloody little Trabant door hitting me on the pavement, that you have been granted permission for your trips to Beijing and London. Because the timescale is in such close proximity to each other you will find two sets of documentation, visas et cetera for both of your journeys." A large brown envelope was pushed over the desk toward an anxious-looking Dr Grachev. "Make the most of your journey for it will be your last trip to China... ever! And as for your annual scientific conference to London... that's it as well as far as we're concerned. No more junkets globetrotting at the expense of the Russian citizen." Colonel Oleynik seemed to relish giving Dr Grachev the devastating news. All pretence of comradeship had been dropped.

For Dr Grachev it was quite normal to travel to Beijing on a regular basis in a spirit of co-operation between what used to be known as the Soviet Union and the People's Republic of China. No reason had been given as to why these trips were no longer to be countenanced, but Dr Grachev knew enough to reason it was to do with the break-up of the Soviet Union, the secret treaty of co-operation between the two countries now being null and void as the USSR ceased to exist in 1991. If a new Sino-

Russian treaty was to be drawn up; well, that was in the future and from Dr Grachev's point of view it did not really matter for as far as he was concerned there was no future for him in Russia any more.

However, Dr Grachev's forthcoming trip to Beijing, although Colonel Oleynik and his boss General Kovalyev did not know it, had the potential to be the most important visit to China Dr Grachev had ever undertaken. Biological samples were to be brought back which would supply him with the information he required to complete his experiment, hopefully leading to what he lovingly thought of as the creation of The Super Strain. As was the precautionary routine for such transportation from China, these samples were to be brought back to Moscow overland, it clearly being too risky transporting such a dangerous consignment by air in case the aircraft should crash with the resulting consequences being too terrifying to contemplate. These consignments being transported in a spirit of mutual co-operation with the Chinese were always covertly escorted to their destination in Russia by a Soviet scientist and armed guards. As for his journey to London, Dr Grachev only really required a one way ticket, though he knew provision had been made for his safe return to the Motherland. As he prepared to take his leave and nodded toward Colonel Oleynik, Dr Grachev was stopped in his tracks.

"Haven't you forgotten something?" For a fleeting moment Dr Grachev was taken aback and raised his eyebrows with a quizzical expression upon his face.

"Your signature... you must know it is required Grachev." Dr Grachev grabbed the proffered pen and scrawled his signature on an official-looking piece of paper – the receipt in triplicate for his travel documentation.

A wave of relief swept over the scientist as he retreated hastily, brusquely murmuring his goodbyes to Colonel Oleynik's secretary. He was surprised at just how light his steps were as he once again entered out into the bright sunlight, clutching his ticket to freedom and making his way back to his battered old Trabant. He had never liked Colonel Oleynik and this meeting had just confirmed his suspicion that the feeling was mutual. Calling him Grachev like that only confirmed this suspicion. And when informed of his truncated travel arrangements, Schadenfreude had been written all over Colonel Oleynik's features.

CHAPTER 40

It was three o'clock on Saturday afternoon when the couple walked from the direction of the Royal Crescent, ambling along Brock Street before passing the house designated number 8, the property once owned by the British Prime Minister Benjamin Disraeli, renown for ensuring that in 1875 Britain bought the controlling stake in the Suez Canal. Bearing right, the couple then turned into the Circus, so-called because of its circumference being based on that of Rome's famous amphitheatre known as the Coliseum. The word 'circus' related to the entertainment enjoyed by the ancient Romans, such as throwing Christians to the lions.

If they had taken themselves around the perimeter of the Circus to the left, the couple would have passed both numbers 13 and 17 respectively; the former house of David Livingstone, famous explorer of Africa, and that of the equally famous English landscape and portrait painter Thomas Gainsborough.

As it was, they bore right, walking slowly past number 9, former residence of Lord Leighton – painter and sculptor; his painting entitled 'Flaming June', being of such fame. Number 7 the Circus was the one time residence of William Pitt the Elder, British Prime Minister in all but name and father of William Pitt the Younger, very definitely Prime Minister – the youngest ever at the tender age of 24.

Another sharp turn right took them downhill along Gay Street, and past the former residence of the Gay household, elaborate stone carvings of foliage and swags of fruit above the street door earmarking that particular Georgian property in which they had resided, and after which personage the street had been named. At the time of their residence however, the etymological significance of the name Gay, did not bear any sexual connotation or proclivity to the aforementioned.

After a while they reached the Roman Baths, famed for its hot water springs which the Romans had so cleverly exploited two thousand years before, transforming them into places for bathing and worship of the water deity Aquae Sulis. The Roman Baths had been written about by such luminaries as Samuel Pepys and the city of Bath itself immortalised by Jane Austen. The Georgian honey-coloured buildings framed against the dazzling bright blue sky looked splendid, soaking up the warmth of the sun.

The couple made their way toward the Roman Baths this particular afternoon, not because of any leanings toward Roman and English history, although both Professor Richard Lambton and his wife had a keen interest in that subject.

Walking beneath the stone pier colonnade, where two hundred years before, porters had collected and put down their fare paying passengers, including William Pitt père, ferried in enclosed sedan chairs, Professor and Mrs Lambton now paused within the shadow of the impressive Bath Abbey before veering right through a doorway where the sign on a tall thin tripod read 'Cream Teas'. This was Mrs Lambton's bank holiday as much as her husband's and she was determined to enjoy it. Moving smoothly from Abbey Churchyard, through the glazed swing doors into the Pump Room – some six metres above the original Roman temple precinct and sacrificial altar, the professor and Mrs Lambton entered to the strains of a string quartet situated at the other end of the large room which had been opened for the first time in 1795 by the Duchess of York.

The quartet performed upon a stage set into one wall. Beneath this charming picture of cultural musicianship waitresses bustled to and fro around the occupied tables, taking orders for cream teas, as well as sandwiches, hot scones and buttered teacakes. It was a very English scene and both Mrs Lambton and her husband found it quite a novelty, getting away from the trials and tribulations for a short while. The couple had only recently moved to Bath in preparation for the professor's imminent retirement, his wife now being on the verge of obtaining what she had been dreaming of for a very long time. In the early years of their marriage, long before Mrs Lambton's husband had been awarded his professorship, they had lived in London, south of the Thames, and hated it. They hated the traffic and its ensuing pollution, they hated the noise of the neighbours and most of all they hated the crime. So ever since, whenever she had at the slightest opportunity, Mrs Lambton badgered her husband about moving to Bath, always extolling its virtues and pointing out that if it had been good enough for her favourite novelist, Jane Austen, to write about in her novels... and to actually live in the place, then it was certainly good enough for them to settle down in.

After entering the tea room and Mrs Lambton having lowered her ample form onto one of the dining room chairs, her mind became momentarily occupied with the theatre play booked for that particular evening, until her train of thought was interrupted.

"Do you want the full works darling? The waitress is waiting."

Mrs Lambton raised her head from the local newspaper, bought specifically for details of forthcoming events in and around Bath, smiling broadly.

"The waitress is waiting? That's a pun darling... yes please dear, the full works. Tea, cream, scones, strawberry jam, the full works. Oh! And would you be so kind as to make sure the tea is piping hot? I do so hate tepid tea. Oh, and could we please have a large pot of boiling water? I mean really hot dear." A beaming smile was flashed at the waitress who responded in like manner.

Michael had decided to mow the lawn early the following morning, being a Sunday, before driving outside Bath to find "a nice little pub for a spot of lunch." Like all well laid plans he had not taken into account his cell phone. As it began to ring with a shrill high pitched tone, the professor could have sworn that he had purposefully left it indoors on the sofa so as to avoid anyone contacting him from his office as they invariably did when he attempted to take time off from his demanding roll. Now his wife produced the cell phone from her large handbag and held it toward her husband.

"Well, go on dear, answer it. Good job I lifted it from the sofa before we left this morning. It's probably Caroline. I guessed she would ring.

***

Two hours later Mrs Lambton was very definitely not in a good frame of mind as her husband sat on a London bound train reading a copy of the in-house journal 'Nuclear, Biological and Chemical Warfare', issued by the government agency at Porton Down, of which professor Lambton was Deputy Director General. When Mrs Lambton was asked by friends precisely what her husband did, she took pains to point out that it had something to do with noses and the common cold. "His job is very boring dear. He's always suffering with his nose. Why he couldn't find a better job than that I don't know. Not pushy enough I expect. You have to push to get ahead, don't you? How he became a professor doing what he does I don't know. They still haven't found a cure for the common cold have they?" It was a misunderstanding with his wife relating to a conversation about his work years before, a misunderstanding which he had been quite happy to let stand, having adopted the philosophy, *anything for a quiet life*.

Porton Down, Britain's centre for experimental research into chemical and biological agents, concerns itself with the defence of the realm by attempting to counter the very real threat of chemical and biological warfare. The Down itself having long ago been covered over its many acres with a motley assortment of buildings incorporating outlying storage facilities; concrete bunkers, tall tower like structures – a sure sign of its ungodly and dangerous work – and also two-storey high red brick offices, as well as the all-important laboratories.

This highly secret government complex was very convenient for professor Lambton as it was no more than forty miles from Bath as the crow flies.

At the rear of Hillfort Road, Mrs Lambton sat alone in their long flower-strewn garden on that balmy spring afternoon, dwelling on the fact that it had not been the first time and no doubt would not be the last, that her husband had been dragged away on urgent business at the weekend. For her, his retirement could not come soon enough.

The particular page of the in-house magazine professor Lambton was reading bore the title 'Biotechnology: The dawn of a new era.' It was an extract of an article taken from a well-known American scientific publication and written by one Dr Grachev, a Russian scientist.

CHAPTER 41

RUSSIAN HINTERLAND

"Louder, I can't hear you."

The frail woman with the brown, weathered, deeply lined face, and one protruding buck-tooth digging into her lower lip, sat hunched up looking very uncomfortable, her small dark eyes darting back and forth from Captain Zhizhin to her daughter Marishka and then back to her son as she continued to squirm and look embarrassed. Attempting to clear her throat she found her tongue sticking to her palate. There was a long silence before managing to create enough spittle to free it.

"I'm just an ordinary woman; a widow with a small family to support." Her voice faltered, barely audible. She tried again.

"I couldn't tell you anything about what goes on at the factory. I know nothing about anything. Nothing! You must believe me. You have the wrong person. I am innocent. I don't know any Ivanovich. I have never heard of such a person." Her protestations however, fell on deaf ears. The blank pieces of paper upon which each had been encouraged to write what they knew about the factory and the assistant deputy director, lay untouched on Captain Zhizhin's desk, with the explanation that the whole family were illiterate.

"Speak up. Stop mumbling and answer the questions I put to you. Have you ever seen a man known as Ivan the Terrible?"

The elderly woman became incensed, momentarily forgetting the dire situation she and her family found themselves in, gaining false courage to answer spontaneously. "What is this, some kind of joke?" she whispered, trying desperately to make her voice more audible. "You did not say that before. You just said Ivanovich. Even I know Ivan the Terrible is dead."

Spiritually you may well be right, the captain thought to himself. "So you knew him then?" Her interrogator's eyes widened with pleasure as a faint softness crept into his features. "Now we are getting somewhere."

"Knew him? Yes I knew of him, of course I did."

"And when was the last time you saw him?"

Her face now registered both disgust and disbelief. A bony finger swept back a few grey hairs which had become dislodged from behind one of her red ears.

"I don't know how you can ask such questions. I may not be able to write or read and I only knew him through a few history lessons at school but how could I have met Ivan the Terrible? He's been dead for hundreds of years."

"Not that Ivan you stupid woman: the Ivan I am speaking of works at the factory as you very well know. Ivan Sobolev. Word is that you are very close to this man. Do you deny it?" The room fell silent; each of the interrogator's victims aware of their own laboured breathing, amplified by the stillness. Suddenly this air of calm was shattered by the screaming disjointed voice of a man possessed.

"Do you not understand who I am – what power I have over you?" A large hairy fist banged down heavily upon the solid desk top, making the blank sheaf of papers bounce. "You think you can play games with me? I could have you all locked up. Now answer my questions." Mother, daughter and son stared in terror at the enormous man with the thick hairy arms and red flushed face.

Captain Zhizhin realised he wasn't getting anywhere so tried another tack.

"Your name is Marishka isn't it?" His voice had now become suitably modulated for conversing with the young girl standing beside her mother's chair. She stood in such close proximity, partly to give her mother support, partly for her own imagined protection.

"Yes sir, Marishka Petrova." The young girl's heart was beating so fast that she thought she would faint.

"Such a pretty name, Marishka – the same as your mother's I note." Captain Zhizhin stared down at the piece of paper with the family's names upon it, then up at the ceiling for a moment, formulating the next question in his mind before speaking again. He did not like children being present at such interviews, but had over the years gleaned some interesting titbits of information from a suspect's offspring.

The last piece of information proffered by Yevgeny before returning to Moscow with his two colleagues had been a snippet of gossip gleaned from a high ranking official within the factory. It related to the fact that Ivan had been seen several times in the company of one Marishka Petrova. To Captain Zhizhin it presented a lead – if only a tenuous one, a window into the private life of someone who on the surface, seemed not to have had any life at all outside that of his work at the factory.

"Now then Miss Petrova, do you think your mother is telling the truth?" The captain turned his gaze upon the teenager's mother, looking at her in a friendly fashion.

"Am I to understand that your mother had never entertained this Ivan at home eh? What do you think?"

"Yes sir, she is telling the truth." The pretty headscarf knotted around her delicate white throat made Marishka look even younger than her seventeen years; even her demeanour belied the fact that she stood on the verge of womanhood, her long black hair flowing down her back in a girlish sort of way.

Slowly the truth began to seep into Captain Zhizhin's head – that what he had been pursuing was a phantom leading him up a blind alley – just malicious gossip. That was not uncommon. Ivan after all was somewhat younger than this small unattractive woman with two children to look after. The scientist and fellow GRU officer could have taken his pick. Surely there were more attractive women out there whom Ivan would have been attracted to. It was beginning to appear that the information Konstantin and his colleague Pyotr required would not be forthcoming; certainly not from this quarter. He had suggested as much before they set out on their return journey to Moscow.

Captain Zhizhin peered at each member of the family in turn before focussing his undivided attention once more upon the mother. There then followed a silence of perhaps three minutes. It might have been longer. For Marishka senior it felt like a lifetime. Her face grew redder and redder as she lost eye contact with her interrogator, slowly inclining her head toward the floor, working the buck-tooth back and forth along her nether lip.

Sometimes the trick worked, sometimes it didn't. Keep staring at a perceived guilty person for long enough and they might just break. But this was one time when Captain Zhizhin did not have any conviction in that particular ploy.

"You are free to go." His voice visibly startled the shrivelled woman standing before him, her head jerking up and backwards as if attached to an invisible thread controlled by a puppeteer.

Captain Zhizhin lifted the piece of paper from his desk bearing the family's details and proceeded to ceremoniously tear it in half before dropping it into his wastepaper bin nearby. He looked up at the mother and then at both children once more, the children remaining where they were, the trio unable to comprehend that their ordeal was finally over.

"Well what are you standing there for? Go! Get out of my office." After gesturing with his large hands, Marishka's mother finally moved from the spot where she had been guarded on one side by her daughter and on the other by her small son.

"I would like to have been of more help." The sentence was flung at her interrogator out of sheer relief as the small woman stepped toward the large door. Opening it quickly, her daughter was the first to make a rapid exit, passing in front of her mother into the long corridor, happy to be leaving the stifling atmosphere behind her. It was only as she moved out of sight did her small insignificant looking brother, a scaled down version of his mother, with skeletal looks and painfully frail body, turn back toward his mother's tormentor.

Captain Zhizhin was in the process of fiddling with one of the desk's drawers when the boy tugged at his sleeve. The bear looked down at him with a benign smile, being reminded of his own small daughter's habit of doing just this same thing when she wanted to gain his attention. And as Captain Zhizhin glanced down Marishka's brother stood on tiptoe so as to whisper something into his ear.

A look of puzzlement tinged with relief crossed the Captain's face as he stooped even lower to retrieve the two torn pieces of paper he had just consigned to the bin.

CHAPTER 42

LONDON

As a practical measure it had served its purpose well over the years, and being located so close to the Ministry of Defence it was perfect. If the weather was fine Professor Lambton would take a leisurely stroll down to the Ministry. If the weather was foul then there was always a taxi at hand.

The professor had no need to proffer his name to the porter, he being acknowledged by a slight nod of the head and a welcoming smile as he explained that he was expecting two visitors before passing through a grandiose portal, soon to be ensconced within the elegant surroundings of his club situated just off Trafalgar Square. After removing a copy of the Times from an array of other newspapers laid out neatly upon a sofa table beside the reception desk, he ordered a large whisky before making his way into the lounge.

The mahogany fielded panelled walls, pink marbleised columns topped with gold leafed Corinthian capitals, and red plush deep pile carpet upon which stood sofa tables similar to the one which held the newspapers supporting elegantly proportioned chinoiserie-style table lamps with silk bowed drum lampshades, gave the cavernous room an air of luxury and comfort, acting as a retreat from the chaotic pace of city life not a stone's throw away from where he now sat in a brown soft leather armchair. A cloistered sanctuary of calmness in the heart of a noisy polluted London. It had yet to turn five so there was time to kill.

Most of the seating, be that of the scattering of tall winged back chairs upholstered in dark green leather, matching button-backed sofas or the informal groups of damask covered low-backed easy chairs and sofas, was vacant. Just one elderly white-haired gentleman, with a red and yellow paisley-coloured silk handkerchief peeking out from the top breast pocket of his dark suit, sat in the far corner of the room, quietly nursing a whisky whilst perusing a distinctly pink copy of the Financial Times. This gentleman had preceded Professor Lambton into the club just seconds before, having deposited his now very dated bowler hat and neatly furled umbrella with the porter for safe keeping. Within two hours or so the club would begin to get busy with the prospect of dinner and fine wines.

The professor's mind rankled on the fact that the call from his daughter

Carol had spoilt Mrs Lambton's holiday weekend. But he also knew that Carol would not drag him up to London on a whim – it must be important, whatever the reason. His daughter had also imparted to him a piece of good news relating to a prized object for which he had been searching, thus softening the blow of having his bank holiday plans interrupted. As the professor's whisky arrived carried by a porter on a small silver tray Carol appeared, trailing in her wake a large rugged-framed man looming in Professor Lambton's peripheral vision. The scientist half eased himself out from the armchair without straightening his back and proffered his hand.

"Daddy, this is Stryker. Stryker meet my father Professor Lambton, deputy director general of Porton Down."

The professor's eyes met Carol's. "Yes dear, I think we can dispense with the formalities."

Tactfully Stryker ignored this rebuke to Carol by her father by taking his hand and shaking it warmly.

"Good to meet you Professor, I've heard a lot about you."

Carol scrutinised her surroundings, satisfying herself it was safe to speak. Once the elderly man in the far corner reading his newspaper was deemed not to be within earshot or a security risk she carried on. "Sorry to be so cryptic on the telephone Daddy. I did hate making that call but I felt it was important to see you urgently."

"Yes, I guessed as much, but could it not have waited till after the holiday?" Even as he spoke, he wished he hadn't. Carol was a good daughter and as long as she was happy that was all that the professor and his wife had wanted. He knew she worked for the government doing some sort of secret work but had no idea she was a spook. He had met lots of Foreign and Commonwealth Office and Ministry of Defence people over the years through his work as a government scientist, but had been given no reason to believe that he and his wife had a bona fide spy in the family. Since abandoning her modelling career Carol would occasionally pick her father's brains, Professor Lambton knowing that she was a civil servant and had been positively vetted by Special Branch, it having been accepted as par for the course. The professor had been made aware of the vetting procedure because of the two plainclothes men that had paid a visit to his wife Gloria when he had been at work, asking all sorts of questions as to their daughter's political leanings and what newspapers she read as well as more intrusive questions. Therefore when matters of a sensitive nature came up, impinging on national security, professor Lambton knew he could answer them frankly and honestly without shying away from awkward topics. The tea which had been missed earlier in Bath because of the telephone call from his daughter was now duly ordered, minus the cream and scones that his wife had so much been looking forward to.

Thinly sliced sandwiches of smoked salmon, chicken and beef sat between the three of them on a low mahogany butler's table, giving each of them the space to feel more comfortable, as most English men prefer. Caroline began talking in as quiet a voice as was possible though not even a waiter loitered nearby. Leaning forward over the sandwiches toward her father, she spoke in a confidential manner.

"Daddy, I don't think you know Stryker – he's Richard Truman's nephew." A look of dismay clouded professor Lambton's face.

"So you're the son of my ex-wife's ex-husband?"

"For my sins, that is so, sir."

"And you are familiar with my daughter's work?"

"Yes sir, I am." Stryker attempted to modify his accented American drawl but to Carol's ears it just grated.

"Well, that's more than I am."

"Daddy, you know that I work for the government and Stryker here is also working for the same bunch so is vetted." Then in an attempt to pacify her father further Carol added, "Stryker worked in Seattle as a detective. Anyhow, we are now collaborating together on something which you should be able to help us with: information on biological warfare!"

Professor Lambton gave a benign smile. "Yes, I had a communication from some civil service department or other to that effect. Go on, I'm listening." Notwithstanding the smile there was a faint hint of hostility in his voice, as though he had been put out by this American upstart who had ruined his wife's weekend and possibly also because of the filial relationship between himself and his daughter having been sullied by his ex-wife's tenuous family connection with this American detective from Seattle.

"It's possible we have a potential Russian defector on our hands who says he is a scientist. If he is telling the truth, then he's in the same business as you are daddy – chemical and biological warfare. As I say, it is very urgent as we are both off to Moscow soon so need some background knowledge, otherwise I would not have dragged you back to London. You're not annoyed with me are you?" Carol had noted with some concern the pointed question from her father as to why their meeting could not have waited until after the holiday, and had wanted to let him see that this was no frivolous request. She searched the professor's face for any sign of hostility.

"No, of course not darling – you'll just have to make your peace with your mother the next time you see her." After a few more pleasantries had been exchanged between the professor and his daughter, they moved on to the real reason why the three of them were having tea in such grandiose surroundings.

"As your daughter says, sir, we require some background on Russia's development of biological weapons. Time permitting, we could of course go ask my countrymen for this information but I'm sure anything that you can tell me would be of help."

"Well it's a big subject Stryker, as you can I'm sure imagine, but I will give you some pointers on the seriousness of such weapons. So we speak of Russia. In 1972 there was a Biological Weapons Convention banning the stockpiling and use of such weapons which we know the Russians didn't stick to. Russian experiments have been ongoing into the effects of such biological weapons ever since." Professor Lambton half stood and half leaned to the right as he fumbled for his spectacle case, finally locating it in one of his crumpled dark suit pockets. Once retrieved, he sat down heavily and after extracting the thick-lensed glasses proceeded to toy with them without actually putting them on.

"Yes. We know of course because of the recent defection to America of another Russian scientist, one Dr Kanatjan Alibekov, former Moscow scientific researcher into biological and chemical weapons," Carol interjected, looking pleased with herself, being able to show she had some knowledge into the background of these things.

"Precisely," retorted the professor, giving his daughter a slightly quizzical look. "And we have learnt from this scientist that ongoing experiments are still being carried out by the Russians into a long list of agents including smallpox, glanders, plague, anthrax, Marburg, Ebola, and the list including other haemorrhagic fevers goes on. As an example, take this last one I mentioned Ebola, named after the Ebola River and one of the deadliest viral diseases known to man for whom there is no known vaccine as yet and a fatality rate of as high as 90 per cent. The flu-like symptoms of the disease such as headache, sore throat, high temperature and aching limbs may not even be noticed for up to three weeks, though a rash might appear after just a few days. This of course presents many problems in this age of air travel where one may theoretically travel the globe without even being aware of carrying any highly infectious viral disease. The only positive thing to say about this particular virus is that as far as we know it can only be transmitted by body fluids as opposed to the flu virus, but there again, this is not really good news at all when you consider it can also be spread by vomiting, diarrhoea, saliva, sweat from many different parts of the body including hands and forehead, and possibly also by sneezing. There is no known cure for this Ebola disease whatsoever – none. For many people they're history within two weeks. Just this year in Zaire there was an outbreak. Many people haemorrhaged to death. Do you understand what it is to die by haemorrhaging?" The professor looked at both his guests in turn. "Bleeding to death. One's veins in the body act as if they had been punctured, leading to unimaginable leaking of blood from eyes, ears, mouth, and rectum – most people have no idea just how much blood is held within the human body – need I go on? And concerning the adaptation of the Ebola virus into biological weapons for warfare against an army or even a civilian population come to that, well under research conditions it has been proven that this virus is ideal for use in encompassing aerosol technology. Can you just imagine Ebola turned into airborne particles? They would be breathed into the lungs, get into the eyes – no hiding place. The thought is horrendous. Biological weapons such as viruses are invisible to the naked eye, possessing neither smell nor taste yet are living entities with characteristics of having DNA and RNA. The common template of DNA and RNA, you might be interested to know, is the same template that you and I and all other life forms on the planet Earth possess. But the thing you must understand about viruses is that there is one way in which a virus differs from all other life forms, and that is that whilst many viruses possess DNA in their make-up, many others employ RNA. This established fact was only initially made possible by the work of the now world famous countryman of yours," here the professor looked at Stryker, "the American scientist James Watson who together with the Englishman Francis Crick made their breakthrough whilst at Cambridge University, here in England, in 1953 at the Cavendish Laboratory doing research in molecular biology. For this they were both awarded, together with Maurice H. Wilkins, the Nobel Prize for medicine and physiology in 1962. This of course led to scientists specialising in this field of medicine, being able to decode life as we understand it – many would say the greatest biological discovery in the last hundred years. But I digress. To return to the subject of being infected by a virus, the fact is, you might not know for days or even weeks that anything was amiss. But once these organisms take hold of your body – boy oh boy! You wish you were dead, and of course ultimately you are granted that wish. It's just that in the meantime the suffering can be unendurable. Pus in the lungs, blisters and ulcers all over your body including the inside of your mouth and the soles of your feet which can also ooze with blood and pus. The skin itself can turn into something resembling wafer thin parchment which has the propensity to crack exposing raw flesh. Fingernails drop off. A living hell is what I'd describe it as."

Carol glanced down at the sandwiches sitting between them and felt nauseated.

"There is all this talk about Russia developing germ warfare weapons, but is there not an even bigger player in this field of research?" Carol queried, describing a giant arc with her hands and arms.

"Are you suggesting that Mr Stryker's country is as involved in this as is Russia?" came Professor Lambton's rejoinder, turning his spectacles over in his hands and peering at them with half closed eyes as if inspecting them through one of Porton Down's high powered electron microscopes. Carol stared at him.

Stryker looked on bemused to see father and daughter in such an animated discussion, the professor playing with his glasses and his daughter playing devil's advocate.

"No. Of course not Daddy! You spend enough time in America yourself to know that. Who mentioned anything about America?" Carol glanced at Stryker. "No, as you know, America and Britain gave up the idea of using offensive biological weapons years ago with respect to treaties it signed. It is true that there has been ongoing research programs into defensive studies here, but we, like our American cousins," here she gave Stryker a pointedly knowing look, "really do not have an offensive capability regarding biological weapons, do we?" Carol turned her head to her father for an answer she already knew. The professor raised his eyes from the now minutely examined glasses for a moment and shook his head in a negative fashion, slightly put out by the question.

"No Carol, we certainly do not carry out work which in any way, shape or form could be described as offensive. The only work we carry out on these nasty microbes is for the defence of our citizens and country. In fact, we carry out work which I hope can help the whole world by attempting to discover what and how infectious diseases, which I might add are sent to us from places all over the world, can be detected and combated." His eyes darted back to the plastic and glass he held gingerly in his fingers.

Carol carried on. "Anyway, as I say, why mention America? What about Libya, Syria, Cuba, India, Iran or Iraq or Israel, Germany and France. Not necessarily involved in developing these microbes for offensive purposes but certainly it is said they have the capability if they put their minds to it. There are just so many countries aren't there. North Korea, South Korea, Taiwan. Why go on? It is appalling. No, I mean China, the country with the largest population on this planet – though population wise, India will not be too long in overtaking China so I'm told."

Professor Lambton pursed his lips for a moment before resuming his conversation with his daughter and American guest. "It is certainly true that China have made great strides in many fields. So I suppose it would be arrogant to believe a nation of its stature knew nothing about such matters."

A twinkle came into Carol's eyes. "Of course you are right. I suppose it does not take a great leap of the imagination to realise that the Chinese are involved. The point is the Secret Intelligence Service has proof that they are working in conjunction with the Russians, is that not so Stryker? What do you say to that?"

Professor Lambton smiled. "I'm really not surprised. Though it's frightening to have it confirmed. I heard through the grapevine some time ago for instance, that the Russians had become second to none in the field of fermenting and drying microorganisms for use in biological warfare. Now that type of knowledge would be the sort of thing that could well be traded by the Russians for some of the scientific secrets that the Chinese might well possess. After all, they are both communist states aren't they, and might see a certain similarity in their joint striving."

It was a canny guess by the professor, and one that Stryker believed was not too far short of the mark. He leaned imperceptibly closer to Carol's father so as not to miss anything this top class British scientist said, knowing that any morsel of inside scientific information might possibly come in handy at some future date when dealing with his nemesis quaintly named the Red Chameleon.

The professor was now getting into his stride and warming to the subject. "I think the consequences could be terrifying. D'you know Stryker, when we, the United Kingdom that is, during the Second World War faced the possibility of gas attacks on this great country of ours, over 97 million civilian respirators – gas masks to the layman – were produced on the orders of the government? Just on the off chance that poisonous gas might be dumped on the civilian population plus our troops abroad by enemy aircraft. Fortunately that did not happen. I know we were on a war footing, but today, to be frank, we could not possibly protect our population if biological attacks were launched against it in the next few months. I can't speak for America of course. But even in the longer term there would be massive insurmountable problems. Just supposing that we knew in advance, which is extremely unlikely, what the biological weapon consisted of – for once the disease has taken hold it is almost impossible to treat, and many of the viral diseases have no known antidote with which to protect the population anyway." At this point Professor Lambton took a sip of his previously ordered whisky before continuing.

"Yes, as I say, even if we had prior knowledge of such an attack, it would be a false assumption to say that we could produce enough antidote to treat the population at large, assuming there was an effective antidote, which in any case would be horrendously expensive... prohibitively so. For example, to give you an indication of how insidious these viral diseases are, there was one laboratory accident in this country, I think it was in 1976. It was the Ebola-Sudan strain of virus. One person was infected but thankfully survived. But it just goes to show you that even in a carefully controlled environment such as a laboratory these viruses are tricky things to deal with. There again, take pneumonic plague. When people get struck down with pneumonic plague it is almost one hundred per cent certain that you are going to die a very horrific death – one hundred per cent."

"Daddy, to hear you of all people, an insider with your scientific background, say that the consequences of Beijing's collusion with Moscow in such matters could be terrifying makes me wonder if it's sensible to bring babies into such an unstable environment. Did you know that America and Russia hold between them enough anthrax powder, about one thousand small glass vials, to wipe out the entire world's population if they were able to distribute it properly, which of course would be a tremendous logistical problem to say the very least, and that these vials have the same status as a nuclear capability and are treated as such? They are held under what they call the triple key lock system. Three different people, each with their own key must be involved before they have the capability of gaining access to this plague of dust."

Professor Lambton smiled benignly. "Yes, I know. It was I who told you. And remember this; anthrax is very easy to propagate."

Carol carried on regardless, ignoring her father's last comment.

"But don't you think that's obscene?"

"Of course it's obscene," replied the professor. "But not wishing to split hairs, it's also a bit of a sweeping statement to say that the entire world's population could be wiped out. I know you inserted the caveat regarding distribution but let's face it, there is no way one could be sure of infecting everyone upon this planet. And even if there were – say if all the possible sources of the world's drinking water were contaminated, well what would be the point? I know your next question: 'What if there was an accident and the drinking water did become contaminated? What then?' Of course I get what you're driving at, and yes darling... you have good cause to worry about these weapons... most of the world's population don't really have an inkling of just how serious the situation is. Even you Stryker, not wishing to sound disparaging, unless you are a scientist working within this highly specialised field dealing with viruses and biological weapons... well, no one else can truly comprehend... begin to understand the horrendous ramifications. And governments have done absolutely nothing to educate the population on the frightening consequences of biological warfare. Sometimes Stryker, in my quieter moments, even I become fearful of just what we're up against... dabbling with Mother Nature. Who knows where it will end? The consequences never seem obvious when you're really just on the threshold of coming to terms with something like this, for in truth we've barely scratched the surface. Think of the expansion in world population. Just a hundred years ago there were estimated to be about one and a half billion people living on this planet Earth. Today, just one hundred years later there are six billion people. Exponentially the population explosion is terrifying regarding the unknown consequences of such numbers. I tell you this because plague spreads a lot faster in confined areas. Think of potential killer diseases like E. coli or Legionnaires' disease. Think of the world's biggest pandemic – 'Spanish flu', caused by a type 'A' influenza virus – claiming between 50 million and 100 million lives between 1918 and 1919. With air travel today these diseases evolving into an epidemic can be spread to the other side of the planet within twenty-four hours, ending up as a pandemic, and the source virtually untraceable. And speaking of statistics, did you know that in the last two hundred years the plague of tuberculosis has killed approximately one billion people – yes, one billion. Are you shocked? You should be."

Carol came back with another question, knowing there was really no need for a reply but carried on regardless.

"Did you also know that in over one thousand centres around the world there are virus and bacteria banks where one can obtain samples of the deadliest diseases known to man? It is true to say that these banks serve the science of the world by supplying samples for respectable and lawful research a lot of the time, but there again, no one can say with any certainty that one day the security of these banks will not be breached. I mean, just look at the proliferation of countries with nuclear weapons and their fissile material. These communicable diseases would be a pretty powerful tool in the hands of terrorist organisations wouldn't they?"

"Yes they would. And I suppose it needn't even be an organised group. One misguided and determined maniac is all that it would take. I suppose one comforting thing regarding a nuclear weapon strike on these reinforced facilities holding such plagues of microscopic dust is that they are built to be virtually indestructible against a nuclear strike." Professor Lambton looked at his daughter and felt great sympathy with her previously expounded soul searching regarding whether to bring children into the world. He had gone through the same thought processes in the nineteen-sixties when the possibility of nuclear war hung like the Sword of Damocles over everyone – especially when the Cuban Missile Crisis took the world to the brink of nuclear war with Russia. Yet his daughter had been born regardless and thank God for it. Then the thought struck him that there might have been a lot more people around now it had not been for many prospective parents putting off having children because of the perceived inevitability of a nuclear holocaust to come. Strange to think of a nuclear device acting as a contraceptive, he mused.

"Daddy, do have some more sandwiches. Stryker, help yourself."

Stryker responded to Carol's entreaties by grabbing another four salmon filled offerings before gratefully dropping them onto a side plate.

"In some ways it might have been better to have lived in medieval times sir. At least they didn't have to worry about biological warfare."

"Now that's not quite true. Apparently they used to hurl bodies contaminated by plague into besieged cities using catapults. Can you imagine the effect that had on such a confined community? It must have decimated them. Look at what happened to people during the so-called Black Death – thrown into plague pits; many people being hastily nailed into wooden coffins whilst still alive. That's borne out by fingernail scratch marks discovered on the inside of coffin lids hundreds of years later. I wonder if many of the scientists who produce these deadly biological warfare agents dwell on the potential suffering they can cause."

"Civilisation hasn't moved on much since then has it?" replied Stryker.

"Morally we're no better than hundreds of years ago are we?"

"I'm afraid you're right Carol. No further advanced in that field. But Britain has made great strides over the years in attempting to produce antidotes to counter biological diseases. One of my fellow scientists died, it must be thirty years ago now, in just such an endeavour. He was accidentally exposed to *Yersinia pestis* – more commonly known as bubonic plague. Poor fellow suffered unimaginably painful glandular swellings under his armpits as well as in his neck and groin...also painful black lumps appeared all over his skin. His lungs gradually filled with fluid. It was a slow suffocating death preceded by agonising convulsions. I never want to see anything like that again. Of course he was put in total isolation – treated like a leper, which of course is what he was. In a way, that's what drives me now. If I can do something to alleviate the sufferings of other people afflicted in such a manner... that would be something wouldn't it?"

Carol looked at her father, eyes twinkling with compassion.

"You shouldn't feel guilt ridden. After all, you're only doing your job."

Stryker broke in. "What specifically are biological warfare agents anyway?" Having already been given virtually nothing on biological aspects regarding the potential for weapons by Carol at his Swiss Cottage condo he felt pretty well ignorant as to what they were dealing with so felt amplification from the expert a prerequisite when the potential Russian defector the Red Chameleon might contact him and speak about such matters.

"Well, biological agents tend to be living microorganisms as I have already mentioned, like for example, bacteria. They can also be a toxin.

Even though they are not living organisms, toxins originate from microorganisms, for example animal or plant life. Now viruses which cross from birds and animals – another example, bats can be infected but do not die themselves – to humans, a process known as zoonosis, could and unfortunately most probably will eventually wipe out the whole of civilisation without us even getting involved in manufacturing biological weapons with sophisticated delivery systems. And that scenario might happen at any time – today or tomorrow – this year or next, we just don't know when – but the late eminent scientist and Nobel laureate Joshua Lederberg has postulated that the biggest threat to mankind's survival on this planet is the virus. But to speak of biological warfare, there are over thirty microorganisms and toxins suitable for wrapping up into a biological bomb. These biological agents can be in powder form as in the case of anthrax held by the Americans and Russians, or they can be held in a liquid suspension of live microorganisms or toxins. For example, powdered anthrax would be added to a small amount of water and distributed in aerosol form." Professor Lambton took another sip of his now tepid tea then drained his whisky glass before carrying on.

"The frightening business with biological warfare is the fact that you cannot see the weapon, as I have already mentioned. You can see the delivery system, as in a rocket or the physical casing of a bomb, but the actual thing that attacks you is invisible. It can be in the air we breathe, but like flu, one would not know about it until the symptoms appear, which could be many days or even weeks later. Or one could feel the effects pretty much instantaneously. It might also be in the water we drink. That's why it is so insidious and frightening. Even insects may spread a viral disease. The point is, we have developed systems to be able to detect *some* airborne pathogenic agents capable of being used in biological warfare, but there are just so many different types, and by the time they have been detected it is more often than not too late to do anything about it. Quite a problem isn't eh?" Stryker could see that Professor Lambton was now well into his subject by the absent-minded way he now swung his glasses to and fro between forefinger and thumb mimicking a pendulum.

"What if I get more sandwiches for the three of us? Would you like a few more rounds of chicken, and say some roast beef? Oh, and we'll order more tea too. That lot will be cold by now." Professor Lambton craned his neck, his eyes sweeping around the room laser-like before catching the attention of an elderly waiter unobtrusively padding toward them. No avoiding eye contact here and pretending they had not seen you, he thought, sinking even deeper into his comfortable leather armchair.

"Take smallpox for example. In 1763 Sir Jeffrey Amherst, English commander of the army in North America, was instrumental in ordering that blankets distributed to the Pontiac Indians were deliberately contaminated with smallpox. This of course is certainly a form of what we would now term germ warfare. You being an American might already have heard of these episodes concerning the red Indians. And there is no known cure once you have it you know. It's caused by a virus; the most severe form is known as *Variola major* and will kill up to sixty per cent of people infected. Anybody who survives is either left blind and disfigured or is able to view their disfiguring scars. After breathing in the invisible virus you would not know anything about it for approximately twelve days while it is spreading to infect the internal organs. Then after this come the backaches, headaches and fever. Then three to five days after that a rash appears on the arms, face and hands before spreading to the legs, feet and ankles and the trunk of the body. You end up with large bloody ulcers oozing yellow liquid. Scabs cover the ulcers, eventually falling away leaving horrific scars. A cough is enough to infect another person within their vicinity. It is said that sometimes by design and sometimes by accidental spread of contamination over time approximations of fifty-six million native inhabitants of America have been killed by various plagues."

"That sounds like something out of a horror movie." Carol's face registered disgust and gave an involuntary cough.

"Of course, we're going on about deadly viruses as if there weren't other pathogens already attacking people right now at this very moment on a vast scale. If I have given you that impression then it would be a very misleading one."

Stryker moved imperceptibly closer so as to catch every syllable uttered from Carol's father's lips. "You mean there are already large scale epidemics working their way through the population?"

"I mentioned it just now for I am alluding of course to tuberculosis, which can be spread like many other pathogens, simply by being in the vicinity of someone sneezing, coughing or just breathing, is now the biggest killer in the world today. Millions are dying every year, some drowning in their own bloody fluid filled lungs. And I do not use the term 'bloody' by the way, in a pejorative sense. Your lungs can really fill up with blood until you become asphyxiated. Of course, that is an extreme example, but still... thank God there are not too many cases in this country. In certain parts of the world, such as on the Indian subcontinent, it is endemic. Did you know by the way that viral diseases kill twice as many people as cancer?

"And one more thing for you to dwell upon: Your countrymen know this as well as we scientists do in this country and it terrifies all scientists, doctors and microbiologists. Antibiotic resistance to many of these diseases is becoming rife. If one of these killer diseases gets out of control and it proves to be resistant to antibiotics there could be a pandemic of such proportions that – this might sound dramatic – but I'll say it anyway, life on this planet as we understand it might very well come to an end – and it could happen very quickly indeed because of the way we travel around the globe – in a blink of an eye – in other words within months or even weeks. If it happens then God help us."

The government scientist, his MI6 daughter and Stryker sat in their genteel surroundings, the three of them feeling physically divorced from their topic of conversation in a surrealistic sort of way, all three knowing, though not voicing their fear, that these trappings of luxury they were now surrounded by could not act as a citadel if such deadly viruses were ever visited upon them. And for all the words spent upon the subject of biological warfare that late afternoon, it was still hard to take in the very real possibility that such a catastrophe could ever truly happen. After all, it was always other people who were the victims – wasn't it?

CHAPTER 43

Chen Hsu, propped up by one elbow, remained lying on the spot where he had fainted earlier, surveying upturned chairs and the broken table from which the largest assailant had slid down to the floor before making a quick getaway with his fellow bully boy. Plates and food lay scattered across the intricately designed carpet depicting a Chinese motif representative of good fortune. As with the first attack, the few customers who were witness to the melee had dissipated into thin air, except that this time half of the waiters had vanished along with them. It had felt like a kick in the stomach seeing the two arrive, their long black coats now harbingers of violence. In Chen Hsu's frequent nightmares, the black garments became interwoven with glinting steel choppers and bloody severed fingers. He knew that neither he nor his business could survive much more of this. Once word got out, people would avoid his restaurant like the plague. There was only one chance left and that, borne out of desperation, was to fight fire with fire.

Monday morning came early for Chen Hsu as he carefully spelt out in large black letters on a piece of white card: CLOSED FOR FAMILY BEREAVEMENT. He did not like to tempt fate by putting such a notice in his restaurant window but felt no other option had been left open to him. Having given his few remaining staff the day off so as they might try to recover from the trauma of the night before, his ulterior motive was to sort out the situation the only way he could figure it out.

This time the journey to Brixton was premeditated. It did not take Chen Hsu long to locate the barber shop in Coldharbour Lane which had been mentioned on his last visit. A seedy, semi-detached building, with red paint flaking from around a blue door, it bore the legend: BAR, the second part of the word 'Barbers' having been crudely sprayed out graffiti-style. Through the large, grimy, plate glass window could be seen a couple of white-haired West Indians sitting in worn out armchairs, the whole scene resembling someone's dilapidated front room as opposed to a barber's shop. He was in two minds whether to enter when the door flew open and a wizened man, his clothes much too large for his frail body, half stepped out into the street, holding the door open and blinking as the daylight hit him.

"Only two to go mate."

Chen Hsu now felt obliged to enter, apprehensively making his way to one of the easy chairs now left vacant and sat down with trepidation. The

175

man who had just vacated the chair he now occupied was sitting bolt upright in an old fashioned cast iron framed contraption which must have seen much hair fall onto its now cracked and dried out leather upholstered arms. A collector's item, Chen Hsu mused as he scrutinised the open fire beneath a mantelpiece facing the man in the barber's chair. The barber was dressed in a soiled black silk dressing gown, the stitching giving way at the side seams in a one sided contest to contain various fatty bulges.

The only attempt at decoration within the room was a vase of plastic flowers set on a deep windowsill, the red and yellow petals now bleached by the sun into a pale imitation of poppies and daffodils, lovingly preserved in a thick blanket of dust. An empty glass display box kept the flower display company with the word DUREX stencilled across the front in bold letters. Chen Hsu's eyes settled on the other customer, an elderly man of around eighty waiting his turn by filling in the time by quietly studying the pages of a well-thumbed copy of a 'Men Only' magazine.

"Next!" The word was barked out as though by a Sergeant Major, loud and clear, but Chen Hsu kept his eyes trained on the old man who was transfixed by two naked women cavorting in some far away exotic location which he could have only experienced in his dreams.

"You, you're next. Leave that ol' git to fantasise. 'E's me farver. 'E sits there all day. Good as gold 'e is."

Chen Hsu ambled up to the hairy collector's item which had now been vacated and stood waiting for the last client to leave the shop. As the door finally banged shut he struggled to find the right words. In his mind he could formulate very concisely the simple sentence: "I have been told that you can supply me with a gun," but instead the words stuck in his throat. Whilst still attempting to garner up the courage he eased himself into the chair.

"'Ow dew like it sir, same as last time?" Chen Hsu had been fighting the onset of baldness since his teens and had now succumbed to the ravages of time and worry. His restaurant may have been up and running but it had taken its toll. Just recently hair had been coming out at an alarming rate, clogging up the teeth of his black nylon comb with each pull through.

"Yes, the same," he answered wearily, biting his nether lip in disgust at his inability to overcome the formalities. He also hated the insinuation that he had visited this particular barber shop before. After having his remaining hair washed, a damp fetid-smelling mid-grey towel was lifted from a pile lying in a corner on the floor, then wrapped around Chen Hsu's face as his head was lifted back from the cracked crescent shaped porcelain sink. The stench of other men's sweat from the filthy towel made him retch, the nauseous smell filling his nostrils and making him gag for air. Overcome by a feeling of deep frustration and hatred of the situation in which he now found himself Chen Hsu clutched at one end of the towel and ripped it from his face.

"I require a gun with bullets," said Chen Hsu.

The barber stared down at the top of Chen Hsu's head, shifting his weight imperceptibly from one foot to the other.

"Why, what else would they fire, bleedin' peas?" His mouth had a limpness about it as though it were not quite coordinated with his upper face. The next few minutes were taken up in silence as the ritual of seeking out the last few remaining hairs began, snipping at them with a ferocity which only a maniac with a hefty insurance policy would dare imitate. He then pointed the blow dryer at the nape of Chen Hsu's neck, extracting the last vestiges of moisture out of the remaining wispy fluff.

"There sir, 'ows that? Bleedin' alright ain't it, even if I do say it meself." A mirror was positioned behind his head revealing more red scalded scalp than hair.

"Yes that's fine," Chen Hsu sighed. "Now, about that gun."

"All in good time sir, Rome weren't built in an 'urry, if yer git me meanin'. Anyfing on it?"

"No, nothing on it, thank you." After charging for what vaguely passed as a haircut and turning the notice around in the window to 'CLOSED', the barber held an indeterminate blue limp curtain to one side as he ushered Chen Hsu through the impromptu doorway at the back of the shop and up some rickety wooden stairs to what appeared to be a bedroom. After the incongruities of listening to a West Indian speaking with such a thick cockney accent nothing could surprise Chen Hsu any more, he thought. He was wrong.

"Wot yer looking for? Kalashnikov. I can git me 'ands on one of those in a couple of days. Israeli submachine guns, no problem – as many as yer want. Only seventeen inches long in total, but don't be fooled by that. Used by Special Forces the world over. Pack some punch they do. Cut a fella in 'alf."

"They're too big. I want a hand gun."

"I can even git yer a bleedin' rocket launcher given enough time."

"A hand gun will do nicely thank you."

The West Indian's eyes hardened. "Eighty quid on the nail – no bargaining, take it or leave it." The formerly friendly barber's banter came to an abrupt halt as he mentioned money.

"Here." Chen Hsu pulled out a bundle of ten pound notes and peeled off eight. The barber's eyes lit up.

"Plus twenty for the ammo. That's a ton altogether."

"When can I pick it up?" The barber moved to the bed covered in discarded clothes and boxes of shampoo, hair conditioner and other hair product paraphernalia to be found in even the most run down barber shop. Suddenly he disappeared beneath, ferret like, before surfacing with a small bundle of rags which he laid on top of one of the boxes. The cloth was unfolded slowly to reveal a piece of thin, almost transparent greasy brown-coloured paper which made a crackling noise as it was opened up, Chen Hsu's eyes focussing for the first time on a small metallic-coloured gun.

"It's a nine millimetre snub-nosed five shot revolver. 'Ere, lift it up and feel the weight. An 'evy little fing ain't it? Abaaht six an' a 'alf inches in lengff. Small fer a gun but longer 'n' yours eh!"

Chen Hsu ignored this personal jibe at his expense and stared at another small package just visible beneath the gun. There nestling between the paper folds lay a small cardboard box.

Sweeney Todd could see what had caught Chen Hsu's attention.

"Ere... they're the bullits. Just push 'em in the revolvin' bit, close it an' press the trigger. Bobs yer uncle an' Fanny's yer aunt." Chen Hsu noticed that the barber had not touched the gun himself, only handling it through the brown greaseproof paper; he supposed so as not to leave any of his own fingerprints. For one hundred pounds he had bought himself a gun with bullets. Now for the first time since his troubles began he felt in control of the situation.

The Chinese restaurant owner left the property which had been earmarked for demolition, with the black cockney barber's parting words still ringing in his ears: "An' don't effin' bring it back 'ere mate. I don't wanna know. Toss it in the River Thames if yer afta."

CHAPTER 44

MOSCOW

Having just arrived back at Biomedico from his trip to Beijing, Dr Grachev had to work fast, the one thing he hated to do. Science for him was a slow academic business. It was, as he saw it, a contest between his fine intellect and the very essence of nature itself.

It was late. He knew that working into the early evening at the institute might very well cause raised eyebrows with the watchers, no matter what pretext might be used. He was not a stupid man and realised that the Institute had Federal Security Bureau agents within it: Russia's Internal Security Service. The FSB Counter-Intelligence, part of the former KGB, monitored his and everyone else's movements. That was just the way things operated. However, he did not know just who the watchers were, so had to be very careful as any one of his colleagues could be an informer for the FSB. Ever since a fellow Moscow scientist had defected to America last October, paranoia had become prevalent within the Institute, whilst gossip and innuendo was rife. However, this was a very special day for Dr Grachev, because the breakthrough he had been seeking for so long had happened earlier that very morning thanks to his short trip to Beijing and it was imperative that no time should now be wasted.

Having gone through the ritual of robing-up as a prerequisite for gaining access to Zone Four by inserting his personal security card and tapping in a special eight digit code, another three doors had to be passed through before hooking up his oxygen supply hanging from the ceiling allowing Dr Grachev to be able to stroll over to a sterile laboratory bench. Above this work surface was a small, white, wall-mounted safe which was locked. After punching in another series of numbers and opening the door of this wall safe he removed a tiny hollowed out bead of clear glass with a miniscule aperture incorporating a cleverly constructed microscopic delivery system in the form of an atomiser, similar in function to that of a perfume spray though this one only just large enough for a hypodermic needle to pass into. The size of this ampoule incorporating within it the atomiser was only one and a half centimetres in diameter. Wearing rubber gloves, it proved a delicate operation within the negative pressure cabinet to grip the small glass bead between his thumb and forefinger, whilst in the other hand holding a syringe filled with a small amount of yellow fluid which he had also removed from the cabinet held in a sealed test tube. This fluid acted as a suspension for the live virus Dr Grachev had been working on. These particular self-propagating pathogens, as indeed all viruses are, embraced within their modified structures the living blueprint which could be turned into the world's deadliest strains of virus ever known to man. This operation of filling the glass bead and sealing it had to be carried out with extreme caution within this specially constructed glass-fronted cabinet incorporating a carefully designed series of filtration systems so as to catch any stray organisms that might otherwise escape into the atmosphere, which in this case would lead to an epidemic, and if not caught in time, conceivably a pandemic.

Dr Grachev took a deep breath as he held within his left hand, now pushed deep inside the special one-way air flow filtration laboratory cabinet, aided by the air pressure within the room, the minute glass orb and steadied his slightly trembling right hand now holding the filled syringe. If he missed the tiny point of entry with the needle, he knew it would be relatively easy for the very sharp tip of the metal needle to slip along one side of the glass bead and penetrate his thin protective gloves and one of his fingers, releasing the killer toxins straight into his bloodstream. He could be dead within the hour if not sooner. It had happened before to one of his colleagues. The sight of his friend writhing in agony and dying a horrible death before his eyes had left him with terrible nightmares for months and he had even toyed with the idea of giving up his job, which meant everything to him, although others had done so for sometimes the stress was almost unendurable. But in the end, he knew he could not survive without his precious science; without that feeling of elation when another border of discovery had been traversed. It gave sustenance and meaning to his life.

Gingerly locating the needle sized hole on the surface of the glass bubble he slowly inserted the tip of the needle and gently applied pressure to the plunger on the syringe, pushing the selective killer virus into its new receptacle drip by drip. This very delicate operation carried on for half a minute before the ampoule was nearly full and ready to be sealed. Once it had been made safe by sealing the minute hole, through which the syringe had delivered its lethal dose of microorganisms, with a specially formulated reddish-coloured cold sealant, and the glass capsule sterilised and withdrawn from the cabinet, Dr Grachev gingerly held the sealed glass ampoule within his clenched fist, the microscopic triggering delivery system itself covered in the cold sealant thus making it safe to handle.

The security zones a Russian scientist must pass through to be able to work with the most infectious and dangerous biological agents known to man were numbered One to Four. Zone Four was the most dangerous of all to work within, which is why it was so very well protected. To reach it Dr Grachev would strip naked; leaving all his clothing behind, then undergo a vigorous fingertip inspection by a doctor, searching for any cuts or abrasions on every part of his anatomy through which a deadly micro-organism might enter, before donning a biohazard suit complete with Perspex headgear similar to that worn on space missions. Also worn were tall white boots sealed at the thigh and protective gloves.

The next step would be to wade through a series of sealed chambers housing sophisticated air filtration systems similar to the laboratory cabinets used for scientific experimentation, and containing antibacterial and antiviral solutions before finally emerging into the laboratory itself. This routine served a dual function. The most obvious one was that of guarding against the real possibility of contamination of any scientist who happened to be working with such dangerous microorganisms, thus eliminating the possibility of an outbreak within the community of some highly contagious and nightmarish disease, which might possibly have no known antidote to counter its often gruesome effects upon the human body and central nervous system, more commonly referred to as CNS. The second function served the FSB's internal security service purposes well – making it seemingly impossible to remove these deadly organisms from Zone Four without the consent of higher authorities.

He retraced his footsteps back through the various sterile chambers until it was once again safe for him to remove his protective helmet which had been plugged into various lines of oxygen supply dangling from the ceiling within the protected zones. As he did so his right hand moved rapidly to his mouth which opened wide before placing something upon his tongue, carefully avoiding his teeth and the all-seeing video surveillance cameras. He swallowed hard.

This second function relating to security Dr Grachev had now circumvented. His relief produced a thin film of perspiration over his forehead. This was unusual, for Dr Grachev rarely felt nervous except in very dangerous circumstances. This happened to be one of those circumstances. Within his body he now housed a sample of the cloned virus which with a minimal amount of preparation had the potential for destroying not millions of lives but possibly billions, for a micro-organism such as this would be able to spread swiftly throughout a whole population. One had only to think of outbreaks of influenza to realise just how insidious and rampant such invincible killers can be. And for this particular micro-organism there was no known antidote because it had been carefully constructed within Dr Grachev's laboratory with just such a purpose in mind; to kill with as much suffering as could possibly be conceived without any way of alleviating that suffering. A haemorrhagic fever which up until now had never seen the light of day, but when that day came, would be compared to Nagasaki and Hiroshima all rolled into one and then multiplied a million times – a holocaust of unimaginable dimensions. A large proportion of humanity could be wiped out.

It was a feeling that for Dr Grachev was not possible to put into words. But somewhere within him he sensed a power, a great strength he had never experienced before. He was so overwhelmed by the magnitude of his achievement that dizziness gripped his whole body and for a while he stood in a stupor. To hold the destiny of the world within his hands had in an instant changed his perception toward himself. Before this moment he was just a scientist. Now he was a God.

Calmness descended upon him as he stepped out into the cool evening air and walked toward his car. There was a silent stillness, the sounds of birds and other creatures having dissipated – being absorbed into the night. He released the clutch and the small black car moved swiftly through the darkness. The only thing left for Dr Grachev to do now was to telephone the Institute and explain he was feeling unwell. He would remain at home for a day or so to let nature take its course, gingerly examining his own excrement until the tiny glass orb once again made its reappearance.

CHAPTER 45

NORTH WALES

At the Black Crow, Dr Kenneth Jones had been keeping his own company for over an hour before David made his presence known by standing in the as yet empty saloon bar and shouting from the doorway, "I see you recovered from last night then!" It was a genial if frequent war cry, to which the warden responded in kind.

"Oh yes boy, takes a lot of drinking to keep a good man like me down. What'll it be, the usual?" It was still early and the other regulars had not yet made their way down from their dinner tables, wives, or mistresses. After buying David a double whisky they made their way to a small circular table in the corner. It was a cosy pub and the warmth was inviting. David's skin began smarting from the cold left outside and he grabbed the small glass gratefully. Dr Kenneth Jones looked at him with a searching smile. "Well, where is she?"

David had been a regular drinking partner for over six years and had never once in all that time missed the appointed hour for early evening carousing unless something very important had come up, as when he had spent all his available time with Penny for that glorious two weeks last summer. And tonight, as far as Dr Kenneth Jones was concerned, was one of those epoch-making occasions. Whilst waiting for an answer he stubbed out the tiny fragment of what had been a cigarette just five minutes before and extracted yet another from his seemingly endless supply. Like some conjuror who performs the impossible task of producing from his top hat an endless array of colourful flags of all nations, his silver cigarette box always appeared to contain just one more. David had often wondered whether it might have started out as some party trick which had now been adopted out of habit. As Kenneth lit up, his eyes seemed more rheumy than usual and his face bore a greyness which encroached upon his ruddy complexion.

"Ken, you're not looking too well, are you feeling alright?"

"You're avoiding my question boy," Kenneth countered. "Where's Penny?"

"I left her at the cottage to recover from that ghastly journey. An hour extra it took her because of some accident somewhere just outside one of the stations. Instead of the usual excuse of leaves on the line, this time they announced it was because of two bodies on the line."

"I suppose they don't give details about something like that. To paraphrase, one is carelessness, but two! It's bloody awful – poor sods." The tip of Kenneth's cigarette glowed red as he breathed in.

"Of course it might have been a suicide pact!" David thought back to when he had been living in London and how he had regularly travelled by tube train. This particular morning, after arriving early and walking onto the all but deserted platform, he noticed that a train had been stopped just inside the tunnel with only half a carriage in full view. Then his eyes had wandered down to the edge of the platform opposite the half visible carriage. There, where it had been dropped, lying conspicuously isolated on that grey platform was a long, black, tightly furled umbrella and nearby an unopened copy of a neatly folded *Times* newspaper. Obviously the train had run over the man, not having had time to stop, and the body was presumably still beneath the train. That this stark image of those two inanimate objects – the newspaper and umbrella – could convey such horror had remained with David for weeks after, and with it, the question of just why someone who was going to commit suicide should go to the trouble of buying a newspaper. In retrospect, the poor fellow, working on the assumption that it was indeed a man because of it having been a man's umbrella, must have made the decision on the spur of the moment that life had lost all its allure and that death was his only salvation. Of course, it may have been a more mundane reason for the fatality such as the poor fellow having had a heart attack and fallen on the tracks.

David raised the glass of whisky to his lips, hoping to erase the image of that platform, but the vivid picture remained. "I can't stay for too long Ken, just came in to invite you round for dinner tomorrow evening."

Dr Kenneth Jones's face dropped. "But you've only just arrived. It must be love I'd say. Well, she's a beautiful girl is Penny. I'd like to accept the invitation but I would feel as if I was intruding. No, you make the most of your time together by yourselves. You don't want some old fuddy-duddy spoiling your fun now, do you?"

"Well, if you change your mind. Anyway, let me get a round in before I leave."

"Yes, you do that, an' then scurry home to that lovin' woman of yours."

David had never discovered whether Dr Kenneth Jones had ever been married, as the wily old academic always changed the subject no matter from which angle it might be approached; but he suspected that he hadn't. He also suspected that, for Ken at least, the booze in conjunction with his books, acted as a surrogate wife, comforting him when he needed his spirits lifted and consoling him when all else failed. In many respects they were kindred spirits but in one respect they were worlds apart. David had a woman's friendship which meant more to him than anything and he wanted to convert that platonic friendship into something more, something which would eventually lead to marriage.

***

The lights in front of the cottage were out when David arrived home. But at the rear of the house it was a different matter. A blazing fire greeted him and the two side table lamps were also lit, with Penny curled up on the sofa reading a book. She was wearing a pink dressing gown and he could smell her freshly applied perfume as he entered.

"David, you're back earlier than I expected." Penny's face glowed with a healthy radiance, her long silky hair wrapped up in a small hand towel, turban style. "I hope you don't mind but I took the liberty of having a bath while you were seeing Kenneth. You don't mind do you?" David was touched by the way Penny constantly looked for reassurance. Somehow it added a childlike innocence which he found very endearing. "Shall I get you something to drink – make you some tea perhaps?" Penny laid the book down beside her and unfurling her long bare legs stood up. "You look absolutely frozen, come over here by the fire."

"You don't have to ask permission to bathe. Of course I don't mind." As he spoke Penny reached out and unbuttoned his jacket, slowly slipping it from his shoulders and gave him a light kiss on his cheek. As she walked out to the kitchen David conjured up the shape of her bottom, slightly visible through her bathrobe. Her figure would do justice to any catwalk, he thought. Ten minutes later they were both settled down on the sofa with the tea tray lying between them.

"Shall I be mother?" Penny raised the teapot and David resisted saying that she looked far too young to be a mother figure. After they had both sipped the tea Penny's voice took on a more serious tone. "Can we see if my sister is able to be located through your hypnotising me?" The hand towel had been removed, her long tresses of hair now glistening in the firelight as it lay across her shoulders.

"If you really want to try and you think that I can help you."

"Dear David, since I saw you last I've thought of nothing else. I'm sure you can help me. You're the only true close friend I have. I know we haven't known one another very long, but that means nothing, does it? I just know that you can help me gain some peace of mind." The look of pure confidence on Penny's face made David feel humbled.

185

CHAPTER 46

MOSCOW

It was unheard of for General Kovalyev to visit the Institute. The fact was, Grigulevich had never met him so had not known what he looked like up until now. He knew of him of course; that he worked for the Fifteenth Directorate which came under the auspices of the Ministry of Defence responsible for dealing with biological weapons for the armed forces and that sort of thing, very much in the way they did here at Biomedico. He also knew of his fearsome reputation. Had he, Grigulevich, not often passed on requests to Professor Anton Cherenkov or Dr Anatoly Grachev through General Kovalyev's secretary?

Grigulevich was impressed with General Kovalyev's presence. He was impressed with the way he dismissed his chauffeur with a quick flick of the wrist, making it obvious that giving orders came naturally to him. Grigulevich liked the power the general exuded. He also admired his smart military bearing, the straight back in his grey uniform with red epaulettes and rows of medals to match. He was to Grigulevich's mind, every inch the soldier. These thoughts ran through his head as the two guards just inside the large entrance hall snapped to attention and were intent on escorting the general to the lift which he shunned, opting instead for the stairs. That had impressed Grigulevich even more as he mentioned to one of his colleagues later.

The general had a grave look upon his face as he removed his peaked cap, setting it down upon the large desk separating himself from Professor Cherenkov. Through the thick window set into the office wall opposite his desk, the professor could observe a team of his scientists, all clad in white cotton coats, busying themselves with different ongoing experiments alongside a bank of high-powered microscopes. Test tubes and other attendant paraphernalia, which one would expect of a scientific biological warfare institute, were scattered around in a seemingly haphazard manner. These scientists however, were well insulated from the outside world Professor Cherenkov could view if he looked to the right side of him through the other three tall windows of his bright, airy office.

Outside, below the windows, a rectangular gravel courtyard large enough to house an army parade ground funnelled into a wide roadway leading to a set of heavily fortified gates topped with razor sharp wire and a forest of trees beyond. In the immediate vicinity a huge transporter had pulled up, ferrying what looked like an oversized metal tumble dryer with various tubes emanating from it. This was in fact the latest acquisition in a long line of fermenters, capable of breeding biological viruses on a grand scale. There were various teams of scientists and engineers working within this particular complex of buildings dealing not only with deadly viral infections but also carrying out research into microbial genetics and the growth of bacteria.

This bulky piece of equipment now being offloaded very gingerly using a hydraulic crane, could however, to the untutored eye, have easily been mistaken for some sort of industrial clothes dryer. A layman would not have been too wide off the mark in making such a guess, as machines for drying microorganisms were certainly used, as well as machines for milling the deadly spores of diseases into a size acceptable to the mucous membrane within the nasal passages and thence into the lungs themselves, thus precipitating death in a truly heinous and agonising fashion.

"To what do I owe the pleasure of your company Comrade General?" Professor Cherenkov knew this visit from the general must presage something serious.

"You have been here a long time now have you not?" General Kovalyev posed the question as more of a statement than a genuine enquiry as he stared at the professor from beneath his red bristly eyebrows. Professor Cherenkov looked at the deep lines etched into General Kovalyev's weather beaten face and nodded.

"Twenty years, give or take. I suppose some would call that a long time. Yes."

"And in that time how many assistants have you had?"

"I have had only two assistants; Doctor Grachev of course and his predecessor. But why do you ask me of these matters? You know all this. Besides, this information is in my files. And you knew my old colleague Doctor Asimov very well before he retired." Professor Cherenkov could not help his irritability getting the better of him but also knew it would be to no avail.

"Of course I did Comrade. You got on well with him didn't you? You trusted him, yes?" Professor Cherenkov began to wonder where this line of questioning was leading but carried on attempting to answer the questions in as affable a way as possible.

"Well yes. Comrade Doctor Asimov was a very capable scientist – very capable."

"Capable scientist! Well yes. But could you trust him?"

"What are you driving at General?"

"What I am driving at professor is, did you ever suspect Doctor Asimov of doing things which perhaps were not quite, how shall we say, correct?"

"No, never. He was very trustworthy."

"And how about Doctor Grachev? Is he in your opinion a trustworthy scientist?" Professor Cherenkov shifted his feet beneath the table in an attempt not to betray his emotions as he wondered whether General Kovalyev had heard the rumour of plagiarism levelled against himself regarding a recently published scientific paper on Human Genomes, which just happened to be one of Dr Grachev's pet projects.

"He is also a colleague of mine, only having recently arrived back from a trip to Beijing." The general's questioning was beginning to irritate. "What do you want me to say? It is true that maybe we do not have quite the same close working relationship that Doctor Asimov and I had. There again, Doctor Grachev is a lot younger than myself. But, yes General, I trust him."

The general's eye's narrowed and his mouth tightened, making a small star-like scar on his right cheek stand out white against his florid colouring.

"Then you are a fool, Professor."

As he pursed his own lips, now white with anger, Professor Cherenkov tried desperately to keep his emotions under control, his stomach muscles tightening involuntarily. To be insulted like this was unheard of. His next words were measured but uttered with as much indignation as he could muster.

"Comrade General!"

"I have reason to suspect our Doctor Grachev may very well be working for a foreign power – spying for the West." General Kovalyev studied the professor's features closely, searching for the tiniest indication that the information he had just imparted might already be known to him.

Behind his thick spectacle lenses held in place by a gold-coloured wire frame, Professor Cherenkov's deeply sunken eyes had for the past few seconds been idly peering over General Kovalyev's shoulder observing one of his scientists adjusting a long glass tube within the rubber-lined jaws of a clamp, his attention having drifted slightly from what the general was saying and focussing more on the possible accusations and ramifications of submitting his colleagues ideas as his own. Now it was as if the scientist he had been so carefully scrutinising did not exist – that he had actually vanished before his eyes. He could not believe what he was hearing and asked the general to repeat what he had just said.

"I am telling you all this for a good reason Professor." To give his words extra weight the general had wagged his stubby finger at the professor with the precise timing of a metronome, all the while maintaining eye contact.

"Colonel Oleynik will arrange for Doctor Grachev to be given extra help in this project he is working on for me, so as to ostensibly speed things up. His assistant will be a GRU agent, you understand – Russian Ministry of Defence Intelligence. He is also a doctor and scientist, so his cover should withstand scrutiny. I should like to arrange it so that this GRU agent will be in place when Doctor Grachev arrives back from England. It will be his last trip anyway, whatever the outcome."

For Professor Cherenkov at that particular moment General Kovalyev's face took on a look as inscrutable as any Chinese diplomat. He knew that to question a high ranking military man, especially a man such as General Kovalyev was foolhardy in the extreme, but he just could not contain himself.

"This whole story is so incredible. But tell me, who is this GRU agent who is to spy on Doctor Grachev? Have I met him?"

"I am not at liberty to tell you that at this moment; but yes, I am sure you have made his acquaintance at some of the regular scientific meetings held here in Moscow. However I will let you know that a wire-tap carried out on Doctor Grachev's flat by the FSB men from the Twelfth Department have found out that a meeting between our Doctor Grachev at his flat in Moscow and someone calling himself Stryker will take place soon. Your resident senior intelligence officer Vladimir Stalnov is being kept informed. That's just between you and I you understand."

"You say Doctor Grachev... is spying for the West? But what possible evidence...?" The professor's sentence was never finished as the general interrupted him.

"Good morning Professor. Remember, silence is a virtue." With that final facile remark, General Kovalyev retrieved his peaked cap from the desk and was through the door and out into his chauffer driven car whilst Professor Cherenkov remained rooted to his chair, feeling shell shocked and still taking in the enormity of the unwanted revelation.

What really puzzled Professor Cherenkov was why he himself had been informed of such a secret regarding Dr Grachev? After all, there was a counterintelligence unit operating within this particular institute for biological weapons, as indeed there were in all other such locations. Why hadn't General Kovalyev sent Colonel Oleynik on his behalf to approach the resident senior FSB intelligence officer Vladimir Stalnov? Stalnov was not a particularly likeable person, rather what Professor Cherenkov would call a wheedling supercilious ignoramus, but certainly a man who one had to stay on the right side of and certainly not have as an enemy. And why come to him? In a society where everyone was constantly trying to read between the lines it was easy to feel paranoid, and Professor Cherenkov felt that today he had been given more than ample grounds for just such a notion.

CHAPTER 47

In his office situated on the other side of the Biomedico Institute building, Vladimir Stalnov lay sprawled across three chairs pushed together with his door firmly locked, his knees pulled up into his pot belly and retching violently on what was by now an empty stomach. After a heavy night's drinking the evening before, it had only been by the grace of God that whilst still nursing his hangover he had managed to evade the inquisitive eyes of Grigulevich as he staggered through the lobby and into the safe confines of the lift. Safe, for it only required a few strides, once he exited the utilitarian device that whisked him up to the very top floor, before he could lose himself in the single corridor which ran the length of the main building, having been used originally by the installation team who built the complex, but which was now regarded as off limits and only used by security. It also had that cold, damp feeling, typical of an area isolated from the rest of a building, giving off a fetid odour of stale food, sweat and nicotine. The office itself was small and cramped, but very secure.

Vladimir Stalnov's predilection for vodka was a closely guarded secret and he intended it to stay that way, which is why the large grey steel cabinet pushed into one corner of his office bearing its liquid contents was like his door, always kept securely locked. This was his only weakness which he acknowledged to himself. There was one other however, and that was for a secretary who worked within the Institute. That he regarded her as more of a professional matter than anything relating to affairs of the heart was only because he would not openly admit to himself that he was deeply infatuated with Marina – Dr Grachev's secretary. It was she who now mopped his brow with her handkerchief as his legs dangled unsupported over the edge of the third chair, not quite reaching the floor. In the normal scheme of things Vladimir would have been regarded as a rather tall fellow, but viewed from the angle at which he now lay it was difficult to acknowledge such a fact.

It is a strange truth that quite often beautiful women – and Marina was no exception to this quirk – fall for ugly oafs of men who seem not to have any social attributes except that of being forward with their opposite gender. This was particularly so with Vladimir Stalnov. He was neither handsome nor had the mitigating intelligence for what might be described as normal pleasing conversation. His language could be profane, scattered as it was with expletives when the need arose, which in his role as chief security intelligence officer for this particular building was quite often as he saw it. Also his mood swings would regularly mimic that of the proverbial English weather, but at this particular moment, lying prostrate on his back, he was very subdued.

"My poor, poor darling, how are you feeling?"

"Wretched. I'm fucking wretched."

"Please Vladimir, don't swear like that. It's not nice."

"Oh! I feel so ill."

"You mustn't drink so much. You know it isn't good for you. Why do you do it?" A look of genuine concern crossed Marina's pretty face.

"I'll tell you why, shall I? It's because of your little bloody genius Doctor Grachev. He's enough to drive anyone to drink."

"Vladimir Stalnov! Why do you say such things?"

"I say them because it's true." And the truth it was, except that in Vladimir Stalnov's case, no excuse for drinking was required. He had used up many man-hours placing a team of watchers on Dr Grachev's every move outside the confines of the Biomedico Institute without anything being turned up. Nothing! He appeared as clean as a whistle. But then, as he knew only too well, appearances could be deceptive.

Guilt by association with someone in London going by the name of Stryker possibly working for the British Secret Intelligence Service had been the initial trigger a few weeks earlier for keeping an eye on Dr Grachev's movements, and if there was anything to unearth, Vladimir Stalnov was determined to find it, except that Dr Grachev's lifestyle did not appear to be out of the usual for someone in his position. The fact was that his social life in Moscow was, at least in Vladimir's eyes, as dull as ditch water. Frequent travel abroad may have made for a more interesting life, which was pretty obvious to anyone who had been incarcerated within a country such as the Soviet Union. But that part of Dr Grachev's life was of course out of his hands, being taken care of by the SVR, many of whose agents of the post-Soviet Russian foreign intelligence agency were based overseas.

The premise 'give a man enough rope and he will hang himself', was a ploy Vladimir Stalnov had employed many times in the past, but in this instance with regard to Dr Grachev, it was not bearing fruit. Besides which, he found it unsavoury that such a nice young woman such as Marina, being only in her early twenties, should have to work for such a skunk. Behind his back nobody had a good word to say about him. Dr Grachev treated his staff with contempt and now there were suggestions that he was consorting with a suspected spy. Marina glanced at Vladimir Stalnov and uncannily echoed his thoughts.

"You know Vladimir; I would happily work for you if the opportunity arose. Is it not possible to arrange?" This same idea had crossed Stalnov's mind more than once, and although Dr Grachev held enormous sway within the Institute, having access to Colonel Oleynik without prior notice, now the situation was changing imperceptibly in as much as he was suddenly being viewed as a potential traitor. It appeared well within the realm of possibility to have Marina working for himself. But viewed from another aspect it served Vladimir Stalnov's purpose to have someone on the inside, so close to Dr Grachev – in the short term.

"No Marina. At this moment it cannot be done. Give me time though and I'm sure something might be arranged." Lying for Vladimir was second nature, but in a way it was not such a lie. He was determined to pin Dr Grachev down if it was at all possible and he thought he would see if there wasn't something he could do personally rather than always relying on his subordinates. After all, it was not by chance that he had recently secured his position as Senior Intelligence Officer within the research institute. Also, the sooner Dr Grachev could be sorted out, the sooner he may well be able to bring about a transfer for Marina to his own office. Vladimir retched once more, wishing that he had excused himself from duty, just for one day, but his conscience would not let him. Not until Dr Grachev was once and for all truly nailed to the cross.

Marina abruptly stopped mopping Vladimir's forehead and stood up from her squatting position. "I'd better get back to the office as Doctor Grachev will be in soon."

Vladimir's eyes focussed upon a large metal ring with a bunch of keys hanging from it, one of which was planted firmly within the keyhole of the locked steel cabinet. Maybe, he thought to himself, as Marina made her exit, just one more drink wouldn't hurt. After all, he had been suffering for the cause, and the cause had driven him to it. As he twisted the key in the lock he suddenly felt buoyed up by prospect of having Marina in such close proximity to himself during working hours, and perhaps, who knows, possibly even after working hours as well, though just what his wife would make of it all God alone knew. She could be an understanding woman, granted, though they did not really communicate any longer. But, Vladimir thought, even she would balk at such a prospect. "Not in my flat you don't. Not 'till hell freezes over," would be her predictable sentiment.

His head began throbbing again as he poured himself a full glass of vodka and pulled out a thick sheaf of papers relating to Dr Grachev's background. Attempting to shake off his flights of fantasy regarding Marina he sat down gingerly, so as not to upset the delicate equilibrium brought about by the previous night's drinking and lifted the brimming glass to his lips. His trembling hand spilt a little vodka onto the desk while in the process of struggling to bring his eyes into focus, scouring his papers once more in the hope that some quick solution to his problems might present itself. It was then that his prayers seemed to be answered as his attention was caught by the latest wire-tap carried out on the orders of General Kovalyev by the FSB men from the Twelfth Department relating to an impending meeting between Dr Grachev at his flat in Moscow and an English man named Stryker – the same name mentioned by the general several weeks earlier at one of the usual security meetings.

For Vladimir results were everything and in Grachev's case the results had not been materialising. Buoyed up by the prospect of being able to move matters along with regard to Marina he made up his mind there and then to dispense with the watchers and do the job of keeping watch on Dr Grachev's flat himself that very night, hoping this new approach might somehow give fresh impetus to the investigation and perhaps prove a way of getting rid of the one obstacle to his own happiness plus even possibly move his own career prospects further up the greasy pole.

CHAPTER 48

NORTH WALES

"Ken, I'd like to ask you a question. It's about Penny."

"Marry her boy. Best thing you could ever do. She's a lovely lass." David knew Ken had a soft spot for Penny ever since he had first introduced her to him the year before.

They were sitting in Dr Kenneth Jones' study, sunshine streaming in through the tall narrow window situated on David's right hand side, the slanting rays washing out the delicate rose colours carefully woven into the worn Aubusson carpet beneath their feet. Dr Kenneth Jones sat facing him in his usual chair with his usual glass of whisky placed beside him on a small side table. He was wrapped up in an untidy bundle of brown dressing gown three sizes too large, held together by a silk tasselled cord with a chunky cream coloured Arran knitted sweater peeping from the neck to counter the early morning chill within his private rooms.

"Come on David, join me... hair of the dog!"

"Why, it's only half past ten; too early for me Ken." David looked at the scholar's features. The skin was pale and his eyes watery as though he had been peeling onions.

"What I want to ask you is, can you translate verbatim from the Russian language straight into English? Like they do at the United Nations?" He thought Ken could do with a decent holiday but he also knew that this was his whole life; his ivory tower of academia. That and the Black Crow.

"What's this all about then David? You say it's about Penny, but what's the connection?" His nicotine-stained moustache required trimming and several globules of whisky were hanging off the edge like early morning dew. Kenneth reached for his cigarettes, extracted two from the box and proffered one to David.

"You're a good friend Ken and I know I can confide in you." David took the cigarette and carried on. "Well, Penny has agreed to my using my hypnotic skills in an attempt to unravel the mystery of the whereabouts of her missing sister. By the way, Penny said I could tell you because you may be able to help in that attempt."

195

"But you're the hypnotist David, not I. How could I possibly be of help?"

"With your knowledge of the Russian language you may be able to serve as an interpreter. You see, last night we had our first hypnotic session and Penny went under very quickly. She is obviously a good subject. I even managed to regress her which is rushing things on the first occasion, but it worked like a dream – literally. I managed to regress her back to when she was nine years old without any problem at all. The trouble began when I took her back in her mind to when she was eight years old. In her waking state, you know; when she is not hypnotised, Penny can remember everything back to when she was nine, but her memories before that are zilch. Nothing!"

"You mean under hypnosis you really took her back to when she was nine years old and that she could remember being that age in some detail?"

"Oh! Perfect recall down to what clothes she had been wearing on her ninth birthday. Not to get too technical, I use a technique harnessing what is known as her Ideo Motor Response. It's a very powerful tool. Whist under hypnosis I ask my subject to choose one of their fingers on the right hand – it can be either hand actually – and I suggest to them that whilst I am counting backwards from their present age, every time I mention a number, for example nineteen, that particular number will represent the nineteenth year of their life. The amazing thing about this is, if there are any emotional disturbances in whichever year I mention to them under hypnosis their chosen finger they have previously nominated will twitch. For me this then pinpoints the year where they have experienced some trauma in their lives. After that I can delve deeper into their subconscious mind which has been unconsciously shielding them from some trauma so as to explore that problem in some depth, perhaps because at the time those problems were too painful to face up to. Sometimes there are many years in a person's life which have affected them, although as I say, they themselves may not be aware of this, for often these emotional disturbances have been locked away deep within their subconscious mind. That's where hypnosis can help; to gain access to those sometimes terrible traumatic events which have been pushed safely away from the conscious memory. It's a way of dealing with memories they would sooner forget about. Except that the consequences of seemingly successfully erasing such sometimes painful memories from the conscious mind can come back to haunt you many years later – and in a variety of ways – such as skin conditions for instance; psoriasis, eczema. Also, to name another condition: hyperventilation – that's uncontrollable rapid breathing to you.

"I had one such case whereby this particular person's hyperventilation was the result of having been in a German concentration camp as a young girl and of being forcibly separated from her parents within that camp – and that had happened sixty years prior to her fits of hyperventilating. But through IMR… sorry – Ideo Motor Response, I was able to discover her debilitating problem while she herself had never imagined it was because of her time spent in the infamous Auschwitz concentration camp all those years previously. Bad memories stay with you whether you are aware of them or not. It's like a hard drive disk on a computer. You may think you have erased that disk but actually the unwanted information always remains there, even when new information has been written over the old, layer upon layer. You can always get to it if you know how. That's why hypnosis can be so powerful.

Clouds of smoke swirled around both their heads as David continued to explain the finer points of hypnotherapy. Kenneth's glass had been drained, and as he stood up to get a refill David fell silent. Kenneth turned his head so as to look at David. "Go on, I'm listening. You sure you won't indulge?"

David held up his hand and shook his head in a negative fashion. "No thanks Ken, not just now."

Dr Kenneth Jones walked unsteadily toward the glass decanter perched on a heavily carved sideboard and filled his glass before gingerly making his way back to the armchair, carefully placing the whisky onto the side table and pulling his dressing gown a little tighter around his bulky body before dropping like a stone onto the horsehair stuffed seat. The leather arms of the chair were pockmarked with perfectly formed holes burnt by half-forgotten cigarettes dangling from Kenneth's fingers when in one of his many intoxicated stupors. He raised his head and leaned forward, looking into David's face as a signal to carry on speaking.

"As I say, everything worked out well, taking Penny in her mind back to the time when she had been a young schoolgirl in England. Then as I regressed her back to the age of eight, Penny began speaking in, what was to my ears anyway, an unintelligible language. And that language I took to be Russian. Now although I was speaking to her in English and she could understand my questions, she was obviously unable to answer in English as from her perspective up until the age of eight she could only speak Russian."

"I see. And you think by using my linguistic skills in the Russian language you would be able to discover the root cause of her problem of total amnesia before the age of nine."

"Precisely," David retorted, smiling at Kenneth, hoping that it was possible for his old friend to take on the role of interpreter.

***

"I'm now going to count from five to zero. When I say zero your eyes will close and when I say sleep, you will go into a very deep sleep. FIVE... FOUR... THREE..."

Dr Kenneth Jones sat transfixed by the scene in David's living room, hardly daring to breathe. The temperature inside was quite warm compared with the frost clinging with a vengeance to the windowsill outside; the fire crackling nicely in the grate had been kept going for several hours now by the judicious choice of logs, being neither too green nor too dried out. Penny lay slumped deep into one of the comfortable armchairs propped up by numerous plump cushions. David was perched by the side of Penny on a hard dining chair looking down at her soft features.

"TWO... ONE... ZERO..." Upon muttering the word 'zero', Penny's eyelids snapped shut as if by magic. Kenneth let out his pent up breath and stretched his arm, fumbling blindly behind the sofa for his tumbler, not daring to avert his eyes from Penny's recumbent form. Eventually he located the glass and took another swig of whisky.

"SLEEEEP!" As David uttered this command in his soft soporific tones, Penny's shoulders slumped imperceptibly a fraction.

"Well done my boy; why that's the best display of..."

David put a finger up to his pouting lips gesturing for silence.

"I'm now going to use a technique called regression to take her back to when she was eight years old. But before I do so I shall build a safety device for her into my instructions so as not to let her become too anxious if there is something lurking in her subconscious mind which might disturb her."

Reverting to a flat sonorous tone David leaned toward Penny and spoke.

"Penny, I want you now to imagine a place in the past where you once felt comfortable and happy – any place. It might be a place on a beach with friends or anywhere else you choose. Can you see that place now?"

Penny responded in the affirmative with a soft "Yes!"

"Now Penny, if at any time you are becoming upset I shall say: 'QUICKLY SLEEP' and you will immediately go to this safe place, do you understand?"

Again Penny's soft "Yes" echoed around the small cottage under the watchful eyes of Kenneth. After testing the phrase to satisfy himself it was firmly instilled within Penny's subconscious mind, David now stood on a precipice, unwittingly ready to ignite a revelatory train of events, the ramifications of which were to lead to repercussions he could not possibly have foreseen; nor could he have known how the revelations would touch the lives of so many people with such disastrous consequences.

"Penny, I want you to go back to your eighth birthday. Nod your head if you understand." Although Penny's eyes were tightly closed as if she was fast asleep she gave a definite nod of her head.

"How old are you Penny?"

"I'm eight."

"What do you see? Describe where you are." Penny began speaking, but it was not in English but in what David took to be fluent Russian. And it was not in her usual adult voice but in a high pitched childish one. She spoke in a breathless state of euphoria, Dr Kenneth Jones doing his best to keep up with the torrent of words issuing from Penny's lips, translating as fast as was possible for him under the circumstances.

"She says she is very excited. She loves horses and has been promised a visit to the Moscow state circus."

"Penny, who are you going to the circus with?" David had an intent look upon his face as he spoke to her, enunciating his words clearly and injecting a firmness into his voice which was not usually there.

"Masha will take me. It's my birthday and she takes me every year." It is a strange quirk of the mind that even though David was speaking to Penny in the English language and that she could understand everything asked of her, she herself was not able to respond to any of his questions except in anything but Russian.

"Who is Masha, Penny?"

"Why, my sister of course."

"And how old is Masha?"

"I think she is sixteen."

"And what are you doing now?"

"I'm walking toward the circus tent. My sister is holding my hand too tightly. It is hurting."

"Did you receive any special presents for your birthday?"

"My mamma gave me a doll and a pretty blue bow for my hair. Masha is wearing a new dress. It is white and has puff sleeves with a little red decoration around the neck and waist. Mamma says for my next birthday she will buy me a dress like Masha's."

David smiled at Kenneth and mouthed the words "Thank you."

Kenneth had placed the tumbler down onto the carpet by his feet and turned his head around to stare at Penny, spellbound. He found it hard going translating verbatim but felt he was managing much better than he had anticipated.

"Penny, I want you to go into the circus with your sister. What are you doing now?"

"I'm sitting with Masha and looking at people flying through the air in pretty sparkling dresses. They are very high and twisting through the air, swinging backwards and forwards." Ken leaned toward David, tapping him on the shoulder.

"I think she is speaking of trapeze artists." David nodded and carried on with his interrogating.

"What is happening now, Penny?"

"A man wearing a black cape lined with red silk is now asking for a volunteer. It's very noisy, everybody's shouting and clapping."

"Who is the man in the cape Penny?"

"Why, everyone knows who he is. He's the famous hypnotist: The Mystic. Oh, I'm frightened. Where has my sister gone? She has left me sitting on my own. Now The Mystic has made a girl standing in front of him fall backwards as if she was made of wood. I cannot see my sister, where is Masha?" Penny began displaying signs of distress and David uttered soothing words to calm her down. Then her whole body lurched forward. She was wide eyed as though seeing the events happening within the room where Kenneth sat rapped with fascination while David attempted to control the situation.

"What do you see now Penny?

"The hypnotist has laid the girl on her back on a bed in the middle of the circus ring. Now two large steel rings, each held by a rope, are descending from the roof of the tall circus tent. The rings have been lowered just enough to slip the girl's head into one of them and her feet into the other. Now the rings are being raised by two big muscular men pulling upon the ropes, raising her body as if it were a stiff plank of wood. She is only supported by her neck and her heels resting inside the rings with nothing beneath her. It's like she is floating upwards toward the pointed fabric ceiling of the tent. Everybody has stopped talking. It is very quiet now. Higher and higher she goes, becoming smaller and smaller."

Penny fell silent and Kenneth looked up at David, waiting for his next instruction to her. Never having experienced anything like this before, it was to him an enlightening experience of just how powerful and complex the brain was. To know that all the facets of one's life and experiences are stored away in the subconscious mind just waiting to be re-activated, like replaying a tape recording. Taking advantage of the temporary lull and his throat feeling like sandpaper, rough and dry through attempting to keep up with Penny's fluent Russian vocabulary, Kenneth furtively snatched another mouthful of whisky, settling down again for what was becoming a fascinating insight into the mind. "It seems that this Russian hypnotist used the same technique for making Penny's sister as stiff as a board as you did in that lecture you gave at the college recently David."

David acknowledged this remark by once more raising one of his fingers to his lips before carrying on with his hypnotic session.

"Penny, just relax. I want you to describe what is happening now."

A look of terror crossed the young woman's face as her throat emitted a short high pitched scream before speaking. "Oh! There is a loud cracking noise like a whip. It is echoing all around the tent. Oh! The steel ring supporting the girl's neck is beginning to slip from her head. Her body is tilting downwards with her head pointing toward the sawdust on the ground far below. A rope has snapped and her head has slipped out of the giant steel ring and she is like an arrow flying down from the roof of the tent but it is like watching it in slow motion. I can't look. I can hear people crying and someone has put their hands over my eyes so that I cannot see what is happening but I'm standing up now and running towards the circus ring. I see a girl lying face down. Her head is at the wrong angle and her dress is torn. It is a white dress with puff sleeves and a little red decoration around the neck and waist. Oh no! Oh no!"

Penny's Russian words articulately translated by Kenneth poured out in a torrent as in a waterfall, and as in a waterfall, they rapidly followed one another in quick succession, flung out and suspended in mid-air for a moment or so before crashing down and being painfully impaled onto the rocks of her consciousness, her face mirroring all the signs of torture and agony of what she was re-experiencing, seemingly for the first time, floods of tears now gushing down her cheeks.

It was at this debatably late stage that David interceded with his prepared verbal antidote fashioned so as to theoretically ease any unforeseen anxiety "QUICKLY SLEEP." Concealed by the mind, these words relating to Penny's distressed state might well have been immediate and salutary, though outwardly their effect was not patently obvious.

As David's soothing words removed Penny from the veiled tortured world she had unwittingly inhabited just a short while before, her tear-stained eyes opened as the full implications of what she had just revisited sank in.

"So I do not have a sister after all, do I David? She's dead isn't she?"

David looked at her heartbroken face and gently put a comforting arm around her shoulder.

"It very much sounds like it I'm afraid. Yes Penny. That's what it looks like."

Dr Kenneth Jones averted his eyes, unable to face the distraught young woman whose words he had so faithfully attempted to translate by keeping as much to the tenor of the situation laid out before him as well as to the strictest meaning. To see so much mental suffering displayed by Penny had left a lump in his throat and he made a vow to himself that he would never again carry out such a chore; not for David, not for anyone. He had been so much affected by the whole experience that half a glass of fine malt whisky had remained in its tumbler beside the sofa as he quickly made his way back in the dark to his cold rooms immediately after taking leave of his now two subdued hosts.

CHAPTER 49

As they stood in their first queue at Sheremetyevo II, Moscow's International Airport, Carol clinging as tightly onto Stryker's arm as she did to the relished role of fictional lovers, she whispered her excited words: "We'll see everything, won't we?"

When one catches the travel bug it bites hard. It was no different for Carol. And it was not just the tourist sights of Moscow which now ignited her imagination even though she had visited Moscow twice before in her modelling days, but standing here with Stryker it was the attractions of the rest of the world that now seemed so appealing.

Carol savoured every minute of the journey, even including waiting for the suitcases at their destination. Everything was now such a new experience for her – gone the jaded memories of tight schedules to keep for agents and clients alike. The taxi journey – setting out for the heart of Moscow along the St Davidsburg Highway, passing the large anti-tank memorial made out of huge criss-cross structures denoting the limits of the Nazi incursion into the heart of the Russian Empire during World War II, even the apartment blocks, dismal as they were, scattered along the once open fields. Her nose pushed hard up against the hoar frosted taxi window. Carol looking for the entire world like the little girl she was at heart, drinking in the sights and sounds she was witnessing as voraciously as though she were a virgin traveller, except that the images looming up before her appeared so much more in focus than the usual familiar sights of London.

After checking in at their hotel situated on the Krasnopresnenskaya Embankment, Stryker and Carol immediately left to explore Moscow in the ankle deep snow. The sky was grey and pregnant with yet more snow as they began slowly moving along Zemo Renova, eventually entering the Kremlin through Trinity Gate. Carol did not want to waste a minute and was full of questions about this and that memorial although she already knew a lot of the history.

Carol knew that just like herself Stryker had been on several trips to Moscow when he was a student so as to familiarise himself with the Russian language. But even so, he was so knowledgeable about Moscow in general and the buildings in particular. It is a very large city but around the centre he seemed so familiar with all the little backstreet shops and cafés that it was as though they were strolling through London, so confident of his bearings was he, which impressed her immensely.

Then she thought of the fight in the Chinese restaurant and how Stryker could take care of himself – and of her! Of how he had treated her with such understanding and tender loving care after returning to Belsize Park and putting her to bed. For Carol in her imagination, Stryker took on the persona of her protector and also her imagined lover. This unalloyed happiness did not last long however.

Later that first evening in Moscow Stryker explained that he had to meet a friend on some business and would be away for a couple of hours. Carol, feeling tired, had thought that they would spend the rest of the evening together and had put up a thousand reasons why he should stay put but to no avail. The friend whom Stryker was determined to meet was Dr Grachev, but it was not going to be just a social call. He was curious as to why Dr Grachev had befriended him and wanted to subtly probe Dr Grachev's motivation on his home turf. Stryker felt that people were always more vulnerable to the truth while in familiar surroundings with their guard lowered.

The last image Stryker had of Carol before he vacated his hotel was of her lounging on the small sofa switching between the limited television channels.

Within minutes of leaving their hotel Stryker began walking out of the immediate vicinity. It was while he was making his way toward a taxi rank that out of the corner of his eye he thought he saw someone in the shadows trailing him. Moscow is a big place but there are areas in any city where the streets are quiet, so this is where Stryker made for. Just as he turned into one of the deserted side streets he spied someone, confirming what he suspected. Walking slowly, he acted as if he did not know quite where he was headed and quickly turning he again caught a glimpse of the person about twenty meters away loitering in the shadows. Attempting to find transport for his journey to see Dr Grachev, it suddenly became a cat and mouse game. If he stopped so did the figure trailing him. He knew that the Russians were past masters at tailing their target and was also aware of their sometimes employing something known as the dolphin technique. This was a technique whereby the Russian agents made it only too obvious they were following their target by flooding the area with their agents before lulling them into a false sense of security by then fading away, giving the impression of having been shaken off. Except that they hadn't lost their target at all – they had just given that impression – it was an illusion. That was the spying game. When he began walking quickly away this particular follower too quickened their pace. Stryker kept this pretence up for another fifteen minutes before he finally decided to take a chance by shaking off his pursuer for the clock was ticking. It was not difficult and within a few minutes he was on his own, this time heading toward Dr Grachev's apartment hoping that his own particular tradecraft learnt at home as a detective in Seattle had stood him in good stead.

CHAPTER 50

MOSCOW

In Moscow it was becoming colder, any warmth of the sun having been leached by the frozen earth hours before. So as to repel the chill as far as was possible Vladimir Stalnov had been studiously plying himself with vodka since having left the Institute and was now distinctly unsteady on his feet, though in his intoxicated state he hardly noticed. His long suffering wife and three daughters had given up on him many years ago, knowing better than to enquire of his movements. His matrimonial status was more akin to a lodger in some stranger's home. He would eke out the few hours from his office either sleeping or eating but not communicating either verbally or otherwise in what should have been a happy family environment. With some judicious use of the space provided he had managed to secure a small room for himself, almost living as a hermit in isolation from the rest of the household within the small cramped flat. For a few hours the booze enabled him to cope with the unhappy situation he found himself in, but it would never last. Existing in a state of numbed euphoria one moment and despair the next, his vicious mood swings at the Institute were becoming legendary as his actions became more unpredictable.

In his intoxicated state at this moment, there was only one thing on his mind – and that was the scientist unwittingly keeping Marina away from him. As he twisted his feet into tall, fur lined leather boots and heaving his heavy standard issue greatcoat over the leather shoulder holster housing his Makarov 9mm pistol and donning the sheepskin shapka before pulling it down firmly over his greying hair, he thought of the long cold night before him, adjusting his scarf before adroitly tossing one more shot of vodka to the back of his throat before leaving the warmth of his cheap abode and entering the dark, gloomy street awash with deep snow drifts. Up along the sides of the surrounding buildings soft snow had blown into all the hard right-angled brick and cement strictures, ignoring the architect's inward vision by sculpting them into gentle curves. Giant heavy stalactite-like icicles clung precariously from gutters, a bluish tinge glinting in the intermittent moonlight, occasionally dropping into the deep white snowy carpet beneath, making sharp cracking noises as they broke under their own weight.

As Vladimir sat in his car, grateful to be out of reach of the stiff icy breeze, it took a few minutes to get the cold engine started, and even longer to regain some semblance of warmth back into his chilled toes. After driving gingerly through the almost deserted snow-swept streets of Moscow for nearly forty minutes he pulled the vehicle into what he approximated to be a kerb and unwillingly got out, standing in the inhospitable climatic conditions, knowing he had a few more streets to trudge through before reaching his destination. Almost immediately he began hankering after the remaining dregs of vodka intentionally left behind in his flat, knowing that it would probably be a good few hours before he could pour himself another deep glass to revive his circulation. Vladimir stamped his feet as he walked, occasionally stumbling and already beginning to have his doubts regarding the wisdom of setting off on an unplanned mission about which he had not informed any of his colleagues.

It was as his misgivings were beginning to take hold that something happened to sweep all self-doubt away. For through the evening's settling gloom a tall figure wearing a trilby hat climbed out from a taxi and approached Dr Grachev's abode, and though Vladimir was gripped by the urge to follow in pursuit, instead raw instinct took over, willing him to hold back. He was perhaps fifty feet from the Russian scientist's residence so slipped behind some trees in the vicinity to keep watch and see what new developments might occur. Removing his gloves, he scribbled the taxi number in his notebook then pulling on his gloves once more, waited in the numbing cold, cursing his foolhardy decision to go out on a limb with no backup.

CHAPTER 51

The bell to Dr Grachev's small flat rang three times before the door was answered.

"Ah Stryker, bang on time as you say in England. Do come in out of that freezing weather. I apologise for my homeland's greeting – that time of year I'm afraid – totally different country in summer, but of course you must know these things being a frequent visitor."

"Thank you, I caught a taxi as you suggested." Stryker's face glowed with the intoxication of warmth after the arctic conditions outside. "I don't know how you stand this cold."

In the cramped lobby Stryker stamped his feet to get the circulation going again and removed his brown trilby hat with the matching brown band. It was now damp with rapidly melting snowflakes which had quickly accumulated upon the well-worn brim in the short time between vacating the taxi and making his way to Dr Grachev's street door.

Stryker's host gave a broad grin. "Do come in. Good to see you comrade."

Stryker ignored the communist overtones of the word *comrade*, holding out a brown paper bag clearly outlining the shape of a bottle.

"Here, I brought you a little present, a thank you for that pleasant meal in London." A broad grin on Stryker's face now mirrored that of Dr Grachev's.

Dr Grachev detected a genuine note of warmth in Stryker's voice, a friendliness he was not used to. His own smile grew even wider to show a perfectly formed row of white teeth as he grasped the proffered bag gratefully and ushered Stryker through into the living room, motioning him to an easy chair. From this low vantage point Stryker was in the act of lifting his head to meet Dr Grachev's gaze when he became aware of a deep husky voice uttering the word 'SLEEP'. The trigger word 'SLEEP', a post-hypnotic suggestion which had been surreptitiously planted deep within Stryker's subconscious mind during their tête-à-tête in the secluded dining room back at the London hotel, instantaneously sent Stryker into another world, a cosy world where all was perfect bliss. Not so in reality.

After being taken to an even deeper hypnotic level Stryker lay quite still,

Dr Grachev knowing just what words to use to keep him in this state of suspended animation, using them now to great effect, pouring suggestions into Stryker's subconscious mind as one might pour wine into an unsuspecting victim's mouth, with the same intention; to gain complete control. Dr Grachev used suggestion to anaesthetise Stryker's arm, then after applying a rubber tourniquet he produced a readily prepared syringe and capped needle, removed the cap and plunged the sharp needle within the now distended blood vessel unloading a full syringe of the strong sedative lorazepam, the same sedative used by hospital anaesthetists for putting patients to sleep. There was no response. Satisfying himself that he had indeed put Stryker initially into a deep trance and thence a drug induced sleep, he set about his grisly business with elation mixed with caution.

CHAPTER 52

LONDON

Chen Hsu sat at the front window of his restaurant forlornly watching in a distracted manner the shoppers moving up and down the street, neither seeing them as pedestrians, nor as people at all, just objects moving along the pavement. As usual his mind was on the two men asking for protection money. They had now become a permanent fixture of his every waking moment and were slowly driving him mad. His once square shoulders now hung limp, giving off a dejected air of helplessness and despair. His boyish good looks had become haggard, the two days' growth of stubble making him seem a lot older. In an attempt to shake off the apathy which had led to him recently closing the restaurant – a temporary measure as he had explained to his remaining staff, and in an effort to forget for a while about his few remaining assets being drained away in lieu of the restaurants now defunct profits – Chen Hsu had decided to visit his injured waiter recuperating at home.

On the way he stopped at an off-licence to buy an extra-large bottle of Bell's Whisky for his friend. It was then that a sudden sense of guilt overwhelmed Chen Hsu's senses. The man behind the counter could see how distracted he was, as though mentally disturbed. Chen Hsu's eyes, red raw with sleepless nights, had a vacant look and his clothes were dishevelled. He walked with the gait of a haunted man.

CHAPTER 53

MOSCOW

Having incapacitated his victim, Dr Grachev now preceded to half carry, half drag Stryker toward the two tables prepared earlier – pushed together and lined with a heavy blanket. Dr Grachev struggled with difficulty to lift Stryker up onto the makeshift bed, which now took on the form of a doctor's examination couch, being only too aware of the doubling of body weight under such circumstances. It became a great effort to carry out this necessary chore, momentarily draining him of all energy. As his victim lay in a supine position upon the makeshift examination couch, the situation reminded Dr Grachev of his time as a newly qualified medical doctor when he had carried out so many diagnostic examinations. He had of course eventually specialised in biology and genetics, a choice which was to lead to his being transferred for work on secret Soviet government projects, and with that transfer his ultimate realisation of working for Biomedico under the auspices of Biopreparat.

Momentarily breaking off from his labours, Dr Grachev made a beeline for the kitchen and pulled out from his tiny refrigerator a bottle of Baltika beer, its label boasting of having been brewed in St. Petersburg. After a moment's hesitation it was replaced, being substituted by the bottle wrapped in the brown paper bag which Stryker had brought as a present. This would help give Dr Grachev the required Dutch courage for what he was about to do. Unscrewing the top from the bottle of fine malt whisky, a liberal glass was poured. The scientist then sank it in one go and pulled a face. Another glass would have been nice but the doctor knew he could not take a chance, aware that the task which lay ahead required steady hands.

CHAPTER 54

Vladimir Stalnov was also attempting to steady himself after having imbibed too much alcohol whilst making his way in the snow toward his quarry's abode. Half hidden behind one of the snow-clad trees by Dr Grachev's apartment, the senior FSB intelligence officer for the Biomedico Institute swayed involuntarily, his head having lost the capacity to think clearly as the cold seeped through his heavy overcoat. Yet even in these uncomfortable wintry circumstances he had the lucidity to realise that Dr Grachev's guest must be Stryker, the man mentioned in the wire-tap installed on the instructions of General Kovalyev. This realisation determined his resolve not to move a millimetre from the spot where his feet were taking on the same temperature as the frozen ground he stood upon. And for that very reason, rather than taking a short stroll to get his circulation going, he stamped his feet for a while before resuming his statue-like stance, the trained eyes of the secret agent not wavering for a moment from their target's abode.

CHAPTER 55

The tables were judged to be just the right height for the purpose Dr Grachev had in mind as he propped Stryker's head up at a slight angle, inclining it forward by using an old embroidered cushion to support the neck. Then, turning to a corner cupboard he retrieved a small, old, worn leather-look cardboard suitcase. From this modest case he extracted a wad of cotton wool, a black rubber pump bearing a tiny half-cupped suction pad attached to one end of a length of thin rubber tubing, and finally a wooden spatula. These items were methodically laid out in a neat row on the edge of the blanket in the space between Stryker's head and shoulder. The scene was now beginning to take on the sinister aspect of a quack's makeshift operating table, with only a bare lightbulb throwing its meagre illumination upon the patient's prostrate and defenceless body.

Removing his jacket and then rolling up his shirt sleeves, Dr Grachev changed his mind, deciding that one more glass of whisky could not possibly make any difference. After pouring himself another measure and setting it aside he pulled on a pair of long rubber gloves reaching up to his elbows. These gloves had been removed from his laboratory the day before.

Dr Grachev had only known Stryker a very short time and yet he had grown to like him. Stryker's present of booze was a touching gesture. *If circumstances had been different*, he mused, *perhaps I would not be doing this*. He had detected an almost palpable affinity between himself and the Britisher; Dr Grachev felt he could really sense this kinship.

He gazed down at Stryker and felt compassion for him, lying there so helpless and vulnerable. Yes, in different circumstances... he had detected that Stryker was a good man, an honest person. Maybe he would even understand why this had to happen. Stryker was going to be helping his Russian friend as well as protecting the West. To that end he was certain Stryker would agree with him. To some people in life there falls a responsibility to help one's fellow man. It had not been an easy decision, but if things turned out right... he felt sure Stryker would thank him one day. With that in mind, he raised the second tumbler of whisky toward Stryker's tired-looking body and toasted his guest – "Here's to a successful outcome – *Budem zdorovy!*"

Stryker, now in a very deep drugged state, was breathing heavily but evenly. Dr Grachev also took a deep breath in unison and steadied himself, not so much because of the alcohol-induced effect upon his lean frame but because of the operation he was about to perform – something he had never attempted before. Gripping the wooden spatula between thumb and forefinger of his right hand he gently raised Stryker's left upper eyelid with his other thumb. He could feel the tension break between the membrane of the watery red inner eyelid and the smooth surface of the glass orb. An involuntary tear trickled from the corner of Stryker's eye and Dr Grachev murmured more soothing words using his natural deep voice directed at the victim's subconscious mind out of instinct, for of course the true binding which shackled Stryker to his confinement was the sedative lorazepam. Removing a small piece of cotton wool he dabbed at Stryker's tear duct.

The scientist steeled himself before easing the wooden spatula beneath the lower eyelid, past the multifarious layers of fatty tissue, it made a rasping sound as it scraped the glass surface like sandpaper on teeth. Putting pressure on the spatula, he began easing it down in between the posterior of the lower eyelid and the glass eye, levering at the same time. Suddenly he could feel the rubbery-like resistance to the long wooden tool.

He pressed the flat side of the spatula hard onto the lower eyelashes, crushing them as it dug deeper into the puffy flesh within the eye socket. As Dr Grachev applied a little more pressure, using the cheekbone as something to lever against, the eyeball made a soft sucking sound before shooting out of the now gaping red hole in Stryker's face, The prosthetic eye rolled across the floor, skimming along the brown linoleum before ending up under the worn out easy chair. Dr Grachev realised his mistake immediately. Becoming so consumed with his efforts he had forgotten to use the rubber suction pump to secure the false eye whilst in the process of removing it.

Dr Grachev rarely swore, but now he let out a string of abuse under his breath, all his invective being directed at Stryker. Crouching down, he removed the glove from his right hand and felt gingerly beneath the large overstuffed chair. He was in luck first time – if luck is what one might call it – his fingers making contact with the sticky glass orb. It felt as though it had been covered in wet saliva and his stomach churned. He felt sick as waves of nausea rolled over him.

Removing a large piece of fluff from one side of the glass eye he grabbed a handkerchief and quickly wrapped the orb within its folds. He was surprised at how much it weighed as he slipped the still warm object into his overcoat pocket. Stryker lay motionless, Dr Grachev knowing he had the vulnerable Englishman just where he wanted him as he readied himself to put the next part of his plan into operation.

CHAPTER 56

In the suburbs of Moscow it was now dark and the snow made a muffled crunching sound underfoot, being two feet deep in places. The small block of flats he was searching for was hard to locate. They all looked the same to Dr Grachev, who had never visited this particular area before. He did not use his old Trabant and it seemed to him a great distance, having to change local buses twice. Moving through these unfamiliar back streets the area took on an unfriendly, even hostile air at this time of the evening. Most people were in the secure confines of their abodes by now, eating their supper or more likely preparing for bed. The cold was beginning to bite into his hands and feet. He could feel the shape of his hard fought for treasure nestling in the deep sheepskin jacket pocket, pressing it now and then to reassure himself that he did indeed have it within his fingers.

A half-eaten moon appeared intermittently through ragged cloud formations, periodically dusting the snow with an eerie blue tinged softness, dark sky merging with the earth as twilight displayed one of nature's grand illusions permitting huge shadows to loom out at him suggesting harbingers of impending doom.

It had started snowing again with a light breeze blowing the feather-like snowflakes into Dr Grachev's face. Now he pulled his scarf higher, so that only his eyes were visible. Past two more blocks of nondescript housing and there it was. Through the deteriorating weather he could barely make out the giant number painted on the side of the crumbling block of flats. As he drew closer it was just discernible that at one time the building had been rendered a battleship grey, but the hostile elements had eroded most of the paintwork save for the odd patch, leaving it now in a shoddy state of crumbling decay. Large lumps of concrete lay at the base of the building as if it were in the process of shedding its skin. The area he found himself in was a slum. The contents of rubbish bins vomited amid graffiti-strewn walls.

For some inexplicable reason Dr Grachev's mind drifted back to the conversation he had with Professor Anton Cherenkov a few days previously after returning from his very successful trip to Beijing. It had been engineered with a view to informing Dr Grachev that an assistant would be assigned to him on the orders of Colonel Oleynik in the "vain hope that it might speed up your work here on the virus."

Having had it pointed out to him that these were the words of Colonel

Oleynik and not the professor's own, Dr Grachev could not fail to notice however, that Professor Cherenkov appeared to enjoy conveying this message. What Professor Cherenkov did not know was that Colonel Oleynik had already informed him of this impending proposal and even named the scientist who was to act as Dr Grachev's assistant. Colonel Oleynik had sworn him to secrecy regarding the identity of his proposed new assistant, explaining that it should be kept from Professor Cherenkov for the moment. Dr Grachev suspected that this secret between them was just a ploy to gain his confidence. He could feel the noose tightening around his neck.

The last thing he had wanted was someone watching over him whilst he plotted his escape to the West with a sample of the deadly virus. Dr Grachev's steps through the snow grew stronger as he offered up a silent prayer of thanks to one of the saints, grateful that Colonel Oleynik had left it too late to install an informer to see what he was up to. And he was sure that his proposed assistant would indeed eventually turn out to be that of an informer if Oleynik had anything to do with it.

Dr Grachev dwelled upon his impending trip to London. The fact was that if all went well within twelve hours he would be on a plane bound for England, and tonight would be the culmination of his entire well thought out plans; plans that had become an obsession over the past few weeks. He was also determined that especially tonight nothing should impede those plans, absolutely nothing.

CHAPTER 57

Vladimir Stalnov heard a distant clock striking twelve, acutely aware of sharp freezing breath stinging the deeper recesses of his lungs, chilling his body from within. He had been on the verge of succumbing to the idea of bursting in on Dr Grachev and his guest when a shadowy figure slipped out from the doorway of the scientist's abode. It was the doctor himself and this posed an awkward paradox for the intelligence officer of the Biomedico Institute. Did he stalk his quarry Dr Grachev at the very same time as losing sight of Stryker, the doctor's guest, in incriminating circumstances, who may or may not also possibly vacate the premises, thus presenting Vladimir Stalnov with another target to follow, a man who to all intents and purposes had been designated a spy in his own right? He was beginning to curse his decision of dispensing with other agents for backup in his self-imposed task, instead going it alone, not foreseeing such an occurrence.

Perhaps if it were not for the inclement weather conditions his decision may have been different but he needed to get the circulation going in his body and glean a little warmth in the process so decided to follow Dr Grachev instead.

CHAPTER 58

Tom left work early, concerned that he had not seen nor heard from Li Cheung for the last two days – not since their decision to get married, and of her stated intention of informing her parents. Attempting to ring Li Cheung at home in Camberwell and discovering the telephone line dead, he had been informed of a possible fault on the line. But now today, after attempting to get through once more, a telephone operator at the local telephone exchange said that the line had been disconnected.

As Tom drove toward London his imagination began to run riot. He had attempted to ring Li Cheung at her place of work but was informed that she had not been in since the last time he had seen her himself. They were adamant that her personal details could not be given out to anyone. Nor did he have her parents' telephone number. In fact, he didn't even know where Li Cheung's parents lived. He was frantic. It was possible, he supposed, that she had been getting nuisance calls and that her private line had been changed and was now ex-directory, but why then had she not called him? After all, they were getting married weren't they?

He was double de-clutching like a racing driver as he pushed his old wreck through the heavy traffic. The heater had packed up ages ago and there were cold draughts coming into the car from all directions. He caught himself repeatedly touching his chin with his index finger like some nervous tennis player going through the routine of bouncing the ball eight times before each serve. It was a compulsion he could do nothing about. In his peripheral vision he caught a glimpse of an ambulance on the other side of the road with a police car in attendance. As he turned his head to look closer there were two cars smashed into one another, head on. Then he saw the dirty brown scar cut deep across the dual carriageway where the car on his side of the road had slewed across diagonally, churning up the road surface before hitting the other car with presumed gut wrenching force. He shuddered and hoped it was not an omen.

A black depression settled over Tom but he still coaxed the car into going as fast as possible whilst weaving in and out of the traffic around him. His mind was so fixated with the mystery of why Li Cheung had not contacted him that time became condensed, until suddenly he found himself standing in front of the house where she lodged. Tom looked up and something, he could not quite understand what, filled him with foreboding. Something was different but he could not put his finger on it. Ten times he rang the bell with no response. All was eerily silent. He tried the other three bells of her neighbours, No answer. Feeling in his jacket pocket he curled his fingers around the two keys Li Cheung had given him and wondered whether he should just open the street door and walk in. Tom stepped back to take one more glance at Li Cheung's room from the street, and as he did so a man in his early twenties came up the steps.

"Excuse me but I'm looking for Li Cheung but there's no answer. Would you know where she might be contacted?" The young man stared at Tom and then a look of recognition crossed his face.

"You were at Li's birthday party weren't you? Come in and wait for her if you like." Tom followed. The young man lived on the ground floor because he moved straight past the stairs and disappeared along the hall passage leaving Tom to climb the stairs. In his mind, Tom planned to sit on the floor outside her room until she arrived. The hall lights were not working thus leaving the stairway shrouded in dark shadows. As he reached Li Cheung's landing he changed his mind, instead deciding to enter her room with the keys she had pushed into his hand. The keys had been warm from the heat of her own fingers, and he attempted once more to conjure up the feeling he had experienced when she told him that, from now on, her room was his as well as hers. "Use them anytime... just like we're married."

A thick wedge of bright sunlight roused him as it cut through the darkness from her half open door. Tom's heart raced as he moved quickly toward it, expecting to find Li Cheung inside, perhaps swaying in time to some of her favourite music pumping through earphones connected to her Sony Walkman. Or possibly a towel had been wrapped around her head after washing her hair, covering the ears like a turban, which would explain why she had not heard the doorbell.

Knocking on the half open door with his knuckles, it swung inwards, Tom suddenly understanding what had been so puzzling as he had looked up toward Li Cheung's room from the street. Facing him were the large windows, now stripped bare of the curtains which had previously adorned them. That explained the intensity of the light streaming onto the landing. Taking two paces inside, he cast his gaze around the room, which was devoid of almost every piece of furniture except for that bed – the bed they had shared together. It still retained the pillows and blankets and sheets on which they had travelled in ecstasy to heaven and back. The room looked dishevelled; as though Li Cheung had just left it in that state before rushing off to work, with the intention of straightening it when she arrived home later – except she never did come back.

The wardrobe was also still there, although now empty, matching the feeling in Tom's stomach. He could not believe his eyes. Not a stitch of Li Cheung's clothing remained, nor the little colourful pieces of bric-a-brac which had been scattered everywhere around the room like confetti. It was as if she had never existed. The only clue to Li Cheung having lived here was the faintest trace of Miss Dior, which hung in the air – tantalising his senses. He thought of the last time he stood at the window holding Li Cheung's hand, admiring her birthday present sitting down in the street, waiting to whisk them to the coast where Tom had proposed to her. He could not take it in. He felt sick. How could someone just disappear? He stepped outside of her vacated room, dropping the latch as he closed the door, it made a clicking noise as the spring lock engaged the brass plate set within the door jamb.

***

"When was the last time you saw her sir?"

"Two days ago."

"And you say she had left the flat where she'd been living?"

"Well, room actually. But yes, she's gone – just disappeared into thin air."

"But that's not anything to be worrying over sir. People living in London are constantly moving. It's a well-known fact sir, a multifarious population constantly on the move. That's the attraction for a lot of people of living in a big city. Anonymity – it's normal in a place like this. And if you don't mind my saying so sir, two days – well that's nothing is it, in the scheme of things I mean, sir? Don't worry – I'm sure she'll turn up." The policeman at the desk had a kindly manner and was doing his best to reassure Tom, but his reassurances fell on deaf ears.

"But all her furniture and clothing have gone – everything."

"Well, that sounds pretty normal to me. People would take their belongings when they move wouldn't they sir?"

"But we were going to get married!"

"When was that sir?"

"Well, no date had been fixed."

"I'm sorry, there's nothing we can do about that I'm afraid. People leave London all the time. It's normal, nothing to worry about sir. I'm sorry."

Tom left the local police station feeling dejected but slightly placated by the policeman's reassuring manner. Maybe Li Cheung had got cold feet and disappeared to avoid the embarrassment of telling him that she had changed her mind about getting married. But deep down he knew he was clutching at straws. He felt that he knew Li Cheung well enough to know that she would not do such a thing. It was impossible. There had to be another explanation. He had already questioned everyone in Li Cheung's house and they had all expressed surprise at her leaving without saying goodbye. And no, nobody had seen her leave. The landlord said the lease had another six months to run on her room, so he had no problem with her vacating and suggested that she might be on holiday somewhere at this very moment. The more Tom thought about it the more worried he became.

CHAPTER 59

Dr Grachev had never knowingly been followed; that is to say, he had never witnessed anyone tagging along in his footsteps, but his sixth sense told him that tonight was different. He suspected he had been shadowed before now because of what had unwittingly come out in conversations with other people, though he had not been too surprised because that was the way it had always been living in such a closed communist state such as Russia. But tonight he definitely knew. Maybe it was because he normally used his car to travel everywhere and would not notice such things, but tonight he had decided to leave his transport parked back at his flat. As he came to the building he was seeking, momentarily standing on the threshold, he spun around quickly in as nonchalant a manner as he could as though in deep thought. This was so as to make sure he was not being followed, a thing he never usually did but he was feeling nervous because of Stryker lying inside his flat. At that very moment he caught a fleeting glimpse of what he thought was someone darting back around the street corner he had passed not a minute before. Dr Grachev struggled to keep calm and tried vainly to push the stranger to the back of his mind, intending to deal first with the urgent business at hand.

Mikhail shuffled along the dimly lit passage where an old worn out lightbulb shed its meagre yellow glow onto the drab walls. Dr Grachev banged for the third time upon the upper panel of the weathered door partially split by neglect and the inclement weather over the years. It creaked open but was held fast by a chain, just long enough for Mikhail to put his head around, craning his deeply lined neck so as to see who had been banging with such impatience.

"Yes, who are you?" His tone was abrupt and unfriendly. Dr Grachev stared at the old man's half hidden face.

"I was informed you could do a little job for me. Sergei suggested you did favours." This was partially true. Sergei, whom Dr Grachev had met only once, in a wine cellar in the middle of Moscow, did indeed mention that there was an old jeweller living on his own who could do favours like making small pieces of jewellery to one's own design. Also that he occasionally acted as a fence for stolen items. It had been two years ago when this was mentioned, but Dr Grachev had made a mental note and filed it away for possible future use for to survive in Moscow, even for scientists, one used the black market. It was a way of life.

"Go away. I don't know you," the old man replied in a frightened voice.

Dr Grachev had come prepared for such a hostile reception and pulled out a packet of American cigarettes brought back from his last trip to London.

"Here, take these, it's only a small favour I require. It won't take up much of your time." The sound of a chain falling from the other side of the door signalled grudging acceptance, the old man's scrawny hand beckoning him in.

"What is it you want?" he enquired suspiciously, greedily snatching the cigarettes from Dr Grachev's hand.

Dr Grachev produced the prosthetic trophy he had removed from Stryker's head less than an hour before and explained in some detail the diameter and depth of hole he wanted drilled into it.

"It must be at the rear of the glass eye, exactly opposite the front. And don't drill too deep, that's an order." Being a scientist at Biomedico he was used to giving orders to pharmaceutical suppliers for his experimental equipment. But this was no pharmaceutical supplier and at once he knew it had been a mistake talking to the old craftsman like that.

"I've been a jeweller for over sixty years and you can get out now if you don't trust my workmanship."

Dr Grachev's eyes became expressionless and as hard as the one proffered to this master craftsman. "I trust you. It's just that I want a good job done, that's all. No offence."

The old jeweller shuffled into a tiny back room and Dr Grachev followed uninvited. Taking up the whole length of one bare wall was a well-worn oak workbench, heavily scarred with all manner of tools scattered upon it. Electric cables, blocks of wood, drills of different sizes, metal files, yellowed paper, dust and dirt. A large vice was held firmly to the bench by thick rusted nails, the heads not quite hammered home but bent sideways. There was also a range of different sized hammers, some as small as a little finger and covered in grime. When Mikhail was young and just starting out in the jewellery business every tool had its place, hung from hooks or lay neatly in a cabinet, but as the years passed, he had grown lazy and could see no reason for expending so much energy walking back and forth so as to retrieve one tool after another. For the last year or two he had grown used to the idea of putting off cleaning until he felt up to it.

These days he never even felt up to washing his grimy vodka glass which had been a special present on one of his name days. He could not remember which year it had been given to him by his wife, now long dead. His children had flown the nest too many years ago for him to remember them either, except in a hazy sort of way, as his memory played tricks on him now. Ah! What a life he had led when he was young. Living in the country and playing on the banks of the Volga, watching from the levee as the boats passed by with all those people working on them. It had seemed so romantic as a child, lying in the grass through those interminably long hot summer months watching the birds soaring above those boats. He would often hear the boatmen singing old Russian folk songs which caught on the breeze and wafted across the pastures, as they had across the centuries, Mikhail sometimes being inspired to wave at the boatmen and receiving a wave back in acknowledgement.

"You'll be careful not to damage it won't you?" Dr Grachev's words seeped into Mikhail's consciousness bringing him back to the present.

"You worry too much," the old man replied, lifting two small hollowed out pieces of wood, covering each with a piece of soft grubby-looking lint cloth. The glass eye was gingerly placed in this sandwich of wood and lint, the pupil set away from his gaze. The wooden supports with the eye nestling between them were now inserted into the jaws of the vice.

"What are you going to drill it with?"

"What do you think? A diamond-tipped drill of course, that's what." His manner was edgy and Dr Grachev decided to remain quiet. He watched closely now as the right sized bit was inserted into an electric drill. Then some small pieces of wood were drilled through. Now the bit was replaced with the diamond one with the wood, the holes freshly drilled, threaded onto this diamond bit. A ruler was used to measure the remaining length of this drill bit and pieces of wood added until the remaining exposed length was that of the depth Dr Grachev had wanted drilled.

The high pitched drill rent the air with a whine as it was lowered down onto the back of the glass eye and skidded over the surface, leaving in its wake a shallow channel. Mikhail uttered a curse and started again. Dr Grachev's fingernails dug deep into his palms as he swore aloud. The tip of the diamond drill let out another high pitched whine as this time it cut deep into the glass, sending up a sparkling cloud of fine glass dust. This time it had not skidded but pushed through the glass orb until the wooden collar would not let it go any further.

"There, it's done." Releasing the jaws of the vice and with a smirk upon his bloodless thin lips Mikhail handed the drilled glass eye back to the doctor. "Would you like to measure it?"

Dr Grachev produced a thin pencil which was inserted into the depth of the freshly drilled hole. Keeping his thumb nail upon this mark he then measured it against the ruler.

"Congratulations my friend, you've done a good job." He smiled weakly at Mikhail. "How much would you like? Say fifty roubles?"

The old man stared at Dr Grachev and continued grinning. "Well, if that's alright with you. Sure... sure." Now he became more expansive and animated, not being able to contain himself. "I could have done that with my eyes shut. Oh! You should have seen some of the jewellery I've made in the past. You would not believe it. And if there is any other job you have in mind for me sometime – well, you'll let me know won't you? Just anything. I can do anything for you – it's no trouble at all, no problem for you my friend."

Dr Grachev's hand reached into his inside jacket pocket and produced another packet of cigarettes. He took one out, the only one remaining, and pushed it into Mikhail's bony fingers.

"Have a smoke old man, go on. I'll light it for you. You deserve it."

Being called an old man irritated Mikhail but he nevertheless put the cigarette to his lips. Dr Grachev pulled out a lighter. A yellow flame licked around the end of the cigarette.

"Inhale old man, inhale to seal the deal." As Mikhail's cheeks sucked in, taking the smoke deep within his lungs his eyes became dim. The cigarette slowly slipped from his fingers and his mouth opened wide as if about to yawn. Then his eyes took on a look of sheer terror as his features froze. This was toxic shock. He remained in that position for a full thirty seconds before his frail body crumpled to the floor. His chest gave one frantic enormous heave and he was dead.

Before leaving, Dr Grachev retrieved the poison cigarette from the floorboards where it had been stubbed out with his foot, carefully replacing it in the cigarette carton. He also removed the full packet of American cigarettes he had given to the old man earlier. Then, with the drilled glass eye safely back in his possession, he walked over to the workbench and lifted a long handled razor sharp chisel which he gingerly slid halfway up his overcoat sleeve, the cold steel blade nestling flat against the palm of his hand. On his way out he dropped the catch of the front door lock, slamming the door hard to make it secure from intruders.

It was only as the cold outside air hit Dr Grachev's face that it sunk into his consciousness just how much the cramped abode had reeked of staleness, a certain smell, which was hard to describe. The odour imbued a faded sense of helplessness, of memories encapsulated within a time warp – of an old man who had been unwittingly waiting for death.

CHAPTER 60

For Anthony Lovejoy-Taylor things were very definitely not looking up. Since his dalliance with the floater, known in certain circles as lithesome June, word had come to his ears that a spate of malicious gossip about his sexual prowess not living up to expectations engendered by his own boastful excesses was going the rounds, causing him a lot of soul searching. Also the ambassador was on his back.

Sir John Postlethwaite was usually a very easy going man, though some of the embassy staff viewed him as an old maid. An imposing figure at six feet three inches tall, he looked every bit the archetypal diplomat that the British were only too eager to foist upon other unsuspecting countries. Happily married with three children back in England: one daughter at university and two younger sons at boarding school, Sir Anthony did not take kindly to his staff's dalliances with the opposite sex at his embassy, nor for that matter a liaison with one's own sex either.

Sir John, a cautious man, liked to run a tight ship. Carrying the metaphor to the extreme for the uninitiated, he was often heard whispering to his staff at cocktail parties, his drink-induced pink tinged jowls quivering as he sailed through a sea of faces like a turkeycock: "No waves please," meaning, hold your tongue and be courteous to all and sundry, even if they are boring the pants off you, which tended to be par for the course. Cocktail parties were generally boring affairs, like the annual celebration of the Queen's birthday, having to constantly circulate, which could be murder on the old pins, another one of the ambassador's favourite expressions.

Conversations were also pretty limited, in Moscow being for the ex-patriot community a much closed fraternity, diplomatic staff tending to stick to themselves for the sake of security. The US embassy was a source of fraternisation acceptable to HMA which the staff at the British Embassy used mainly for their own purposes; namely to gain access to their American cousins' NAFFI, the luxuries obtained there being offered on a very generous discount.

Many Foreign Office personnel were heartily sick of one another's company if the truth were known, other peoples wives being the exception to the rule, and unfortunately cocktail parties were just one more vehicle for retelling the same old well-worn stories for the umpteenth time; the more adventurous tending to add a new character here for effect or introducing a whole new extra set of circumstances there. No wonder so many Foreign Office staff became secret budding authors. The inane conversations could become very tedious, plus seeing the same faces day in, day out could also put a strain on previously very successful relationships, including that of the plain incestuous.

The ambassador was not known for being a particularly vain man, although the grade four Minister did notice at the regular morning prayer meetings, preceded by a long line of sober suited senior diplomats trooping through the corridor to HMG's office like so many undertakers, that the ambassador's longish sideburns were sometimes greyer than at other times, suggesting something other than worry was colouring his hair.

This thought was also running through Anthony Lovejoy-Taylor's mind as he found himself facing Sir John Postlethwaite on a one to one basis across his imposing desk. Then, as if to read Lovejoy-Taylor's thoughts, the ambassador slowly ran his fingers through his hair. Lovejoy-Taylor could not take his eyes off Sir John Postlethwaite's hand, and as hard as he tried not to look, he found himself scouring the ambassador's fingers for the slightest telltale signs of black hair colourant or whitening which might have been added to his sideburns suggesting a more dignified persona.

"Pogo, old fellow, you seem to be miles away. I said how's your daddy getting on? The last time I saw him was at the Beagles club in Mayfair. Do you know it?" Anthony Lovejoy-Taylor did indeed know of the Beagles club, as he had been forcibly ejected from the premises on more than one occasion when violently drunk and hurling abuse at all and sundry.

"Yes, been a member for years – a quiet place. My father's keeping well." Anthony Lovejoy-Taylor's eyes were rooted to the ambassador's fingers until the next question set his mind ticking.

"And how are you Pogo, old boy, any problems eh?" From most people, such an enquiry might have been construed as innocent enough, but for Anthony Lovejoy Taylor it contained a coded message. He did not think of himself as a suspicious man, notwithstanding his being a member of MI6, but thought he knew exactly what the ambassador was doing... he was fishing. He knew Sir John placed family values and morality at the top of his list and sensed he was now being got at. He also knew that the ambassador's wife had formerly been his secretary and that old Postlethwaite had felt obliged to marry her because of 'putting her in the club', to use the vernacular. The ambassador was full of hypocrisy. Lovejoy-Taylor had been confided in by his father, that as a young man, Sir John had dabbled in homosexuality before, as he put it, 'discovering women.'

Anthony Lovejoy-Taylor stared at the very conservative-looking man opposite, giving him an indignant look borne out of petulance. "If you mean did I have a run in with one of our floaters, well then, the answer is yes."

The ambassador's face clouded, taking on a pained expression as he reached over the thirty thousand pound highly ornate mahogany desk, which sat in stark contrast to the homilies delivered to his staff on the virtues of frugality, acting as they were on behalf of the British taxpayer, and patted Pogo on the back of his hand. "I believe she is due to be replaced actually. Perhaps we'll expedite matters." A knowing smile crossed Sir John Postlethwaite's face before suggesting that Pogo come to dinner later in the week. Lovejoy-Taylor fleetingly wondered whether the ambassador had renounced the last vestiges of homosexuality, or if some traces of such feelings remained, as he tactfully withdrew his hand from beneath that of Sir John's.

Summoning up as much good grace as he could muster, Anthony Lovejoy-Taylor replied "Thank you Ambassador," before beating a hasty retreat out of the ambassador's office, thinking that he had been dead right to suspect HMA of fishing; only to Anthony Lovejoy-Taylor it had seemed more like whaling. He was now surer than ever, that the scurrilous rumour of his performance with the lithesome June not living up to expectations, had definitely reached the ear of HMA, though even Lovejoy-Taylor himself thought he might be a tad paranoid. As he ambled down the corridor away from the big chief's office, he casually glanced at the back of his hand and noticed, not without a touch of pique, that there was no residue pertaining to hair colourant, wryly observing that it was obviously of a type that stayed where it was put, which was more than could be said for the ambassador's hands.

CHAPTER 61

By the time Dr Grachev arrived back at his apartment it was after midnight and the streets were now deserted, but from the corner of his eye, lurking within the shadows opposite the building he noticed something move, adding confirmation to his suspicions that someone had been following him. As he turned to see what it was a loud gunshot rent the silence, echoing in the cold, crisp night air and he froze momentarily, straining his ears. The sound came from a few blocks away, someone was perhaps shooting a stray cat or maybe settling an old score with a drug dealer; a common enough occurrence now since the foreshadowed fall of the Soviet Block.

Law and order to Dr Grachev's mind was rapidly disintegrating in what was once a police fearing state, where under Joseph Stalin you could get sent to one of hundreds of Gulag prison camps scattered around the country for ten years just for stealing an ear of corn. Stalin, a pseudonym retained out of habit through his being a revolutionary – a man who was arguably the worst tyrant the world had ever known, whose real name had been Joseph Vissarionovich Dzhugashvili. Dr Grachev instinctively knew that when he looked back to check the shadows from where the movement had caught his eye, the secret policeman would be standing there. As he glanced around, true to form, merged within the gloom was a man of more than average height, and dressed in a greatcoat.

With a purposeful stride, Dr Grachev made his way through the freshly fallen snow toward the imagined agent, brandishing the packet of American cigarettes he had used with such devastating effect upon the old jeweller earlier, now calling out to his adversary, asking if he had a light.

As Dr Grachev drew close, the agent, his hands now fumbling in his heavy service issue greatcoat pockets to meet this request, looked totally surprised. It was this air of being caught off guard which registered in Dr Grachev's mind. At the same moment as the stranger stepped out of the shadows, Dr Grachev recognised the face as that of the FSB security officer from Biomedico, Vladimir Stalnov as he himself recognised the face of Dr Grachev. After a sharp intake of breath, Dr Grachev drew close enough to detect that the FSB man's own breath reeked of vodka as his mouth opened on the verge of saying something, and noticed his body swaying slightly. After a brief moments' flurry of activity a quizzical expression passed over

Stalnov's face as he slowly withdrew both hands from his pockets, in the process dropping a box of matches onto the freshly fallen snow before clasping Dr Grachev's arms just above the elbow, as in a gesture of solidarity with his fellow man. They both stood there transfixed, looking like lost souls in a hostile environment, gazing intently at one another, no words being exchanged, just staring at each other, searching one another's faces for what seemed like eternity.

In reality it took only a few seconds before the agent's strong grip slowly loosened, sliding onto his knees through the snow and staring down in disbelief at the old jeweller's long, worn wooden handle of the steel chisel which had cut so cleanly through several layers of clothing before burying itself deep within his heart. There was no violent struggle, no attempt to get away, not even a scream, just a muffled gurgling sound emitted from the agent's now quivering bluish lips as his eyes clouded over. Then unexpectedly, he appeared to rally back to life, a furious struggle set up within his body as with great effort, eyes rolling backwards into his head, he managed to softly enunciate with a hoarse whisper one final word: "*Mama.*"

Dr Grachev, anxiously looking around him to make sure there were no witnesses, caught Vladimir's cadaver beneath the shoulders, dragging him to his car parked nearby. He struggled for ages before eventually managing to push the rapidly cooling body onto the back seat, still leaving the jeweller's long handled chisel protruding from the FSB man's chest so as to help stem the flow of blood. After quickly scouring the scene for any clues linking him to the murder he jumped in behind the steering wheel, quietly closing the door to avoid drawing any unnecessary attention to himself before moving off. He drove slowly at first so as not to awaken the local residents, but quickly gathered speed until soon he was well outside Moscow, heading through the suburbs toward an isolated part of the river. This was to be the FSB agent's watery grave, Dr Grachev having first removed from Vladimir's bloodstained overcoat the barely decipherable notes relating to his own previous movements. Dr Grachev did not stay to witness the body sink rapidly beneath the dark water and become entangled in the weeds and roots. He only remained long enough to scoop up handfuls of snow with which to clean the rear seat of his old Trabant which had become covered in copious amounts of Vladimir's blood leaking from the chisel wound through his greatcoat. Dr Grachev was acutely aware of having crossed his own personal Rubicon for which deed he knew there could be no going back. Yet he thought it strange that he felt no remorse, which worried him more than the actual fact of killing both Vladimir Stalnov – the Federal Security Service Officer plus the old jeweller.

Time was now critical for Dr Grachev. Disposing of his watcher had become an inevitable consequence from that first moment he had glimpsed him when setting out on his quest for the jeweller's abode earlier in the evening. There had been no option. How could he have possibly explained to Stalnov about Stryker remaining in his apartment all evening while he himself was out, for the agent would undoubtedly have seen Stryker arrive? Hopefully there would be nothing to link him with the FSB agent's death, not immediately anyway; and by then he would have been granted political asylum with a new identity.

The unlit common hallway led to six apartments. Dr Grachev was fortunate in living on the ground floor. As the communal door leading off the street slammed shut, isolating him from the cold outside, Dr Grachev stood for some seconds attempting to compose himself in the gloom, letting the warmth seep back into his now tired body. From the stairwell he opened the door which led into his flat from where he had initially greeted Stryker only a few hours earlier. He walked with leaden legs into the lobby and passed through into the sitting room before switching on the light. The room where Dr Grachev had left Stryker had grown cold; the unreliable antique radiator must have packed up soon after the doctor had vacated his abode. Stryker still lay on his back looking for all the world like a sleeping child, oblivious to the frenetic events of the past few hours – oblivious to his forthcoming ordeal.

Dr Grachev immediately set about his grisly task of re-inserting Stryker's false eye, but not before carefully placing his lethal glass capsule containing the micro-organism taken from his Institute within Mikhail's carefully drilled hole; this glass capsule being held securely in place by a small amount of sealing wax. The jeweller had done his job well, leaving a slightly burred edge at the opening so as to give the sealing wax something upon which to grip. All the while Dr Grachev worked, a crystal clear image was held securely in his mind. Having already collected the necessary documentation and travel tickets from Colonel Oleynik for his visit to London, the image was of himself leaving Moscow by aeroplane the very next morning and arriving at London airport three and a half hours later, his precious sample of toxic microbes following him shortly after, transported in a place where nobody would dream of looking for it, even if anyone knew of its existence – in the safe keeping of his friend Stryker's head.

CHAPTER 62

Supplementing food by setting snares in the woods was second nature for those who lived in and been brought up in the rural areas. To know how to trap small wild animals and birds had saved many people from starvation, especially during the time of Stalin and after. It had certainly been the case for this particular elderly man as he crept about between the trees, checking the traps and snares set the previous day. As he scoured the undergrowth his eyes lit up at the prospect of a tasty meal after spotting a bundle of fur held by the serrated steel jaws of a trap, the small animal, whatever it was, still quivering as it struggled to free one of its half severed hind legs, its life force not quite ebbed away.

It was whilst during the process of bending down to aid his failing eyesight, to see more clearly between the shadows of trees cast by the large bright moon that the vehicle pulled up almost beside him, the thicket by which he crouched fortunately lending enough cover to make sure he could not be seen. Not that the driver of this particular vehicle was in any state to notice much that was going on around him, so engrossed was he in his chore of pulling a body from an old Trabant.

Remaining as still as he could, he watched as the body was dragged the small distance to the snow covered bank. The car's engine had been cut and there was not much sound, just the gentle swish a sleigh might make before the dead weight was pushed over the side, cracking the thin sheet of ice as it landed before disappearing into the dark, freezing water. While observing the car being given a cursory clean with handfuls of snow, he made a mental note of the number plate. He was also fortunate in getting a clear view of the man's face. *What a stroke of luck*, the elderly peasant mused, his eyes twinkling with elation in the bitterly cold night air, barely able to contain his joy at the prospect of being given a few roubles for doing nothing more than inform on a fellow citizen. That was second nature to him, having done that all his life, so that was nothing new. And for someone who had known nothing but existence on the breadline it was indeed like manna from heaven.

CHAPTER 63

It was gone one when Stryker eventually arrived back at his hotel where Caroline had been waiting up for him. Not being a state run Intourist hotel, the chances of its rooms being bugged had decreased significantly, but not impossibly so. It was therefore with the utmost caution that anything which Stryker felt might be of any interest to the Russian Intelligence Service, was written down upon a special notepad, which had the facility to be obliterated in seconds ready for the next message to be shown to his partner. That worked well in theory, but did not take into account the situation he now walked into.

"Stryker, why were you so long? You ostensibly take me on holiday and then leave me in a foreign country and I was terrified something bad had happened to you, you shit." This took Stryker totally by surprise. It was out of character to speak in such a manner. Although he had not seen her for a few hours he knew that something must have unsettled her. It is true Stryker had anticipated a bad reception, perhaps some sulks or a few hastily misjudged words tossed in his direction, but nothing like this. Carol was beside herself. Fear is a terrible animal when let out on a long leash and it was now snapping at Stryker's heels.

"Why? Why didn't you call? You knew I'd be worried. You could have been dead. Look at me. Look at the worry you've put me through." Stryker suddenly felt ill. He had experienced many relationships with women but nothing as intense as this. He knew it was their close friendship that sent the nearest object to hand, which happened to be his electric razor, hurtling toward his head, only narrowly missing it's mark as he swiftly ducked, it making contact instead with the wall and shattering into a thousand pieces of plastic and metal parts. It may have been friendship but to Stryker it felt more like hate.

"I'm so sorry, I never meant to..." Words, it seemed, were no match for real life flying objects as they came sailing fast and furiously past him as he ducked and weaved his body into unbelievable shapes of contorted athleticism. It not only made him realise just how fit he was, but also raised the question in his mind of how the hell he was going to be able to meet his contact in Moscow later that evening. Things were definitely not going to plan and he began to wonder if it had been a wise decision to bring Carol with him on such a mission.

There was also another niggling question beginning to grow like a cancerous tumour in the darker recesses of his mind. It related to the meeting between himself and Dr Grachev in London at the hotel. Then, the lapse in his memory of just what had gone on earlier that particular evening he had put down to over tiredness. Now he felt distinctly uneasy. As before, he had a distinct feeling of euphoria, yet this time it was mixed with foreboding. Perhaps he was suffering from some debilitating illness which affected the senses. The most frightening thing was that he could not even remember how he had arrived back at the hotel. He began to wonder if he was beginning to lose his mind,

Stress, he knew, could do strange things to people, and as of late he had begun to ask himself too many questions about just where he was heading – something he had never done before. His laid back attitude to work and life in general was beginning to dissolve. He felt his whole character was changing, only it was not for the better. Not only that, but his false eye was also starting to give him a lot of pain. So much so that he had been compelled to take a couple of painkillers – something he rarely did.

It was whilst he stood in the bathroom sorting out the painkillers that Carol entered, feeling full of remorse.

"I'm sorry Stryker," she said, performing a complete volte-face. "I didn't mean what I said and know you have things to do and it was also silly of me to throw your razor and other things at you like that. I guess it's stress. But I think you'll understand when I show you this." It was a copy of the latest English broadsheet newspaper.

Stryker took it and stared hard at the front page in disbelief. Then without saying a word he held his finger up to his pursed lips, before dashing into the sitting room and lifting the magic pad before scribbling a quick message which was instantaneously rubbed out as soon as Carol had scanned it. Moments later they both pulled on their overcoats and hurried from the hotel out into the now almost deserted streets.

Here they could talk with complete candour without fear of being eavesdropped upon. It was Stryker who kicked off proceedings with a question.

"The restaurant in Villiers Street – the one you met Brenda in that lunchtime. Thinking back over the situation, can you now recall if you thought it was prudent to have spoken of such matters as you did or could someone have possibly overheard Brenda tell you about us being considered *persona non grata?*"

"Not unless the whole place had bugs built into the walls of the basement – that's where we went for privacy. If I had not considered it safe

I would as you suggest, have kept quiet about department work. Not even the waitress was around – she had gone upstairs when Brenda confided in me. There was just no way that anyone could have eavesdropped on our conversation. Oh and I remember there was some classical music playing in the background. Can't remember what it was though." Here Carol gave her inimitable rendition of softly pealing bells, her nervous laughter making Stryker realise just how vulnerable she must be feeling.

"OK. Now you say she told you she had nearly been caught taking a peek at the Dubai file."

"Well, yes Stryker, but the operative word there is nearly. It's just that the guard came and looked over at what she was doing. She didn't think he actually caught her doing anything. She said she had other files out on the table so I don't think Brenda was what you might call caught in the normal sense of the word."

"Right. And can you remember what Brenda told you on the telephone that final time you spoke to her?"

"Only that she would try to have another peek at the Dubai file."

"Nearly, but not quite. Do you remember you were on the telephone at our flat and so as to allow me to follow Brenda's part of the conversation you reiterated what she told you? To quote: 'You say you will definitely try to get another look at the Dubai file and this time even possibly see who signed the papers relating to Stryker and I being classified as *persona non grata*?' Then you added: 'Do please be careful Brenda. For your own sake.'"

"God Stryker, are you trying to impress me with that feat of eidetic memory? Anyhow, I must admit I am impressed. You got it verbatim. But how does that help solve anything?"

"It's what you just told me about that basement in the restaurant where you and Brenda met. You said you didn't think anyone could eavesdrop on you unless the whole place had bugs built into the walls."

"So!"

"So if anybody heard that piece of your conversation with Brenda that might explain what happened to her – sealed her fate."

"Are you telling me you really believe that basement was bugged?"

"Of course not. But what I do believe is that when we arrive back at Swiss Cottage and search our flat we should not be too surprised to discover a bug or two planted there."

"Oh Stryker!"

"Oh indeed. And if I was back in Seattle working as an ordinary detective I should get a fingerprint job done on Brenda's apartment as well as getting forensics involved."

"Well, there's no point in travelling along that path Stryker. Not if it has anything to do with the SIS anyway. They would get a dry-cleaning job done."

"Dry cleaning?"

"Yes. That's Secret Service slang for what they do to any accommodation or place where they require a thorough clean up. They're a meticulous lot. Fingerprints. DNA. They're gone in a flash. Well actually a few hours."

"Yeah, I can imagine."

CHAPTER 64

It was beginning to snow again as Anthony Lovejoy-Taylor left the secure confines of the British Embassy compound and made his circuitous way to the pre-arranged meeting in Gorky Park, eventually driving himself over the frozen Vodootvodnyj canal and turning right along the Bol. Jakimanka. The lengthy detour used anti-surveillance tactics best known to MI6, being employed to make certain he was not followed. It took him more than two hours. Even after parking the car he had taken an unlikely route on foot, doubling back on himself so as to make quite sure he had shaken off the inevitable FSB followers before finally making contact. The face of the man standing beneath the snow-clad weeping willow was only familiar from the passport photograph he had been supplied with at the British Embassy a few days earlier, except now he was sporting a stylish brown trilby hat. The man's partner was a young attractive woman. She looked glum.

"Aha! Mr Smith. We have to be quick you know. I did not realise you were bringing this delectable pretty young woman with you. I admire your taste."

"May I introduce you to Carol, my good luck charm? Carol, this is..."

Stryker chortled, smiling broadly as he displayed more than usual of his immaculate white teeth. It had not been such a hoot earlier that morning however, when upon learning of yet another of Stryker's assignations, Carol had hurled yet more insults, the indomitable detective come spy consoling himself that they were only verbal and not of the more tangible type, hazarding a guess they had been motivated more by fear of being left alone because of what had happened to her friend Brenda rather than by anything else.

"I'm known as the reprobate Anthony Lovejoy-Taylor," the Englishman said, putting out his hand in greeting. "Just call me Pogo, all my friends do." As he said this he surreptitiously handed Stryker a small sealed brown envelope. "I believe this is yours deah boy."

"Ah yes, thanks Pogo," Stryker answered, staring into Anthony Lovejoy-Taylor's eyes with a conspiratorial look, having never been let into the confidence of such an inane nickname before.

Stryker's false eye was playing up, feeling a little gritty, which he put down to the exceptionally cold weather, his irritability compounded by

Anthony Lovejoy-Taylor's rich, nasal, upper class accent.

"Well, we must push on. Goodbye."

"Goodbye old chums," replied the embassy spy, then just as Stryker was in the process of turning hard on his heels Anthony Lovejoy-Taylor's voice floated over his shoulder.

"Carol, I don't suppose you would like a solo guided tour around Moscow this evening – whilst your friend's tied up with that client, would you?" This final piece of news relating to yet another of Stryker's secret assignations proved the final straw. Carol had known their sojourn in Moscow would not last long, so this was just too much for her to bear.

Carol's response could not be ascertained by Anthony Lovejoy-Taylor, only what sounded like the beginnings of a hearty quarrel erupting from the couple as they disappeared into the snow laden gloom.

***

Settled once more back in their hotel, Stryker now knew it had been a mistake letting Carol tag along with him to rendezvous with his contact Anthony Lovejoy-Taylor. The idea was that the embassy official would supply detailed written instructions to enable Stryker to collect a bagful of secrets from outside Moscow. The details were in code, innocuous for anyone seeing the missive. Once the code had been deciphered by feeding it into Stryker's seemingly normal computer the instructions would become clear – then burnt. He had only acquiesced to Carol's request for her to be taken along with him when meeting Anthony Lovejoy-Taylor because of the unsettling effect the front page newspaper article had had on her. It was the harbinger of something that spelled bad news for both of them. It was the revelation that Carol's work colleague and friend Brenda had been discovered dead with a broken neck four floors below her flat balcony in Pimlico, just days after confiding in Carol that she would have another go at gaining access to the restricted file on Dubai with a view to discovering who actually gave the go ahead for classifying Stryker and herself to the Dubai British Embassy as *persona non grata*. Her body had been discovered sodden with alcohol. The obvious excuse that she had drunk too much and fallen to her death from her own balcony had been dismissed by Carol as pure fantasy, having been informed earlier by Brenda herself at the Vauxhall Cross Christmas party that she was teetotal. Therefore the news of her friend's death had shaken Carol to the core.

Stryker suspected Brenda's attempt to get another look at the Dubai file held in Registry at Vauxhall Cross had led to her death, and for that he blamed himself, bitterly resenting the fact that he had asked her to do it.

Spying and acting as nursemaid to Carol did not go together either. Drastic action had to be taken if he wanted to get her back to England safely and by the same token not put in jeopardy the security operation he was specifically here for. Within the last hour since their meeting with Anthony Lovejoy-Taylor his false eye had become much more painful. It had never affected him before but now, coupled with the possible ramifications of Carol's work colleague having more than likely been killed by the people she worked for, they both agreed they had to be extra vigilant.

***

It was an open secret known by certain people in the news media that Pimlico, only a stone's throw from Victoria station, was a designated area for safe houses used by members of the Secret Intelligence Service. Brenda had happened to occupy one of these flats and so discovering her body in suspicious circumstances in that particular area of London the press had had a field day. Worried that a 'D' notice would be promptly slapped on the case and thus stifling any comment by the news media, pre-emptive speculation had been rife. A blanket ban on the police and members of the intelligence community from speaking to the press had resulted in unnamed sources being quoted as factual evidence of skulduggery amongst the spying community and supplying a list of suspect countries as long as one's arm. There had even been swift newspaper speculation penned by one old seasoned cynical hack speculating that when it came time for a coroner to examine the case there would inevitably be a Public Interest Immunity Certificate issued precluding any substantive information relating to the case being put into the public domain.

It was these considerations that now prompted Stryker to remove his jacket from the bed and walk into the bathroom, leaving Carol to scour and scowl through the Moscow tour guide she had optimistically brought with her. After quietly securing the bathroom door and rifling through his pockets he came across two items he had been searching for. The first was a small gold lighter, bought for him by an old flame he had split up with a couple of years before.

The second item was a small packet of cigarette papers, the name Rizla emblazoned upon the flimsy cardboard box. Removing a Rollerball pen from inside his jacket pocket, he seated himself down upon the rim of the cast iron bath, extracted a wafer thin rectangular piece of paper from the Rizla dispenser and proceeded to write a cryptic message in neat but very small letters. After completing this tiny notification Stryker grasped both ends of the gold lighter and with a sharp tug pulled it apart, revealing a tiny space. Before replacing the two halves with a sharp snap the tightly folded message had been secreted within the lighter's inner cavity with just enough room to spare for the now exposed lighter's mechanism. Getting Carol to deliver this lighter to the British Embassy on the pretext that it was the property of Anthony Lovejoy-Taylor, had been accomplished with the promise that for the next two days Stryker would be all hers. Once she heard this news her mood lightened, confiding in him with a look of mysteriousness.

"I knew you wouldn't understand but I had been warned that something bad was about to happen to you. That's why I acted the way I did. Please forgive me."

Stryker looked at Carol in disbelief. "Who warned you? What's this all about?"

"A little bird told me – an omen. I know it sounds irrational but that's what happened."

"An omen? Are you serious? Are you telling me you have conversations with birds? Come on, you gotta be joking. Tell me you're joking."

"No Stryker, I'm not joking, though it is not quite the way you put it. Of course I don't speak to birds. What do you think I am – crazy?"

"Well, I must say you had me going there for a moment."

"The bird in question was one that landed on the windowsill just after you left the other evening, you know – for your assignation with that Russian friend of yours, Dr Grachev." Stryker put his finger tips to his lips. Caroline moved a little closer and scrawled something on the pad and then immediately wiped it clean.

Stryker looked intently at Carol. "You mean a bird landed on the windowsill and pecked at the window pane. And you think that is an omen that presages doom and disaster. Good God Carol, first you rearrange my bedroom resulting in my nearly breaking my neck and now you tell me about a little bird that was pecking at the window. Are you superstitious or what?" He let out a loud booming laugh, smiling broadly. "But nothing has happened to me. The only problem is that my eye is playing me up that's all. Anyhow, it's rather fortuitous for you. It means that for the next two days we'll be able to spend more time together before we head back to the UK."

"But what about this evening?"

"Don't worry about that. It's all taken care of. There's just one little thing I'd like you to do for me." Stryker held up the lighter he had just removed from his jacket pocket and gave a wry smile. Carol frowned, screwing up her face, to Stryker's mind, in a very attractive way.

CHAPTER 65

The dacha stood out against the clear frosty night sky, lit up by the intense brightness of the full moon. The line of the roof and outbuildings suggested that it had not been built in one go, but instead had metamorphosed like some ill-defined creature over many years, flanked on all sides by ragged hawthorn bushes and stunted trees, now devoid of foliage due to the harsh inclement weather.

Clambering up the steep wooded hillside, it had taken Anthony Lovejoy-Taylor an exhaustive half hour of intense effort to reach the perimeter of this lonely abode from the roadway far below, obscured by the dense pine forest covered in a soft blanket of snow. The only hint of any movement around this silent area was the brief intermittent flickering from vehicles' headlights spied through the occasional gaps in the trees he had left far behind him as he periodically halted, fighting to catch his breath in the freezing night time temperature and occasionally turning his head around to look back over his shoulder, mentally calculating the distance he had already travelled.

Breathing heavily, ghostly ectoplasmic-like shapes emanated from his mouth and nose as if his whole body were inhabited by an alien lifeform. He cursed the cold and the snow now making inroads into the top of his expensive boots and beginning to soak through the double layer of thick socks. His thin leather gloves fared no better, only serving to hold within them the dampness of the Arctic night. Under his breath he damned the man responsible for his present predicament. He had never met Smith, a.k.a. Stryker before during his two-year secondment to the British Embassy in Moscow, so never realised that Stryker might be capable of dropping him in the shit.

Once he had received the secreted message hidden inside Stryker's lighter, which read: '*POGO – CANNOT MAKE PARTY TONIGHT AS FEELING UNWEL. MIGHT PUT OPERATION IN JEAPORDY. APOLOGIES. S.*' Anthony Lovejoy-Taylor had been left with no option but to stand in for Stryker. Unfortunately he knew from his own experience that operations like this could so easily get out of control if they were not set up and prepared for meticulously. Everything was in the planning and that included the fall-back position. He was aware that Stryker, by bailing out so late in the day, could put him in a hazardous situation, knowing all along that even the information he had now come to collect was only a back-up and not virgin. He now felt like kicking himself. Why hadn't he ignored the gift of Stryker's lighter, taking it on face value as a friendly gesture instead of the receptacle of an unwelcome message, which it had turned out to be, being proffered to him by Stryker's girlfriend as an object having been mislaid earlier by himself? If Stryker didn't want to carry out this task, he should have said so earlier in the day, when he was in the process of parading his female acquisition in front of him in Gorky Park like some rare Dresden doll. He might even have been escorting Carol himself this evening, instead of which the roles had been completely reversed. If he was Moscow Head of Station things might have been a lot different but he was only his deputy dogsbody – all the shit dumped on himself. And if the Department knew what had happened – well... what real difference would that have made? Realistically – none! All these thoughts were tumbling through his mind at breakneck speed in complete antithesis to the progress he was now making up this damned obstacle-laden hill. And all the while his body felt as though it was losing its core temperature. He was so cold he found it hard to stop his teeth from sounding like Spanish castanets.

"Well, I'll get my revenge in the long run – you see if I don't," Anthony Lovejoy-Taylor mumbled softly to himself as he slowly inched his way through the trees to the perimeter of the clearing, where to his right the silhouette of a large wooden chicken hutch came into sharp focus. Peering up at the dacha he thought he detected a shadow pass one of the windows, but was not sure. With these situations in strange surroundings he knew the mind could play artful tricks.

Having been briefed on what was supposed to be Stryker's party the arrangement had been to wait for a signal in the form of light being briefly shone twice through one of the dacha's windows. The British agent should then reveal himself and wait until contact was made outside the dacha where the documentation would be handed over. That would be the most dangerous part of the whole operation for at that moment he would be as naked as the day he was born, with no protection whatsoever. If there were not two flashes of light, then after a short period of making sure the area was clear, the hidden papers could be retrieved from a pre-determined burial place within the garden. Anthony Lovejoy-Taylor had left the detail of the precise burial spot back at the embassy, having committed it to memory. The Russian agent he might or might not meet was someone who had been cultivated over a number of years by the British SIS, treating their Muscovite like a game of pass the parcel. Except this was not the usual contact zone and this Moscow man didn't even reside in the city. It was thought that by varying his British handler's routine, the less risk there was that this particular Russian informer would have his cover blown.

A muffled sound like a car backfiring coming from somewhere far off in the distance brought Lovejoy-Taylor's senses to a heightened fever pitch of awareness. He instinctively dropped his body down low into the deep snow, the cold pricking at his eyes, making them water as he opened them wider, desperately searching for any danger signals. Suddenly a bright light flickered briefly through one of the windows on the ground floor of the dacha and was then swallowed up by the blackness again. To his eyes it seemed like there was only one brief flash of light instead of two but he convinced himself that this was the signal he had been waiting for. Raising himself from his prostrate position he stood up and now brazenly walked out from the safety of the cover of the trees toward the dacha before coming to a halt in front of the six wooden snow-laden steps leading up to a creeper-strewn balustrade veranda. Standing stock still he slowly surveyed the scuffed indentation of footprints leading in the direction of the raised platform, and another deeper, heavier set of footprints, leading away in the direction of the chicken coop.

From where he was standing, Anthony Lovejoy-Taylor could not see the dark bulky outline of a figure clad in a padded windcheater, spread-eagled from the waist up lying across the wooden table within the large room overlooking the veranda. Nor did he see the small calibre pistol which the victim had not been able to bring into play quickly enough, it now lying on the dust-strewn floor at his feet.

The table was bare, save for a rubber torch with its plastic lens split down the middle lying in a growing pool of blood, and a bullet shattered vodka bottle. The missile which had caused the damage laid buried deep within the table top, fired from a gun fitted with a silencer, having first passed through the base of the victim's head. The muffled noise of the gun's silencer is what Anthony Lovejoy-Taylor had taken to be the dampened sound of a car backfiring. In its dying moments, the victim's hand with the partially missing index finger, had involuntarily clutched a shard of broken glass from the shattered vodka bottle, slicing open the soft skin of Ivan Sobolev's palm, and for a brief moment a fragment of this curved glass inadvertently caught a reflection of the full moon shining so brightly amongst the stars. This flash of reflected moonlight is what Anthony Lovejoy-Taylor mistakenly took for the pre-arranged glare of a torch beam signalling safety through the window. This flash occurred just seconds before another bullet from the direction of the chicken coop took Anthony Lovejoy-Taylor's head off, exploding in a fiery ball.

The assassin broke cover from inside the low wooden hut, slowly approaching the now prostrate body of Anthony Lovejoy-Taylor with a caution which appeared out of all proportion. As he bent low over the headless corpse, a hand on his shoulder spun him around, the rock hard fist crashing into his jaw and sending him flying through the air, landing in the snow, away from the body which was now furiously pumping blood from the neck.

"You fucking fool, you've just wasted an asset. We were supposed to interrogate him back at HQ before killing him. Now we're really in the shit. You can kiss your career goodbye." The light from the full moon cast long, deep shadows over the features of Konstantin, making him look like the ogre Pyotr had always believed him to be. Pyotr, a quizzical look upon his face, could already begin to taste the warm, salty tang of blood where his lip had been split by the ferocity of Konstantin's blow.

***

It was some time before the British Embassy learnt of the fate which had befallen Anthony Lovejoy-Taylor. When the news did come through, it was taken badly, especially by a floater named June who requested a transfer, which was granted immediately. Many others were also devastated at losing one of their more lively companions to an unfortunate road traffic accident as the assembled coterie of staff had been diplomatically informed by the ambassador.

After secret protracted negotiations with the Russian authorities, the body was eventually released to the British Embassy where it was placed in a coffin, one of a consignment recently sent over from the UK. British embassies around the world generally carry a small stock of coffins for emergencies with regard to British nationals. At that particular moment however, the stock had been running low, so it had proved coincidental that just prior to Anthony Lovejoy-Taylor's demise and only one day after June's disastrous sexual encounter with this Lothario, she had been the one to send a requisition to London through the diplomatic bag for a top-up.

The sealed remains of Anthony Lovejoy-Taylor were flown home by military plane to Brize Norton and handed over to his immediate family. He now rests in a small picturesque village graveyard deep within the English countryside, so familiar to him as a boy before eventually leaving home and selflessly doing his duty for Queen and country. The details of his death were never released, not even to his closest relatives. Only within the meticulously kept archives of MI6 are the facts laid bare and only then on the standard need-to-know basis.

Anthony Lovejoy-Taylor was posthumously awarded a medal for bravery which his aged father now carries deep within his breast pocket of whichever suit he happens to be wearing. Such are the diverse ways people cope with death. His wife survived her son by just over a year before succumbing to terminal cancer, brought on, some believe, by the stress of her grieving.

CHAPTER 66

"Comrade Colonel Oleynik, it would seem there is only one thing you can do... have him killed." There was a long, calculated silence so as to let the unexpected words sink in. "You understand just as well as I do that we are no longer in the ascendancy... politically speaking." Here he furled up his fingers to make a fist, bringing it down hard upon the desk top. "But cheer up, we still wield a lot of power."

General Kovalyev dropped his closely cropped head back onto the black leather swivel chair's headrest, his large bulky frame making it groan beneath the weight. As he stared from across the desk at Colonel Oleynik he toyed with a buff folder, turning it over and over in his powerful hands. Occasionally, as happened now, he would shun his visitor by spinning his back toward him and staring out of the fully glazed floor to ceiling window – down upon the Moscow traffic six floors below. His large well-furnished office was soundproofed against the strident noise of a city in full flow, making every pause in their conversation a significant contribution to what had gone before. A long silence followed, eventually broken by the now subservient tone struck by Colonel Oleynik.

"I was hoping you would say that. Yes, I have already formulated a plan. It was a stupid mistake, informing Doctor Grachev of my idea to foist Ivanovich Sobolev upon him." For Colonel Oleynik to admit to any mistake on his part was unheard of, but he did so in the hope of gaining sympathy from the general, entertaining the thought that the two of them might see eye to eye, and it appeared to be working.

"If that got around I might be thought of as a fool, trusting someone in the form of Ivanovich Sobolev, scientist and GRU officer with the Fifteenth Directorate who turns out to be a spy. My credibility would be destroyed." But Colonel Oleynik had his own secret agenda to follow. The real reason he could concur with the general on having Dr Grachev killed was that Dr Grachev's friendship with Stryker, a known British spy, would lend itself to making Dr Grachev a prime suspect for passing classified information regarding the Chinese connection on to Ivanovich Sobolev, thus making Dr Grachev the perfect scapegoat; whereas, in reality, Colonel Oleynik realised that the information passed to the west had been innocently given to Ivanovich by himself in unguarded conversations between the two of them.

It had never entered his thoughts for one moment that he could not trust Ivanovich. After all, had not Ivanovich's father, a lieutenant-colonel, been one of his closest friends until an unfortunate accident with fatal consequences befell him on an island being used to test an anthrax bomb resistant to antibiotics? The bomb had been constructed to one of Colonel Oleynik's own designs as it happens. It may well have been that the unfortunate accident had helped him draw closer to Ivanovich; perhaps a guilty conscience had led him to overcompensate for Ivanovich's father's death, the colonel becoming after that tragedy something of a confident to him. With no offspring of his own, it had felt good having an ally in the form of Ivanovich. If it now got out that he had confided to Ivanovich, that revelation would not only bring his career to an abrupt end and leave him in penury without a state pension, but would at the very least put him in prison for being the source of that information; at worst he might be viewed as a spy himself and shot as a traitor. He shuddered, breaking out into a cold sweat as the thought hit him.

The general turned his chair to face Colonel Oleynik once more. "Don't be too hard on yourself colonel, after all, you were not to know Ivan was spying for the British, were you?" General Kovalyev raised his thick, red, bushy eyebrows to emphasise the point. "But what do you make of this peasant coming forward, linking Doctor Grachev with the death of Vladimir Stalnov?" He now placed the folder on his desk in front of him. "A stroke of luck eh? The bastard deserves to die."

It was true. There was another long pause before General Kovalyev spoke again, this time with a hint of malice in his voice. "I'm sure your friends will do a good job on Doctor Grachev to avenge a fellow officer." The general swung his chair once more to face the window.

Colonel Oleynik savoured the point made. That was neat. He knew that the murder of Vladimir Stalnov, a fellow intelligence man, would indeed spur them on to do a tidy job. He may not have been from the GRU, but to all intents and purposes, he was still one of them. After all, what is sweeter than revenge? Growing bolder, Colonel Oleynik warmed to the theme.

"Well, as you are aware, Ivanovich Sobolev has already been presented with a little gift from one of my team... Pyotr to be precise... in self-defence I hasten to add. The bullet did not weigh much, nor did it require a large box with a bow of ribbon to fit into," here the colonel's face became wreathed in a broad grin, "but we'll require a large box now for this traitor to fill."

"And what about this Englishman Stryker? What about him?" The general's face was unsmiling.

"Unfortunately I happened to be on leave when my office found out what Ivanovich Sobolev was up to. Then a colleague discovered that a meeting had been arranged between Sobolev and Mr Stryker at the dacha – his aunt left it to him apparently. As you know we have one of our deep cover agents working within the British Embassy."

"Yes, been there for years. Still in their visa section I believe."

"That's right. Well, we had already been watching Mr Stryker because of his arranged meeting days earlier with Doctor Grachev."

"The evening when Vladimir Stalnov was killed?"

"Correct. And it was Vladimir Stalnov himself who had been responsible for watching Doctor Grachev. If Stalnov had not decided in his misplaced wisdom to stand our team of watchers down for that particular evening and presumably taken on the task himself for whatever reason, he would very likely still be alive now. And until that peasant turned up yesterday with his eyewitness account of Doctor Grachev disposing of our colleague's body it had been assumed, understandably, that the intrepid Mr Stryker – I use the word in a derogatory sense you understand – that our Englishman had been responsible for Stalnov's death. Then soon after, when we discovered that a meeting had been confirmed between Mr Stryker and Ivanovich Sobolev at the dacha the opportunity was too good to miss. We sought out revenge for Vladimir's death and we achieved it."

"Or so you thought."

"Yes, it's a pity the peasant couldn't have let us know earlier that it was Dr Grachev who killed Vladimir Stalnov, instead of us thinking it was Stryker. Stryker would not have been killed if we had known. Anyway, there you go, that's life."

"Or death!"

"Quite."

"And now you're off, I speak metaphorically of course, to settle matters once and for all."

"Well… obviously not myself."

"No, as I said, metaphorically you… but not you in reality of course, but a team, shall we say, seeking retribution?" The general still had his back toward him and it began to irritate.

Colonel Oleynik knew that what he had just told the general was not the truth about the death of Stryker. There was no revenge. It had been a balls up as so often happened, and then history had to be changed to suit the event. A common enough occurrence in the old Soviet Union. But it had a certain credibility; enough anyway to get him and his team off the hook. In reality, if Pyotr had not acted so hastily they might have been able to extract a lot of interesting information from the Englishman. But that was now all in the past, and he was hoping that his assassination team would be successful in putting an end to the whole affair.

"You know that Dr Grachev is already in London? One step ahead of us I'm afraid." The colonel failed to mention that it was he himself who had only recently given Dr Grachev the documentation, including an exit visa, for him to visit London. "But our people from the London Embassy will have him under twenty-four hour surveillance until I get my team out there."

"But surely the Foreign Intelligence Service should handle this," General Kovalyev remarked frostily.

"It's true that the SVR would normally deal with these cases, but we know the background to all of this, we're in deep... let us finish the business ourselves. After all, as you say, we still wield a lot of power and times are changing. Everything is in a state of flux. And we didn't find anything in or around the dacha at the time Ivanovich was killed, It must have been verbal information... we turned the place over, including the garden – nothing was discovered. From that point of view I'd say it was a GRU matter – internal. I think we should keep it in the family."

"Yes, state of flux," the general repeated, looking thoughtful, as though his mind was on other things.

"Who are you sending?"

Colonel Oleynik felt intimidated having to talk to General Kovalyev's back. As if reading his thoughts, the general spun his chair around to face him, with an intent look upon his gnarled features.

"Three fellow GRU officers," Colonel Oleynik replied. "You may know of them, Comrade Konstantin and Comrade Pyotr – the very same agent who killed Ivanovich in self-defence. Oh! And Comrade Yevgeny Kotov." As luck would have it, all three spoke a smattering of English, however stilted, to smooth their way if the occasion arose.

"Ah! Am I thinking of the same Yevgeny. Eighty-nine – Afghanistan?"

"That's the one. Specialist in unarmed combat."

"Ah yes, I know of him. A good man. Fast with his hands."

"That's why I thought he should be part of the team. We don't want to cause a furore over in England do we? Bullets will be avoided if at all possible."

"Good... good." General Kovalyev turned to the window again. He did not care if it seemed ignorant to turn his back on people. It was a technique learnt years before. By concentrating upon the voice, to the exclusion of all else, one might learn a lot more than from a normal civil conversation. He could tell, for instance, if a person was lying.

"Of course, the information that found its way to the West through Ivan – it might not necessarily have been Dr Grachev who gave it to him. We have to bear that in mind Colonel Oleynik."

"Yes, as you say, we have to bear that in mind." Oleynik froze, his brain becoming sluggish as he wondered if General Kovalyev suspected.

"Well, I'd better be going. Must brief Konstantin and the others as soon as possible. Want to get them to London quickly. Documentation to prepare, that sort of thing." As Colonel Oleynik rose to leave, General Kovalyev positioned his chair once more so as to face him with a view to posing yet another question, but it was obvious he already knew the answer.

"Ivanovich Sobolev… he was an acquaintance of yours wasn't he?" The general's face now had a stern look about it.

"What? Oh yes, an acquaintance. Saw him occasionally at ministry meetings. Apparently tried to pull a gun on Yevgeny. Yevgeny shot him dead in self-defence unfortunately."

"Yes, so you said… self-defence. But why do you use the word unfortunately? Are you saying that out of friendship for the man?"

"Of course not. I meant that now he has been killed we are not able to interrogate him."

"Quite. Keep me informed won't you?" General Kovalyev turned once more to stare out of the window, keeping his thoughts to himself, while idly following with his weary eyes the slow stream of traffic in the congested road far below. Then, as if as an afterthought, he reached for a remote control handset from behind his desk.

Immediately a full bodied sound flowed through two concealed speakers, flooding the room with music. It was a piece from Tchaikovsky's Sleeping Beauty suite by Rostropovich and thus signalling the end of a meeting that Colonel Oleynik had been dreading all morning.

Nodding stiffly toward the back of General Kovalyev's chair, the colonel finally left the imposing building far behind him, as he too joined in the long line of traffic in the early afternoon sunshine, chauffeured by his regular driver, wishing that Dr Grachev was already dead.

CHAPTER 67

It was three days after Anthony Lovejoy-Taylor had been shot that Smith, a.k.a. Stryker, was buttonholed inside Sheremetyevo II airport at the very moment when Carol had become distracted nearby, browsing through some Russian fashion magazine.

He was a tall, smart-looking young man in a well-cut black suit with a large white handkerchief peeping from the top of his breast pocket. Stryker did not recognise him and was keen to get on the flight out of Moscow as soon as possible, explaining that he was in a hurry to catch the plane and that time was not on his side.

However, the man in the dark suit with a very English upper-class accent persisted, not about to be put off that easily, whispering something into Stryker's ear before he could escape. Stryker froze, his features fixed in an expression of shock and surprise. It was then that the announcement came over the public address system in English, incorporating within it a thick Russian accent: *"Would all passengers for British Airways flight BA Eight Three Seven to Heathrow please go to gate four as the plane is now ready for boarding."*

This announcement had already been broadcast in Russian. The harbinger of bad news clasped Stryker's arm tightly, whispering a few more carefully chosen words close to his ear, before proffering something with his other hand after first conspicuously polishing the hidden object meticulously with a white handkerchief, the handkerchief he had deftly whisked from out of his top breast pocket as a magician might before performing some sleight of hand trick. Stryker, not accustomed to being accosted like this, knocked his assailant's arm away sharply, but not quickly enough to avoid the proffered object being pressed into his hand.

When it suddenly dawned upon Stryker just what it was the dapper English man had palmed off onto him, his grip upon it grew momentarily stronger until his knuckles became white with the effort. Then, moving to the nearest rubbish bin within the concourse he opened his fingers, letting gravity take the object swiftly down in a straight trajectory to join the empty Coke cans, fast food wrappings and other detritus to be found in all the airports around the world. Except this was not rubbish, but a keepsake which had symbolised the last vestiges of his smoking. The neat gold lighter, now devoid of its cryptic message which had sent Pogo to his death, looked out of place nestling by the side of a half-eaten sandwich.

A minute or so later, even as the tall young man from the British Embassy was still making his way out from the confines of the airport, the trophy had been recovered by a plainclothes officer and within the hour was undergoing fingerprint tests at the FSB's Third Main Directorate offices situated in the centre of Moscow.

Meanwhile, Stryker had joined Carol as they finally headed toward their designated departure gate, guiding her by the elbow through very familiar surroundings. Carol did not notice the small tear trapped within the corner of Stryker's one good eye, nor the look of remorse writ large upon his face.

An SVR man stood transfixed, staring after the couple just long enough to see them disappear through the boarding gate to catch their plane back to England. He had also watched his unsuspecting FSB counterpart retrieving the lighter so hastily discarded only moments earlier. The watchers were watching the watchers.

If Stryker had not become so distracted by the news of Pogo's death, he might have been aware of three gentlemen who were also boarding the same flight and who, as chance would have it, happened to be given seats immediately behind Carol and himself.

The first gentleman was a rather tall-looking middle-aged man, dressed in a badly cut dark suit with a fixed stony expression upon his face. He carried a small black briefcase which was carefully tucked beneath his seat immediately in front of him before settling back for the three and a half hour journey. Sitting next to him was the second gentleman, who proceeded to read the in-flight magazine from cover to cover, studiously ignoring his colleagues. The third member of this group was of rather short stature with a blank look upon his face and bearing a faint trace of dribble upon his long chin. All through the flight not one word was spoken between the three of them except in relation to the proffered plastic airline food which they all accepted with good grace and ate with ravenous appreciation.

Stryker on the other hand, declined his sustenance, the black dog shutting out all communication between himself and Carol, and as hard as she tried, she could not break through his sullenness. To her it was a complete mystery why Stryker's mood had changed so suddenly, having thought that their final few days together in Moscow had turned out to be the most wonderful holiday she could possibly have imagined. Finally, letting her head settle into the awkward position that airline seats dictate, Carol closed her eyes, attempting to rid her mind of all the negative thoughts that she was now surrounded by, and drifted off into a light sleep.

CHAPTER 68

Meanwhile, in the centre of Moscow within the Yasenevo building, Stryker's file had once more been brought to the screen virtually instantaneously, and was now being amended at the bottom with the words in capital letters: 'DECEASED – FILE CLOSED.' It would take another day before the fingerprints lifted from a gold lighter retrieved from the litter bin at Sheremetyevo II airport, disclosed the revelation that Stryker had not in fact had his head blown apart. It had been General Kovalyev himself who guessed – wrongly as it turned out – that Stryker had been the victim of the shooting when reviewing the tapes from Dr Grachev's bugged telephone conversation with him. When eventually the truth came out, there would be two questions posed for the Third Chief Directorate, military counter-intelligence. The first one was, put simply, just who had been killed at the dacha? The second question, and in many respects of far more importance, how could it be covered up? By the time Stryker's file had been resurrected he was safely on his way back in London.

There were also humorous moments for the FSB men working on the Dr Grachev case. These agents of the state worked for the Twelfth Department specialising in eavesdropping. This levity was brought about by listening to a tape originating from Dr Grachev's bugged flat. It had been made on the night Dr Grachev had entertained the British spy Stryker, offering him a glass of whisky before extolling the virtues of sleep and explaining how wonderfully relaxed he would be upon waking. The consensus of opinion, to howls of laughter, was that Dr Grachev must be a closet faggot. This tape was taken out and played quite a few times that first day it came into their hands, becoming something of a diversion from the usual round of more mundane conversations gleaned through their planted listening devices.

CHAPTER 69

As Dr Grachev sat in the cafeteria staring through the giant plate-glass window watching depressing wave after wave of torrential rain sweep over the tarmac, and the occasional plane rise up and disappear into the low cloud hanging over London, he thought about his future. Keeping one eye on the trolley carrying his luggage, he absentmindedly ripped open a sachet of brown sugar, tipped it into the white froth which passed as coffee and mechanically stirred it using a small plastic stick, unwittingly creating a burnt umber tone matching that of the dull monochromatic sky outside.

The doctor was feeling tired after the journey. The flight had not been improved by the plane having been buffeted by severe turbulence initiating an infectious wave of nauseousness amongst the travellers, many passengers having recourse to the sturdy brown paper bags held fast to the back of the aircraft seats by elasticated ribbon for just such an emergency. Although clocking up many thousands of air miles, Dr Grachev had never witnessed anything quite like it before. For most of the journey, his fleeting glances through the aircraft window were met by a dirty grey mist from the other side. The one consolation was that he himself had managed to avoid being sick, though his stomach felt distinctly queasy.

Continuing to stir his coffee he thought about the telephone kiosk conversation he had just concluded immediately on touchdown at Heathrow with the stand-in for his contact Smith. The news had lifted his spirits, having been informed that the situation looked optimistic regarding his acceptance as a candidate for political asylum. However, being back in London gave him no peace of mind, every day bringing with it a fear of being arrested at the behest of the Russian Embassy, or even more frighteningly, receiving a bullet to the back of the head from an unknown and therefore unseen SVR Russian Foreign Intelligence agent.

He knew killing the jeweller in Moscow could not possibly have any repercussions for him, as the likely outcome of an investigation into this particular death would be put down to natural causes. He was certain of that, because the toxin used to treat the cigarette had been developed by himself for use by the KGB whilst carrying out work for the Third Main Directorate, which laughingly came under the jurisdiction of the Ministry of Health.

The FSB man's death however, posed quite a different problem; that was of course supposing that his body had been found by now. Having had

254

time to consider the situation in a calm manner he now felt sure that this murder would be linked to him, not only by circumstantial evidence, but more certainly by forensic evidence. Working closely, if only sporadically, with these KGB specialists over the years, and also from his intimate knowledge as a doctor, he knew very well what clever techniques were at the disposal of such forensic experts. That is why time now became all consuming. He had to set up a meeting with the British Secret Intelligence Service just as soon as possible so as to demonstrate to them how valuable and indispensable he would be; not only now, but in the future. But he also felt his time was running out fast. He was also mindful of keeping to the usual routine as far as possible regarding his attendance at the symposium's meetings, which had ostensibly been the reason for him coming to London in the first place.

After having manoeuvred his suitcase onto the underground tube station at Heathrow, and whilst sitting patiently waiting for the train that would whisk him back into the heart of London, he began turning over in his mind the letter he had just posted to Smith, hoping to ensure that his acceptance by the authorities as a bona fide asylum seeker would be no more than a formality. With the letter he also enclosed the lapel pin given him so many years ago by his father.

"*Yes,*" Dr Grachev mumbled to himself, as he dragged his case between the rubber door seals into the carriage. The pin bore the red enamelled flag of the old Soviet Union, and in one corner a small gold hammer and sickle design. For a symbol of domination and suffering I shall gain in exchange an infinitely more valuable commodity: my freedom.

CHAPTER 70

Captain Zhizhin had been wondering for the past few weeks when he would receive the paperwork back from the factory and finally here it was at last. If there was one thing he prided himself on it was keeping his paperwork up to date. He loved systems. Rules and regulations to him were everything.

Once he had notified the hospital through its directorate that a subversive had been allocated to them, things were taken out of his hands and everything then became a mere formality, like signing the form which now sat on his desk staring back at him. As his large hand reached out for a cheap ballpoint pen sitting amongst another half dozen within a small clay pot made at school by his six-year-old daughter, he thought of her forthcoming birthday organised by his wife for a little later that day. The arrangement to take the afternoon off for the sake of his only child and to the delight of his wife had been made several weeks earlier, confirming the impression that here was a family man who took his responsibilities seriously. Although he was a man of large stature, he possessed the patience of a saint as far as his daughter was concerned and could tolerate all sorts of misadventures, indulging her in the most spoilt manner.

After signing the official-looking document with a flourish, a satisfied expression settled upon his face as he went to a filing cabinet standing to one side of his dusty office window. Slamming the metal drawer with a bang he proceeded to lock it using one of the keys attached to his key fob. Then, removing an oversized raincoat from a hook screwed to the door he walked swiftly outside, gliding down the corridor and stairs to reception with a deftness which belied his heavy bulk.

Once outside, he pulled his collar up to prevent the rain from getting at his freshly laundered shirt and made a quick sprint to the government supplied car parked in a side street nearby. He glowered as he thought of the empty promises of a car parking area for the staff – promises made for as long as he could ever remember, but he was still waiting. Now it was too late. How times change, he mused. One minute everything is rush – rush – rush. Now… Now nothing meant anything anymore. The whole fucking set-up to be dismantled, a few more weeks, possibly, but then – nothing.

Like the rest of the Soviet Union, everything was falling apart, or had already done so. Even his own methodical way of doing things had come unstuck at the seams. Like this piece of paper he had just signed and filed away. It had been initiated by him weeks before, the same day that the urgent request came from Moscow – a round robin to the factory – the hospital – to him. Its orders were to begin closing everything down immediately. He remembered the precise time; it was midday. A mug of black coffee had been set before him just like any other day, except it was not like any other day. He had been in the very act of lifting a pen to sign a warrant for the detention and removal to the hospital of yet another subversive and had been placed in a quandary. For the first time in his career there seemed an impossible conflict to be resolved. Should he ignore the Government edict and finish the job already begun? Or, should he take the order literally and cease everything he was doing from that very moment. Like the good soldier he had always obeyed orders without exception – but this was different. Perhaps, he now reflected, if time had not been so pressing. If Konstantin had not insisted that a report on Ivan be completed and sent to him in Moscow that very day. Well, his decision might have been different. But as things stood, time was of the essence. Therefore he had indeed made a snap decision. Pushing his large right hand into the trouser pocket, his fingers fumbled around until he found what he had been searching for.

The dark stained coin bore on one side a hammer and sickle, and on the obverse, a side profile depicting Joseph Vissarionovich Dzhugashvili's head in relief, Stalin's pseudonym adopted during the Russian Revolution. The coin lay in the palm of his hand. He would let fate make the final serious decision of his career, under the aegis of what had until recently been the KGB, and on behalf of the State. If upon landing, Stalin's head appeared, then the bloody deed would be executed to the letter as it always had been on his watch. But if the hammer and sickle should take precedence, then the paper about to be initiated against his final victim would end up as so much confetti in his wastepaper bin, just as if these very symbolic implements representative of industry and agriculture had themselves destroyed the document, and the person would be free to live out the rest of their natural life span within the New Order; though what that New Order held in store for its citizens, only God knew. As Captain Zhizhin thought of these words he crossed himself being, as he was, a very devout man.

With one flick of his fingers the coin was sent spinning. It appeared to hang in the stale office air for eternity with Stalin's eye seemingly winking in the dull glint of sunlight before dropping rapidly and spelling out the fate of a subject residing barely a mile from where the captain now stood, unaware of this game of chance being played out in such a casual manner of which the old dictator himself must already have known the outcome. There was a heavy thud as the coin landed upon the papers scattered about the desk, before rolling and catching its edge on his daughter's childish efforts in the shape of the clay pot holder, flipping itself over at the very last moment and lodging under the form he had been about to sign. Taking a sip from his coffee mug he curled a large finger beneath one corner of the flimsy piece of paper before gingerly raising it to reveal a sombre-looking Stalin.

Even in death the tyrant was poised to take yet one more of his victims, not satisfied with the tens of millions he had already dispatched to their maker during the mass purges of the Great Terror. Captain Zhizhin paused to stare into space and dwelt on this irony for a moment, before quickly appending his initials to the document, feeling absolved and distanced from the final act of cruelty and hoping to catch the midday post, a figure of speech really as the *midday* post always left his particular office at twelve-thirty precisely His conscience was clear. Now, for this unwitting victim, the only thing that had landed metaphorically in the wastepaper bin was the legal concept of *parens patriae*, the protection of the state.

Climbing into his car for the short distance to the hospital, Captain Zhizhin dwelt upon how that heavy coin had flipped itself over. Of course, he understood there always had to be a final casualty in any war. He wondered though if this particular victim was the instrument of fate, or if his young daughter's attempt at pottery had influenced the outcome; the clumsy small hands of a child full of innocence. Then the question begged itself; was it innocence or ignorance? And if it was innocence, where did that innocence come from, and how is it so slowly ground away that one day without realisation it has disappeared? The change as subtle as moving from boyhood to manhood; that subtle, he told himself.

CHAPTER 71

The house Konstantin and his colleagues had taken over for the duration of their mission in England was situated in a leafy suburb of North London. It had been arranged by the Russian Embassy through a Russian émigré who owned several properties in that neck of the woods. The émigré's only stricture placed upon the agents staying there was that, at all costs, a low profile must be maintained.

This strict proviso was insisted upon because she had been a member of the Soviet intelligence service and put in place by the KGB some twenty years before as a sleeper, and to all intents and purposes, a law abiding citizen of the United Kingdom. In reality she was what is known in MI6 parlance as an illegal, working under an assumed identity arranged by the KGB and a fully paid up member of the Communist Party, a lifelong supporter who had remained ready to be called upon by her mother country to do its bidding. With the passing years she had become pretty much anglicised, and with a change of name coupled with a now very English accent, she could have passed muster as the genuine article anytime. After this long period she was not about to let her cover be put in jeopardy by a bunch of transient agents.

To help things run smoothly for the three undercover agents and with a view to expanding on the low profile format, their hostess had left them a list of do's and don'ts. Topping this list was the stricture: "Don't do anything to annoy the neighbours."

As luck would have it, this particular property had become vacant only a few weeks previously, the former tenants hailing from Australia and having now returned home to Sydney. It being detached and secluded, with tall evergreen trees shielding the front and back garden from prying eyes, the large red brick house was the ideal location for the Chekisty, as former KGB officers liked to refer to themselves. This was an allusion to the first Soviet intelligence organisation, the Cheka, set up in 1917 at the time of the Russian revolution.

Besides this property, the one other necessity which had also been supplied by the Russian Embassy was a small van taken from their closely guarded motor pool. This was no ordinary van but had been adapted by their security team for keeping a twenty-four hour watch on the Normanhurst hotel where Dr Grachev was staying. This was so as not to draw attention to them over a protracted period of time. Dr Grachev's movements could now be carefully monitored until a plan had been formulated on just when and where Yevgeny might deal with his quarry. It had also been decided that to be able to sustain a round the clock cover, each of the three Russian agents would do an eight hour stint. Konstantin, being the team leader, would begin the day shift starting at eight in the morning and ending at four in the afternoon. Yevgeny had been given the next shift from four until midnight and Pyotr would work the graveyard shift. It seemed to Pyotr that once again he had drawn the short straw, or rather, been handed it by Konstantin.

After Pyotr's very first stint from midnight through to eight the next morning, he was only too happy to be replaced by his boss Konstantin. Nothing had been seen of Dr Grachev through the wee small hours; he would most likely have been tucked up in the luxury of his hotel bedroom during the night while Pyotr had been freezing his balls off. If, before the job started, he had not harboured any particularly strong feelings either way about Dr Grachev – ignoring the fact of course that an FSB man had been killed by him – all that had now changed over the last eight hours. It had been a cold night sitting in the cramped van, with only thin metal walls of the specially converted vehicle between him and the inclement weather outside, the temperature having dropped to almost zero. He was therefore very relieved at the end of his shift to be able to return to his own comfortable, if only temporary bedroom, where he fell upon the bed fully clothed and tried to sleep.

Unfortunately, in contrast to the fact that while in the van at around 2 a.m. he had been fighting a hard battle to keep his eyelids from automatically sticking themselves together, as if they had a mind of their own; now, as his head lay upon the soft down pillow which had occupied his thoughts incessantly throughout the night, it was in vain. For as he lay there, not having had time to adjust to the night shift, his body rebelled against any suggestion of sleep he might try to inculcate within his mind. Then he began thinking about a conversation he had held with Konstantin. It was really more of a lecture crouched in the form of a threat. Or was it a threat couched in terms of a lecture? Whatever. The gist of it revolved around his shooting of Ivanovich Sobolev. Konstantin's words to him, relayed in soft tones of friendship, had magnified the message a thousand fold, making his hair stand on end. He recalled verbatim the stinging sentences.

"Times are changing at a rapid pace in this country of ours, fortunately for you. Until recently I would not have hesitated to send you to a hospital like the one attached to Experimental Sector 205 – you know – the one we visited recently. Yes my friend, they would have worked on you in one of the operating theatres, in the interests of science, you understand, until there would have been nothing left but your bones to dissect. As I say, lucky for you that on the surface at least, times are changing and the powers that be are going soft."

Even if Pyotr had succeeded in dropping off however, it would not have lasted long. For as he lay there a loud banging interrupted his grisly train of thought, the sound coming from the room next door. This particular room happened to be the one that Yevgeny had been allocated. Wearily, Pyotr rolled off the bed in one smooth movement and slipped into his shoes with the intention of telling his neighbour to cut the racket, then at the last moment he changed his mind, instead climbing back into the bed and holding a pillow over his head to stifle the sound.

Initially the loud grunting and groaning accompanied by rapid banging emanating from Yevgeny's bedroom had been put down to some kind of ritualistic self-debasement, and though the pillow failed to do the trick, Pyotr still shied away from his intention of intervening, attempting to ignore the noise and trying to keep his mind occupied by getting some refreshment and retiring back into his own room. But after a while he could stand the rumpus no longer, banged on Yevgeny's door and strode in.

There before him stood the short stocky GRU agent in his vest and baggy pants, the perpetual dribble upon his chin, beating the hell out of a rolled up carpet, strategically placed against one wall and propped up by the end of his bed. Head, fists, knees and feet flailed the carpet as though it were a mortal enemy, the makeshift dojo reverberating with a staccato sound as he worked himself up into a frenzy. When he realised that he was being observed, he stopped what he was doing and reverted to his usual placid self, portraying a mildness of manner in stark contrast to his previous demonic efforts as he enquired as to how Pyotr's shift had gone. Pyotr was astonished by the almost instantaneous transformation. As Yevgeny stood there sweating and breathing heavily from his exertions, the lightness of mood between them was palpable for the simple reason that Konstantin was doing his stint, thus taking the ogre away from the house and off their backs for a few more precious hours.

CHAPTER 72

The guard manning the gate gave a smart salute and snapped to attention as it was opened by one of his colleagues, whose blanket like overcoat soaked up the rain like a sponge, torrents of water pouring from his peaked hat as if from a tap. A dog's long snout poked out from its kennel, too lazy or too dry to get wet in the torrential downpour. The steel links of its chain were visible, being attached to a diagonally running line stretched from its cramped shelter to the guard's hut.

On the threshold of the building, Captain Zhizhin removed his wet outer garment, shaking it furiously before handing it in at the cloakroom to a young girl in her late teens sporting an unusually fresh complexion. She draped the coat carefully onto a hanger bearing a small metal tag with a number etched onto it.

"Comrade Captain Zhizhin. You have not been here for some time have you?"

"No indeed. Where is Maria Schedrin?" The woman he enquired of was a good friend whom he had known since his first visit to the hospital over ten years before. When his wife or daughter had any ailments, the first person he would come to was Maria. Originally from Moscow, she was always his initial contact at the hospital and had a ready access to drugs outsiders were unable to obtain.

As he stood there watching his limp raincoat being hung up whilst still shedding rivulets of water down along the seams of its sleeves, Captain Zhizhin questioned his motives for breaking his journey home to visit perhaps the last sacrificial offering in the interest of science and humanity. He knew that once experiments on these people had begun there would be – could be – no turning back – no going home. It could not be, for how would the authorities possibly explain the hideous scars and missing limbs, removed for all manner of experiments from their originally healthy bodies? How could anyone possibly explain the inexplicable; the strange rashes which would appear periodically without any warning or obvious reason, or the mental anguish and odd behaviour more reminiscent of inmates from a lunatic asylum?

Nor would the 'normal' outside population have been able to accept the constant screaming brought on by terrifying nightmares, whether in their waking state, or those lucky enough to be allowed to sleep, though fitfully. And all this was supposing that what they harboured within their bodies was not contagious, a supposition which would have been totally erroneous. Why otherwise would doctors and surgeons who worked upon these poor wretches, dress in clothing resembling spacesuits? The answer was of course, to reduce any risk to themselves of catching the hideously debilitating diseases introduced to and harvested within their bodies by doctors, who at the beginning of their medical careers had sworn *Clyatva Geppocrata* – the Russian version of the Hippocratic Oath.

No, once you had been received into this particular institution you would never leave, only as so much ash, incinerated at an unimaginably high temperature in the hope of destroying toxins whose mutations were manufactured at the factory for use against the presently perceived enemy of the time.

It was as these depressing thoughts wormed themselves deep into Captain Zhizhin's mind that a willowy woman of about forty appeared, dressed in a white tunic. Her blonde hair was in the process of attempting to escape from beneath a tiny white starched hat perched precariously toward the back of her head, held in position by two light brown hair clips. Although the rules forbade lipstick being worn, a faint trace had been wiped across her full lips adding much needed colour to her pale complexion, common throughout the indigenous population. She resembled one of the euphemistically termed 'patients' who had just been through the practice sometimes carried out on them whilst still alive, that of exsanguination.

"You look deep in thought Comrade Captain. And where are we going today?" Captain Zhizhin's mind had switched to his wife and daughter who would at that very moment be waiting expectantly for him at home.

"Ah Maria, I should like to have a quick peep at my latest catch, just for a few moments. It's my daughter's birthday. I promised to be there." Doubts now began to creep into his voice as he realised that it might have been a mistake coming here. What had been his motive – to do penance? He was not sure of anything anymore.

CHAPTER 73

Pyotr usually found Yevgeny hard to talk to, never managing to elicit much of a response to his own attempts at conversation. But this particular morning Yevgeny seemed to be fired up, and if not quite garrulous, at least amenable to a little verbal communication. Pyotr knew that the success of this mission hinged upon Yevgeny's skills as a trained killer, and supposed that this was his way of preparing himself, both mentally and physically.

"Ever see any real action, Pot?" Yevgeny for some reason insisted on using his own pet name for Pyotr, but Pyotr understandably made allowances.

"How do you mean?"

"Kill lots of people?" Yevgeny was short on long sentences.

"Just that one out at the dacha," Pyotr responded, a little indignant that such a question should be put to him. He liked to think his usual method of dealing with situations was by using his higher mental powers as opposed to firepower. He was also suffering dreadful nightmares after the episode and so in some respects, in the short term at least, it made it easier for him when he did not sleep.

"I have – many, many people." There was a long silence while he reinstated the carpet in its rightful place and adjusted the bedclothes.

***

It was some time later, as Pyotr sat nursing his second cup of black tea in the lounge, that he heard the front room door bang and there was Yevgeny standing before him, beaming broadly and clutching a scrawny black and white cat by the nape of its neck. Kneeling down, he gingerly placed the small animal on the floor and stroked its head around its ears. The cat nuzzled up against Yevgeny's knee, arching its back in friendliness.

"Look," Yevgeny half whispered in Pyotr's direction. As Pyotr lazily gazed over the brim of his tea cup pressed firmly to his lips, he saw through his now tired eyes Yevgeny's hand, fingers slightly splayed in a vertical position poised two inches above the silky arched back.

Pyotr told friends later when back in Moscow that his eyes never

264

detected one slight movement of that hand. But as if like magic, the cat collapsed into a heap. He blinked his eyelids, not being able to believe what he had witnessed. The move had been executed so fast, like watching a performance by a master card sharp, or a concert pianist's fingers trilling the ivory keys in a pink blur. Except that there was no blurred movement of Yevgeny's karate chop. Pyotr had not seen the thick, muscular hand move. Later he discovered the cat's back had been cleanly broken, urged upon Yevgeny's insistence to feel both ends of the backbone beneath the soft fur. A neighbour put up posters on many trees around the area, but never did discover the fate of his cute pet cat.

With regard to the list of do's and don'ts which had been left by their landlady so as to ease themselves into the situation – that disappeared the same night as the cat.

CHAPTER 74

Maybe it was the perceived hypocrisy of the clean snow white sheets upon which her body lay, naked as the day she had been born, the vulnerability of such a young girl being worked upon by not one surgeon, not two surgeons, but three; three large men in space suits dealing with one very small creature. She lay silent, except for her neck, nervously straining it to see the sharp bladed instruments and forceps being prepared – and following the long pointed needle with her eyes. The needle designed to deaden any pain she might otherwise feel as her body was taken apart, piece by piece, until there was nothing left to dissect. Or it could have been the sight of her left hand clutching at something with all the remaining strength she possessed. It might even have been the fact that now Captain Zhizhin's own work was coming to an end, the scales were dropping from his eyes, letting him see afresh just what he had consigned so many people to over the years.

Tiny white fingers gripped the treasured possession within her smooth palm until a sensation of pins and needles overwhelmed the slender arm and wrist, making it impossible for her to hang onto the object any longer. Now everything slowed down, the sudden spasm of her body, the painfully thin back supporting half developed breasts, arching upwards, her fragile-looking spine forming the acute angle of a bridge before dropping back stiffly, revealing the exaggerated extent of her slightly bloated stomach, The colourful object rolling out of her grasp and falling onto the sheets, reminded him so much of his own daughter, then it hit the hard, bright, shiny floor before splitting into many pieces and scattering beneath the hospital bed. Except for one small image, about the size of a fingernail carved in the shape of a brightly painted doll with a yellow and blue babushka; the headscarf of the type worn by Marishka the day she lay down with Ivan beneath the tall pine trees, unsuspectingly watched over by her little brother.

One of the surgeons removed a protective glove before stroking her forehead, the long, lustrous jet black hair having been shaved off in preparation for the first of perhaps many operations, her now bald head shining beneath the excessively bright overhead bank of lights. The anaesthetic had not yet taken hold and perspiration brought on by fear glistened on her forehead, sparkling like diamonds. The surgeon who was about to participate in the desecration of this young woman's body looked into her eyes so as to detect signs of drowsiness before removing a tissue and with the humane action of someone full of compassion and contradiction, gently wiped her brow. Captain Zhizhin also looked into her eyes and saw within them terror and fear, but also an aura of beauty that transcended this place of incarceration.

CHAPTER 75

Tom drove around Trafalgar Square with a heavy heart. Under normal circumstances he would have viewed it as a break from the routine of Porton Down, however because of Professor Lambton's plans regarding his imminent retirement, Tom had recently been handed more of his bosses chores and responsibilities, and one of these was to attend a bi-monthly discussion group in Whitehall on Professor Lambton's behalf. It was mostly run-of-the-mill stuff and Tom would have no difficulty in giving his little spiel, this particular talk updating the eminent group regarding future directions relating specifically to biological Research and Development. Tom's mind right now though was not on such lofty matters as national security, but on his missing bride to be. Since the disappearance of Li Cheung the week before, Tom had kept in touch on a daily basis with the eye hospital where she worked as a laboratory technician, but they had not had any contact with her either.

As he was about to leave Trafalgar Square and turn into Whitehall, slowly moving through the morning traffic, a sports car coming from behind cut him up as it roared past. It took a few seconds for it to sink into Tom's now numbed mind that although he could not be sure of the registration number, it looked just like Li Cheung's red convertible. Switching lanes at the last moment, Tom nearly hit another car as he attempted to follow.

The traffic as usual was dense, and after momentarily losing sight of the distinctive-looking vehicle Tom glimpsed it once more as it weaved through the myriad of cars and lorries. Attempting to keep a safe distance so as not to be spotted, he finally slowed down as the red sports car came to a halt in Soho. Tom watched from a safe distance as a burly Chinese man got out and stepped into one of the many Chinese restaurants dotted along the road, Tom's pulse was now racing as he waited and wondered what he should do. He was due to keep his appointment with the discussion group in fifteen minutes. As he considered his options he spotted the man come out of the restaurant again, but now there was a middle-aged woman standing at the restaurant door talking with him. He seemed to know her and leant down to kiss her before walking alone toward a newspaper shop and disappearing inside. The woman returned inside the restaurant.

Trying to remain as calm as possible so as not to draw attention to himself, Tom jumped out of his own car and sauntered over to the red convertible, scouring the wheel hubcaps as quickly and as unobtrusively as he could. Sure enough, there staring back at him was the scuff mark on the shiny hubcap, damaged when Li Cheung had archly tossed the ignition keys in his direction and he had missed catching them. This then was definitely Li Cheung's car. In the windscreen he noticed a local resident's parking permit. Tom was now late for his meeting. The only thing for it was to return later, reasoning that if the person was a local resident then he should not have too much trouble locating the car again. After writing down the car's registration number Tom sped off once more in the direction of Whitehall, and his impatient audience, knowing that Professor Lambton had probably never been late for such a meeting in his life. Pushing his foot down hard upon the accelerator Tom cursed his luck at not being able to hang around and find out just what was going on.

CHAPTER 76

It had been a few days since Stryker and Carol had returned to the UK and were now slowly climbing the hill toward Hampstead Tube Station, veering right as they passed Whitestone Pond on their left, the main shopping thoroughfare having petered out, giving way to the wide open spaces of Hampstead Heath. It was Carol who broke the gap in their conversation.

"Was that a coincidence or what? The very day we arrive back in the UK our Russian friend rings the office."

"Yes, as you say, what a coincidence. It's a good job someone was on the ball, making such an excuse to our elusive fugitive. We might very well have been at Heathrow at the very same time that our asylum seeking Red Chameleon friend put the call through. He might even have been on the same flight come to that. Yesterday I requested all incoming and outgoing passenger lists for Moscow flights over the last week to be faxed over to Vauxhall Cross."

"Why for a whole week when we know which day he rang from Heathrow?"

"Could have been a dry run for some reason or just arranged so as to put us off his trail."

"But he did mention that he was concerned that he might not be granted his request for political asylum."

"Well his mind was put at rest on that score. At least he's beginning to lose his shyness about contacting us."

"And you were right about our place being bugged – one in the bedroom and two in the sitting room."

"Yes, but I feel sure there are more bugs we haven't even discovered. Anyhow, it's a good job we know because now we are on our guard."

"I suppose it might just be that they had been placed there earlier for an entirely different purpose – for someone else that had previously occupied the place in the past and that the bugs were just forgotten about. I don't understand why we don't just dispose of them and do a thorough search for any more that might be planted – get our boys in to see what they can find!"

"Because as I told you before, it might be one of 'our boys' as you so quaintly put it, who planted them there in the first place – to eavesdrop on us. If the bugs are left in situ then we might be able to use the situation to our advantage."

"But Stryker, I can't believe that our own SIS would want to do such a thing. What would be the point? Besides which, I feel as if I'm living in a police state having to watch every word I say when we're there. It's like being back in Moscow. I feel uncomfortable. And if there are hidden cameras installed in the flat – well. It would be like having to live with a peeping tom. It gives me the jitters just thinking about it."

"Don't worry I've already taken care of the situation regarding our being bugged. Your modesty will remain safe." Stryker pushed one hand deep into his overcoat pocket and pulled out a plug with a small black box attached to it. "This will give the boffins at SIS a few headaches. At least I hope so."

"What is it Stryker? It looks like a computer charger."

"You're half right. Got it sent to me from Seattle by a police friend of mine. We make sure it is plugged into one of our wall sockets at home and it will interfere with any planted bug signals within the condo. It's not something you can buy off the shelf in the States but my friend has very good contacts. Don't forget that in America we have something called Silicon Valley – some very impressive people put this little thing together for me."

A stiff breeze got up so Stryker gave a sharp tug to the felt brim of his adopted trilby hat. By keeping Whitestone Pond to their left they hugged the perimeter of Hampstead Heath. It was now quite dark and chilly, but Stryker had suggested the stroll would be good for both of them and Carol had acquiesced, explaining that now they were out of their flat she had something important to tell him about the Red Chameleon.

"Beautiful isn't it?" Stryker murmured, nodding to their right. A vast panoramic scene was laid out before them. It was one of those clear, crisp nights when one could see for miles, the moon lighting up London as if it were a jewel displaying all its artfully cut facets, searching out every last vestige of reflected moonlight and multiplying it a trillion times. Set against the soft blackness it looked magnificent.

"It's strange to think of the millions of people down there, their lives being played out against such a vibrant city backdrop, all separate and yet when you see it like this, all together like an amorphous mass of humanity." Carol felt safe and happy as she walked along with Stryker beside her.

Gravel and twigs crunched beneath their feet as Stryker led her off the main road and onto a steep narrow path carved out of the hillside. As they stepped cautiously down the side of the damp grassy bank, Stryker felt the occasional sharp nudge in his ribcage from the leather shoulder holster which held the Browning high power 9mm handgun tightly to his body. He'd been informed It was unheard of and strictly taboo to carry such a weapon in Britain except on live missions, but since the death of Carol's friend from Vauxhall Cross he knew he would use it if the occasion arose, though he thought that most unlikely.

It was at this particular juncture that things began happening fast. By now they had cut deep into the heath, past the ironically named Vale of Health and were surrounded by trees. Because Stryker had been so engrossed in his thoughts he had not noticed the large figure about to step out from beneath the shadows just half a metre away and grab Carol by the arm, putting it in a hammerlock by wrenching it up behind her back and at the same time slapping a large fleshy hand across her mouth.

CHAPTER 77

All through the afternoon Tom found it hard to concentrate, his mind repeatedly returning to Li Cheung and just why she had not been able to contact him, if indeed she wanted to, though of this he had no doubt.

At his Whitehall meeting time hung heavily, some of the questions being aimed in Tom's direction were of a very puerile nature. He felt that valuable time was being wasted with all these questions, that most of his audience were probably dwelling more on what type of biscuits were going to be served with the optional tea or coffee as to the finer points of aerosol delivery systems for dispensing highly contagious toxins. It was always the same. One person would ask questions just to show how knowledgeable they were, turning the whole proceedings into something akin to Mastermind. After lunch the meeting dragged on and on, until finally the chairman scrutinised his wrist as though he had never seen a watch before and with a look of astonishment upon his face, acted as if it had arrived by magic.

"Ah! Gentlemen, time appears to have caught up with us." As he shuffled a few pieces of paper in front of him, half of those assembled were already making for the exit.

It was getting dark and Tom began to feel hungry, his stomach having made one or two rumbling noises while still answering questions within the conference room. Hurrying to his car he banished such considerations from his mind, concentrating instead on what he would do when he finally confronted the man driving Li Cheung's car.

The roads were busier than ever as Tom found himself caught up in the rush hour traffic, cars blocking every side road and clogging up the main arteries. It was bedlam, a cacophony of horns synchronised to the ever changing traffic lights. Tempers were becoming frayed and he began to feel paranoid as many hand gestures from other frustrated drivers were aimed in his direction. Luckily Tom spotted an opening, and quick as lightening he was through, heading back toward Soho, an area which his mind had never completely left since being there earlier that morning.

Twenty minutes later he was manoeuvring into a gap between two large Volvos parked opposite where Li Cheung's car had last been seen. There was no sign of it now, but Tom felt sure it would return and had little option but to wait. After a while his stomach began rumbling again as acid came up his throat leaving a bitter taste in his mouth. Having noticed a fish and chip shop whilst driving along the same road earlier and reasoning that fifteen minutes would not make much difference, Tom left his parked car and headed in search of food. He made it back to his vehicle in ten. The hot chips burnt his fingers as he ate ravenously, keeping his eyes peeled. An hour had passed and it was now gone eight. Tom screwed the soggy paper from the meal up into a ball but rather than alight from the car into the cold air dropped the paper into the foot well adjacent to the passenger seat. Pulling up the collar of his jacket to fend off the chill now seeping through the car, he dug his body deeper into a more comfortable position and rested his head back onto the padded neck rest.

It was the familiar roar of a car engine that kicked Tom back to life with a jolt, wrenching his eyes open just in time to see Li Cheung's car pulling away from a long line of stationary vehicles. He must have nodded off and missed its arrival, but now all his senses were alert as he rapidly fired up his own car and swung out into the road, peering through the darkness and trying to see which way it had gone before catching a fleeting glimpse of its tail lights turning right up ahead. The long queues of cars had disappeared hours before, the traffic flow much lighter now, but it was still difficult keeping up with such a nifty sports car as compared with his second-hand effort.

Tom endeavoured to maintain a safe distance between himself and the car up ahead as they sped west through Slough. Not vacating his own vehicle since getting out to buy his fish supper hours earlier, his back began aching severely as he remained in the cramped position that his old banger dictated, so different from that of the soft leather seats of the sports car speeding away from him up ahead. The car also stank of oily fish batter and vinegar. His head felt stuffy so he wound down the window, a wall of cold icy air hitting him full blast in the face with the ferocity of wind whistling off the tundra. To his surprise they were now driving through Reading, the same route he had taken earlier that day, which now felt like a long time ago.

His eyes were sore with the effort of keeping the little red sports car in his vision as it hurtled through the night at crazy speeds, Tom's car engine whining as it strained to keep up. At this late hour there was hardly any traffic to speak of as they sped through Newbury and on toward Marlborough, Tom felt as though he were caught in a time warp, that he must be dreaming, for the route being taken was in the same direction as that of Porton Down. Was it possible that the person driving the car was Li Cheung? That she had discovered where he worked and was now desperate to see him so as to explain why she had not been in contact.

Tom struggled to keep his anxiety in check, as the car he was following slowed down and came to a halt in front of the large security gates – the entrance to Porton Down which he knew so well. All the way from London the black hood to the sports car had been up and the interior lights off, so he had no way of knowing whether it was a man or woman driving. Now as the car door was opened, although Tom was staying well back, he could just make out a silhouette in the darkness. However, his hopes of setting eyes upon Li Cheung step gracefully from her car were dashed; instead a shadowy figure of a man clambered out and stood stock still for a moment before speaking to what Tom took to be one of the night time security officers. But even from where he stood staring through the darkness, Tom could also see that the figure of the man was not that of the burly Chinese gentleman who had initially parked Li Cheung's car in Soho earlier that morning.

To Tom's utter astonishment, the sturdy gates slid open, Li Cheung's car gliding smoothly inside the secret establishment before parking a short distance within the security compound. Tom's viewpoint, half obscured by trees gave him some cover, so he remained where he was, absolutely stunned. What on earth was Li Cheung's car doing at his place of work, and who the hell was that man driving her car, and why was he allowed access to a British government top security establishment?

CHAPTER 78

Before Stryker realised what was happening to Carol, a hard blow caught him across his right shoulder, making his body judder and his head spin. His knees buckled before hitting the damp leaf-strewn floor on Hampstead Heath, shaking his head as he rolled over onto his back. Although still groggy his training automatically took over, sliding his hand inside the bulging jacket, searching out the hard lump of cold steel strapped to his breast. The Browning pistol slid into the palm of Stryker's hand as his mind changed gear; thirteen bullets in the clip. Devastating accuracy at a range of up to thirty metres in the right hands, and Stryker's were definitely the right hands.

Stryker's accuracy was excellent because of his having belonged to one of the best Special Forces outfits in the world, the American SEALS, and his shooting skills had been tested by some recent competition shooting at Bisley in Oxfordshire – just to keep his reflexes in tip top condition – famed for its renowned shooting range where some of the best marksmen and women in the British Armed Forces vie for recognition and trophies. And while waiting for news of the Red Chameleon, Stryker had also paid the occasional visit to the shooting range at Fort Monckton, Hampshire, used for training SIS agents, amongst other things, in the highly specialised art of small arms shooting. But there was one other particular reason why Stryker was such a good shot. Because of his having lost an eye his other eye seemed to have compensated and therefore when he focussed on a target it appeared twice the size it should have looked, just as if it was right there in front of him.

As his index finger located the trigger he saw the heavy log, which had felled him seconds earlier, whistling through the semi-darkness once more, this time it was aimed at his taught stomach. At the same moment Carol was lifted off her feet, legs flailing the air as her abductor half ran, half stumbled through the gloom. Stryker summoned up all the athletic agility he could muster, swiftly rolling over twice to avoid the log before quickly drawing a bead on his target, illuminated by the moonlight being filtered through the branches of the trees. Training took over as he rapidly squeezed the trigger to bring the single-action high power Browning into play, letting off a bullseye shot at his attacker who was whipped backward by the exploding force of the bullet slamming into his forehead, removing the back of his skull with a flash of bone fragments and matter. Stryker scrambled to his feet, this time in a crouching position, making himself as small a target as possible, momentarily squatting on his haunches, straining his eyes and ears.

After the loud retort of the Browning there was silence, but his acute senses now amplified every sound. A twig snapped, maybe twenty feet away. Stryker turned his head and saw Carol lying prostrate with the big man's knee in the middle of her back and one hand still clamped over her mouth. At that moment a terrible rage entered Stryker as he quickly took aim once more. The moon made the large Chinese man's face glow with a white luminescence, presenting a perfect target. Another thunderous bang exploded, making Carol's body tremble. At this same moment the large clammy hand smothering her mouth dropped away limply, enabling Carol to let out a shrill scream. Running toward Carol for the second time within weeks, Stryker took her in his arms and comforted her, burying her head deep into his shoulder muscles and moulding her body tightly to his.

***

Having left the two bodies where they lay Stryker and Carol quickly made their way back to their flat in Belsize Park. Now the weather had deteriorated and it was raining. Soon a smell of Rum laced coffee with a heaped teaspoon of sugar wafted from the kitchen as Stryker attempted to calm Carol's nerves.

Carol sat in Stryker's king sized bed propped up by two extra-large pillows covered in white starched pillowcases. A box of paper tissues nestled within the folds of the thick duvet, Carol's pale tear-stained face bearing witness to the evening's earlier events.

"I think I'd better explain about the gun."

"What do you mean? You don't have to explain anything to me about carrying a gun. Part and parcel of our job isn't it?" Carol responded between sobs.

As Stryker knelt down to plug his cell phone into a charger located in the skirting board of the bedroom wall, he detected a note of false bravado in Carol's voice, regretting having to put her through such a frightening experience. As far as his gun was concerned he guessed he was safe. To match bullets to a gun you require a gun. He had learned in one of his obligatory lectures that the Metropolitan Homicide Branch initially dealt with these things and would never approach the security services for anything like that, and he also knew that they would get short shrift if they tried. The now steady drizzle might also be in his favour, for many clues could easily disappear in such inclement weather. But there again, people do get caught, and sometimes through seemingly inconsequential pieces of evidence as his police work in Seattle had taught him.

"Carol, you know as well as I do that it's not common for a British secret agent to carry a gun in this country. In the States we do things differently. I'm so sorry to have had to put you through that terrible experience tonight. I shot those people to protect you. I didn't have any choice. You saw what they were doing. I hope you understand."

"I know you were protecting me," she muttered mechanically, looking at him through mascara-smeared eyelashes. It was the first time she had witnessed someone being killed and hoped it would be the last. Outside, Carol could hear the wind howling and the windows rattling as if in a storm on the high seas. The darkness viewed through the basement bedroom window obscured peeling white painted brickwork supporting half dead desiccated roses trailing against it. Remnants of decayed leaves flew through the chill air, snapping at the glass as if fingernails were drumming upon it. For Carol, the last few hours had been like living through her worst nightmare, except that this one was real. She blinked back yet more tears welling from beneath her long, thick eyelashes.

"But why were you so worried about me so as to carry a gun over the heath against department rules?" Carol suspected she already knew the answer but wanted to hear Stryker put it into his own words.

"Because I feel responsible for your protection while doing this particular job, that's why. And after your friend Brenda's body was discovered – well obviously things are definitely getting more dangerous so I figured a gun might come in handy – and I was right wasn't I?"

"Oh Stryker, you're so sweet. I worry about you too. After that Anthony Lovejoy-Taylor chap was shot dead outside Moscow I worried that it might very well have been you."

"I've had the same thought myself. I believe someone set me up as a sitting target in Moscow."

Carol looked wide-eyed. "You mean someone planned to have you killed. But why would anyone do that?"

"The question to ask is not why anybody would want to kill me, but who? The why seems perfectly obvious to me. It is because I saw something in the Persian Gulf I should not have seen. That Russian registered sunken shipwreck containing potential biological weapons grade viruses together with a connection to the Chinese is explosive knowledge. That's enough to get anyone killed."

"Your two friends from the Special Boat Service for example – they were decapitated weren't they? Oh Stryker, I suddenly feel very frightened." There was a gap in the conversation while Carol took another sip of her sweet rum-laced coffee. "Surely the only people who might want to keep the things you saw on that shipwreck secret are the Russians and the Chinese. So to me the question would be, how would their spies know you even existed?"

"Good question. I suppose there's a chance that we have a Russian agent working within the British Embassy in Moscow who could have tipped them off regarding my movements and proposed secret meeting with Ivanovich Sobolev."

"Really Stryker, is that what you think?"

"No. But it's the sort of conclusion some people might come to after that force majeure whereby Anthony Lovejoy-Taylor was, let us say, possibly mistaken for me and killed. Anyhow, as I see it, there were only a limited number of people who would have known about my meeting with SIS's asset Ivanovich Sobolev – six to be precise. First there would obviously be Anthony Lovejoy-Taylor. I think we can definitely rule him out. Then there would be his station boss. He would obviously have known what his underling was up to and would therefore be an obvious candidate for interrogation about the shooting by Vauxhall Cross later, so I believe he can also more than likely be ruled out as someone who might have tipped off the Russians. The third and fourth people in the loop would be myself and you Carol. Then of course the fifth person would have been the British Ambassador Sir John Postlethwaite. I believe he would have known because again the 'need-to-know' thing would have come into play." Stryker stopped speaking and looked at Carol with a smile fixed firmly upon his face.

"And the sixth person?" queried Carol, impatient with the pause in Stryker's conversation.

"Firstly let me say that the people I have nominated for being leak proof, excepting us two of course, might or might not bear too much scrutiny. Having said that, I believe that the people named would be a fair summary of people we should be only too happy to entrust with our lives."

"Come on Stryker – don't tease me – who is the sixth person?" insisted Carol, more impatient than ever.

"The sixth person is obviously the spy who informed the Russians of my existence which nearly cost me my life but unfortunately cost Anthony Lovejoy-Taylor his instead."

"So it was a spy within the British Embassy."

"No, I don't believe it was a spy within the embassy."

"So you do not know who this sixth person is – be it a he or a she?"

"I do not know who he is at the moment – suffice it to say that yes, I believe it to be a man and I have my suspicions as to who that man might be. But to help with my own enquiries I have solicited help from a trusted source in Seattle."

"Seattle. But how would anybody in Seattle know about any of this? Don't forget you have signed the British Official Secrets Act, Stryker. That's a very serious business. You can't go telling outsiders about the goings on in the SIS."

"My dear young lady – might I call you that?"

"Yes please Stryker – dear is a word I like very much coming from you."

"Well yes, anyway, I am very aware of the British Official Secrets Act and would not wish in any way to infringe its code of ethics for anything in the world."

"I'm very glad to hear it. So who is this contact in Seattle?"

"That I am not at liberty to say at this moment in time but suffice it to say, it is an impeccable source."

Just then the telephone rang. Stryker stepped into the study and answered it. After a couple of minutes he stepped back into the bedroom. The call had been from Dr Grachev. The scientist wanted Stryker to meet him at a doctor friend's surgery in Harley Street tomorrow at midday, which was Saturday, being informed something very important had come up and he needed to discuss it with his friend. It all sounded a little dramatic to Stryker but Dr Grachev was very persistent, saying he was not prepared to explain over the telephone but implied that it was a life and death situation, although those were not his precise words. Stryker had been given the address and instructed to ask specifically for a Dr Grey.

"Have you heard of this Doctor Grey before?" enquired Carol when he returned to the bedroom.

"No, I've never heard of the guy. But Grachev sounded worried and said it was urgent."

"He's not the only one who's worried," replied Carol.

"You don't need to worry. You're safe here. Before all the trouble on the Heath you said that you had something very important to tell me?"

"Ah yes. With all this happening I completely forgot. 'C' intercepted a letter at H.Q. It was intended for you. It contained an elaborate gold pin fashioned into the Russian red flag with the hammer and sickle symbolic of the Soviet Union. Of even more interest is the fact that the letter purports to come from the Red Chameleon. Would you be a darling and fetch me my handbag from the sitting room?"

As Stryker got to the sitting room door the telephone rang once more. Slipping into the study he quietly lifted the receiver. This time he held a whispered conversation for some minutes before wearily dropping the handset back onto its cradle. The clock on the mantelpiece was in the process of striking nine times when Stryker came back into the bedroom carrying Carol's handbag as requested, his Browning pistol once more strapped to his chest within its leather shoulder holster and hidden from view by his suit jacket, the dark overcoat draped casually over his arm.

"That was a wrong number. Don't worry Carol, as I say you're safe now. I've got to go and report the deaths to the police," he lied. "I will probably be some time, so don't get worried if I'm not back for a few hours."

"God Stryker, what a mess. Please do be careful. I mean, just because you're now a bona fide member of the British secret services it means what it says – secret! You can't go shooting people just like that without a stink being raised. You've signed the official secrets act don't forget. I mean what I say Stryker – be careful. They could disown you – or do God knows what. Remember my line manager and good friend Brenda, poor thing. Have you thought of that? I must dash off myself now. Did I not mention that I'm due to work a night shift at Vauxhall Cross and daren't make an excuse of not feeling up to it by explaining to the powers that be that it's because I've just witnessed two men being shot dead – one of them in my arms? Can you imagine?" Impulsively Carol ran up to Stryker and flung her arms around his neck and kissed him hard on the lips. "I do love you Stryker. Please, for my sake, be careful." Then with moist eyes she released her grip and said, "Just wait a moment; I've got something to show you."

Carol delved into her handbag and handed a crumpled photocopied piece of paper to Stryker. It read:

I am now in a position to supply you with a sample of that recently mentioned newly constructed pathogenic and selective virus with no known antidote. This powerful deadly virus housed in a glass vial and developed with the unwitting help of Chinese geneticists in Beijing, will be exchanged for my safe conduct throughout the United States of America, Britain and Europe, once you have graciously granted me political asylum. I have enclosed as a token of comradeship this gold lapel pin, the symbolic red flag of the Soviet Union representing the hammer and sickle.

It was signed – *Red Chameleon.*

"Have you got the pin? I'd very much like to see it."

"Sorry Stryker, I believe 'C' has it in his safe. It was 'C's' secretary who got me the photocopy on his orders. She knows that I'm working on the case with you."

With the Red Chameleon's words in the letter hanging heavily on his mind, Stryker lifted his adopted trilby, flashed Carol a beaming smile and was gone, quickly making his way out on to the lonely deserted street of Belsize Park now glistening with rain. As he scanned the immediate vicinity, his left hand planted firmly on top of his hat to prevent it from being blown away in the strong breeze, there was only one condo with a light shining through the darkness, and that was his own. Stryker felt happy, safe in the knowledge that Carol would not now be in danger from the two Chinese men ever again. Nor would she be in any possible danger relating to the mission on which he was now embarking upon. Leaving this beacon of comfort behind he pointed his finely tuned Morgan in the direction of Berkshire, wondering what other ugly surprises the cold night held in store for him. His cell phone lay forgotten on the bedroom floor where he had left it, still being charged.

CHAPTER 79

The cold was biting into Tom's body as he sat shivering in the darkness, not only with the cold but through gut wrenching fear. Fear for the safety of Li Cheung. His eyes were beginning to feel sore with the strain of staring through the blackness, attempting to keep a close watch on events across the other side of the road. Several minutes passed before Tom eventually made out a figure slipping back into Li Cheung's car. Once more the security gates were opened, the driver leaning out of his now wound down window and shouting something toward one of the security officers, the words being carried away in the distance before once more speeding off, carrying on in the direction which Tom had been so steadfastly following.

This part of the journey was unfamiliar to Tom so he tried to keep as close as possible to the other car which was moving faster than ever. What the hell was going on? What conspiracy was it that led Li Cheung's car to Tom's place of work? And who was the driver luring him on yet another mystery tour? Now and then Tom pinched himself just to make sure he was not dreaming. Was this really happening in England in 1993? He could hardly believe his senses.

Soon they were speeding through a place called Melksham, now at this late hour just a ghost town, lit up with the minimum of street lighting. Twenty minutes later they were passing through Bath when the little red sports car pulled up in front of a row of immaculate Georgian terraced houses with which Bath had become synonymous. This was the moment Tom had been yearning for, to finally confront his protagonist and discover what had happened to Li Cheung. Tom drew up as close as possible behind the car and jumped out with the intention of confronting the other driver who had not yet had time to open the door.

Tom's heart was pounding as he rushed to grab the person clambering out. Tom let out a muffled shout.

"Good God it's you! I nearly had a heart attack."

CHAPTER 80

The street was deserted as Carol swiped her security card through the metal device before keying in her personal security code to gain entry to Vauxhall Cross, arguably for the uninitiated, Britain's most secret installation, on a par with G.C.H.Q. To reinforce this axiomatic truism the words *Semper Occultus* – in translation meaning approximately Always Hidden or Secret – were there to remind everyone who entered this building just what their business was about. As the green 'go ahead' light flickered she pushed her way in out of the chilly night air, catching her reflection in the Perspex security screen as she ran her fingers through her thick hair whilst nodding to a security guard at the reception desk. A few minutes later after being transported in one of the numerous high speed lifts she stood gazing out from her high vantage point, scanning the twinkling lights of the London skyline, clutching a piping hot coffee just extracted from an automated drinks dispenser situated nearby. Carefully balancing her hot concoction she walked through a nondescript unmarked corridor which in turn led to her office. At that particular moment she was thinking of visiting the staff canteen later which was situated in the basement. It boasted hot meals around the clock cooked by civil service employees, some of whom held cordon bleu certificates. There was not half so many staff working during night-time hours, but enough to deal with any emergency which might arise, bearing in mind the different continents and time zones the British Secret Intelligence Service agents' operations covered.

Carol had not been at her workstation for more than a few minutes, half tuned in to a little friendly banter going on between two junior desk officers. She was on the verge of retrieving some documents from her safe when the call came through. It was 'The Red Chameleon' and he wanted to speak with 'Smith'. The large clock on the wall was showing 10:30 p.m.

Carol put the call on hold and quickly rang Stryker's cell phone. Then she remembered seeing it lying on the floor in the sitting room being recharged. There was no response to Stryker's cell phone. She tried again. Once more, still no response. It now seemed an opportune moment to do something she had discussed with Stryker just days before.

CHAPTER 81

"Tom, what the hell were you doing following me like that? You nearly gave me a heart attack. You had better come in and explain yourself." As a key entered the front door of an authentic three hundred year old Georgian townhouse, a light came on in the hall.

"Hello darling, who's this you've brought home with you?"

"This is my assistant, Tom." Professor Lambton's face was flushed with barely concealed anger and adrenalin as his smiling wife led the way into the drawing room. The professor stared at Tom, and in a very menacingly low voice almost growling, said, "You had better sit down and explain what's been going on, and it had better be a very good explanation,"

Tom stared at his boss in disbelief, seeing him in a totally new light. He had never heard the overt trace of menace in the professor's voice before and was astounded. "But sir, why were you driving that sports car parked outside?"

"What the hell's that got to do with you?"

Professor Lambton's wife caught her husband's eye and looked as stunned as Tom was at his rudeness, her face registering amazement and outright disapproval. "Please don't speak like that darling," she said through gritted teeth.

"Do you know what this young man has put me through this evening? If I were a cat I should have used up my nine lives tonight through sheer shock." Seeing the quizzed expression on his wife's face he repeated the word. "Yes, shock. He's been following me at breakneck speed all the way down from London. And you…" he gave Tom a withering look. "You ask me why I was driving that sports car standing outside. Well, because I own it that's why – it's mine."

"But you can't own it. That car belongs to Li Cheung."

"Li Cheung? Isn't that your girlfriend, the girl that disappeared?" Professor Lambton's face was as flushed as ever.

"Yes. I was driving that car myself just a few weeks ago."

"Well, I bought it earlier this evening from a Chinese fellow in London."

"I know where you drove it from because I followed you all the way.

285

But how did you come to buy it? I mean, it belongs to Li."

"Yes, so you keep telling me." There was a tone of irritation in Professor Lambton's voice. "My daughter saw it standing in the street last week; in Soho to be precise. It had a 'For Sale' notice on it and she knew I was on the lookout for a little sports car for when I retired. Also it was the colour red, which is what I wanted, so she gave me the telephone number. I made an offer and took a train down to London this evening to pick it up. You really worried me, tailgating me like that. I drove like a maniac to shake you off."

"I'm sorry about that sir. I know I drove like the devil because I could hardly keep up with you." Tom's eyes wandered over the exquisitely furnished drawing room, with its antique furniture and pale green silk draped curtains. In normal circumstances it would have had a calming effect on anybody sitting in such surroundings, but Tom's mind was running riot.

"You say it belonged to Li Cheung," the professor noted, still with a barely concealed note of exasperation in his voice, "but I have the log book and registration documents here – yes, see here, a Mr Xing Cheung."

"Well, that's Li's surname so it must be her father who sold you that car. But why would he do that? He bought it for her birthday just recently. It doesn't make sense."

Mrs Lambton stood up, brushing the creases from her skirt as if swatting a fly.

"I'll make you both a nice cup of tea," she said, disappearing from the room and leaving the two men, whose faces were now creased with anxiety, staring into space.

***

From where he lay, Tom watched the colourful hot air balloon, framed by the widow against a dazzlingly blue sky, as it drifted slowly over the rooftops. He could make out the miniature figures as they stood clinging to the leather-trimmed wicker basket suspended in mid-air just inches from the adjacent Georgian houses' chimney pots on a scale reminiscent of a doll's house. Moments later the balloon had disappeared, leaving the blue sky crystal clear once more, without a blemish.

It was a comfortable bedroom, though the flower motifs running riot along the wall, across the down duvet and stencilled upon every hand painted piece of furniture, from the chest of drawers to the bedside cabinet was somewhat excessive. It brought to mind the Pre-Raphaelite painting executed by John Everett Millais – the one depicting Ophelia drowning in a flower-strewn watery grave.

A light tap on the bedroom door was followed by the substantial figure of Mrs Lambton bearing a wooden tray containing a cup of tea and plain biscuits scattered around an inevitably floral decorated china plate.

After emitting soft cooing noises Tom was duly informed that breakfast would be ready within half an hour and the question posed as to whether he would prefer poached or soft scrambled eggs with his bacon. During breakfast Mrs Lambton attempted to lighten the strained atmosphere between her husband and the unexpected house guest without much success, both men's minds being preoccupied with the days forthcoming events, attempting to penetrate the seemingly impenetrable.

CHAPTER 82

MOSCOW-BOUND TRAIN

Beneath winter's dark low slung clouds, the exodus of factory workers and other residents alike had been gathering pace for days, gradually turning into a stampede. People crowded the ancient railway station which had not seen such activity since its inauguration so long ago that there were few who now remembered the occasion. Women with plump red arms and even larger hips carrying giant sized bundles of personal effects in brightly coloured fabrics; small children hanging onto their mother's skirts, others being carried by men who had not had time to shave, such was the urgency to abandon the place where so many had spent all their working lives. Relocation! To the bureaucrats in Moscow it was expedient. To the uninitiated workers of Experimental Sector Two Oh Five it was, of those destined for the Urals, a nightmare, though ignorance brings its own salvation.

The few Moscow-bound trains that passed were crammed to overflowing, battered old cardboard suitcases blocking the corridors, squeezed cheek by jowl with the enormous fabric bundles ready to be used as improvised seating and bedding for the long journey which lay ahead. Those who were lucky enough to occupy the caravan of carriages with wooden seats were seemingly pinned in for the duration of the journey. People pushed and shoved one another with an infectious frenzied air of activity. Excited yells and screams from children pierced the dank air as they looked forward to the great adventure ahead, and harried women rushed around trying desperately to locate loved ones.

The carriage in which the man and his family sat was crowded like all the others, so much so that the old carriage door, inset with glass panels, could not be closed. Vast plumes of acrid smelling smoke from cheap Russian cigarettes, of those who still had room to move their arms in the corridor, swirled uninvited into this straightjacket environment. Chilled fresh air from open windows helped alleviate the heady mixture of bad breath and sweating bodies packed in such close proximity to one another, at the same time drawing in yet more noxious fragrances from children who had successfully evaded their parents' attempts to clean up the small feral beasts for the journey of a lifetime.

Seated or standing, even the youngest nursed bottles of various coloured liquids to help sustain them on their thousand mile journey to Moscow. Loaves of bread and dried meat of an indeterminate nature were distributed amongst the throng, giving the impression of a mass picnic about to be indulged in. The lucky few also clutched fruit, cheese and other luxuries, wrapped mostly in newspaper, the print of which carried such stories as the Russian Mafia making millions of roubles out of others' misfortunes, and carrying pictures of elderly, half-starved Muscovites selling what few possessions they held dear, so as to be able to supplement their meagre dwindling pensions being eaten into by rabid inflation. As the train gathered speed it began rocking, the momentum throwing passengers standing in the corridors off their feet and onto one another, turning them into a great writhing mass of humanity.

Pushing her forehead up against the dust ridden window, the woman gripped her husband's arm tightly as she looked out upon the rapidly vanishing panoramic view of the small city which had once upon a time started out as a former penal colony in the Stalin years, before serving its purpose later on as a biological warfare outpost, the factory's former auxiliary workers now being shipped out.

A new beginning dawned for a people whose grossly inflated hopes would inevitably lead to disappointment, viewed as outsiders in a society where the rule was now the survival of the fittest. Gone the communist doctrine of egalitarianism for a people who always appeared to live life on the edge in a constant state of flux and hardship were in for just one more shock amongst the many heaped upon them as they strove to survive yet another chapter in their miserable lives.

The woman's grip grew ever tighter as she witnessed her private hopes and aspirations bulldozed and razed to the ground. Flames and acrid black smoke from the distant blocks of housing and tightly knit complex of factories licked the air hungrily as they devoured the wood and other combustible matter strewn across this wasteland, having no respect for imagined high political institutions nor humble hovels – all being laid to waste in a grey carpet of ash. This woman knew that very soon there would be no visible trace remaining of the previous life which had seen their daughter blossom into the young lady of six years old that she now was, a bright red ribbon tied tightly into her auburn hair enhancing her cherubic plump face, which resembled that of her father.

Once again the train lurched, jolting the occupants forward with the momentum of a rocket, sending Captain Zhizhin's mind reeling backwards. The car, his cherished prized possession, had been smashed to pieces through his lack of concentration, dwelling more upon his daughter's forthcoming birthday party than on his driving. The miraculous escape, walking from the wreckage with barely a scratch or even a bruise; the feeling of relief and immediately after, a powerful sense of superstition overwhelming his senses, making him feel that there must have been a reason why he had been spared. Then, the image of a vulnerable frail-looking Marishka Petrova, whom he had just left at the hospital, engulfed his mind. Although he was conscious of his wife and daughter waiting for him at home he now knew he had a far greater function to fulfil. Retracing his route, this time on foot, he made his way back to the building surrounded by barbed wire, patrolled by armed guards and ferocious-looking dogs and which bore the oversized red cross painted on its exterior wall.

This time Captain Zhizhin had not waited for an escort but quickly negotiated the corridors and located the glass partitioned operating theatre where the surgeons were still preparing their charge for an operation his imagination could only reel against. It did not take long for him to draw attention to himself by banging hard with his large fists upon the specially insulated observation window. Then the slow movement of the tallest surgeon and even slower opening of the air sealed door to confront Captain Zhizhin with a sharp accusation of interrupting an important operation about to take place, and his equally sharp rejoinder that the operation must cease at once.

"But it is too late, we have already begun."

"Late or not, the orders are from the top. Stop it at once," Captain Zhizhin yelled. His face had grown red with anger as the surgeon made a move back into the safety of the theatre – but not quite fast enough. Zhizhin's hand grabbed the green clad shoulder and spun him around. Eyes bulging, Zhizhin now spat out the words that as a GRU officer he could have the surgeon imprisoned for ignoring his orders. That appeared to do the trick, yet he had not won the day – yet.

"Comrade I told you, you really are too late. She has already been given a shot of mifepristone."

"What the hell are you talking about? Will that kill her?"

"Well no, not her."

"What do you mean, not her?"

"She was four months pregnant. What we have just given her will abort the foetus." There was a pause while Captain Zhizhin digested this information.

"But she's only a child." He thought of his little daughter and a tear appeared in his eye.

"Yes, as you say, only a child herself. But then you should have thought of that before you consigned her to this hospital." Before the information had filtered down to the medical staff regarding the imminent closure of their establishment the surgeon now conversing with Captain Zhizhin would never have dared speak like this but all authority was now quickly ebbing away.

"You mean experimental institute. I want her out of here immediately."

"We have already started the procedure to abort. That alone will take a little time."

"Take the time you require, then I want to take her away from here. Do you understand?"

"If this girl is released, who knows how she might talk? It could cost us our lives."

"This is a naïve young girl you are speaking of. She is illiterate like her mother and brother so there is no chance of her making a written statement."

"And you think she will not speak to her mother and brother of what she might have witnessed here?"

"She could not speak of what she might have seen because her mother has abandoned her. Her mother and brother fled the area as soon as she was arrested. It was stated that they would not be seeing her again. They were terrified. I told her mother that her daughter had consorted with an enemy of the state which for them would mean prison. They are ignorant people." In fact, both mother and son had been transported on Captain Zhizhin's orders to the infamous Perm-35 labour camp situated in the Ural Mountains.

The surgeon removed his heavy headgear, deep in thought with the intention of speaking with Captain Zhizhin in a more intimate manner. Now relieved of this restraint, he moved a little closer.

"If we let her walk out of here there would have to be a serious condition attached." The surgeon's closely cropped head of snow white hair and his gnarled sun kissed features belied the fact that he was one of the top surgeons within the institute. He would not have looked out of place leading a team of mountaineers on an assault of Mt Everest, so weathered was his skin. The straight nose and brilliant white even teeth leant him the looks of someone who might have made his career in films. Beneath this façade however lay a ruthless streak, as Captain Zhizhin was soon to discover.

A whispered monologue now took place, the surgeon's mouth so close to Captain Zhizhin's face that the policeman could detect a sour miasma of sausage and garlic. After the surgeon had concluded his diatribe there was a long silence while he waited for a response. Captain Zhizhin stared in disbelief.

"But that is not ethical. You are a monster."

"Are we not all monsters my dear comrade captain? If you want your precious girl, those are the terms."

"It is an impossible situation you place me in," Captain Zhizhin replied. He had begun to entertain the thought that for the first time in his life he could feel noble in his attempt to save a young, undeniably pretty, girl's life; a novel experience, quite alien to him. Yet what he actually felt, listening to the doctor's suggestion of how to circumvent the impasse between the two of them, by setting out before him a solution in all its sordid detail, was repugnant, and he had a feeling of being tainted by the corrupt system he was now attempting to fight back against. Except of course, he had been inured by the state's day to day operations both metaphorically and literally for too many years to stand any real chance so late in the day of being absolved of the heinous crimes which the system had heaped upon the unsuspecting masses.

CHAPTER 83

Tom was thankful that the proposed journey back to London from Porton Down that Friday morning with a view to resolving the mystery of the whereabouts of Li Cheung and the rightful ownership of Professor Lambton's coveted sports car would necessitate him driving his own old banger and not have to travel with the professor. At this moment in time he preferred his own company.

It had turned midday by the time they reached the environs of Soho's Chinatown, the myriad of Chinese restaurants beginning to fill up with the usual motley assortment of tourists and members of the indigenous population. Searching for a place to park both their cars they crawled at a snail's pace past an area of pavement illuminated by arc lights which was in the process of being cordoned off from the public by two surly-looking uniformed policemen. Adjacent to the freshly tied red and white plastic tape setting out the boundary of this cordon sanitaire another two policemen, this time attired in white overalls, were erecting a tall screen of blue plastic sheeting around a badly parked car set at a forty-five degree angle to the kerb.

The offside wheels were still visible as the sheet was stretched taught over a framework of light metal bars. Tom glanced from his car window toward the temporary structure being assembled, a feeling of foreboding beginning to overwhelm him as it sank in that this police activity was taking place immediately opposite the Xiang Wah Wei restaurant – the same restaurant that the burly Chinese man had entered the evening before after vacating Li Cheung's red sports car. The same car Professor Lambton was now in the process of parking with such careful consideration.

It was at that very moment a sudden gust of wind caught an as yet unsecured flapping edge of the blue plastic sheeting, shroud-like, billowing in the breeze, revealing an image so graphic as to sear itself upon Tom's mind as a red hot cattle branding iron might burn the hairs and flesh of a young steer.

Moments later Tom cruised to a halt, parking his vehicle just behind that of Professor Lambton's with barely an inch to spare. The blood drained from his face as he sat there in a state of shock. It was the professor who quickly opened the old car's passenger door.

"Tom, you look like you've just seen a ghost." Tom's knuckles were as white as his face as he sat gripping the steering wheel and staring straight in front of him between the broken windscreen wipers. Closing his eyes, the uncannily clear snapshot image reappeared. The slight body of a Chinese man stretched along the front seat – his head and the windscreen splattered in a mass of blood. Lying on the passenger seat beside his head, a gun was clutched tightly in the man's right hand. There had also been an extra-large bottle of Bell's Whisky keeping the gun company. It looked as though the bottle had not been opened. It was also spattered with the victim's brains and blood.

Professor Lambton could see how upset Tom was. He leaned over the passenger seat to put his hand on Tom's back in a fatherly show of comfort and understanding. He had witnessed the same bloody scene at the same time as his assistant. Tom looked thoroughly miserable as he spoke.

"Why, when he had decided to commit suicide, would a man buy a very large bottle of whisky and then not drink some to give himself courage?" His whole body began to tremble involuntarily as the shock of seeing the carnage hit him. Rather than make eye contact with Professor Lambton, he continued to stare at the road ahead.

"Maybe he didn't need courage," replied the professor, reflecting that a measure of whisky was ironically just what was required at this particular moment.

CHAPTER 84

Konstantin and his two GRU cohorts had kept Dr Grachev under close observation for the preceding five days and during that time one or other of the Russian agents had constantly watched and trailed him, but to no avail. Dr Grachev's routine had been so precise one could have set the proverbial clock by it, which in normal circumstances would have been a bonus for anyone intent on killing him. Unfortunately for the would-be assassins every hour of Dr Grachev's day would see him in the company of someone. When not at the symposium listening to papers being read on genetics or discussing the finer issues inherent within that field of science, he was confined to the hotel; be that for dining, reading or otherwise enjoying the company of similar minded people in rooms set aside for just such communal relaxation. It appeared that the only time he was actually alone was when he walked to his room, the route taking him through frequently busy corridors at the end of an invariably convivial evening's drinking. The idea of spiking his drink had also been considered but finally dismissed as being too difficult to gain access to.

Friday had been the final day of Dr Grachev's symposium and he was due to leave the hotel on Saturday for his flight back to Moscow; though no one expected him to attempt to catch that plane; not after having killed the FSB officer Vladimir Stalnov. Konstantin had calculated that Dr Grachev would therefore make his break for freedom soon after the scientific conference, which is why it had been decided that Yevgeny would do the job *tout de suite*. A plan of action had been decided upon and today, Friday, would see that plan put into operation.

CHAPTER 85

It was Friday and the end of Dr Grachev's symposium. It was a rush to pack his Gladstone bag, a souvenir from a former trip to London, and leave the hotel without being detected by the hotel staff. His bill was to have been settled tomorrow morning but that didn't matter as his life would be changed forever once his asylum had been settled. But now it was just a case of being selective about which of his meagre collection of items to take with him.

It had never been an option to take many belongings when Dr Grachev fled Moscow. The Russian internal security service in the form of FSB agents were everywhere, and any sign that he might be planning to leave the country on a permanent basis would have triggered his immediate arrest. So the paucity of his wardrobe had to be accepted as part and parcel of defection and freedom. However, he had chosen two particular items to bring with him. The first of these was a small *name day* icon which always accompanied him whenever setting foot abroad. It was over a hundred years old and painted on a wooden panel and held within a decorated silver frame. This was now removed from the bedside table and carefully placed inside his Gladstone bag. The second item, a lucky charm from his days as an officer in the Russian armed forces, a 'dog tag' with his army number stamped upon it, was now dropped into his jacket pocket. His symposium's scientific papers were left in a neat stack on top of the dressing table. The few clothes he had brought with him on his trip were left hanging in the ornate wardrobe while other smaller items of insignificant worth lay at the bottom of his now abandoned suitcase. He had made up his mind that he would not be returning to the hotel. His money was running out and it was getting too risky to remain for another night.

This desire to suddenly vacate the hotel had been singularly brought about over the course of a few days when he had initially spotted one, then possibly two men dressed in Russian style suits which had caught his attention as they were not so well finished as the other guests at this establishment and they both looked too Russian for his liking, and both men seemed to be loitering about the hotel reception every time he came back from his trip to the university. He had his doubts but had worked with such people and had also been spied upon by them all his life. Like many Russians he had a highly developed sense of being in the company of secret police and could almost smell them. Dwelling upon these facts over the last few evenings when alone in his bedroom, dark thoughts had crowded in upon him triggering a state of mild paranoia.

It was also in this paranoid state that he had decided to retain his guise as an elderly gentleman and forsake his own clothes, leaving them hanging in the hotel wardrobe, giving credence to anyone who might be interested that he would be returning shortly.

CHAPTER 86

MOSCOW-BOUND TRAIN

It had been broad daylight when the train journey began – now it was dark, and in direct measure the people's mood dark with it. The fortunate ones, the young children, had been lulled to sleep hours before by the rhythmic chugging of the wheels over old stretches of track, mile upon mile of it, seemingly stretching into infinity. For the adults however, the monotony had dampened their ardour which had preceded the journey. Now it began to dawn on them that the homes they had inhabited for so long were no more, hundreds of miles away and in ruins as they hurtled helter-skelter toward a very uncertain future, their lives hanging over an unfathomable void.

It was in this sombre frame of mind that Captain Zhizhin looked first at his wife, now dozing with her head resting uncomfortably against the ice cold carriage window and nursing in this unconscious state a half-consumed bottle of water. Next, his eyes travelled to her left, picking out the dark shawl covering the unseen head of his young daughter moving fitfully as she turned first this way and then that, struggling to find that state of bliss called sleep. Finally his gaze settled upon that of a young lady. It was a pretty face, but her dark lachrymose eyes stared straight back into his with an innocence which concealed a feeling of helplessness. Her lustrous dark hair now replaced by a thick brown shawl similar to his daughter's, hiding a closely cropped head and framing her features in what little illumination there was, Captain Zhizhin thankful that his own features must surely have remained partially concealed in this gloom. Yet as he looked upon his charge, even in these furtive shadows he could detect what he had attempted to avoid in the glaring light of day.

Just beneath her chin leading down to the neck of her old tattered blue dress, rescued in the nick of time from the relentless flames of the hospital incinerator, a fresh scar was visible – a token of the one terrible concession to a future life for this innocent victim of the state.

If Marishka Petrova's little brother had not turned around at that last moment, just as he was about to leave Captain Zhizhin's office, standing there on his toes, craning his neck so as to whisper about his sister's liaison with Ivan, a known spy. If that heavy old coin had landed with the hammer and sickle up, inscribed with the letters CCCP, instead of that tyrant Stalin's image. If the one condition of releasing Marishka Petrova from that nightmarish experimental institution had not been to give free rein to those butchers, resulting in the cordectomy operation, the removal of her vocal cords so as to silence her forever! The cruel consequences of that operation and pact with the surgeon would live with him as well as with her for the rest of their lives. He dropped his head so as to avoid the anguished look in her eyes, knowing that the shame he now felt would never leave him, even in sleep.

Nobody except Ivan knew about Marishka's pledge to keep the Matryoshka dolls until the day she died, and now Ivan was dead: except of course nobody had explained to her about Ivanovich Sobolev having been shot in the back of the head at his aunt's dacha. Sometimes ignorance can indeed be bliss.

Marishka knew the tiny wooden Matryoshka doll, clutched tightly within her childlike hand beneath the heavy brown shawl, had helped to get her through the operation. Captain Zhizhin, she now understood from experience, to be a kind man, having explained to her that the operation upon her throat had been necessary because of an infection she had somehow contracted. Yet sometimes she still tried to understand why he had initially treated her so badly; or questioning her for hours without letting her eat, neither drink nor sleep, every question having been about Ivan. In the end she had broken her pact of secrecy and explained to Captain Zhizhin how Ivan had told her about his inheriting the dacha on the edge of Moscow – she even told the policeman of its location, as Ivan had related it to her. Captain Zhizhin had said she could trust him and that the information she divulged would remain secret – just between the two of them.

Now she was treated like a second daughter by both he and his wife, having been informed that her mother and brother had abandoned her but that she could live with them in Moscow. Within her heart though, she knew there was only one person she wished to live with, and that was Ivan.

Although her yearning for Ivan could no longer be expressed in words from her pale, delicate lips, her heart ached for the moment when she would once again push that intricate wooden symbol of love she felt so earnestly for him, into his strong, tender hands.

CHAPTER 87

Friday had not arrived quickly enough for Pyotr, anxious as he was to get the job done and fly home to Moscow, once again picking up his life as a single man with at least a semblance of independence. This view persisted, even though the crazy hours Pyotr had worked over the last week meant Konstantin had not dominated his life in the UK quite as much as he had feared.

Having already completed his eight hour shift through the night, Pyotr had felt tired earlier in the day, but now since overcoming the first signs of sleep deprivation he was in a state of euphoria in his twentieth hour of wakefulness.

All three GRU men had now moved into the hotel foyer, poised for their final act of exacting retribution on Dr Grachev for their colleague's death. But Konstantin had a worried look upon his face. Had Pyotr missed him? The same way as he had lost sight of Ivanovich Sobolev – 'Ivan the Terrible' – at the airport in Moscow? After all, on the face of it, Dr Grachev had not been seen by any of them since checking back into the hotel about tea time yesterday afternoon, returning from his scientific conference. He had arrived by taxi, Konstantin having witnessed the event himself. Was it really possible that Dr Grachev had slipped out of the hotel again without their knowing? Konstantin knew that the unsocial hours had begun to take their toll on all three of them, and once or twice, through sheer monotony, he had even caught himself momentarily losing concentration himself.

Konstantin had tailed Dr Grachev along the various corridors within the hotel several times during the last few days, attempting to see where the opportunities might lie with a view to waylaying him. Unfortunately there were always people milling around and it had been decided that the best opportunity would be to trap him when he was inside his hotel room. The plan had been to wait for Dr Grachev to leave the hotel this Friday morning with one of them trailing him to make sure he did not disappear and then, when he returned, the three of them would follow and grab him as he entered his room; but he had not appeared and they were beginning to wonder whether he had already flown the coop.

Konstantin surreptitiously beckoned Pyotr over, whispering that he should have another look around the ground floor reception rooms, just in case Dr Grachev was hanging about killing time. He also threatened that if by any chance he had let Dr Grachev slip out of the hotel without their knowing, he would personally make sure Pyotr was kicked out of the service.

Pyotr thought what an irritable bastard his boss could be as he trailed behind the short stocky figure of Yevgeny, making yet one more foray around the various ground floor reception rooms, searching in every possible place in as unobtrusive a way as possible, while Konstantin kept his eyes glued on the entrance hall's large revolving doors.

Within ten minutes they returned once again to their respective strategic vantage points, attempting to merge in with the rest of the hotel guests. Unfortunately, what passed as smart suits in Moscow tended to look rather old fashioned, compared with the other hotel guests moving in and out of the foyer. The cut of the three agents' clothes had a certain cheapness about them so it was difficult to appear entirely inconspicuous. Pyotr caught the eye of Konstantin, slowly shaking his head in a negative manner. With the evening fast approaching, Konstantin's patience had run its course as he summoned his two colleagues over. He just hoped Dr Grachev was still in his room. After gazing at both men in turn, he whispered his sophisticated instructions: "Go up there and kill the fucking bastard so's we can all go home."

As Yevgeny lead the way by staircase to the third floor, Pyotr noticed a look of disgust on his colleague's usually blank face, and he thought he knew why. Yevgeny hated swearing. Pyotr knew this and guessed it was because of his strict religious upbringing.

CHAPTER 88

Professor Lambton cupped both hands up to the window, while at the same time pushing his nose firmly against the glass pane. The restaurant was closed and it was dark inside. To one side of the frosted glass door was a small cheap plastic bell push. He pressed. And waited. Tom, who had pointed out to professor Lambton the location of the Chinese restaurant from where the driver of Li Cheung's car had emerged the previous evening, stood beside him looking dejected. Suddenly the door opened and Tom found himself staring at a woman wearing the traditional light samfu suit worn by Chinese women – high necked jacket and loose fitting trousers, the same woman he had seen being kissed by the burly Chinese man. An uncanny feeling took hold of him, an undefined knowledge that he had seen her somewhere before – somewhere else besides the restaurant he was now standing beside. The hair was tightly swept back from her forehead in a severe style, grey flecks marring the otherwise jet blackness of it. Her face was very pale and her eyes puffy as though she had been crying.

"Yes, what do you want? Are you the police?" Her manner was both sharp and cold.

"Is your husband in? We would like to speak to him." Professor Lambton purposefully evaded her last question, hoping to give the impression that they were indeed the police without actually claiming to be so.

"Why do you torment me so? Are you mad? Do you not talk with your colleagues?" Tom was surprised at her command of English for a woman who had obviously not been born here. He figured that out because of her accent.

"Is your husband's name Xing Cheung?"

"His name was Xing Cheung," she replied. Tom's eyes widened, but it was Professor Lambton who carried on with the questioning.

"How do you mean? I bought a car off him yesterday."

"Oh! So you are not the police. You don't know? My husband is dead."

"Dead!" It was Tom who spoke now. "Where is Li Cheung? What's happened to her? Is she safe?"

The frail-looking woman shrunk back into the passage under this barrage of questions, merging into the shadows as though the daylight

302

might turn her to dust.

"What business is it of yours?" She stared hard at Tom before answering her own question; now softening her tone and taking her inquisitor's breath away with her next statement. "You're Tom aren't you?"

Tom replied falteringly. "You are Li Cheung's mother, and you know where she is don't you? Please tell me where she is." Tom's voice was beginning to crack with emotion. "Please tell me she is safe."

The diminutive Chinese woman took another step backwards into the gloomy hall avoiding eye contact. "Yes, she is alright."

Tom gave a huge sigh of relief before detecting light footsteps brushing against the carpeted floor. From the gloom of the passage a shadow became visible as Tom's eyes adjusted to the darkness. Then the shadow slipped quickly past Li Cheung's mother before appearing in the sunlight. The tear-stained face looked as fragile as the woman she had just passed but the eyes, blinking in the glare of the sunlight were very familiar, the smile in them radiating joy and love.

"Tom my dahlin'!" With those words ringing in his ears, Li Cheung threw her slender arms tightly around Tom's neck, her pouting lips feverishly searching for his, her eyes streaming with tears, both now oblivious to the man and woman staring at them with such acute embarrassment.

CHAPTER 89

Upon reaching the third floor, Yevgeny held up one of his powerful hands to bring Pyotr, who was fetching up the rear, to a halt. Rapidly scanning the length of the corridor Yevgeny spied an elderly man vacating the room which, by counting the door numbers, he figured to be that of Dr Grachev's. In a flash, before the door could be pulled shut by the gentleman vacating the bedroom two Chekisty sprinted forward, pushing the old man to one side and leaving him stupefied as they furiously charged past.

It all happened so quickly that the man carrying his Gladstone bag stood momentarily frozen to the spot as the two thuggish-looking men stared hard at his features before dashing into the room. Pyotr took the bathroom, while Yevgeny scoured the bedroom looking for any possible escape route. Scuttling to the window he threw it open and looked out for the half expected fire escape, but to no avail.

Pyotr gave a breathless yell, "He's not in here."

"Nor here," Yevgeny shouted, before responding to the loud ringing of the bedside telephone. As he raised the receiver a smooth young man's voice came on the line.

"Dr Grachev?" There was a pause before Yevgeny answered.

"Yes!"

"Is that who I think it is?" A different voice had come on the line. Yevgeny was surprised and shocked at the same time. "Konstantin!"

"Where the hell is Dr Grachev? Is he there?"

There was a pause as Yevgeny gathered his thoughts.

"Nooo… he's not."

Even as Yevgeny spoke, Pyotr had already dashed toward the wardrobe and found what he was looking for. A coat with a maker's name printed in Cyrillic. That was the confirmation.

"This is definitely his room," Pyotr shouted. But then a nagging question arose in his mind. Who was the elderly man leaving with that holdall? "Quick, downstairs, that old man, that's Dr Grachev!"

Yevgeny looked surprised. "Nooo…" he responded once more, still hanging on to the telephone receiver until it was yanked out of his hand by

Pyotr as he was half dragged by his shoulder through the still open door, out into the now deserted corridor.

As the stooped figure of Dr Grachev sloped out of the lift clutching his Gladstone bag in one hand and the silver-topped walking cane in the other, he quickened his pace making his way through the lobby still disguised as an old man. Then, just for a split second, he was halted in his tracks by a deep male voice with a thick Russian accent on the telephone at the reception desk asking in Russian, "Where the hell is Dr Grachev?"

Upon hearing his own name, Dr Grachev swung his head up in a conditioned reflex to see a tall, grey-suited man whom he did not recognise. But he did recognise the familiar bulge beneath the interrogator's jacket as he shifted the weight of his body from one foot to the other. He knew instinctively it was a gun. Dr Grachev felt a chill run through his body as he forced himself to walk and not sprint toward the swing doors. His legs already having lost their co-ordination when coming face to face with his potential executioners only moments earlier, now felt like lead weights as he strove to hurry self-consciously across the large hall.

Konstantin watched absentmindedly as the old man passed him by unsteadily, crossing the hotel reception area with a rolling gate. If he had not been so preoccupied with his telephone conversation he might also have noticed the agitated look tinged with fear etched on the surprisingly smooth-complexioned face. Sporting long grey hair and carrying the silver-topped walking cane lent a certain elegance to a figure that was seemingly well past his prime. Everything then took on a surreal aspect as the revolving doors spun quickly, spewing the stooped figure out into the evening air, Pyotr now running in front of Konstantin, bellowing at him to grab Dr Grachev.

Once outside, nerves gave way to blind panic as his eyes swept frantically up and down the street for a taxi but there were none in sight. Suddenly the situation hit him with all the force of a volcano erupting: his worst nightmare was unfolding before him – not only was he being pursued by a hostile British Secret Intelligence Service but also by Russians from his homeland. Dr Grachev knew he was now running for his life.

Only as Pyotr and Yevgeny moved toward the now empty spinning panes of glass making up the door to the hotel did Konstantin grasp the situation. Rapidly following his subordinates out onto the street and without thinking, automatically drew his Russian Makarov 9mm service pistol before taking aim, managing to fire one round at the dark silhouetted figure receding into the distance of the gathering gloom.

CHAPTER 90

After paying off the taxi driver, who in Professor Lambton's estimation had been gifted with a remarkable talent as a raconteur, using his soft Irish brogue to such good effect even though it had been wasted upon himself, and still brooding about the loss of the sports car to which he had so quickly become attached, it was decided to delay entering his club in favour of a stroll.

The chilly night air was agreeable, clearing his mind as he turned over the events of the last couple of days in an attempt to come to terms with his assistant Tom tailgating him all the way to Porton Down the day before and then having experienced the suicide in front of Tom's girlfriend's house. The professor passed one of the lions in Trafalgar Square, reclining peacefully in the long shadows of the encroaching night. Years before, as a young man toward the latter part of the nineteen-fifties, there had been a coffee bar on the corner of the square, just down from St Martin's in the Fields, where all the so-called beatniks used to congregate. Young girls, many in their early teens, wearing hessian sack cloth for dresses and masses of dark eye shadow, making them appear as though they had not slept for a week.

Even in those days there had been a ready supply of soft drugs to smoke, but nothing like cocaine or heroin as there is today. Where were all these young people now? Probably with children and grandchildren of their own, he mused. Crossing the road he strolled along the Strand and passed Charing Cross railway station before doubling back on himself after reaching the Savoy Hotel, pressed to do so by too many memories from his youth. The day had been a long one. It was getting late and the professor was feeling tired and hungry.

Returning to his club and signing the member's book, he wearily made his way into the dining room. Scouring the menu he decided on a medium rare pepper steak with a good bottle of vintage red wine to complement it.

It was not long after draining the dregs from his second glass that he decided to retire early, so as to be able to make an equally early journey back to Bath the following morning, a Saturday. The idea of getting home to Bath raised his spirits considerably. Before decamping to his room he had dutifully telephoned his wife to let her know where he was staying and said he would be home as early as possible in the morning. Professor Lambton then asked one of the porters for a train timetable for just such a journey. A taxi had also been booked on his behalf to ferry him to Waterloo Station and the hall porter generously recompensed.

The thought of placing his head upon a crisp white pillow seemed like heaven as he heaved his tired body between the cool linen sheets. The room temperature was just right as the professor fell into a light slumber. It was not a slumber however, which was to get any deeper, and not one to last all through the night.

CHAPTER 91

Dr Kenneth Jones had made a vow to himself not to translate Penny's Russian words ever again, having been put off by the sight of her distraught face under hypnosis and the very real suffering which she had obviously endured. It was Penny herself who had managed to sweet talk him into going back on his word and attending another session; a session which was to have startling implications for himself as well as Penny.

It began in a similar manner as before, a roaring fire having been lit in the cottage some time previously, so as to make the sitting room warm and conducive for the hypnotic regression which was to come. Dr Kenneth Jones had made sure before coming over from his college rooms that he carried an ample supply of whisky in the form of a full bottle, and was dressed up well to combat the sleet, the weather having turned nastier in the last few days. Residing on the coast and being exposed to the harsh wintry winds sweeping in from Cardigan Bay had given Dr Kenneth Jones a slight chill, so the whisky in this instance, could be viewed as medicinal. As he stepped gingerly over the threshold he was greeted by David as usual, like a long lost brother.

"Great to see you remembered your medicine." David's eye had caught sight of the bottle almost hidden from view in the deep poacher's pocket of Dr Kenneth Jones's voluminous overcoat. This remark by his friend was followed by a swift nudge in Ken's fatty region where the ribs should normally be residing, and a knowing wink.

As there was no hall to walk through, it was easy to spy Penny already lying on the sofa, the plumped up comfortable pillows strategically placed around her, giving the impression of being in a boudoir as opposed to David's front parlour.

Penny was reclining adjacent to where Dr Kenneth Jones had now placed himself and he was taken by the skilful way she had swept up her long silky hair from the nape of the neck, securing it with a tortoiseshell comb; her smooth pink skin exposed beneath the usually flowing tresses, suggesting an innocent nakedness. Penny was also wearing a piece of jewellery upon which the doctor complimented her.

It did not take David more than a minute or so to induce Penny into a very deep trancelike sleep, and not long after that Dr Kenneth Jones was

308

putting his translating skills once more to the test.

For Penny, the intervening weeks had done nothing to dissipate the mixed feelings regarding her long forgotten sister, nor quell the still raw emotions. Neither did it dim the yearning to find out more about her recently discovered stepbrother.

The story began unfolding with David's first question. This time though, there were no more tears, just revelations – both shocking and surprising in their matter of fact way of delivery. Then something in Dr Kenneth Jones's mind clicked and he suddenly stared at Penny as though he had seen a ghost, quickly terminating his translation in mid-sentence. David looked at his friend in astonishment as the words dried up. Had it been something that Penny had spoken of in Russian but Ken had omitted to translate? Or was it something else? Something perhaps which David had mentioned? Whatever it was, it brought to an abrupt end the evening's truncated proceedings, almost before they had a chance to get into their stride.

Dr Kenneth Jones muttered something about the chill getting the better of him, and after making his excuses, left in a hurry. He had attended two hypnotic sessions with Penny and both times they had been terminated abruptly. This time however, the situation which caused such concern for the academic had nothing whatsoever to do with the perceived stress or otherwise of Penny, but more to do with Russian defectors.

After returning to his rooms, Dr Kenneth Jones made a quick telephone call without even bothering to remove his overcoat first. His face was very flushed and he needed to sit down to let his heaving chest settle back into a more rhythmic pattern before he could get his words out. The person on the other end of the line gasped with amazement – the type of emotion Kenneth had to suppress in David's cottage only a short while before. After the telephone call had been concluded, he grabbed a few items of clothing and quickly tossed them into an overnight bag, then grabbed a bottle of his favourite brand of whisky before jumping into his car, knowing that it would be a good few hours before he reached his destination.

CHAPTER 92

The image of an elderly gentleman tearing along the street away from the Normanhurst Hotel at breakneck speed whilst carrying an elegant silver-topped cane in one hand and clutching a Gladstone bag in the other, coupled with white hair trailing in his wake would have presented a bizarre image for anyone fortunate enough to witness such a spectacle, but the thoroughfare had been deserted and it was dark as Dr Grachev raced to put as much distance as possible between himself and his pursuers before eventually managing to flag down a passing London cab and quickly hop aboard.

It did not take long for his taxi to arrive at the deserted Harley Street premises and soon Dr Grachev was safely ensconced within his surgery, where climbing upon the examination couch, he was determined to get some rest, for he was expecting Saturday to be arduous in the extreme, though even he could not have imagined just how true that was to prove. There was only one more thing to do – search out a telephone kiosk far enough away from Harley Street and ring the special telephone number he had been given months before at Victoria railway station, so as not to give the location from where the call had been made, and then hunt for something to eat – but that would keep for a few hours.

CHAPTER 93

Remnants of an Indian chicken dhansak takeaway lay scattered by the bed. Small silver-lined boxes which had until recently held rice and other bits and pieces including two naans, were now residing in a brown paper bag used to carry the welcome home feast back to Li Cheung's flat in Camberwell. One of the large windows remained open so as to remove the spicy aroma synonymous with Indian restaurants.

Because of Tom and Li Cheung's reunion taking place such a short time before, there had been no opportunity to reinstate the table and other furniture which Li Cheung's father had been instrumental in having removed. Only a small suitcase containing a few items of clothing and overnight things occupied the room which now appeared so cavernous. She and Tom were just grateful for the bed with sheets, blankets and pillows. It was also a shock hearing from Li Cheung's mother that her husband and another Chinese business associate had been discovered shot on Hampstead Heath. Li Cheung had loved her father dearly and could not understand why anyone would do such a thing. Under the tragic circumstances professor Lambton said that it was only right that Li Cheung should have her car returned, her father having sold it to him without Li Cheung knowing anything about it. Because it was so late Professor Lambton also made the decision to stay at his club and took a taxi back to Trafalgar Square. It was then that Li Cheung had asked Tom to spend the weekend with her at the room in Camberwell.

Only now, as Li Cheung lay beside Tom enveloped in his arms, did he broach the subject of her mysterious disappearance. Snuggling into the warmth of Tom's body, her soft voice began to relay the events of the past few days – days, she said, which she hoped she would never have to endure again – ever.

It began after paying her parents what had been planned as a brief visit. Li Cheung explained to her mother that she was going to get married. Her mother had suggested that she was too young and that perhaps she should wait a while. "That was when my father arrived home from some business trip in Hampstead. Once he had been told the news by my mum he went berserk, saying that he had lavished the sports car on me as a birthday present and that this was how I repaid him.

"No, he would never hear of my marrying a white man – he did not

311

condone mixed marriages. That's when he grabbed me by my wrist, pulled me up to my old bedroom, the one I had occupied before moving here in Camberwell, pushed me inside and locked the door. I have remained there ever since; that is, until today. I had no opportunity of contacting you. I was so depressed. I never knew that my father had sold my car either, until your boss Professor Lambton explained what had happened. Oh my dahlin', I'm so happy to be with you again. You'll never leave me will you Tom?"

Li Cheung looked softly into Tom's eyes, the scent of her body overwhelming his senses. Her tender white hands moved to the nape of his neck, sending waves of ecstasy flooding through him as her fine fingers ruffled his hair.

"I love you Tom, more than anything in the whole wide world. You'll love and protect me, won't you dahlin'? And when the time comes, we'll die together won't we, so that we never miss each other? I couldn't bear to be without you again." Tom wrapped his arms around Li Cheung's slim body, holding her tight to his, and feeling the warmth of her flushed face upon his cheeks.

"Yes, darling, I'll love and protect you for always, but I don't want to think about dying, we've got too much love to live for."

Li Cheung smiled contentedly, certain in the fact that Tom was truly the man she had been searching for all her young life, and now without her father, he was the only man of any importance to her.

CHAPTER 94

The office was situated on the top floor which must have been assigned to make a point. It was late, but as Carol approached 'C's' door it was ajar with a wedge of light spilling out onto the dark plush anteroom carpet which she had just crossed after having obtained permission from one of the uniformed duty security officers on late shift. Before letting her enter the chief's office the guard had carefully scrutinised her security badge hanging from a thin chain around her neck. The office was larger than the rest of the ones on this particular floor except for the conference room of this post-modern building.

"Why, hello again Carol. What can I do for you?"

"Hello Sam. Sorry to disturb you but it's to do with that gold pin sent by the Red Chameleon which 'C' let me have a peek at earlier. Would it be breaking the rules if I had another quick look and perhaps also at the letter our Russian friend sent? I think it might be useful. I have just had another verbal communication from him and hope to contact 'C' as soon as possible."

"Are you on a late shift?" There was a quizzical look upon her face – but then she often bore a quizzical expression as though not quite understanding what you were saying.

"Yes, I'm doing my bit. But it's quite important that I get another look, Samantha." Carol ameliorated the secretary's name, hoping that might lend a little more gravitas and possibly even a touch of authority to the situation she now found herself in.

"It's really more than my life's worth and it is late. But 'C' is around himself this evening stalking the building so you should be able to contact him soon I'm sure." Then she frowned. "I'm on my way home myself in a few minutes so if you're quick I'll make an exception. But you will really have to be very quick. I should have left hours ago. Some start to the weekend eh?" she smiled. 'C's' secretary moved effortlessly between strategically placed pieces of reproduction office furniture scattered about the room, making a beeline toward the large safe let into an alcove in one wall. An eight digit number and some letters were rapidly punched into a mounted pad on the heavy safe door which opened with a smooth swish before displaying serried rows of grey steel shelves. Each shelf held bundles of files and one slim file clearly marked upon its spine with the name 'Red Chameleon' was removed by Samantha and handed to Carol.

Cradling the file in her arms whilst scanning the documents for the Red Chameleon's letter, a loose piece of paper floated gently to the floor and in the midst of attempting to retrieve it Carol became aware of a third person who had quietly walked up behind her. Quickly making a grab at the document labelled SECRET in bold capitals, Carol knew immediately who had penned the missive even before seeing the signature: Carol just had time to speed read the words *"Persona non grata – Attention Dubai Embassy staff –* CAROLINE LAMBTON *and a man calling himself* STRYKER *to be treated as* PERSONA NON GRATA *if they should attempt to contact this embassy or the American embassy."* It also had the signature of the person who she now knew had written the missive.

As Carol struggled to return this piece of paper to its file tagged 'Red Chameleon', a hand reached out and snatched it. But just before it had been removed from her grasp Carol noticed that the person who had signed the indictment was the same person whose eyes she was now staring into.

'C' stood stock still, clutching the paper marked secret within his fist and staring hard at Carol.

Without waiting to make any excuses for having the classified file or the piece of paper which had fallen from it Carol quickly handed the file to 'C', and with a coolness which she did not think she possessed, said, "Thank you sir," turned on her heels and left the office slowly, fighting the impulse to look back or hurry.

CHAPTER 95

The deserted streets of Bath lay in silence, except for an occasional straggler who had taken advantage of the Friday evening public house extension to its drinking hours. Occasionally a peal of laughter or shrill scream rent the stillness but did not ruffle the sleep of Mrs Lambton. The fresher air of Bath, compared with that of London had a beneficial effect, of which dividend a good night's sleep each and every night was paid in full. So it was with some irritation that she felt compelled to leave her two fur lined hot water bottles beneath the swan down duvet and wander into the kitchen to boil yet another pot of water.

This situation had been brought about by the very late night telephone call from some government department emphasising the necessity of getting in touch with her husband. So once she had been roused and taken the cryptic message, there was no option but to dance attendance on her blossoming insomnia by making a cup of tea before putting a call through to her husband's renowned gentleman's club.

Like his wife, Professor Lambton had also been sleeping particularly well when a persistent ringing seeped into his consciousness, wrenching him away from his pleasant dream of driving a new red-coloured sports convertible. Opening his sleep ridden eyes and fumbling for the telephone sitting on top of the reproduction Louis XV1 bedside cabinet he was not immediately aware of his surroundings, it taking him a few seconds to come to terms with the reality of being safely installed in one of his club's bedrooms. Only then did he catch sight of the luminous clock face set into the radio. It was precisely half past midnight as his wife bellowed down the other end of the line with some urgency. Friday had now merged seamlessly into Saturday.

Within half an hour he had cancelled his pre-arranged taxi ordered for the following morning, and was outside his club climbing into a shiny black government limousine which quickly whisked him away into the night, still desperately trying to shake off his groggy tiredness which had enveloped him. He was not happy about the situation and nor was he used to being dragged out of bed at such an unearthly hour of the morning.

CHAPTER 96

The large house situated not far from Wokingham in Berkshire was set well back along a winding potholed bitumen track. It was hidden from prying eyes and the Finchampstead Road by a mixture of tall evergreen trees and high privet hedges mingling with overgrown bushes. The sturdy black entrance gates gave no hint of the electronic wizardry that operated them, though in fact they were top of the range with built-in safeguards. Nor did the entrance bear any house number. Instead, to the left of the plain metal seven foot high gates, was an old weathered piece of wood about eighteen inches in width nailed to one of the tree trunks bearing the legend in white paint, 'St. Kildare'. Unsuspecting motorists would not have given the sign a second glance, so unprepossessing and more importantly inconspicuous did it appear.

By happy coincidence, the very first school that the occupant of this comfortable, spacious, six-bedroom country house, protected by state of the art security systems, had attended at the tender age of three years old, happened to be just a stone's throw away, adjacent to a place known locally as Nine Mile Ride. That was before his parents had taken the decision to move to an area between Bristol and Bath, where his father had accepted a job with the Ministry of Defence.

Working behind tall fences topped with razor wire in buildings which resembled rectangular concrete bunkers, the child's father's job had involved something to do with armaments. So it seemed in keeping that this particular family for two generations at least, were destined to be linked with security in one way or another.

His son, having turned eight, was then installed in a large old granite structured school, just outside Bath, named 'Monk's Temple'. It was from here ten years on, at the age of eighteen that he went straight up to Cambridge to read history and modern languages. Three years later, after obtaining a double first he took a year out to 'see the world'. He actually ended up working for two years in Washington, assisting a well-known American historian with his research for a book. He then returned to England where he was clandestinely recruited by MI6.

While still relatively young, the position of MI6 Controller Middle East fell into his lap; then Europe. Eventually he crossed the pond once more, this time destined for Washington to head MI6's liaison staff. Kim Philby,

British traitor spy, who arguably passed more of his county's top secrets to the Russians than any other British subject had once held this same position. After a successful stint there, he returned to London to become a Director of Operations, in other words, one of two Deputy Chiefs under 'C', except that he was the one who four years later became known as 'C', stepping into the shoes of one of the most powerful men in the country. Along the way he picked up a CMG and an OBE. That seemed all a long time ago now and was the last thing on his mind as he prepared for his late night meeting.

***

The room in which the man known as the Chief or 'C' was seated possessed a certain faded grandeur. Oak linenfold panelling, removed at one time from an old mansion destined to be pulled down to make way for a new housing estate, looked as if it had resided here for centuries, so skilfully had its size been reduced to fit into the much smaller space of this particular house. With bump interlined heavy drapes at the windows to help keep out the chill of the night and act as sound proofing, the room's furnishings were what one might call 'Old Style'; consisting of an assortment of six comfortable easy chairs, now pushed together into a semicircle with a low, outsize heavy mahogany wooden coffee table placed in the centre. A seventh tall wing chair, upholstered in rich, deep, red velvet, sat facing this semicircle. Beside this tall chair stood a piecrust table upon which lay two well-thumbed files labelled TOP SECRET. The first file came from SIS personnel with the name of the individual it concerned discreetly printed upon the cover in neat capitals. The second much smaller file bore the pre-printed word: *OPERATIONS* on the front. Beneath this in longhand was scrawled the words: *RED CHAMELEON*.

'C', as he was known to all but his closest friends and those who knew no better, disdained the thought of unexpectedly travelling at such a late hour to his well-regulated office in Vauxhall Cross, situated on London's South Bank of the River Thames. The idea of holding this late night meeting at the beginning of the weekend did not appeal to him, so instead he had ordered the relevant files for this special occasion to be whisked post haste to his country retreat by one of SIS's couriers. It was not unusual for such occurrences and his wife, daughter and three grandchildren knew the drill, though tonight, being of such a late hour that was academic. But still, the rules were: Never in any circumstances, unless the house was in flames, should the head of MI6 ever be disturbed when he sat in conference with his colleagues. That was absolutely sacrosanct.

Donald, 'C's' man-servant-cum-bodyguard and occasional chauffeur, ex-

2nd Battalion Paratroop Regiment, known colloquially as the Red Devils and member of the Troop (SAS), a sergeant who had specialised in close quarter protection, was now recognised as a peripheral member of MI6, or more correctly termed Her Majesty's Secret Intelligence Service. In actual fact he was on a two-year secondment from his unit. He had already sorted out the coffee machine situated in one corner, which now sat bubbling away nicely. Beside this black bubbling nectar stood a large, circular, white bone china plate divided into four segments, each one–holding a different variety of biscuits. This sustenance was frugal by the standards of the daytime restaurant housed within the plush new postmodern offices of MI6, only recently transferred from the decidedly misleading cramped and dingy offices long used by SIS at Century House in Lambeth, its location not far from the Elephant and Castle.

The blazing log fire, started only an hour earlier, warmed the back of 'C's' tall wing chair and cast its dancing shadows onto four of the six people who had already taken their places in this semicircle opposite, now perched like birds of prey on the edges of their chairs gazing inquisitively at their host. Staring right back at them was a heavy set face with piercing blue eyes. This was not the Chief however, but one Admiral Mansfield Cumming who had founded the Secret Service Bureau, the forerunner to the Secret Intelligence Service in the year of our Lord nineteen hundred and nine. That is where the designated 'C' came from: Cumming. The large portrait executed in oils staring back at the four seated gentlemen from behind 'C' and above the ornate marble fireplace was only a copy, but it could still put the fear of God into anyone who was unlucky enough to have to endure its gaze for any length of time. Or perhaps it was because anyone unfortunate enough to be incarcerated with 'C' for a long session in the early-hours of the morning knew that heads might very well roll – figuratively speaking of course; mostly.

'C' proceeded to introduce each of the four guests making up this semicircle who had already arrived, ignoring the fact that there was one more gentleman sitting stony faced outside this semicircle with his back to the heavily draped curtains merging into the shadows, which even in this very important meeting is where 'C' preferred him to remain. He was attired in an expensive grey crumpled suit. Even though it was very creased, it bore the impeccable low key style and cut of Savile Row. Stryker adjusted his adopted old school tie and gave a muffled cough. Throughout the meeting he was neither referred to nor acknowledged as being there though all who sat within the room were aware of his existence, but none had the temerity to question the fact of just who he might be.

'C' began the meeting by giving a verbal thumbnail sketch of the Red Chameleon using the facts as far as was known, including a psychological profile on what little they had to go on in the form of his Vauxhall Cross taped conversations and an overview of the potential Russian defector's offer of supplying information relating to biological weapons. It had been deemed more suitable to get the meat of the subject to be discussed out of the way before moving on to who the prime movers in the room were.

Working from 'C's' right, the first person to be introduced was a Sir Samuel Dogson. Sir Dogson wore a pinstriped suit and sober tie fastened with a small tight knot beneath a white starched collar, perfectly matching his smooth anaemic complexion. He bore a rather snooty expression planted on his angular but otherwise unremarkable features and looked every inch the senior Civil Servant and member of the ultra-secret Joint Intelligence Committee, or in Westminster parlance JIC, on whose behalf for tonight he was here to represent. This particular secret coterie of high ranking officials hailed not only from the Foreign Office and Cabinet Office, but also the Home Office and of course the leading member of this highly secretive group was from the SIS. Sir Samuel Dogson himself actually hailed from the FCO.

The spy committee which Sir Dogson represented, whose penumbra touched many different government departments, was so secret that even ministers were kept ignorant of its activities, as was its expenditure – although on this particular occasion the Permanent Undersecretary for such matters would duly be informed of the meeting. Government ministers did not receive regular reports either, except on a very irregular basis, and then only at the whim of some civil servant who represented one or other of the Offices or SIS itself. His attire was very formal and business-like. Even his steel-rimmed glasses gave off an air of cold detached officialdom.

During this meeting Sir Samuel Dogson listened with rapt attention, but unlike the others, he never voiced an opinion, except to thank Donald for the proffered coffee which was received gratefully and biscuits, which were declined because of having earlier indulged himself in a late night snack, knowing through similar occasions how this meeting might drift on well into the night. He had arrived at 'C's' meeting by using a standby government chauffeur from the pool to drive him down from London. He was there in his capacity as an observer and therefore took no part in the proceedings, although it was noted by 'C' that a few rapidly scrawled aides-memoires were consigned to a small red notebook, withdrawn earlier from his inside breast pocket. Having arrived before the others he had already been briefed by 'C' over a stiff whisky.

Seated next to Sir Samuel Dogson was a legal advisor from SIS Administration who had been invited to the meeting on the off-chance that his advice might be required. The next chair was still vacant.

The fourth chair was occupied by a man who stood out not only because of his physical size but also because of his military bearing, and possessed a ruddy complexion hinting at a life spent as much outdoors as inside pushing a pen and who was indeed a very senior officer in the Special Air Service, a brigadier named 'Dick' Jordan. In fact this brigadier was not only a valued member of one of the greatest fighting units the world has ever witnessed but he was also a very senior member of an even more anonymous and shadowy team drawn from the Special Air Service, together with that of the other group of distinguished special forces, the Special Boat Service, otherwise known as the SBS to which Stryker's two buddies who had been killed by the Russians had belonged.

This anonymous team of fearsome fighters were chosen for possessing exceptional and specialised talents, not just for their prowess in foreign languages and knowledge of medicine, but also for such diverse skills as computing and electronics. Many had degrees and put their exceptional talents to great use on a daily basis around the globe. All had seen much active service and all worked beneath the radar of public scrutiny, this being as much for carrying out successful covert operations as well as for their own personal security. This shadowy group of well-trained men was whispered to be known as The Increment, though no one outside of a very select and privileged group of people could be sure.

The fourth man sitting at one end of this semicircle looked totally out of place amidst the civil servants and ramrod-backed soldier next to him. In fact, being positioned next to the high ranking officer with perfect deportment had the effect of amplifying the bad posture of this gentleman as he slouched with a tired-looking demeanour in the very comfortable chair he had been allocated. He was dressed in a pair of baggy brown corduroy trousers, so stained that they had the appearance of having been lifted straight out of a skip, and upon his shoulders sat an ill-fitting tweed jacket. There was one other vacant seat still waiting to be filled next to this shambling image but for now it was this last person who resembled a vagrant with which 'C' initially made eye contact as he began speaking.

"Gentlemen, we are expecting two other people, but so as not to keep you up too long, having now entered the early hours of Saturday morning, and because time is of the essence, let me introduce you to an old friend of mine who also happens to be a house guest just now, Dr Kenneth Jones. He is a Russian translator par excellence and a long time Soviet watcher and analyst specialising in logical semantics."

Ken gave an imperceptible nod of his head and looked slightly embarrassed, his cheeks flushed by the heat of the fire and a lifetime's dedication to old malt whisky.

"Now Ken, tell those assembled what you told me just a few hours ago." 'C' smiled at Dr Kenneth Jones, nodding as he did so to give him encouragement. The doctor slowly rose to his feet, walked slowly to stand beside 'C' and looked purposefully at each of the gathered guests in turn before speaking.

"I shall not waste your time here delving deeper into the background which the Chief has already expounded upon, but suffice it to say that through the good offices of fate I have discovered – no, stumbled upon the fact that 'THE RED CHAMELEON', the Russian scientist and potential defector, has a stepsister." As he looked around him for some reaction there was none whatsoever. Then he dropped the bombshell – "...And she is a naturalised British subject residing in London." This time there was an audible collective gasp.

Ken continued. "We know that the person using the alias THE RED CHAMELEON is really an eminent Russian scientist. The surname of my friend's stepfather, who is, or rather was, because he is now deceased, the father of this Russian scientist, was a Mr Grachev. So the person we are dealing with, that is to say, our target, is therefore one Dr Anatoly Grachev, and according to our records a foremost Russian scientist known throughout the international scientific community."

At the mention of the Russian's name, Stryker's ears pricked up. Although he had requested some background information from Registry on any information they held on Dr Grachev he had never pursued the matter. A little earlier, when closeted with the civil servant who resembled a shop window mannequin, for a cursory briefing of the facts by 'C', the actual name 'Grachev' had not been mentioned, only the fact that a Russian agent was in their sights. The revelation by Dr Kenneth Jones that the name now appended to the Russian scientist being hunted was a Dr Anatoly Grachev – who just happened to be a friend of Stryker's – put a completely different complexion on the situation, the ramifications for himself possibly far reaching – and if the Russian knew that he, Stryker, was working, even on a temporary basis, with Britain's Intelligence Service, then it could be very dangerous indeed. In fact it would seem quite likely that he, Stryker, had been targeted by Grachev just because of his connection with the British SIS. But these fatuous ideas were instantly dismissed for what they were – crazy. There was no way that Dr Grachev could possibly know any of this.

Ken carried on speaking to the assembled group of grey-suited men. "This stepsister of Dr Grachev, she is known to me as, well... Penny Churchill, a good friend. The connection only came to light, as 'C' says, a very few hours ago. "

That was the truth. It had happened whilst David was closely questioning Penny under hypnosis. It appeared that her stepfather had once been a famous stage hypnotist and that it was he, who whilst giving one of his performances at a Moscow circus, had been responsible for the death of Penny's sister. It had been the joint grief of Penny's mother and of Dimitri having caused her death which in a strange way had brought them together. Dimitri, having left his first wife and son, had eventually married Penny's mother. They then decided to live in England. But before leaving Russia, Dimitri had arranged for a Moscow jeweller to produce two identical lapel pins, crafted in red enamel and gold. It was in the shape of the Soviet Union's red flag bearing in one corner the symbolic hammer and sickle fashioned in gold.

These two facsimile copies of beautifully crafted pieces of jewellery were disposed of in the following manner: one had been given to the now eminent Russian scientist Dr Grachev, and the other to his stepsister Penny. Both of them were young children at the time. Penny had previously mentioned to Kenneth that the only existing letter from a friend of her mother's in Moscow mentioned an elderly jeweller who had once made this very piece of jewellery, and that he had recently died of a heart attack. His name was Mikhail. Dr Kenneth Jones, having only the week before been given a description by his old friend 'C' regarding an elaborate pin sent to one of his agents, Kenneth suddenly realised that Penny herself had sported such a pin in his presence and correctly deduced from this that the potential Russian defector must of course be Penny's stepbrother. It was whilst acting as translator in David's cottage that he made this connection between Penny and THE RED CHAMELEON, leading to the decision to contact 'C', resulting in Dr Kenneth Jones's late night dash to explain matters first hand. The chance connection between Penny and Dr Grachev must have been millions to one – it was incredible – but, c'est la vie.

Kenneth had not mentioned the connection to Penny nor David, but instead feigned illness, so as to be able to get away to ring his old chum 'C' – head of MI6 – to let him know the real identity of THE RED CHAMELEON. Even now, while they were at this meeting in the early hours of the morning, MI5 were working on behalf of SIS, searching London for Dr Grachev's whereabouts. As yet, he had not been located, but then London was a vast place to search.

Just as Dr Kenneth Jones finished speaking the soundproof door swung open to reveal a tall, stooped, grey-haired figure in his sixties who looked as though he had been put out by being summoned to such a late night meeting. 'C' welcomed his new guest and introduced him to the assembled group.

"This is Professor Lambton, Deputy Director of Porton Down, an establishment of which I am sure you will all be familiar." As 'C' spoke, he motioned the professor to the vacant chair in between the legal bod and the soldier. The scientist had never sat in the presence of 'C' before, but being a person with such intimate knowledge of the subject to be discussed it was deemed that his presence would be invaluable. As the professor took his place and in the process of retrieving his spectacles, he felt more than a little stunned as he turned his head to catch a glimpse of Stryker sitting in the shadows, acknowledging him with yet another brief nod before being offered a cup of coffee and biscuits by Donald and settling down to the matters at hand.

For the benefit of his coterie of advisors 'C' briefly set out the background to Dr Grachev's plea for asylum. Professor Lambton was then given the opportunity to explain the significance of just what Dr Grachev was offering and how dangerous such a selective virus could be to the population targeted. However, Professor Lambton proffered the thought that, "Because this particular virus had been developed in Russia and considering the experimental nature of the particular toxin used, Dr Grachev's killer virus would presumably have been created using strands of DNA obtained from supplies of blood donated by his fellow countrymen. Therefore, based on this educated guess, unless one possessed the DNA of Russian extraction, it would more than likely be perfectly safe to handle. After all, if this Russian would-be defector has developed such a selective virus, that would be the whole point of the exercise – for the virus to be selective. So in other words, unless you are Russian, or of Russian extraction, and we do not have too many of those people in this country at the moment, you would in theory be perfectly safe inhaling Dr Grachev's microbes as opposed to dealing with them in a bio level safety four facility or in the case of Porton Down, an upgraded BSL – 3."

A smug look crept over a section of the assembled group, confirming perhaps what some of them had always believed, that they were inviolate to any horrors visited upon other sections of the population.

'C' interrupted the professor's discourse.

"Professor, for those of us who are not au fait with the terminology in such matters, would you please elucidate on this bio-level safety issue – of what significance is that?"

"I apologise. For the layman then; when dealing with the most dangerous viruses known to man, BSL – 4 describes the highest maximum-security laboratory. Out of interest there are only five of these facilities in the world – six if you include the modified facility here at Porton Down. Russia has two facilities, America two and Canada one. These facilities deal with the most dangerous viruses that could conceivably wipe out the entire human species on planet Earth if distributed in the right manner – and I do not exaggerate. Many are termed plague microbes which I believe is self-explanatory, and have been used for centuries in what I would call the invisible armaments business. It goes without saying but I shall say it anyway, these deadly microbes are treated as one would the storage of nuclear weapons – with extreme caution and security. When working with these infectious agents they are prevented from escaping into the environment by using what is known as a negative pressure system within the laboratories – that means that air flow can only move one way – inwards toward special filters away from the corridor one enters by so that the air is always being sucked into the laboratory and cannot flow outwards, thus avoiding any contamination outside these laboratories. Not only that, but one has to be attired in all the protective gear for working with these killer microbes – for that is what they are. These scientists are obliged to wear disposable gowns – gloves – masks – glasses – footwear – the lot. For what they are dealing with are the most highly contagious infectious diseases on this planet. So it is not surprising that the scientists that deal with them, when attired, look as though they are on a space mission – and in some respects I suppose they are." At that moment the door to the study opened once more.

Professor Lambton's assertive discourse was interrupted by Donald – 'C's' bodyguard –whereupon 'C' made a cursory apology to those assembled and a rapid exit. Ten minutes later he was back with his final guest.

This was the person who had been responsible for the summoning by 'C' of all those, except Stryker who had arrived on a totally different mission, to the hastily arranged meeting, and who even now as this integral figure was ushered into the large study was creating something of a shock for two of those in attendance.

CHAPTER 97

"Why Dad – Stryker…!" After that brief cry, the rest of her sentence was never completed because of Carol's growing awareness of other soberly attired people inside the room, but the remaining unuttered words, already framed within her mind would have been, *"…What on earth are you doing here?"*

Professor Lambton looked not a little nervous as he announced in a loud, clear voice to the heads now staring in the glamorous stranger's direction, "Gentlemen, this is Caroline Lambton… my daughter." For a moment or two the atmosphere was lightened as a humorous chuckle rippled around the room. That was, except for one particular man who sat in the shadows and who was definitely not smiling, but whose face instead registered a look of complete amazement. Carol was wearing the same attire as Stryker had noticed when saying goodbye to her just a few hours earlier. Skin tight black leggings, a rather loose lilac top with frills adorning the low cut neck and voluminous sleeves from another era, obviously one of her haute couture designs she had modelled when she had been the belle of the catwalk. Stryker had guessed right when he assumed the chuckles had been brought about by Carol's titillating mode of dress. But as he had learnt to his cost, the maxim 'never judge a book by its cover' certainly held true for this particular young lady.

After introducing Carol to the grey-suited men whose eyes had rapidly lost their sleepiness as they now sat agog in that semicircle, momentarily letting their attention waver as 'C' invited Carol to recount the events she had expressly contacted him about less than two hours previously, and which in the process would make it crystal clear as to just why they were all assembled here in the early hours of the morning.

At that introduction 'C' then handed the floor over to Caroline for what was to be an intriguing and revelatory session, surpassing most events that had ever taken place in that room since it had been given over to its present function by the head of Britain's Foreign Intelligence Service. A hush descended upon her captivated audience as an angelic-faced Caroline began speaking.

"Gentlemen, my name is Caroline Lambton and earlier this evening whilst carrying out my duties at Vauxhall Cross as an officer of SIS I received a telephone call from the Red Chameleon, which since having arrived here a short while ago, I now understand to have been unmasked as a Dr Grachev." At the mention of Grachev's name Carol's eyes momentarily rested on Stryker sitting in the shadows at the rear of the room. She omitted to say that the Russian scientist had requested to speak with one of their agents, cover name Smith.

Carol knew all incoming calls to Vauxhall Cross – SIS HQ – were recorded for security reasons, and that this particular call would be scrutinised very closely once the words 'Red Chameleon' had been filtered out by dedicated computer software designed to isolate key targeted words pushed into its memory bank. This was one of the reasons why Carol already had a plan of action worked out with Stryker for just such a situation as now presented itself. She did not want to be perceived as being caught on the hop because of not having done her homework. Therefore, when it was suggested by the Red Chameleon, a.k.a. Dr Grachev, that the ampoule containing a deadly biological virus would be ready for delivery to Smith, a.k.a. Stryker the next day in the afternoon, one of many predetermined scenarios had been put to the would-be Russian defector.

Carol supplied chapter and verse for the edification of the people assembled regarding her conversation with the Red Chameleon, explaining that she had suggested to the scientist requesting political asylum in exchange for his stated living sample of a newly constructed selective pathogenic virus with no known antidote, that he should meet Smith the following afternoon beneath the statue of Eros, Piccadilly Circus at 2 p.m. Being such a famous landmark, it had been reasoned that the potential Russian defector would have no difficulty in locating the area. Also, unbeknown to Dr Grachev, this location would make observation easier for MI6 agents sent to monitor the meeting from vantage points in nearby buildings overlooking the statue and a vehicle had been supplied so as to visually cover all entrances and exits to Piccadilly Circus, even on a busy day like Saturday. Carol was loath to speak on the open landline, so had to keep the information for the would-be defector as cryptic as possible, whilst not jeopardising the operation by giving garbled instructions which could possibly result in any misunderstanding.

"Bring the promised ampoule with you," she had instructed. "Everything you requested has been agreed to. You will recognise Smith by something he is wearing – a visual sign of friendship. If you are delayed for any reason and do not show at two you have one more chance at five pm; do you understand?"

Dr Grachev had replied in a firm voice *yes*, but was puzzled by the words, "*You will recognise Smith by something he is wearing, a visual sign of friendship.*" He had then quickly replaced the telephone receiver.

***

After a question and answer session lasting barely half an hour, 'C' let the legal advisor raise certain points pertaining to defection and go into some detail of the pitfalls. It was a well-worn theme which had been gone over many times before, but 'C' felt that everybody in the room ought to be made aware of such facts once again. 'C' always liked to bear in mind the basics before moving on. Once the legal aspects had been looked at in a cursory fashion the legal advisor was dismissed. By his happy demeanour it was obvious that the words of dismissal were music to his tired body. He rose slowly and nodded his goodbyes, which was more akin to briefly nodding off and being re-awakened with quick jerks of the head. He was very grateful for having at his disposal a driver drawn from the pool of government chauffeurs to ferry him back to London and his flat overlooking the Thames close by Vauxhall Bridge.

***

'C' took the floor once more. It was a smooth if somewhat lengthy performance, explaining the Government's attitude to détente with Russia. It was explained to the assembled guests remaining that the latest Russian defector to America had made it almost impossible to accept another defector at this time of rapprochement because it would not bode well for the new détente, now jealously guarded by the Western Powers. Good relations with Russia let Western governments cut back on their defence budgets which would be heartily endorsed within the precincts of Westminster and the country at large – namely the voting electorate.

"That is why it had been decided in the even earlier hours of this morning by a hastily convened meeting of a truncated COBRA Cabinet committee, made up of people who sit in judgement upon such things, that for reasons over and above that of the usefulness of the potential information, well… that no resettlement package could, nor indeed would be considered." By mentioning COBRA, which was made up of Cabinet Ministers, MI5 and MI6 Officers plus defence staff, 'C' was anxious to let his colleagues know just how serious this particular situation had become, and what terrible repercussions might follow if it all went haywire. "This is being treated as top priority – the Prime Minister is being kept briefed. The very safety of this nation – that of Europe, NATO – and of our friends across the pond, hangs in the balance."

After a moments murmuring, a heavy silence ensued. It was then from the shadows at the rear of the room that Stryker, in his barely detectable soft American accent, broke the tranquillity by posing a few "What if?" questions, having been emboldened by 'C's' reference to "our friends across the pond."

"What if the Red Chameleon, or rather Dr Grachev, does not turn up at either of the times mentioned? What if he never shows? What if word got out about losing someone as valuable as this?"

'C' interjected with a raised hand. "I respect forward thinking, but don't you think that's being just a little negative? I mean, we're the ones ostensibly doing this Russian chap a favour by promising him political asylum. I do not think he would have taken the risks he obviously has if he weren't prepared to see it through to the end, do you? Besides, as our colleague Sir Samuel Dogson will no doubt understand, now that I have informed him of course…" here there was an attempt at lightening the heavy atmosphere beginning to develop which elicited another ripple of stifled mirth, "this discussion tonight, err… correction, this morning, remains within these four walls. In other words, on a need-to-know basis, and quite frankly as far as I'm concerned, until I decide otherwise, no one else needs to know. Is that quite clear Sir Dogson?"

Sir Samuel Dogson blushed and nodded in the affirmative and backed this up with a barely audible "Yes." Stryker noticed that having the spotlight turned upon this civil servant in such a way in front of these other men within the room, Sir Samuel Dogson looked as if he had been slighted by being made the butt of a joke, and he did not like it.

Stryker had asked in the most direct way possible what the future might hold for Dr Grachev if this particular operation went pear shaped, but he knew in his heart even before posing the question, that nothing would come of it. In normal circumstances he would never have considered such an obvious ploy in Seattle and it only confirmed what he had been dwelling on too frequently recently and hinted at in confidence by various other Six men, namely that it was time for him to be moving on while he still had the chance. Being an American citizen he was patently an outsider and no matter what happened that was not going to change.

The loss of his two SBS friends had left its mark and it was for this reason Stryker had posed the questions that patently irritated 'C'. It had only been because of the loss of these two Brits that he had agreed to go along with his own government's request by acquiescing to the pleas for help by the British Secret Intelligence Service in an attempt to discover why they had met such a grisly end. But now an idea was growing in the back of Stryker's mind, being formulated even while he attended to the meeting in progress, knowing that whatever decision was taken by 'C' at the end of this session, he – Stryker – would be expected to accept that decision stoically like some automaton… yet, on another level, for the first time he was beginning to see things in a totally different light. He was beginning to develop a conscience about this guy Dr Grachev. That was bad news for Stryker and his adoptive department which he had no say in being seconded to. That had been decided with no input by him but by shadowy men from the American Embassy based in London – or so it had been hinted at. Everything relating to this case seemed to Stryker to be on a need-to-know basis which would normally be understandable coming from a very professional police force in Seattle, except that to his mind it seemed to be taken to the extreme. He had been kept totally in the dark about the involvement of his own countrymen and made to feel an outsider by the grudging acknowledgement that his input might somehow be of value. So even before 'C' had made any definite decision, Stryker knew what he would do later that same morning and he could not wait for that time to arrive.

'C' focussed once more upon the conclusion of his preamble regarding Dr Grachev's application for political asylum, adroitly explaining for the benefit of Stryker, who had raised the follow up question of whether he was to be granted this favour of political asylum, that the answer was an unequivocal "NO."

Stryker tried as best he could to hide his feeling of Dr Grachev's betrayal by 'C', who only hours earlier had given the go ahead to let the Red Chameleon, now known by his real name of Dr Grachev, have a promise of the four things he had required – namely; asylum, money, plastic surgery and safe accommodation in the UK. Stryker had come to the conclusion that Dr Grachev was not responsible for his two British friends' deaths, for why would the Russian scientist knowingly send them into a trap if he had wanted their host country to look favourably upon him for the granting of his asylum? There must be another reason why his two friends had been put in that dangerous position but as yet he had not figured it out.

"Dr Grachev, " 'C' said, "was to be held on the understanding that his wish for political asylum would be granted, but that once he had been "sucked of all knowledge pertaining to biological weapons until he was as dry as a husk – this being carried out by a scientific committee headed by professor Lambton of Porton Down – he would no longer be of any use, and as I mentioned earlier, would in fact become a liability."

'C' then made direct eye contact with the SAS officer before carrying on. "The lieutenant here will deal with the matter once our team of British scientists have picked this Russian's brains as clean as a whistle, thus absolving the British taxpayer from the burden of keeping this potential Russian traitor in the manner he would no doubt wish to become accustomed, whilst at the same time protecting our embryonic détente with Russia mentioned earlier and thus gentlemen, killing two birds with one stone." Stryker gave a wry smile as he thought about the irony of 'C' having used the same phrase Dr Grachev had attempted to use, though on this particular occasion in the correct manner.

Brigadier Jordan looked at 'C', grew two inches taller in his chair and nodded confidently before supplying in a clipped accent, perhaps a little too much information than was required, "You will be familiar with the fact, sir, that wetwork is my specialty."

CHAPTER 98

After those assembled began to make their separate ways home, or in the case of Professor Lambton, returning once more to his club, acquiescing to 'C's' request of remaining in London for the time being, Stryker hung back to have a few private words with 'C' as he had requested a little earlier, handing his car keys to Carol, asking her to wait in the Morgan parked outside on the long gravel drive.

It had turned four and although still dark outside, there was the feeling that dawn was not far off. Certainly this was the thinking of 'C' as he dismissed Donald, his bodyguard, and walked back into the large, now empty room which had begun to exude that peculiar stale smell of warm bodies and half consumed cups of coffee.

Stryker could detect a coolness creeping into the room. It had nothing to do with the first rate central heating system malfunctioning, but rather the manner of 'C', from whom Stryker wanted some clarification.

'C' had already switched off the lights so as not to sustain eye contact and motioned Stryker to sit down. The only illumination now came from the hallway.

"Now then, take this and keep it safe until required." 'C' pushed a sturdy-looking brown envelope into Stryker's hands. "That is the gold lapel pin sent by Dr Grachev and is to be worn in your lapel in a highly visible manner when the moment is suitable. I believe Carol Lambton has already shown you a copy of the letter enclosed with this ornamentation so it has been omitted. I also had a word with Carol at the Office last night about the whole set-up. No doubt she will put you right about a few things which I don't have time to deal with at this moment as you might or might not appreciate."

Stryker pocketed the package without speaking and stood waiting.

"What is it you wish to say? It's been a very long day and you have work to do later so you'd better get some sleep." There was no emotion in his flat, monotone voice, just words.

Stryker broached his subject falteringly: "Am I to understand that after I have made contact with the Red... err... Dr Grachev, that he will no longer be granted political asylum as he had been promised?"

As opposed to 'C', Stryker found it impossible to keep emotion out of his voice. 'C' picked up on this attitude and rounded on him with vehemence.

"It's no good getting uptight. Nobody but nobody questions my decisions. You know perfectly well what I said earlier and it is imperative that this operation is carried out professionally. You have been tasked to help us out because of the unfortunate situation which has arisen through no fault of your own I admit, but tasked you have been and I expect you to hold up your side of the bargain, is that clear? You cannot afford to empathise with this traitor, for that is what he is; a traitor to his own country – to your country and to ours. And as you were informed from the word go America, well to be more precise the Central Intelligence Agency actually," the word *actually* was pronounced syllable by syllable to reinforce his coming point, "has been kept in the frame. They know all about your mission so do not neglect your duty. Miss Lambton has already furnished you with all the details required for meeting this Russian chap – the times and everything. You know there will be a strong back-up and everything is tight and leak proof.

"A special van will monitor your every movement as you meet up with the Russian so as to keep you safe as well as protect our target. Eros has been chosen for the initial contact and once that contact has been confirmed by our colleagues you and the target will then be taken to a safe house where the Russian will be thoroughly debriefed by a team led by Professor Lambton. Whatever happens thereafter is of no concern of yours. We will have fulfilled our part of the bargain for you have been paid handsomely and as an American citizen you will be shipped home to Seattle, and because of your signing our official Secrets Act which will not conflict with your being an American citizen, you will never mention this operation to anyone ever again and as far as I am concerned, when all this has finished, no matter how it turns out you will be regarded from then on as *persona non grata*. In other words, I shall wash my hands of you Stryker – is that clear?"

'*Persona non grata*' was a phrase that set Stryker's pulse racing. He could feel the blood surging to his face, a sensation akin to it being on fire.

"But I gave my word to Dr Grachev through Carol Lambton that he would be granted these things he asked for in exchange for the virus, the main request of which was political asylum." He knew he had gone too far in questioning a decision made by the Chief but felt he had to make a final attempt to reverse the outcome. He knew it would be on his conscience for the rest of his life if he did not at least try, in his own way he had always striven to behave with honour toward his fellow man, even his adversaries.

Now he began to feel dirty.

"In this situation I'm afraid your word cannot be your bond. And don't play the innocent with me, my boy. Did you not learn anything in your brief stay at Fort Monckton? Surely they told you that as a serving officer of the realm, even as a temporary one I hasten to add, that any promise you make cannot override the security of the state. It's standard procedure to make promises we can't keep. We all make them in this job. Promise the world. Anyway, I make the decisions and my decision is final." Those last few words were constantly reverberating around the environs of Vauxhall Cross, mimicked by the men and women who would prefer not to hear them from their Chief's own mouth.

"Oh, and before you leave there is one other thing – well several actually. Two men of this realm died within your vicinity in the waters around the Persian Gulf. After that came the suspicious death of yet another one of our men, namely British agent Anthony Lovejoy-Taylor, which could be put down to your mishandling of the situation in Moscow. Then again there were the two Chinese civilians you dealt with on Hampstead Heath. And what about that woman in Registry – what was her name – Brenda Watkins? There have just been too many people associated with you in one way or another who have ended up dead."

"Excuse me but I have – had, never met Brenda Watkins."

"No. But Carol was close to her – a good colleague of hers by all accounts. Neither do we forget your boast to one of our officers when this whole operation began that you killed four Russian Special Forces with your bare hands. You are not James bloody Bond you know. We don't give our agents carte blanche to go around killing people willy-nilly. Maybe as a detective in Seattle you can get away with such actions but not in this country. If you were a cat you would surely have used up your nine lives many times over. We in the SIS do not take these things lightly. Anyhow, the end result of this forthcoming operation must be successful. That, Mr Stryker, is imperative." Uncharacteristically 'C's' voice had risen to a crescendo before he brought the meeting to a rapid close by rising to his feet without saying goodnight. Stryker followed the Chief from the darkened room, slamming the door harder than he should have in the early hours of the morning.

***

Stryker was still seething as he climbed into his red Morgan sports car, Carol leaning over the passenger seat and opening the door for him as he continued turning the unexpected events of the past few hours over in his mind. It was Carol who spoke first.

"Sorry I couldn't warn you of that message I received from Dr Grachev. I'll bet that came as a big shock. I rang you on your cell phone from Vauxhall Cross as soon as I heard from him but there was no reply."

"Yeah, I left my cell phone at the condo recharging. Signal was getting weak."

"As I've told you a thousand times Stryker, we here in England don't call it a condo but a flat, darling. But how did you manage to be at tonight's meeting? You said you were going to see the police about those two Chinese men you shot?"

Stryker ignored her calling him darling and continued. "Well, that's being taken care of. I mentioned it to 'C' who was not exactly pleased with the outcome. Of course what I am saying is he went ballistic. I visited 'C' because there were certain things I wished to clear up with him but as soon as I arrived your telephone call came through and all hell broke loose – telephone calls galore as you can imagine. So my chance to speak with him was lost. Once you had mentioned the fact to 'C' that the Red Chameleon had been in touch then anything I was going to question him about paled into virtual insignificance. But there are more pressing things to deal with now. I trust you didn't mention that I knew Dr Grachev on a personal basis?"

"It's just mind blowing isn't it?" Then Carol patted Stryker's muscle-bound arm. "You know I wouldn't do anything to compromise you sweetie. I'd never let you down, you know that."

"No, I'm sorry to ask but I just had to know what you may have told him. In fact, as I mentioned last night, I'm expected to have a meeting with Dr Grachev at midday today – Harley Street to be precise. He said it was urgent. I'll bet that was heartfelt. He rang me to arrange the meeting just before I left Swiss Cottage.

"But 'C' thinks you're going to help capture Dr Grachev later on this afternoon."

"Yes, that's rather awkward isn't it? But I have a plan and not too much time to arrange things. I require your help though. I'll tell you all about it on the way. There's a lot to do."

Carol gave Stryker a sideways glance at his cryptic reply but nodded in the affirmative, the black drop pendant earrings she had worn that first night at the flat danced around her flushed cheeks, contrasting with the flawless complexion which quickly turned into a broad smile. Looking hard into Stryker's eyes she said, "I'm your girl Stryker, you know that... anything, just ask."

Stryker inwardly winced as he slid the sports car into gear for the long haul back to London, wondering what pitfalls lay in store for him in the ensuing hours ahead. Then the conversation with 'C' came to mind. *"I also had a word with Carol at the Office last night about the whole set up. No doubt she will put you right about a few things..."*

"What's this I hear about you and 'C' having a heart to heart about the gold pin and the Red Chameleon's letter?"

"Oh Stryker, its good you reminded me, though come to think of it, I shouldn't have needed reminding should I? It was last night. 'C' caught me red handed looking at the Dubai file lying in his safe together with the gold pin which I had persuaded his secretary to let me have a look at after having arranged with the Red Chameleon, a.k.a. Dr Grachev, for his meeting to take place at Piccadilly Circus. Samantha knew I was involved with the case so I thought it might be a good opportunity to get another sneak look at the file and maybe see something of interest as you requested. And as it happened I saw who the person was who signed off the order to designate both of us with the tab: *'Persona non grata.'*"

"Who was it?"

"You'd never guess in a million years. It was signed in green ink. That should tell you everything."

"Why should that mean anything to me? Red, green, blue, black. I haven't the slightest idea what you mean," Stryker replied.

"It was 'C' himself who gave the order. I recognised his distinctive green ink he had used all over the document. Not only that but he really did catch me red handed with a piece of paper in my hand from that secret file, whereby he describes both of us as persona non grata. I could have died of embarrassment. Did you not know that he is the only person in MI6 who is allowed the use that particular coloured ink? Makes it that much more distinctive to pick out from all the dross that crosses one's desk I suppose. I'm surprised you haven't come across any of his missives yourself. Anyhow, don't worry Stryker. He explained that it had come about because of the situation regarding the Dubai incident. He said everything had to be kept what he termed 'in house'. He said that he had been obliged to keep an open mind about the whole case. He apologised for the order and said we should be relaxed about it. That it was just normal procedure in such cases. That is, to err on the cautious side. He said that after all, those two men who went diving with you had lost their lives and that you were the only witness, so of course things had to be done in a certain way – that it was just Six's way. Mentioned tradecraft and that one must never rule anything out or conversely, to read too much into that order. He also told me not to be paranoid."

"'C' said that?"

"That's what he said, Stryker."

"Then I hope you will bear that in mind when I tell you that just a few minutes ago when mentioning this problem I have with all these people dying who had been associated with me in one way or another he mentioned your late friend Brenda Watkins from Registry."

"What did he say?"

"He said that you were close to her – 'C's' words not mine – and that she ended up dead."

"What the hell is he insinuating?"

"Carol, to reiterate 'C's' advice, you must not become paranoid?"

"Huh! Oh, and you will be shocked to hear that there was something else which poor Brenda told me before she died, though that sounds stupid putting it that way doesn't it? I mean, it had to be before she died otherwise she couldn't have told me could she?"

"Carol, please do get on with it, and tell me what it is that Brenda told you."

"Well, I did not tell you this before, because we had no immediate plans to travel anywhere and I did not wish to worry you, but the other thing that Brenda told me she saw when she looked through the files a little while ago was something called a restrictive order placed upon you and I forbidding us to be allowed to leave the country. I worked out the dates and figured that it was only after we had returned from our disastrous trip to Moscow that that particular order had been instigated.

***

The roads had been pretty much empty and with the speed limit being ignored it was only just over an hour later, pulling up at the kerbside outside their flat, that Stryker awoke Carol, who had slept fitfully and uncomfortably using Stryker's shoulder for a pillow and announced: "Home, sweet home." Carol opened her smeared mascara-lined eyelids and smiled dreamily.

"What would Mummy say now if she could see me with my American hunk? She never met you did she?"

Stryker gave Carol a long look and moved onto a more pressing subject. "I received a return call from my American friend in Seattle and he has been able to confirm what I suspected. It makes me even more certain that I was set up to be a sitting target, Anthony Lovejoy-Taylor being killed in

Moscow by mistake instead of me. As I mentioned to you before, if it wasn't for my eye giving me problems it could so easily have been me taking that bullet to the back of the head. When you've caught up on your beauty sleep I want you to do some more ferreting for me at Vauxhall Cross – I think the whole episode stinks – the whole caboodle. But you must be very careful. You wouldn't attract so much attention asking questions today because of 'C's' planned operation to catch Dr Grachev. My guess is that everybody involved in it will have their mind on that and not on other things. That's just human nature at work when a large scale operation like this is mounted. Don't forget, everything in that building is done on a strictly need-to-know basis so do be careful. Remember that. Promise!"

"Come on Stryker, I'm not silly you know. There's a lot of sympathy for my friend Brenda out there right now. But tell me, who is this person in Seattle and how have they helped you?"

"I can't say at the moment, but I shall let you know later. Just do a little ferreting as I suggest and let me know what you can find out, if anything?"

"What do you want me to look for?"

"Well for instance, you could begin with my initial interrogator where this all kicked off. That Welsh guy Hughes for instance, our elusive naval attaché stationed at the British Embassy in Dubai and his sidekick – what was his name? Yes. Stephen, that's it. The Duty Officer – see what you can find out about them, where they are now. Someone must know what has happened to them. You're familiar with the background so anything you can get a look at relating to this case would be a great help. If you are able to breach the need-to-know security aspects for instance – by getting your hands on any files like you did from 'C's' safe – use your imagination. Back in Seattle I have a good Indian friend called Danny whom I use on occasion – he'd know what to look for. Has a nose for these things."

"I can do this as well as your friend Danny, I'm sure."

"Well don't let hubris get in the way of your safety. Be careful Carol – please!"

"I will Stryker, I will. Maybe someone familiar with this failed operation might be able to tell me something. They may even have a direct line to MI6's head of station out there in Moscow. After all, Anthony Lovejoy-Taylor may not have been their head of station but he was their number two."

"Just be careful. These people can be very dangerous. Consider who you talk to – remember how your friend Brenda ended up. And if anybody asks you about anything – well tell anybody that enquires absolutely nothing."

One of the attributes required of an Intelligence officer working for the British Secret Intelligence Service as it is to its counterpart in the U.S. is the ability to adapt to situations as they arise, and to live by one's wits where necessary. Stryker thought of the US Navy Seals' stratagems – Improvise. Adapt. Overcome. As he and Caroline had driven back into London in the early hours of the morning, dwelling on his forthcoming meeting at midday with Dr Grachev, he had formulated his next move in some detail.

During the last few hours at 'C's' house, Stryker had learned of something about his so-called Russian friend which had taken his breath away and put a totally different complexion on everything about the case that had gone before. Stryker might not have been focussed one hundred per cent on the Russian scientist in the run up to that late night meeting, but Dr Grachev certainly had his undivided attention now.

It was broad daylight by the time Stryker had dropped Carol off at Swiss Cottage, and after pocketing his cell phone, reached his destination in Regent Street fifteen minutes later. It was still too early for what he had in mind. Pulling his car into one of the side streets near Garrard, the royal jewellers in central London, he fed a parking meter and settled down to catch up on a few hours' sleep before putting his plan into action, which would entail him making his way up to the second floor of the Swiss Centre to see a contact he had made whilst in London and who owed him a favour.

He was awoken over two hours later by knuckles rapping on the car window. As he opened his eyes, he was greeted by the sight of a pretty young woman beaming down at him. It had always been a thrill awakening to find a pair of alluring eyes belonging to a beautiful woman looking at you first thing in the morning, even if it happened to be, as in this case, that of a traffic warden.

After ploughing yet more money into the parking meter, his appetite, like that of the ravenous meter, now required appeasing, it still being too early to do much else. So without a moment's hesitation, after having had a quick shave with his battery operated razor which lay in the dashboard, he secured the car and made his way into Oxford Street and up towards Selfridges Hotel where he knew he could indulge himself in a full English breakfast; eggs, bacon, sausages, fried tomato and bread plus numerous cups of coffee to help him stay awake for the rigours of the day ahead which was about to unfold, culminating in his meeting with Dr Grachev and the mysterious Dr Grey.

CHAPTER 99

As they lay with their heads supported on pillows lightly scented by the fragrance of Li Cheung's perfume, Tom could not have envisaged a more perfect end to the day which had begun with so little hope. They were on the verge of falling asleep when Li Cheung broke the news to Tom.

"I've decided to spend a few hours at the hospital in the morning. I hope you don't mind. See someone in administration if possible – just so that they know what's happening. I shall tell them my father has died and I require a few days off – compassionate leave. They must wonder why I have not been in touch. I'll think of something to tell them. I can hardly say I was kidnapped can I?" She gave a little nervous laugh. Tom turned his head sideways to look into Li Cheung's tender eyes, already missing her as his hand came to rest on her smooth, taught belly.

***

Tom was asleep. His chest rose up and down in a slow rhythmical manner as his breath came free and regular. Just once was there a slight flicker of the eyelashes, caused by some dream which Li Cheung would never be able to divine as she sat naked upon the edge of the bed, closely scrutinising his face.

After what seemed like an eternity, she quietly lifted her bare legs, one at a time, pushing first her right foot and then the other, through into the holes of her pink, lace-trimmed knickers. Planting her tiny feet firmly upon the carpet, Li Cheung took the full weight of her trim body, gently leaning forward, her calves bulging slightly as she endeavoured to stand, rising to her full height of five feet two inches. The sinews in her back became more pronounced momentarily as she lifted and stretched her arms akimbo, letting blood gorge into her slight shoulder muscles.

Li Cheung leant forward once more, bending her knees and letting her arms drop, her fingers gripping the elasticated waist of her knickers as she yanked them up with such force that they cut sharply into the crotch, her mound of Venus bulging like a grassy knoll under the nylon fabric, simulating the appearance of a second skin.

Tom was still oblivious as Li Cheung crept with feline grace toward the bathroom. Proud, hard, rose-coloured nipples enhanced the flawless, smooth, milky surface of her firm, well-proportioned breasts. Her arched back reversed its gentle curve as she leaned over the taps, splashing cold water, first on her face, then onto her breasts. For a moment she gazed at her reflection in the mirror as water formed rivulets on them, trickling down to the erect nipples before cascading back into the ceramic sink.

Finally Li Cheung awoke Tom by placing one hand upon his chest, caressing it from shoulder to shoulder, until he opened his eyes. She was kneeling by the bed fully dressed. Her dreamy expression said it all – they were deeply in love. Still half stupefied by sleep, Tom begged her to take her clothes off and come back to bed.

"My dahlin', you know I love you. Please do not ask me to prove it right now at this moment. Meet me at one o'clock at the eye hospital." Li Cheung kissed Tom softly on his cheek and bade him a final farewell.

"See you dahlin'. I love you." Then she was gone.

CHAPTER 100

At precisely midday the stillness within the Harley Street consulting room was broken by a buzzing sound, and as the button was depressed, a flat voice came over the intercom: "A Mr Stryker is here Dr Grey, shall I send him in?"

The consulting room carried the musty smell of stale air which even the opening of the window had done little to ameliorate. The odour was trapped deep within the fibres of the curtains sitting in front of the neutral-coloured venetian blinds. It was also in the old worn carpet, badly frayed immediately in front of the desk where two patients' chairs had been moved to and fro over many years

"Yes?" came the fractured tinny voice over the cheap intercom. The disinterested receptionist pointed her freshly lacquered fingernail toward the room which Dr Grachev had recently rented in the name of a Dr Grey. She did not bother to speak to Stryker, instead keeping her eyes firmly glued upon an article in one of those give away magazines with the enticing title: 'How to combat stress in the workplace.' Stryker caught sight of the heading and smiled to himself, thinking that she might so easily have been the author.

Stryker moved toward the door, rapping twice with his knuckles. The heavy door opened and he walked in, not immediately seeing the person who had opened it. When the door had been closed, without any preamble Stryker was swiftly ushered to one of the strategically placed chairs set up for him. Sitting down he thought the grey-haired man with the moustache, whom he now turned to look at, seemed vaguely familiar, but had no opportunity to voice such an opinion as Dr Grachev incorporating a sonorous tone emanating from deep down within his throat, issued the command, "*SLEEEEEEP!*" Stryker's eyes instantly glazed over.

After uttering a few more soothing words designed to take Stryker into an even deeper trance he pushed up his victim's jacket and shirt sleeve and once more applied a rubber tourniquet to Stryker's arm as he had in Moscow so many months before. A syringe was produced and after locating the blood vessel the syringe's needle flooded the detective's bloodstream with lorazepam, a strong sedative. That would knock him out for hours.

At the same time as this was happening, Stryker's shoulders dropped and his body swayed forward, the trilby remaining precariously perched upon his head which now lurched to one side. The loose two buttoned jacket fell open. Dr Grachev gasped as he caught sight of a glinting metal gun handle peeping from the top of the leather gun holster. This was Stryker's pistol on loan from the SIS, a Browning high power 9mm automatic, favourite of British undercover agents and the SAS alike.

Dr Grachev collapsed backwards, stretching his arms out to support himself on the edge of the desk as he stared in disbelief, attempting to come to terms with Stryker carrying such a weapon. His mind raced. Was Stryker an agent working on behalf of the Russian Foreign Intelligence Service – the SVR, successor to the KGB? A chill ran down his spine. He was certainly not a businessman in the accepted sense of that word as Dr Grachev had been led to believe. Many Russian businessmen carried guns as far as he was concerned, but not in his mind, an Englishman trading in icons.

Dr Grachev removed a handkerchief from his pocket and using it as a barrier against fingerprints, gingerly removed the gun from its holster. From his national service days within the then Soviet Army, he knew immediately that it was not of Soviet origin. He replaced it just as carefully, not wishing to have an accidental discharge as he had witnessed back home in Moscow, when one of his fellow army recruits had shot off his own scrotum by accidentally firing his weapon. Upon this young man being invalided out of the armed forces, one of his fellow soldiers had suggested with a grin planted upon his face the oxymoron he had a lot of courage but no balls.

So who really was Stryker? Dr Grachev already instinctively knew that this particular question was now a purely academic one as far as Stryker's future was concerned. For whomever he was, fate had now run its inexorable course. He, Grachev, had been preparing himself for this moment since first setting eyes upon Stryker all those months ago at the Easter service of the Russian Orthodox Church in Ennismore Gardens, Knightsbridge. His plan had been worked out down to the last detail. How he would finally relieve Stryker of his false eye and extricate the tiny glass ampoule containing the deadly virus, the culmination of his scientific research into the world's deadliest killer disease. He had rehearsed the procedure in his mind a hundred times: how the process would be the same as the one he had used in his Moscow apartment; levering the false eye from its socket, and this time melting the sealing wax and removing the glass ampoule for which he had put his life in jeopardy before reversing the process and re-inserting the false eye once more. Stryker himself would have been none the wiser.

It had been a stroke of genius to use Stryker as the unsuspecting mule to carry his biological agent through customs without any suspicion being aroused. Only one person knew of this plan and that was Dr Grachev himself. Much to the consternation of Dr Grachev, his plans had now been thrown into disarray. Anyone carrying a gun could not be trusted. He felt drained of energy as he began to consider his next step. No matter which way he looked at the situation, he knew that the gun secreted in that leather holster beneath Stryker's left breast had sealed his fate – just as surely as if Stryker had inserted the barrel into his own mouth and pulled the trigger. He had grown to like Stryker, as someone he could instinctively trust, but now...

With a feeling of being divorced from reality, soothing hypnotic words were spoken in a gentle *sotto voce* as Dr Grachev slid his hands around the front of Stryker's throat. The hypnotically soothing words which would normally only be used for taking the subject deeper into a trancelike state were in reality totally irrelevant as the sedative lorazepam would put anyone into an unconscious state ready to be operated on but not used to kill them. The sedative he had used only moments earlier would have been for another scenario but now that particular situation he had envisaged had been changed irrevocably. He began by delicately loosening the maroon coloured tie. It was silk, the Windsor knot sliding easily out of its compact shape. Then, his nimble fingers undid the top three buttons of Stryker's blue and white striped Asser and Turnbull cotton shirt. Dr Grachev moved deftly behind the bolt upright figure of Stryker, who at this stage was compliant to the gentle tugging at the back of his collar, offering no resistance at all.

This gentle tugging continued, allowing Dr Grachev enough room to manoeuvre his long slender fingers beneath Stryker's collar, searching out the base of his neck. Trailing his hands across the smooth surface of skin lay bare; he eventually located the two pressure points with his thumbs which would cut off the supply of blood to Stryker's brain. Although having never carried out such a procedure before, Dr Grachev knew from his medical training that once he applied enough pressure with his thumbs upon these two throbbing arteries for only a matter of seconds, Stryker's brain would begin to die of oxygen starvation, and that if he were not revived by a vigorous slapping across the face, Stryker would lose consciousness and any semblance of life within two minutes.

Gradually at first, Dr Grachev applied pressure within the neck muscles, standing on his toes so as to gain leverage. Then the pressure grew ever harder to sustain until it began to feel as though Stryker's throbbing pulse had been transferred to that of Dr Grachev's own thumbs. Ten seconds, twenty, thirty – one minute. Dr Grachev blinked back the tears in his eyes. It was very emotional for him, as if he were a mere spectator, not able to intervene on his friend's behalf, but instead, feeling an immense amount of remorse as he noted the relentless pressure of those white tipped thumbs. The only visible sign of Stryker's inward struggle was a brief flicker of his fingers; that was all.

CHAPTER 101

Carol raised the receiver from within her office at SIS Headquarters in Vauxhall Cross then reconsidered and dropped it again just as quickly. It was a quarter to one in the morning and time was running out to let Stryker know just what she had discovered. She had, as promised, succeeded in contacting a colleague from Central Registry and as a favour had actually been allowed to sneak a glance at the restricted file on Anthony Lovejoy-Taylor relating to the fiasco in Moscow culminating in his being killed. In normal circumstances Carol's lowly grade should have made it impossible to do such a thing but thinking it worth taking a chance to help Stryker as he had asked, Carol had persuaded a colleague of Brenda's who, feeling sorry for Carol losing a friend in such a horrific manner, had acquiesced. The scrambled line on the other phone was a better option because Carol wanted to make sure the call was secure so she lifted that receiver and dialled again. She knew that Stryker's meeting in Harley Street was scheduled for twelve o'clock so he should have done whatever he intended to do hours before and left the surgery.

Stryker's telephone rang incessantly but there was no response. Where was Stryker and what had happened to him? The information she had was terrifying and burning a hole in her mind. She just had to communicate what she had recently learnt before it was too late. It regarded the two British men Stryker had been interrogated by at the British Embassy in Dubai whilst on holiday there. Namely the naval attaché, a Mr Hughes, and his subaltern Stephen, the young Duty Officer who had held Stryker captive at gun point while his apartment had been searched. Both of these men she had learnt to her horror had been killed whilst travelling together in a suspicious car crash. The other thing, though of less importance, was the fact that 'C' had blocked all Stryker's requests for any incoming information on the Red Chameleon until 'C' himself had vetted it. Why? It seemed that 'C' wanted a very hands on approach relating to this whole affair.

***

Not being able to concentrate on anything else, Carol had returned from SIS headquarters to her shared flat in Swiss Cottage and once more attempted to ring Stryker – it had now gone half past one and Carol was becoming very concerned. The meeting with Dr Grey and Dr Grachev was scheduled for midday and this had passed some time ago so where was Stryker? From the information she had gleaned from one of the other SIS officers she now knew that they were both in grave danger and Stryker had to be informed. Was he carrying out the charade they had decided upon in the long chat on the drive back to London? Was he at that very moment loitering in Piccadilly Circus attempting to convince SIS that he had indeed meant to follow 'C's' instructions and rendezvous with Dr Grachev? Maybe! But she did not think so. He had promised to stay in touch with Carol during the day and he hadn't. She trusted Stryker with her life and knew that the feeling was mutual. But where was he? She now began to fear that something was drastically wrong.

Without an address Carol decided there was no point in visiting Harley Street. She looked in the telephone book to discover if a Dr Grey was listed. There was only one Dr Grey and he was south of the River Thames. He said he had never worked in Harley Street and knew of no one by the name of Dr Grachev. Carol was becoming even more worried now. It seemed that this doctor Stryker had been going to visit did not even exist. Dr Grachev was not listed in the general telephone book or in the Yellow Pages either.

Nevertheless Carol donned her Gucci leather jacket and made her way to Harley Street, striding up and down with a heavy heart, dreading what she might discover but it seemed a futile waste of time without an address. She glanced wistfully up at the many buildings, thinking that Stryker had been in one of them earlier in the day, but which one, and might he still be there being held against his will? Hoping that at any moment she might see him step from one of the houses Carol attempted once more to contact Stryker yet again using her cell phone. Then from the middle of Harley Street an elderly gentleman with flowing white hair and carrying a black walking cane topped with a silver pommel passed her, she thought how agitated he looked and how lucky he was not to have to bear her heartrending situation – there was still no answer to her telephone call and the information she had to impart to Stryker was weighing heavily on her mind. She just had to find him.

CHAPTER 102

Whether one believes in such things or not, Hubert Golightly's sixth sense played a major, although it should be said an unspoken role in his life. It was not that he did anything strange like attending séances; nor going to meetings in a spiritualist church with the aim of contacting a long dead relative through the ether of time and the good offices of some Indian spirit guide. It was rather this feeling of doom and gloom which every so often overcame him. What smarted was not only so much the fact that this feeling quite often acted as a precursor to disaster, but that it was becoming more frequent as the years rolled by. The subject had been mentioned by him only once and that to a work colleague as it happened, his closest friend, only to be informed in a light hearted manner that half the population probably felt the same. In a more serious frame of mind he had wondered if his now negative attitude was influencing the way he reacted to situations and that it was this which was actually screwing up his life. Anyhow, today was definitely one of those days when he just knew things were not going to go his way. It had begun soon after parking up the large white transit van. This manoeuvring of the van was carried out early, so as to be able to gain the best vantage point for scanning Piccadilly Circus and also, very importantly, the positioning of it above one of the drains in the road. Within minutes, a tubby puce-faced parking meter attendant was drawn to the vehicle as a magnet is drawn to metal. Golightly knew straight away that the confrontation was not going to be easy.

"What are you doing parked here?"

Golightly thought he would try a little friendly banter and take him into his confidence.

"You are right of course to question the matter of my parking, but quite honestly there is a very good reason for it. It's a matter of security." With the word 'security' Golightly also gave a knowing wink.

"Out!"

"Out! How do you mean?"

"Please wind the window down a little further so that I can speak with you more easily." So Golightly, thinking he was making progress by gaining the warden's confidence, complied, reaching over the passenger seat and winding the nearside window down even further. Unfortunately that was when the long blue-sleeved arm of the traffic warden whistled through the aperture and caught Golightly by the throat. "Don't play games with me sonny. I'm not one of your enlightened masses."

This was one character Hubert Golightly had never come across before: a psychopath. What was worse, here was a psychopath in uniform. Covert surveillance is a very sensitive issue with the general public and as such, has to be treated with due respect. Those were the thoughts which ran through Golightly's mind as he gripped the assailant's wrist with his left hand and twisted it rapidly, in the process releasing the traffic warden's fingers from around his throat and gripping the smallest of these digits with his not insubstantial right hand. The snap was clearly audible as the little finger sprang out of its socket, now angled sideways to the hand. But that noise was nothing to the scream the traffic warden would have emitted had not Golightly had the foresight to pull the head of his antagonist inside the driver's cab and muffle his screams with his gloved fist shoved deep inside the now gaping mouth.

Because it was still early and lashing down with rain, keeping most sensible people off the streets, and also because the situation was handled with such alacrity, nobody in the vicinity noticed the fracas nor the unmarked SIS car rapidly summoned to remove the person who might otherwise jeopardise the covert operation. The traffic warden was rushed straight in to some private doctor who re-set his little finger using a splint and was then immediately relieved of his traffic warden's job and uniform, as well as being threatened not to speak of his ordeal to anyone, not even to his wife. The oversized goons who did the threatening took their jobs to heart, leaving the ex-warden seriously terrified.

Except for this piece of drama which served to ease the tension for all of five minutes, time hung heavily in the cramped vantage point of the van filled with state of the art telephoto lens, powerful bi-directional listening equipment together with sound and other recording paraphernalia which had the nasty tendency to generate even more heat than the five bodies ensconced within it. The drain beneath the van acted as a place for the judicious use of a flexible plastic tube which the watchers would utilise to unobtrusively relieve themselves if the occasion arose. Golightly had to make do with a strategically positioned plastic bottle.

Golightly was partitioned off from the others although in microphone contact, so was not affected like his colleagues by the lack of good air conditioning, although he was obviously vulnerable to the attention of nutters as this episode amply illustrated. As covert surveillance went, this room on wheels was stuffed with the most up to date equipment money could buy, but without that special ingredient called luck, the best paraphernalia in the world couldn't guarantee success and this just happened to be one of those occasions hence Golightly's premonition.

CHAPTER 103

A shrill bleep shattered Dr Grachev's reverie as Stryker's cell phone began ringing. Dr Grachev watched in a dissociated state as his thumbs released their tension, his fingers slowly sliding down from Stryker's limp neck as though he were himself mesmerised. In another minute it would have been too late to reverse the situation. It was as though Grachev had been awoken from some deep slumber and suddenly had his wits about him as he made a momentous decision – he would not kill Stryker after all, but instead let the powerful sedative work its magic by keeping his friend incommunicado for many, many hours. That would ease Dr Grachev's conscience. He felt so tortured inside – his head was ready to explode.

Dr Grachev knew from his experience with the FSB man he had killed in Moscow, that it was not a fallacy about dead men weighing more than when alive, but still had difficulty manoeuvring Stryker's body onto the examination couch so he had been dumped upon the floor instead, lying there peacefully in his drugged stupor as though asleep. His brown trilby hat lay nearby. Dr Grachev consoled himself with the thought that at least Stryker had not suffered, and Dr Grachev should know about suffering. Watching animals, especially the monkeys, slowly die through his experiments visited upon them with viruses and bacteria; their writhing in absolute agony and screaming in pain as blood would ooze out of their mouths, their primate's eyes pleading in vain for mercy. Dr Grachev had never gained pleasure from watching these animals die, and yet had striven over many years to produce toxins which would have a similar effect upon *Homo sapiens*. He realised just how paradoxical that was, and had tried many times to justify it to himself by saying it was for the greater good of mankind, to protect the Motherland. And to an extent it had worked.

He was now battling against the clock; the ringing from Stryker's cell phone had not ceased but to Dr Grachev's ears was becoming more persistent as time passed so he had been driven to turn the cell phone off, wondering if the caller might know of Stryker's appointment in Harley Street. He then rolled Stryker's body onto its side, positioning it so as to gain access to his inside jacket pocket. It was hard work, but slowly, and with some effort, he pushed his right hand into the pocket and managed to extricate three objects. The first was a large black leather wallet. The second was a long brown envelope – sealed. The third was Stryker's diary, the very one into which Dr Grachev himself had written down his own Moscow address and telephone number when he had first hypnotised Stryker at the Normanhurst Hotel. This little diary would link him to Stryker so he carefully stashed the three items in his Gladstone bag. Then he paused, taking stock before removing the long black wallet again and opened it up. There were five twenty pound notes neatly tucked inside. These Dr Grachev removed before pushing them back into Stryker's jacket. The scientist had put Stryker out of action to preserve his own fragile security, not for his friend's money.

Dr Grachev dragged Stryker by his armpits toward the double pedestal desk, propping him up against it as he set about carrying out the final part of his task. Preparing to remove Stryker's eye the shrill intercom buzzer stopped Dr Grachev in his tracks. Steadying Stryker's body with one hand, he reached up from his crouching position, his fingers fumbling for the black button and jabbing at it with a ferocity borne out of panic.

"Yes?" A few moments passed before the receptionist's voice crackled from the tinny sounding speaker.

"Do you want any tea for yourself and your patient? I shall be locking up at two o'clock sharp as there's nobody else here except you today." Dr Grachev attempted to gather his thoughts. *Be at Eros by two o'clock to meet your contact.* Time was pressing.

"Err, no. That's alright, its fine. We don't want anything."

As hard as he tried to control his irritation it had revealed itself in his voice. Returning to his grisly task once more, the receptionist's voice was heard under her breath muttering: "It's alright, I was only asking."

Before the receptionist's sentence was completed, Dr Grachev's fingers were already digging into the soft puffy skin beneath Stryker's false eye as he attached the suction pad to it, then using a wooden spatula he began trying desperately to angle it so as to lever the heavy glass orb into the palm of his hand. His mind was still on the receptionist's query about tea. She could just as easily have walked into the consulting room to enquire. It would have been unethical to interrupt a doctor with his patient, but what were ethics to a stupid woman like her? He grew nervous, knowing that time was pressing. He had turned Stryker's cell phone off but knew there was a possibility that the person ringing Stryker might arrive at the surgery. He should get out as soon as possible, leaving Stryker's heavily sedated body somehow hidden, but with what?

As he pondered this last question the warm prosthetic eye dropped into his cupped hand. Retching, he quickly wrapped it into a large linen handkerchief brought for the purpose and stuffed the damp linen ball into his Gladstone bag before snapping the brass locks with a click. Walking over to the musty smelling curtains he grabbed one in each hand and gave a sharp tug. There was a sound of wood splitting as the cheap plastic curtain rail flew off the wall, the curtains coming down in a cloud of dust. Dr Grachev held his breath, not only to stop the dust from entering his mouth but also to listen for any sound outside. The noise of the curtains with the rail being ripped off the wall had made a racket and Dr Grachev felt almost sure that the receptionist must have heard the noise. He waited for perhaps half a minute, but nobody came to the door. Then just as he stooped to pick up the bent rail with the curtains half hanging off, the air was again rent with the shrill noise of a buzzing sound. Dr Grachev dived for the button once more.

"Is everything alright in there? What was that noise? Has something broken? What was that bang?" The questions tripped off the receptionist's tongue as bullets from a gun aimed at a foreigner, in whose suspicious activities the receptionist's imagination knew no bounds.

"Nothing to worry about... just tripped over a chair. It's alright." There was more silence. Dr Grachev quickly crept up to the desk carrying the bent curtain rail and one of the curtains, opened the cupboard in one of the pedestals and after manipulating the rail pushed it inside, followed by the screwed up curtain fabric now rolled into a small bundle. With great effort, Stryker's body was doubled up before being pushed unceremoniously beneath the desk between the twin pedestals. When that was done the body was covered with the remaining curtain before making sure that no body part peeped out from beneath the edges. Scanning the room he saw there was a little mess where the curtain rail had been screwed to the top of the window frame, but not too noticeable. And the dusty venetian blind had not been damaged, thus giving the room a semblance of normality when viewed from the street. Sooner or later of course, Stryker's body would be discovered or Dr Grachev's friend would regain consciousness, but hopefully not before the person known as Dr Grey was safely many miles away from the scene.

***

The receptionist would later tell detectives that just before Dr Grey vacated his surgery that Saturday lunchtime she had heard raised voices from within though she could not make out what was being said – then the door opened and Mr Stryker had come out with his back toward her, his brown trilby hat perched at what she termed a jaunty angle, shielding the nape of his neck. He did not say goodbye to the woman taking in every detail of his departure but within minutes Dr Grey himself then made his own exit, carefully locking the surgery door behind him. The time had just turned ten to two and within another ten minutes the receptionist herself would make her way out into Harley Street to begin what was left of her weekend.

***

The police questioning went as follows:

"What was Dr Grey's age?"

"About seventy."

"Colour of hair?"

"White."

"His demeanour?"

"Demeanour... what does that mean? He looked normal to me. Christ, he was a very frail-looking doctor. He had a stoop. Why would he break the door down to get into his own surgery if he had a key? Yes, frail's a good word. I don't honestly think he could hurt a fly so no. I don't think he would have had the strength to break the door down. Besides, come on... as I say, he's a doctor." The Harley Street receptionist also patiently explained to the detective investigating the break-in that the noise coming out of the surgery on that Saturday morning had made her suspicious. With all the banging going on it had played on her mind. So when she opened up the surgery on the Monday morning and discovered the door to Dr Grey's surgery smashed open and the curtains lying on the floor by the double pedestal desk with no one around she had telephoned the police. And it was as the police sealed off the premises that the secretary had left for the rest of the day with her prognosis ringing in their ears.

"Although I think it's a real mystery, I also think it was someone attempting to get their hands on drugs."

But the police knew different. Dr Grey's surgery door had obviously been broken from the inside because of the positioning of the splinters and plaster from the door frame and wall and the door itself had been found lying on the carpet in the entrance hall and not in the surgery itself. To the detective dealing with the case it did not add up. If Dr Grey and his patient Mr Stryker had both left the surgery and the door and window had been locked how it was possible for the door to have been broken from the inside was a complete mystery as the secretary had stated.

Later on that Monday the police had got around to questioning builders who had a skip positioned just two houses away from the Harley Street practice on the off chance that they may have seen something unusual. It was then that they discovered Dr Grey had asked these builders for the loan of a ladder so as to assist the elderly doctor to re-enter his surgery through his half-open window on the pretext of having locked himself out. The investigating detective did not conclude that it would have been a simple matter for Dr Grey to have created the illusion of being Stryker, the doctor using Stryker's trilby hat perched at just the right angle to hide his features, leaving the premises by posing as his patient before re-entering the surgery using the builder's ladder and then making his second exit as Dr Grey, re-locking the surgery door behind him and once more in the street handing the ladder back to the builders. And why would the detective have made such a deduction? For even if the police had made this connection it still did not explain how the surgery door came to be smashed from the inside, and why?

CHAPTER 104

Having accomplished his illusion which even the great Houdini might have regarded with some admiration, Dr Grachev now made his way out of the surgery and along Harley Street. On his way he noticed in passing a young woman wearing a rucksack upon her back holding a cell phone and wearing a fashionable black leather cagoule, the hood pulled down revealing a face that seemed lost deep in thought with a forlorn expression upon her beautiful features. He made his way into Cavendish Square and picked up a taxi so as to be in time for his meeting with Smith at two o'clock that Saturday afternoon. Ten minutes later he was once again on foot, moving quickly around the perimeter of Piccadilly Circus, still clutching his silver-topped cane in one of his gloved hands with his Gladstone bag in the other. It had proved awkward to stem the blood from his hand where the bullet shot from outside the Normanhurst Hotel from the previous night had caused more damage than at first thought and it began throbbing.

The cane had been purchased with only one specific purpose in mind. The hollow silver pommel had been intended to act as a receptacle for the glass ampoule containing his killer virus, once this ampoule had been removed from the prosthetic eye within his room at the Normanhurst Hotel. But because of his having to flee the hotel the night before and due to the discovery of Stryker carrying a gun into the consulting room at Harley Street, there had simply not been enough time to carry this procedure out before his arranged assignation with the SIS man at Piccadilly Circus. Thus, the heavy exquisitely crafted detachable silver pommel at this moment in time had no discernible use, save for that of decoration and lay concealed beneath Dr Grachev's glove clad damaged palm.

At precisely two o'clock the doctor had located a vacant table at a window inside an expensive-looking café overlooking Piccadilly Circus. The vantage point was excellent. From where he sat he could see anyone approaching or leaving the area. To help in his identifying the agent who he was going to meet beneath Eros, Dr Grachev extracted from his Gladstone bag a pair of high power binoculars. Even when ordering his coffee he dared not take his eyes off the scene outside for a second. The waitress thought him totally ignorant not to look up when speaking. The only time he averted his gaze was to occasionally snatch a glimpse at his watch. "*You will recognise Smith by something he is wearing, a visual sign of friendship.*" The phrase rolled round and round in Dr Grachev's mind as he scanned the constantly shifting crowds moving as bees around a beehive, no one person standing still for long enough to enable the Russian scientist to be able to spot that 'visual sign of friendship', he so longed for.

Time was passing – a storm was gathering – dark clouds reflecting Dr Grachev's uneasiness. It was now two thirty and not one person carrying or wearing the mentioned *"visual sign of friendship"* had materialised. His eyes were feeling the strain of keeping up the surveillance as he continued to use his binoculars to scan the few people now hanging around in the inclement weather, his body taught with nerves, ready to dash out the door at the slightest hint of an SIS agent waiting for him. Another coffee was ordered – the same waitress who served him as before. Another twenty minutes passed. It was now nearly three p.m. Dr Grachev's stomach rumbled and he realised that no food had passed his lips all day.

***

Since parting with Stryker earlier that morning Carol had not been able to make contact to find out what was going on. Stryker did not answer his cell phone because for the last hour or so it had been switched off. That never usually happened. Stryker always kept his cell phone switched on. Stryker's idea had been to behave as though nothing was changed as far as the plan to catch Dr Grachev was concerned and Stryker had told Carol that he would turn up at Piccadilly as pre-arranged to meet the doctor. But that was hours ago and Carol could not understand why she still hadn't been able to contact him. As far as she was concerned it now seemed that she was in it for the long haul.

CHAPTER 105

Piccadilly was always going to be full of unidentifiable people, as all the watchers knew only too well. Surveillance can be a very time consuming business and a strain on the senses. There were twelve sharp A4 size black and white photographs. Two had been supplied to each MI6 and SAS officer. This was for positive identification purposes. What Stryker would have thought of his portrait being scanned frequently by the covert team was open to conjecture. Some of the operatives were on nodding terms with their fellow spooks, but as there were over two thousand staff working for MI6 plus over three hundred intelligence officers, the order that each one of this particular surveillance team was to be issued with his photograph so that there were no mistakes, made sense. The second photograph, only able to be handed out to each man at the very last moment, was that of Dr Grachev; a blown up version lifted from his visa application. It had been a rushed job, carried out just hours before, but as usual the specialists in the photographic and image intensifying section had come up trumps.

The plan had been for Stryker to make contact with the RED CHAMELEON somewhere in the middle of London where the Russian could be positively identified, so the famous landmark of Eros, God of Love, had been selected. Then Stryker and the Russian scientist would be approached by two of the designated officers from the surveillance van. The operation, which had taken account of the rules of the SIS charter, meant that both SAS officers drawn from what is known as The Increment, were to transport Stryker and the target back to a safe house where the debriefing by a group of scientists was to be carried out. It was the SAS officer's duty to make sure the Russian was kept secure while being debriefed and then await orders. These two officers had no inkling at this juncture that it had already been decided they were to be the escorts who would lead Dr Grachev to his executioners. That had been the plan.

CHAPTER 106

A light meal was ordered consisting of an omelette and chips served with yet another coffee. Four o'clock came and went. Dr Grachev ate the food with an air of dejection. It was beginning to feel like the last supper. Time dragged heavily as he ordered yet more coffee, seeing his waitress speaking to one of her colleagues and gesturing with her head toward him. At ten to five – the final opportunity to make contact with his saviour loomed large as he nervously scoured the few remaining pedestrians but to no avail. Five o'clock, the designated hour for his final chance at making contact with the one person who could solve all his problems, came all too quickly and passed in a flash without any new faces appearing. At a quarter past six, having consumed even more coffee, he quickly paid his bill and received a withering look from the waitress, tipping being the last thing on his mind.

Exiting the café, he walked through the initially light shower of rain and lingered for a while at the base of Eros, still hoping that Smith would eventually turn up and that he would be easily recognised. A few grey pigeons stumbled around by his feet pecking at dirty pools of water. He looked up at the rain-laden sky, then at the grey buildings before dropping his head again, to see his refracted image in the thin film of water accumulating on the grey pavements. Everything had taken on a drabness which began to depress Dr Grachev as never before. He bit his lower lip, attempting to summon up all the optimism that he possessed. The crowds of people which were there earlier had dissipated. This was the twilight time when it is too late for the day's shoppers and too early for people seeking the night life. Dr Grachev noticed the white van some distance away which had not moved since he had arrived to keep his appointment at two. He wondered at the patience of a driver who could sit there for so long. There were only four people loitering by the base of the winged cherub poised as if to let fly his arrow of love, an earlier downpour having driven the hordes of tourists into nearby shops and cafés. Two young women chatted away in a lively animated fashion beneath their makeshift canopy consisting of a shared raincoat; another young woman was wearing a black hooded leather anorak with a rucksack upon her back. The cagoule which had a gold tassel hanging from its peak was pulled up over her head keeping out the rain and making it almost impossible for street cameras to see her features except when using her cell phone which she seemed to do constantly, whereby a glimpse of her pale pink complexion could be detected or a wisp of chestnut hair could be seen peeping out from beneath the rain sodden hood. The fourth person was an old man, a vagrant sitting by the steps consuming a bottle of something, seemingly oblivious to the steady incessant drumming of rain. Dr Grachev felt desolate. It was now half past six.

In a state of acute agitation he re-entered the café and ordered yet another coffee while wondering what to do next. Then Dr Grachev remembered Smith's diary, removed from his body earlier in the day. It now seemed such a long time ago. Extracting the diary from his Gladstone bag Dr Grachev began leafing through the pages coming across an entry at today's date which leapt out at him.

What he read next instantly removed any saliva lingering in his mouth, making it as dry as the Gobi Desert.

CHAPTER 107

Dr Grachev stared hard at Stryker's diary and could hardly believe his eyes. He looked out of the café window where he was keeping watch and then once more scanned the page open at today's date. It was a cryptic message written in Stryker's neat hand. It read:

Meet R.C. at Eros – 2/5.

Dr Grachev continued to gaze at the handwritten note in Stryker's diary, attempting to make sense of it. Could it represent 'R' for 'RED' and 'C' for 'CHAMELEON'? Then there were the figures 2-5. Might these numbers in Stryker's diary mean 2 for 2 p.m., 5 for 5 p.m.? His mind raced – questioning! How was this possible? Why was this information in Stryker's diary? Had Stryker been spying on Smith? Was Stryker somehow privy to information Smith might have had on Grachev himself. Who was spying on whom? Then as he held the diary up for closer inspection a small shiny object fell from its leaves into the Gladstone bag.

The Russian scientist distractedly pushed his hand back into the Gladstone bag and retrieved a gold pin bearing a miniature symbol of the red Russian flag. Dr Grachev's body slumped back in his chair at the enormity of finding this symbol of the Russian flag in his possession. For a fleeting moment he doubted his own eyes. It was the same symbolic piece of jewellery in the form of a flag he had been given by his father as a young boy. His father had left home shortly afterwards and Dr Grachev had never set eyes upon him again. It was also the same carefully crafted piece of gold jewellery which he had sent to Smith in a gesture of comradeship. And now it was in Stryker's possession. Again he questioned himself. *How was it possible? What were the circumstances in which Stryker came to possess it? Had it been stolen?*

His mind swam in confusion; a thick fog clouding his vision before the heavy shades of reality came crashing down with all the force of the Revelation. The gun he had gingerly held with his handkerchief and so carefully replaced in Stryker's shoulder holster only hours before. Of course – Stryker was working for the security service. Now it suddenly became clear why Smith had not been able to keep his appointment at Piccadilly. How could he, when Grachev himself had drugged him? *Stryker was Smith and Smith was Stryker – one and the same person!* Stryker had been his potential saviour and now he was in a deep stupor, put there by himself. He had been Moses leading Grachev to the Promised Land. And now he had carried out the ultimate betrayal of both Stryker and himself. He had put Stryker out of action in a chemical straitjacket, as in a Greek tragedy. Stryker, the unwitting innocent victim he had targeted at the Orthodox Easter service because of his glass eye, being inspired to use him as a mule for unwittingly transporting his deadly virus!

Stryker, the one Englishman he had truly come to look upon as a friend. The only one who could save Dr Grachev had been put in a chemical straightjacket by Dr Grachev's own hands. The irony was that the place where he had first made Stryker's, or was it Smith's acquaintance, he was not now sure of his name, was the Easter service to celebrate the raising of the dead of Jesus Christ. Dr Grachev thought with bitterness that he could have done with such a miracle today. Stryker might not be dead in the strictest medical definition but to Grachev he might just as well be for it would be a good few hours before he regained any semblance of consciousness. If only he had seen Stryker's diary and the pin that fell out of it before he injected his quarry with the strong sedative. He began to dwell on the chance meeting with Stryker at that Easter Service. That, in retrospect, is where all his troubles had begun. Inspiration as a scientist had contributed to so many of his discoveries, helping him to achieve a certain status within the scientific community, and yet that same inspiration had now led to his having isolated himself, as far as he could see, with no way out. He felt dead inside.

He stared at the hard, shiny, red enamelled flag, symbol of Mother Russia with the gold representation of the Hammer and Sickle shining within his fingers. This was the '...*mutual sign of friendship*', hinted at by Stryker's stand-in – the pin which Stryker was going to wear, so small, and yet in symbolic terms, so huge. The symbol which he had been betrayed by all his life and that he himself had betrayed. His mind reeled, barely able to take in the consequences of his actions. His heart was pounding. Nausea swept over him, settling in the pit of his stomach. He now knew that he was beyond redemption.

Dr Grachev wondered if it was really still possible to salvage something from his nightmarish situation. Absentmindedly, perhaps subconsciously attempting to regain something of what he had lost, after having replaced Stryker's diary into his Gladstone bag he lifted the miniature symbol of the red Russian flag and pushed it into his lapel. In the distance an unseen bell tolled seven times, a thin sound which for Dr Grachev resonated with gloom. It was then that he decided to make his way back to the only temporary safe haven he had at that moment.

CHAPTER 108

Looking back on her day, it had been a series of futile gestures as far as Carol was concerned, not being one jot closer to locating Stryker than when she had begun her desperate search. And in the final few hours sitting on the rain sodden plinth of Eros surrounded by an eddy of slow moving traffic attempting to contact him by constantly using her cell phone had also been to no avail. Desperation had now set in and she was beginning to believe that the confidential file she had been shown relating to the deaths of the two British men from Dubai Stryker had dealt with might very well hold the secret to Stryker's disappearance and possibly even his demise. She felt lonelier now than she had ever felt in her whole life. The only thing to stick out in her mind was the surprise at seeing what she thought was that same white-haired old man she had spotted in Harley Street earlier in the day wandering past her just moments before as he moved slowly around the base of Eros. It had just turned seven o'clock. It was a depressing sight viewing the surrounding area of Piccadilly through the rain dripping down in rivulets from the hood of her cagoule. Carol thought that if it wasn't the old man she had set eyes upon earlier in the day then her imagination was playing tricks, though she felt in the back of her mind that there was something strange about that elderly gentleman, something troubling, but she could not bring to her consciousness just what that disconcerting feeling signified or what it might presage. Perhaps it was because she was overtired. That she could believe. The fact was she felt absolutely drained of energy. Taking a leaf out of the elderly gentleman's book she began to make her way home to Swiss Cottage, determined to carry on ringing Stryker's cell phone from there.

CHAPTER 109

The rain had eased as Dr Grachev shuffled slowly across the road away from Piccadilly Circus, attempting to avoid the traffic and static lakes of water as best he could, whilst playing his role as a decrepit old man to perfection, a role which after all that had happened over the last few hours now came to him so naturally. For a moment he was stopped in his tracks as his eyes honed in on the white van, or rather the person in the vehicle. The driver's body appeared to be frozen, the posture upright with both arms jutting out from his torso holding the steering wheel at the recommended position of ten to two. Dr Grachev began to wonder if this particular driver had fallen asleep, but as he crossed immediately in front of the van the upright figure's eyes were wide open, and without moving his head actually followed Dr Grachev with his eyes for a few seconds before once more returning to stare straight ahead. *Very strange*, Dr Grachev thought. Could the van have anything to do with his own meeting with Stryker at this particular location? A silly notion, the sort of thing one read about in spy novels, but not in real life; well, in Russia perhaps, but not here in London. So shortly after the shattering revelation that he had drugged the one person who could have helped him gain political asylum, Dr Grachev made his way through the damp early evening gloom, across the grey rain-splashed pavements in the direction of Regent Street with a view to catching a taxi back to his consulting room in Harley Street.

***

It was not until several weeks later that the elderly man caught on film by the street camera as he had moved slowly along Harley Street was matched to the same figure viewed hanging around the base of Piccadilly on that gloomy Saturday. This second film however was shot from one of the many disguised spy holes in the white van in which Dr Grachev had taken such an interest and which, unbeknown to him, was actually occupied by two film crew, two SAS specialists in unarmed combat and one very senior SIS officer plus a highly skilled driver trained in close protection and evasion techniques. Needless to say that after being cooped up in this vehicle for over seven hours in a very stuffy atmosphere, it was with great relief that the team had finally been ordered to stand down, knowing that their quarry had not materialised, at least, not as far as they were concerned.

CHAPTER 110

The door of the consulting room having been firmly locked behind him, the first thing that Dr Grachev did was to make sure Stryker was in the same condition as when he had left him all those hours before, taking his pulse to confirm that he was still alive. Satisfying himself that the sedative he had pumped into Stryker would remain effective for a few more hours, Dr Grachev sat down at the patient's side of the desk, resting his Gladstone bag upon it, knowing that he would be safe from any intrusion as he began to inspect the bag's contents.

The first of the objects Dr Grachev stared at was the sealed long brown envelope removed earlier from Stryker's inside pocket together with his wallet and diary. Whilst sitting in the café he had been so devastatingly shocked at the implication of discovering that piece of jewellery which had been given him by his father, nursing the hope, albeit tenuously, that somehow the SIS agent would still turn up, so much so that he had completely forgotten about this large envelope.

Dr Grachev's hands trembled as the sealed end of the envelope was torn open and the contents extracted along with a short note. As Dr Grachev unfolded this note written in a neat hand and began to read, his jaw literally fell open. He raised his head, gazing up at the window in an effort to clear his mind and take in the simple message, but each word dragged him down like a millstone around his neck. He re-read the note several times, hoping to glean a different interpretation from the indisputable one set before him, his spirits sinking lower with every reading, until his disbelieving eyes finally had to accept the simple but awful truth. It stated that Dr Grachev was about to be betrayed by the British Secret Intelligence Service. That the powers that be had decided he would not after all be granted political asylum in Britain as he was viewed as a liability, not wishing to put in danger the fragile arms agreements between Great Britain, America and what was the Soviet Union, and that Dr Grachev's life was in great danger, making it necessary for him to leave the country immediately.

Dr Grachev was also informed that he should forget about attempting to make any deals with the British security services as he would end up dead if he attempted such a thing. Ultimately, better to try America notwithstanding what he had mentioned earlier, Stryker reasoning that the biological weapon Dr Grachev had been willing to trade for political asylum

364

would be just as safe in American hands as with that of their British cousins and that they might conceivably have a different attitude to these things. Concluding his note, Stryker said that it had been only a few hours earlier, that very Saturday morning in fact when he had first learnt about the true nature of Dr Grachev's business – of his intention of seeking political asylum in exchange for, to quote, 'information regarding Russia's ongoing experiments into biological warfare', and of the fate awaiting him if he attempted such a thing here in England. This final line of the note dispelled any false optimism Dr Grachev might have harboured about striking a bargain with the British security services.

It was like a powerful blow to the solar plexus. Details of a safe house in Switzerland and a contact name were also written down. It stated he should remain there until contacted by himself. The letter was signed – 'Smith, aka Stryker' and he trusted the doctor to burn his incriminating note after reading it.

The contents inside that long brown envelope, removed along with Stryker's note, was a one way business class plane ticket to Zurich, Switzerland, timed for departure from Heathrow airport that very same Saturday at seven p.m. He scanned his watch, knowing it was a futile gesture. It had already turned eight. Too late, the last opportunity had literally flown. Stryker had visited the Swiss Centre earlier that morning to collect the ticket using his contacts through SIS after taking his English breakfast at the Selfridges Hotel, just off Oxford Street whilst Carol helped to obtain a passport for Grachev in a false name. When Stryker learnt in the early hours of Saturday morning, at the meeting with 'C' and his colleagues, that it was his friend Dr Grachev who was the Russian scientist seeking political asylum he had been left momentarily stunned. But once he had come to terms with this situation he had decided to tip his friend off as he felt sympathy for Grachev's predicament and determined to help him escape the death sentence imposed upon him by 'C'. However, Stryker had not bargained on 'C's' resolve.

It took a while for Dr Grachev's mind to cope with the initial shock and disbelief, only reinforcing just what a good friend Stryker had been. Stryker, the Good Samaritan, a counterpoint to Dr Grachev's Judas Iscariot.

Dr Grachev was only too aware that this was not the time to dwell upon the finer aspects of human nature and his own undoubted treachery toward Stryker. Now he was on his own – out on a limb. He knew the safe house in Switzerland, organised by Stryker for a friendship which seemed to know no bounds, could not be used – not now that he had left Stryker barely alive with his administered sedative delivered by injection. Nor would it be of any use attempting to change the airline ticket. Like everything else, it was too late for that. The most pressing question was, to whom could he now go for help? There was no one. He had burnt his boats and there was definitely no going back. It was impossible. He felt sure that it was a member of the SVR who took a pot shot at him the day before as he fled his hotel. He reasoned that they had to be from Russian Intelligence. He also knew that they must have linked him with the death of Vladimir Stalnov, a dedicated FSB man.

As Dr Grachev distractedly took from his pocket the linen handkerchief and carefully removed the false eye he had taken from Stryker earlier, he stared at the pupil of it for some time, his thoughts now overwhelmed by seemingly insurmountable problems and unendurable stress. He could be excused for momentarily thinking he was losing his mind. For there, held between his thumb and forefinger, the iris of the glass prosthetic eye he had been staring at, did the one thing most people would think impossible – it dilated as a real eye might if a light were to be shone onto it. The black hole in the middle of the glass eye became smaller.

Dr Grachev quickly swept such notions of derealisation away and swung back to reality as his mind reeled back to when his interest in hypnosis under his father's tutelage first took hold, and how his father had initiated him into the secrets, at a very young age, of a mystery which very few people could begin to comprehend. The KGB had experimented with hypnosis over many years, as have various other secret organs of the state, both in Russia and elsewhere in the Western world. For to have an intelligence agent, who through the use of hypnosis, can soak up an unimaginable amount of information as a sponge soaks up water, and regurgitate it at will, is an asset which any country's self-respecting secret service would prize highly. To hypnotise an unwitting subject as he had hypnotised Stryker, was a tool of the greatest value for those in the higher echelons of spying. To be able to turn around an agent working for a hostile country into an asset, in the form of a programmed automaton, and get him or her to do the bidding of one's own secret service unwittingly and against their will, was something else – what might be described as the Holy Grail for spy chiefs around the world. The research into the boundaries of hypnosis as well as brainwashing techniques to be used as a tool to be harnessed for intelligence purposes was an ongoing, if well-kept secret.

Dr Grachev knew that so-called 'Brainwashing' methods in conjunction with hypnosis had been used and refined over many years. Through the grapevine he had also heard accounts of a hypnotist, Dr Vladimir Zukhar, who had been placed in the audience ostensibly watching a game of chess yet used by the KGB in the 1978 World Chess Championships held in the Philippines, employing a fixed gaze technique to distract and unsettle the Soviet dissident chess player Viktor Korchnoi, so as to enable their own man, a politically correct Soviet world champion, Anatoli Karpov, to win. No hands on approach – this was carried out from a considerable distance.

To hypnotise a person, that person's interest has to be captured in one way or another so as to fascinate and hold their attention. There are, in fact, a myriad of ways this can be achieved, some obvious, many more not so obvious to the often unsuspecting subject whether that be face to face, on television, on stage or over the telephone. This use of a false eye was one of the more obvious techniques. The hypnotist would place the false eye upon a small piece of black velvet cloth to help focus the subject's concentration and instructions would be given to gaze at the centre of the eye. Sooner or later, because of the phenomenon of optical illusion the iris would indeed eventually appear to dilate. This is precisely what had just happened, but without using the black cloth. It was while pondering this phenomenon that Dr Grachev now received the biggest shock of the day.

CHAPTER 111

Mr O'Connell had grown up just a few streets away from the Falls Road in Belfast. His childhood had been one of poverty and deprivation and because of his being a Catholic, as he saw it, was viewed in his own country as a second-class citizen. He knew that all the decent jobs were handed out to the Protestants and he had been raised on the tales of anti-Catholic discrimination in the workplace. The noise of riots and of bombs exploding had become synonymous with his childhood memories and had led to the decision as a young man to escape the violence by forsaking his birthplace for a quieter life on the mainland as many had done before him.

When he had first arrived in England with hardly any money in his pocket, a single room in one of the more run down parts of London was the only lodging he was able to afford, shared with five other of his Irish compatriots. Soon he was labouring on a small building site south of the River Thames and within six weeks had managed to afford his own tiny bed-sitting room where he no longer had to endure the nauseating smell of sweaty socks mixed with the heady aroma of fried food.

Now in his early thirties he had succeeded in carving out a successful living as a taxi driver. Working for himself had always been his ambition and he had achieved that ambition by hard work and long hours when others were out enjoying themselves. Owning his taxi had signalled the final step to independence and a better lifestyle. Now he was married with two children and another one on the way. True his mortgage was high, but with twenty-four hours in the day and youth still on his side, it could be managed by judicious planning.

Experience had taught him that children were not cheap to clothe and feed so his working hours had risen even more steeply in preparation for the day when yet another voice would be heard screaming for attention and food. In a good week he could earn nearly a thousand pounds; however before managing to scrape the money together to buy his own taxi he had to give half of his takings to the firm he worked for. Yet he found that by some mysterious law, the more he earned the more money he required. Even so, he knew that by the time he had reached fifty the large house with an even larger garden for the kids would be paid off, and then he would be able to sit back and take things easier than he could at the moment. That was his dream and he was well on his way to attaining it. His wife Michelle was not qualified for

368

any particular work and before meeting Patrick O'Connell had spent her time in an electronics factory carrying out menial tasks with a soldering iron, which had taken her all of half an hour to get the hang of. She was therefore only too happy when Mr O'Connell, as she had known him then, proposed marriage within three weeks of their meeting.

Michelle felt an instant attraction toward the young man with the dark curly hair, a lithe body and soft Irish brogue who never tired of telling a stream of jokes, many of them aimed against his own tribe. His memory for these often long, convoluted jokes, and his general good sense of humour delighted all around him, and so he became known in his local pub as the life and soul. Very rare was the occurrence when a passenger who entered Mr O'Connell's taxi did not end his or her journey in peals of laughter, often tears streaming down their face; the young women especially identifiable as having been one of his fare paying passengers by the long muddied streaks of mascara running down their faces through tears of joy and amusement.

Notwithstanding this joy and amusement that Mr O'Connell spread liberally over the often drab lives of his clientele, he had something else of value in common with taxi drivers the world over: knowledge – a certain type of knowledge. Not the testing examination which all London taxi drivers have to pass before they are granted a licence to carry their fare around the myriad of streets to be found in London, known to all aspiring taxi drivers as THE KNOWLEDGE. No, the knowledge referred to here is of the type often divulged to cabbies by people who inhabit that nether region of society unknown to law abiding citizens. Information unsolicited but often very valuable in monetary terms – knowledge gained over many years of experience with John Doe.

People often open up to taxi drivers in a way they would never dream of doing to their doctor, dentist or builder. It may be the certainty that more often than not the meeting will never be repeated. It might possibly be for the simple reason that the passenger is often at the mercy of the driver for their destination if not their destiny and feel beholden to them. It may very well be that people divulge more than they ought out of sheer loneliness or more often than not, intoxication. But whatever the reason, the plain fact is that over many years, that friendly taxi driver who will stop for you at the nod of a head or the raised hand will often know the areas, and more particularly the addresses pertaining to the underbelly or seedier side of life to be found in all urban conurbations. In this respect Mr O'Connell was no exception.

The understanding of human nature and the frailties within people's make-up came easily to someone who knew what it was to struggle. Not that he was a saint – far from it. He had often used the weaknesses of others to gain advantage for himself in one situation or another. Being something of a cynic he also believed that ambling down the transitory corridors of life appeared to be solely a case of self-gratification, nothing more, and nothing less. It was just that he knew from experience that the thin veneer of respectability for many people hid vices freely spoken of in the back of his cab. It was as if some of his clients viewed the closeted interior of his taxi as akin to the confessional. This very aspect was to lead to Mr O'Connell understanding that a trouble shared was not necessarily a good thing.

CHAPTER 112

Using his fingers to roll Stryker's prosthetic eye over in the palm of his hand, Grachev realised that the telltale red dot at the rear of the glass orb had vanished. Then it slowly dawned upon him that for the weight of a glass eye, this one was just not heavy enough. This false eye was made of plastic, therefore not the one holding the ampoule of deadly microorganisms upon which his safe future in the West had depended and which had now become his only tangible bargaining chip. To his horror he realised that the prosthetic eye must have been switched. For a brief moment he felt a sharp pain in his chest. A faintness came over him as he arched his body in an attempt to catch his breath, desperately trying to figure out what could possibly have happened and more pertinently, what could be done to survive this new catastrophe. Dr Grachev had reasoned that even with all that had gone before, the vial containing his deadly concoction might still represent his passport to a new life if not in the United Kingdom as Stryker's letter had suggested, at least in the United States. But how was this to come to pass if he did not possess it?

Still in a daze, Dr Grachev retrieved Stryker's long black leather wallet from his Gladstone bag hoping to find a card from an eye hospital. He was in luck. It was green and folded in half. On the front was printed in black lettering: 'Eye Hospital Appointments', with a telephone number below and instructions to give at least twenty-four hours' notice if an appointment had to be cancelled. Inside were three columns. In the first column was the appointment date. The last date entered for Stryker being just four days previously. In the next column was the time for the appointment: Two-thirty. In the final column was the name of the eye specialist, a Dr Thompson. Dr Grachev raised the telephone and in the process of fumbling with the receiver dialled the number on the card. After a few clicks from the handset a verbal message informed him that he was being transferred to an emergency number for the eye hospital. After several conversations and delays on the line, he finally managed to introduced himself as a Dr Grey speaking from Harley Street, it still taking another five minutes before he was informed that although Dr Thompson had gone home long ago it might still be possible to find the paperwork for Mr Stryker, though it was highly unusual for such an occurrence as everything was locked up for the weekend – but seeing as he was a doctor telephoning from his Harley Street practice...

Dr Grachev hung onto the receiver as though his life depended upon it. The silence was interminable as he visualised the rifling of a myriad of patient's notes. After what seemed like an eternity a voice came back onto the line. "I'm afraid I am having difficulty locating the name but I shall keep trying." It was then Dr Grachev out of desperation had a brainwave.

"If you cannot locate the name Stryker then try Smith. That's right. SMITH."

A few more minutes passed before the voice came back on the line. "I've found the records. Yes, it was the first name you gave me – a mister Stryker."

It was then explained that in his notes it said that Mr Stryker's prosthetic eye had been replaced because of the irritation it had caused. It was also explained that some people remove their false eye daily for hygienic purposes and that others leave them in for weeks, and yes, the whereabouts of the original glass eye was possibly known. From the paperwork it looked as though it was with the ocularist who made and fitted the replacement just recently. His full name and address was then passed over the telephone. Partially relieved, Dr Grachev could only hope that the false eye had not been tampered with and much more importantly, that his bargaining chip for being granted asylum in Britain – the virus he had created with the potential of causing a deadly pandemic – remained still encased within its glass ampoule.

CHAPTER 113

The traffic had been heavy around Hyde Park, black rain clouds turning the sky even darker and it was still raining hard when Carol arrived home to Swiss Cottage, so the first thing she did was to climb out of her wet clothes into a heavy towel bathrobe. Then she tried ringing Stryker's cell phone. To her utter surprise it rang three times before a strange voice answered. It was a woman and she sounded breathless.

"Hullo, who's this? Can I please speak to Stryker?" No sooner had she finished pronouncing the name Stryker than the phone went dead. "Hullo, hullo. Is anyone there? Please answer." The line remained dead. Carol now grew even more worried than she had been all day. Surely if Stryker was alright he would answer his cell phone and who was that woman? All sorts of ideas ran through her mind and not all of them complimentary to Stryker. Carol attempted to ring the cell phone number again but this time it had been switched off. She sat clinging onto the handset, frozen with fear tinged with jealousy. The time had just turned eight o'clock in the evening and it was pitch black outside.

Carol was suddenly gripped by a desperate urge to ring any number where Stryker might possibly be located. The thought struck her that Vauxhall Cross would be a good place to begin with but then had second thoughts, reasoning she would not be able to trust what they might tell her. So she tried the local police station without success. Then she decided that maybe the hospitals would be a better bet, so grabbing the local telephone directory she set about ringing all the hospitals in the local area beginning with Hampstead Royal Free, the first to elicit a negative response regarding Stryker's whereabouts. Three hospitals had been rung before desperation began to cloud her judgement. Maybe Stryker was dead. Maybe she had accidentally missed Stryker at the Eros landmark. It was a possibility for a sea of people had been milling around at lunchtime though toward evening the rain had acted as a deterrent to the many tourists who had flocked there earlier.

It was whilst Carol was figuring out which hospital might be her fourth on the list to try that the idea of ringing Vauxhall Cross became more insistent within her head, like some nagging thought she could not get rid of. The number she now dialled had been given to her in strictest confidence, and was only to be used in an emergency. Her hands began trembling as she lifted the receiver, with so many emotions running through her that she hardly knew where she was. Some tablets found in Stryker's medicine cabinet used to ease the soreness of his eye had somehow helped to calm her racing pulse. She now experienced a great sense of lingering fear and unreasonable guilt over Stryker's disappearance and overriding all these emotions was a vast void of loneliness, something she had never felt before. Carol had been expecting Stryker's comforting looming image to appear at any moment but he had not and the loneliness had gotten worse. Why had Stryker's cell phone been answered by a woman and then switched off?

After dialling the number and feeling full of trepidation, she waited for the line at Vauxhall Cross to be answered. However when Carol's call was eventually responded to it was not sympathy that she received but an irascible voice on the other end, cold and accusative. "We've been trying to contact you for the last couple of hours – of course we don't know where Stryker is." Then a barrage of questions came fast and furious. When had been the last time she had seen Stryker? What had he said to her? Had he not been home yet, possibly to get a change of clothing and did she not have any possible idea where he might be and who he had seen?

Carol gave a negative answer to all of these questions, remembering what Stryker had instructed her to say. "Nothing! Tell anybody that enquires absolutely nothing."

The voice on the telephone then barked out the order, "Stay where you are, we're coming over." It sounded like some trite phrase from a 'B' movie. "*Keep your hands on the table where we can see them.*" Carol stood in Stryker's sitting room, the unexpectedly soporific qualities of the drugs she had gratefully taken earlier now beginning to lose their potency but still leaving her a little unsteady on her feet.

CHAPTER 114

Michelle had suffered bad stomach cramps all afternoon but had managed to hang on until her husband arrived home around tea time. Mr O'Connell drove to the maternity hospital using his knowledge to find the quickest way, occasionally jumping red lights. His wife had been in some distress and so it was with a great deal of relief on both their parts when she was finally handed over into the care of a maternity nurse.

To keep his mind occupied and stay busy, Patrick O'Connell had left his two children in the care of friends who also happened to be neighbours, and was now plying his trade around the West End. It would also bring in a little more money for all the things that a new addition to the family required. He dwelt on the rising crime rate against taxi drivers in that part of the London area he was most familiar with and the expenditure on improving his safety by just having had a steel sheet fitted within the back of his taxi seat. Many of his friends had done the same after a young colleague plying his trade around the same area had been stabbed and killed, knifed through the back of the insubstantial upholstery after picking up a late night fare. Now he felt easier sitting in his cab late at night with a total stranger sitting immediately behind him.

Intermittently he would ring the maternity hospital to ask how his wife was doing. Michelle's first two children had been born in the same hospital, during which time she had become close friends with a nurse named Zoe who happened to be on duty that evening. She had taken Patrick O'Connell's mobile telephone number, promising to keep him informed of any developments. That was why, as he drove around the streets of London this particular evening, Patrick O'Connell was in a quieter, meditative frame of mind than usual.

***

The old man might have been dozing in his favourite armchair, as had often happened over the last few years, but he was not asleep. Now and then he would mutter something, not in English but in a foreign tongue, though there was no one to answer him. In one of his frail hands he held a faded sepia-coloured picture of two young people, obviously very much in love. You could tell by their body posture, both lovers, their arms draped so naturally around the other's waist, gazing into their companion's eyes with that faraway wistful look. The well-thumbed photograph had transported him within a split second over a gulf of half a century. The only clue to his emotions as he took in that romantic episode, enacted so many years before, were a few tears which rolled down his cheeks and became trapped in the crevices of his now heavily lined face. Sammy Weizmann had always been an intensely private person without any close friends, and so had become a broken man since the death of his wife. With no children of his own and in his late seventies, he now channelled every remaining ounce of his energy into his work. There was nowhere else for it to go. It was all that he now possessed.

The only child of Jewish parents, having originally come from the city of Cracow, situated on the River Vistula, the family had lived in Munich, Germany, until the outset of the Second World War. Attempting to flee across the Swiss border to safety and freedom, Sammy was the only one of his family not to have been rounded up in the mountains and transported to the infamous German concentration camp Dachau, in southern Bavaria where they had all been gassed or worked to death.

Eventually managing to cross the English Channel to find sanctuary in England, he did not seek out fellow refugee as many others had done but remained an isolated figure, even as a pilot. Just before war broke out he had gained his flying licence in Munich and so had been welcomed with open arms by the British.

After the war, shunning advances by neighbours with a view to striking up friendships, he concentrated upon the specialist skills he had developed with his father. It was also since losing the love of his life that he had become something of a miser. Although driving a hard bargain for his special skill, he was not interested in anything which cost him money, having nothing to do with his well-deserved earnings but keep the money locked up in his safe. As soon as he was paid by cheque he would change it into bank notes and add it to his accumulated hoard.

Sammy Weizmann had been so traumatised by the war, having lost all contact with his remaining cousins after fleeing from Munich, that one possession had kept him company throughout the ravages of time for the last fifty years. This was his old battered leather suitcase which remained stuffed with a few personal belongings which included old yellowed newspaper clippings, faded family photographs and a few clothes plus some essential items such as his treasured British passport. This suitcase, kept under his bed ready to be dragged out at the first sign of trouble, represented to him the sum total of the things that really mattered. He had managed to escape the clutches of a tyrannical power once, though he had not been prepared for it. Next time he would be.

CHAPTER 115

It was very late on Saturday evening by the time the Russian doctor arrived at the address of the ocularist. The rain had now abated, replaced by a cold dampness in the air as a cloak of darkness descended upon London. The part of West Hampstead Dr Grachev now found himself in was not the Hampstead where the affluent resided. Small terraced houses passed only minutes before, gave way to larger detached properties in a sorry state of decay. Gaps appeared where once a continuous line of these formerly prosperous houses stood. This had been the result of German bombs overshooting their targets on bombing raids during the Second World War as they searched out the railway lines. Spaces in between their rubble-strewn structures, now long vacated, were overgrown with weeds and shrubbery and used as a dumping ground for detritus such as old broken beds and other garbage.

To Dr Grachev, peering through the dark, the old houses resembled a mouthful of decayed teeth, some of them missing, some yet to be extracted. The taxi pulled up at one of these large houses, the two either side having been blown away by high explosives from German bombs or just fallen down years before. This solitary house stood facing a tall eight foot high brick wall directly across the road, running in both directions for as far as the eye could see – except the eye could not see very far, due to the surrounding street lights having been put out by vandals, but even in the dark the Russian could still make out thick wedges of grassy tufts in between once pristine paving slabs.

Dr Grachev asked the taxi driver to wait, hauling his Gladstone bag out after him whilst in the other hand he clutched his walking cane. Making his way up the steep row of rain sodden concrete steps he continued to mimic an old man's discreet pace, feeling the eyes of the driver boring into his back.

For Sammy Weizmann, the doorbell rang unexpectedly, shattering the usual Saturday evening silence. It unsettled him, his first thought being to ignore it. The ringing persisted, completely blotting out the task he had been about to perform. Curiosity eventually got the better of him as he slowly made his way out from the darkened room, along the hall to the sturdy street door and peeped through the spy hole. To his surprise he could see an old man approximating his own age standing on the doorstep doubled up with what he himself knew so well to be osteoporosis. His own condition had grown steadily worse and so felt some empathy with this stranger. Nevertheless, he shuffled back along the hall toward the adjoining room where he had been busy, sticking his arm out and yanking the door handle hard so as to shut it firmly behind him. But as he did so the shrill bell rent the silence once more and not quite yanking the door hard enough it had remained ajar, letting the illumination from the hall filter into the room just vacated whilst he let the stranger in over the threshold.

With a grave air Dr Grachev explained that he was a doctor, here on behalf of a Mr Smith, to collect the prosthetic eye which, he had been informed by the eye hospital, had been delivered to this address. It was then that Sammy Weizmann assured Dr Grachev that no such eye with a red dot on its posterior had been delivered and that the eye hospital was always making these mistakes. "Usually," he smiled, "because of their sloppy administration." He also explained that because he was now a widower, he alone kept track of every transaction made between the eye hospital and himself.

As Dr Grachev stood there listening to this explanation his eyes drifted over Weizmann's shoulder, noticing something through the partially opened door leading off the hallway, the one thing that Sammy Weizmann had determined his unexpected guest should not have seen. Weizmann caught this fleeting glance of Dr Grachev's gaze and continued to smile as he took a few steps backwards so as to close the door behind him whilst still maintaining eye contact with his unexpected late night caller. But in the process of attempting to casually close this door something else, something frightening, caught the attention of the ocularist.

CHAPTER 116

'C' sat in his study with a scowl planted firmly upon his face. He did not like failures and this was calamitous. MI6 had just lost their biggest catch for years and one of his agents had done a bunk – even if the said agent had been co-opted unwillingly, which he had, and perhaps was feeling the collar pinching when the lead was metaphorically tugged, but it was only on a temporary basis. That initial assessment appeared to be the only explanation. That was it in a nutshell. Dr Grachev's claims for his virus were now unable to be substantiated by respected scientists, but if his claims were true, his own elevation to the Lords with a life peerage, which had been hinted at on more than one occasion, could be kissed goodbye. Funds were tight as usual, and though he had pulled out all the stops to get as many Secret Intelligence Service Agents onto the streets of London as was possible for a weekend, he knew it was going to be like looking for the proverbial needle in a haystack. To paraphrase, losing one valuable asset in a day is definitely bad luck, but two is carelessness.

"Ken, you go ahead and have another whisky. I unfortunately, must try to keep a clear head." Dr Kenneth Jones had remained in the county of Berkshire on the insistence of his friend 'for support' as he had put it. Ken on the other hand felt there was more to it than that. The two men had known one another for more years than he cared to remember. Ken could remember when 'C' had been a Six case officer (MI6), and even then liked to confide and hypothesise and knew that Ken was good at playing devil's advocate. But that was not what he was looking for from Dr Kenneth Jones on this late damp Saturday evening.

"We agree that this Russian fellow Dr Grachev, for some reason or other, has decided not to turn up for his rendezvous by the famous London landmark of Eros. Or he did turn up but our agent Stryker, a.k.a. Smith, by not materialising himself, again for God knows what reason, sent our Russian friend scurrying. We are at this very moment scanning film shot from our van placed in Piccadilly Circus plus CCTV coverage taken from buildings overlooking the area, attempting to find a match with Dr Grachev's passport photograph."

There was a gap in the conversation whilst 'C' went through the ritual of removing a long black cigarette holder from his dinner jacket pocket before inserting one of his gold tipped Black cigarettes taken from an intricately carved wooden box inlaid with mother of pearl – a souvenir from one of his many trips abroad. After lifting the heavy gold cigarette lighter from his desk and lighting up, he inhaled deeply before throwing his head back and blowing a perfectly formed heavily fragranced smoke ring toward the ceiling.

It was a ritual Kenneth was very familiar with, knowing that 'C' was not usually given to prevarication, so was immediately put on his guard, ready for some unpalatable suggestion. Then in a futile attempt to divert the course of this impending conversation he used the simple expedient of changing the subject.

"I've never bothered to enquire before but where do you get those smelly things from? Christ they reek."

"Don't you like the fragrance? Gillian buys them from Harrods. They do them in cartons of two hundred. They're Russian you know." 'C' said this with a mischievous twinkle in his eyes.

"They're like those bloody Turkish things we used to smoke. Do you remember, ten pence a pack? Smelt like camel shit."

'C' cleared his throat and attempted to pick up the thread of his conversation, determined not to be side tracked.

"Well, of course it may be that Dr Grachev's fellow Russkies have got to him first." 'Russkies' was not a term 'C' would normally use but he had heard the hackneyed expression so many times from his cousins across the pond that the word just popped out. Ken interjected.

"I hope you don't think I'm being too inquisitive old friend, but do we not have our own inside information leaking out from the Russian Embassy here in London?"

"Oh, you mean agents?" 'C' gave a roguish grin. "Unfortunately at present we do not. Though we do have a few bugs planted here and there, the ones they've not discovered." He chuckled and winked knowingly before hastening to add, "But not in the important locations I'm afraid Ken."

Dr Kenneth Jones lifted the whisky toward the direction of his lips, pausing in mid-air, waiting for 'C' to carry on speaking.

'C' liked Dr Jones for a number of reasons. One reason was for his intellect. Another had been for his intense patriotism fighting the Nazis during the Second World War. The third, and most important attribute, was that of trust. He knew he could trust Ken with his life, and on more than one occasion had done so.

Just then there was a light tapping on the study door made by a woman's hand, It was 'C's' wife Gillian declaring dinner would be ready within five minutes. Both men raised their heads and smiled before being left to continue their conversation.

"A woman's intuition Ken is infallible."

Ken looked at 'C'. "You were saying?"

"Ah yes. Well, we know this Dr Grachev was hell bent on gaining political asylum, yet if we assume that he was not grabbed by the Russians and is still a free agent – excuse the pun – then he might well still be open to another inducement."

"Another inducement?" Ken swirled the whisky around in his glass for an instant before taking a sip.

"This is where you might be able to help," 'C' replied in a barely audible voice.

Ken swallowed hard. He knew it: 'C's' prevaricating had given it away. Hang a woman's intuition – his own wasn't so damn bad either. His mind was now working overtime wondering how on earth he himself could possibly be of any assistance in catching this Russian fellow, Dr Grachev. Ken swirled the whisky around in his glass once more before finally draining the dregs, readying the glass for replenishment.

CHAPTER 117

It was late on Saturday evening as Stryker climbed out of the taxi and as Carol heard the street door open she gasped. "Stryker, you look like a pirate." Stryker's left eye had been occluded with a black eye patch.

"Don't you think it has a certain cachet?" he beamed. "I have to wear this until my new eye is ready for service which they tell me should take about a week."

"What happened? I've been trying to contact you all day. I was so worried. Some of Six's boys have only just left – I'm surprised you didn't run into them. They wanted to know where you were."

"What did you tell them?"

"Nothing. What could I tell them? I'm afraid they went through your stuff with a fine tooth comb – searching for God knows what. They didn't take anything away though so I assume they didn't find anything worth their while." Then her eyes narrowed. "And by the way... who was that woman who answered your mobile?" As the questions flowed Carol ushered Stryker indoors, her eyes glued firmly onto his back as though she half expected him to disappear before he had a chance to answer her unanswered questions and before she had time to impart to Stryker what she had learnt about their situation regarding MI6.

"That woman was a nurse at the eye hospital who gave me succour." Stryker said, his face wreathed in smiles.

"You make that sound sexy," Carol responded over her shoulder as she made her way into the kitchen, Stryker himself making his way into the living room before easing his large frame into one of the large easy chairs.

"Is it just my imagination or can I really smell rum-laced tea being prepared?"

"Just the way you made it for me after you shot those two Chinese men. I'm returning the compliment. Then when I have sorted out the drinks you can fill me in, chapter and verse, on why you didn't make it to the rendezvous at Eros and how you came to end up at the eye hospital? Then I shall reveal what I discovered from Vauxhall Cross," Carol shouted from the kitchen. "I promise it will make your hair stand on end." These final sentences were only uttered once the anti-bugging device disguised as an ordinary three pin plug had been inserted into the skirting board socket and activated, but not before Stryker yelled out to his partner in crime not to go easy on the rum.

CHAPTER 118

Under normal circumstances the familiar sound would signify nothing more sinister than a dripping tap. But tonight… to the sharp ears of Sammy Weizmann it had the steady resonance of a tom-tom drum, the beat magnified within his head a thousand fold like an acute attack of tinnitus but in this case signalling danger.

Beneath the Gladstone bag which Dr Grachev held tightly in his left hand a steady stream of blood had begun dripping onto the black and white marble tiled floor, rapidly forming into a small crimson pool by his left foot. It was only then that the realisation that the wound sustained when he had been shot the night before outside the Normanhurst Hotel had been worse than he had thought. Now he could hear the tape recorder in his head replaying the sound blotted out as he attempted to climb into the taxi; the one sharp crack of a pistol being fired in his direction as he fled as fast as his legs would carry him from the pursuing Russian agents. It had been a lucky shot by his hunters, creating more mess than deep damage to his hand. Removing his sodden glove he could now see the superficial flesh wound caused by the glancing bullet once more reopened.

Looking up, Dr Grachev became aware of the fear now reflected in the old man's yellowed eyes as he took in the blood dripping from Dr Grachev's hand, flowing down the handle of the Gladstone bag, adding to the steadily expanding pool by his feet. Instinctively, though knowing in his heart that it was a futile gesture, the old man turned his back once more on Dr Grachev to make sure the door of the room housing the heavy safe was secured. Dr Grachev brought the heavy black cane bearing the silver pommel down hard across Weizmann's frail shoulders, the brittle bones giving way with a snap. As his thin body hit the floor, Dr Grachev thought he detected a soft whimper.

Stepping over the wizened form, the now dull eyes still open and sunk deep within the pallid skeletal features, Dr Grachev moved on through into the next room to confirm his notion of what had been fleetingly glimpsed over the old man's shoulder. There before him in the gloom, illuminated only by the light filtering in from the hall, was at least a partial answer to his prayers – a heavy safe about two feet high with a key in the door swung wide open. Beside it stood neat piles of banknotes consisting of twenty and fifty pound note denominations. Inside were lots more bundles. He estimated each bundle of bank notes was worth one thousand pounds. After stemming the flow of blood from his injured hand with a scrap of material lying nearby, Dr Grachev counted how many bundles there were: it came to nearly two hundred thousand pounds. Without rushing, he opened up his Gladstone bag and methodically crammed the tight bundles of money inside, then locking the safe door he removed the heavy key and began to take in the details of the darkened room.

He was pulled up with a start as he peered through the gloom for no matter which way he looked he was met by the luminescent whites of dozens of eyes glaring straight back at him – accusingly. *Something with scales and sharp legs then began crawling slowly down Dr Grachev's spine.* He fumbled for the light switch before illuminating the area.

This room was evidently where Weizmann had carried out his delicate business of crafting the prosthetic eyes out of plastic resin. It was furnished as a small laboratory, shelves holding samples of his work. Everything was white: white walls; white shelves; white work surfaces where all the tools of the ocularist's trade were laid out neatly on a dark blue piece of fabric. There were large thick brown paper bags holding clear crystals, which Dr Grachev took to be that of a plastic compound, and ceramic moulds in which to pour the resin. A gas ring and Bunsen burner also sat on the pristine work surface next to various sized metal clamps, and a microscope. It took a while for Dr Grachev to examine all the false eyes, lifting each in turn out of their drilled wooden holders, but without locating the one he had put his life in such jeopardy for. After dropping the safe key down the back of a central heating grill beneath the window he lifted up the telephone sitting nearby, and rang the eye hospital once more.

A rough male voice answered the switchboard: "The hospital is now closed. Please ring back on Monday morning."

Dr Grachev replaced the receiver and swore. He leant over the blue cloth holding Weizmann's tools of his trade, slowly scrutinising them before carefully secreting something into the palm of his hand before returning to the waiting taxi, but not before dragging a large terracotta flower pot across the tiled floor in the hallway, to be used as a wedge, preventing the heavy street door from closing completely.

The taxi driver had been sitting with the interior light on patiently reading a newspaper as Dr Grachev climbed into the rear seat. While in the process of putting the engine into gear, the driver heard an urgent tapping on the glass partition separating himself from his passenger. As he slid the partition back, Dr Grachev leant forward, putting his mouth very close to the driver's ear and spelt out his request in words of one syllable.

CHAPTER 119

Earlier in the day, just as Dr Grachev had been preparing to meet Smith in Harley Street, not yet having set out upon his ill-fated rendezvous beneath the iconic statue of Eros, the Greek god of love, Li Cheung had been in the process of discovering to her dismay though not to her surprise, that the staff administration section of the hospital was closed all through the weekend.

So rather than becoming involved in a heavy conversation regarding her unscheduled week away from the eye hospital and requesting compassionate leave, Li Cheung found herself filling in the time until one o'clock, when Tom was due to meet her, by spending the morning tidying up her particular section of the laboratory in which she worked and categorising various tissue slides – a job that had been put off for many months. In reality, for the last few hours, all her thoughts had been unintentionally taken up with the sort of wedding dress she had dreamed about since she was six years of age. In between these idle thoughts Li Cheung chatted to a colleague who also happened to be in the laboratory that particular Saturday morning.

It was nearly one o'clock and time was pressing. Li Cheung worked as a prosthetic technician, a position she had held for the last two years. Rising from her tall swivel chair she was just about to remove her freshly laundered white cotton laboratory coat and get ready to meet Tom, when something caught her attention, something that she had been staring at without realising just what it was that she found so interesting. Then it dawned on her. The item of her fascination, lying on a shelf just inches away from her head, happened to be a false eye. The glass eye itself looked perfectly normal in all but one respect. Viewing it sideways on, what was so uncommon was the small red dot at the rear.

After giving the large circular clock mounted on the wall above a row of filing cabinets a cursory glance, Li Cheung sat down once more at the laboratory bench, carefully removed the prosthetic eye from its resting place and began to examine the object now set before her.

Being very aware of the time and knowing that Tom would be kept waiting if she was not careful, Li Cheung worked quickly. It was not that unusual to have a fixing, a protuberance at the back of plastic eyes. Indeed, not all false eyes were even orb shaped but only partially curved. However, the one she was now staring at was made of glass and was indeed spherical with nothing but a tiny red blister to disfigure the otherwise smooth surface. Lifting a sharp instrument akin to a compass point she scraped at the shiny red blemish. It left a mark, scoring easily. Pushing the point deeper into the hard substance a flake chipped off. To Li Cheung's eyes it resembled sealing wax. Moving to the other end of the work surface some six feet away, Li Cheung lit a Bunsen burner, and using a pair of steel tweezers offered the tiny red fragment to the blue flame. It formed into a molten bead and splashed upon the white worktop, mimicking the miniature tip of a fiery volcano. It was indeed sealing wax. Intrigued, Li Cheung adjusted the flame until it had turned orange, losing much of its heat. She then raised the glass orb once more using the stainless steel forceps incorporating a ratchet device, this time ensuring the glass orb was clamped firmly within its grip as it was held over the tip of the flame.

A thin film of carbon began to form on the surface, slightly discolouring the posterior of the eye before the heat from the flame had the desired effect. The red wax dot softened, quickly turning into a thin red molten stream flowing from the eye's posterior cavity, taking with it the miniature glass ampoule holding a clear yellow fluid compound which Li Cheung was not quick enough to catch. Even if she had been able to prevent it from hitting the hard top of the laboratory workbench, the heat from the Bunsen burner had already cracked the ampoule, spilling the yellow fluid onto the white worktop, floating in pools between the hot shiny beads of red wax and tiny glass splinters. A fine mist immediately began to form. Within seconds the pathogenic substance had evaporated, a minute amount of it being sucked hungrily into the air conditioning unit and transported through the silver coloured tin ducting before being spewed out into the street and mingling with the heavy shower of torrential rain.

CHAPTER 120

Even though the accent was pronounced, the taxi driver had no difficulty in understanding what his passenger required.

"It will cost you." The driver found it easier to make such a request for money without turning his head around. "Give me five hundred quid," came the demand in an off the cuff manner.

"Quid?"

"OK – pounds if you don't understand."

Dr Grachev counted out the money from his Gladstone bag and after snapping it shut, pushed his hand through the glass divider into the front of the driver's cab, his upturned empty palm gesturing for the information.

"Print it so that it is legible." Dr Grachev ordered, dropping all pretence of friendliness.

"Okay mate, he's an expert, so it's not cheap. But the other piece of information you wanted you should find it easy to remember without me writing it down for you. It's a large expensive building you're looking for and it's very close to here so it's not too hard to find."

After a few seconds the taxi driver passed over a crumpled piece of paper with the name and address written out neatly in block capitals and whispered the other piece of verbal information which included the word 'hospital'. Dr Grachev pushed the five hundred pounds in twenty pound notes through the opening where the sliding glass partition had been a minute earlier, with the advice that he had better count it. As the driver now jubilant with his good fortune bent over the money and licked his thumb before beginning to work through the bundle of notes, three things happened in quick succession.

Firstly, the taxi's mobile telephone crackled into life. Secondly, the driver flicked a switch and made a deep growling sound, which in turn elicited a response from the warm voice now resounding around the cosy dark cab interior with crystal clarity.

"Mr O'Connell, its Zoe here. I've good news for you – it's a seven and a half pound baby girl." It is debatable whether or not Mr O'Connell actually heard this last piece of exceedingly good news because of the third event happening when he appeared to be smiling at his good fortune.

It is quite often impossible, just by looking at a person's contorted face from even a relatively short distance away, to differentiate between tears of joy or tears of agony and suffering. Thus it was in the case of Mr O'Connell. The thin top lip drawn back exposing the regular upper line of white teeth and partially visible pink gum could just as easily be construed as a smile, whereas in reality, there resided a frozen snarl at the final moment when death gripped his features.

The only clue as to why such a grimace was visible on Mr O'Connell's face lay in the thin steel glittering implement so discerningly removed by Dr Grachev from the blue cloth upon which lay the ocularist's array of instruments within his workroom. This particular implement had been selected with all the expertise of choosing a really special diamond amidst a gem dealers sprinkling of mediocre offerings. This long slender stainless steel rod used in the construction of false plastic eyes, having been chosen so meticulously only minutes earlier, now sat firmly implanted between the second and third vertebra at the base of Mr O'Connell's neck, having skilfully severed the spinal cord with its razor sharp blade just as surely as the Spanish expert, who will garrotte a prisoner sentenced to death on behalf of the Spanish state at the behest of a judge. In this instance though, there was neither judge nor jury, only a small seemingly frail man with long flowing white hair and a stoop, and bearing a small indentation in the palm of his gloved right hand, caused by the terrible exertion of pushing the steel shaft so deep into Mr O'Connell's neck between the occipital condyle just above the hairline.

The act of flicking the switch to receive the radiophone message from Zoe, and the deep growling sound made within his throat, had both been caused by the involuntary reflexes of Mr O'Connell at the precise macabre moment of his death.

It was as if death had also visited the surrounding houses, for the whole area lay in darkness and silent as a graveyard. Dr Grachev struggled with the body, dragging Mr O'Connell out of the cab by his armpits and up the house steps, the now lifeless legs limply following on behind, scuffing the heels of his trainers in the process. Dr Grachev felt a great sense of relief as the body was deposited in the hall out of sight before he made his way back to the taxi. Opening the driver's door he reached inside to remove the ignition keys and the five hundred pounds scattered upon the floor, the money he had paid the driver only minutes earlier, before carefully re-locking the doors and returning to the house.

Once inside, Dr Grachev worked fast, stripping the clothes off the taxi driver until he was completely naked. The thin steel shaft of the craftsman's tool, which Dr Grachev had taken such care over selecting, remained firmly implanted within the now purplish area of the neck, only the faintest trace of blood visible around the base of the shaft where it had penetrated the skin. After this task had been completed, he began to undress himself.

A casual observer might have been forgiven for thinking that what they were about to witness was some ritualistic form of necrophilia. They would however have been mistaken. It now looked and felt like a refrigerated abattoir within the tiled hall, Dr Grachev shivering uncontrollably as he removed the last vestiges of his own clothing. But it was not just because of the cold that Dr Grachev's body trembled; his heart was now pounding furiously as he desperately tried to control the powerful emotions that were taking over. For a moment he stopped what he was doing and drew enormous gulps of oxygen deep within his lungs, attempting to regain some of his lost composure before reversing the disrobing process by getting dressed again, this time however, using the clothing removed from his victim. Even the taxi drivers' undergarments were exchanged, only too aware that each item of his own clothing held telltale labels in Cyrillic script which could help convince the authorities of someone's identity. Once this task had been completed he began to feel a little calmer and surveyed himself in the hall mirror.

What Dr Grachev saw pleased him. Gone were the grey wig and moustache, replaced now by a man in his mid-thirties dressed in a pair of white trainers, blue designer jeans, a grey silk polo-necked shirt and topped by a leather fur lined flying jacket. It was indeed fortunate that the man lying spread-eagled on the floor wearing Dr Grachev's cast off clothes, including his dark conservative style suit, was approximately of similar stature, only the ill cut trousers being a little on the short side, but nothing too obvious, and Dr Grachev's shoes could have been tailor made for Mr O'Connell.

To add to the authenticity, Dr Grachev pulled from the jacket pocket of the suit a mojo in the form of his lucky dog tag. He draped this tag – which bore his old army identification number – around the dead man's neck, gingerly lifting the cord over the steel device which had been used so skilfully to terminate Mr O'Connell's life, before tucking it beneath the shirt collar. The Russian identification tag had replaced the silver St Christopher and chain given to Mr O'Connell in happier times by his wife Michelle. This silver talisman seemed to Dr Grachev a fair exchange as he slid it over his own head.

Once his clothing had been traded with the corpse, Dr Grachev looked carefully through his own wallet before switching it with that of Mr O'Connell's, also sliding his own passport inside the dead man's pocket to accompany it. All documentary evidence of Mr O'Connell's identity had now been removed. The switch was complete. After casting a critical eye over his freshly attired victim, he moved into Sammy Weizmann's laboratory, dragging Mr O'Connell's body behind him to carry out his final grisly task.

Before setting to work on the body with his fine fingers which had concocted so many variants of deadly biological weapons of mass destruction, Dr Grachev lifted a pair of rubber surgical gloves lying on the workbench and pulled them on, temporarily removing his own leather gloves, one of which was damp with his own blood from the bullet wound. They were a little tight but would serve their purpose. He also found an apron Sammy Weizmann had obviously worn over many years, it being quite frayed and soiled. After donning this item of clothing he half dragged, half lifted Mr O'Connell's body up onto the workbench into the close vicinity of the Bunsen burner which had been used to heat up the ceramic prosthetic eye moulds. Once the gas had been lit, it took a comparatively short time to completely excoriate Mr O'Connell's hands and facial tissue, thus removing almost the last vestiges of identification. This left only the teeth to be removed, a job which Dr Grachev set about with uninhibited gusto, using a hammer and pliers to accomplish his grisly task.

After glancing down at the two crumpled bodies, once more reunited in the hall, Dr Grachev looked satisfied with his messy but to his mind necessary handiwork as he made a foray into the other rooms, now suffused with the smell of burnt flesh, in search of the kitchen and food. As a doctor he knew stress could do funny things to people. He felt ravenous. Walking around the prostrate body of Weizmann, his attention was drawn to the ocularist's left foot which twitched momentarily. It might have been an involuntary muscle spasm. It might not.

CHAPTER 121

Tom found the traffic heavy going. Driving around central London any day was a bit of a nightmare, but on a Saturday morning! Everything was crawling at a snail's pace because of the rain hitting the road surface so hard that it appeared to be climbing back up from whence it came. It also felt like an obstacle course, attempting to avoid the spate of roadworks which seemed to have appeared overnight like a bad rash of measles. To add to his misery, every time Tom approached the traffic lights they were against him and time was running out. He hated to be late.

It was nearing one o'clock when he finally approached the imposing building, the façade made up of solid grey slabs of stonework and topped off with a large pediment, creating an air of heaviness and stability which the Victorian architects seemed to adore. It did not take long to spot Li Cheung's car. Here his luck changed. Li Cheung had used the staff parking area and the parking space adjacent to hers was vacant, so without thinking twice he manoeuvred his own vehicle into it, trying to look confident as though he always parked there. Not that anyone was taking much notice in the torrential downpour. He glanced at Li Cheung's car and felt happy that she had been reunited with it. Tom then glanced at his watch. It was precisely one. Because of the rain he decided to wait in his car until he caught sight of Li Cheung before getting out to greet her. As he sat there, his eyes straining to see through his own partially misted window, he was blissfully unaware of the events taking place not a hundred yards away from his vantage point.

CHAPTER 122

Dr Kenneth Jones leaned toward 'C' as if drawn by an invisible magnet, elbows on knees, searching his colleagues face for any possible clue as to how he might be of assistance in catching this Russian scientist who they figured was now on the run. As he should have guessed, with regard to all matters pertaining to state security and intelligence, things were never that straight forward.

They both sat there as 'C' gathered his thoughts, pondering on how best to put such a plan to his friend. As the French saying goes: *"Les amis, des mes amis, sont mes amis."* The friends of my friends are my friends. Well – not quite. Having worked for SIS on and off for over half a century he knew very well that in the final analysis expediency ruled. Dr Kenneth Jones also knew only too well that so-called friends can often be hung out to dry. That was why, when the suggestion was put to him, it could be truthfully said he was not overly enthusiastic. It took a good few hours and many more glasses of whisky before he agreed to at least consider the proposition. Not that the whisky clouded his judgement. It would have taken more than a bottle of Scotch to do that.

"You do understand that I would not ask you to do something to put anyone's life in jeopardy, don't you?" A look of hurt solidarity replaced one of pure selflessness. Another ball of camel shit fragrance took to the air, the dark cloud wafting gently away over the desk, away from the black Russian cigarette, dissipating into the ether, conjuring up the smell of rotten eggs; a metaphor for 'C's' suggestion.

"Last throw of the dice old boy – trying to rescue the situation, that's all." 'C's' face had a pallor to it which Ken had not noticed before. Fine cobweb-like lines were spun around his mouth and eyes, rendering him very old.

"We've known one another for a long time and I know you would not knowingly put a civilian in the same line as a professional soldier," Ken retorted, more in hope than belief. "That's why I question these things. The problem I have is that this is a close friend of mine we're talking about. You know as well as I do… probably much more so than I, that the best laid plans can go awry. This is a very vulnerable person we are speaking of. Nevertheless I shall put your proposition forward and see what their response is. I can do no more than that. But what I will not do is to put pressure on them. That would not be fair and I do not think you would expect me to do so."

"Ken, my dear boy, please do not feel put upon to push the suggestion against their will, for that is all it is, just that, a mere suggestion."

Dr Kenneth Jones knew that on the surface what he was being asked to suggest was a seemingly very straight forward request. As simple as simple can be – but without laying all the cards on the table. Well, half-truths were often worse than no truth at all. Smoke and mirrors, that's what he and his companion had traded in for a lifetime – in many respects they were no better than conjurors – charlatans, performing a sleight of hand with the dexterity of a card sharp. Yet deep down he loved his country and would in exceptional circumstances do absolutely anything for it – anything. He would, if pushed, describe himself as a true patriot – a son of the soil.

CHAPTER 123

All was quiet inside the small laboratory. The friendly banter bounced to and fro between Li Cheung and her colleague Fay had ceased minutes before. A slide beneath Fay's powerful microscope was being brought into sharp focus as she became aware of the eerie, heavy silence that had enveloped the laboratory. Only the soft steady hum of the metallic air conditioning unit snaking across the ceiling hinted at a vague sense of activity.

At first Fay thought that maybe because of her own intense concentration upon the sample now being studied under the microscope she had not noticed her colleague slip out to the hospital reference library, situated as it happened in the next room but one. It was a common enough occurrence. But then a snake-like viper hissing sound impinged upon the silence, drowning out the faint hum of the air conditioner. Fay's head twisted sideways, away from the microscope, and was on the verge of remarking upon the strange sound to her colleague when what she saw next momentarily paralyzed her.

Li Cheung had not slipped out of the high ceilinged laboratory as Fay had assumed. Instead she sat immobile on her high stool, her body tilted stiffly at an unnatural angle over the laboratory worktop. Unlike Fay, there was no discernible life in her. She sat there rigid, paralysed in her posture like one of the waxwork dummies Fay had seen in Madame Tussauds.

Fay's initial reaction had been to assume that Li Cheung was fooling around. Then she saw it, a thin red biro line running down her cheek. Initially the trickle of blood appeared to be flat; two dimensional. Slowly it took on a thickness and life form resembling that of a worm, oozing from Li Cheung's ear and dripping from the exceptionally smooth skin around her jawline onto the white cotton lab coat. The sickening stain was spreading fast. In panic, Fay half jumped, half fell off her chair, intending to administer first aid. When she got closer, she realised it was too serious to tackle on her own. What Fay failed to notice was a fine sliver of glass, one of many fragments lying scattered about the laboratory worktop. This particular piece had ruptured one of Li Cheung's delicate fingertips, allowing the deadly viral cocktail to enter her bloodstream.

Li Cheung's now waxy-looking face had taken on the frozen demonic look caused by toxic shock. Her rapidly jaundiced eyes suddenly began bulging beneath swelling bags of red pus, staring with horror into the middle distance, the result of the deadliest strain of virus ever known to man, attacking her immune system in the most immediate and terrifying way imaginable. It was then that Fay became aware of blood haemorrhaging not only from both ears, but also from the swollen lower rims of her eyes, nose and mouth. On her pale lips, tiny pink bubbles were forming, half choking her. It was from Li Cheung's lips, rapidly turning a bluish colour, that the soft urgent hissing sound emanated, a noise which was to haunt Fay's dreams and memory forever.

CHAPTER 124

So eager was Tom to see Li Cheung again, he could wait no longer. His watch read ten minutes past one when he left his car and made a dash through the heavy rain across the courtyard and into the reception area of the eye hospital. Dripping wet, he asked to be put in touch with the department where Li Cheung worked. It was after giving his name that he was handed a note, the message being taken over the telephone only moments before. Tom stared at it in disbelief. It said that Professor Lambton required Tom to get in touch A.S.A.P. It stressed that it was very, very urgent. The telephone number of his club had been written down at the bottom. As one of the switchboard operators put Tom through to this number, he began to wonder just how on earth the professor had found him.

"Hi! It's Tom here."

"Yes Tom. I couldn't get you on your cell phone. Something has come up and it's a matter of national urgency. Meet me at my club. I'll explain when you arrive. Come straight away." After taking down the address of Professor Lambton's club the line immediately went dead. Tom cursed under his breath for not having charged his mobile telephone and asked for the second time to be put through to Li Cheung's laboratory. He was informed the line was busy as there was some unspecified problem. Before leaving he scribbled a note for Li Cheung and handed it over to the receptionist.

As Tom left the eye hospital's parking lot he was forced to swerve to avoid colliding with a speeding ambulance coming in the opposite direction. Thinking no more about it he soon found himself sitting in the company of Professor Lambton at his club whilst being filled in on the previous night's meeting with 'C'. The professor explained to Tom that he had been instructed to co-opt a handful of top scientists who were specialists in biological warfare. These scientists were required to help debrief a fellow Russian scientist by the name of Dr Grachev that coming evening and wondered if he himself would like to accompany him. Tom was crestfallen, knowing that he would rather be seeing Li Cheung.

"When do we go?"

"I don't know Tom. I have contacted four other scientists, very eminent in their particular field of specialisation, who have agreed to co-operate.

They are just sitting tight waiting for my telephone call, the same as we are waiting now for a call from the intelligence services. In the meantime, let me offer you a late lunch."

"How did you locate me at the eye hospital by the way? I was amazed."

"That's quite simple. Li Cheung's mother said her daughter might be at her place of work. From then on the deduction was rather obvious my dear Watson." They both laughed as they made their way into the dining room, Tom happy that his working relationship with the professor had not been dented after the fracas over the late night car chase. Just as they were entering the panelled dining room with its sea of starched white linen-covered tables laid with silver cutlery and empty wine glasses, Tom explained that he would like to ring the hospital to find out if Li Cheung had left and whether she had been given his note. He said he would follow the professor shortly.

It did not take long for Tom to discover that Li Cheung had been rushed to the local hospital as an emergency, the result of some unspecified accident in her laboratory.

On the way to the hospital, professor Lambton tried to keep Tom's spirits from sinking by uttering all types of platitudes, hoping words would somehow help, instead of which they just irritated. Although the eminent scientist felt great empathy for Tom's distraught frame of mind he also found it very difficult to cope with such situations. Once they were at the hospital, Tom explained to the Admission's Officer that he was Li Cheung's fiancé and that he had to see her. Tom was told that was impossible as she was in Intensive Care and that the whole area had been isolated. Professor Lambton then stepped in, introduced himself and enquired as to why that was.

"Perhaps you would like to speak to a doctor," the Admission's Officer said, looking at Tom and pointedly ignoring the professor. If you are engaged to Miss Li Cheung then perhaps someone will speak to you."

It took several more minutes before a grey-haired, grey-faced man in his early fifties appeared, wearing a dark suit accompanied by the *de rigueur* rainbow-coloured bow tie.

"Doctor Jordan, Consultant Epidemiologist." He stuck out his hand in the direction of the older man.

"Ah, Doctor Jordan, I'm Professor Lambton and this is Doctor Thomas Dart. His fiancé is in intensive care; why the isolation?"

"Come into my office and I'll explain. I'm afraid we've just lost one of the people rushed into admissions from some type of haemorrhagic fever, meaning bleeding from the body orifices though I am sure you are familiar with that terminology already, so I am rather busy right now. Just as a matter of interest he happened to be a young man in his mid-twenties."

"You mean he's dead?" It was Tom who spoke with an air of disbelief.

"Yes, I'm afraid so."

They were led through a maze of corridors, green, red, blue and white lines of plastic tape covering the floor leading to areas such as x-ray, ENT clinic, oncology and haematology. This last area must have been right at the other end of the building from where they had entered. It was a windowless room they found themselves in with stark white fluorescent ceiling lights outlined through white opaque plastic sheets of Perspex.

"I'm sorry to hear about the loss of this young man. But how is Li Cheung? When can I see her?" Tom could hardly contain himself as the consultant carefully positioned himself behind his desk.

"Well, that depends. To be absolutely brutally truthful, Li Cheung is in a critical condition. She has been intubated and put on a ventilator. Blood samples have been taken and have already been sent for analysis. As you can appreciate there are many microbiological tests being conducted right at this very moment. The man who has just died – an autopsy is being carried out on him by a local pathologist – Rupert Adams as we speak. A lung biopsy is the thing to tell us more – one of the tests our team is working on beside mucoid smears and other things is something we call fluorescent antibody tests – to search for bacteria as you will be aware." The doctor gave a nod in the direction of Professor Lambton. "According to the doctor carrying out the autopsy in the mortuary it would seem that as well as his lungs weighing over twice as much as would be expected, his spleen is also enlarged."

"As would be expected? My God – you don't think there is a possibility of…" it was Professor Lambton who broke into the doctor's sentence, his brow furrowed with a worried look.

"Yes Professor, it is only an educated guess, but yes, some of the symptoms resemble that of *Yersinia pestis,* the bacterial cause of… "

"Plague! You mean that because of the lungs being affected like that you are referring to what would be known as pneumonic plague."

"Correct Doctor Dart. Many people don't realise that plague is still alive and out there in this big world of ours. The other plague of course would be that of bubonic – cause of the Black Death in Europe and Asia in the Middle Ages, the worst epidemic the world has ever known, but we see no evidence of the telltale buboes or swelling of the lymph glands which give their name to this dreadful disease. In any case, we suspect she may have a viral condition so have asked for viral culture tests but these tests take a long time to produce results as I've no doubt you are aware of – I suspect she may have a virus within her body for which as of this moment we have no antidote to counter its effects. If it is plague we are dealing with it can be cured if caught and treated quickly enough. We have sporadic outbreaks in New Mexico for instance. However, we are still screening in an attempt to eliminate many possible factors. And some of the symptoms do not fit the bill. The prognosis is not looking good I'm afraid. We are trying a broad spectrum of antibiotics hoping it may be an infection and this may help but…" Whatever the doctor was going to say, he held back.

Tom was on the verge of interjecting once more, having so many questions rapidly forming like bubbles in his mind. The consultant lifted the palm of his hand to halt him in his tracks.

"If this is a virus we are certainly not familiar with the particular strain – we have not as yet been able to find anything in our arsenal of antidotes to stop it dead in its tracks. But to be on the safe side we are already attempting to trace any primary and also secondary contacts these poor victims may have come into contact with, though as yet we have only been able to isolate it to one particular person in the eye hospital."

"Why would it be a virus? Could it not simply be a bacterial infection as you suggested earlier?" There was a note of panic in Tom's usually measured tone of voice.

"Well, I did say we are still in the process of screening for the possibility, carrying out a series of toxicity tests and such like. But so far all have proved negative. A virus would seem to be the most likely cause. But I must add the caveat that in all my years of practice I have never seen anything quite like this. Her symptoms are not responding to anything we try. There just does not seem to be any antidote to treat this. There are many viruses out there today which no penicillin drug or any other antibiotic such as vancomycin seems capable of being any help. For example vancomycin is an antibiotic that is really only used to treat bacterial infections, not viral disease. But in desperation we are trying it anyway and anything else we can think of. We must just hope that whatever it is, it is not hardy enough to cause a pandemic. Only time will tell."

Whilst Dr Jordan waited for a few seconds to let the full implications of what he had told them sink in the telephone rang. Another case had just been admitted with symptoms of a severe haemorrhagic fever similar to that of Li Cheung. The patient had come from the same eye hospital where Li Cheung worked as had the young man who had just recently died. At this point Tom once again insisted on seeing Li Cheung, Professor Lambton being very surprised when Dr Jordan this time acquiesced but just before letting the Porton Down scientist go he whispered into his ear: "I'm afraid this requires urgent action. Because of what is happening I am letting the central register for serious infections at Colindale Communicable Diseases Centre in North London know of this outbreak. It's important we get this information out there as soon as possible."

"I was going to suggest the same procedure myself. Also, because we may very well be dealing with a viral outbreak, I would advise any cleaning staff be supplied with sodium hypochlorite instead of using Dettol. That will kill any viral contamination."

Both Tom and Michael were then dressed for entering what would now be known as the quarantine zone in what to them was familiar protective clothing consisting of a white gown, gloves and a mask containing something known as a particulate filter – designed to trap viruses, before being led into the now cordoned off Intensive Care Unit. There was not too much to see of Li Cheung as she lay beneath a white sheet and blankets, even her very pale face only partially visible, being mostly covered by an oxygen mask. Tubes were everywhere, some hidden beneath the blankets running to her now frail arms and another tube inserted into her neck. Her eyes were half closed, the long jet black eyelashes contrasting vividly against her chalk white cheeks, the only sign of life a barely discernible movement in the region of her chest as she struggled to gain her breath. Blood still seeped from her ears and mouth, partially filling up the next to useless oxygen mask with a dark fluid caused by Li Cheung's liver, heart, spleen and kidneys slowly falling apart, molecule by molecule just as Dr Grachev had designed the virus to behave toward its host body, as if the vital organs had begun to take on a similar form as the red molten wax Li Cheung had so casually let drip from the posterior of the prosthetic eye in her laboratory. The internal organs were liquefying inside Li Cheung's body while she was still barely alive.

It was the professor, who whilst lacking words which might have eased the agony, placed his hand on Tom's shoulder and slowly guided him out of the glass partitioned room housing the Trexler tent, a plastic cube totally isolating Li Cheung from the room it had been erected in, it maintaining a negative pressure so as to contain any virus contamination, both men fighting back the tears which would flow later when they were alone.

CHAPTER 125

Penny stared at Ken, not quite believing her own ears. "You mean my stepbrother is in London?"

Dr Kenneth Jones had fixed it so as to be alone with Penny whilst David had gone into Barmouth, a small town on the coast approximately ten miles away, on some pretext dreamt up by his mentor. It was becoming a regular occurrence for Penny to spend the weekend in North Wales as frequently as work would allow, which made contacting her relatively easy.

There was one problem though. 'C' had insisted that whatever Ken told Penny, it could not possibly be the whole truth. It was to be done on the old 'need-to-know', premise. To protect Penny, she would be told as much as was required to get results – but no more. That however, was a tall order. How on earth was he going to explain to her that the seemingly innocuous gold pin bearing the communist symbol of the red flag might possibly reunite Penny with her stepbrother? He took the easy way out by using guile, for he felt sure he could depend on her.

"Penny, there are some things in life which just have to be taken on trust. That is what I am going to ask you to do now. Trust me. Can you keep a secret?" It sounded clumsy and patronising, and he wished he had been given the chance to rephrase it.

"Of course I can." Penny gave Dr Kenneth Jones a trusting smile. "But what is this about? Can't you give me my stepbrother's address so that I can visit him myself?"

"Like life my dear, it's not quite that simple I'm afraid, for I do not know where he is at this precise moment."

"But you just told me he's in London." The declaration of trust had now given way to puzzled anxiety.

"Well, I think he *may* be in London. But I'm not sure of his whereabouts. However, I have influential friends in the publishing business and after explaining your problem to them they have agreed to help locate your stepbrother if possible." The doctor knew a supplementary question was now on the cards and he was right.

"How could a publisher help to locate him? You're not making sense."

"I'm sorry Penny, please let me explain. You remember that last session when you were hypnotised. You wore a small brooch."

"Ah, you mean the pin given me by my mother... sorry, stepfather. It has a small red flag at the top with a gold hammer and sickle."

"Yes, that's it. Well, my friends in the publishing business, newspapers actually, well, they would be willing to print the picture of it in the hope that your stepbrother sees it and gets in touch. I understand that he also had one of those pins as you call it."

"How did you know that? Did I mention that under hypnosis?"

"Well, yes. Yes, that's right; you said it while under hypnosis." *He lied.* "The point is, would you let me have this decorative pin so that it can be photographed and used in an attempt to locate your stepbrother?" Ken already knew the answer would be in the affirmative coupled with an effusive display of gratefulness.

After thanking him with a kiss placed upon his forehead which took Ken by surprise, Penny quickly disappeared into the spare guest bedroom and soon after reappeared with the small piece of jewellery, handing it over to Dr Kenneth Jones with all the reverence she could muster.

"This will work, won't it?"

"I hope so." Those three words brought a look of pure relief to Penny's face.

"You know Ken; I really do appreciate what a good friend you are and how you have tried to help me. Thank you." Penny stooped down once more, this time planting another kiss on his cheek. Dr Kenneth Jones smiled weakly, trying to hide the acute feelings of guilt he was now experiencing.

***

Two days later, Rear Admiral Thomas Watkins, secretary of the Defence Advisory Committee, better known as the government's D notice committee, had, upon instructions from one of 'C's' minions, contacted an up-market newspaper and gained their co-operation in printing in the next day's edition's front page a picture of Penny's pin plus a London telephone number beneath. No caption was used, it being reasoned that if Dr Grachev saw the photograph his curiosity would get the better of him and after a while he would undoubtedly get in touch. Then, on 'C's' bidding, a D notice was also slapped on the newspaper for good measure, to prevent any disclosure relating to the cryptic display. The trap was set. The question was, would curiosity get the better of Dr Grachev to take the bait?

A telephone warrant was also obtained so that the SIS could intercept all calls to that special telephone line installed by vetted British Telecom engineers. The interception would be carried out around the clock from MI6 offices situated not far from the Tate Gallery, London's modern art museum on the side of the River Thames at Millbank.

A team of female listeners would monitor the specially set up telephone line ready to impersonate Penny at a moment's notice, hoping for that one clue as to where the Russian might be in hiding. The telephone line was also monitored by electronic specialists who had been seconded to SIS, hoping to get a fix on the location from where the call had been placed if it was ever made by using a special technique known as triangulation.

A backup team of seconded SAS men were also put on standby, ready to snatch Dr Grachev at a moment's notice if the opportunity arose. It was quite usual for these Special Forces to be used in such covert operations by SIS but this particular operation was deemed number one priority. The secret biological weapon Dr Grachev held could very possibly mean the difference between life and death for a whole nation. The search was now stepped up as all major main line train stations in London, as well as docks and airports, including those in the private sector all over the country, were watched. Agents were put on the highest alert as they searched for the Russian scientist. Every hospital – public and private, hotels, social security exchanges plus police stations were being checked to see if any word of Dr Grachev had surfaced. His photograph had also been faxed to any other conceivable place where he might be located.

CHAPTER 126

Tom having decided to remain at the hospital all through the weekend, Professor Lambton let his wife know that he would keep him company. The SIS had contacted the professor within hours of the aborted mission in their search for Dr Grachev, informing him that his services and that of the scientific team he had assembled would no longer be required and should be stood down.

In the middle of Sunday morning, while Tom was being urged by his boss to try and eat something, another two casualties of the virus were brought in on trolleys, being rushed through the same corridor in which the two scientists had gone to stretch their legs. Professor Lambton caught a glimpse of one of the patients and said he was going to try and get more information out of Dr Jordan. Tom insisted on coming with him. As they moved in the direction of the isolation ward, Professor Lambton seemed on edge and enquired if Tom himself had noticed either of the people's faces on the two trolleys being wheeled in at a frantic pace. Tom said he hadn't.

"Tom, I've got a hunch, but I can't say what it is until it can be verified. Come on." Tom scurried behind Professor Lambton, wondering what was going on, but only too eager to be doing something.

Rushing along the corridor, the professor cast his mind back to the early hours of Saturday morning and his meeting with 'C' and the other members of SIS. He thought of what he had told that assembled group barely thirty hours previously and it made him feel physically sick as he mentally reviewed his words: "*...because this particular virus has been developed in Russia... Dr Grachev's killer virus would presumably have been created using strands of DNA obtained from supplies of blood donated by Russians. Therefore, unless one possessed DNA of Russian extraction, it would more than likely be perfectly safe to handle. After all, if this Russian chap has developed such a selective virus that would be the whole point of the exercise – to be selective. So, in other words, unless you are Russian, or of Russian extraction, and we do not have many of those people in this country at the moment, you would in theory be perfectly safe even drinking Dr Grachev's compound.*"

Professor Lambton bit his nether lip, hoping against hope that he had not been wrong in his assertions, and that his words would not come back to haunt him and that this new hunch was just that, a hunch and not fact.

As they arrived once again at the office of Dr Jordan, professor Lambton turned to Tom: "What I told you in confidence about that meeting with 'C' and other members of the SIS – well, this meeting with Dr Jordan must also be regarded in the same vein, no matter what is said, it is said in the strictest of confidence."

Tom looked perplexed but answered in the affirmative.

The consultant was sitting at his desk with files scattered all over it, an x-ray pinned up on the wall behind him. The x-ray itself showed a pair of lungs but not the healthy-looking type with air-filled alveoli sacs but what in medical terms would be described as a 'whiteout' – the lungs filled not with oxygen but the delicate air sacs being completely blocked with its own body fluids presenting a solid white mass allowing no illumination to shine through. Professor Lambton hoped his resultant conversation with Dr Jordan would be profoundly different.

"Professor Lambton and Doctor Dart, please do sit down. How may I help you?"

"Doctor Jordan, do you have the latest admission figures relating to this haemorrhagic disease?"

The consultant shuffled his files around the desk top before coming up with a slip of paper. "Yes, here you are. Five patients admitted to this hospital, the first of course being Li Cheung, same symptoms in each case. Bleeding from all orifices; toxic shock symptoms, identical. As he spoke the consultant turned behind him to tap the x-ray pinned to the light box. "This should demonstrate what we are up against. There is hardly any oxygen entering the air sacs of these lungs. They are filled with liquid quite literally drowning the patient. Of course there are another eleven casualties distributed among two other hospitals. Well, that was up until nine this morning. That's when I was given the latest count."

"You say another eleven casualties elsewhere?" It was Tom who spoke now, unable to mask the shock in his voice.

"Well, we don't have the facilities here to cater for such an outbreak. You know – isolation and intensive care. We're pretty limited. Our facilities are really stretched. Of course I have already been in touch with a consultant from the communicable diseases unit and also the School for Tropical Medicine."

Professor Lambton nodded. "Tell me Doctor Jordan, you have a list of all the patient's names?"

"Well, only the cases admitted to our hospital. Why, what is the point you are driving at professor?"

"I cannot say at the moment. Could you get me that information quickly? It may have a bearing."

"As you are aware Professor, with this outbreak my time is..."

"It *may* have a bearing." This time Professor Lambton spoke louder in a very assertive manner, emphasising the word 'may'.

"I'm terribly sorry Professor, but I really think you are overstepping the mark. You might very well have some academic sway over..."

"Read this." What was now pushed into Dr Jordan's hand was a security card bearing the professor's photograph with the heading: *Deputy Director General – Porton Down.*

"But that's the top secret chemical and biological weapons place. My god, you don't think...!"

The professor looked the doctor straight in the eye and held out his open palm. "Please Dr Jordan, the names."

Within a few minutes Dr Jordan's fax machine sprang into life, rapidly spewing out the names which Professor Lambton, so out of character, had become unconscionably insistent upon being given. In between time, Professor Lambton and Tom had been settled with cups of coffee by a medical secretary. Not having had any proper sleep for the last forty-eight hours, both men's eyelids were beginning to droop. When the list was finally ripped from the fax machine Dr Jordan gave an audible gasp.

CHAPTER 127

"It's all a bit of a blur really. I remember entering the Harley Street practice where I was supposed to meet Dr Grey and Dr Grachev as I mentioned to you and then for some inexplicable reason I must have blacked out because the next thing I remember is coming round in one of the consultation rooms. It had grown dark and I realised that I'd been locked in and had my prosthetic eye removed. There was no one around so I had to break the door down to escape the premises and then made my way to the eye hospital – hence the temporary eye patch which you see here." Stryker tapped his silky black eye patch with his forefinger. "When I initially arrived at the eye hospital there was some sort of brouhaha over a fire alarm or something like that so I was transferred to another hospital nearby. Whilst at this hospital I discovered that my plan to help Dr Grachev escape to Switzerland must have gone like clockwork because the airline tickets I bought for him earlier had been removed from my jacket pocket – whether those tickets were removed by Dr Grey or Dr Grachev, at least that part of the plan had worked, though why anyone should want to remove my prosthetic eye remains a complete mystery." Carol stared at Stryker with disbelief written all over her face.

"You bought Dr Grachev an airline ticket for travelling to Switzerland? But Stryker, why would you want to do that? I mean, you were supposed to help catch him weren't you?"

"I'll explain my reasons in a minute, but I can see you're just bursting to tell me your piece of news that's going to make my hair stand on end so spill the beans." Stryker gave Carol an encouraging smile and took another sip of his tea laced with rum. Carol shot Stryker a quick glance and bowed her head as if not wanting to make eye contact with him – perhaps not wishing him to see the fear which must have been etched into her face.

"It's about those two British Embassy officials in Dubai – they've both been killed in a car crash."

"What!"

"Yes. I picked up that piece of information by chance from a Vauxhall Cross SIS agent who has only recently returned from a posting there; said he had been seconded to Registry for a short spell. He says he was called home to replace my friend Brenda on a temporary basis until something more permanent can be sorted out. He also said he'd been told by the First Secretary at the Dubai Embassy that both men had been killed in a car accident and that he knew one of them as the British Embassy's naval attaché." Stryker's facial muscles grew taught.

"The naval attaché who initially interrogated me in Dubai was in Naval Intelligence – I'm sure of it. He almost told me as much."

"Well, do you remember that night when I took a curious telephone call from that stranger – when you were in the bedroom? It was a man's voice, softly spoken with a soft Welsh accent asking to speak to you Stryker."

"Remember! How could I forget? That was the night after you nearly killed me re-arranging the bedroom furniture. I ended up in bed with concussion. Oh I remember alright."

"Please don't start that again Stryker. My heart weeps for you – truly," she responded in a mocking tone. "Anyhow, that man claimed that someone was trying to kill them. 'THEM'. Remember! Not him, but them! He asked me if you had a secure line – said he could not speak on an open line but that it was very serious. He was adamant about the line being secure. Not the sort of question you would ask unless you're in the security business is it? Don't you agree Stryker? Anyhow, it was then that the telephone was cut off. Maybe he worked for our bunch in Six. The SIS agent standing in as a temporary replacement for Brenda in Registry told me that a friend at the embassy in Dubai thought the two British officials had been killed in a car crash in suspicious circumstances because they had both been in a similar near fatal car accident only the day before and only escaped that time by the grace of God. Not that it did them any good mind you. And after I had worked out the dates when they supposedly had that near fatal car accident, well – it seems that it was the very same evening when we received that strange telephone call. So if the telephone call for you was from the British Embassy's naval attaché in Dubai, well maybe if he had been able to talk to you that night, Stryker, the two of them might still be alive. The SIS agent in Registry made some sort of sick comment about there definitely not being safety in numbers. And he said his suspicions had been further raised regarding their deaths when a blanket ban had been imposed forbidding anyone at the embassy from talking about the two men's demise, so he said he shouldn't really be talking about it to me, even though he obviously knew I also work for MI6. His hunch was that an assassination of the two of them had been carried out by a foreign power, thus the blanket ban on speaking about it. I'm frightened Stryker. It sounds to me very dangerous for both of us."

"Yes, it sounds as though we're skating on very thin ice here. But you do see the implication in all of this don't you Carol?"

"Well, it's obvious really. First of all there's my two unfortunate diving buddies who were decapitated by those Russians; then there's the naval attaché and his assistant – you remember the young man I mentioned who guarded me with a pistol whilst my hotel room was being searched, plus that SIS agent who was skippering the yacht and had his throat cut. I'm the only one still left alive who can testify first hand as to the events regarding that Russian ship carrying its secret toxic cargo. Before I was flown to Britain I was absolutely forbidden to speak to anyone about the events which had occurred off the coast of Dubai. No one! Need-to-know basis was quoted to me chapter and verse. With me out of the way now these events would just metamorphose into hearsay. No witnesses."

"Concentrates the mind doesn't it Stryker?"

"Sure does Carol. Then there's the information I requested from Vauxhall Cross including background information on Dr Grachev."

"What happened?"

"Nothing – that's the whole point. Do you remember how on my first making the acquaintance of Dr Grachev I was tailed home in the early hours of the morning from that night-time Easter church service by a suspicious-looking car and how I requested detailed information from the office regarding that car and was informed by the department a few hours later that it was registered to the Russian Embassy in London? Well after that enlightening piece of information I then requested a background check on the Russian national Dr Grachev to be left on my desk by the following morning. Well that request seemed to have fallen on deaf ears because I have never received that nor another morsel of any other intelligence worth speaking about since. It seems that my being supplied with that piece of information regarding the Russian connection with the car that tailed me that night was the catalyst for my not receiving any more requested information. Not another crumb of intelligence was ever passed my way after that. Why would that be do you think?"

"I've no idea. Why would that be Stryker?"

"Well I suppose in a strange sort of way it's beginning to make sense."

"To my mind it makes no sense whatsoever – a non sequitur if you will."

"Well, let's look at it from another angle. That naval attaché from the British Embassy in Dubai warned me that the watchword was secrecy! He said to quote: 'I have been instructed from the very top echelon in London, and I really do mean the very top, that these things which you say you saw must remain between ourselves, just the three of us.' That third person he was alluding to of course was his assistant. In retrospect that statement by the naval attaché coupled with the fact that certain unfortunate events have since befallen me has confirmed my suspicions that someone is pulling the strings as if I was an expendable puppet, or if you will, just a pawn in a game. In Moscow when I could have been killed instead of that poor fellow Anthony Lovejoy-Taylor during that failed operation – it was a classic set-up that went awry. In other words, this secrecy thing can lead to an absolute abuse of power. Remember the phrase power corrupts – absolute power corrupts absolutely? 'On a need-to-know basis' is a phrase I keep hearing banded around Vauxhall Cross. That sentiment can be used to stop anyone interested in asking pertinent questions. But the real question it raises is – who watches the watchers? In other words – by quoting the secrecy law the person quoting it is given carte blanche. You can make up the rules as you go along and no one is at liberty to question you because they don't even know what they're supposed to ask questions about. As I said, I'm the only one still alive to tell of just what did happen in Dubai and what I saw on the deck of that sunken cargo ship the *Little Murmansk* – the only witness to those events!"

Caroline's face clouded over as she strode over to Stryker, leant down and taking him by surprise flung her hands around his shoulders. "Do be careful. Please." Her eyes backed up her heartfelt rendition.

Stryker smelt her intoxicating perfume which had the effect of making him feel light headed for a moment before taking a sip from his cup of tea laced with alcohol then spoke once more.

"Another thing I've discovered is that as opposed to what 'C' told me, the American Government has no knowledge about my helping the British Secret Intelligence Service. I discovered this after asking my Seattle policeman friend and ex-boss Captain Billy Stoker to investigate using his confidential sources because I suspected it was a lie. Let's just say it was a detective's gut instinct. It might just be that 'C' himself has been led up the garden path, if you will excuse the expression, and that he did believe that the cousins across the pond knew all about my co-operation with the British SIS but it does stretch the imagination if the boss of Britain's Secret Intelligence doesn't know what is going on."

"So that's who you got in touch with in Seattle. Your old policeman pal," Carol replied.

Stryker said his friend had informed him that through a highly placed American source he discovered that Stryker's application form for his visa application to Britain had been filled in on his behalf by the now deceased British naval attaché in Dubai, giving the reason for Stryker's stay as an extension to his holiday and that as far as the American Intelligence

Services were concerned he was certainly not down as assisting the British Government with anything.

"That was the reason why I decided to help Dr Grachev escape from England by supplying him with papers to get to Switzerland. Don't forget, if he had been detained at Eros he was earmarked for assassination. He's a scientist for Pete's sake, not a killer in the accepted sense of the word. If you Brits killed everyone involved in the arms trade you wouldn't have much of an army would you?"

"Well Stryker, I guess that's one way of looking at it. But knowing what I've been told by my father about biological weapons capable of mass destruction that's not to say I agree with you."

"Remember 'C' intercepting that letter delivered to Vauxhall Cross which had been intended for me containing an elaborate gold pin fashioned into the Russian red flag with a hammer and sickle in one corner, symbolic of the Soviet Union. Why would he do that? And I never managed to obtain information regarding the aeroplane passenger lists from Heathrow I requested so as to possibly be able to trace the Red Chameleon through them. It feels to me as though someone has been blocking my requests. I suppose it's possible that someone was protecting Dr Grachev."

"What, here at the SIS? Why that's impossible... isn't it?" Carol looked downcast. "By the way Stryker, that's the other piece of information I gleaned at Vauxhall Cross and meant to tell you about. Apparently all requests for intelligence placed by you have to go through 'C' first. I also got that piece of information..."

"From your new friend in Registry. He must like your face."

"Now don't be jealous Stryker. You know there's only one person for me." Before Stryker had a chance to interject Carol quickly carried on. *"Persona non grata."*

"What?"

"Persona non grata. I told you that's what 'C' has designated both of us as and it would therefore make sense his vetting all your requests for information."

"And blocking them?" Stryker interjected.

"Well, as he says, a lot of people have died since you came onto the scene."

"You sound as though you agree with him about putting a block on all my requests."

"Of course not, you know that. But as far as 'C's' concerned, he has a right to be suspicious of you."

"Yeah. But still, right or not, I think right now I can do more outside the British Intelligence Service than within it. I obviously can't trust what I am told at Vauxhall Cross by the powers that be because the way I see it, omitting information is as damaging as lying, so I'll resign." Just then the cell phone rang.

Carol answered and handed it to Stryker. "It's for you."

"Yes, Stryker speaking." There was a gap in which Stryker looked baffled. "Sure, sure. I'll get over there. Happy to oblige."

Carol gave Stryker a quizzical look. "Who was that?"

"It was 'C'. He said to get over to Vauxhall Cross pronto. I'm to report to the security desk with my security pass. He must have second guessed me – apparently I'm fired."

CHAPTER 128

It was Porton Down's Professor Lambton who spoke first, staring hard at Dr Jordan who was standing holding a faxed list just ripped from the machine. "Just as I thought, they're all Chinese names aren't they?"

"How did you know that?" enquired the doctor, full of curiosity. "I haven't given you the list yet."

"They are though aren't they?" enquired Professor Lambton.

"Why yes, here take a look." As the list was proffered to the professor, Tom impatiently snatched it from Dr Jordan's hand, scouring the list headed with Li Cheung's name and spontaneously let out a cry.

"The selective virus!"

"The selective virus? What the hell's that?" The doctor's curiosity was now at fever pitch. "You know something about a selective virus?"

Just then a pretty young nurse dressed in a blue and white uniform pushed her head around Dr Jordan's door to ask if she might have an urgent word with him. Whilst Dr Jordan and the nurse stepped outside for a moment, Professor Lambton's mind reeled back to a conversation he had had with his daughter Caroline, who told him what Dr Grachev had said:

"I can supply you with a sample of a newly constructed pathogenic and selective virus with no known antidote."

"Selective virus – Dr Grachev said he had worked with the Chinese." Tom looked at Professor Lambton who continued: "My god! The Russian scientist had used the DNA of his Chinese host nation to splice a sample human genome removed from a person of Chinese descent onto a killer virus – a virus that would therefore only attack people of Chinese extraction."

When the doctor returned he wore a worried frown upon his face.

"Bad news I'm afraid. It seems that one of our own medical team working in the ICU has just succumbed to what we now believe to be a viral infection. It's what I was beginning to fear – nosocomial spread. That is, from patient to staff within a hospital environment... and yes, before you ask, he was of Chinese extraction. The pathological mechanism whereby people can succumb to this disease so quickly is something I have never

STRYKER'S HOUSE OF SPIES

witnessed before. It is truly terrifying."

"Dr Jordan, I am swearing you to utmost secrecy regarding what you are about to hear." Professor Lambton then recounted to the consultant a story about a mystery virus which might have selective properties only attacking people with a certain type of DNA. He left it at that, leaving out all reference to the Russian Dr Grachev, the Chinese and biological warfare.

"You mean there is a virus out there with the capability of storing racial genetic information? Why, that's not possible... is it? Jesus! Tell me I've misunderstood you. I've got that wrong."

"I'm afraid I wish that I could put your mind at rest but it is a distinct possibility. May I have a sample of Li Cheung's blood? It might help."

"At the moment she is receiving intravenous antibiotics in the ICU – she is on life support, as you saw for yourself. You know our laboratory does not possess a laminar flow cabinet in which to inspect this virus if that is what it turns out to be. When do you want the blood sample?"

"Well, as soon as possible. I'll take it back with me to Porton Down and see what we can find out there. I'll also notify the Ministry of Defence, also the Health Authorities – they must be put on full scale alert. Also COBRA must be notified straight away. Tom, if this is an outbreak on a massive scale we will require the secret stockpile of vaccines against smallpox and other diseases distributed very quickly indeed. I worry about the stocks we ourselves hold. They are not nearly enough to cope. Let's hope the emergency plans which have been laid down by the government for just such an eventuality stand up to scrutiny if they are put into practice – for all our sakes. What I don't like is the fact that as yet we are not sure what type of virus, if indeed it is a virus, we are dealing with here. Smallpox vaccine is no good in fighting something completely different. I shall explain the situation to the authorities and get them to search for the source of this contamination, beginning with the area where Li Cheung was taken ill – at her laboratory, and get it quarantined."

"I'll remain here and keep an eye on Li," Tom said. He looked a crumpled man, his shoulders sagging with anguish.

Before the two scientists took their leave of Dr Jordan, Professor Lambton left him in no doubt about the dire need to keep any staff of Chinese extraction away from the isolation unit and any of the other hospitals where the victims were being treated. That, it was explained, could be a matter of life and death.

Beads of perspiration laced the consultant's brow as he broke out into a cold sweat. His imagination was beginning to run riot.

CHAPTER 129

It took nearly three and a half hours before Professor Lambton finally reached Porton Down, Europe's leading viral diagnostic laboratory, with his special consignment of Li Cheung's blood samples held in plastic vials, plus other swabs taken from various parts of her body and some biopsies kept fresh in dry ice. Being Sunday, only a skeleton staff kept an eye on the ongoing experiments taking place there. He had already sent a message ahead of him so that a team could be assembled for the demanding work that lay ahead. Some of the best scientific brains in the country were already preparing for the task in hand when he finally arrived at the fortified government establishment.

Within minutes of his arrival, Professor Lambton's team were searching for the particular destructive virus which had taken hold of Li Cheung's now ravaged body in a vice-like grip. They were also racing against the clock. Professor Lambton knew, as did Tom, that the key to the possibility of saving Li Cheung's life was to discover which virus was causing such massive devastation to her immune system. The best clue lay in the fact that vital organs within her body, including the liver and kidneys, appeared to be in the process of being dissolved. The prognosis, as Dr Jordan had stated on Saturday, was not good. Every hour Professor Lambton's team of scientists worked on the mystery virus was another hour for the virus to wreak even more havoc on Li Cheung's now very frail body.

The breakthrough came in the early hours of Monday morning. Professor Lambton had gone home to Bath, hoping to get a little sleep. It seemed like déjà vu when his wife roused him from his deep slumber – the similarities of being woken early on the previous Saturday morning were too obvious to mention as he stumbled, still half asleep, to the telephone. It was one of his team of scientists on the line with the unsettling news that virus number one had been located and that it was a member of the filovirus family. He had not expected more than one virus to be involved and asked the person calling to double check, at which point he was informed that had already been done. Yes, it was definite that another virus was also involved. That came as a blow to the professor. When told the name of the particular virus already discovered he dropped his head in despair. It was Marburg, a haemorrhagic fever virus and for that there was a fatality rate of twenty-three to twenty-five per cent. The complications could also prove severe.

It was in 1967 that Marburg, a very rare type of virus, was first recognised as such by laboratories in Frankfurt and also in Marburg, Germany, after which the virus was christened. The outbreak was seen simultaneously in laboratories in Serbia and is derived from African green monkeys, which is why Marburg is also known as Vervet monkey disease. The odd thing about the way Li Cheung had been affected was the almost instantaneous haemorrhaging of the blood vessels. Usually there is an incubation period of five to ten days before any symptoms appear in the form of chills and headaches, followed by a rash on the stomach, chest and back. If that were not enough, this would be swiftly followed by sickness, pains in the stomach, diarrhoea and weight loss, becoming delirious with massive haemorrhaging. Many of these symptoms Li Cheung possessed, but within hours, not days!

Professor Lambton's order to his staff was unequivocal: "Take every precaution but carry on searching for an antidote to this new variant of the virus. It might very well be that the virus can spread through aerosol delivery – i.e. coughing or sneezing, so either way it is very dangerous; biohazard protective suits and masks are *de rigueur*. I'll be there as soon as possible." He then rang Tom at the hospital and explained the seriousness of the situation for those dealing with Li Cheung. Because of the nature of the virus, extra precautions would now have to be taken to protect the nursing staff, as Marburg was highly contagious even without the extra deadly properties of Dr Grachev's modifications to it.

As the professor was about to depart from Bath and make his way to Porton Down the telephone rang once more. It was a very distraught Tom on the line. Li Cheung was dead. Within another day all the other victims of Dr Grachev's virus would also be dead.

Around the time that the final casualty of this double edged virus had yielded to the devastating effects of having the immune system blown to pieces and their body ravaged, Professor Lambton's team had come up with the name of the second virus grafted onto the same human genome as the Marburg virus. It turned out to be the Ebola strain. The symptoms would normally be flu-like and the virus usually passed on through contact with other victim's body fluids including sweat, vomit, urine, diarrhoea, possibly even sneezing. The incubation period for Ebola is normally two weeks.

The Ebola River located in the Congo, situated in central Africa, is the area from which the Ebola virus took its name after the very first outbreak known to man occurred in 1976 where two hundred and eighty people fell victim to the first onslaught of this truly horrendous and devastating disease which has no antidote or known cure. This was just nine years after the first outbreak of Marburg. The really frightening thing was that the dual modified virus grafted onto this human genome had become so virulent that there was not even enough time to attempt treatment. All the victims had died within days. If the genetic make-up of this virus had been different and not targeted the specific gene for Chinese people, it could have had an even more devastating effect than the Black Plague, possibly wiping out most of Britain. Perhaps next time it would. And there surely will be a next time, for what people forget or do not realise is that Mother Nature is not a particularly philanthropic creature. What is the irony that an area within central Africa is designated as the cradle of mankind? The irony is that many horrendous killer diseases now threatening the future of mankind itself emanate from that very same African continent which gave birth to our civilization.

Diseases such as Vervet monkey disease derived from African green monkeys; Marburg virus, another haemorrhagic fever although only noticed in the German cities of Marburg and Frankfurt during a small epidemic in the 1960s, the virus also appearing at the same time in the Yugoslavian capital of Belgrade. This species of virus known as MARV has also been discovered in Rhodesia, Kenya, the Congo, Angola and Uganda as well as Koltsovo in the Soviet Union. Lassa fever, another haemorrhagic fever, was again only discovered in1969 in the town of Lassa, Nigeria. In parts of Africa Lassa fever has become endemic.

Twenty-six people succumbed to Dr Grachev's virus, all of Chinese extraction. If the weather had not been so atrocious whereby the viruses' ability to remain stable in such a hostile environment had prevailed that particular Saturday afternoon, making it possible for the virus to survive and spread, a full scale epidemic could have very easily occurred amongst the Chinese population. As it was, the usual platitudes were rolled out by the government of the day, the excuse this time was of an outbreak of Legionnaires' disease within the air conditioning ducting. This lie was used, "So as to keep the general population from panicking," as it had been explained to 'C' by the Prime Minister. Thus the danger was covered up, more for political expediency 'C' suspected, than through any real concern for the health of the general public.

However, what the scientists could not explain was how a pathogenic viral solution was able to escape into the air conditioning unit straddling the ceiling of Li Cheung's laboratory. For it would have been almost impossible for the virus to have arrived there by evaporation. For although the filters within this ducting were found to be grossly contaminated and some faulty installation of these filters had allowed unobstructed air flow, more likely was the theory that Li Cheung herself had somehow spread the virus through her respiratory tract.

The whole hospital was sealed off from the public and quarantined while squads of scientists and decontamination workers searched for the virus reservoir, suspecting Li Cheung had been the index case and spent several weeks eliminating any trace of the viral outbreak overseen by eminent epidemiologists from the School of Tropical Medicine whilst collecting samples from what was termed the *hot zone* for future investigation at Porton Down.

With Marburg, Ebola, Aids and Lassa Fever all being comparatively new viral diseases, only discovered in the last third of the twentieth century, and able to inflict a truly heinous suffering and death upon whole populations, there may be great truth in what the eminent scientist and Nobel laureate Joshua Lederberg has postulated, that the biggest threat to mankind's survival on this planet is the virus.

CHAPTER 130

It was a long drive to the coast. At first it was an easy route to follow, but the daisy chain of street lights finally ran out and Tom had to instinctively feel his way along the top of the cliff in the blackness. Tonight there was no moon to ease the way, just two insignificant white rods of light from the car's headlamps to guide him. After stopping the car he got out, standing still, ears straining to capture the sound of the sea, also becoming aware of the soft ticking coming from the rapidly cooling engine, the repetitive sound being carried away on the stiff sea breeze. It took time, stumbling as he did in the tangible darkness to pick his way around the uneven ground, seeking out small recognisable clues to the unrecognisable landscape.

Occasionally he would stumble, but in the dark Tom eventually found what he had been searching for. Pushing his hands flat against the oak tree, his fingers made contact with the one palpable sign that Li Cheung had existed. The edges of the broken bark, smashed with so much loving force such a short time before had not yet begun to heal... like Tom's broken heart; that would take time. He felt very lonely as his fingertips sensed the areas of deep wounds within the tree trunk which Li Cheung had wanted to last for a thousand years. *"That will be there for a thousand years as a symbol of our love won't it?"* He could hear Li Cheung's plaintive voice so clearly in his head – seeking reassurance, before being extinguished by the sound of the wind gusting in from the sea. Was it also his imagination, or could he really feel her soft fingers beneath his hands as he desperately clung to that oak to prevent himself collapsing into a pit of despair? Then the loneliness seemed to evaporate, but in its place came the tears.

CHAPTER 131

Dr Grachev stood by the window, peeping through the flimsy net curtains on that early Monday morning, having felt like a virtual prisoner all day Sunday, not daring to venture out into the daylight. It was still dark as he began to initiate his rapidly formulated plan of action.

One thing Dr Grachev had found on Sunday, while searching the large house, was a battered old suitcase pushed beneath one of the beds. Rummaging through what he took to be cheap trash, he came across something which was to raise his spirits considerably. It was Sammy Weizmann's passport. This he stuffed into his jacket pocket. He had also located a box of candles and brought them down to the entrance hall. Melting the ends of each one in turn, Dr Grachev stuck them onto the black and white tiled floor, the area now resembling a small shrine to the two victims of Dr Grachev's machinations. Then, walking once more into Sammy Weizmann's laboratory, he turned on the gas tap which gave off a noxious smell as it gushed from the rusted metal ring, used over so many years to heat up the ceramic eye moulds. After closing the door to the laboratory, he stepped over the two prostrate bodies and stooping down, gingerly lit the candles. With the gas in the laboratory turned on Dr Grachev knew it would take only a matter of time before this gas eventually seeped beneath the door leading into the hall and became ignited, setting off a conflagration equalling that of a sizeable bomb similar to the Nazi ones which had destroyed the neighbouring houses.

Dr Grachev hauled the body of Mr O'Connell out into the cold night air, leaving him momentarily lying on his side at the top of the cement steps in the darkness, his now featureless face resembling that of a burnt oven baked potato. Making one last foray into the hall, Dr Grachev grabbed his leather Gladstone bag before finally leaving the house for the last time. After carefully closing the heavy door behind him, so as not to cause a draught which might possibly snuff out the myriad of candles, he grabbed hold of Mr O'Connell's shoulders, sitting him in an upright position with his back against the street door and the forthcoming explosion that could now be only a matter of minutes away.

Sammy Weizmann's body, lying so peacefully in the hall amidst the candles which had taken on the semblance of a holy shrine, would eventually be consumed in the huge explosive ball of gas and fire to come.

Mr O'Connell's cadaver however, was to be saved that indignity, leaving him in better shape to make it easier for the taxi driver to be wrongly identified as Dr Grachev, the Russian's army identification tag aiding this deception. By then, Dr Grachev would be far enough away not to hear the panic and frantic activity of neighbours gripped by fear and terror.

One final task remained before Dr Grachev could finally walk away. Pushing his hands deep within the pockets of his newly acquired flying jacket, he pulled out the grey wig, eyebrows and moustache, which had probably saved his life, and proceeded to adorn Mr O'Connell's disfigured head. The resulting portrait was macabre.

In the cold, deserted street, dawn was tantalisingly close as he quickly slid into the driver's seat and pushed the key into the taxi's ignition. Dr Grachev gripped the steering wheel tightly with both hands in an attempt to steady his nerves. In his quest for a better life in the West he had now killed five people.

With mixed emotions he moved off slowly, as quietly as the engine would allow, following the high wall in the semi-darkness, retracing the route along which the taxi had brought him less than two days before. He was grateful to be wearing the fur lined flying jacket, removed from the shoulders of the dead taxi driver, the large collar of which was now pulled up around his neck, helping to keep out the cold and shield his features from any possible prying eyes. Dr Grachev heard a faint rumbling sound in the distance. It was coming from the other side of the wall. It grew louder as he pulled away from the old house now rapidly filling up with gas, the pot holed road shaking with the vibration of an unseen train whistling past, shattering the stillness. He knew it was only a matter of time before the British security service would be on his trail searching for him. To have the security agents of two countries hunting him required drastic measures. Dr Grachev drove without lights with one hand firmly clutching his Gladstone bag placed on the passenger seat beside him, until at the end of the long curving wall he felt secure enough to switch them on, their powerful beams of light slicing laser-like through the seemingly tangible darkness as he gathered speed, attempting to outrun the coming light of day, moving purposefully toward the one place where he felt sure his immediate problem of security could be solved. Three roads away there was another strong vibration similar to the one the train had caused just seconds before, but this time it was followed by the dull hollow rumble of a distant explosion.

Being unfamiliar with the area, it took time and a few wrong turnings before finding his way into the vicinity of St. John's Wood, just down the road from West Hampstead. He had found what he was looking for before leaving the main road and parked at the other end of a quiet side street, still under the blanket of darkness. Daylight was fast approaching as he doused the interior with half a can of petrol siphoned from the taxi's fuel tank before starting out on his perilous journey. Now removing the taxi's fuel cap he trailed a prepared fuse from the remaining tank of fuel. Once more, as with the candles, he set light to the end of the wick, made from a piece of Sammy Weizmann's pyjama cord, hoping that the ensuing flames would destroy any forensic evidence.

Without wasting time, Dr Grachev fled the scene as fast as his legs would carry him with his Gladstone bag stuffed with money, surprised at his own athletic ability. It was as he neared his destination that a second muffled explosion reached his ears.

CHAPTER 132

"It's for you Stryker." Caroline's voice expressed surprise, experiencing a sense of déjà vu having spent the previous day talking with him about nothing else but the department at Vauxhall Cross and forcefully castigating it. Her particular sentiment being that she and Stryker were working in a dangerous organisation in respect of her friend Brenda having died suspiciously, and also berating an ungrateful institution for dispensing with Stryker's services and at the same time empathising with Stryker's prior intention of handing in his resignation only to be pipped at the post by 'C'.

Caroline stood mimicking one of her many poses she had struck on the catwalk, dressed in a fashionable black outfit donned with the intention of cheering Stryker up and handing him her cell phone as she had done on Saturday evening, which had unwittingly presaged the news of his dismissal from Britain's Secret Intelligence Service.

It was unusual on a Monday morning, having just turned eight o'clock, to receive a call so early. It came from the administration section of the eye hospital where Stryker had spent the early part of the previous Saturday evening. After interrogating Stryker with a view to ascertaining his identity the caller explained the reason for her unsolicited call.

"I felt you should be informed about an enquiry regarding the ocularist who had initially made up the prescription for your false eye. Apparently on late Saturday evening, just after you had discharged yourself from this hospital a security guard here took a call from someone who purported to be a Dr Grey of Harley Street."

"Purported?"

"Yes Mr Stryker, purported. I use the word advisedly because we belatedly took it upon ourselves to check this doctor's credentials and can find no trace of him ever having worked in Harley Street."

"What did he want?"

"The so-called doctor requested information about your false eye and we are sorry to say that because of the upheaval here during the last forty-eight hours the security guard had misguidedly supplied Dr Grey with the ocularist's address who had been dealing with the matter as I mentioned. Because of the problems we have been experiencing at the hospital the security guard, in the confusion of the moment, gave out to a complete stranger what we regard as private and confidential information and as I say we can only give you our heartfelt apologies for what has been a terrible lack of professionalism."

"And was there anything else this Dr Grey wanted to know concerning me?"

"I'm afraid to say there was. Apparently, because the security guard was having trouble locating your name in the records and because of the furore here on Saturday, Dr Grey, if that is his real name, informed the security guard that if it was not possible to locate the name Stryker then he was to try looking for the name Smith."

"That's it?"

"That's it."

"Thank you. Oh, just one more thing. Would you give me the ocularist's telephone number and his address?" Stryker motioned to Carol for a piece of paper to write this information down upon before handing the cell phone back to Carol with a grimace.

Just as Stryker had finished relaying his conversation with the hospital administrator to Carol she handed the American detective a broadsheet newspaper which had only minutes before dropped through the letterbox. "Look at this."

The banner headline screamed 'Mystery Killer Disease' and beneath it ran an article stating that there had been an outbreak of a mystery illness – quoting the Government Health Protection Agency suggesting it was possibly an outbreak of Legionnaires' disease and that it had broken out at a famous London eye hospital causing some fatalities, and that many other people had been rushed to another nearby hospital and kept in isolation. The article also stated that the Communicable Diseases Unit based in North London had also become involved.

When he had finished reading this article Stryker sat peering into his freshly brewed mug of coffee Carol had just poured as if it were invisible and he was carved out of a block of stone, not moving a muscle. Then without warning he spoke.

"Carol, get me this number." Stryker then recited the ocularist's telephone number from the piece of paper he had been given a little earlier. After tapping in the proffered number Carol responded.

"Can't get the number Stryker – it's signalling out of order – just a continuous bleep."

Stryker picked up the black plastic hand control for the television set and turned it on. "Maybe there's some new information about that supposed outbreak of Legionnaire's disease at my eye hospital."

"That's a bit of a coincidence isn't it, the outbreak being at the same hospital you attend? But supposed outbreak of Legionnaire's disease! What do you mean by saying supposed?"

"I mean that Dr Grachev's deadly virus might already have been unleashed on an unsuspecting public – that's what I mean." There was an irritable tone to his voice.

Carol sat down on the sofa, closer than usual beside Stryker, just in time to catch a newsflash – not about the viral outbreak Stryker had been hoping for but something totally different. An announcement was being read out by a female newscaster to the accompaniment of a picture filling the whole screen depicting a burnt out building. Wisps of smoke could be seen corkscrewing up from the gutted building with two fire appliances and firemen carrying long hoses in the foreground. The voiceover was announcing: "Two bodies have been found at the burnt out premises situated in West Hampstead which neighbours say was owned by a Mr Sammy Weizmann, some sort of eye specialist."

"That's your eye chap isn't it?" Carol interrupted.

Stryker responded with a nod, putting a finger to his lips before whispering, "Hush!"

The newsreader continued: "Apparently the two bodies had been burnt beyond recognition and it is thought that a team of forensic specialists will be carrying out a thorough search of the premises once it has been made safe. Foul play has not been ruled out at this stage in the investigation though it is too early to say more because a strong smell of gas could be detected in the immediate area so there is speculation that a gas explosion might have been the root cause of the devastation. There was also a second explosion nearby just minutes later when a taxi burst into flames. There is no suggestion at this stage of it being linked with the explosion at the house nor is there any suggestion of bodies being discovered in the taxi, though the police have cordoned off the vehicle and are remaining tight lipped about the possibility."

Stryker switched the television off and turned to Carol. "Smith. That's the other name Dr Grey mentioned to the hospital security guard – my Six cover name. How could he possibly have known that?" Stryker grabbed his jacket and pushed his hand deep inside a pocket to retrieve his personal diary.

"Gotcha! That's how he knew both my name and my pseudonym. I wrote my projected meeting with Grachev at Eros in cryptic terms. See, there." Stryker handed his diary to Carol and pointed to the page carrying the entry. "Look." Sure enough there it was:

Meet R.C. at Eros – 2/5.

"Whoever saw that in my diary might have been able to put two and two together – especially the R.C. for Red Chameleon. I mean, Dr Grachev was supposed to meet someone named Smith from MI6 and he sure as hell knows me as Stryker."

"Eureka!" shouted Carol.

"What?"

"I didn't mention it earlier, Stryker, but I've just remembered something which I think might be very important. During last Saturday when you were supposed to keep your appointment with Dr Grey I desperately wanted to get in touch with you to let you know about those two people I discovered who had been killed in Oman. So because it was impossible to contact you on your cell phone I paid a visit to Harley Street. It's awful to think that you were laid out cold in that very same vicinity I was searching yet I couldn't find you."

"What's the point you are making Carol?"

"Well, while I was standing in Harley Street in the middle of the road around lunchtime looking about wondering what on earth to do and hoping against hope that I might catch sight of you – a silly notion I know, but in desperation I believe one might do absolutely anything. Anyhow, whilst I was standing there an old man came out of one of the houses and later I realised just what a coincidence it was when I could swear I caught a glimpse of that very same old man wandering around the statue of Eros at Piccadilly Circus later that evening. It was raining but I caught a fleeting glimpse of his wearing something which has just sprung into my mind as having been impossible – yet I remember it now as definitely being the same as the one sent to Vauxhall Cross and given to you so as the Red Chameleon would be able to identify you."

"You're gabbling darling; you mean he was wearing that same gold pin in his lapel – the flag of Russia with the symbolic hammer and sickle set in red enamel?"

"Yes, that's what I said. That's precisely what I saw in his lapel."

Stryker looked at Carol and smiled indulgently. "Yes, I'm sure that's what you said. Anyhow, it must be the same pin I carried between the pages of my diary because as you can see the indentation is still there upon the paper but the gold pin has vanished. He must have taken it while scrutinising this diary. But why should the old man you describe be wearing it?" Stryker was now on his feet and in full flow as he paced the room speaking as he went. "Unless!"

"Yes Stryker, unless what?"

"Unless that old man you saw Carol... What did he look like – could you describe him to me?"

"Well, he was wearing a worn dark suit and had long grey hair down to his shoulders. And he looked quite old because he had a stoop. He would stand out in a crowd. He looked as though he had just stepped straight out from a bygone age – like someone you might see in a museum. If he was wearing a stovepipe hat it wouldn't have looked out of place."

"Stovepipe hat?"

"Sorry Stryker. A stovepipe hat looks a bit like a top hat but much taller."

"And what height would he have been approximately Carol?" But Carol was ahead of the game. "Well, if he hadn't had a stoop he might have been the average height of a man – like – like..."

"Yes, like Dr Grachev. That must have been his disguise when I visited him in Harley Street. It's coming back to me as if in a dream. Now I can remember seeing his face as I entered the surgery. He had long white hair hanging down to his shoulders just as you describe him but there was something vaguely familiar about his face. That's it. That's why he proffered the other name Smith at the eye hospital as well as Stryker. He didn't know who I really was did he? I might have been either person."

"But why would he go to all that trouble of dressing up?"

"That's a good question Carol. Why indeed? I'm sure there has to be a connection with that enquiry regarding my ocularist at the eye hospital. Dr Grachev told me he was initially a medical doctor before he went on to specialise in his field of genetics so I feel certain he would be capable of removing someone's prosthetic eye if required. But again the question poses itself – why?" Stryker ceased walking to and fro in front of the sofa and settled himself down once again beside Carol.

"You got to know him a little didn't you, Stryker. I mean, you had that snack with him at his hotel here in London and then met him again in Moscow for the evening. What did you talk about?"

"Well as you say, I met him twice and come to think of it, each time after my meeting him I remember having a feeling of wellbeing – elation and pretty much total amnesia. I know it sounds strange but maybe he drugged me for some reason. In fact, when I think about it, if he had removed my false eye he unwittingly saved my life; for if he did tamper with my eye, maybe that was the cause of the irritation I felt so shortly afterwards, which of necessity precluded me from making that pre-arranged meeting with my contact just outside Moscow to act as bagman and consequently that poor guy Anthony Lovejoy-Taylor who acted as my replacement ended up dead instead of me.

"Do you think that's why Dr Grachev befriended you at the Easter Russian Orthodox Church service, so as to be able to get close to you?"

"Well done Carol, that's precisely what I'm beginning to think. First there's the occurrence of some mysterious disease which the Government Health Agency is calling an outbreak of Legionnaire's disease, though that is a bacterial disease isn't it? And then there's that fire at the ocularist's house."

"You're right about the bacterium because our asylum seeking scientist spoke about his concoction as being some sort of virus, not bacteria. But anyhow, were splitting hairs. The real question is how all of this is connected with the possibility of your prosthetic eye having been removed by Dr Grachev?"

"I think I have the answer to that too. I believe Dr Grachev befriended me at the Easter Church service just because of my eye. He mentioned the faint scar I have and therefore raised the issue himself. I believe he had this obscene idea of using my prosthetic eye as a vehicle for transporting his selective virus out of Russia and into England without being detected. And of course, if that's what he did it was a brilliant idea really. I very much suspect that front page newspaper article means that somehow Dr Grachev's virus has escaped and those poor dead people are the end result."

"If you are correct, do you think you will ever find him now that the virus is out there?"

"Like a bad penny he'll turn up sometime and when he does... But tell me again, when did you last set eyes upon the old man whom we now know to be that of Dr Grachev at Eros wearing that pin?"

"I last saw him at about seven o'clock on Saturday evening."

"Then he must have kept his appointment at Eros and was waiting there for me to turn up – except of course he was expecting someone called Smith, not myself, who he had unwittingly left incommunicado back at the surgery. In my note I warned him not to show himself at Eros because the secret service was going to kill him. It seems he ignored my advice, though being in disguise probably saved his life like my eye irritation in Moscow saved mine. Chance seems to have decided whether we lived or died and we were both very lucky in that respect. Anyhow if you saw him at seven by Eros then it would have been too late for Dr Grachev to execute his escape I had arranged for him, for by being seen by you loitering around Eros at that time he had obviously missed his opportunity to catch the plane using the airline ticket I purchased for him at the Swissair offices situated just by Piccadilly, for the time of that plane's departure was at precisely seven o'clock. Therefore," Stryker reasoned, "Dr Grachev must have remained in the country not having taken the opportunity I gave him to flee."

"But Stryker, why did you give him that opportunity to escape?"

"Because I thought he was a decent man and needed a break. Now I see I made a big mistake. And because of my bad judgement people are dead."

"Stryker, no one is infallible, no one. I respect you for what you tried to do for Dr Grachev believing him to be a friend."

"Oh Carol, you'd defend me against anyone and anything. I don't deserve such blind loyalty." Carol blushed and said nothing, but inside she felt only love for Stryker.

"Stryker, I'm going to resign. They treated you abysmally and I hate the organisation. I feel as though they are treating me as a pariah and after losing my friend Brenda I can't see the point of working for such an organisation any longer. One doesn't know who one can trust there. No, I'm leaving and that's that."

"Hold your horses; let me counsel you on this decision. Don't be hasty. Do what wise men do – sleep on it. Just take a few hours to make sure you feel the same way tomorrow."

"OK Stryker, I'll do just what you suggest, but believe me, it won't make any difference to the way I feel now. I just think of my friend Brenda and hate the organisation."

CHAPTER 133

The entrance to the expensive modern-looking exterior, a four-floor box-like structure made up of white travertine and dark tinted glass gave way to a spacious black marble foyer strewn with Persian carpets. Charles Eames reclining chairs with matching footstools in Rosewood and soft black leather hide, over a thousand pounds each, sat amidst rich tapestry-strewn white silk walls. Onyx ashtrays on silver-gilded stalks perched adjacent to each chair. Crystal coffee tables displayed the latest high style magazines and heavily illustrated books on Arab related matters – many in the Arabic language. But the real object of this opulent façade, for that is all it really was, a façade, lay hidden behind this sumptuous air of luxury designed to impress, out of sight of the clients who actually funded this over the top display of riches. It was not in any sense a restaurant, though the meals and wines served here were of the highest quality which might be found in any top class London restaurant. Neither was it a hotel, though the service lavished upon the wealthy clients inhabiting this environ could not be bettered by any five star establishment. Nor suffice it to say was it a high class bordello, though for a price almost anything or anyone might be procured.

In fact, the real reason why the clients, or rather private patients, entered this institution was for the array of expensive medical equipment such as kidney dialysis machines. There were of course still many operations, such as open heart surgery, which could not be performed here and instead had to be carried out using other private hospitals. The Clinic, as the hospital was informally known, was an exclusive preserve of the rich and famous situated within the heart of St. John's Wood, North London. One of the best money spinners was that of varicose vein operations. Although there was a permanent staff of doctors, surgeons and other specialists on call twenty-four hours a day, many consultants worked here part time in between their NHS obligations. That was the way of the world – that was the way to make real money.

There had been a time in the nineteen-seventies when Arabs came to the hospital in their droves carrying suitcases stuffed with large denomination notes. A hundred thousand pounds would be commonplace. If you have a life threatening complaint and are worth tens of millions, hundreds of millions or even billions of pounds it makes sense. On home visits, nurses from the Clinic came back with tales of very young Arab children in nappies sitting on potties playing with fifty pound notes while hundreds more were scattered around like confetti on inch thick white pile carpets, their parents in another room playing with their own pot, theirs containing twenty or forty thousand pounds. In its heyday, consultants at the Clinic were handed heavy solid gold ornaments by these satisfied patients after operations, in appreciation for their services. Alas, those days were no more, the Arabs eventually sensing the sheer greed of these medical men which had been engendered by what they perceived to be their own foolish generosity.

Consequently, many of these Arabs now took their business to the continent instead, perhaps feeling more comfortable in the knowledge of being fleeced by someone with a soft French accent. The good old days, as those doctors and specialists often referred to these heady times, had slowly, inexorably, come to an end and now it was back to reality. There were still exceptional episodes of generosity, like the rich Arab who recently gave a fully furnished flat in Knightsbridge to one very happy recipient, but these cases were now few and far apart.

It was in these circumstances then that Nurse Beckett found herself as she signed the staff book and changed into her uniform for the night shift, first making a cup of tea in between scanning the night duty roster, looking to see which patients had been discharged during her weekend away. As usual there was a shortage of nurses, so the local nursing agency had been contacted and the shortfall made up with three young women, one of whom was a very experienced regular. Her name was May and had been re-booked in for the coming week and probably for many more weeks after that.

Although it was a private hospital, the Clinic could still not overcome that problem particular to institutions for the sick; that all-pervading smell of disinfectant which infused the operating theatre, post-operative recovery rooms, offices, staff canteen and anywhere else that the air conditioning unit might infiltrate. Halfway through her night shift Nurse May had decided to relieve her nostrils of this particular odour and slipped outside into the lush garden situated at the rear of the building for a quick cigarette. It was while re-entering the hospital and climbing to the next floor that she heard voices coming her way. The long corridor with patients' suites of rooms leading off either side made it impossible not to be seen coming from the direction of the garden. Nurse May quietly slipped into the first room that presented itself and softly closed the door behind her.

The only illumination available within the private room she found herself standing in was from a small light beside a very large flower display. She moved a few paces toward it before her body froze. It had taken a few moments for her eyes to adjust to the gloom before spying among the shadows a body lying on the bed, not under the bedclothes, but on top of it. Although the temperature outside in the garden was quite wintry still, inside it was more like the tropics. When her eyes did eventually become accustomed to the darkness what she saw made her heart skip a beat. The face was completely hidden, swathed in bandages save for slits to accommodate the patient's dark eyes which were open. As she edged back toward the door the eyes followed her, reminiscent of some old horror film where the ancient Egyptian mummy comes to life. May let out a scream, shattering the silence whereupon the door behind her flew open and she was grabbed by a strong hand forcibly pulling her out of the room backwards. May had both arms pinned behind her back by a doctor who had not yet finished his duties for the day. Staff Nurse Beckett closed the door quietly, revealing a notice pinned to the outside of it: 'STRICTLY NO ADMITTANCE – PRIVATE.'

Whilst Nurse May was being given a stiff dressing down in one of the offices into which she had been dragged, having explained to her that she had worked there long enough to have realised that one of the most important things the hospital prided itself on was patient anonymity, the patient in the semi-darkened room slowly raised one of his heavily bandaged hands up to his similarly swathed face, carefully tracing as best he could the outline of his jaw, before the sedatives had the effect of dropping his arms heavily once more onto the bed.

His jawbone felt as if it had been shattered into a thousand pieces, as did his cheekbones and nose. Even his forehead felt painfully sore. While waiting for a nurse to answer his call for painkilling tablets, initiated by his pressing the button at the end of a white plastic lead within reach of his round ball of bandaged hand, the figure constantly whispered something to himself as though his mind was wandering. Over and over again as though his life depended upon it, his lips repeatedly formed two words though hardly any sound could be heard. But within his head these two words were crystal clear. Around and around they went, burying themselves deeper and deeper into his brain like worms feeding off a rotting carcass. It was a name he whispered and it was that of Nikolai Petrov, an old friend from his days at the University of Moscow.

Lying on his hospital bed in the gloom, slipping in and out of consciousness, Dr Grachev whilst attempting to review the past few weeks tried to put into context what had happened to him. He was mentally and physically exhausted. It had been a week since vacating Sammy Weizmann's house and leaving the two dead bodies in his wake. Mr Carol, the surgeon whose business card Dr Grachev had so gratefully slid into his wallet just an hour after the taxi had exploded, had not wanted to perform such a dramatic facial operation; at least – not in one go.

Dr Grachev was told there would have to be a gap of two weeks after operating on the nose before considering anything else to have done. It could take up to four months after that particular operation for the swelling of the mucus membrane to go down, which would very likely impede his breathing in the short term. But Dr Grachev had been determined. Nose-chin-cheeks: all in one go. The surgeon said it was not ethical. Dr Grachev said he felt sure his money would help the surgeon come to terms with the problem over ethics. He also explained that he too was a doctor and understood the problems. The pièce de résistance were to be the slivers of skin cut from his toes to transplant upon his fingertips, thus supplying him with a new set of fingerprints. The surgeon was too interested in money to ask questions' regarding the reason for Dr Grachev's required wholesale change of identity.

It had taken about half an hour to talk the surgeon around to performing the commando surgery. To help with identification he had proffered the surname of his unwitting benefactor, Weizmann. Now he lay suffering in the darkness. And as he lay there on the bed, feeling totally alone, he became aware of the deathly silence broken only by this steady sound of soft laboured breathing. It took him some time before it sank into his fuzzy brain that it was issuing from his own lips. He could feel the irregular flutter of his heart as it beat beneath his thin, bony chest. As he waited for the nurse, the fingers and thumb of his right hand made a barely perceptible jerking movement. One-two-three-four... four people had died by his hands. Biological warfare was easier – that was not at close quarters... but this!

One of Dr Grachev's very earliest childhood memories was of being able to perform what he then thought of as some kind of magic; similar to the kind of magic his father used on people he had put under hypnosis. When his parents threw the occasional theatrical party, he would sit on the perimeter taking in the whole scene before shutting his eyes tightly, completely blotting out the light. At that age, not much more than a baby, he had not been able to disassociate his personal experiences from that of the people sat around him. He had believed everyone would be left in darkness. It was always disappointing upon opening his eyes to discover that the party-goers had not been affected and remained at his parents' house long after he himself had gone to bed. As he scrunched up his eyelids now in a futile attempt to blot out his bad memories, the four dead faces welled up out of the darkness before him vying to haunt his soul. It had not helped then and it did not help now. Trying to blot everything out was useless.

Mikhail, the old jeweller, egged on and cajoled into smoking the doctored cigarette designed to precipitate a heart attack. The steel chisel, so sharp it had sliced cleanly through four layers of clothing before piercing FSB Officer Vladimir Stalnov's heart. The taxi driver and ocularist had also both been killed by him. Then Smith. Christ... Smith. Smith-Stryker. Stryker-Smith. It was too hard to even begin to contemplate the possible woeful tragedy of having nearly killed this person whom had turned out to be a very good friend indeed. Dr Grachev's mind spun in a vortex of mixed emotions. Self-pity and loathing at the same time. How could he have been such a fool? Jesus, even though he was so well wrapped up in his head shroud, the sweat on his forehead felt unbearable, like needles puncturing the flesh, similar to that of a crown of thorns, making the thick shroud-like layers of bandages damp with perspiration. He was feeling feverish, his whole body shaking uncontrollably. Dr Grachev lay there for what seemed like ages in this mental state of anguish, before his bandaged hand managed to hit the button again and this time almost immediately a nurse arrived.

This nurse had a soft face; her features denoted a kind person. But the surgeon Mr Carol, whom he had approached the week before, whose dull eyes only lit up when Dr Grachev showed him the money in his Gladstone bag and explained his request for facial reconstruction – his expression was hard. That was why Dr Grachev had no compunction about putting a plan which had been gnawing away at his imagination for the last six hours into operation; he just needed a piece of good fortune – a piece of good luck to help resolve his problem. It appeared to him that it really was the only way of solving a dilemma which had arisen that first night he had been admitted to the hospital. It was something which should have presented itself to him much earlier but because his mind had been so preoccupied on his immediate salvation of total facial reconstruction it had been totally overlooked. But now that the operation was over his mind was fully occupied with searching for a solution to the episode which had occurred whilst being examined for his operation. Mr Carol, the surgeon, had seen Dr Grachev without the hood of the deceased taxi driver's jacket obscuring his face and so had the anaesthetist plus the two perioperative nurses, known as such because of their assisting the surgeon in the operating theatre and who in fact had both assisted in Dr Grachev's very own operation. One of these perioperative nurses of which he had later discovered to be named May.

Because May bore a soft-featured face and had a kind way of treating him, Dr Grachev had marked her out as an unwitting assistant in a plan he had as yet to formulate – but he felt certain that at some stage an assistant would be required. She was the one who had supplied him before his operation with a very helpful patient information booklet including line illustrations of the various zones within the building. This booklet also

435

showed, amongst other things, the layout of patient designated rooms of which his lay on the first floor just a few metres up the corridor from the main Otis lift, large enough for porters to wheel patients on a gurney for their operations in the basement operating theatre adjacent to the post-operative/recovery room.

CHAPTER 134

It was around midnight; nearly a week after the reconstructive surgery on Dr Grachev's face had been completed. Whilst recuperating in his hospital bed he became aware of the noise. His painkilling drugs had been reduced to a smaller dose and in a light stupor the loud exaggerated metallic sound of something being ratcheted up just outside his bedroom door had unexpectedly rent the deathly quiet of the hospital corridor, shattering his sleepiness. It was an incongruous sound as though a clock was being wound up. Sliding gingerly out of his hospital bed and creeping to the door he managed to open it with some difficulty and was startled by a large black man standing well over six feet tall in a peaked cap and black uniform, reminiscent of his own lifetime spent in the stifling authoritarian atmosphere of Russia and its secret police. What was unusual about this stranger's eyes was that they were fleetingly tinged with terror and equally startled to be confronted by what Nurse May had witnessed the week before – what to all intents and purposes was a living corpse whose head and hands were swathed in bandages resembling the return of the mummy from a Boris Karloff film. Both men let out a reflexive yelp before regaining their senses and remembering where they were. After Dr Grachev had taken in the image of himself being confronted by this very large man whom he had initially viewed as a potential threat to his wellbeing he then noticed the giant had an epaulette badly sewn on either shoulder with the words Elite Security emblazoned in red on a white background with the same tag mirrored on his peaked cap.

Whilst all this information was in the process of being absorbed into Dr Grachev's still groggy consciousness the security guard had already apologised twice in quick succession for alarming the patient, worried now that his job would be on the line if it got about that he was going around putting patients' lives at risk of having a heart attack through frightening them.

For the third time the security officer apologised profusely. "I'm very sorry, sir. As I said I was doing my security rounds here in the hospital. I am sorry if the clocking device positioned just outside your room disturbed you and I have already mentioned the positioning of this particular key point before to the company who employ me. They will just have to reposition it now. I shall make another report in my log and it will be attended to A.S.A.P. Sorry if I have caused you any trouble, sir." The device of which the security officer spoke was a long key attached to a flexible piece of twisted wire screwed to the wall just outside Dr Grachev's door. This key would be inserted into the keyhole of a heavy special metal clock about six inches in diameter locked in a tamper proof metal and leather case the security guard carried with him on a leather shoulder strap. The key, when inserted into this keyhole, registered on a thin inked paper roll recording the time the key had been turned thereby providing proof to his supervisor of his security officer having carried out his inspection or 'round' as it was called, and not fast asleep in the early hours of the morning. It was a clever device and virtually fool proof, though Dr Grachev immediately spotted that there was a simple way of circumventing such an obstacle.

To Dr Grachev's mind the security officer was apologetic to the point of obsequiousness, and attempting to calm him down by assuring him that nobody would be informed of the occurrence, he was invited into Dr Grachev's room and fell into conversation with the doctor. It transpired that the man's name was Philip Ojuku, a Nigerian student of twenty-nine years of age with two degrees to his name and who was now in the process of studying for a third in pharmacology. Eventually wishing to go home to his own country to use his talents as a teacher, he explained that the security job at the hospital had been a boon because it gave him time to study his textbooks whilst also getting paid – a small sum it was true, but enough to cover his rent and food. Then he informed Dr Grachev of something which made the scientist's ears prick up, attempting to impress the doctor by boasting to him that he had the run of the place at night and could obtain the keys to the hospital pharmacy and all other areas such as pathology. Suddenly it appeared to Dr Grachev that the possible resolution of a problem which had been taxing him since coming around from his surgical operation might well be in the offing, and that the student Philip Ojuku would unwittingly join May as a good second candidate for helping in what was beginning to take shape in Dr Grachev's mind.

***

In the ensuing days as Dr Grachev continued to recover from his commando surgery, he became ever closer to the security officer, sharing a little of his medical knowledge as a doctor and beginning to gain Philip Ojuku's confidence. The Nigerian student could not in his wildest dreams have imagined that the invisible man hidden behind so many layers of bandages was one of the most brilliant genetic scientists the world had ever produced, his scientific pedigree being of the highest calibre, having written papers coupled with insight which had often astounded and mesmerised his fellow scientists working in this same field of highly specialised research.

It had been two weeks since Dr Grachev entered the Clinic and although Nurse May had supplied him within hours after entering the hospital with a patient's handbook illustrating in basic detail the layout of the place, he felt the time had come to use his newfound influence with the security guard. In the course of numerous conversations with Philip Ojuku he had gleaned many snippets of information about the staff routine and the night cleaner's duty roster. The next thing on Dr Grachev's mental list was to engineer a late night guided tour of the basement.

CHAPTER 135

It was nearly one in the morning when Dr Grachev ventured into the deathly quiet corridor immediately outside his room, keeping a wary eye open for any nurse who might be on an urgent mercy mission to answer a patient's bell or just slinking off to find somewhere to rest up for a couple of minutes whilst fighting off the effects of sleep deprivation.

The security officer's room was conveniently situated at the end of Dr Grachev's hospital corridor. As he entered the office the security man himself was not there, although the clock encased in the black leather holder which had awoken Dr Grachev outside his room a couple of days earlier was now lying upon a bare wooden table amidst a line of used empty plastic coffee cups taken, he guessed, from the free drinks dispenser on the ground floor.

The doctor picked up the security man's clock and was in the process of minutely examining it when the security guard came into the office from behind, taking Dr Grachev by surprise.

"Hello Sammy, how you feeling tonight?" he enquired with a grin planted on his face, displaying a row of pearl white teeth made even whiter by his pitch black skin. The formal surname Weizmann, to be found in Dr Grachev's newly acquired deceased oculist's passport, had been dispensed with and the Christian name Sammy had been proffered to Mr Ojuku instead, allowing the security guard a sense of familiarity, dispensing with all formalities as the doctor knew he had to if he was to become sufficiently close to his prey. So the two unlikely friends bonded during the small hours of the night while others slept.

Part of this bonding experience came in the form of a night-time tour by security officer Mr Ojuku using the hospital stairways and avoiding the lifts in case they got stuck, so as to explore the hospital's different floors which included the basement's operating theatre. During this guided tour Dr Grachev noticed the planned dates of the weekly operating duty lists detailing the surgeon, anaesthetist, theatre assistants and nursing staff involved pinned just outside the theatre doors and the patient recovery area.

Whilst Mr Ojuku enthusiastically though ineptly extolled the many aspects of the hospital to Dr Grachev the scientist closed his mind to what he regarded as the security man's inane chatter, only mentally taking in the salient visual points of the tour so as to fulfil his resolution, noting that there was for instance only one key point on each floor, the actual key on a long wire attached by a screw to the wall for Mr Ojuku's security clock. He discovered from the security officer the details and number of cleaners allocated including when their shifts began, which was early in the morning, and when they finished plus where they kept their cleaning materials and more importantly to the scientist, the location of the cupboard housing all the keys to the different rooms of the hospital.

Sometimes in life chance steps in to make ones plans so much easier – so thought Dr Grachev to himself as he stalked Mr Ojuku along the hushed hospital's corridors on his illicit guided tour; rooms giving off to the left and right where the very best equipment lay ready for use, paying close attention to the large, white, circular disc-shaped laminar flow unit measuring approximately a metre across attached to the ceiling of the main operating theatre. This piece of equipment designed to remove any bacterial or viral contamination within the air was very familiar to Dr Grachev, though because of the specific scientific work he had been obliged to carry out in Russia the filters he dealt with were on a much larger industrial scale.

For the rest of that night Dr Grachev could not sleep for the adrenalin coursing through his body, his mind working hard during those twilight hours driven by what had materialised into a tight time factor after spying the lists of operations schedule pinned just outside the operating theatre's swing doors, putting together the finishing touches to a plan that would solve the pressing problem of how to make amends for the necessary but troubling fact that four people had seen his features before and during his face changing, nay life changing operation. The people involved were in pecking order the surgeon Mr Carol, the anaesthetist Dr Rogers, Nurse Beckett and Dr Grachev's unwitting helper Nurse May.

Following Dr Grachev's night time guided tour of the private hospital by the security officer and as a pretext to testing her willingness to obtain certain items, the Russian scientist enquired of nurse May if she could possibly obtain a steel tape measure for him.

CHAPTER 136

A day later after May had bought Dr Grachev the steel tape measure as requested, he reciprocated by handing her a detailed shopping list with the explanation that he was an amateur inventor and felt it would help keep his spirits up if he had something with which to occupy his mind in the small hours whilst recuperating, having suffered a lifetime of insomnia. He also explained that it would be better if she did not inform anyone else of the list or what he was doing because if word got round about his activities he might be thrown out of the hospital, quickly adding that he would make it worth her while.

The list he handed to May requested electrical items from Radio Shack on Tottenham Court Road including 70 metres of ducting tape, a small reel of solder and soldering iron and fuse wire plus other miscellaneous items such as a small pair of pliers, scissors and a selection of screw drivers. Also from this shop came something a little more esoteric – a contraption for housing a small lightweight torch so as to allow a beam of light to be shone from an elasticated headband plus the aforementioned torch with batteries.

May was also requested to purchase from another shop two cheap disposable cell phones. And to complete the list, a set of six-inch aluminium containers similar to the type found in Indian restaurants used for takeaway foods plus a packet of large coffee filter papers from a local supermarket. May was handed one thousand pounds in fifty pound notes and as an inducement for keeping quiet about her shopping trip she was informed that after purchasing these items she could pocket the change plus he would give her another five hundred pounds. Dr Grachev had also asked May to buy a him a very large black fabric zipper bag with which to place all the items in plus a padlock to secure it and something from a photographic shop, plus a box of matches with long stems and several tubes of quick drying glue, the type used for sticking fabric and metal and card.

The final request necessitated a trip to an art shop where a large stiff artist's board was purchased, with the board being cut to the requisite dimensions so that it could be slipped flat inside the large black zipper bag plus a sharp craft knife. All this happened just after Dr Grachev had been informed that his face would have healed enough for him to be discharged the following weekend.

442

It had taken May another two days before she was able to garner all the items requested by Dr Grachev, plus as an afterthought, a small reel of nylon fishing line.

CHAPTER 137

Now thoroughly familiar with Mr Ojuku's set routine of the security clocking times, Dr Grachev chose the following evening at a moment when the security officer had completed the second of his night time rounds, knowing that unless something untoward happened he had two hours of being uninterrupted before Mr Ojuku normally repeated his routine, though tonight the doctor would not be taking any chances. Dr Grachev had been confided in by the security officer that the only real point of walking through the building at night, as far as Mr Ojuku himself was concerned, was to push the hanging key screwed to the wall, one to be found on each floor, into the clock slung over his shoulder and giving it a twist to record the time he had been there. In between this trivial task, set up to prove that he was not sleeping, he would devote himself solely to his studies.

It was late as Dr Grachev, sitting on the side of his bed, set about gingerly removing the bandages from his hands and fingers before creeping from his room so as to satisfy himself that the security officer had returned from his clocking round and was safely ensconced within his office, confident of this fact by peeping along the corridor to witness Mr Ojuku once more at his studies. Dr Grachev now set about locating the key cupboard situated on the ground floor by the reception desk, and after removing a couple of labelled keys he made his way to the cleaner's cupboard, and using the first key removed a pair of step ladders before revisiting the basement operating theatre with the steel tape measure purchased by May. From the hospital's *gratis* white towel dressing gown pocket he now removed an elasticated band with a small torch attached which was switched on before sliding it upon his head. He now entered the dark operating theatre lit only by his head torch and carrying the pair of step ladders.

After positioning and climbing the step ladders he began carefully examining and measuring the interior dimensions of the disc-shaped laminar flow unit fixed to the ceiling set to one side of the operating table, making copious notes and sketches. Because the main lighting had not been switched on as a precautionary measure so as not to draw any attention, he was surprised when footsteps were heard coming from the vicinity of the corridor. Almost tumbling off the step ladders he just managed to fold them and crouch behind the operating table before the whole room was illuminated. Whoever it was who had entered the room must have given it just a passing cursory glance before the lights were doused once more. Dr Grachev had caught one of his fingers in the process of folding the ladders, cursing silently under his breath.

Relieved not to have been caught with the step ladders in his possession, he finished what he had been doing and eventually managed to replace them in the cleaner's cupboard before returning to the sanctuary of his own room. He then waited for maybe twenty more minutes before stepping along the corridor, and confident of finding Mr Ojuku still at his books, engaged him in conversation whilst surreptitiously slipping into one of his interminable plastic mugs of coffee a sachet of a powerful sleeping draught he had prepared; the drug having been stolen from the hospital pharmacy just the day before.

Fifteen minutes later, satisfying himself that Mr Ojuku was now dead to the world with a few sharp slaps across his face using the Russian scientist's freshly un-bandaged palm of his hand which made it sting ferociously, and thus ensuring that the security officer would be out of action for a good few hours he lifted the officer's heavy leather encased security clock lying on the plastic cup strewn table before creeping out of his office, and after making another quick cursory visit to collect his black cavernous bag from his room, once more made his way down to the basement, this time avoiding the operating theatre. Instead he moved on to a room marked PATHOLOGY and unlocked the door before entering and securing it from the other side. Here he donned his headlight, careful not to switch on the bank of fluorescent lighting should it attract any passers-by, though at this time of night the chances of anybody wandering by would be most unlikely. And instead of carrying a pair of step ladders he now carried something he had removed from the cleaner's cupboard – this was in a bottle marked 'Tile Cleaner' though he was not here to clean the pathology lab. He also had with him some other bottles and items which had been purchased on his behalf by May.

After familiarising himself with the layout of the laboratory he found some heatproof glass beakers, clamps for holding them and other miscellaneous equipment he would be using. The coffee filters obtained for him by May and other bottled liquids were produced from his cavernous zipper bag. But before he could begin on the next phase of his work there was something else to be done and that is what he set about doing next.

Grabbing an assortment of different sized screwdrivers he left the pathology laboratory which now held all his paraphernalia and made his way floor by floor carefully locating each key point Mr Ojuku had pointed out to him on his first night time tour and removed the wire holding each key ending up with a bunch of twisted flexible steel stalks bearing a key at the end of each like a bunch of flowers. Quickly scrutinising his wrist watch and making a mental note of the time, he knew he had just over an hour.

Adjusting a selection of the metal clamps found in the pathology laboratory he slid the Pyrex heatproof dishes in position one by one before filling them with some of the chemicals he had brought with him. Making another mental note of the time – it had just turned one o'clock in the morning – he began.

It was time consuming work and could also be very dangerous if he did not keep his wits about him – which he did by getting the extraction air filtration system running within the laboratory as his first priority. After this he arranged one of the coffee filters he had brought with him, placing it on the rim of a large glass heatproof beaker so as to filter out the hoped-for solution he would be producing. All this was now slow going as adding to his difficulties everything had to be done in near darkness with only the pencil beam from his small torch as his sole source of light affixed to his forehead by the elasticated band affording him his only basis of visibility. He was very aware of the time and when his self-allotted hour was up – it had now reached two o'clock – he lifted the heavy security officer's clock ensconced within its leather case and grabbing his steel bunch of flowers with the keys from the different floors of the hospital hanging limply from the end of these storks, inserted them one by one, leaving a few minutes in between each before insertion in their correct order into the keyhole of the clock and twisted once. This had the effect of leaving an indelible mark upon a paper reel locked inside the clocking machine, notating the time and which key had been used, the said marked paper reel only being accessible to the supervising security officer using his own special key. It was foolproof – except of course it had been proved otherwise by the Russian scientist Dr Grachev.

By the time Dr Grachev had completed his work within the pathology department it had turned three allowing him enough time to clear up the mess he had created and for Mr Ojuku's to be ready for his next clocking round at four a.m. After hiding the chemicals and other materials in his large holdall bag and making his way back to the safety of his room he locked and secured the holdall bag in his wardrobe, before quickly wandering the corridors where he began replacing the security keys he had removed earlier with a screwdriver and finally entered Mr Ojuku's office returning the heavy clocking machine to the table amidst the coffee cups before finally making sure that the security officer was roused, estimating that his grogginess would last for the best part of another hour. If Mr Ojuku wasn't fully awake until much later, well, that didn't matter; the assumption being that the security officer was just feeling a little sleepy –

probably put down to the singeing of the candle at both ends as Dr Grachev thought the saying went. He felt good about his perceived mastery of the English language and the use of the idiom. The Russian scientist also knew that this particular aspect of his job had been successfully completed but that the really important work was still to begin.

CHAPTER 138

Two nights later in his bedroom, assisted by the help of copious notes taken earlier on his solo visit to the operating theatre and with his bedroom door now safely secured, Dr Grachev began gingerly assembling the various items purchased by May from her shopping trip made on his behalf. Within a few hours the carefully constructed unit had been completed before being concealed inside the newly purchased voluminous black zipper holdall bag which he then gingerly placed into his room's wardrobe, the scientist breathing easier now the bag had been carefully locked away out of sight from prying eyes.

CHAPTER 139

Fortuitously it had been Hobson's choice when Dr Grachev was presented with the prospect of the weekend when staff numbers were at their lowest ebb and where, as was scheduled, all the hospital staff he wished to deal with would be gathered together in one place down in the operating theatre to carry out an operation on Abdul Hussein, one of their foreign paying patients.

It had also been fortunate that the one thing Mr Ojuku, the night security officer was quite definitely not cut out for was his particular way of subsidising the studies that would eventually take him back to his homeland with good qualifications. He was a man of habit and that to an opportunist such as Dr Grachev was like manna from heaven. Due to Mr Ojuku's clockwork routine one could set one's proverbial clock by and which by dint of having to record his hospital rounds every two hours, nothing could dissuade him from such practice. And in between these clocking rounds he would give every second of his attention to the textbooks that would eventually prove his salvation from the perceived poverty he was so eager to escape from.

So it was with a certain justified confidence that earlier on that particular morning, before the cleaners had arrived, Dr Grachev chose the time when the security officer would be at his studies before surreptitiously carrying his large black holdall bag containing his extramural handiwork in the dead of night down to the hospital basement, where after carefully avoiding any night staff, he ended up once more in the operating theatre.

Here in the silent darkness he pulled onto his forehead the elasticated band which held the night torch ready to install his self-assembled piece of technical hardware. He switched on the torch, its slim beam making it difficult to see as he peered along its slim pencil beam through the darkness before eventually managing to remove the grills of the operating theatre's ventilation system with a screwdriver and placing ducting tape behind these grills so as to block the air flow, thus effectively ensuring that the room was now a sealed unit once he had replaced the covers. From his black nylon zipped holdall bag he lifted out the carefully constructed Heath Robinson-like structure mounted on a base made rigid by using a double thickness of card and cut into a semicircle. This he placed to one side before disconnecting the electrical wiring of the laminar flow unit and then setting to work ripping out all the internal electrical components and fans making up the filtration system until it was just a shell before placing the detritus inside his cavernous bag to be disposed of at a later date.

Dr Grachev now knelt down beside the structure he had created whilst alone in his private hospital room and began the task which had taken so much of his time and ingenuity. The structure itself essentially consisted of three shallow modified aluminium containers positioned one above the other, held in place by a framework of thick balsa wood struts May had obtained from a craft shop, the top two containers being ingeniously hinged.

Dr Grachev now proceeded to tip crystals from a plastic bag into the top tray. These crystals had been created by Dr Grachev in the pathology department just three days earlier. Then he gingerly unscrewed a bottle containing a mixture of liquid chemical compounds removed from within the hospital pharmacy which he proceeded to gingerly pour into the middle tray. A common household bleaching agent discovered in the cleaner's cupboard was the final item to be tipped from another bottle into the lowest container.

When all this was completed his meticulously constructed creation was warily lifted, positioned and fixed with clips inside the now empty metal shell of the laminar flow unit. At this juncture Dr Grachev was working blind, not being able to see anything but the base of his construction so this point of the operation had to be carried out very slowly, being at pains not to spill any of the silver container's contents including the liquid compounds, and keeping a firm grip with two of his fingers on a spent matchstick used to prop up the top silver container now half-full of crystals. Although Dr Grachev was used to dealing with delicate operations with some of the deadliest viruses known to man he was nervous and a rash of perspiration covered his forehead.

When the semi-circular base containing this structure was safely installed he then carried out his final task of setting up the sister cell phone to the one he had back in his room. This was the most delicate and arduous operation of all, having to do everything above head height.

He then replaced the bottom of the unit and screwed it into position so that on final inspection it appeared that the laminar flow unit which had occupied so much of his thoughts had never been tampered with.

***

It came as a huge shock. Even though he had tried to mentally prepare himself for this introduction to Nikolai Petrov, it was still a weird sensation seeing the reflection of a total stranger staring back at himself, and yet knowing down to the last detail what made him tick. Even his own mother would not have recognised him if she had still been alive. It was true that his face was badly swollen, but he knew about these things, having been a man of medicine. Even so, even allowing for the bruising and swollen facial features which would eventually return to normal, he could see it was a job well done.

Dr Grachev laid the hand held mirror down upon the freshly laundered sheets of the hospital bed, beside the long strings of soiled bandages which had just been removed against the surgeon's advice. He suddenly had a feeling of being totally secure for the first time since he could ever remember. It was a security borne out of total anonymity which had cost him sixty thousand pounds, paid in cash, no questions asked. Dr Grachev did not know it, but a similar facial reconstruction had been carried out not so long before. That particular client though had not been fleeing from both the British and Russian intelligence services. The reason for her facial reorganisation was a serious misunderstanding with the Sicilian Mafia and by virtue of having the money to pay for such an operation one could only guess from where that disagreement arose.

**

Two hours later, after the hospital doors had been unlocked and the early morning cleaners had arrived to collect their pails and mops from the cleaning cupboard, but before the hospital day shift proper began, Dr Grachev put his working knowledge of the routine of this medical institution, gleaned from his newly acquired friend Mr Ojuku, to good use by discharging himself from the private hospital through slipping out of a side door, assiduously avoiding anyone capable of noticing his face, assisted by carefully donning the taxi driver's flying jacket he had arrived in just a few weeks earlier with its large fur collar pulled up, thus hiding his features.

CHAPTER 140

Hampstead's Millionaires' Row, as the large houses grouped around the patch of green sporting a permanent giant target used for archery, was known. These housed many prosperous and successful business people and one of these was a Mr Carol. He was known as self-effacing but supportive of the local community and was well respected. He was also the surgeon who worked in St. John's Wood at the prestigious Clinic, preserve of the rich and sometimes famous.

Quite often he and his wife would spend their weekends away staying with friends in Norfolk when the shooting season allowed, or sailing off the coast of France, weather and time permitting. This weekend – Saturday to be precise, he had a more mundane engagement carrying out an operation on an old Arab friend he had known for the last thirty years. He had promised to carry out this varicose vein operation himself as a favour – something he rarely did for someone he knew personally. He had also said many times before that he was so familiar with the procedure that he could carry out this particular operation blindfolded. Unwittingly though prophetically as one colleague had facetiously remarked – condemned men arc blindfolded.

After parking his maroon-coloured Bentley in the usual place reserved for him he strode into the Clinic, and within an hour had joined his fellow assistants in the hospital operating theatre having by then dressed in his usual blue scrub suit and donned his surgical cap and gloves.

By this time his patient Abdul Hussein had already been given his intravenous dose of propofol to send him to sleep some while before by the anaesthetist Dr Rogers. The two perioperative nurses; Nurse Beckett – a scrub nurse – and Nurse May had already taken up their positions around the surgery table and also like their colleagues were robed up, scrubbed up and wearing their surgical masks ready for surgery.

Soft soothing piped music selected by Mr Carol filled the operating theatre in stereophonic sound as he adjusted his surgical binocular loupes ready to begin. The operation was a simple one and he should be finished within the hour, all being well. He might even be able to make it sooner which would please his wife as they had been invited out to dinner by their neighbours that evening.

Dr Grachev stood on the pavement just a few metres away from the prestigious Clinic and removed a cell phone from the large black holdall by his feet before tapping in a series of numbers. The telephone number entered was to the cell phone secreted within the laminar flow unit mounted on the ceiling of the operating theatre, initiating a train of events, the results of which he could only imagine. Within the white shell of the operating theatre's laminar flow unit an angled piece of thick card had been scored with a sharp knife and glued together, making a pyramid of sorts, but with the point at the top cut off so as to form a ledge the size of a dime, just large enough upon which to precariously balance the cell phone. This cell phone was attached to a nylon fishing line by way of a taught looped lasso held in place by a dab of superglue.

To the other end of this short length of fishing line was attached one of the long spent matchsticks May had purchased, this acting as a support beneath the topmost of the three aluminium containers, the top two of which possessed hinges made out of paperclips taken from Mr Ojuku's office. These straightened paperclips acted as miniature metal rods passing through holes punched into the sides of the silver foil containers and greased with butter left over from one of Dr Grachev's meals.

These modified containers had been constructed so that as the cell phone rang its reverberations toppled it from the apex of the pyramid, the cell phone toppling and sliding down the side of the thick card just as it was designed to do. At the same time the weight of the cell phone yanked the supporting matchstick attached to the other end of the fishing line away from its position of propping up the top silver-weighted container, setting off a sequence of events by tipping its contents of cyanide salts – the fruits of his labours within the hospital's pathology laboratory three nights earlier – into the second hinged container housing a viscous solution made up of various chemical compounds. The weight of this noxious solution coupled with that of the cyanide salts tipped the second hinged container, spilling its contents into the third and largest silver metal container holding phosphoric acid removed from the cleaner's cupboard in the form of a propriety tile cleaner which acted as a catalyst for setting off a chain chemical reaction.

The cyanide salts had been created using potassium hydroxide found in the hospital's dispensary along with potassium ferricyanide obtained by the judicious reclamation of the compound obtained by using materials May had purchased from a photographic shop nearby the Radio Shack store off Tottenham Court Road. The resulting deadly hydrogen cyanide gas – similar to that of Zyklon B, a form of hydrogen cyanide as used in the Nazi gas chambers during the Second World War – formed by the cyanide salts' chain reaction led to the deadly gas silently, slowly, seeping unnoticed into the air through the open vents of the laminar flow unit.

CHAPTER 141

The soft piped music in the operating theatre drowned out the noise of the cell phone's banging sound as it was toppled from its cardboard pyramid, the surgeon's attention as that of the anaesthetist and the two young nursing assistants was now firmly fixed on their patient as the second incision was made just below the knee, slicing through the skin and flesh seeking out the varicose vein that was to be disposed of. A puff of vapour from the open circular grill of the laminar flow unit began forming into a more substantial cloud as it spread, taking on the semblance of a thick fluffy white duvet creeping outwards along the ceiling unobserved by the hospital theatre staff whose rapt attention was now fixed on the task at hand.

The first sign of anything untoward, though nobody else at this stage had noticed, was the laboured breathing of Nurse May and the beginnings of a headache as she went to apply a swab in the area around the open wound created by Mr Carol's razor sharp scalpel. Although the operation was known to the hospital authorities as a bread and butter affair one still had to be on one's guard for anything going amiss so that when by chance the scrub nurse Beckett gave a fleeting glance in the direction of Mr Carol she noticed that he was in the process of adjusting his binocular loupes, something she had never seen him do before. The surgeon himself caught sight of scrub nurse Becket's fleeting glance as his own breathing became laboured, beginning to inhale so deeply that his mask was sucked right into the vicinity of his mouth forming the shape of an O.

Things then began moving in very quick succession as the anaesthetist Dr Rogers let out a muffled yell before ripping away his face mask and violently vomiting. At that very moment a warning alarm attached to the oxygen machine he was monitoring began a high pitched wailing noise, indicating that something was dreadfully wrong with the gaseous mixture being pumped into the lungs of patient Abdul Hussein.

It might have been the position Nurse May had taken up in the operating theatre which determined that she was the last of the operating staff to become effected by the hydrogen cyanide gas but never the less she swiftly succumbed to giddiness followed by the similar headache and quickening of her heart rate and vomiting as had struck her colleagues. Mr Carol succumbing to the noxious gas as it tore at his lungs, blindly struck out with his sharp surgical scalpel, slicing a long gash in the patient Abdul

Hussein's arm which unlike his leg had not been secured with a tourniquet, thus allowing his blood to flow freely, spurting in a red stream over the surgeon who was now on his knees in the grip of convulsions as he too retched like the other members of his team, ejecting the contents of his stomach over the prostrate body of his friend and patient Abdul Hussein who himself was in his death throes evidenced by the whole operating table quivering with a ferocious rattling noise due to his own violent convulsions. However Dr Rogers the anaesthetist, totally unaware of all that was happening, lay sprawled unconscious beside the steel controls and dials of his trade, seconds away from his own certain death.

CHAPTER 142

Oblivious to the unimaginable horrors unfolding inside the Clinic's operating theatre Dr Grachev replaced his cell phone and retrieved a crumpled piece of paper onto which Mr O'Connell had so carefully printed the name and address of the person who would be able to change the details and photograph on the passport stolen from Sammy Weizmann's house. The only people now who could have borne witness to his face since the operation were all dead.

Dr Grachev also hoped for false documentation leading to a birth certificate, driving licence and social security number in the name of Nikolai Petrov. With a final backward glance, he made his way onto the street and hailed yet another taxi. However this taxi driver was more fortunate than Mr O'Connell, not only surviving the trip to the address handed him on that crumpled piece of paper by Dr Grachev, but also after having arrived at the destination, actually being given a tip.

Because of the temporary disfigurement of Dr Grachev's face resulting from the major surgery carried out, he would have to wait a couple more months before being able to supply photographs of himself to the person who would furnish him with the necessary documentation. The going rate was five hundred pounds up front, plus another five hundred when everything was ready.

Dr Grachev also handed over another five hundred pounds as a deposit and first month's rent for a cheap but cramped bed-sitting room nearby and eventually, when his face had healed, obtained four passport sized photographs, printed from one of the many photo booths dotted around London, ready for transferring onto his new identification documents, including that of Weizmann's passport which now became his own.

Within six months, the old Dr Anatoly Grachev had ceased to exist, now replaced by a Dr Nikolai Petrov. The forger who had supplied the new documentation had succeeded in doing something which medical science had so far been unable to deliver. In minutes he had rejuvenated the old Dr Weizmann by slicing at least forty years off his age – on his passport. On this passport too, Dr Weizmann's profession had changed from that of Prosthetic Eye Technician to the more prestigious one of scientist.

At thirty-five years of age, the newly naturalised Dr Petrov, a.k.a. Dr

Grachev had a good profession. The world, as the saying goes, was his oyster – so long as he was able to curtail his new found lust for life – other people's that is. Sadly this had not been achieved immediately in the case of his master forger, who had by accident or design been knocked down and killed by an unidentified car – hit and run as it had been termed on the police record – just days after supplying Dr Grachev with his own life saving papers. And what a fortuitous coincidence that the only people at the Clinic who would have been capable of identifying him to the authorities – Dr Grachev's surgeon, anaesthetist and the two nurses who had witnessed the transformation of his face in the operating theatre – had also met with untimely deaths, having unwittingly ingested a concoction which might have been dreamt up by a practising doctor with a certain knowledge of chemicals and their effect on the immune system, if one were available. As a scientist, until recently, he was used to directing his specialist knowledge toward the destruction of man on a mega scale by the harnessing of biological weapons. More recently he had taken it down to a very personal level. He was determined to reverse this factor however, just as soon as he could sort out new job prospects for himself. He was beginning to feel tainted by the closeness of death. It was much easier to kill people from a distance. He also felt sure that arms dealers would be able to empathise with this particular point of view. And yet there was a certain emotion he had never experienced before when killing someone... could never have encountered in the cold clinical environs of a laboratory... something indefinable that however he looked at it had, in his eyes, a certain cachet, a certain appeal. The thought made him uneasy and he shuddered – just a little.

PART TWO

CHAPTER 143

It was late afternoon and everything was green in Gorky Park, the ice on the river Moskva being just a distant memory. Crowds of people were out enjoying the weekend break. But for the two men diligently following one of the tracks which cut through the trees the extensive park could have been deserted. The taller man, his back held straight, stared ahead, looking neither left nor right, acting as though he was on his own as he tried to ignore a ceaseless verbal onslaught. In stark contrast, his companion, shoulders hunched, arms flailing the air, shot occasional glances of detestation in his companion's direction.

"So it's my fault we screwed up yet again? Yes, blame it on me once more. I'm surprised you've tolerated me for so long."

"Don't push your luck Pyotr... let it drop. I was just saying that maybe if we had all acted in unison, well... things might have turned out differently that's all. Anyway, it's too late now."

"You're damned right it's too late. I want that transfer."

"Oh! Not that again. You begin to sound like a parrot."

Pyotr was about to continue his verbal tirade then checked himself, still barely able to contain his emotions as a small group of frayed-looking middle-aged men came jogging up from behind them, all dressed in maroon tracksuits and passing at a sluggish pace. Each without exception sported an expensively cultivated beer gut swaying to the rhythmic pounding of their feet as they chased distorted memories of their half-forgotten youth. Even though it was the tail end of spring on this late Saturday afternoon, the air still bit into Pyotr's face, making it look like a ripened tomato, tears streaming from his eyes, the effect of the blunt wind blowing in from the north.

Pyotr pulled up the collar of his overcoat, trying to protect his ears and wind chapped neck as best he could against further denudation by the stiff breeze, and also so as to isolate himself from his boss. As he was caught up in this particular action he noticed one of the joggers turn swiftly on his heels and head straight for him out of the sun's dying rays, creating a contre-jour effect.

"Konstantin, Pyotr... how are you? What a surprise." It was a scarcely recognisable Captain Zhizhin, looming like a maroon-coloured bear. Both Konstantin and Pyotr gave a genuine smile at this unexpected piece of good luck as they mentally thanked their patron saint for such an intervention.

"Why, you look so prosperous. Have you changed jobs?" It was Pyotr who spoke, possibly a Freudian slip or just pure wishful thinking for his own predicament. Captain Zhizhin stood panting with a bemused look upon his scarlet perspiration-covered face then gave a low growl of laughter. His heart still pumping furiously, even though his body was not moving now, and it took some time before he could gather his breath.

"You joke my friends. But no, pay no attention to this." Here he tugged at his jogging top. "I am still in the security business. Stepped into Vladimir Stalnov's shoes, God rest his soul." At this point he crossed himself. "You know... at Biomedico. He was the Chief Federal Security Bureau officer."

"I heard you were transferred to Moscow – that they destroyed that place of yours," Konstantin replied with a grave look.

"It's really not so bad. In fact, I like it here. Things are changing, how shall I put it – unfettered?" Both Konstantin and Pyotr repeated the word in unison.

"Unfettered?"

"You know?" Captain Zhizhin lifted his right hand and rubbed his forefinger and thumb together in the age old international gesture. "Money! As I said, things are changing."

The two agents of the Russian state had now become three. They found themselves standing by a large black car, a driver sitting behind the wheel with the synonymous telltale bulge visible beneath his left breast.

"I believe, if my memory is correct, that neither of you are married." Captain Zhizhin made this remark in a casual enough manner, half leaning against one of the passenger doors with one large hand resting upon the car's roof. It was Konstantin who innocently answered that it was indeed true.

"Then gentlemen, you will be my guest for the evening." It was not what either man had planned nor wished for as they were ushered into the spacious back seat, corralled like cattle, murmuring pleas of prior engagements, but all to no avail. The maroon bear hauled his sweating torso into the front passenger seat next to the driver-cum-bodyguard.

"First time I've been to Biomedico unaccompanied. No... I lie! I did use this place to change into my running gear a little earlier today. Officially, I start work on Monday morning." Captain Zhizhin fixed his guests with a toothy grin as he set about removing his soft running shoes before padding across what had until recently been Vladimir Stalnov's sanctuary within the Institute. Standing in his socks he leaned toward a tall grey cabinet and fingered the heavy padlock. Then, turning his attention to the desk, he ran his fingers beneath the wooden edge. A knowing look of satisfaction flashed across his face. Smiling, he raised a large hand revealing his palm like a conjuror does when showing the audience a trick. Sure enough, dangling from his thick hairy fingers was a key. It glided into the grey cabinet's steel padlock smoothly. A minute later three grimy-looking glasses set before Konstantin, Pyotr and the conjuror himself were being filled to the brim with a well-known brand of vodka.

"To Vladimir Stalnov – Budem zdorovy!" The three men downed their glasses in one gulp and crossed themselves like Captain Zhizhin had done in the park, their eyes immediately moist, not with sentiment, but with proof of the distiller's skill at making fire out of liquid... nearly the full two hundred per cent proof.

The three glasses were immediately set up again and filled to the top with the same actions as before; three glasses momentarily suspended in mid-air in preparation for another toast to one another and three more repeated shouts of "To Vladimir Stalnov –Budem zdorovy!" before being drained.

"What happened to your friend Yevgeny Kotov? Is he still around?" Three more shots of vodka were being set up as Zhizhin posed the question.

"Yeah," Konstantin answered. "Transferred to another department. You may have heard – our trip to England was a disaster – he was the fall guy as they say in those American films. Someone had to carry the can."

Lucky bastard, Pyotr thought as he glared in Konstantin's direction before grabbing one of the replenished glasses, a little unsteady now as he joined his two comrades in once again downing the hot fiery liquid in one go as before, but this time attempting to drown out the other two voices by shouting very loudly, "Budem zdorovy!" Then after a considered pause he said, "I might quit."

"What did you say?" Zhizhin enquired in a slurred voice, looking at Pyotr. Pyotr himself was as surprised as Zhizhin how his words had tumbled out without giving too much thought to them.

"Well," came the retort in an equally slurred voice, "I keep hearing about all these changes taking place in this great country of ours. Maybe it's time to change course. Be like everyone else; branch out."

In between pouring the third round of spirits, Captain Zhizhin had slowly disrobed and was now standing in a grubby white string vest, loose fitting underpants and black knee length socks. As the conversation rambled on, Pyotr thought that in his youth Captain Zhizhin might have had an athletic figure, but now it had definitely gone to seed.

Two great tree-like lumps of white flesh supported his fat trunk, the enormous belly hanging down so low it was stretching the waistband of his underpants to breaking point, so much so that Pyotr feared he might soon witness the Goya-like figure resplendent in all its nakedness in the nether regions. What Pyotr had failed to notice was the expensive-looking loose-fitting black suit suspended on a hanger to one side of the makeshift steel drinks cabinet. Once he had dressed again, Captain Zhizhin's now amply covered figure looked almost respectable.

"If you are serious, I have friends who might be able to help you out."

"What, you mean offer me a job?" Pyotr's face was becoming flushed with excitement and the effects of the unexpected consumption of alcohol.

"He's drunk," interjected Konstantin. "He doesn't know what he is saying," he slurred. "Of course he won't leave the service. He's got his pension to think of." Konstantin was feeling groggy after three large shots of vodka, each one swiftly following hot on the heels of the other.

"Fuck you. I know exactly what I'm saying. I'm very interested." It was the first time in ten years Pyotr had sworn at his boss Konstantin and he didn't feel a twinge of anxiety or regret. It was as though he had already left the service. The vodka had worked its magic. Konstantin was so taken aback he did not even respond, instead he remained silently swaying.

***

It was still early morning. The bodyguard-cum-driver had been dismissed, leaving Captain Zhizhin alone with his two colleagues loitering outside one of the many new clubs which had sprung up within the centre of Moscow. This was when Konstantin made his move, insisting that a prior engagement really could not be broken, as sweat that Captain Zhizhin had displayed upon his brow earlier brought about by his exertion of jogging now appeared on that of Konstantin's brow. Pyotr knew it was a lie but was only too happy to go along with it – glad to see the back of him.

After Captain Zhizhin rapped with his giant's knuckles onto a very small door painted black a tiny hatch was lifted and he proceeded to have a short conversation with a pair of eyes which Pyotr took to belong to that of the doorman peering out from the other side of it. Captain Zhizhin appeared to be on very familiar terms with this guardian of iniquity and Pyotr followed his newfound friend as they stumbled into a dimly lit room scattered with tables. At the far end on a tiny circular raised platform not much larger than a table, a scantily dressed young woman wearing black fishnet tights swayed to the bleak discordant notes of a saxophone under the searchlight beam of a spotlight which would not have been out of place on the perimeter fence of a gulag. This thick tube of harsh white light beneath which the femme fatale danced accentuated the gloom in which the two intelligence officers now sat. It took a while for Pyotr's eyes to adjust to their surroundings. They were seated immediately beside the raised stage and furnished with a couple of chilled beers by a skinny guy sporting a thick moustache.

Quickly scanning the room, Pyotr realised that all the people sitting at the other tables drinking beer were men. On closer inspection, most of them looked nervous and ill at ease. To his surprise, a few of the early morning night clubbers – a contradiction in terms – wore dark glasses as if they did not wish to be recognised. What baffled Pyotr was how anyone wearing dark coloured lenses could possibly see anything in such dark surroundings. There was only one woman. She was the one performing a series of impossibly contorted positions with her skeletal body. The saxophonist did not accompany his young accomplished gymnast upon the stage but sat slouched over his instrument within touching distance of Captain Zhizhin. He seemed to know him because between numbers the musician leaned forward and in a very familiar manner uttered lewd comments about the girl strutting her stuff, comments at which they both laughed out loud.

Pyotr began to wonder if this was a place which gay people frequented and began to feel as nervous as the men he now observed at the other tables. Maybe this was Captain Zhizhin's predilection? It was possible. He recalled one particular Moscow policeman, known as the human battering ram. Twenty-two stone of solid muscle and six feet five inches tall in his bare feet – a mountain of a man. He was always in demand by his colleagues for raiding parties, smashing through doors like they were made of matchsticks – a real man's man. Then suddenly it was rumoured he liked nothing better than to lounge around in a skirt, wearing stockings and suspenders. Suddenly that phrase 'man's man' took on a whole new meaning.

As Pyotr prepared to beat a hasty retreat, the skinny guy who had placed the two beers on the table a short while before, came over and whispered something to Captain Zhizhin, upon which, the captain got up from the table and beckoned to Pyotr. "First of all, would you like a Moscow Mule?"

Pyotr shot Captain Zhizhin a quizzical glance as though he was high on drugs. "What do you mean – are you telling me you are trading in exotic animals now?"

Captain Zhizhin bellowed with laughter. "My friend, you have a wicked sense of humour. I suppose you could call what I have upstairs an exotic animal in a way. But no my friend, a Moscow Mule is a type of cocktail the Americans liked to drink in the nineteen-fifties. I learnt that from our secret files." Here Captain Zhizhin tapped the side of his nose. "Vodka, lime juice, ginger beer. You're so unsophisticated Pyotr – I'll teach you how to live like you've never lived before if you stick with me." Pyotr felt very embarrassed and also belittled – something he had often felt in the company of Konstantin – was there no end to his troubles? Here he had just escaped from the company of one maniac only to find himself in the company of another.

Pyotr mentally crossed himself as he was led up two steep flights of stairs and along a narrow claustrophobic corridor, not being given a hint by his host as to where they were headed, except when Pyotr attempted to enquire he was brushed off with a cheery smile coupled with a cryptic, "You'll soon see."

At the end of this narrow passage Zhizhin came to a door marked – 'Private – Keep Out.' On being told to wait, Pyotr looked around the corridor but could not find anything to focus his eyes upon. There were two other doors, both labelled in a similar manner with the same message upon them on a similarly dirty coloured piece of cardboard. Then a muffled commotion was heard and what sounded like a high-pitched yelp as if a puppy dog had been hurt. Then Pyotr recalled what Captain Zhizhin had said just minutes earlier: "I suppose you could call what I have upstairs an exotic animal in a way." *Some type of snake, or maybe a monkey?* Pyotr was suddenly becoming very curious. Was it possible that Captain Zhizhin really had begun illegally trading in rare animal species?

Another five minutes passed in silence before Captain Zhizhin's lumbering frame reappeared in the doorway and placed a friendly hand upon Pyotr's shoulder.

"Before I leave, you may be interested to know that a little earlier I found a job to suit your talents – that is, if you are interested. We can double your present salary and it would still be in the same field of business you're in now – security."

"We can double your salary – who's we?"

"I own a tangible share of this new enterprise. Anyhow, let me know. You said you were keen to branch out. See you later. By the way, this is on the house." He motioned Pyotr to enter the room he had just vacated. With that, Captain Zhizhin disappeared, leaving a puzzled seasoned state security officer to explore with trepidation the dimly lit interior.

***

All rooms have an atmosphere. This one was no different. It was spiced with a cheap perfume. The sole source of light spilled grudgingly from a small table lamp fashioned from a grubby wine bottle which blended in with its surroundings fairly successfully. Pyotr could just make out a single bed bearing the languid figure of a young woman with something draped around her body. Once inside the room he stood stock still, having quietly closed the door with his back while still gripping its handle. He felt incriminated and embarrassed just being there. To cover his embarrassment he took a step closer without saying a word. He could see now that she was wearing a crumpled diaphanous nightdress which barely covered her thighs. Two more soft steps brought him to the edge of the bed, allowing him to stare down at the near naked body of a childlike figure, her head slightly inclined as though too heavy to support it. But the eyes looked up at Pyotr from beneath her brows, large saucer shaped eyes – pleading – yet vacant – pupils dilated. Then he saw within the crook of her right arm a tattoo of tiny pin pricks gathered around the dark swollen vein, her fragile hand raised in a futile reflexive action, shield-like, to protect her face. She looked as delicate as a moth's wings. A smudge of mascara marked one cheek – but it could also have been a fresh bruise just coming out. He sighed, thinking how wise Konstantin had been to make his excuses and leave when the opportunity arose.

Pyotr felt as a spectator might when watching a film in the cinema, divorced from the real emotions going on behind the fragile façade of a beautiful young woman. The defensive gesture of her arm movement was in reality a very drowsy subject succumbing to a liquid tranquiliser; stretching her limbs, and in the process stifling a yawn. It was in this act of raising her delicate neck that Pyotr saw in the dim pool of light what appeared to be a ridge of knitted skin, which he knew from experience to be a scar from a recent operation.

"What's your name?" Pyotr desperately wanted to help this pitiful figure watching him with suspicion; Captain Zhizhin's *'tangible share'*. He repeated the question, attempting to elicit some kind of response, but there was no answer. *Such a simple question*, Pyotr thought to himself. *How can I help if you're not willing?* His eyes scoured the room searching for some detail, but there were no details of any note. There was the bed and a small cheap table supporting the lamp. In one corner a dirty sink stood upon a cracked ceramic pedestal, and in another, a simple wooden high-backed chair – a grubby-looking towel draped over the back. Pyotr felt a great surge of helplessness well up within him. He knew they were both trapped in different ways; trapped in a country which had lost its very shape, and its identity. She had rekindled feelings he had not experienced since childhood. The crystal clear image of a pathetic creature he had once seen in a pit. Kept down a hole in the ground, even when the emaciated brown bear was offered some paltry sustenance it had looked wary, as though its confined world was more tolerable when left alone, even in such abject circumstances.

This room was also a tiny cage – her world. And like the animal in that bear pit, she would never escape. She would be looked at and fed and used, but never would she see the normal outside world; just as Pyotr would never be able to sever the bonds of his childhood which wedded him to his country, no matter how corrupt that country might be.

There was only one piece of decoration within that bare room, the brightest object because of its position, placed as it was, directly beneath the faint rays of the yellowed lamplight. It was a tiny Matryoshka doll, no larger than a fingernail. Without saying anything else Pyotr shrugged his shoulders in a gesture of helplessness and at the same time averted his gaze, finding it too painful. Four paces and he was once again out into the hall, away from the stifling oppressive atmosphere, pulling the door shut on his turbulent emotions as he desperately attempted to expunge the harrowing scene from his mind, yet deep within his heart knowing that it would always remain locked there somewhere in his subconscious mind, filed away as a harrowing experience never to be forgotten.

CHAPTER 144

Dr Kenneth Jones removed his copy of the *Times* newspaper from reception, a tiny area of the college set aside to be used not only for signing in new students at the beginning of the academic year, but also for holding letters and parcels, and even more mundane matters such as general enquiries regarding course tutors and the like. In the process of removing his paper he managed to give the bursar the slip. The bursar, Old Scrooge, as he was affectionately known, had been trying to nab Dr Jones for several days with regard to expenditure on the partial external renovation of the college. His epithet was an obvious if somewhat misleading description for someone with his pecuniary talents.

After climbing the vast oak staircase which led to his rooms and closing the door upon the rest of academia, Dr Jones entered his personal library, carrying the newspaper over to his chair and laid it down upon a well-used mahogany coffee table. He then made his way to the sideboard where he proceeded to pour himself his usual liquid breakfast consisting of a large whisky before scouring the front page.

What then took place had become something of a ritual of late, as he delved into the old battered briefcase set beside him and pulled from within it a rather tatty copy of the newspaper he had been about to read. However, this particular newspaper was nearly a year old. Gingerly sipping the ten-year-old malt whisky he ran his tongue around the rim of his lips and moustache, so as not to let the merest drop of nectar escape his taste buds. After doing this, he pushed his toes deep into the soft brown leather slippers before staring at the old newspaper's front page, absorbed in his thoughts.

It was not the main headline he was so taken with, but the black outlined box above. He knew the coloured photograph held within its black borders so well that every detail had become etched within his mind's eye. The shiny enamelled red flag inset with the hammer and sickle. This was the piece of jewellery worn by Penny so long ago, whilst enduring David's attempts to draw out from her mind all that had been locked away in another lifetime. And with every month that passed by since its publication, Dr Kenneth Jones had given a deeper sigh of relief than the month preceding it.

Even though the operation had been wound down months earlier, it remained an uncomfortable feeling for Dr Jones, knowing that Penny had been set up as the unwitting bait to catch Dr Grachev. Viewed as a 'costly fiasco', as 'C' had so eloquently put it, the dedicated telephone number expressly set up and monitored by specialist telecommunications experts was now just a bitter memory, and the agents assigned to the task of vetting the calls had now been transferred to other assignments. The calls that did come through had been checked out and ascertained as being either from cranks, mischief makers, or the just plain curious.

Another thing that weighed heavily on Dr Jones' mind was the fact that Penny had been kept in complete ignorance of the search for her stepbrother Dr Grachev by the British Secret Intelligence Services for their own purpose. There was nothing philanthropic about their motives.

Maybe he had become too paranoid about the Russian scientist. After all, what possible harm could befall Penny? It was now six months since Dr Grachev had disappeared. And anyway, if that picture in the newspaper had been spotted by the Russian, surely he would have been only too happy to get in touch with his stepsister after all this time. That is of course, if he remembered her: and if he knew about the identical piece of jewellery which she had been given. 'C's' words came flooding back, so succinctly summing up the situation at the time – *"Last throw of the dice, old boy."*

On impulse, Dr Kenneth Jones screwed up the tattered newspaper tightly and flung it with some vehemence into the wastepaper bin with the intention of laying that particular ghost to rest. He felt a burden lifted from him as it hit the side of the basketwork and dropped inside. He definitely felt lighter and within just a few hours was looking forward to greeting his old friend and confidant 'C', who until now had never set foot within the Welsh college precincts.

CHAPTER 145

Dr Grachev fingered the torn off piece of newspaper for the umpteenth time. There were two items which held his attention. The first was an article featuring Saddam Hussein and his supposed stockpiles of chemical weapons, and fears voiced by Israel of the Iraqi regime's possible research into biological weapons of mass destruction. The second feature was not so much an item in the accepted sense of the word. It was a black framed photograph in the top left hand corner on what had been the front page. This photograph was a facsimile of the pin Dr Grachev had been given by his father. Cryptically, below this picture without any explanation, was a telephone number.

Unlike Dr Kenneth Jones, Dr Grachev was unaware that he had a stepsister or that her name was Penny. Nor that she had been handed by his father an identical copy of the pin bearing the red flag of communism, the identical copy of which he himself had unwittingly passed on to Stryker, a.k.a. Smith and then been reunited with in such disastrous circumstances. He had however guessed correctly that the photograph inserted on the front page of a national newspaper was an attempt to lure him into the hands of the British security service, and thanks to Smith, a.k.a. Stryker's tip off, that was the one thing he was now determined to avoid.

Yet even in the knowledge that the British security service was after him, he had on many occasions lifted the telephone receiver in the desperate hope that Stryker had been wrong; that he would be just a telephone call away from his dream of gaining political asylum in Britain. It had taken a great deal of self-control not to give in to this self-delusion, so that just as quickly as he had raised the handset, reality kicked in and he had always dropped it again as if it was red hot. Under his newly acquired identity of Dr Nikolai Petrov, Dr Grachev was now living in a bed-sitting room at St. John's Wood; behind the hallowed Lords cricket ground in North London and just a stone's throw away from the private clinic where his facial features had been so dramatically changed. He had striven to keep a low profile and had so far succeeded. The facial scars from the commando surgery carried out on his face to obliterate his former features had not had time to heal, but the operation had made him virtually unrecognisable.

CHAPTER 146

Attending the Easter service with thousands of other people inside the Russian Orthodox Church at London's Ennismore Gardens, a trio of men were beginning to feel the sleep inducing effects of their night time vigil after having just hours earlier stepped off a three-hour flight from Moscow to Heathrow airport. The three Russian agents were wearing cheap cagoules, the hoods pulled up so as to obscure their faces for they did not wish to be recognised by the man they had come to seek out on the off chance that his religious bent would overcome any paranoid lingering fear from secret agents of the Russian state. And Dr Grachev would surely have recognised them as his potential killers from the fracas at the hotel the year before when they had taken a pot shot at him.

They stood in a huddle, vainly hoping to share the gifts they had brought with them like the three wise men following a bright star, except that their particular star was coloured red and to be found on the front page of the Russian daily newspaper *Izvestia* – and they were out of season. Nor did their names correspond to the Magi... Melchior, Caspar and Balthasar. To their Russian mothers they were simply known as Konstantin, Pyotr and Yevgeny. Their strained and furtive glances swept back and forth like the searching beams of a lighthouse over a sea of faces – Yevgeny Kotov being so short he occasionally resorted to standing on the tips of his toes in a seemingly futile attempt to see over the heads of those surrounding him. Pyotr on the other hand occasionally touched his secreted pistol for reassurance, knowing that if their target was located it could be eliminated within a split second.

It was during the Liturgy that Dr Grachev first noticed two people standing immediately in front of him and who were obviously deeply in love. By their body language, and the tender way their fingers were entwined said it all. But it had been as the voices of the choir rose to a crescendo that Dr Grachev had noticed something about one of them that made him doubt his eyes.

Unaware of this particular incident and at almost the same moment of Dr Grachev's shock at seeing something he dared not believe was possible, there was also a faint stirring between two members of the congregation just a couple of rows behind him. They were attired in monks' robes consisting of voluminous brown habits secured around their waists by thick cords coupled with loose-fitting cowls hiding their faces, these shapeless hoods effectively performing the same function as the cagoules worn by the three Russian would-be assassins. The synchronised movements of these two heavily robed people signified a hint of recognition as one of the lessons began, read by a member of the clergy, his deep bass voice resonating with conviction as he began dealing with such weighty topics concerning love, sin, repentance, hope and forgiveness.

During that long night service, through snatched opportune moments of whispered conversation mingled with potent exhilaration of prayer and the choir sans any musical accompaniment singing with gusto, the two hooded figures watched Dr Grachev closely, not daring to let him out of their sight.

Dr Grachev, blissfully unaware that he himself was being observed, stood totally entranced by the two people within touching distance mingling amidst the throng of other worshipers inside the Orthodox Church – two people who had joined the throng of several thousand others holding their flickering candles illuminating the congregation's faces, as well as making the gold and silver religious relics shimmer and sparkle, adding a touch of magic to this Easter service. They could not possibly know that it was here, a year to the day, that the person who now found them of such interest had first made the acquaintance of Smith, nor of the many lives which had become tainted in the intervening months because of that fateful meeting.

Oblivious of Dr Grachev's eyes moving from Penny to David and back again, Penny stood gazing around her in wonderment, wide-eyed at the beautifully painted icons adorning the walls, just as Stryker had so many times felt spiritually uplifted by the myriad of voices and the inextricably linked fragrance of heady aromas, so evocative of eastern religious worship.

It had been a desperate last ditch measure – a hunch dreamt up by Colonel Oleynik. All three knew the colonel was clutching at straws, but orders were orders. And so their eyes had not been closed for the last twenty-four hours, travelling all the way from Moscow in the vain hope of catching sight at this religious festival of their avowed arch enemy and traitor, Dr Grachev. After all, had not Dr Grachev been spotted leaving this religious Easter service by one of their comrades from the Russian Embassy in London just the year before?

Immediately after the service, as David and Penny were making their way out of the church, a thick accented voice caught Penny's attention. It was coming from behind her and sounded familiar. When she turned around however, she could not place the face associated with the voice into any context. As she stood there, her body half turned, the person whom she was looking at moved sideways behind one of the other congregation. Then it came to her. The resemblance was of someone who had resided at the hotel where she still worked. But that had been the year before and his face was not that of the person she now remembered, but was heavily scarred. He had been a Muscovite and she had secured a small private dining room for himself and one guest.

Dr Grachev's new persona as Dr Nikolai Petrov had completely fooled her, but something had caught his own eye. It was the sole remaining link which Penny possessed to remind her, if indeed she needed reminding, of her Russian homeland – the small, seemingly insignificant piece of jewellery she now wore in the lapel of her coat. The same piece of jewellery Dr Grachev possessed in the form of a photograph from the newspaper cutting which now lay carefully secreted inside his wallet. He had come to the conclusion very early on that whoever inserted the photograph must have had ties with the British secret service, and that it had been their way of attempting to trace him. Having heeded the written warning from Smith that the Intelligence Service had been on the verge of killing him, he was not about to reveal himself now. He knew that with the British Intelligence Service his fate was sealed.

He also knew that only one person, other than himself, possessed that identical piece of jewellery illustrated in the newspaper photograph. He knew too, that this same woman who had just turned around to look at him with such curiosity was the same person who worked as the receptionist at the hotel where he had first hypnotised Smith. She may have recognised him, or certainly his voice, for why else had she turned around to stare at him? It was even more than likely that she was an agent working for the security services and had followed him to this Easter vigil, or had been recruited as an informer at the hotel. It happened frequently in Moscow so why not here in London? And if she had followed him it meant that she knew where he resided! All these thoughts flooded in upon him as Penny attempted to take her leave. Dr Grachev was now feeling very vulnerable. This woman wearing the symbolic red flag of Soviet Socialism could so easily betray him. And she was at this very moment with a man just a few paces away from him, no doubt another agent.

Dr Grachev mingled with hundreds of other worshipers as he struggled to keep the location of this imagined traitor in the shape of Penny within his range of vision as the three of them were momentarily swept away, being hidden by the milling crowds and jostled down the worn steps of the Russian Orthodox Church and out into the cold air of the street. As Penny and David strolled across Hyde Park in the chill of the early morning with a view to locating their car, they were blissfully unaware of the stalker who was now tracking their every movement. Large trees stood silhouetted against the lightening sky like tall black sentries along a myriad of paths cutting across the park, enveloping in their shadows another pair of spectators who with some effort were pushing a Harley-Davidson motorcycle. These two spectators had been spying on Dr Grachev and not the doctor's own targets, the young man and woman too interested in one another to notice they were being hunted down as a panther hunts a smaller defenceless animal, and with that same intentioned deadly resolution.

These two curious spectators who just moments before had been attired in long brown hooded robes were now transformed into leather clad motorcyclists replete with visored helmets. This alteration to their appearance having been brought about through the good offices of the church authorities, aided by the two strangers, having earlier flashed an MI6 security identification card used to secure a side room where quickly divesting themselves of their loose priests attire – without losing sight of their own quarry – they had revealed beneath their cassocks two sets of motorcycle leathers and having donned their helmets, making them look for all the world like an ordinary couple of motorcyclists.

It might have been supposed that this motley group of assembled characters would have made up a full complement of unusually curious people for whatever reason, trailing one another at a discreet distance, but that assumption would be wildly misplaced having not yet taken into consideration the three secret Russian agents Konstantin, Pyotr and Yevgeny. These three surrogate wise men having brought gifts of bullets and destruction had only at the very last moment before being swept along with the milling crowds vacating the church spotted Dr Grachev, by the one thing that he himself had overlooked when attending the Clinic; his hair bore a distinctive small, white, cross-like birthmark upon the back of his head. So this was to be the unwitting coterie of strangers destined to spend the next four hours on the roads headed toward a place only two of them had ever been before.

CHAPTER 147

"Did you sleep well?" This seemingly innocuous question would normally be posed in the course of events out of politeness for someone who had just spent the night at a friend's abode but was in this instance pointedly directed by the college warden Dr Kenneth Jones toward his good friend 'C', who had just appeared in the drawing room looking rather tired and distracted as though he had other things on his mind.

"Thank you for enquiring. I am afraid you know me only too well. I didn't inform you when I arrived yesterday but apropos to the elusive Dr Grachev a few days ago I instructed my office to have two of our agents attend last night's Russian Orthodox Easter church service, just on the off chance that he may have put in an appearance. I suppose in a way it could be described as clutching at straws but I felt there might have been a chance! I hope you don't mind but I'd left your number with my office just in case there were any developments. I would have expected some sort of news by now so it seems to have been a wasted ploy." Before Dr Kenneth Jones could posit an adequate response they were interrupted by an unusual din outside.

It began with an almost inaudible sound akin to the resonance of waves breaking gently over the sand dunes echoing with the swish of the sea, but without being followed by that inevitable sigh. Dr Kenneth Jones had imbibed his first nip of the day and felt warm and contented inside before refilling his tumbler. And although it was the first time 'C' had visited the Welsh college since his friend had been appointed warden many years before, he had declined the offer of an early morning tipple before breakfast notwithstanding. As Dr Jones firmly placed the second full glass of whisky down upon a side table the sound outside metamorphosed into a harsher discordant screech of wheels emanating from the rapidly moving line of cars as though from a train of railway carriages, the reverberation of which entered the confines of the warden's apartment, gradually worming its way into his consciousness and for some inexplicable reason extinguishing his general feeling of wellbeing by presaging a deep seated state of gloom.

It was still early, just a few hours having passed since dawn had displayed its first nourishing glimmer of light from behind the Welsh mountains when beyond the stone mullioned college windows, the seat of learning itself now bereft of staff and students alike due to the Easter holidays, Dr Kenneth Jones spotted from a distance through his pair of high powered binoculars a convoy of three cars slowing down as it crawled past the quadrangle toward the ruins of Harlech castle. Snatching the pair of binoculars from the warden's fingers, 'C' saw the one thing he had always feared, though not in such a location as this, the scene creating in his mind a dichotomy, a disjuncture of place and event as his attention focussed on the wound down window of the third car, a limousine displaying *corps diplomatique* plates. A thickset man, the driver, sat cradling a gun upon his lap. 'C', like that of his friend Dr Jones, was unaware that this convoy had travelled in the early morning from London's Russian Orthodox Church all the way up to North Wales.

After quickly consulting with 'C', Dr Jones lifted the telephone receiver and rang a Welsh number. A brief conversation ensued before handing the receiver over to 'C' and after a few more words were exchanged the handset was replaced upon its cradle. A couple of minutes later 'C' and the college warden were out in the courtyard, striding toward his own rather decrepit transport, but did not have far to drive beyond the college confines before catching up with the now stalled caravan of other more robust vehicles.

The first thing to be spotted by both 'C' and the college warden in this sleepy Welsh village, usually deserted due to it being a Sunday, was not the expected tail end of the convoy; it was not even a car at all, but the unexpected rear view image of a large and powerful American Harley-Davidson motorcycle which had not been spotted earlier, neither by the other cars it had been trailing having remained at a discreet distance all through that early morning, nor by 'C' himself from his vantage point within the college. The gleaming powerful red and chrome motorbike had carried its two riders from London dressed in black leathers, sporting atop their heads matching black motorcycle helmets with their reflective visors pulled down, successfully hiding their features in the crisp early morning light.

Without warning the incongruous set of vehicles making up this convoy slewed left, ending up within the confined ruins of the 13th century Harlech Castle hugging the perimeter of the sand dune strewn coastline. Dr Jones and his colleague kept their distance, waiting and watching. To Dr Jones' great surprise, he now recognised the leading car in the procession to be that of David's and saw him and Penny Churchill rapidly climb out, glancing back over their shoulders with what appeared to be puzzled expressions on their faces. Then quicker than would have been expected, another man in his thirties opened the door to his own much more substantial and faster black Jaguar being parked immediately behind David's. Climbing out, he began running toward the couple, one hand pushed deep within the breast pocket of his jacket as though going for a gun. The couple, seeing this, began running away from their pursuer. Then Dr Kenneth Jones noticed that the man chasing David and Penny Churchill rapidly performed a complete volte-face responding to one of three men who had now themselves alighted from their own sleek limousine, the stocky man with the gun shouting out Dr Grachev's name in Russian. Then to the utter astonishment of the college warden and 'C', Dr Grachev was literally lifted off his feet and once again spun around.

The delayed crack of a pistol shot was heard above the shouting which would account for Dr Grachev being turned by the force of a bullet. *So that was Dr Grachev!* 'C' thought – the man he had been searching for and had attempted to lure out into the open by placing that picture of Penny Churchill's pin in the newspaper. And that shot, would have been fired from the gun he had witnessed lying within the limousine driver's palm. And in that fraction of a second of hearing that pistol shot, the youngish man whom he now knew to be Dr Grachev, without as expected turning away from his assailants, then did something even more unexpected, moving rapidly backwards toward the remnants of a section of the castle wall, as if propelled there by an invisible wire, clutching his chest as he went. He had been shot and in the process his hand dropped something glinting in the early morning sun on the uneven stony ground – an object 'C' had not seen. But one of the motorcyclists had witnessed it being dropped and it was not a gun.

At this juncture the whirl of a helicopter's rotor blades overhead could be heard, creating such a distraction and downdraft that everyone looked skyward – everyone that is except for the two people on their Harley-Davidson motorcycle, clad in leathers and wearing helmets. It took just a fraction of a second for the Harley-Davidson's engine to be revved up and the clutch let out, aiming the heavy, shiny, roaring piece of machinery at Yevgeny, the gunman who had been mesmerised by this unexpected turn of events, knocking him off his feet and in the same manner as Dr Grachev, sending him flying backwards, his gun spinning in the air and out of reach. David, who with Penny had been watching all this commotion, moved cautiously from behind one of the castle's walls before tentatively reaching out for the dropped firearm. The pillion passenger rapidly leaping off the motorcycle and being faster than David, had kicked the gun away with his foot before quickly retrieving it himself.

'C' and Dr Kenneth Jones were also transfixed by the sight of the helicopter but appeared more circumspect than the other people, though smiling as if half expecting this intrusion into what was now turning into a very ugly situation.

The pair of friends' reason for being wary was the sight of what was slung beneath the helicopter's fuselage just above their heads, swaying menacingly. One of the Harley-Davidson motorcyclists also recognised the army Land Rover painted in jungle green camouflage as it was swiftly lowered mechanically by steel cables onto the uneven patch of stony ground from the helicopter next to the castle walls, though they did not realise that it was the One-Ten model used by the SAS for its manoeuvrability in all terrains. After being lowered to the ground and following hot on its heels was a contingent of Britain's Special Air Service troop abseiling down ropes suspended from the tactical transport Puma helicopter's doors whilst continuing to hover as if fixed by some giant puppeteer's unseen hand, neither veering by a foot this way or that. The whole operation worked like clockwork and was carried out in seconds.

CHAPTER 148

The three Russian agents sent to liquidate Dr Grachev were now frozen by the sight of the cream of the British Army appearing to multiply every few seconds until there were twelve large, ferocious-looking, battle-hardened soldiers, faces streaked with war paint and carrying weapons ready to be deployed at a moment's notice with magazines full of live ammunition, not blanks. Dr Grachev lay on the ground where he had been felled after being shot disbelieving what he was seeing.

A tall barrel-chested man dressed in combat fatigues, the first soldier whose feet touched terra firma after vacating the helicopter, let out a cry of greeting as he ran toward Dr Kenneth Jones and his house guest 'C', snapping to attention and throwing a smart salute.

"Why Dick, you're the last person I expected to set eyes upon today," shouted 'C'. The soldier was brigadier 'Dick' Jordan, a member of the Special Air Service who had attended the late night meeting held at 'C's' house 'St. Kildare' in Berkshire to discuss Dr Grachev, at the time intimating to 'C' that he would be only too happy to carry out a 'wet job' on the Russian. He then acknowledged 'C's' colleague Dr Kenneth Jones.

"You're the Harlech college warden who initiated the call I take it? I've heard a lot about you. Dick Jordan." The smiling soldier, his face streaked with green and black camouflage war paint stuck out his large fist and grabbed Dr Kenneth Jones' hand, unwittingly almost crushing it in the process. The brigadier's other hand dangled by the side of his left leg clutching a menacing Swiss made P 228 SIG Sauer, his personal choice of handgun as favoured by many SAS troop for its reliability and accuracy. "We were on one of our exercises on the Brecon Beacons. Soon as I heard what was happening after your call was patched through to me from HQ I grabbed a chopper and brought a contingent of my troop. It was very fortuitous us being on hand. Good timing eh? Look!"

But Dr Kenneth Jones had no need to look far as two giants of soldiers came running over in full battle dress with their icy, cold, staring eyes fixed on the doctor and 'C' in a threatening manner with rifles cocked and pointed straight at both of them.

"It's alright lads; these two people are friends of mine," shouted the brigadier. While this conversation was going on, numerous other SAS soldiers, having been rapidly ferried from the Welsh Brecon Beacons to relieve the plight 'C' and Dr Kenneth Jones found themselves in, had after abseiling from their tactical transport Puma helicopter fanned out, running toward the other unidentified people brandishing their weapons and covering each one with an MI6 assault rifle as they yelled, "Get your effing hands in the air."

Yevgeny meanwhile remained lying on the ground with a broken shoulder where he had been felled by the Harley-Davidson's front wheel, but as opposed to having earlier been intimidated by two black leather clad motorcyclists standing over him wielding his own gun which had been knocked from his grasp, and with his image reflected in their mirrored visors pulled down over their faces so as to keep their identities secret, as would be expected of the Secret Intelligence Service, all three were now even more intimidated through staring down the barrels of three gun-toting soldiers who looked as though they meant business. Yevgeny's gun, a Makarov 9 mm pistol had once more changed hands with that of a more than capable SAS soldier, the gun itself being very familiar as many foreign small arms are to the British SAS because of their vigorous training methods.

David, who along with Penny had ventured out from behind their perceived safety of the castle walls, also had unexpected army escorts and clung to each other as if their lives depended on it.

For the remaining two Russian FSB security agents Konstantin and Yevgeny, English was not their second language of choice, but even they gave the impression of understanding the international gesture for 'get your fucking hands in the air' by the way the elite team of SAS paratroopers gestured with their rifles together with their blood-curdling shouts.

There now appeared to be a moment's reflection by all those participating in this melee before 'C' gestured to the two motorcyclists, guessing that these two were the MI6 officers ordered to stake out the London Orthodox church and as if to read his mind, even before they got within hearing distance, one of them flashed their Six security card.

Dr Grachev now stood before 'C', sandwiched between the two motorcyclists; his face still blotched with the red surgical scars inflicted upon him in his patently failed attempt at disguising his identity.

'C' squared up to the Russian scientist, looking him straight in the eye. In English he enquired: "You are Dr Grachev?" The question was immaterial for there was no reply.

"You are the Red Chameleon!" This time it was a statement of fact and repeated in the Russian language for good measure. Still there was no reply. Then 'C' looked at the two motorcyclists. "I want you two to escort this fellow back to London. Our friends here will transport you by helicopter. MI6 headquarters – straightaway! You are in charge of him and his safety. Don't let me down." The motorcyclist who had flashed his secret service security card nodded.

Brigadier Jordan spoke. "Shall I uncouple the Land Rover first sir?"

The terse reply came back. "I said straightaway. Forget about anything else. This is top priority. ASAP. That's an order."

"And what about the other three Russian men sir?"

"They are to be transported to SAS headquarters at Hereford and held there incommunicado until you hear from me personally."

CHAPTER 149

Within minutes the troop carrying tactical transport Puma helicopter was once more filling up with SAS soldiers who had scared the shit out of the three Russian FSB officers.

The two motorcyclists watched intently as Konstantin and Pyotr were being manhandled onto the helicopter along with Yevgeny, who kept his mouth firmly closed, presumably not wishing to join in their conversation and whose only sign of life at this stage being a thin trickle of slime slowly running down his chin. Konstantin was raving in his mother tongue; a whispered tirade aimed at Pyotr. "I just knew we would end up in some fucking mess because of you. You botched up the other operation killing Anthony Lovejoy-Taylor instead of that British guy called Smith who we were tipped off about. What an idiot you are Pyotr. You knew that Ivanovich Sobolev was revealed as spying for the British by our man from British intelligence in London and yet you lost him at that airport just outside Moscow and then you later fucked up by shooting him before we'd even had time to interrogate him. I used to call the operatives in First Directorate our arch rivals – well, I now see that you are even worse than them – you idiot. You work in Intelligence – ha! That's a laugh. I should have gotten rid of you years ago. You're useless."

One of the motorcyclists within earshot who freely admitted speaking a smattering of the Russian language heard their conversation, but for the moment had decided to keep it to himself.

The three Russians: Konstantin, Pyotr and Yevgeny – notwithstanding his broken shoulder – now lay spread-eagled on their bellies on the floor of the helicopter, trussed up like doomed chickens destined for the slaughterhouse with restraining zip tie plastic cuffs binding their ankles as well as their wrists. If they raised their heads with effort they were able to make out in the gloom four figures with their backs against the metal structure of the fuselage, looking not a little uncomfortable themselves. These were Brigadier Jordan, Dr Grachev, plus the two motorcyclists with their darkened visors still firmly pulled down, masking their faces.

**

Soon after the helicopter had lifted off, one of the motorcyclists separated from Brigadier Jordan by Dr Grachev was asked by his colleague: "That big fellow in charge, what's his name?"

"The brigadier's name? Why do you ask? His name is Jordan."

"I'll bet nobody's ever crossed him."

The motorcyclist was just about to acknowledge his colleague's sense of dry wit when he noticed something was terribly wrong. He saw that Yevgeny, still lying on his stomach opposite in the same manner as his two Russian compatriots with their hands and feet firmly secured behind their backs, had managed to arch his body so as to be able to raise his head and was craning his neck. The strange thing was that Yevgeny's mouth was agape as though in the process of yawning and to the motorcyclist's horror a red laser beam was pointing straight into it. Swivelling his own head sideways to see where this beam was coming from he traced the line of the red beam back to the direction of the unknown source. To his puzzled horror it appeared to be coming from the centre of Dr Grachev's forehead, centred right between the eyes. Could it possibly be a trick of the dim light inside the grey fuselage or could there be some other explanation? Was it really being generated by something he himself had read about? Was he witnessing some form of ectoplasmic manifestation emanating from Dr Grachev's head? It was known in the Hindu religion as kunkumam, a common enough sight in India, being a red dot formed between the eyebrows used in meditation and also known as the Third Eye relating to the sixth chakra system. Was it really possible to generate enough latent energy from within the body for others to actually witness something materialising into a form resembling that of a red laser-like beam? The motorcyclist had heard of ectoplasm supposedly pouring forth from the mouths of spirit mediums but as far as he was concerned he had dismissed that phenomenon as pure hokum and stagecraft. But this was totally different. At that particular moment as Stryker was having grave doubts about his own cognitive ability to understand what he had just witnessed the helicopter felt as if it were falling from the sky and from the bottom of the fuselage beneath his feet came a loud bang, causing the whole aircraft frame to judder as though it had hit the top of a mountain and not as had actually happened an air pocket. Then a succession of events followed swiftly one upon the other.

Disbelieving his own eyes, though concomitant with the evidence placed before him, was the realisation that the red beam of light had been replaced by something that caught the ambient glow inside the fuselage of the Puma helicopter, appearing to shine as a silver hair might shine when catching the light for a nanosecond before disappearing straight in the direction of Dr Grachev like a bolt of lightning. It travelled fast but remained silent, any sound having been masked by the noise of the motors driving the helicopter's rotor blades.

While all this was going on and with a sudden innate realisation and understanding of what he had just witnessed, he now did something in that fraction of a second that coincided with what he took to be turbulence momentarily affecting the stability of the helicopter. He instinctively nudged Dr Grachev hard, resulting in the scientist tumbling forward in a heap thanks to the motorcyclist's quick thinking of thumping him in the solar plexus, though it might also have been due to the momentary pitching of the helicopter caused by the turbulence.

Then, too late, he caught sight of Brigadier Jordan just as he was also in the process of keeling over in the same manner as Dr Grachev, but this time with one of his hands firmly clutching his neck. And between Brigadier Jordan's thick fingers flowed a copious amount of blood spurting from what the motorcyclist guessed to be a severing of the carotid artery. The leather clad motorcyclist saw all this through his motorcycle helmet's darkened visor which was now rapidly removed to gain a clearer view. A second later his colleague followed suit, letting out a high-pitched scream as their own helmet was removed before swiftly keeling over in the same manner as that of Dr Grachev, though this time the reaction was caused at the sight of brigadier Jordan's blood and not by the sharp nudge applied to Dr Grachev by the motorcyclist.

The SAS soldiers who were scattered around the Puma helicopter let out a collective volley of expletives as their heads turned in unison to see what all the commotion was about and the sight that met their disbelieving fixed gazes was something to make their hearts beat faster. For the initial object of their oaths was the sight of a very young, pretty, dark-haired woman slumped along one wall of the Puma helicopter who had just fainted. The next thing to capture their attention was the voice of the man into whose arms she had collapsed as he attempted to revive the woman who resembled a catwalk model. He was yelling her name but what was so unexpected here was that he had a soft American accent.

"Carol, you OK?" Before waiting for a reply he had turned to Brigadier Jordan who was by this time being attended to by the troop's medic, who was shaking his crew cut head in a negative manner, making it obvious that Brigadier Jordan was already dead.

CHAPTER 150

Whilst all this commotion was going on Stryker noticed that Yevgeny had somehow managed to roll over from his stomach onto his back, but now with his mouth firmly closed and he was no longer craning his neck. While Stryker was still trying to make sense of what he had just witnessed Dr Grachev had recovered his posture and was tapping Stryker on the arm, notwithstanding the restraining plastic cuffs limiting his movements.

Dr Grachev whispered something into Stryker's ear but spoke so low that on his first attempt Stryker could not make out what he was saying. It was also because of being drowned out by all the frenetic voices of the soldiers surrounding them shouting at one another in such a confined space. Stryker inclined his head toward Dr Grachev who spoke again in his broken English, now in a more urgent voice and kept his attention focussed on Stryker, who had this time managed to tune into what was being said to him, the scientist not letting his eyes settle for a moment upon his three Russian compatriots trussed up on the floor of the helicopter just twelve feet away.

"I said I never expected to see you again." Then he enquired: "Smith, or is it Stryker?"

Stryker responded quick as a flash: "Dr Grachev! Or is it Dr Grey?"

Then they both stared at Carol as she shouted above the din inside the helicopter to make herself heard: "Or is it the Red Chameleon?" The three of them gave a wry smile.

Dr Grachev spoke in broken English which Stryker no longer found endearing, but noticed a look of terror in the Russian's eyes.

"You must me help Mr Stryker or whatever your name is." His vocal chords were taught with stress, raising his voice an octave or two higher. "Those three Russians lying over there – they tried to kill me when I was staying with my hotel in London. You remember? I give you a meal there. I'm certain they are FSB agents sent to England for my purpose." But what he then whispered into Stryker's ear was pure dynamite. After Stryker had time to digest this information and while the soldiers were coming to terms with what had just happened to their commander, something clicked in Stryker's mind as he stood up and moved toward Yevgeny before leaning over him and to Carol's utter disbelief gave him a hefty thump in the solar plexus, resulting in a loud breathless gasp from the Russian. Although

Stryker had his back toward Carol and his broad shoulders obscured her view of Yevgeny she could see his elbows moving like pistons and saw enough to know that Stryker had seemingly once more struck out, this time hitting the Russian in the face which was confirmed when Stryker made his way back to his position in the fuselage of the helicopter with a fixed smile of satisfaction on his face. And now that usual thin trickle of slime running down Yevgeny's long chin, so familiar to his comrades, had been replaced by a stream of bright red blood.

After the rumpus had settled down amongst the SAS soldiers within the helicopter's fuselage, Stryker eventually sat down beside Carol, having surreptitiously pushed something into one of his large motorcycle trouser pockets before zipping it with a flourish. Then Carol vented her anger in no uncertain terms as she whispered: "How could you do that Stryker? How could you? What barbarity. Did you enjoy beating up that poor defenceless man?" She was incandescent with rage and did not attempt to hide her feelings.

Things took on an even worse aspect when she heard Stryker's retort to her question: "Did you enjoy beating up that poor defenceless man?" with the reply: "Well, I know you won't believe this Carol, but in a strange sort of way I did."

"Believe it. I am thoroughly disgusted by your actions. You're an ape – a monster, you, you…"

"Come on Carol, now that's not fair. You've known me long enough to understand that I would not do anything unfair."

"Unfair. Unfair," she repeated for emphasis. "You've just beaten up a man who couldn't move because of his plastic wrist restraints. A sitting target! And you call that fair! Urrghh!" The deep noise emitted from the back of Carol's throat was more akin to a growling bear than anything Stryker had ever heard before.

"Trust me, I have my reasons and when they are revealed I'm sure you will see things are not as they seem. Really!"

"Well, I'll suspend my judgement. But you'd better not go beating up any more people."

"I did not go beating up anyone. Anyway, let's forget about this episode for the moment because we've got work to do."

"OK," Carol responded, unconvinced by Stryker's protestations of innocence, for she had just witnessed the event with her own eyes and was not about to forget nor to forgive him in a hurry.

CHAPTER 151

"How did you fix that?" Carol asked irritably, peering into Stryker's pale blue eyes with a quizzical look.

"Oh Carol, you look a sight. You've got grease from that helicopter all over your face."

"Gee, thanks Stryker. But you've not answered my question."

"OK! Well, after Brigadier Jordan was killed inside that helicopter Dr Grachev told me that the three trussed-up Russians were an assassination squad sent over here to eliminate him – Dr Grachev that is – for whatever reason, but failed to carry out their assignment."

"No!"

"Yes! Those British soldiers knew that we were to be given top priority as far as making key decisions as to what to do with the Russians after Brigadier Jordan was killed, knowing that we were members of the British Secret Intelligence Service. So I gave orders to transport the three other Russian captives back to the soldiers' headquarters at Hereford as 'C' had requested, but explained that Dr Grachev must accompany us to a special destination as he was a VIP and for that we must also take charge of the jeep."

"Well I am anyway."

"You're what?"

"You said that we were members of the secret service. Now that is not strictly true is it Stryker. You were fired, remember?"

"I'll bet you are now glad that you took my advice and slept on your decision to resign from the service after I was given my marching orders. And if you hadn't changed your mind and decided to remain in place, well, I don't suppose we would have located Dr Grachev. Wise decision if I might say so."

"Stryker, what can I say? You are a genius. Is that what you want me to say? Dressing up in monk's habits; that was fun I'll admit. But I haven't forgiven you yet for the miserable treatment you dished out to that poor Russian in the helicopter. Oh yes, there's something else I wanted to tackle you about." Here Carol leant forward and whispered in Stryker's ear. "How did you recognise Dr Grachev when we were at the church service in

London? After all, he had had plastic surgery hadn't he? He looked quite different."

"Oh! That was easy." Stryker simulated the same posture of confidentiality as Carol had before he replied: "I spotted Dr Grachev as soon as I saw him because of his hair."

"His hair! How do you mean?"

"I noticed it upon my first meeting with him at the Russian Orthodox Easter church service last year. At the back of his head he bore a distinctive birthmark on his hair in the form of a small white cross. I thought at the time how apt. His being at the church service I mean. I suppose when Dr Grachev had plastic surgery on his face to disguise his appearance he must have overlooked this birthmark. Otherwise he would possibly have used black hair dye."

"No wonder you are a detective. Bravo. Now tell me about this special destination we're headed for."

"Well, I have decided upon our destination because of being given a particularly puzzling and worrying piece of information from Dr Grachev concerning a British agent, something he mentioned to me just before we vacated the helicopter. He said he recognised one of the men he had just seen in North Wales. A British man!"

"You mean 'C'? Well I suppose it is possible that Dr Grachev saw the head of MI6 before today because of 'C' being in charge of searching for Dr Grachev? I mean it's unlikely, but still…"

"Yes, as you say, that's pretty unlikely. Especially when I tell you the person he was referring to was first seen by Dr Grachev in July two years ago! That's a year before Dr Grachev even came onto the scene and therefore to the attention of the British Security Services through his request for political asylum."

"And just where was this sighting of the mysterious British person two years ago?"

"That's the strange thing. Dr Grachev says he saw him in Moscow – at the Ministry of Defence!"

"No!"

"Yes. In Moscow!" Carol looked perplexed.

"The whole thing sounds fantastic! Maybe Dr Grachev is a plant – sent here by the Russian FSB to sow disinformation."

"I agree that's a distinct possibility. But I also think right now we have to take Dr Grachev's word at face value and believe what he says until proven to the contrary. Now I'll tell you about our special destination. This is where were going but I'll need your help."

When Carol heard the news she nearly fainted and at first objected vehemently, but under Stryker's constant heckling she relented with the words: "Under duress we'll go because I trust you implicitly – but don't take advantage of me because of that silly sentimental streak, Stryker."

"Huh, would I ever!" With that retort they sorted themselves out, Carol taking the steering wheel and Stryker keeping his eyes firmly fixed on Dr Grachev in the back seat who seemed pleasantly resigned to the fact that at this particular moment at least he was not about to be disposed of at the behest of Britain's Security Service, though as Carol erratically meshed the Land Rover's gears, bumping and jolting down the country road with an enthusiastically determined look upon her face, Dr Grachev began to have his doubts.

CHAPTER 152

It had been a long journey by the time of their arrival and Carol was feeling very tired because of having had so little sleep over the previous thirty-six hours. Stryker himself appeared impervious to such hardships and had some uncanny knack of dealing better with sleep deprivation, possibly due to his having been in the American Seals and the training he had received with this indomitable group of sailors, seemingly having the metaphorical spring restored to his step as they reached their destination. Just before this Stryker and Dr Grachev had had a heart to heart conversation about the virus sample trapped in Stryker's false eye and the revelation of how the virus may have escaped in Li Cheung's laboratory, causing so many deaths to a section of the Chinese community in London. Dr Grachev said it was just a theory but that it was because of a matter of expediency that at the time of his trips to Beijing and in the spirit of Chinese mutual co-operation with Russia that he had used blood samples for his experiments taken from some of the indigenous Chinese population there, and that might possibly be the explanation.

Stryker, Dr Grachev and Carol now sat in an annex of the Porton Down facility adjacent to the main entrance through which they had passed under the hard scrutinising gaze of many armed guards. The Russian scientist's plastic wrist restraints had already been removed by Stryker before attempting to enter the highly restricted area so as not to raise any suspicions about just who he was or as to why the three of them were there. After demanding the keys to their Land Rover one of the guards had parked it in a specially designated visitor's area with ease as though he had carried out such manoeuvres on a regular basis, being very familiar with the vehicle's controls.

Being the daughter of Professor Lambton who was Deputy Director General of the highly restricted Porton Down facility based in Salisbury, Wiltshire, the government military experimental chemical and biological warfare establishment into which they had just entered cut no ice with the security man who acted as their escort, even though Carol had added to this power play of hers by also smiling sweetly and flashing her MI6 security identity card, which in any other circumstance would have ridden roughshod over every rank in the armed forces that could be mustered. This time however, for some inexplicable reason – it was just after one of the security personnel had put a call through to a colleague with some explanation and passing on of their names – the expected and desired effect suddenly vaporised in an instant together with the formerly almost friendly atmosphere, which had now been replaced by an openly hostile one. When Carol had a second stab at drawing the guard's attention to her filial relationship with the Deputy Director General, she assuming the guard had not fully appreciated the unspoken benefits this should have bestowed upon her; this apparently was not so, the guard's response being: "I know who you are. You are now in our custody and the three of you will not say another word, either to one another or to anyone else who might enter this room without my express permission. Now, don't say another word, got it?" And that was that.

Dr Grachev took all this in his stride after being half shaken to death in the ride of a lifetime by Carol's erratic driving, anything else appearing to him as something of a bonus. So he stretched out his long, thin legs and settled into the hard red plastic seat and dozed off.

The room in which they were now incarcerated did not have any windows, the only illumination being three bare fluorescent tubes emitting a glare of intense white light being bounced off plain whitewashed walls, and the armed guard standing just inside the door giving no hint of just what sort of facility they had entered except for the fact that it must be of a restrictive nature and not at all welcoming. The four moulded red plastic chairs, the legs of which had been firmly cemented into the bare concrete floor had been fused onto what appeared to be a heavy RSJ beam, screaming functionality not comfort. Minimalistic décor was the watchword. As Carol also fell into a light slumber, taking her cue from Dr Grachev, Stryker, little realising just what a commotion was about to ensue and that he would be the unwitting architect of it, became aware of the rhythmically soft snoring being emitted from Dr Grachev's direction before casually removing from his jacket pocket what was to be the cause of this imminent furore; a fist sized object made of polished steel, glinting for a moment as it caught the room's extreme illumination, the large white linen handkerchief judiciously placed so as to cover this strange piece of engineering having partially slipped, revealing what was hidden beneath as Stryker gingerly placed the object upon the red Formica-topped table by his knees.

That action was to be the trigger for an almighty rumpus as soon as the guard saw it, he letting out a ferocious yell and nimbly springing forward toward the table at the same time blowing a whistle attached to the lanyard in his shirt breast pocket which had the effect of instantaneously summoning half a dozen armed guards with rifles, which to Stryker's trained ears were cocked and ready to fire. As for Dr Grachev, he appeared to visibly shrink in size as though attempting to fuse in with the red plastic material of the chair upon which he had been lazing.

CHAPTER 153

"There's no question about it. It must have been Stryker. Who else has an American accent? And because I myself fired him and he has no MI6 identity card because I, not personnel, had him relieved of it, the only other person with him who fits the description of his female accomplice perfectly and does have MI6 identification must be Stryker's relative Caroline Lambton as the name on her security pass confirms. Besides which, Stryker was apparently seen in the helicopter sitting next to Dr Grachev who just happened to be sitting next to Brigadier Jordan only moments before he was killed. Stryker and the Russian scientist must therefore have been in collusion. Well – don't you think?"

From his strategically placed vantage point the Assistant Controller of MI6 Charles Kingdom sat gazing out from the large plate-glass window at Vauxhall Cross. He was absentmindedly watching the snarled-up traffic as it vied with the maelstrom of London taxis crossing Vauxhall Bridge, and sombrely nodded in agreement with 'C'.

"That's why I called you in. I want an Alerts Ports Notice issued for Stryker and his accomplice Miss Lambton, together with that of the Russian scientist Dr Grachev. We must locate these three people as soon as possible. Circulate their photographs to include places such as all police stations and security establishments as well as hospitals and to all the usual places at which they might be seen such as hotels and boarding houses. Oh! And we might as well try the cinemas too. And I want an hourly progress report. Also mention the jeep and Harley-Davidson motorcycle. This is a national security matter. My orders are to shoot on sight, no questions asked. If it is them, my orders are shoot to kill. Understand? Let the relevant people know. That American Stryker has killed before and he may well kill again. I'm not prepared to give them another chance. Got that?"

The Assistant Controller answered 'C' without hesitation. "Yes sir, I understand. Kill on sight."

CHAPTER 154

"What is it? Can you guess Stryker?" Professor Lambton sat in his office at Porton Down examining the contraption with all the curiosity of a geologist who might have been holding a piece of moon rock in his hands. Or as a physical anthropologist might hold the jawbone of some ancient *Homo sapiens*, except that this particular jawbone bore no resemblance to humankind but rather to a robotic facsimile of one.

"All right, I'll put my cards on the table Professor, and say I'm as baffled as you. You asked me earlier from where I obtained this object and I told you from a Russian man sitting opposite us in the helicopter. His name is Yevgeny."

Carol's eyes narrowed. "Yes Daddy, that's right. I saw Stryker beat up this defenceless Russian man with my own eyes, I promise. I'm sure that contravenes something like the Geneva Convention. I mean, you just can't start beating up someone who is tethered by wrist restraints. It's just not right, it's spineless and it's definitely not British to act in that way." Here Carol turned around to face the American detective with a look of pure contempt. "I never thought I'd say this of you Stryker, but it is the mark of a true coward, what you did."

"What a load of nonsense you talk sometimes Carol. The Geneva Convention details the treatment of captured and wounded military and civilian personnel in wartime. Might I enlighten you to the fact that as of this moment the West is not at war with Russia – at least, not as far as conventional warfare is concerned and I most certainly did not 'beat up' as you so diplomatically put it, this Russian fellow named Yevgeny."

"Please children, stop arguing!"

"But Daddy I'm not arguing, I'm just telling the truth."

"You wouldn't know the truth if it bit you on your bottom. I did not beat up that Russian. What you presumably saw is me leaning over Yevgeny and extracting this object we have here from his... mouth."

"So you didn't actually sock him in the mouth?"

"What colourful language you possess Caroline. I'm sure you never spoke like that when you were at university," interjected Professor Lambton.

"No, I didn't 'sock him in the mouth' as you so tactfully and fancifully put it. The contraption must have cut his lips as I removed it." Stryker then relayed the tale of the red laser beam which he had initially thought was shining into Yevgeny's mouth until he came to the realisation that the red beam was not shining *into* Yevgeny's mouth but instead, as impossible as it had seemed, it was shining *out* from his mouth onto Dr Grachev's forehead just as a sniper's rifle might have a laser beam fixed to a telescopic sight for pinpoint accuracy.

"I'm so sorry doubting you Stryker," cried Carol, looking crestfallen. "I just knew you couldn't be capable of carrying out such a heinous act."

"That's not what you were saying just a moment ago."

"Now stop it you two. Yes Stryker, I gathered all that from this detailed report written for me by one of our Porton Down technicians. But now, after you have read this report, you will see how and why Brigadier Jordan came to be killed." The professor handed the American detective a sheet of paper.

It read:

AFTER HAVING SPOKEN BY TELEPHONE TO SEVERAL SERVICE PERSONNELL WHO WERE IN THE PUMA HELICOPTER AT THE TIME OF BRIGADIER JORDAN'S DEATH I HAVE COME TO THE CONCLUSION THAT THIS STRANGE LOOKING METAL OBJECT REMOVED BY THE AMERICAN NAMED STRYKER FROM RUSSIAN NATIONAL YEVGENY'S MOUTH WAS THE ITEM THAT LED TO THAT SAD INCIDENT. THE ITEM ITSELF CONSISTS OF TWO IDENTICAL CRESCENTS IN THE FORM OF A BOXER'S GUM SHIELD HELD IN PLACE AT THE POSTERIOR BY A THIN STEEL AXEL ACTING AS A HINGE RUNNING BETWEEN THE TWO COMPOSITE RUBBER AND STEEL UPPER AND LOWER MANDIBLES, LENDING STRENGTH AND STABILITY TO THE WHOLE STRUCTURE AS WELL AS CREATING A PLATFORM UPON WHICH IS MOUNTED AT RIGHT ANGLES TO THE STEEL AXEL A SHORT, PARTIALLY FLATTENED METAL TUBE UPON THE TOP OF WHICH IS PLACED A TINY RUBY STONE SET BEHIND A SERIES OF MINIATURE MAGNIFYING GLASSES ALL HELD WITHIN A SECOND TUBE, THIS TUBE MADE OF DARKENED GLASS RUNNING PARALLEL WITH THE FIRST AND HOUSING A MINITURISED BATTERY AND BULB AT IT'S POSTERIOR, SO AS TO PROVIDE A LIGHT SOURCE TO SHINE THROUGH THE

RUBY STONE FOR CREATING A SOURCE OF LIGHT FOR THE LASER BEAM.

THE SECOND ITEM IS A SMALL SPENT GAS CYLINDER WITH A THREAD AT ONE END THAT HAD PREVIOUSLY BEEN SCREWED ONTO THE CROSS-SECTIONED OVAL-SHAPED METAL TUBE INTO WHICH THE TINY GAS CYLINDER FIT SNUGLY. THIS PARTICULAR TUBE WAS DESIGNED TO HOLD THE SHARP DISCUS-SHAPED METAL PROJECTILE WHICH WAS LATER DISCOVERED FIRMLY EMBEDDED IN THE INTERIOR METAL SKIN OF THE MILITARY PUMA HELICOPTER AND I BELIEVE THIS DISCUS-SHAPED METAL PROJECTILE IS WHAT KILLED BRIGADIER JORDAN BY SLICING THROUGH HIS CAROTID ARTERY. IN TRIALS IT HAS BEEN DEMONSTATED THAT BY INSERTING IN THE MOUTH AND BY USING THE TONGUE ONE CAN ACTIVATE A HAIRPIN TRIGGER MECHANISM BY MOUTH AND A DEMONSTRATION HAS BEEN LAID ON TO DEMONSTRATE JUST HOW LETHAL IT IS. THE TOOLING OF THIS MECHANISM IS OF A VERY HIGH STANDARD. THEREFORE, FROM WORKING OUT WHERE PEOPLE WERE SEATED IN THE HELICOPTER I BELIEVE THAT IT WAS DR GRACHEV WHO WAS THE INTENDED TARGET BUT DUE TO BAD LUCK DUE TO SUDDEN TURBULENCE WITHIN THE HELICOPTER IT WAS BRIGADIER JORDAN WHO ENDED UP BEING KILLED.

Just then there was a sharp knock on Professor Lambton's office door before one of the security guards entered with a grave look upon his face and whispered something into his chief's ear. After remonstrating with the officer in a similarly whispered diatribe he briskly dismissed the unwelcome intruder and turned his attention back to Stryker and Carol. His face was ashen.

"I have just been informed by one of my security staff that both of you and that Russian fellow of yours, what's his name, Dr Grachev, are on the highest priority wanted list in this country. Orders are to shoot you on sight." He looked at Carol. "My own daughter, can you believe it!" Professor Lambton's face registered disbelief as if to reinforce his point. At this statement Stryker looked decidedly twitchy.

"Before you do anything drastic sir, may I make a telephone call to Sir Samuel Dogson? I have something very urgent to discuss with him. He's the…"

"I know precisely who the man is and that's the first sensible idea I've heard all day." Stryker was surprised by Professor Lambton's acquiescence to his suggestion. "But to reiterate what you yourself just said, before *you* do something drastic you might regret and in light of the unbelievable bombshell just delivered by my security contingent here at Porton Down, please remember that there are armed guards all around this location and they will fire if they must."

"But before I try to contact Sir Samuel Dogson for you, answer me this Stryker; what was the purpose of your coming to this place? Surely it wasn't because of this strange metal object was it?"

"No it wasn't. You'd never guess in a million years, and anyway it's too late now."

Professor Lambton looked very concerned for his daughter. "Tell me anyway, I insist."

"As I say, it is too late now, but it was for one reason and for one reason only – to seek temporary sanctuary – for both of us."

"Well, to use the American vernacular, I'd say that was a bad call."

CHAPTER 155

"Sanctuary! Sanctuary from what or from whom?" 'C' was glowering.

"I don't know. That's all I was told," replied Charles Kingdom, assistant controller of MI6.

"Well someone didn't attain what they were seeking did they?"

"No they didn't, not for long anyway, sir."

The enlarged photograph lying on 'C's' mahogany double pedestal desk showed two blooded bodies in grotesque postures, the woman's arms impossibly set behind her head as a puppeteer might carelessly discard a jointed mannequin with one incongruously undamaged elbow smeared with what looked like axel grease pointing through a ripped piece of clothing. Two sets of legs draped over the side of the blood-spattered vehicle; twisted, dented doors half hanging off their hinges. It was evident that the massive force of impact as the Land Rover had smashed into the concrete wall was one reason for such devastation. It was also obvious why the attitudes of their bodies were so distorted when on closer inspection of the photograph, the other reason became apparent – their shredded, bullet-riddled clothing. Many bullets must have been expended; spent shells lay around the vehicle like confetti. The woman's neck had obviously been nicked by one bullet having veered a few millimetres off course, resulting in a flap of her skin hanging just below the dark hair line. A wisp of blue smoke could also be seen curling lazily away from the jeep's wreckage, supplying a timeline and at that same moment acting as a precursor to the next instant's devastating explosion. The photograph had obviously been taken just seconds after the crash. That piece of visual information providing the reason as to why such a conflagration ensued.

"Have we any other photographs?"

"No, sir. That photograph on your desk was faxed through just a couple of minutes ago. I was told that the whole episode ended in a fireball just after the three fugitives had made a bolt for it."

"And what about the other body? There are only two bodies in this photograph, both with their backs toward the photographer. Was that also consumed in the conflagration that followed?"

"The other body you enquire about was thrown clear of the vehicle but had been shot twice through the back apparently. It was a male and surprisingly he survived – just! He is already on his way to the London Hospital by air ambulance. E.T.A. next ten minutes. And to pre-empt your next question, no sir, we do not know if it is Stryker or that Russian fellow. As you can see by this photograph it would appear that the young dead woman was Caroline Lambton."

"Mmm. Well, I'd better hotfoot it over to the hospital and see for myself if it is the Russian or the American Stryker who survived. You stay here and hold the fort. If there are any developments let me know A.S.A.P. It's been little more than a week since I issued my order to shoot on sight. Well at least we now know where they ended up. Mind you, choosing Porton Down – I mean that's a government establishment with armed guards. What were they thinking? What was their intention?"

"Quite so sir – what indeed? Alas, now we'll probably never know unless the one that's still alive pulls through."

'C' ignored this final remark from his second in command, striding from the rosewood-panelled office with a determined gait, dispensing with the usual formalities regarding his secretary by barking a couple of orders in quick secession before hastily entering his reserved high speed lift which at that moment stood awaiting his departure from the top floor of Vauxhall Cross.

CHAPTER 156

Arriving within the vicinity of East London's Whitechapel and being set down by an unmarked chauffeur-driven car, 'C' scurried up the steps of the extensive London Hospital where a burly armed plainclothes policemen was waiting to greet and escort the chief of MI6 into an elevator. Three floors later, after entering a ward in the private wing of the hospital, the boss of MI6 flashed his pass at two more large uniformed policemen who were also awaiting the arrival of the VIP, this time accompanied by a doctor clutching a small Gladstone bag and wearing a long white cotton coat as well as sporting the de rigueur stethoscope dangling from his neck, the three of them acting as a cordon sanitaire being stationed just outside the door to a single room. After being ushered inside by the doctor the secret service chief was pulled up sharp by the scene that met his eyes.

The sterile room was large and housed banks of electrical sockets; connections for oxygen supply, monitors on trolleys attached to bundles of coloured cables snaking along the length of one wall – the usual myriad of hospital paraphernalia which had been expected by 'C', but his attention had quickly been drawn to the focal point of the room's medical environ – a hospital bed and a visitor's chair beside it. What came as a surprise, though not totally unexpected, was the fact of just who occupied this bed with a white sheet pulled right up to their chin. It was not the face of the American Stryker but that of Dr Grachev, whose eyes were closed. The clear plastic tube from a suspended saline drip in close proximity to the bed snaked beneath the sheets and blankets covering the Russian scientist.

The medical man who had entered the room with 'C' was now dismissed without the VIP enquiring of him as to the patient's condition. That came as a complete surprise to the MD. The two policemen, having never entered the room they were guarding, remained just outside, the door itself being left slightly ajar within hailing distance should their services be required.

As the visitor took a few hesitant steps toward Dr Grachev's bed he lowered his head, listening to the patient's laboured breathing – it was irregular. A smile curled around the corners of 'C's' mouth. Suddenly he was alone with the one person he had been hunting for so long.

'C' reached out his arms and began tampering with the saline drip next to Dr Grachev's bed before his making what appeared to be a minor adjustment to the clear plastic tube. It was then that the smile which had lingered upon 'C's' face vanished completely as the other end of the plastic tube he had been holding fell from beneath the sheets and clattered onto the floor. It had not been connected to Dr Grachev – it was just tucked beneath the sheets to give that impression. But unbeknown to the chief of Britain's Secret Intelligence Service a tiny camera had been secreted amongst the various hospital monitors. 'C's' movements were being recorded; his every move relayed to an adjacent room.

A second later the room's door burst wide open and even as 'C' was in the throes of being enveloped in a bear-hug, for a fleeting moment and to his utter astonishment he had recognised just who was applying that vicelike grip to his body.

"I can hardly believe my eyes – so you're not dead!" he exclaimed in disbelief.

"Full marks for observation," drawled the soft American accent. "Yes, I'm very much alive and fit, as you can see," Stryker continued as he tightened his bear-hug grip around the region of his victim's chest, expelling the last vestiges of oxygen from 'C's' lungs, leaving him gagging for air."

CHAPTER 157

The hospital doctor who had followed Stryker into the room quickly rummaged through his leather Gladstone bag before producing a viciously long, sharp pointed needle, the 5cc syringe already attached, filled and ready to use. Without warning he tugged at 'C's' shirt exposing the flabby anaemic-looking stomach and with a practised eye inserted the needle, plunging it deep within the subcutaneous fat and thence into the flesh with considerable force before pressing down hard upon the plunger, expelling the contents from the glass vial. Very quickly, even before the recipient had time to reconstruct his facial expression from the shock of seeing a syringe being pushed deep into his belly, Stryker felt the weight of 'C's' body collapse in his arms. There also appeared a tiny bright red bead of blood where the needle had been withdrawn.

"It's only a fast acting sedative – same as I gave Dr Grachev at Porton Down, except that this dose is much less and should only keep him quiet for an hour or so." The doctor carefully replaced the syringe back into his Gladstone bag with the needle still attached and snapped the bag shut. Addressing Stryker, he said, "Hey, haven't I seen you somewhere before?"

"Yeah that's right. I was sitting alongside Brigadier Jordan when he was killed in that helicopter," replied Stryker. "And I recognise you too. You were one of his platoon training in the Brecon Beacons."

"Yes. I'm Sergeant Bell sir. And if I ever get my hands on the bastard who killed him…"

"I'm sure that goes for all your team."

"Ain't gonna quibble 'bout that," replied the soldier. Then gesturing to Dr Grachev, who had remained out for the count in his hospital bed, oblivious to the dramatic scenes played out only moments earlier concerning the chief of MI6, the soldier said, "My orders are to guard this geezer. Apparently he's a very important asset." He then let out a barely audible wolf whistle as a nurse wearing a surgical face mask entered in a blue and white uniform, wheeling a gurney with a folded sheet placed on top and positioned it next to Stryker, who was too preoccupied with holding the now comatose sagging figure of 'C' to notice the object of Sergeant Bell's desire. The intelligence chief was hoisted bodily off his feet by Stryker and placed upon the wheeled stretcher before unfolding and draping the supplied white sheet over 'C's' whole body, face and all, as if he was in the throes of being taken down to the morgue. Instead the gurney supporting 'C' was then wheeled by the nurse into the lift and his now not inconsiderable cortege of grey-suited escorts, including Sergeant Bell, once more carrying his Gladstone bag in the gurney's wake walked toward the helipad sited atop the hospital building. Five minutes later and all were aboard the waiting helicopter, its spinning rotor blades already beginning to cause a powerful downdraught. It was a tight squeeze with the gurney taking up a lot of the space but even so, although there were eight chattering people now crammed into the fuselage Stryker could hear the whirl of helicopter blades and was aware of the sensation of lift off as they began to sway in the crosswinds. Stryker made his way through the group of people to speak to the pilot.

"How long will this take?"

"Not long at all, sir. We should be there very soon now. However it's best if you remain at the back with the others until we've landed."

"And just to refresh my memory, what's the destination we're headed for again?"

"You're Stryker, aren't you?"

"Yeah, that's right. How did you... aw, of course it's my accent."

There was no lightening up of the pilot's mood as he ignored Stryker's attempt to glean information, saying, "Well I regret to inform you that I have been fully briefed on this mission and have also been given to understand that because of state security you are not one of those persons to whom our destination is to be divulged because – well – you're an American. But as I say, we should be there very soon now."

Stryker gave a wry smile and left it at that.

***

By the time Stryker had taken in the myriad quilted patchwork of greens associated with the English countryside and worked out where the famous landmarks were from what he remembered of his previous visit to England, he figured they were headed due south. A quick glance at the pilot's controls confirmed this fact. The helicopter was already preparing for touchdown as a large ivy clad mansion with crenelated battlements came into view, and they were landing on its manicured lawn the size of several football pitches. Wide stone steps led up to the impregnable granite turreted building. A small reception committee had already been assembled to meet the helicopter which had landed some distance away. As the gurney supporting the body of 'C' held tight by strong leather straps was in the process of being gingerly offloaded with the nurse and army medic who supplied the sedative in attendance, a tall, imposing figure with a clipboard beneath his arm broke away from the coterie of assembled people and striding across the grass toward Stryker, proffered his hand.

"I am Sir Samuel Dogson. Pleased to meet you again. I believe we saw one another at 'C's' place, do you remember? It was at that late night Joint Intelligence Committee meeting set up to discuss that Russian fellow Dr Grachev's request for political asylum. You sat at the back of the room in the shadows attempting to look inconspicuous."

"Well my ploy patently failed miserably," the American replied, smiling broadly.

"Anyway, let's not beat about the bush. That telephone call of yours made from Porton Down, I don't mind telling you it was explosive. Anyway, it's still early. We'll discuss it in some detail later."

Stryker carefully examined the smooth white-complexioned face of the man he remembered 'C' making the butt of a joke for his audience at Sir Samuel Dogson's expense. Stryker also remembered how all those months ago at that meeting in Berkshire the Foreign Office mandarin Sir Samuel Dogson had worn what appeared to be a similar pinstriped suit to the one he wore now and the sober-looking tie fastened with that small tight knot also looked the same – to Stryker's mind a creature of habit. He also remembered those tight anaemic features, as tight as his knotted tie.

Sir Samuel Dogson turned his back on Stryker to gaze at the silhouette of the imposing building just as the sun was in the throes of settling down behind it, creating a stunningly evocative contre-jour – the civil servant's skin stretched taught, parchment-like, reflecting the vermilion blush of the fiery red sinking orb.

"It's like something out of a children's three dimensional pop-up picture book isn't it? A child's fairy tale if you like. Except you see, in this particular building," he nodded toward the looming heavy structure, "we do not sanction fairy tales, though we might be the architect of a few ourselves. We've heard lots of them here you know. But nothing that's stood the test of time." Here there was a heavy sigh. "And now the time has come to take you into my confidence. For a start, I suppose you want to know what this place is used for. I call it Bleak House as I am something of a Charles Dickens fan, though I suppose it's really a mansion. By the way, I should congratulate you on your carrying out the instructions given you earlier by Professor Lambton. You did a marvellous job in conjunction with Sergeant Bell, subduing and placing Dr Grachev on that stretcher. It all went off very smoothly without any fuss I hear – thanks to you. So now I'd like to introduce myself properly and explain just who I really am and what this is all about."

Stryker had come to a halt on the well-manicured lawn beside Sir Samuel Dogson in front of the wide expanse of steps leading up to the great house, his head inclined, not wishing to miss a snippet of this man's conversation now that he was about to be taken into Sir Samuel Dogson's confidence, the American detective having already expounded upon his own theories during the telephone conversation he had with him earlier.

"But before I spill the beans, as you Americans might say, would you please sign this piece of paper? Security, you understand." Stryker accepted the proffered clipboard together with a ballpoint pen. He had noticed moments earlier that the black clipboard clutched tightly beneath the arm of his perceived co-conspirator held an official-looking document, the closely typed screed was on expensive stiff cream linen paper with a black portcullis design. Its motif, centred along the top edge, was used by various government departments. "As you can see by the first paragraph, it is so that you could – indeed would be prosecuted – if anything I am about to reveal should be divulged by you to anyone. And if you are thinking of blabbing out our secrets in court, well I must disappoint you for any proceedings would be held in camera. Sorry old chum, but I'm sure it won't come to that." This unexpected warning was followed by a cold smile, intimating that he was very serious.

After quickly scrutinising and signing the official document with a flourish Stryker handed it back to Sir Samuel Dogson with baited breath, anxious to learn what secrets were about to be revealed.

"Thank you. Now down to business. It is true as was intimated at that late night meeting held at 'C's' house in Berkshire that I am a senior member of the Civil Service working for the FCO. But what neither you nor anyone else at that meeting was informed of is that I also represent one particular section of a certain organisation. An exclusive ultra-secret section of which you will not have heard, so I shall spare you the boredom of going into details, suffice it to say that geographically not a stoncs' throw away from MI6 resides the headquarters and Director-General of MI5, that is to say – Britain's COUNTER ESPIONAGE. As I straddle both camps with multifarious functions in both, you might describe me as a spy-catcher of sorts with an overall bird's-eye view of various departments, taking on a somewhat quasi-judicial role as chief interrogator in a shapeless penumbra of spies and intelligence... and this building you see before you is used as the headquarters and holding facility for this small secret section, of which I am the prime mover. Truth to tell, it is in some ways an organisation that is totally divorced from both MI5 and MI6. Yes there is parliament's intelligence oversight committee of course, but I like to say that we here have the real answer to that age old question – who watches the watchers? And the answer of course is: We do!" Here he gave a little chuckle. "The persuasive stuff is carried out in our deep, rather isolated subterranean vault – no screams can be heard from down there in the bowels of the earth." Stryker furrowed his brow.

"I will have my little joke. Ours, as I say, is an ultra-top secret section operating within MI5, commissioned to keep an eye on MI6 with the sole remit of locating and rooting out traitors or double agents working for Foreign Intelligence Agencies against Britain's interests and all that that entails. Unfortunately, sad to say, that sometimes includes British spies. This section I oversee was created by my predecessors four times removed in the 1960s after the disaster of the infamous 'Cambridge Five' debacle came to light, of which I expect you have been made aware on your induction into MI6. These traitors were recruited from the British Establishment and spied for Russia. They were drawn from within the top echelons of the Foreign Office and the British Intelligence services. There was Kim Philby – who became at one point MI6 bureau chief at the British Embassy in Washington, acting in liaison with the CIA. Then there was Guy Burgess; Sir Anthony Blunt – Professor of History of Art at University of London and Director of the Courtauld Institute of Art and one time Surveyor of the Queen's pictures; Donald Maclean and of course John Cairncross. Together they did almost unimaginable and incalculable damage to this country and probably to your own country America as well. They have almost certainly cost thousands of lives of men and women striving for a safer world in the name of democracy. We ourselves have a far greater understanding of just what damage these despicable people did to this country and to our allies but have foresworn to hold our tongues for certain long term operational reasons – even after all this time. We see that as being prudent." To reinforce his point Sir Samuel Dogson gave Stryker a long look.

Stryker nodded. "You say your secret section has been commissioned to keep an eye on MI6. But just who exactly is the commissioning agent? Surely the problem is that if you are self-appointed for the good of society then where is the democracy in that? In the final analysis, who is the electorate and whoever they are, like any self-respecting members of that electorate, aren't there self-interests to be taken into account, sir?"

"Look here Stryker, let's not get philosophical. And this is no time to be clever. I don't want to veer off course and be drawn into some deep discussion on the finer points of democracy at this stage of the game; so instead, let us recapitulate. Thanks to Professor Lambton, Carol's father and come to that, with your own help too, Stryker, this Russian scientist Dr Grachev has been held incommunicado at Porton Down for the past few weeks. And we can both agree that because of his incarceration within the confines of the secure top-secret Biological Warfare establishment at Porton Down we have managed, I emphasise here *without* the knowledge of the head of MI6, or better known as 'C' for the initiated to interrogate and debrief Dr Grachev about his top secret Research & Development (R&D) work carried out in Russia on Biological Weapons of mass destruction. We have also discovered that after the accident with the sunken vessel in the waters off Dubai the Russian scientist Dr Grachev had been put on board another vessel known as 'the mothership'," – here Sir Samuel Dogson wagged his fingers in the air in an attempt to indicate quotation marks – "to advise on the safe containment and transportation of drums containing biological weapons grade viruses which is how he – Dr Grachev – came to know about that map grid reference location he so cryptically gave us when attempting to gain our attention and credibility for the purpose of his being granted political asylum. And it was also on this same mothership as it happens that Dr Grachev saw your two friends from the SBS meet their harrowing end. I was sorry to hear about that Stryker." Stryker slowly nodded his head in a solemn manner.

Sir Samuel Dogson then glanced in Stryker's direction to make sure he had his full attention before carrying on. "This move of keeping 'C' out of the loop had been decided upon because of something Dr Grachev had confided to you in the back of that Land Rover being driven by Carol. Is that not so Stryker?"

Stryker nodded his head once more. "Yes. It was something so incredulous that at first I found it hard to believe. But I briefly explained the situation to you in that telephone call I made from Porton Down."

"Yes, as you say, you found what you were being told by Dr Grachev hard to believe. Well, that's understandable. You said Dr Grachev told you that he had witnessed a mysterious foreigner in the Kremlin two years ago being given VIP treatment by two army officers who Dr Grachev recognised as both belonging to Military Intelligence. Then a little while later Dr Grachev had been informed, off the cuff as it happens by a General Kovalyev, I hasten to add, another member of the Russian GRU Military Intelligence, that this man seen being given a lot of attention was in fact none other than a British citizen and one of Russia's top agents who the general believed was ultimately destined to join the secret elite of Russia's Great Illegals. So once you and Carol had fortuitously, without any prior arrangement with her father Professor Lambton I might add, arrived at Porton Down with Dr Grachev in tow seeking sanctuary for him, and because of this intelligence regarding an English spy, we arranged for the three of you i.e. Dr Grachev, Carol and yourself, to ostensibly go missing for two weeks for your own protection, letting interested parties assume that you were still on the run whilst in actual fact of course, at the same time as 'C's' cohorts were scouring the streets for the three of you with a death sentence hanging over your heads, Dr Grachev was in fact being successfully debriefed at Porton Down as I have said. We have suspected for ages that there was a traitor in our camp – someone spying for Russia who was deeply embedded within MI6, but of course the problem was, we did not know the name of that traitor, though we had our suspicions."

Sir Samuel Dogson paused to let Stryker take in the fact that the British security services had known all along that there was a top level spy operating somewhere in their midst. "So thanks to Dr Grachev informing you of his seeing this British spy not only in the Kremlin but also recently having set eyes upon him at Harlech castle, Dr Grachev had unwittingly confirmed our suspicion. I think that is a fair summation of events so far don't you?"

"Yes, very fair," replied Stryker, rather bemused on hearing the facts laid out in so forensic a manner.

"Anyhow, a scheme was then hatched to give the impression that both Caroline Lambton and one of her two male accomplices – that of either yourself or Dr Grachev – had been shot whilst attempting to escape from Porton Down, Britain's centre for research into chemical and biological warfare. Don't forget, this was all done for 'C's' benefit. So 'C', having been supplied with photographic evidence purporting to show Caroline Lambton and a colleague shot, unaware that the shootings had been set up and photographed by the Ministry of Defence's special effects department and fortuitously, I might add, being aided by the fact that Caroline Lambton was double jointed, thus ably injecting a note of realism into the said photograph by giving the dramatic impression of her arms having been broken, the question now posed was: had it been you or the Russian Dr Grachev who had been shot dead as there was only one male body on display in that photograph and the face was not visible from the angle from which the photograph had been taken? That answer had been purposefully left hanging in the air for 'C' to ruminate upon. Whose body survived the shootout: Was it Dr Grachev's or that of the American detective Stryker? That was the question."

"Go on. I'm with you so far," Stryker interjected.

"Well this charade was played out as realistically as possible, as I say, so as to lure 'C' to the London Hospital, chosen because of it containing a helipad on its roof, therefore making it ideal for a swift transit to this imposing place whose lawns we now stand upon. Thus 'C' was put in a position where he might compromise himself and he took the bait laid out before him – namely Dr Grachev, who had been sedated – against his will unfortunately but for his own protection – for the ruse to work, which I must say it did admirably. The end result of this ploy being that we now have a pin sharp video film of 'C' tampering with Dr Grachev's hospital equipment, another item to confront 'C' with during his forthcoming interrogation. And the reason for Dr Grachev himself being sedated was just in case he became nervous and unwittingly gave the game away. After all, he is not an actor and he knew that 'C' might very well have wanted him dead because of possibly having recognised him in Moscow. Is that not the case Stryker?"

"Yes sir, I'm afraid it is. Dr Grachev has since confided in me that he felt it had been expedient for him to use a pseudonym when seeking political asylum in Britain so as to protect himself from being exposed as a traitor to Russia for the perceived crime of seeking this political asylum. So he had adopted the name 'RED CHAMELEON' when contacting the British authorities in London because of this English spy he'd seen in Moscow and of his recent sighting of this same man again in Wales, thus confirming Dr Grachev's clever foresight of adopting such a nom de plume. You see, this Englishman witnessed by Dr Grachev receiving VIP treatment in the Kremlin because of his spying for the Russians might possibly have remembered seeing Dr Grachev's face in the Kremlin, and fearing that his cover might be blown, thus identifying 'C' to the British authorities as spying for the Russians. Therefore this English spy might conceivably have been in a position to have Dr Grachev killed if Dr Grachev had not used his wits to protect himself when seeking asylum by acting cautiously. Either way, my letter to Dr Grachev, which he said he found at his rented Harley Street Clinic, just confirmed his suspicions about being targeted for assassination by Britain's Secret Intelligence Service."

Sir Samuel Dogson took up the theme. "Yes. Carol told me that you warned Dr Grachev of dire consequences if he remained in Britain. You told Carol that you had informed Dr Grachev of this fact in a letter to him and that you had also bought Dr Grachev an airline ticket for travelling to a safe house in Switzerland."

"She told you that?"

"Well our scientist never took up your offer anyhow, so not any harm done there."

"No harm done? I thought I could trust Carol so I would disagree with you."

"Look. I understand you thought there was an injustice being committed to Dr Grachev and you hoped to save his life the way Carol tells the story, which is a commendable attitude and as I say, no harm done. As far as Carol is concerned, do not be too hard on her for she is working for us."

"Us! Who do you mean by us?"

"Carol was enticed into working for our secret section at the behest of her father Professor Lambton, who I should say is not only a top flight scientist but also a top-ranking member of MI5, one of its leading lights in fact. I'll give you an example of just how astute he is. Whilst reading a translation of a Russian scientific paper Professor Lambton came across one article by Dr Grachev and realised that key theoretical elements of this Russian scientist's research work on cutting edge virus technology had emanated from Professor Lambton's very own research carried out at Porton Down a year or so earlier – plagiarism in other words. Which meant someone was passing our secrets on to the Russians, which therefore meant that we had a spy in our midst, something we had suspected for some time. Then because you, Stryker, had been on holiday – proverbially in the wrong place at the wrong time, namely Dubai – Professor Lambton saw this as a golden opportunity for you to be involved as an unwitting protector for his daughter Carol. I put my hand up and confess that it was no accident that Carol was assigned to lure you into helping with hunting the Red Chameleon. Mea culpa! It was also at the behest of Carol on the suggestion of her father that you should act as a 'cut out', seeing as you were opportunely on the scene and had no background relating to spying activities as far as the Russians were concerned so you were not on their radar. The idea was for you to collect secret information in a Moscow suburb from that Russian Ivanovich Sobolev, who was in fact working as a spy for the British – though you were not alerted to this fact at the time – all in the hope of uncovering this mysterious MI6 traitor who had passed so many of Britain's secrets to the Russians out into the open. Brenda from Registry…"

"Don't tell me that she was also involved. "

"As I was going to say, unbeknown to MI6 Brenda was also covertly working for our section when she was killed, having been requested by Professor Lambton to help his daughter Carol as much as possible. Unfortunately Brenda must have got too close to the truth."

"Poor Brenda!"

"Yes, as you say, poor Brenda."

CHAPTER 158

The room could have come straight out of one of the renowned Czech writer Franz Kafka's novels inculcating a nightmarish feeling of mind-bending alienation, vulnerability and loneliness. It was situated in the basement of 'Bleak House' and was propped up on some sort of cleverly concealed structure, lending an unreal feeling of being entombed as if in a cloud of nothingness designed to disorientate the mind. Through the padded walls a soft, indistinct voice could be heard, picked up from several concealed microphones and relayed to a more comfortable setting within the room next door.

"What's he mumbling for?" It was Stryker who put the question to Sir Samuel Dogson, couched in disparaging terms of disdain as he adjusted his not inconsiderable weight in a high-backed black leather swivel desk chair.

"If you listen carefully you will recognise it is 'C's' voice that you hear. He has just been revived from his sedation administered at the London Hospital in Whitechapel less than an hour ago." There was a hint in Sir Samuel Dogson's voice of having been here before; a certain world weariness of witnessing such a scenario. "Once he is revived he will be given a psychoactive truth drug administered by injection – you may have heard of it, sodium thiopental. Then he will be read his rights by one of our chaps from Special Branch."

"Rights?" exclaimed Stryker.

"Yes, rights! Basically he does not have any," replied Sir Samuel drily, putting an emphasis on the word 'not'. After a few moments another voice broke into the silence from the adjacent room. It was a soft female voice and it had a coaxing tone to it, the concealed speakers within the padded walls picking up every nuance.

"Everything is going to feel very relaxed – you are very relaxed. How are you feeling now?"

"I am very relaxed," 'C's' voice responded, clear as a bell.

Sir Samuel Dogson looked at Stryker and winked. "The sodium pentothal is kicking in now. This will take a little while so bear with me. In the meantime I'd like to discuss your earlier telephone call regarding that so-called British agent working for the Russians. After all, that's why we're both here isn't it Stryker, to help us clear up this whole sorry state of affairs. And don't worry, nobody can hear you in this room down here in the basement – nobody. This conversation is strictly between you and me. And you have carte blanche to voice your opinions freely and frankly."

"Of course I understand and thank you. Well to kick off, may I ask you a pertinent question first Sir Dogson? Have you shown Dr Grachev any photographs of 'C' yet, so as to verify his identification? After all, everything hinges on Dr Grachev having seen this British man in Moscow as he so adamantly states."

"Well, no – no I haven't as a matter of fact. But hopefully one of my colleagues is at this very moment arranging for transportation to view what to those from the archive section of Five and Six refer to as the rogues' gallery – that is, a selection of photos which are categorised as ultra-secret, which reminds me, I have had you reinstated as a bona fide Six operative." That statement came out of the blue and not a little shocked, Stryker responded accordingly.

"That's a surprise – when did that happen?"

"I gave orders that it was to be actioned the moment we had 'C' incarcerated down here in this basement and to obtain your clearance I vouchsafed for your integrity, so don't let me down Stryker." Here Sir Samuel Dogson gave Stryker a piercing look as though looking into his soul. "I thought you should be reinstated, seeing as you were and still are an integral part of this operation, which brings us full circle to that telephone call you put through to me from Porton Down."

"Well, I should by rights now be supplying you with details of what I hinted at in that telephone conversation we had. It was something which came straight from Dr Grachev's lips just before we vacated that army helicopter in North Wales and he can confirm the conversation verbatim for you later if necessary."

"Go on." Sir Samuel Dogson's face at that moment bore a broad smile mixed with curiosity.

"It apparently concerned a foreigner Dr Grachev said he had spotted two years previously at the Kremlin in Moscow. It was an English man whom Dr Grachev said he saw climbing into the rear of a black Zil with blacked out windows being escorted by a couple of men who Dr Grachev said he recognised as belonging to Russian Military Intelligence. Just minutes after witnessing this English man and his two cohorts speeding off, Dr Grachev, who as you undoubtedly know is a Russian scientist and biological weapons expert – well that's how he came to know these military figures – who had been informed by General Kovalyev, another member of the Russian GRU Military Intelligence, who works for the Fifteenth Directorate under the auspices of the Russian Ministry of Defence, said that this Britisher – that's what he called him, 'Britisher' – said that this VIP was a British spymaster. General Kovalyev told Dr Grachev that one day this man was destined to join the secret elite of Russia's Great Illegals. I must admit that phrase threw me."

"Stryker, in this Russian context Great Illegals is axiomatic for spies."

"Well anyway, Dr Grachev had been warned not to speak of seeing this man. It was, as the general had informed him, a state secret and to forget what he had seen."

"That doesn't surprise me at all." Sir Samuel Dogson fell silent for a while then carried on by playing devil's advocate.

"Who would you say Dr Grachev had been referring to? A British man was mentioned. And he was described as a spymaster. I think that could only point to 'C'. What do you think?"

"Yes, but the problem here is the fact that a member of the Russian GRU Military Intelligence also described him as a spy. As you just said so yourself, sir, Great Illegals is axiomatic for spies, no?"

"Yes Stryker, that is correct. So we have a big problem here, n'est pas?"

"Well to me the whole thing sounds fantastic! Maybe Dr Grachev is a plant – sent here by the Russian FSB to sow disinformation."

"Well of course, that must always be borne in mind as a possibility, but there again…" Sir Samuel Dogson's thoughts trailed off. Silence reigned supreme for a few moments before it was broken once more, this time by a sharp buzzing sound. "That'll be relating to those photographs I spoke of. Just give me a minute, Stryker." Sir Samuel Dogson spoke briefly into an intercom and without waiting for a response pressed another bell-push, this time it was a large brass one. Almost straight away loud voices could be heard in the hallway and then a door closed with a loud bang.

"Whilst you and I were discussing the possibility of 'C' spying for the Russians a little earlier, I had already arranged for the speakers in the next room to be switched off in here so that we could not hear what questions our interrogators were asking 'C'. It was for your benefit really old boy – secrecy and all that – and it seems that we have hit the jackpot. Apparently sodium pentothal has eased our chum's tongue. 'C' now admits to his spying activities on behalf of the Russians over several decades."

"Well you certainly don't hang about do you? Congratulations."

"No Stryker my friend, it is not quite as simple as that. You see, although 'C' admits to spying for the Russians as a double agent he is adamant that he was not in Moscow two years ago when Dr Grachev swears that he saw him there with his own eyes being treated as a VIP. This makes Dr Grachev's statement tantamount to a lie."

"Or does it, sir?"

"How do you mean Stryker?"

"Well, either 'C' is not telling the truth, even under the drug sodium pentothal for whatever reason, for let's face it this so-called truth drug sodium pentothal is not infallible is it? Or conversely, as you say, Dr Grachev himself is lying. There again, why should 'C' lie when he has already admitted to spying for the Russians? What is there to be gained? What could be worse than betraying one's own country?"

"I think we'll wait till we get a definitive decision on Dr Grachev's photo recognition of our British spy before we become tangled up in half-baked theories and fly off at all sorts of acute tangents. And as for the drug sodium pentothal not being infallible, well that is true of course. This so-called truth serum has on many occasions been used by the CIA, and not always to good effect I might add. There again we, or I should say your countrymen in America, have used it against Al-Qaeda with varying degrees of success so it is not to be dismissed out of hand as something totally unreliable.

"Anyhow, we'll let Dr Grachev take a look at our rogues' gallery now. He might be able to visually identify this British man who General Kovalyev informed him in Moscow is working for the Russians. You never know! It's a risk of course, showing him classified photographs of many of our current operatives, though we shall obviously insert many random photographs of nobody in particular, just in order to muddy the waters you understand. Might shake a few apples off the tree at the same time eh! Just excuse me for a moment Stryker." Sir Samuel Dogson now being fixated upon this idea, pressed a small button adjacent to the main door they had entered and a moment later disappeared through another more inconspicuous soundproof door leading into a short passageway. A few minutes later he returned.

"Grab your jacket Stryker; we're driving down to Whitehall to meet your friend Dr Grachev. Mind you, it's the beginning of the weekend so it might be rather crowded around that neck of the woods." As they swiftly vacated the large crenelated building set in its own grounds with 'C' locked up in its fortified basement sleeping off the effects of the truth drug sodium pentothal, the full ramifications of 'C's' recent confession of spying for the Russians to a grim-faced Sir Samuel Dogson was just beginning to hit home.

***

As Stryker settled down beside Sir Samuel Dogson into the comfortable leather upholstered seating of a large limousine mulling over the events of the past few days the chauffeur himself was not looking forward to the round trip of just over three hundred miles from the government car pool situated at Westminster. Sir Samuel Dogson on the other hand, was mindful of the questions to be put to Dr Grachev and was running through these in his mind as he opened up the polished Burr Walnut faced mirrored interior of the drinks cabinet and poured Stryker and himself a large shot of whisky before leaning sideways toward his companion, and without preamble began speaking of 'C's' confession in a conspiratorial manner.

"What's so baffling Stryker, is the fact that although 'C' has confessed to spying for the Russians, he categorically denies having been in Moscow at the time Dr Grachev said he saw him there. He was in fact in a London hospital having a minor operation and I have incontrovertible proof, certainly in this instance anyway, that he is telling the truth. I've seen the paperwork with my own eyes that prove it. Anyhow, for the time being 'C' will be put back in his house 'St. Kildare'. We're quickly getting some covert listening equipment installed in the different rooms there before that so as to monitor possible conversations that might take place between 'C' and any visitors he might have. Just on the off chance."

CHAPTER 159

Whitehall was crowded with traffic as well as thousands of tourists as they gingerly stepped between the lines of buses, taxis and cars of every description including cyclists and motorcyclists passing the cenotaph, a seething swarm of humanity all heading toward Trafalgar Square for some well publicised pop concert by a world renowned band. There was so much traffic that little notice was taken by the countless pedestrians of a long grey limousine as it slewed to a halt outside the War Office, discharging its cargo of expected passengers, seemingly oblivious to all the hustle and bustle of one of the greatest cities on Earth. It was an unseasonably warm afternoon for the time of year as Dr Grachev stood sandwiched between two burly plainclothes policemen on the worn steps of the large building, and looked very relieved when he recognised the familiar face of Stryker striding toward him. The formalities of introductions were quickly dispensed with as the tall statesman-like figure of Sir Samuel Dogson, Dr Grachev and the American Stryker following up behind quickly made their way inside the impressive white-stone building.

The room into which Dr Grachev and his two would-be interrogators had been ushered by two middle-aged Special Brach officers, one standing outside the door and the other inside the room, gave the lie to the outwardly grandiose architectural features depicted on such an imposing monumental structure, this minor room's interior being devoid of even the barest decoration. It contained three incongruously well-worn, green, high-backed cracked leather upholstered desk chairs and a large wooden trestle table, obviously borrowed for its utilitarian use as opposed to any aesthetic purpose, taking up most of the room's space and upon which lay a scattered assortment of various sized photograph albums and next to these a small pile of loose photographs. Stryker and Dr Grachev sat down on one side of the table opposite the spare figure of Sir Samuel Dogson. They were immediately offered tea by one of the Special Branch policemen and swiftly declined with a gracious 'no thank you' by Sir Samuel Dogson on behalf of the other two, before embarking on their gargantuan task of sifting through these hundreds of photos, searching for the phantom face pointed out to Dr Grachev in the Kremlin two years previously by General Kovalyev of Russian GRU Military Intelligence as being that of the British spymaster. Two pairs of eyes were now firmly fixed upon Dr Grachev's face, seeking the merest glimmer of recognition as their would-be Russian asylum seeker immediately removed the loose pile of photographs from the table, before shuffling them as a card sharp might manipulate cards to perform a sleight of hand trick, scanning them one after the other at breakneck speed. Sir Samuel Dogson uttered in a loud voice, "Slow down," though Dr Grachev ignored his exhortation as he carried on quickly shuffling and scanning the faces as though he had not heard. Shuffling and scanning, shuffling and scanning appeared to be the order of the day.

"No. No. No. No…"

Stryker glanced at Sir Samuel Dogson and whispered, "If we carry on like this we should be done within half an hour. Did you explain to him that should he recognise any face…?"

"Stryker, I have carried out this procedure many, many times. Please, I know precisely what I am doing and Dr Grachev has already been briefed as to what, and more pertinently who, he should be looking for."

"No. No. No. No…" Dr Grachev rattled off in negative terms like sporadic machine gun fire. His fingers worked swiftly through the now diminishing pile of loose photographs before pausing at one of them before assiduously carrying on with the search.

"No. No. No. No…"

Stryker got up from the table and walked behind Dr Grachev before placing his hand upon the doctor's shoulder. "Hold it! Hold it! That photograph you stopped at for a moment, did you recognise it?" the detective enquired, looking at Sir Samuel Dogson. Sir Samuel Dogson licked his lips as he lifted the photograph recently discarded from the pile.

"Well Dr Grachev, answer Stryker's question. Do you recognise the person in this particular photograph?" It was a photograph depicting a short, white-haired, very English-looking elderly gentleman strolling through one of London's parks – St. James's – with the sun shining on the Queen Victoria Memorial in the background, the man concerned seemingly oblivious to the fact that the photograph was being taken. There was a moment's silence before Dr Grachev responded with an answer which took the wind out of Sir Samuel Dogson's sails.

"Why, of course I recognised him – that's 'C' I believe, that's what I heard one of the soldiers call him in North Wales."

"Are you sure you recognise him?" There was a hint of cautious jubilation mixed with sadness in Sir Samuel Dogson's voice.

"Recognise him? Why, as I told you he is the man in Harlech, North Wales who knew I was using the cover name the Red Chameleon. He said so to my face. He was giving orders to two motorcyclists dressed in black leathers."

Stryker lowered his head and whispered into Sir Samuel Dogson's ear: "One of those motorcyclists he's referring to in North Wales was me. He's telling the truth."

Sir Samuel Dogson imperceptibly leant toward Dr Grachev, making eye contact. "And you can definitely say that he is the man described to you by General Kovalyev in the Kremlin as the British spymaster?"

Dr Grachev gave Sir Samuel Dogson a withering look. "What? Of course he's not the man I had pointed out to me in the Kremlin. Are you crazy? I know who I saw in the Kremlin and it wasn't this man 'C'."

Sir Samuel Dogson glanced over at Stryker then looked back at Dr Grachev before pulling one of the thick photograph albums toward him. "It's not my day is it Stryker."

"No Sir Samuel, I'm afraid it seems not."

"I'm sorry if I have not been of any help so far," Dr Grachev responded, looking downcast as he began turning the heavily embossed cover of the first tome just pushed towards him; the first of twelve books containing a voluminous series of British secret agents' portraits.

Sir Samuel Dogson turned to Stryker and whispered, "I had to pull a lot of strings behind the scenes so that we could get this series of highly restricted photograph albums featuring the rogues' gallery delivered over here. It seems as though it might all have been a waste of time."

Each photograph album was then carefully gone through until finally, one and a half hours later the last one was scoured. Dr Grachev finally gave his verdict. "No, the face I saw in the Kremlin was not in any of those albums. Sorry."

The silence was palpable as Sir Samuel Dogson and Stryker sat looking at one another before turning their heads towards Dr Grachev. Sir Samuel Dogson could hardly believe his ears. He had been told by Dr Grachev that the man he had seen in the Kremlin was the chief of the British Security Services. That could only be 'C'. What had gone wrong? It should have been a cut and dried case. It did not make sense.

Whilst Dr Grachev stood up and had a word with one of the Special Branch policemen Stryker appeared to be able to read Sir Samuel Dogson's thoughts by quietly enunciating them for him: "So who was the foreigner Dr Grachev had seen described to him as one of Russia's top spies embedded within the British Secret Service? Was 'C' the double agent? And if it was 'C', had Dr Grachev for some inexplicable reason changed his mind in pointing the finger at him by denying that he was the man described as Russia's top agent? Or was it someone else Dr Grachev had seen in the Kremlin and was now trying to protect, and if it was someone else – who was it?"

As Stryker finished giving his whispered summary Sir Samuel broke into his thoughts: "Did you hear what I just said Stryker? Where's Dr Grachev?"

The Special Branch policemen who Dr Grachev had spoken to just a minute before answered, "He has just slipped out to the toilet, sir."

There were many toilets on the seven floors within the enormous white-stone building so Stryker, closely followed by Sir Samuel Dogson, ran to the nearest one pointed out by the SB officer being situated on the same floor as they were standing, but as they entered shouting Dr Grachev's name it was obvious it was empty, leaving them no option but to search through at least a couple more floors just to make sure, for even on a weekend it was just possible that many of the toilets had been engaged, being used by other staff working unsocial hours. They knew they were grasping at straws but there was no choice. Being a Saturday afternoon the interminable corridors of the building they occupied were eerily silent. By the time Stryker and Sir Samuel Dogson had reached the third floor, forsaking the high speed lift, instead running, taking two steps at a time as they constantly called his name and crashing into doors opening into cubicles, their gut instinct told them it was pointless. They both dashed outside and from the steps of the War Office looked up and down Whitehall, scanning the faces of thousands of people still making their way up towards Trafalgar Square but it was a futile task and they knew they had lost him.

Sir Samuel Dogson was doubled up with both hands on his knees catching his breath when his mobile phone began ringing briefly. Then it stopped before he had a chance to answer it.

"Bloody telephones! I've no doubt whoever it is will try again. Anyhow, there's something much more important than that I should tell you with regard to 'C'. Because of my suspicions that he's not told us all that he could do about himself Stryker, I have persuaded his lifelong friend, a Dr Kenneth Jones, that he might act as an emissary for MI6 by paying 'C' a visit on the basis of his being a good friend and by appealing to his long association with the academic don…"

"…With a view to breaking down 'C's' resolve of holding back certain details of his spying activities, including the most important detail of all – the name of his controller! Yes sir, I'm with you there." Just then Sir Samuel Dogson's mobile phone began ringing once more. This time he managed to answer it in time and spoke for a couple of minutes in a low voice before switching it off.

"How's that for timing? That was one of our watchers. It's also very unfortunate. He says that Dr Kenneth Jones has gone to visit 'C' a day earlier than I had anticipated so that our chaps from Five have not had time to secrete and install all the recording equipment in 'C's' house."

As he was speaking to Stryker, Sir Samuel Dogson tapped him on the shoulder. "That's your phone."

Stryker slid his large hand into his jacket pocket and pulled out his own mobile telephone. "Hello. Stryker speaking. Dr Grachev?" The call was rather indistinct, the conversation being carried on for another couple of minutes before Stryker was heard to say "Hold on."

"That was Dr Grachev. He's at Harrods. I told him to hold on."

"What? What's he doing there?"

"He said that just as he was leaving the Ministry toilet to get some fresh air in Whitehall and stretch his legs for a few minutes after being cooped up with us in that room for so long, he suddenly saw the same person whose face the three of us had been futilely scouring for in the photographs coming out from those same toilets that Dr Grachev was just entering. The same man he had last set eyes upon in North Wales and before that at the Kremlin in Moscow. He said it was this man who had been described to him as the British spymaster by General Kovalyev. On the spur of the moment Dr Grachev said he had decided to follow his quarry by jumping into a passing taxi, asking the driver to follow the man who had himself just climbed into an old black car which made its way through Green Park to Kensington and only minutes later, after seeing the car with the man he was following stop, the man got out and entered Harrods, with Dr Grachev hot on his heels. Apparently it was a little while later that he saw the man again, this time buying some expensive cigarettes – Russian Black Sobranie. Then he lost sight of him."

Sir Samuel Dogson grabbed Stryker's mobile telephone and shouted into it: "Dr Grachev, this is Sir Samuel Dogson. Stay where you are and wait for us. We'll be there as soon as possible." Sir Samuel Dogson turned to Stryker. "He says he will be waiting for us outside Harrods."

***

Within ten minutes of speaking to Dr Grachev by phone, Stryker and Sir Samuel Dogson were climbing out of the limousine they had at their disposal and almost bumped into Dr Grachev on the pavement waiting impatiently for them.

"The man I saw in the Kremlin left Harrods maybe twenty minutes ago and that's when I lost sight of him in the crowd," Dr Grachev said in response to seeing Sir Samuel Dogson and Stryker.

"And where's this man's car?" Stryker enquired, looking around for any sign of a black car.

"It's gone!" Dr Grachev replied sheepishly.

As they scoured the hundreds of faces walking past Harrods department store, hoping for Dr Grachev to spot the man he had set eyes upon only minutes earlier, Sir Samuel Dogson's mobile telephone rang once more, this time the telephone call having been paged through from the covert surveillance team keeping a close watch on 'C's' house in the country. One of the watchers explained that they had just intercepted a telephone call to 'C' which had come from a Dr Kenneth jones, saying that he had something very urgent to discuss with him which could be a matter of life and death and that he will pay 'C' a visit straightaway."

As Stryker and Sir Samuel Dogson were discussing this new development, Dr Grachev interrupted their conversation.

"Did I hear you mention the name Dr Kenneth Jones?"

"Yes," replied Sir Samuel Dogson. "I have asked him to pay 'C' a visit. Though I didn't think he would be going to visit him quite so soon. Why do you ask?"

"Because I saw that name Dr Kenneth Jones, MA Oxon. on a notice board at the office in Whitehall advertising a series of lectures in the Russian language called: 'The language of Politics in Russia for the modern age'. It was beneath the title: 'Russian for civil servants'."

"Well, I don't think we're going to do any good standing here on the pavement in Knightsbridge Sir Samuel," Stryker whispered. "There's no hope of finding Dr Grachev's spy at this moment is there? We'd better get over to 'C's' house 'St. Kildare'. I know you asked Dr Kenneth Jones to make arrangements to visit 'C' with a view to impinging on his friendship for getting him to open up to an old friend, but to say that his meeting with 'C' is a matter of life and death is a little strong. He should have been more diplomatic don't you think? Anyway, I suppose we'd better get a move on."

"Yes, I'm inclined to agree with you there Stryker, life and death is a tad dramatic as you say. And as I mentioned earlier, we can obtain a photofit sketch of the Russian double agent with Dr Grachev's help later. But now there's no time to lose. I'll arrange for a mobile covert surveillance van to collect the Assistant Controller of MI6 Charles Kingdom to join us. Of course there will be you Stryker, and Dr Grachev here. And on our way to 'C's' country house 'St. Kildare' we shall also pick up some other security specialists. Oh and Professor Lambton, as a top-ranking member of MI5, was most insistent that for keeping him up to date with events his daughter Carol should be in on the act.

"I can imagine," replied Stryker, with a pained tone to his voice.

***

"Stryker, why did you spend so much time at Bleak House?" It was Carol who posed the question, but it was Sir Samuel Dogson who answered in a somewhat peremptory manner.

"Because we had to give some of your colleagues in Six enough time to extract information from 'C' on his spying activities before I myself confront him with the devastating news that he has actually been seen in Moscow by Dr Grachev, thereby using this shock tactic to put 'C' under even more pressure to possibly confide more information about his traitorous activities by this unsettling piece of evidence.

"For instance, 'C' has already confessed to the fact that when he was notified of a secret coded message being sent back to London H.Q. by Anthony Lovejoy-Taylor, one of his British agents, and that this secret Russian information was intended to be handed over to one of 'C's' British spies working under diplomatic cover out of the British Embassy in Moscow mentioning a secret location and designated area illustrated in microdot form, detailing a Biological Weapons facility encompassing a mass of information relating to a factory tagged with the abbreviation ES 205, he tips off Russian Intelligence through his control via a dead letter box about Stryker being the person selected to collect the material from a secluded area on the outskirts of Moscow so that he can be eliminated, thus preventing the location of the secret Russian BW factory and techniques on developing these weapons of mass destruction from falling into anti-Soviet hands. Fortunately Stryker travelled on a passport with the cover name Smith and therefore the Russians were not aware of his true identity, and as an oversight 'C' failed to inform them of his true identity. That's how Anthony Lovejoy-Taylor came to be shot by the Russians.

"The fact that 'C' has so far denied having been in Moscow is neither here nor there. We'll get at the truth eventually no matter how long it takes. And through your suggestion of our setting up intrusive surveillance, part of which included hiding microphones behind the oak linenfold panelling at 'C's' house Stryker – the whole house being bugged in conjunction with Dr Jones having been prevailed upon by myself to use his long and close friendship with 'C' in an attempt to loosen his tongue seems to have worked exquisitely, and speak of the devil," Sir Samuel Dogson put an index finger up to his lips as a clear voice emanated from the van's speaker

"*I suppose you know what I've come to talk with you about...*" within the mobile covert surveillance van in which they were now seated, even though they were still maintaining a steady fifty miles an hour along the motorway as they entered the boundaries of Berkshire.

CHAPTER 160

The security cameras mounted high on poles so as to give a good panoramic view and installed for 'C's' security had not yet been dismantled, so even before entering it was easy for 'C' to make out the figure of his friend Dr Kenneth Jones on the security monitor as he sat patiently in his car waiting for the electronically operated gates to be opened. It was a sombre face seen through the windscreen and as the small car slowly made its way up the gravel drive, the sophisticated multi-faceted lens robotically followed every movement. It was also a lugubrious-looking 'C' who answered the heavy front door. Donald, his man-servant-cum-bodyguard and occasional chauffeur had been dispensed with on a permanent basis several weeks earlier.

From the moment Ken entered the house 'C' sensed a stilted atmosphere between them, something he had not experienced since their first days at university together.

"I suppose you know what I've come to talk with you about; I have come as any lifelong friend would in your hour of need and because of our close friendship over the years. Someone you can trust. And if it's not being too dramatic, maybe the *only* person you can now really trust." Dr Kenneth Jones' face bore none of its usual trait of hail-fellow-well-met; instead it had been expunged of all compassion. These were the first words spoken to 'C' since Ken had made his appointment with him over the telephone. "And your wife and three grandchildren, where are they?" Usually Kenneth would refer to 'C's' wife as Gillian. *Not today.*

"As I mentioned when you rang, Susie and her husband are off on a cruise so we are saddled with looking after the grandchildren. Gillian's taken the three of them to visit my mother-in-law for a few hours as you requested," 'C' answered rather pointedly. "It really proved quite awkward to persuade her but she finally acquiesced when I told her what you said about it being to quote: 'a *life and death situation.*'" *No comment from Kenneth.* "Will you have your usual tipple?"

"Not today." All pretence at niceties had been swept away. There was a long frosty silence as 'C' ushered Kenneth to an easy chair and sat down opposite him. Kenneth studiously placed a small parcel neatly wrapped in brown paper on the floor beside his feet before making eye contact with an unspoken hint at being rankled. There ensued another long, awkward silence before Kenneth spoke again, this time letting a torrent of words flow forth as though the walls of a dam had been breached. "What the bloody hell have you done? What's all this talk about you having to retire because of ill health? What have you been up to?" 'C' had never been spoken to by Kenneth like this before, but it was to be expected so he took it with a dose of equanimity.

"I shall not beat about the bush but come straight to the point. It's true I have been pensioned off by the service. Yes, it is also true that the excuse being put around the department is that I was forced to give up my job due to bad health – which is, I might add, pure fabrication of course – easier to feed to the media. Mea culpa old boy, mea culpa. Before facts are distorted by others, which as you know, over time they are bound to become, and before you inform me as to the real reason of your intention regarding this visit, I wish to put the record straight as a form of atonement. I'm not looking for absolution you understand. I know that you could never grant me that, for what I am about to tell you will not put right all the injustices I have committed, nor bring innocent parties back from the dead and no doubt you will come to see me in a totally different light from what you might have perceived me to be from our long friendship." Dr Kenneth Jones fought hard against the desire to interpose with his own views on the subject of their friendship and the tethered vitriolic diatribe held tight on a long leash, its black wings flapping furiously, straining, pecking and tearing at the very fabric of his own outraged nature.

"Firstly let me explain the background to all this. To begin, as with many other men of our generation I was curious in my youth as to the very nature of man and what we might call the human condition. I know that all sounds very grand now, but in one's youth one very often has grand ideals. And as a callow youth I was malleable and open to many different influences and sentiments of the day. Not only British capitalism but capitalism throughout the world was, and still is to my mind at least, the bogeyman of the masses. Like Guy Burgess, Kim Philby et al, I became a committed communist and vowed to serve the working classes through co-operating with Moscow." Dr Kenneth Jones didn't waver in his blank expression aimed at the now former British spymaster.

"I also became an agent of the KGB answerable to one state only – what was then known as the Soviet Union. Not for any pecuniary gain you understand, but for the good of mankind." At 'C's' mention of the phrase 'good of mankind', a hearty laugh from Sir Samuel Dogson interrupted the silence inside the security van. "Though upon introspection my reasons were multifarious and complex, nonetheless the phrase anti-fascist also came into that equation. My sole goal was to undermine the existing capitalist system for a New Jerusalem if you will. In my chosen career with the Foreign Office, I became what is now termed a high flyer and was soon in the enviable position of helping to shape British policy in spheres of influence throughout the world in some small way. Gradually, over the years in the eyes of my spymasters or what I should prefer to call my colleagues in arms, I was given to understand I was one of their kingpins. And so began a long and profitable association over many decades with my true Russian brothers. And I use the term 'profitable' not in a pecuniary way as I say, but in a more abstract manner. I know you must feel betrayed, and I understand perfectly well this sentiment, but there you are, we make our bed and must lie on it as the proverb goes."

Dr Kenneth Jones sat staring at 'C' with an impassive look upon his face, any trace of what he might have been thinking hidden by an indecipherable expression.

"Go on, I'm listening."

"All was going well and I was looking forward to living out the rest of what years I had left in peaceful contentment and tranquillity, for as we both know, I am now an old man. A peaceful retirement in the country was beckoning when one day out of the blue I received an intelligence report at Vauxhall Cross routed through GCHQ apropos our naval attaché stationed at the British Embassy in Dubai. It was suggested that it might be worthwhile investigating a sunken Russian cargo ship off the Persian coast because of rumours of unusual contamination emanating from that particular area. Running in tandem with this, my attention had also been drawn to whispers from one of our agents that a potential Russian defector would be applying for political asylum in Britain; a self-confessed scientist experimenting with biological warfare agents had, with a view to lending himself credibility with us, cryptically supplied a set of co-ordinates without explanation. The problem was that these co-ordinates matched the very same co-ordinates supplied by our embassy in Dubai relating to the location of this sunken Russian vessel. Going against my professed loyalty to Russia and because of my position as the chief of Britain's Secret Intelligence Service I now had no option but to be seen to act; so I sent two of our ex-Special Forces operatives to covertly investigate the shipwrecked vessel, knowing I could never allow them to return to speak of whatever they may have seen. They had to be quickly silenced so I tipped off the Russians. Had it not been for that infernal American detective Stryker's chance meeting on holiday in Dubai with these two former colleagues of his, whom he had known from his own spell working with American Special Forces a few years previously, the situation could have been contained. But although our two operatives were killed as required by the Russians, something I could never have foreseen happened – that damned American, Private Detective Stryker survived the dive to describe the cargo on the sunken vessel in graphic detail as well as admitting to killing four Russian frogmen.

"Now I have two very big problems on my hands. The first of these is how to get rid of Stryker so that he can no longer pose a risk by bearing witness to this toxic Russian cargo of killer microbes with its potential for use in biological warfare, thus breaking all standard protocols and treaties signed by Russia relating to arms control agreements with America and Britain. That's when I formulated the plan to have Stryker assassinated whilst in the process of ostensibly collecting documents from Russian Ivanovich Sobolev, one of Britain's SIS's assets, at his dacha situated on the perimeter of Moscow. This plan was carefully worked out by Moscow Centre and passed on to me through my controller here in England. And again, if it had not been for Stryker having problems with that damned eye of his the plan to assassinate him might very well have succeeded. He truly seems to be indestructible. I knew it would raise a few eyebrows sending what one might call, to use the American vernacular, a greenhorn like Stryker to Moscow to collect this most valuable of information. It went against all the rules of the department – not seen as professional you understand. But I had no option, it seeming to me to be an opportunistic moment to be able to use Ivanovich Sobolev as the way of placing our American detective in harm's way by having the Russians assassinate Stryker and at the same time capture Ivanovich Sobolev, thus killing two birds with one stone, then put it down to our sheer bad luck. Unfortunately the other chap, what was his name? Ah yes, Anthony Lovejoy-Taylor. He replaced Stryker at the last moment and copped it instead. You will be surprised to hear that alas, I am not the infallible spymaster that you might have read about in spy novels, for I did make one terrible mistake which I now bitterly regret and which may have avoided all this trouble. I did not supply Stryker's name, a.k.a. Smith to the FSB, which I should have done rather than just informing them that he was a British spy sent to collect a cache of invaluable documents from Ivanovich Sobolev relating to their top secret biological warfare programme. They might then have known who they were shooting if they had taken the trouble.

"Anyhow, with the best will in the world Moscow Centre's plan never succeeded and Stryker had lived to tell the tale. And along the way two British nationals, i.e. the British naval attaché and a young Duty Officer from the FCO who had assisted him in detaining Stryker at the British Embassy in Dubai also had to die, even though they had been sworn to secrecy, for they knew too much about the sunken vessel from Stryker's own lips – but anyhow they died in suspicious circumstances courtesy of our good Russian friends having once again been tipped off by yours truly – that is, myself. I believe that for whatever reason they both suspected they were targets of an assassination plot and attempted to convey their fears to

Stryker but to no avail." 'C's' breath-taking callousness had to be heard to be believed. "And then of course there was another one of our MI6 operatives who ferried our three divers out to the location of the shipwreck – he too was killed by the Russians – had his throat cut." Dr Kenneth Jones stared in disbelief at what he was hearing but gave a nod as if to say 'well you fooled everyone but carry on with your tale of treachery.'

"Right at the beginning of this operation at our behest one of our MI6 operatives, a girl named Caroline Lambton, being tenuously related to Stryker, wheedled herself into a position of sharing a flat with him – initially, strangely enough, at the behest of a chap on our JIC – sorry Joint Intelligence Committee, named Sir Samuel Dogson who was ostensibly being kept informed as to what was happening with regard to this particular operation because of Stryker having killed the Russians in Dubai with potential international implications. And Sir Dogson also took a close interest because of the two English men also killed in Dubai – so that Caroline Lambton might keep me informed with what Stryker was thinking. She was working in registry so had not been trained for undercover work per se, but I arranged it so that she would travel with Stryker to Moscow so as to keep tabs on him. Sir Dogson didn't realise just what a good suggestion that was from my perspective. Unfortunately Stryker had a stronger influence on this young lady than I could have imagined. Caroline was a raw recruit and got too close to her target. Later I figured that when everything was sorted out she would have to be sent away on a trip to an imaginary spying school in Switzerland to learn a few tricks of the trade, and then she might amount to something. But of course the place I had in mind would have literally been a finishing school in the accepted sense of the word if you take my meaning." Here 'C' gave a knowing wink. "Skiing accidents do sometimes happen, no matter how good you are at the sport – especially if you are skiing off-piste!" Here 'C' made an attempt at a chuckle, but it fell on deaf ears as far as Dr Kenneth Jones was concerned.

"And during all this happening I initiated a smear campaign against Stryker, suggesting to Miss Lambton that it was he who had been instrumental in getting his two so-called diving buddies Des and Terry killed, or maybe had even done the deed himself. That suggestion was planted so that Carol Lambton would keep a close eye on Stryker and tip us off if Stryker ever made a move to fly back to America out of our jurisdiction."

Carol gave Stryker a sweet smile. "I didn't believe a word of it Stryker – honestly."

"Quiet you two, let's listen!" insisted the Deputy Chief of SIS Charles Kingdom, as the van continued to rumble onwards towards 'C's' house.

"In retrospect, even at the beginning of my planned operation things did not bode well. Being the inquisitive type, Stryker had noticed a car following him from the Russian Orthodox Easter church service he'd attended and asked the department to find out who it was registered to. Of course it had nothing to do with us but as bad luck would have it the car was registered to the Russian Embassy. So from that moment on my orders were that every request put through the department by Stryker or his accomplice Carol would have to be initially scrutinised by myself first. I refused to allow any information from Dubai to be passed on to these two people and had the Foreign Office block any requests Stryker or Caroline might make to the embassy by using prevarication on the pretext that they were a possible threat to our national security. So I had Stryker and Caroline designated *persona non grata* as far as the diplomatic staff in Dubai was concerned.

"Here we come to the second problem I had to deal with – that of having a loose cannon in the form of this Russian scientist-cum-possible defector using the *nom de guerre* Red Chameleon."

Dr Kenneth Jones unconsciously shuffled his feet impatiently beneath the chair he occupied, furtively shooting a quick glance at the small package on the carpet beside him. Then imperceptibly gave a slight nod of his head, signalling his friend and now ex-chief of Britain's internal security and counter-intelligence overseas to carry on.

"I made it quite plain to Moscow Centre through my controller that this would-be Russian defector was top of the list to be liquidated as soon as I was able to catch him. Unfortunately, like our American friend Stryker, that was not to be, for he now appears, like Stryker I hasten to add again, to have disappeared God knows where. Then just a few days ago from out of the blue I had been told that there was incontrovertible proof that I was spying on behalf of the Russian state. Something I could not deny under a drug induced confession using the truth serum called sodium pentothal, though the incontrovertible proof has still to be shown to me. But I just knew they had me so threw in the towel immediately. Don't forget I know their methods so didn't want to be dragged through that sort of thing. I'm getting too old for these games, believe me. In retrospect, this whole damned operation seems to have been jinxed from the very beginning."

"Yes, you told me on the telephone that they were keeping tabs on you."

"That's right. They tell me that as things become clearer to them they will undoubtedly have me in for questioning many, many more times until they can get to the bottom of it all but that I could return to live at this place for the time being. No doubt you were logged in by the watchers. You don't see them but they're everywhere you know. Sorry about that but I expect you realised what the situation would be like."

"Yes, I guessed as much. I take it that this would-be Russian defector you spoke of just a moment ago, a.k.a. the Red Chameleon, is Dr Grachev. How could I forget that late night meeting in this very house when you were briefing diverse members of the civil service, including a pale-faced man from the Joint Intelligence Committee, what's his name – Sir Samuel Dogson – and that soldier from Special Forces mentioning being a specialist in 'wet jobs' as I recall? I gathered from that late-night cum early-morning meeting that, at least ostensibly, the plan had been for Dr Grachev to be abducted at Piccadilly Circus. You were then going to use Professor Lambton, Deputy Director of Porton Down, if I remember correctly, to debrief him before having our potential Russian defector disposed of. By the way, if you were so concerned about your brother Russians – comrades in arms so to speak, then why bother having our would-be defector debriefed if he was going to be killed anyway? Surely from your vantage point you would not have wanted the West to know just what your Russian friends were up to would you?"

This attitude of Dr Kenneth Jones – seeing it from 'C's' point of view – took him totally by surprise. Seeing his lifelong friend in a new light led him to assume that he was now softening and entering into the spirit of the problem as laid out for his edification.

"That was pure theatre. Just another smoke screen to show the powers that be I was doing my job. On my instructions he would have been disposed of before he had had a chance of divulging any secrets regarding Russia's BW programme. Pure theatre! Hocus-pocus! That's how I have survived for so long my friend."

"And this secret Soviet agent controller of yours – now that you have finished with all this cloak and dagger stuff, can you not confide his name, not even to me, your oldest friend?"

'C' looked weary-eyed. "Yes, if I could I would surely name this what I imagine is a Soviet illegal known as my controller. I would do it to make some kind of amends for all my transgressions you understand, for I have had a sea change concerning my clandestine activities."

"Oh yes, now that you have been caught red handed – no pun intended – you have re-assessed your values and alliances – bravo my friend – bravo." This acerbic comment was ignored by 'C', understanding only too well how his betrayed friend must be feeling. Nevertheless he continued, ploughing on regardless.

"Truth to tell, I do not even know myself who he – or even she – is, only that he... or she, has been working as a Russian agent in ultra-deep cover for a very, very long time. My assumption – and that of my former colleagues at SIS – is that these requests for my supplying specific information obviously came from Moscow Centre via a legal residency operating from within the London Russian Embassy. That these requests for ultra-secret information were then channelled to an illegal officer stationed God knows where. And I swear to you, I for my part do not know who my controller is. To me he – or she – is and always has been invisible. I know that this may sound impossible but I do not even have an inkling of their alias, legend or anything else. As I say they, he or she, operated in ultra-deep cover. It is strange that I have supplied this agent with information gleaned over many decades by using various dead letter-boxes dotted around the country, though that term is really a misnomer because at the moment they are what is known as LLBs – live letter-boxes, yet even I do not know his or her identity – true or otherwise. Would you believe it – me – the great chief of the British Secret Intelligence Service, totally ignorant of the one man in the UK who could have done more harm to me or possibly even this country than anyone or anything else?"

Dr Kenneth Jones fixed his friend with a quizzical stare. "So you never gave your interrogators anything which might conceivably help trap your controller? Perhaps as you say, to make amends for all your transgressions?"

The people in the white surveillance van keeping up the steady fifty miles an hour on the motorway sat in stunned silence, hemmed in by their own secret thoughts.

"No, I did not say that. I did my best to answer all questions SIS put to me, including how and where I had initially been recruited; information on dead letter-box locations; times of drops; what intelligence including diplomatic, military, political and commercial had been passed on to the enemy – the enemy in this instance of course being the Russians – their parlance, not mine – our intelligence cipher codes, in fact everything I could possibly remember including a list of all my friends and acquaintances over a lifetime. Can you just imagine? Lie detector tests, truth drugs, the lot. That is why I have been incommunicado for the past few weeks and I suppose traces of my controller's DNA might conceivably be discovered at one of these secret locations I have given them. They say they will pull out all the stops. I'm not surprised. That is why I have not been in contact with you recently. They really put me through the mangle. You'll never know." At this point 'C' let out a long, pent-up sigh. "They said that if I am a good boy and am co-operative with them they might consider granting me certain favours, though they are not letting on just what those favours are at the moment. Maybe it's letting me take the easy way out – a self-inflicted coup de grâce perhaps! Perhaps! Who knows?"

Dr Kenneth Jones looked grim as he waited for 'C' to regain his composure, the air of dejection upon his features slowly subsiding before speaking again. "Because of our time in Russia together when we were very young men, just boys really I suppose, I have been closer to you than to any other man. I shall always regard you as 'C' no matter what."

"No my dear friend, in truth the king is dead, long live the king. It was always thus and ever shall be. Do you remember what Nelson was reputed to have said to his flag captain on his deathbed at the battle of Trafalgar?"

"Yes. Kiss me Hardy."

Kenneth smiled and looked even older than usual as he slowly raised his bent frame from the chair he had been occupying, and stooping forward, placed a kiss on 'C's' cheek. Then lifting the brown paper parcel he had brought with him he proceeded to unwrap it before presenting 'C' with a box of his favourite Russian Black Sobranie cigarettes. "Here, take these out of friendship and as a reminder of the old times."

With a tear in his eye 'C' spoke softly. "But, my good friend, you've always referred to these cigarettes as stinking like camel shit." After accepting a proffered cigarette removed by his confidant from the wooden presentation box adorned with a small silver plaque inscribed on behalf of his work colleagues with the ironical words 'For services rendered', Dr Kenneth Jones then raised an onyx lighter from the table beside him and lit 'C's' cigarette.

A click of the lighter was all that could be heard or seen before the transmitter went dead; cutting all communications to the security van carrying Sir Samuel Dogson, Assistant Controller of MI6 Charles Kingdom, Stryker and Carol, Dr Grachev together with a small contingent of security people as it hurtled toward 'C's' country house 'St. Kildare'.

'C' leant back, looked intently at Dr Kenneth Jones for perhaps half a minute before closing his eyes and inhaling deeply, blowing a perfectly formed smoke ring through his pursed lips. But before he had a chance to draw on the cigarette for a second time he learnt in a furious torrent of words issuing forth from Dr Kenneth Jones, the final and most explosive secret that he had ever been party to, notwithstanding that he had been the UK's keeper of its top secrets.

CHAPTER 161

There was a series of explosions just nanoseconds before Stryker jumped out of the surveillance vehicle and ran over the threshold of the mansion closely followed by Sir Samuel Dogson, trailing the vanload of other people after him. The American detective immediately spotted 'C' slumped forward in the wing chair. Dr Kenneth Jones was standing over him clutching the tumbler of whisky still held tight within his shaking fist. A heavy smell of cordite lingered in the air, a pungent smell reminiscent of Stryker's days in the military. A half minute or so later when this noxious smell had given way to the fresh breeze wafting through the holes left in the walls where the doors and windows had just been blown out of their frames and the dust had begun to settle, Stryker fell down upon one knee and took 'C's' head between his large hands before examining his face, then sniffed 'C's' body before placing his hand inside his jacket, feeling his chest. He then carefully picked up the burnt out remains of the distinctive gold-tipped Russian Black Sobranie cigarette lying at the feet of the Chief and sniffed that also.

"What is it Stryker?" It was Sir Samuel Dogson who spoke, asking the question though he had already guessed.

"In Africa it would be called konzo. There is a smell of bitter almonds. The cigarette was obviously tampered with so as to produce cyanide. In medical terms his lips are blue, denoting cyanosis, and his heart has given way through a lack of oxygen. He's dead, sir."

Dr Jones raised the glass of whisky to his lips and took a hefty gulp before addressing the people now crowded around the body staring at him. "There were mitigating circumstances," he stammered. "When I heard that 'C', a close friend of mine, had betrayed my country to the Russians..." As he looked for sympathy scouring their features all he could see was a myriad of faces staring back at him accusingly. In the brief silence that followed he noticed one person in particular, a person whom he had not seen since the time he was with 'C' in Wales and before that the Kremlin. For a moment he stared hard, unable to believe his run of bad luck as he quickly reached inside his open jacket and pulled out a gun which he pointed at Dr Grachev and fired. Carol, who happened to be standing beside Dr Kenneth Jones, screamed as the right side of Dr Kenneth Jones's head was hit by a bullet fired from one of the contingent of six SAS men using a Browning high power 9mm automatic. It was a reaction shot which hit the ear, taking it off cleanly, and with that Dr Kenneth Jones dropped his gun as he fell onto Carol, smearing her with copious amounts of his blood. At that same moment Dr Grachev also fell, hit by the shot fired from Dr Kenneth Jones's gun.

As two of the soldiers ran outside to grab a first aid pack for Dr Kenneth Jones, Dr Grachev beckoned Stryker and whispered something none of the others in the room could hear, then in a louder hoarse voice he said, "Freedom is a precious commodity my friend. And you ARE a true friend. You saved my life more than once – the last time in that helicopter in Wales. I have fought hard to free myself from the invisible shackles the Russian state has imposed on me and yet it has turned out so different to what I had wished. People take freedom for granted but it really does have to be fought for. How do you say – a robin redbreast in a cage, puts all heaven…"

"In a rage," Carol said, blinking back tears. "The English poet William Blake." Dr Grachev then slumped forward.

"He's dead," said Carol, who was in the process of holding her tiny make-up mirror to Dr Grachev's lips.

"Hold on Carol, I hope not." Carol gave Stryker a quizzical look.

"How can you say that Stryker? We all saw him shot by Dr Kenneth Jones. He's dead."

"No, what you see is someone who has been winded by the force of a bullet at close range. It's just shock. Is that not so Dr Grachev?" Dr Grachev opened his eyes and blinked twice before responding to Stryker's question.

"That as you say Stryker, is so. You saved my life once more, thank you for insisting that I wear a bullet-proof vest."

Stryker then turned to Dr Jones, quickly pulling out a large handkerchief to stem the blood by placing it over what was left of his ear and putting pressure there with his hand, saying: "You've confirmed something that Dr Grachev told me just now. He suggested that you were a very close friend of 'C's', more close than even 'C' realised."

"What are you getting at Mr Stryker?" It was the Deputy Chief of SIS Charles Kingdom who posed the question.

"What I mean is that this man standing here before you is as much a traitor as 'C' ever was, and that is why he killed 'C' – to stop himself from being unwittingly exposed. I guess what I am saying is that Dr Kenneth Jones was the controller of 'C' even if the chief himself was ignorant of this fact. For I have just been informed by Dr Grachev that the man he saw in the Kremlin and identified by General Kovalyev from Russian GRU Military Intelligence as destined to ultimately join Russia's Great Illegals, and therefore the British spy we've all been hunting for, the secret agent working for the Russians; the man who Dr Grachev here now recognises is… Dr Kenneth Jones."

Charles Kingdom turned to one of the SAS men. "Arrest Dr Jones and get a first aid lint pad to stem that blood. And where have your two colleagues gone?"

"For the first aid pack, sir."

CHAPTER 162

The new Secret Intelligence Service Chief Charles Kingdom, had never been disposed to wear his heart upon his sleeve, yet even he had found it hard to control his temper as he sat quietly discussing with his deputy the upheaval his predecessor had caused the department and Britain's allies.

Charles Kingdom was only too aware of the parallels with the infamous 'Cambridge Five' drawn from within the British Establishment. They had also been known at the Centre – Moscow's old KGB HQ as simply 'The Five'. Acknowledged as possibly the most successful Russian agent of them all, Arnold Deutsch, a brilliant academic and charismatic Austrian Jew had been instrumental in recruiting in the nineteen-thirties the now infamous five. Of the Cambridge Five it had taken many years before those particular spies had been uncovered as some of the Soviet Union's most successful British agents working for Russian Intelligence. They came from within the top echelons of the Foreign Office and British Intelligence. Kim Philby, Guy Burgess, Anthony Blunt, Donald Maclean and the person known as possibly the fifth man, John Cairncross, although he personally had denied this fact, all managing to inveigle their way into the top posts which they held, all traitors to their country passing untold secrets to the enemy and all misguidedly blind to the inhumane shortcomings of the Russian system. The SIS's discovery, too late, that these men from Cambridge University – all but one of them high academic achievers – had undoubtedly cost the lives of many loyal British subjects and those working as double agents had been a terrible blow to Britain's security service, all of these traitors having been recruited in the early nineteen-thirties and working for decades afterwards against the interests and security of the United Kingdom. And it had not done a power of good for Anglo-American relations either, a chasm of distrust between the two intelligence agencies opening up and taking years to repair, if indeed it ever had been completely forgiven. Not that it was a one-sided affair as the Americans too had their security failures. So the glue known as the special relationship held – just.

The new controller of SIS broke up the meeting early so as to be in good time for a family christening service. As his government chauffeur-driven limousine ferried him to his country residence, he dwelt upon the possible ramifications that might flow from the main topic of discussion that early Sunday morning, namely the discovery that his predecessor had been a Soviet agent covertly working undercover for the Russians, and what steps should be taken to avoid the inevitable fallout which would surely arrive in its wake. With three good years still to go before retirement, Charles Kingdom did not want any idiot fouling it up for him now, especially when he was so close to a knighthood. *And what would our American cousins say?* he thought, dwelling on the imponderable.

So it was with much trepidation that the initial news of his predecessor's double dealings with the service had been revealed to him before being asked by the men in grey suits to take over the job of discovering as much as possible about his former boss.

As luck would have it things had turned out so much easier for the department. 'C' had seemingly died of a fortuitous heart attack. Unusual circumstances true, but nobody could pin that on 'C's' boys. That was all of three months ago and the expected fallout had not materialised. The late controller's files were being gone through with a fine tooth comb but sooner or later they would begin to gather dust in the metaphorical sense as a lot of information was now stored on computer and amen to that, except that the hunt for all the shadowy contacts imagined or otherwise would go on echoing with discordant resonance down the decades long after he had been pensioned off. In the meantime, the hunt was also on for other illegal residents embroiled in this murky affair. One consolation was that the KGB's First Chief Directorate must also be pissed off that one of their star performers had been rumbled.

It had been for Charles Kingdom as it was for the organisation in general a fortuitous thing indeed that his predecessor had died of a heart attack at home. The only reason he had been supposedly let off the leash and returned home in the first instance was in an attempt to discover if his unknown controller might make contact and ultimately lead to the illegal cell operating on behalf of Russian Intelligence being blown wide open. 'C's' house had been staked out by an SIS team and all the rooms bugged with sophisticated eavesdropping equipment whilst 'C' himself had at the time been in custody being interrogated. It transpired that the only person to visit him after his release had been an old friend, an academic named Dr Kenneth Jones who ran a teaching establishment in North Wales.

Charles Kingdom lay back in his chair, and as he had many times before, watched the surreptitiously filmed conversation between 'C' and Dr Kenneth Jones.

Even before the ephemeral fragranced puff of smoke had reached the intricate plasterwork ceiling of 'C's' panelled study his lips had turned blue, the smoke itself vanishing into the air as though it had never existed. The old chief of SIS had succumbed to a massive and deadly heart attack. How

Dr Kenneth Jones wished he could have been in the secret agent's shoes. Through his own moist eyes Dr Kenneth Jones dwelt on that halo of smoke, not only having seen it as 'C's' spirit finally escaping from all the sorrows in this world but also likening it with even more clarity to a noose having been slipped firmly around his own neck for killing his dear friend. Then, as though unaware of the fact that 'C' was no longer alive, Dr Kenneth Jones continued his rambling tirade of self-pity, bemoaning the fact that he had had to sit through Penny's revelation of her own sad Russian history, this story initiated through the medium of hypnosis. Of how her stepbrother Dr Grachev had escaped, even after 'C' had sent two of his SIS men to the Russian Orthodox Church to see if they could locate him and where 'C' had hoped to have him killed on the orders of his controller. And it was ironical that the unmasking of 'C' as Moscow's most important Western secret agent in modern times, had been carried out by an American detective going by the name of Stryker.

Dr Kenneth Jones felt that his own security had been compromised with the confession of 'C' to his British interrogators and that Moscow Centre would now surely brand him incompetent and possibly even have him liquidated. So when Dr Kenneth Jones had finally vented all the anger he possessed upon his now dead friend slumped before him he remembered his host's earlier offer of whisky, usually imbibed upon his clandestine visits to the chief of the British Secret Intelligence Service. Moving to the heavily carved sideboard, he knew precisely where to locate the large decanter of scotch and quickly grabbed a glass tumbler before pouring himself a hefty measure.

And it had been at that precise moment that the whole house had reverberated as though in the midst of an earthquake as doors and windows were smashed into tiny fragments as stun grenades were thrown by men wearing black anoraks and heavy boots as they burst into the living room with their guns drawn and where the Welsh academic Dr Kenneth Jones stood trembling with glass in hand, his triple measure of whisky not having had time to reach his lips.

Charles Kingdom pressed a switch on the machine to turn off the film before dwelling on the fact that he now had a ready-made confession from Dr Jones in the surreptitiously taped ranting tirade aimed at the already dead 'C', the secret Russian agent, revealing both men to be traitors and thus letting detective Stryker off the hook.

CHAPTER 163

Late spring foretold a long hot summer by awakening dormant green buds heavy with the promised rich cornucopia of foliage as Caroline Lambton made her way through St. James's Park; strolling amongst the trees, leaf-strewn branches hanging heavily from high swaying boughs, creating a dappled pattern of strong sunlight on the scorched surface of the path she was following. People were everywhere; sunbathers making the most of their lunch break; secret assignations with colleagues, their whispered conversations intimating a closeness only secret lovers knew. The unexpected heady warmth of half-forgotten beaches in far off holiday destinations created an atmosphere akin to that of relaxation and imagined freedom. Caroline halted at the narrow bridge effectively dividing the pond into two, and momentarily considered stepping out onto it to take in the view from another vantage point, but decided against it. Instead she carried on walking in the direction toward Whitehall and the Ministry of Defence. This route she knew well, having travelled the Jubilee line from Swiss Cottage underground station to Green Park for the past year.

Soon Caroline was walking in Great George Street which ran alongside the Treasury, before turning left heading along Whitehall. Crossing over the busy road, she attempted to remain calm as she entered the hallowed entrance of the Ministry.

After going through all the security formalities and showing her pass, bearing an indeterminate likeness of herself renewed just four months earlier, to some burly man whose broken nose gave the impression that his true vocation might have been a rugby prop forward, Caroline eventually found herself walking along an endless corridor until the right room had been located. It was a male secretary who waited to greet and escort her into the imposing environs within which she had been granted a very short audience with the most powerful person in the British Secret Intelligence Service – a panjandrum of the first order.

"Ah Miss Lambton, do sit down. I'm afraid I have a lot of business to get through this morning so I'll keep it short and to the point." The tall windows had been kept shut since last fall and they had remained shut even though the air bore a fusty smell of recent cigarette smoke. The remains of three or four cigarettes lay at the base of a heavy cut-glass ashtray sitting on the large desktop.

"I suppose I owe you an explanation. We had to know whether our two SIS agents, Desmond Lynch and Terry Moore, were set up. It was a terrible way to go. We just can't lose two men like that without carrying out an internal enquiry. It was Stryker after all, who invited them to join him on that particular dive off the Persian Gulf."

Caroline saw red. She had been used by the department on the former Controller's instructions by attempting to convince her that Stryker had been a stooge of the Russians, and she for one knew that Stryker was nobody's stooge. "I beg to differ, sir, but I believe it was Stryker who was invited by his two friends to go on that particular dive."

"Well yes, I'm sure that is correct, though obviously we are unable to verify it. We only have Stryker's word for that. Anyhow, please forgive me."

The new Chief, wearing a seemingly de rigueur Eton tie, sat impassively behind his overly ornate desk. His small, neat hands, freckled with a liberal sprinkling of brown liver spots, were nudging a red leather blotter bearing silver embossed letters 'HMG' in copperplate. He sat waiting tentatively for some response.

A minute passed, the silence growing in intensity before Caroline changed tack.

"I wish to remain in Belsize Park."

"You must have been endowed with psychic abilities young woman. That is one of the reasons I invited you over here," 'C' replied, reverting to his cold business-like demeanour, "to explain that once a mission has been completed – well, I'm sure you understand what the finance department can be like. The flat was only taken on a year's lease for you to be able to monitor Smith and keep tabs on him. That was of course arranged by my former boss who shall remain nameless." Here the new chief looked up at the ornate ceiling and moved his lips, though this was barely discernible, uttering a silent prayer. "We have the opportunity to extend the lease, but you would have to bear the financial burden. It has already overrun by two months." His heavy eyes bore none of the compassion that might have come from someone in his position, but Caroline had been forewarned against expecting too much. Caroline bridled at his calling her 'young woman'. She felt it patronising.

"Stryker is returning home to America you know."

"Yes. I hear that he left you his Burlington Arcade shop trading in Russian Icons. Perhaps that might generate enough funds to keep the flat going – mind you, I suppose we, by that I mean the Department, helped Smith secure the finances for that business too, out of government funds. Anyway, unless the auditors mention it, we won't say anything." Here 'C'

STRYKER'S HOUSE OF SPIES

gave the merest suggestion of a wink before making some pleasantries signalling the end of their meeting. Then as an afterthought he added, "I understand that Sarah, another of our Six operatives has been helping you with the shop. That must cease forthwith. We need her back at the department. You do understand don't you?" Without waiting for a response 'C' then lowered his gaze to a file which had been placed upon his desk by a secretary just as Carol had entered his office.

Halfway out of 'C's' borrowed office, Caroline came to an abrupt halt, spun on her heel and walked calmly back toward his large desk,

"I suppose it's too late to make any difference now, but this is a resignation letter."

'C' raised his eyes from the file he had turned his attention to. It was regarding a wealthy Saudi. His name was Osama Bin Laden, an Islamic fundamentalist and suspected terrorist and leader of a group called Al-Qaeda, meaning *the Base*. Bin Laden had vacated Britain in mid-march, just a few months earlier. There were strong suggestions that his group was linked to the bombing of the World Trade Centre in New York the previous year, 1993.

"You are resigning?" His face bore a look of thoughtfulness as he puckered up his lips.

"No, I'm not resigning. It's Stryker's letter of resignation." With that parting shot Caroline turned on her heels once more before finally walking out, feeling good that she had wrong footed the most powerful man in Britain's Secret Intelligence Service.

Even as the twenty foot high heavy door was in the process of being closed behind her however, 'C's' attention was drawn to Smith's neat signature at the foot of his resignation letter, and pondered on how, and more importantly, why Dr Grachev's body had supposedly turned up on the steps of an ocularist in some grubby area of West Hampstead, his face and hands burnt beyond recognition, caused undoubtedly by the gas explosion. It was only one of many mysteries surrounding this Russian maverick. True, the missing teeth prevented an absolute one hundred per cent identification being confirmed, but the partially burnt clothing and melted fragment of Dr Grachev's army tag found draped around his neck had helped, as had the documentation found on the body. Thanks to the painstaking work of the forensic scientists, it was now beyond doubt that the remaining fragments of white wig and false eyebrows found at the scene of that gas explosion had been the same as that worn by Dr Grachev within the Harley Street Clinic. Fibres found there had matched the crime scene at West Hampstead.

There were also images of Dr Grachev disguised as an elderly arthritis-ridden man, captured on CCTV within the famous environs of Harley Street, matching the SIS agents' film taken of him from the white van parked in Piccadilly Circus. The charred silver-headed walking cane discovered at the scene of the fire also matched that of the one depicted in both tapes. It had also appeared that the elderly false eye maker had, for some unknown reason, stabbed Dr Grachev in the neck with one of his tools of the trade before being struck a deadly blow by Dr Grachev, though how such a feat had been accomplished after the doctor had had his spinal cord severed was indeed a miracle.

Charles Kingdom searched his pockets before fishing out a slim solid gold cigarette case to extract his first king sized American cigarette of the day, and after having inserted it into an extended cigarette holder balanced between index and middle finger, unwittingly mimicking the Churchillian V sign for victory, lit it and inhaled deeply, feeling much happier now that Dr Grachev's body had been handed back to the Russian Embassy in London, together with the explanation that it had been involved in a car accident.

Before returning the body however, the corpse had been relieved of the thin skewer-like instrument found in its neck, then his boys from the special ops department had incinerated the body even more ferociously in a simulated car accident, removing any doubts the Russians may have entertained about such marks found on the body. By the time this had all been accomplished, however, there really was not that much left to hand over, the main identifying clues being the partially melted blob of the Russian army dog tag and the badly charred remnants of a Russian passport.

Charles Kingdom however, knew that whoever's remains had been returned to the Russian Embassy, it certainly had not been that of Dr Grachev. DNA tests had sorted that one out. Of course, to ascertain the true DNA of a person one first has to obtain a comparative sample – in this case from Moscow. But there again, that is why spies are so invaluable.

The mystery which still niggled at the back of Charles Kingdom's mind was why Stryker had asked for background material on Dr Grachev several weeks before anyone supposedly even knew the potential defector's name. That was a mystery. The request had been logged by Registry, as all such requests are, even though up until then, there was no information held on Dr Grachev within the SIS's very considerable files stored on their computer system. Stryker had given some cock and bull story about having been befriended by Dr Grachev at the Russian Orthodox Church service at Easter a year earlier but the new controller found that very hard to believe – for why should such an approach be made to an innocent American detective? In this case Charles Kingdom thought it wiser to let sleeping dogs lie. Besides which, he had been told so many over the years one more wouldn't hurt. And in the final analysis it was they, the SIS, who had Dr Grachev firmly in their grasp at last with all the inherent information he had shed like some great chameleon lizard shedding its tail. He silently chuckled to himself. The Russians would hopefully now accept that their great scientist was dead and the British Secret Service had gained an asset that was very much alive.

CHAPTER 164

Stryker removed from his jacket the item which had fallen from Dr Grachev's breast pocket in the process of being shot.

"Where did you get that?" It was Charles Kingdom who spoke. He recognised it as the pin Dr Grachev had sent to Stryker as a symbol of friendship. The symbolic flag was misshapen now where it had been hit with the force of a bullet fired by Pyotr.

"I hear tell New Scotland Yard has a black museum housing artefacts of infamous criminals and murderers. Perhaps MI6 would like this little token to begin its own special collection." Stryker tossed the broken symbol of Mother Russia onto Charles Kingdom's desk, the new chief of Britain's Secret Intelligence Service. It was the facsimile pin belonging to Penny Churchill. But this particular pin, with a bent flag struck by the bullet fired from Pyotr's gun, had belonged to Dr Grachev. Penny Churchill did not know and was kept in ignorance of her brother having been hunted by the security services.

And with that Stryker left to collect Carol who was waiting for him outside in the corridor carrying two shiny black motorcycle helmets.

"I think we're due for a holiday, don't you Carol?"

"Oh Stryker, what a good idea! But one more thing that puzzles me before we go. That contact you said was helping you in Seattle. Can you now tell me who he is and how he was helping? I mean, what did he say? "

"Well, he's a very dear friend of mine. His name is Billy Stoker and if you remember, not so very long ago he sent me that gizmo to block any signals from hidden bugs. You remember – we plugged it into the skirting board at our place in Swiss Cottage. He was my old boss when I was still a policeman. Anyway, do you also remember that thing 'C' told me at that late night meeting at his house 'St. Kildare' in Wokingham, Berkshire? After that meeting 'C' said to me, quote: 'And as you were informed from the word go America, well to be more precise the Central Intelligence Agency actually, has been kept in the frame. They know all about your mission.' Do you remember Carol?"

"Well no Stryker, as a matter of fact I don't. You and that eidetic memory of yours!"

"Anyway, that phrase stuck in my mind and I asked Billy if he could find out through his contacts with the CIA over there if they could ascertain the truth of that statement."

"And what did you find out?"

"I was told by Billy that after some time waiting for an answer from the American Central Intelligence Agency that they have never even heard of my name. That's why I have always been suspicious of 'C'."

As the Harley Davidson sped away through the streets of London, Stryker could barely hear Carol as she yelled, "What do you think of Dubai?"

To which Stryker replied, "Dubai? Done that! I think Seattle is a better possibility."

They both laughed.

"Oh, and I'll introduce you to my old friend Billy."

"I can't wait Stryker, I just can't wait."

THE END

Forthcoming novel in the Stryker series:

STRYKER AND THE FOURTH REICH

SEATTLE, WASHINGTON STATE. U.S.A.

In the early hours of Tuesday morning on 13ᵗʰ June 1995, in this particular location and at this time of night, it was an incongruous pose to strike. One leg was jammed firmly behind the buttocks, the other jutted out at an acute angle, arms akimbo as if in the throes of making a heroic effort to soar through the air whilst attempting a high jump. Had the eyes not been sucked out by some inquisitive species of unidentified aquatic creature, they might have been resolutely focussed on an imaginary cross bar.

Immersed for a good while, John Doe's pallid blotchy skin and bloated mud-splattered head resembled that of a puffer fish, the swollen tongue protruding from between surprisingly constricted dark blue puckered lips. Lurking alone beneath the trees' ragged shadows, an icy sensation crawled slowly, spider-like up the mesmerised young girl's spine, inching its way to the nape of her neck, making her fine ciliate hairs stand on end. She shuddered. The outraged moon and stars had hibernated behind a solid mass of thick black clouds, making it a soulless night. A cool breeze ruffled the wide-open expanse of dark brackish water off the desecrated foreshore where the body lay hemmed in between the arthritic contour of land known as Seward Park and Seattle's Lake Washington Boulevard.

A series of portable arc lights had been hurriedly set up surrounding the immediate area. Milling about in this theatrical pool of illumination were four police officers from Seattle's Homicide Unit clad in synthetic fabric boiler suits, specifically designed to avoid cross-contamination of the corpse. Three uniformed traffic cops filled with curiosity stood awkwardly nearby with arms crossed watching intently, occasionally adjusting their position with self-conscious movements as if intruding in someone's private grief. An occasional blinding white light flooded the area. The official police photographer was well into his stride, synchronised flashes breaking up the pulsing rhythm of blinking red and blue strobes emanating from each of two highway patrol cars parked some distance away, the white flashes pinpointing different aspects and features of the aspiring athlete still leaking dirty Lake Washington water from his mouth, ears, and a conservative array of clothing as his body was moved for a cursory examination.

"When was he discovered?" The senior homicide investigator was in his late fifties and bore a passing resemblance to the late film actor John Wayne. He had joined the busy group examining the body and posed the question in his quietly spoken melancholic manner to no one in particular. One of his plain clothed detectives passed him a see-through self-sealing sylthane evidence bag with something nestling in one corner, the article itself having been extracted from the victim's clothing just moments earlier.

"About forty minutes ago, sir. Courting couple spotted him floating close by the water's edge." It was one of the traffic cops who answered. He was a slim, tall, black policeman whose belt was weighed down with gun holster filled with standard issue side-arm, chrome-plated handcuffs, extendable truncheon, stun-gun, pouches for mace, pepper spray, and a thousand other items calculated to subdue the most persistent and recalcitrant aggressor. His short, thickset, white colleague motioned with his head toward a skinny Hispanic-looking kid about seventeen who at that moment was being interviewed by one of the homicide detectives. "He was with that girl over there by the trees. Said they initially thought the body was a mannequin." The senior detective nodded then glanced thoughtfully down at his watch before once more slowly taking in the scene. After a while he limped the short distance towards the young witnesses himself.

"Hi. I'm Detective Stoker. I understand you found the body. Would you like to tell me precisely how you came upon it?" The skinny kid was dressed in loose low-cut blue jeans and trainers with a black hooded parka; the girl's attire mirrored the boys. It was just as his two colleagues had said – nothing more, nothing less. "Want you to come to the station in the morning to make a statement. Give your details to this sergeant." The plainclothes policeman motioned to one of his homicide detectives.

Back at his own vehicle, he yanked the nearside door open wide, climbed in and examined the wallet taken from the evidence bag before extracting a very soggy dog-eared calling card with a heavy sigh, before depositing the evidence bag inside the glove compartment of the dashboard, cursing softly. After climbing out and slamming the door in frustration he stopped to gather his thoughts for a moment before ambling toward a muffled sound emanating from a short wave radio in one of the other police cruisers. Making a circular gesture with his stubby index finger to a sleepy-looking patrolman, the window was lowered.

Without speaking, the detective reached in and removed a handset dangling from the dashboard. Flicking a switch, he spoke into it. "This is

Captain Stoker. I want you to page me through to Stryker Truman – you'll find the number in my book. That's right, Truman." Just as he uttered these words a loud boom echoed around the lake as dark rain clouds exploded in a torrential downpour, seconds later the skyline was lit up by a giant zigzag bolt of lightning. Shadows danced upon the white-faced carcass, theatrically resurrecting him for a nanosecond before the corpse relapsed back into its restless pose. The detective captain had to shout into the microphone above the noisy drumming of rain upon the car's tinny roof to make himself heard. "Ok, I'll hang on!"

The detective took just long enough to settle himself in beside the patrol cop, thus avoiding the worst of the rain, before the person he wished to speak to came on the static-filled line. A hurried conversation ensued terminating with the barely audible words: "Jesus, I'll be right down."

By the time the detective made it back to the his own private vehicle he was as wet as the stiff form still being intently observed from all angles by the forensic scientist, water soaking into his suit and shirt. Another loud clap of thunder and the counting began. And one second, and two second, and three second, and four second, and five second and… Another tremendous flash of static electricity rent the black clouds asunder: Five miles away, coming from the direction of Mount Rainier. Through the streaming windscreen the detective observed distorted humanoid shapes moving in the distance performing the usual dark ritual for the dead, one kneeling, two others facing one another, arms flailing the air in animated discussion through rods of drilling rain reminiscent of a Cherokee war dance in slow motion, occasionally being brought into sharp focus by yet more flashes from the scene of crime photographer.

Scene of crime! More a dump site than scene of crime, the captain thought to himself. From the detective's point of view, a body in water was bad news. A lot of clues can get washed away. Still, at least there would be no need for some poor bloody cop to spend hours checking missing persons reports for the victim's identity, and he had had the sense to keep his clothes on. Even on waterlogged bodies fibres and hairs, whether human or animal, sometimes led to the killer. And there was no doubt, even at this initial stage of the investigation that the victim lying on the foreshore was murdered. Otherwise why else would all his right-hand fingers – or at least, what remained of the stumps, possess telltale signs of being burnt off with a naked flame? He conceded that it was just possible that the person lying spread-eagled upon the shore might have been involved in some sort of boating accident, but no such incident had been reported so far. No, his gut instinct told him it was a homicide – and that he had been tortured. The seared flesh was there for even the untrained eye to see. You didn't need a police pathologist to tell you that. Who hasn't been to a barbecue and witnessed burnt sausages?

It was forty minutes later, shortly after Captain Stoker had made a stab at drying his thinning hair and lined, weathered face with a handful of Kleenex tissues while in the process of pouring himself a second mug of hot black coffee from a Thermos laced with whisky taken from his hip flask, that Stryker Truman rapped on the car window. The rain had eased to a light drizzle but Captain Stoker's friend of many years standing was dressed appropriately enough for such conditions. As he climbed in and listened to his old friend he was handed the sylthane package now removed from the detective's dashboard of his black Ford Sierra RS Cosworth, Stryker's mind reeled at what he saw inside. The captain handed him the hip flask. Stryker took a hefty swig. Slowly recovering from the initial shock, he reluctantly followed Billy down to the freshly taped off area to inspect the body, silently reviewing the past forty-eight hours, attempting to make sense out of something that on the surface appeared bizarre.

"Had a devil of a job raising you – been trying for ages. Don't you sleep at home anymore?"

"Sorry Billy; you know how it is – busy on a new case." His big, soft brown eyes had a puzzled look in them – his face laced with worry.

"Well Stryker, I'm waiting. Just tell me who this guy is and what the hell is going on here. Take your time, I've got all night and I have a funny feeling it's going to be a long one."

Printed in Great Britain
by Amazon.co.uk, Ltd.,
Marston Gate.